Fayte of Blood

Book One
- of -
The Fayte Saga

The Fayte Saga, Book One: Fayte of Blood

Cover design by E.J. Tollridge
Interior map and artwork by E.J. Tollridge

First Edition
Printed in the United States of America

ISBN: 979-8-9999507-0-3

To my son and husband

JCP & JSP

Acknowledgements

To the first readers of this book—Karen A., Sam A., Ryan C., Viktoria K., F. Miller, Amanda R., M.T. Skye, and Mia W.—thank you for your thoughtful insight and genuine reactions to the characters and the story. You truly inspired me to finally publish this book.

Amanda, an ELA teacher I worked with, graciously edited the manuscript. M.T. Skye, Ryan, and Karen provided tremendously helpful feedback during the creative process.

To my friends and family who supported me through hardships and celebrated life's blessings—thank you for being my rock and helping me stay steady.

To the lost friend who once shared this world with me—thank you for helping bring its first iterations to life in our childhood.

To my newest friends from the online community—your wholesome support carried me through the most challenging shift in my career. You gave me the drive to finish what I had started.

To my husband—thank you for all your love, and for putting up with my late-night obsessing over this book, alongside all the other nonsense I've thrown your way over the years.

To my son—thank you for making me your mom. I hope that one day, when you read this, you'll know that you were the catalyst who brought me back to writing. As I waited for you to fall asleep each night, I read *The Legend of Huma* by Richard A. Knaak—and was inspired to rework this story into something I could finally be proud of.

To my future readers—thank you for giving this world, these characters, and this story a chance. *The Fayte Saga* has been a passion project and a labor of love for two decades of my life.

I am incredibly thrilled to finally share it with you.

Contents

The Land of

Moirand

Northern Regania
Aquiad Ruins
Southern Regania
The Sacred Motherland
Ebpeb's Den
Hallowdale
West Erythar
East Erythar
Belluxa
Cobaka's Burrow
Aryekan's Pride
Aetheloth
Tersia
The Pulchid Isles
Arachnian Swamp
The Elkenwoods

“Love is salvation. Love is destruction. Love will endure. ”

-Unknown

A Brief History of Moirand

There once was endless darkness
Until the day that Elodyn came to be.

From the Ether, Elodyn descended to Midthian.
With a burst of light, he shattered the darkness
And wove the Land of Moirand.
From this light came the Saryfim, beings of magic and grace,
Forged the world in his divine vision:

They kindled the sun, the moon, and the stars,
Painted the skies and wove the endless seas.
They sculpted the greens, the mountains, and the beasts,
And gave life to the fayfolk, the giants, and the elves.

Yet Elodyn, in his boundless love,
Shaped mankind with his own hand
And cherished them above all else.
Before he took rest, he gave a final decree:
Guard and guide mankind, for they are the greatest gift.

But among the Saryfim, one turned bitter.
Malaziel, envious of mankind's favor,
Wandered the edges of the world

And found the lurking shadow of the Nether.

The darkness consumed him, body and soul,
And from his former light was born Malcifer the Wicked.
In this monstrous form, he spread his blight,
Twisting fayfolk into Unseelie, mankind into Cruerfel,
And Moirand burned beneath his malice.

The Saryfim, their light vulnerable to his shadow,
Could not face him.
Instead, they turned to mankind,
Bestowing gifts to protect them:
The strength of beasts,
The wings of the sky,
The resilience of the sea.

But Malcifer, unyielding, summoned the dead.
Then from his Cruerfel kin,
He raised a champion of ruin,
The Golviathan, a monstrosity of destruction.

Decades of war scarred the land;
Blood stained Moirand's soil unending.
In desperation, the Saryfim chose their own champions,
Surrendering their divine essence.
Thus were born the Valksha, human vessels of magic and light.

The Valksha stood united,
Breaking the ranks of Malcifer's creations,
Destroying the Golviathan,
And casting down Malcifer the Wicked.

His children fled into shadow,
Lurking, scheming, nursing their hatred.
Though peace returned to Moirand,
Darkness yet stirred in the hearts of monsters and men.

Prologue

Royal Bloodshed

The boy sank his clawed fingernails into his father's throat.

The father's eyes went wide with terror, blood gurgling from his mouth.

As his father fell to his knees, the boy ripped away his hand and let the blood splatter over the marble floor. The father reached for him with trembling hands, but the boy lunged at him. The boy ripped and tore into his father's throat and chest with his claws and fangs. Bits of flesh and wet silk scattered around him.

The father's body dropped to the ground. It fell silent.

The boy was now alone. He breathed deeply, staring at his father's mutilated corpse. His heart raced in his chest and throbbed in his ears.

"Someone please send my mother," the boy called out. "It's urgent."

"Yes, my prince," a male voice answered from the closed door to the throne room.

The boy stood with his back to the door. Moments later, his mother rushed in. At the sight of her husband's body, she let out a horrific gasp—but before she could scream, the boy's claws shredded her throat in one slash. The door fell shut before her body collapsed.

First, his father. Then, his mother. Finally, his brothers.

Now, they all lay at his feet. Four bodies were sprawled out in pools of blood, their royal clothes of silk and wool torn and soaked. The throne room, once a glorious hall of gold and white marble, was stained with red. The boy stared at each body with a satisfied gaze. His golden-yellow irises nearly glowed.

"M...My prince?"

He glanced over his shoulder. He was drenched head to toe, dripping thick red onto the floor. A girl stood at the entrance of the throne room in utter shock, her mouth dropped open, and her yellow eyes large, fearful, and full of tears.

"What did you do?" she gasped.

The boy turned to her and offered her a warm, fanged smile. He began walking to her.

"I've killed them. Now I will be king."

The girl trembled, and tears spilled over her cheeks.

"B-But..." she stammered. "Why?"

The boy reached for the girl's hand and squeezed it tightly. "I did it for you. For us."

The girl ripped her hand out of his grasp and backed away. She shook her head and choked out a sob. "No. No! This isn't...*no!*"

The boy's eyes grew as he stared at her in disbelief. "My love...?"

A piercing shriek erupted from her and echoed in the hall. "You *fiend!*"

The girl whipped around and fled the throne room into the dark corridor.

The boy did not turn away. His eyes remained fixated on the darkness, unblinking, and he tried to retain the last image of her before she disappeared from view.

A voice spoke beside him. It was the same male voice from before.

"Your majesty," he said.

"She will be my queen," the boy muttered. "I will be king. This kingdom will be the greatest of all. I will crush all of my enemies."

The boy's tone lowered into a whispered hiss.

"Kill them all. Kill the Valksha."

Chapter 1

The Last of the Valksha

Year 843 of the Second Age, Eighth Month, Twenty-Fifth Day

A quiet storm rumbled across the sky, dimming the silvery light of the full moon. The forest around the cottage rustled.

Theodin sat by the fire, sharpening his sword with a whetstone. He wore his Kyriegard uniform, though less formal than what the Council chambers demanded. A dark, fitted tunic of heavy woven wool clung to his frame, belted at the waist with a worn leather sash that bore the Order's sigil stitched in silver thread. Over it, he wore a black, sleeveless overcoat—weather-treated and tailored for motion, its edges lined with faded rune embroidery. His breeches were tucked into scuffed leather boots, still damp from patrol, and a cloak hung beside the hearth, its hem crusted with dried mud. A silver pin at his collar marked him as Kaspar's apprentice. Though young, he carried himself with the quiet rigor of someone molded by war stories and expectation.

The rhythmic scrape echoed against the walls, but his attention kept flickering to the window. Framed by a fringe of dark auburn hair, a pair of mismatched eyes—one dull amber and the other blue—peered through a gap in the curtain.

She's close, he thought. The air didn't smell of rain earlier. Lady

Vivian always hid her tracks in the rain. As a master Valksha, she always had the upper hand.

Though it was never quite his preferred method of battle, magic fascinated and somewhat frightened Theodin. He favored the blade—its honesty and its weight. A sword did not falter when emotion clouded the mind. It struck or it didn't. It protected, or it failed. Magic, on the other hand, bent to will. It responded to feeling. And feelings, Theodin had learned, were dangerous.

In order to command magic in Moirand, one must be a Sage, a Pulchid, a Warthrall, or a Valksha.

In other words, you were either born with it or you chose it.

And if you chose it, you either studied it for decades… or damned yourself to be granted it.

Theodin had no patience for shortcuts—or the monsters they made.

Sages were the disciplined individuals who learned how to manipulate the energies of the Saryfim left behind in their creations. Immense study and understanding of the inherent power of their surroundings took years, sometimes decades. Theodin had a light grasp of this due to his Kyriegard training as a Sage *warrior*, but he leaned heavily on the 'warrior' aspect because it came much more naturally to him.

Pulchids were the fayfolk, elvish, and dwarvish, born of two Saryfim to be magical companions of mankind. Theodin dealt with mostly half-breeds and didn't mind their natural ability or quirkiness. He held high respect for the full-blooded ones—namely, two of the current Kyriegard Council members.

Then…there were Warthralls.

They made pacts in exchange for power. Sold something—sometimes their souls, and sometimes worse. Most pledged themselves to Nether demons, creatures who promised strength in return for corruption. Others were vessels for vengeful spirits from the Lither. A few were even bound to trickster Pulchids or to beings from the Ether. Regardless, Theodin had never met one that hadn't lost their humanity along the way.

While it was rare for Warthralls to have a capacity for good, most acted out of selfishness. They took advantage of the weak and preyed upon the desperate. They went against the grain of everything the Kyriegard stood for.

Simultaneously, they caused the most grief in Moirand. There were such things as sour Sages, but they never amounted to the damage that

Warthralls caused. Next were the Unseelie Pulchids—and a combination of them, Unseelie Pulchid Warthralls, were the worst.

Pain. Suffering. That was all they knew and all they shared. Theodin hated them for it.

Valksha, though—Valksha didn't need devotion or decades. The Valksha only needed their faith and family. The Kyriegard did not participate in such things, but they at least upheld the same values. As vessels of the Saryfim themselves, Valksha were naturally inclined for the good and balance of Moirand. They never made anyone slaves or oppressed them.

Yet, the Valksha were the most powerful of them all.

It only took a single drop of blood for the Valksha to wield the power of the Saryfim. That single crimson bead could call fire from the sky, or raise walls from shattered earth. A paper cut could make flowers bloom across a corpse's chest. A gash could silence a battlefield.

Lady Vivian had once told Theodin that their blood was the Saryfim's whisper made flesh. It dwelled in them like a second soul.

But it wasn't just their magic that set the Valksha apart—it was their bond to the Saryfim, an unyielding tether that was as much a blessing as it was a burden. Each Valksha was bound to a specific Saryf, one of the twelve celestial guardians who had once roamed Moirand. This bond shaped not only their magic but their very essence, their emotions, and their instincts. To be chosen by a Saryf was to carry a fragment of divine purpose, but it also meant carrying the weight of their domain.

According to the Kyriegard records, the Saryfim imbued their Valksha with unique abilities—gifts that echoed the traits of their celestial patrons. The Valksha of Abrachiel the Wise, Saryf of Rivers and Seas, could see glimpses of the future on the water's surface. Those bound to Rochiel the Fierce, Saryf of Mountains and Terrains, possessed immense strength but were prone to earth-shaking fits of rage. And then there were Valksha like Lady Vivian, the last known Valksha of Celestiel the Gentle, Saryf of Winds and Clouds, who could summon storms or gentle breezes with her will—or her mood. Theodin remembered reading how even a single misstep in her control could flood entire plains. Yet, despite the overwhelming force she wielded, Lady Vivian was known for her restraint, her command over her emotions as precise as the gusts she conjured.

Theodin often wondered if such control was something innate to the

Valksha or something earned through endless trial and failure. Based on what he'd gleaned from the Kyriegard archives, most Valksha struggled to harness the power that coursed through their veins, especially in the beginning. The bond to the Saryfim was a double-edged blade—granting unimaginable power but requiring unyielding discipline to wield. And for many, that balance was hard-won, if not impossible to achieve.

In the War of Malblight, the Valksha were heralded as saviors—living conduits of the Saryfim's might, wielding magic so potent it turned the tides of battle. But peace had not been kind to them. In the centuries that followed the war, the very power that had made them champions of light became the source of mistrust. To many, they were living weapons, their divine blood too dangerous to let linger in mortal hands. Their numbers dwindled, not from the natural passage of time, but from fear and persecution. Now, only whispers of them remained, scattered like ash on the wind.

And yet… Lady Vivian had endured. She was not merely one of the last Valksha of her Saryf; she was a living paradox—a relic of a bygone era who had carved a place for herself in a world that believed it no longer seemed to need her, yet it desperately did.

Theodin couldn't help but admire her. As a child, he had heard tales of her exploits—the storms she had commanded, the battles she had won. But he had come to see beyond the legends in the times she visited him and his guardian mentor, Kaspar. She was more than a Valksha. She was human. And that, perhaps more than her magic or her bond to Celestiel, was what made her extraordinary.

Theodin watched the shadows deepen through the glass, his nerves on edge. Lady Vivian's presence always carried a kind of gravity, a sense that the world itself had shifted to accommodate her arrival. As a child, he had only known her through the stories—the Valksha of Celestiel who could summon storms and scatter armies with a flick of her hand. But over the years, he had come to see her for who she truly was: a woman carrying the weight of her gift with grace and control that felt almost impossible.

He adjusted his grip on the whetstone, the metal edge of his sword catching the firelight. She made it seem easy, he thought. But control like hers—if it could even be called that—had to be immensely challenging. He had studied the Kyriegard histories and read the accounts of other Valksha losing themselves to their power. Rage, despair, even joy—any emotion could tip the balance. But Lady

Vivian… she was different.

Theodin tossed another piece of wood into the hearth, and the fire sparked and flared. The room brightened, chasing away the shadows that clung to the corners. He leaned back slightly and his eyes flicked once more toward the window.

"Put it out, Theodin."

He jumped, startled by the sudden command.

Kaspar stood in the doorway, his gray, wolf-like gaze sharp as ever. A shadow of impatience flashed across his aged face. His Kyriegard cloak, a silver-embroidered black drape still damp from the mist outside, clung to broad shoulders. Long streaks of silver hair framed a lined face carved by discipline, the creases around his mouth deepened by years of unsaid warnings. Beneath the cloak, his armor was minimal but worn: a dark leather cuirass laced with runic stitching and bracers strapped tight over veined, calloused forearms.

Theodin quickly grabbed the bucket of water nearby and doused the fire. The hearth hissed, and steam rose to fill the room as the warmth was swallowed by the cold night air.

Kaspar stepped closer, his presence commanding even in silence. Theodin glanced at him, waiting for further instruction, but the older man's gaze was fixed on the window.

"She's here," Kaspar said quietly, his voice carrying both certainty and caution.

Theodin followed his stare. Outside, the wind howled softly, and the scent of rain thickened. Whatever storm Lady Vivian had summoned to shield her approach was closing in.

"Kaspar?" Theodin whispered.

"Lady Vivian is being followed by Warthralls. She has someone we need to shelter," Kaspar answered, moving his tall shadow to the window next to the front door. "A Valksha refugee."

"A Valksha refugee?" Theodin repeated. He went to Kaspar's side to peer through the window with him. "How can we shelter a Valksha here in Avasylon?"

"Avasylon is still a stronghold, lad, despite its soft appearance," Kaspar muttered. He didn't take his piercing gray eyes away from the window. "We are still Kyriegard. We are the best warriors and Sages of Moirand. We protect the weak."

The storm outside grew stronger. Thunder rumbled closer.

"The Kyriegard are nowhere near as powerful as the mighty Valksha," Theodin pointed out. "So whatever is hunting them has to be stronger than them and therefore stronger than us. And Lady Vivian is the strongest of them all. Wouldn't this refugee be safer with her?"

"I wondered the same things. We will find out soon enough."

Only nature stirred outside of the cottage. Vast fields of long grass brushed the path to the porch, and the branches of the trees all rustled with the aggravated wind. Theodin squinted to see through the storm's darkness for any other movement.

Abruptly, the door swung open.

Two figures stood there, both in black hooded cloaks. One was tall and slender, and the other was short and petite. Kaspar and Theodin unsheathed their swords, but the taller figure held up a long, elegant hand. A silver-feathered owl swept into the room and landed on ground before them in a defensive stance, its luminous eyes gleaming at them.

"It is I, Nimrod," a mellow woman's voice spoke. She pushed the small figure in, who meekly kept their head down and face covered by the hood. The tall woman shut the door behind them and pulled down her hood. A cape of white hair fell over her shoulder. Her silvery eyes fell upon the owl. "Stand down, Aetheris."

It ruffled its feathers and bowed before hopping aside.

"Lady Vivian," Kaspar huffed, eyes wide and brows creased in concern. His sword lowered. "Your hair...?"

Vivian brushed her fingers through her white hair with a reluctant, wistful smile. "A sign of the times, Kaspar," she murmured. Her voice carried a softness that seemed to calm the howling wind outside. The owl fluttered to her shoulder, its feathers shimmering faintly in the firelight.

Kaspar stepped forward, worry etched into the deep lines of his face. "Does this mean—"

"It means we've run out of time," Vivian interrupted, her tone gentle but firm. "We can discuss that later. For now, we must focus on her." She gestured to the cloaked figure standing silently at her side.

Theodin's eyes glanced toward the small figure, his grip tightening on the hilt of his sword. "Who is she?" he asked, his voice steady but edged with unease.

Vivian's eyes met his. "Her name is Ophelia Bloodworth. She is the last Valksha of Veladriel."

Theodin's heart thudded at the name. Veladriel the Ardent—the Saryf of Spirit and Heart. He exchanged a glance with Kaspar, whose expression had hardened.

"Why is she here?" Kaspar asked, his voice low and measured. "Keeping her in Avasylon will only put her in greater danger."

Vivian nodded. "You're correct. But nowhere else is safe, not now. Warthralls are hunting her. They know what she is and what she's capable of becoming—they want to strike her down before she finds her strength."

Theodin frowned. "And you brought her here? With all due respect, Lady Vivian, this is reckless. Avasylon is a hidden stronghold, but it's not invulnerable."

Vivian's gaze softened as she looked at him. "I brought her here because you are here, Theodin. You and Kaspar are the only ones I trust with her life."

Kaspar grunted. "We'll keep her safe. But the Warthralls won't give up easily. They're bloodhounds—they'll follow your trail."

"I know," Vivian said, pulling her hood back up. "That's why I cannot stay." She turned to Ophelia, who had remained motionless, her face still obscured. "Ophelia, this is Kaspar, and this is Theodin. They are your protectors now."

Slowly, the girl lifted her head, her hood falling back to reveal a pale olive face framed by curly raven hair. Her emerald eyes glimmered with uncertainty but with a quiet determination. She looked at Kaspar first, nodding timidly, and then at Theodin. Something shined in her gaze when their eyes met—curiosity, perhaps, or recognition. Theodin couldn't tell.

Vivian knelt before Ophelia and placed a hand on her shoulder. The owl glided down to perch on the back of a nearby chair, its sharp gaze fixed on the young Valksha. "You'll be safe here," Vivian said, her tone soft but resolute. "Trust them as you would trust me. I will return for you."

Ophelia's expression wavered as she nodded, her small frame tense and trembling slightly. She took an anxious, deep breath, holding it for a moment too long before exhaling. Her eyes flickered with fear and longing.

Vivian's expression softened as she brushed a stray strand from Ophelia's face. "You've endured more than anyone should, child," she murmured, so low that only Ophelia could hear. "But you're stronger than you know. Remember that."

Ophelia leaned into the touch, her quiver easing slightly under Vivian's words. There was a glimpse of something fleeting—a memory perhaps—crossing her features, but it was gone as quickly as it came.

She straightened as if summoning courage from Vivian's presence.

Vivian rose, her hand lingering momentarily on Ophelia's shoulder before she turned back to Kaspar and Theodin. "I don't have much time. The Warthralls are already close. Protect her, and teach her. She is more important than she knows."

Ophelia's hands tightened into fists at her sides, her knuckles whitening. Her eyes followed Vivian as if memorizing every movement, every detail of her pale hair and confident stride. When Vivian reached the door, Ophelia spoke up, her voice small but pleading. "You'll come back, won't you?"

Vivian paused with her hand on the handle. She looked back, her eyes meeting Ophelia's. "Always," she promised, her voice unwavering.

Aetheris hooted with discomfort suddenly and twisted its head to the door, to Ophelia, then back to Lady Vivian.

Vivian remained in the doorway, her hair glinting in the dim light. "They're close," she said softly. "But I've left false trails toward the Elkenwoods—broken branches, footprints, even a decoy fire. They'll waste precious time searching there."

Kaspar frowned. "And what happens when they catch up to you?"

"They won't," she replied with quiet certainty. "I've dealt with Warthralls before and will deal with them again. But Ophelia must stay hidden. She is their true target."

Theodin tensed. "And if they figure out she's here?"

"She is in good hands," Vivian said firmly, her silver eyes locking with his. "You'll keep her safe. I trust you."

"My lady," Aetheris said suddenly. It turned its head to the door. "We must go."

Vivian then glanced back at Ophelia one last time, her silver eyes softening. "Stay safe, child," she murmured, heavy with the weight of both a command and a prayer.

With that, she turned and was gone, swallowed by the storm outside. Aetheris lingered in the doorway for a moment, its silvery feathers gleaming as it cast one last glance at Ophelia before spreading its wings and following Vivian into the storm.

Chapter 2

The Shattered

Theodin exhaled, his breath visible in the cold air left in Vivian's wake. He turned to Kaspar. "Now what?"

Kaspar sheathed his sword and gestured toward the hearth. "Now, we prepare. The Warthralls won't take long to find us."

Theodin nodded and glanced at Ophelia. She stood motionless, staring at the door where Vivian had disappeared. Her shoulders trembled, and her breath hitched audibly.

"You'll be alright," Theodin said. "You're safe here."

Ophelia's green eyes flicked up to meet his, glassy with unshed tears. But then, with a slight, almost imperceptible shake of her head, she seemed to steady herself. She stepped forward, her small frame gathering strength that didn't quite reach her face.

"I want to help," she said, her voice firmer than before, though it cracked slightly on the last word. Her accent carried the odd emphasis Theodin recognized—north…far north, perhaps? It made her words sound formal and deliberate.

Theodin studied her for a long moment, then sighed. "We'll see about that. For now, stay close."

He turned toward Kaspar, but from the corner of his eye, he caught the way Ophelia's gaze lingered on the door again. He didn't say anything, but he couldn't help feeling a pang of unease. The way she looked at Vivian, the way she'd flinched at her departure, reminded him of a wounded animal bracing for the next blow.

As the storm outside raged on, they settled into an uneasy silence. For Theodin, it was the silence of preparation. For Kaspar, it was for calculation. But for Ophelia, it was silent suffering.

Theodin watched the window cautiously while Kaspar moved around the cabin, snuffing out candles and pulling the thick curtains shut. The storm raged outside with the wind wailing like a restless spirit.

"Ophelia," Kaspar said, his tone measured but commanding. "Take a seat by the hearth. We'll need to talk about what's ahead."

The girl hesitated, her gaze flitting toward the door one last time before she complied. She perched lightly on the edge of the wooden chair, her small hands clasped tightly in her lap. Despite the leftover warmth of the hearth, her face was pale, her eyes wide and alert.

Theodin sat across from her, resting his sword across his knees. "Have you ever been to Avasylon?" he asked, trying to gauge her familiarity with the place—and perhaps distract her from the weight of Vivian's absence.

Ophelia's fingers curled tightly around the strap of her satchel as if holding it would anchor her. She didn't move until Theodin's voice cut through her thoughts. She shook her head, her curls bouncing slightly with the movement.

"No," she replied softly. As she continued to speak, her accent was more pronounced now, her vowels crisp and consonants clipped in that distinct northerly way. "I… I didn't even know it existed until Lady Vivian brought me here."

Theodin tilted his head slightly, now fully recognizing the sophisticated precision of her tone. It was the dialect of the northern nobles of Regania—polished and intentional, but slightly at odds in a rugged place like the little Tersian village of Fatum where they resided. Especially here in Olysgard, where Sage warriors like the Kyriegard lived and trained.

"You'll find it's not much to look at," Theodin said with a faint smirk. "Just a quiet place with too many books and an old man who grumbles too much."

Kaspar snorted from across the room. "Watch your tongue, lad, or you'll run laps around the perimeter at dawn."

Ophelia's lips twitched upward, though the smile didn't quite reach her eyes. "It's safe, isn't it?" she asked, her voice barely above a whisper.

Theodin hesitated, glancing at Kaspar. The older man gave a subtle nod before answering. "It's as safe as anywhere in Moirand can be these days," Kaspar said. "But safety isn't something you should rely on. Not entirely."

Theodin leaned forward slightly, his eyes steady on hers. "Do you know why Lady Vivian brought you here? Why she left you with us?"

Ophelia hesitated, her fingers tightening their grip on each other. "She said… she said I would be safe here," she murmured, her gaze dropping to the floor. "She said you could protect me."

Theodin exchanged a glance with Kaspar. They both knew there was more to it, but pressing her now wouldn't do any good. They would have to uncover whatever dangers she carried with her in time.

She was still so frightened. Worried about her safety, though she was reassured many times.

Kaspar walked over and placed a hand on Theodin's shoulder. "Let's give her some time to settle," he said quietly. "She's had enough for one night."

Theodin nodded, rising from his chair. "There's a room upstairs you can use," he said, gesturing toward the narrow staircase. "It's small, but it's warm."

Ophelia stood, her movements hesitant but obedient. She glanced between them, then took a step toward the stairs. She paused, turning back to Theodin.

"Thank you," she said, her voice steadier now but still carrying a meek tremor. "Both of you."

As Ophelia reached the base of the stairs, she paused, glancing back toward the extinguished hearth. Her small frame quivered. The faint light from the storm illuminated her pale and drawn face. Her green eyes darted nervously toward the window, where the storm clawed at the glass. The dimming glow of the hearth seemed to flicker weaker as her unease grew.

"You're safe here," Kaspar reassured her, his tone steadfast but softening at the edges.

She nodded, her trembling hands clutching the strap of her satchel. But before she could step forward, a sudden shadow passed the window.

Her breath hitched. "There's something out there," she whispered, her voice barely audible.

Theodin was already moving, his eyes narrowing as he approached the window with his sword in hand. "Where?"

Ophelia's answer never came. A sharp, searing light erupted from her palms, her fear manifesting before she could contain it. It spilled across the room in searing waves. It wasn't just the brightness—there was a weight to it, a pulse that seemed to shake the air itself. Theodin felt the hair on his arms rise as the magic rippled outward, raw and untamed.

The window exploded in a cascade of glass, the shards scattering across the room as the storm outside surged in. Theodin ducked instinctively, and Kaspar was at her side in an instant, his firm grip steadying her as the light faded.

The silence that followed was deafening. Only the pattering sound of heavy droplets against wood and stone echoed in the large space, and the quiet gasping of the Valksha girl behind the elder Kyriegard.

Finally, Kaspar spoke. He glanced over his shoulder at her. "You don't feel anything, do you?"

A small whimper and a light shake of her head.

Kaspar straightened his stance. "It was nothing. Perhaps a trick of the eye."

Ophelia's eyes lowered to her hands. The receding glow of her magic lingered like embers before snuffing out entirely. Her chest rose and fell rapidly as she stumbled back, pressing herself against the banister. "I didn't mean to," she choked out, her voice breaking. "I didn't—"

Kaspar's hand on her shoulder anchored her. His tone was sharp but not unkind. "Calm yourself, lass. Fear doesn't mix well with magic like yours." His gaze softened as he crouched slightly, bringing himself to her eye level. "Your power is strong, but it must be tempered. Do you understand?"

Ophelia nodded stiffly, tears glistening in her wide eyes. At his touch, the tension in her tiny frame loosened. "I… I didn't mean to hurt anyone."

"You didn't," Kaspar assured her. "But you must learn control. Instinct alone won't keep you or anyone else safe."

Theodin straightened, brushing shards of glass from his sleeve. His gaze lingered on the now-broken window, then flicked to Kaspar. "That wasn't just instinct," he muttered, his tone laced with unease. "That was raw power. That was..."

He glanced at her hands. She never drew blood. Was that possible for a Valksha?

Kaspar leaned in closer to Ophelia with a bit of wisdom. "You're more powerful than you realize. Do you understand?"

Ophelia nodded, though her wide eyes betrayed her unease. "I-I really didn't mean to—I was just scared."

"And that's when magic like yours can be the most dangerous," Kaspar said, his voice gentler now. "We'll help you. But for tonight, try to rest."

Theodin brushed more glass from his shoulder and turned to survey the damage. "Great," he muttered, sheathing his sword. "I'll find something to cover that up."

"I can fix it!" Ophelia blurted, her voice edged with desperation. She stepped forward, her hands trembling. "Please… let me fix it."

Kaspar hesitated, and then he gave a slight nod. "Go on, then."

She knelt by the scattered shards of glass, her hands hovering just above them. Carefully, she scraped a finger against the sharp edge of one of the larger pieces until it pierced her skin and pricked a drop of blood. Her eyes fluttered shut, and she exhaled shakily. The glow returned to her fingers, this time softer, steadier. The drop of blood evaporated and seemed to feed the light festering from her hands. The shards quivered and then began to lift from the floor, drawn together as if by an invisible thread.

Theodin watched in silence, his eyes narrowing as the glass began to reassemble in the window frame. Piece by piece, the jagged edges smoothed and fused until the pane was whole once more.

Ophelia let out a small gasp as the glow from her hands faded. She swayed slightly and her shoulders slumped.

Kaspar reached down to steady her. "Good work," he said gruffly. "But don't overdo it."

Theodin crossed his arms, his gaze still fixed on the window. "Not bad," he admitted grudgingly. "For a first try." Then his strange eyes flicked to Ophelia, his tone sharp but benign. "But next time, think before you panic."

Ophelia's face colored with shame at Theodin's sharp remark. She lowered her gaze, her hands tightening into small fists at her sides.

Before she could retreat further, Kaspar let out a slow exhale and shot Theodin a pointed look. "Enough, lad." His voice was measured, but firm, cutting through the heavy silence. "She's had a rough night."

Theodin's jaw tightened, but he held his tongue. He knew that tone—Kaspar wasn't just scolding him.

Kaspar turned back to Ophelia. "You did well," he said simply, his stern voice softening just enough to take the sting out of Theodin's words. "But that's enough magic for tonight."

Ophelia twitched slightly, as if resisting the urge to curl in on herself. She nodded once, barely more than a dip of her chin.

Kaspar watched her for a moment longer, then glanced at Theodin. "Take her upstairs," he instructed. "She needs rest."

Theodin's head snapped up, his brows knitting together. "Me?"

Kaspar leveled him with a look. "Yes, you. Show her where she's staying, make sure she settles in." His voice lowered slightly. "She's our responsibility."

Theodin hesitated, but Kaspar was already turning away, moving toward the shattered remnants of the window frame to inspect her repair work more closely.

With a reluctant sigh, Theodin glanced at Ophelia. Her exhaustion was more evident now—her shoulders sagging slightly, her breath coming slower, deeper. The faint glow that had once flickered at her fingertips had completely faded. She wasn't just tired. She was drained.

Theodin's frustration wavered slightly, replaced by something quieter. He exhaled and jerked his head toward the stairs. "Come on," he muttered. "I'll show you where you're staying."

Ophelia paused, casting one last apprehensive glance at Kaspar. When he nodded in reassurance, she finally stepped forward, seeming small and tentative.

Theodin led the way up the narrow staircase, his footsteps muffled by the aged wood. He didn't check to see if she was following, but he could hear her quiet breathing behind him. Slower than his. Lighter.

When they reached the landing, Theodin pushed open the door to the small room at the end of the hall. He bowed his head slightly to dodge the top of the door frame as he entered first, lit the oil lamp at the nightstand, and then he ducked again as he emerged.

"It's not much," he said, stepping aside to let her pass. "But it's warm, as I said earlier."

Ophelia stopped in the doorway, her timid eyes scanning the simple space—the modest bed tucked against the wall, the small wooden desk beneath the window, the single shelf lined with a few books that Kaspar had probably left behind long ago.

She didn't speak. But something in her expression shifted, as if the weight on her chest had lessened—just slightly.

Theodin crossed his arms and leaned against the doorframe,

watching her carefully. She still looked small. Tired. How could a being capable of such explosive destruction seem so meek?

He didn't know why that unsettled him.

Ophelia stepped inside slowly, trailing her fingers over the surface of the desk. Then, as if drawn by some quiet instinct, she drifted toward the bookshelf.

Theodin huffed a faint chuckle. "You actually like reading, don't you?"

Ophelia glanced at him, her lips twitching into something that might have been a smile if she weren't so exhausted. "I do," she admitted softly. "Books don't—" She hesitated, as if reconsidering her words. Then, she whispered, "Books don't leave."

Something about the way she said it made Theodin's amusement fade.

She ran her fingers along the spines of the books, reading the titles with quiet reverence. "History of the Kyriegard…" she murmured, pulling one from the shelf and flipping it open. "Lady Vivian taught me about them. But not everything."

Theodin snorted. "That's because she doesn't agree with everything."

Ophelia glanced up at him, eyes sharp with curiosity. "Do you?"

His smirk faded slightly. He wasn't sure if she was asking about Lady Vivian or the Kyriegard. "Doesn't really matter," he muttered, pushing off the doorframe.

Ophelia closed the book, cradling it to her chest like an anchor. "I want to learn."

Theodin eyed her for a long moment. He didn't doubt that. She had a hunger in her—a need to understand, to prepare herself. But for what?

He exhaled, rubbing a hand over his face. "Just… get some sleep."

She nodded, moving toward the bed and carefully placing the book on the nightstand. She lowered herself onto the mattress and tugged the blanket over her shoulders, but even as she settled in, she didn't look at ease. She didn't even remove her cloak. She kept it on like she could still jump up and run if she needed to.

Theodin didn't dwell on it for too long. He turned to leave. "If you need anything, Kaspar's downstairs," he said. "And I'll be—"

"Wait."

He paused.

Ophelia had shifted slightly, clutching the edge of the blanket between small, pale fingers. Her eyes flicked to his, uncertainty pooling in their depths. Then, her gaze lowered and wasn't quite on him, but somewhere near his feet, as if afraid to look directly at him.

"...Will you stay?"

The words were barely more than a whisper, hesitant and fragile, as if she feared they might break if she spoke them too loudly.

Theodin stared at her, caught off guard.

"I just—" She inhaled, like she was gathering courage. "Just until I fall asleep."

He exhaled through his nose, shifting his weight. He should say no. He *wanted* to say no. He wasn't a babysitter, and he wasn't about to coddle some girl who had barely spoken to him since arriving.

But then he *really* looked at her.

She wasn't just a Valksha with untamed magic. She was *tired*. A kid who had been running for her life. A kid who had watched her family die. A kid who had just been left behind again.

And despite everything—the power she had, the magic that had cracked stone and shattered glass—she was still *terrified*.

Theodin sighed heavily. "I'm not going to sit here all night," he muttered. "But… fine. Just until you fall asleep."

Ophelia let out a breath that she had been holding too tightly. "Thank you."

Theodin grabbed the chair from the desk, dragging it closer to the bed. He dropped into it with a huff and leaned forward with his elbows on his knees.

Silence stretched between them.

At first, Ophelia didn't move, her fingers still clutching the blanket. But then, slowly, her breathing began to even out.

Theodin glanced at her from the corner of his eye.

Her face was softer now and the tension in her shoulders eased bit by bit. She still held onto the blanket like it was something precious, something solid in a world that had only given her uncertainty.

For a long time, Theodin simply watched the storm in the window begin to ease. Then, finally, he pushed himself up from the chair, moving as quietly as he could. He reached for the oil lamp on the nightstand and twisted the knob to extinguish it. Silently, he crossed the room in a few steps, pausing at the door.

Something made him glance back. Ophelia was still, her chest rising and falling evenly. But the air in the room felt… different.

A faint hum pressed against the edge of his senses—subtle,

unspoken, something just out of reach. It wasn't the same pulse as her magic earlier. It was quieter. Steady.

His eyes narrowed slightly.

Theodin wasn't superstitious. He wasn't like the diviner Sages who whispered about fate, nor was he like the fools who thought the Valksha were godlings made flesh. But something about the way the air felt right now made his skin prickle. He didn't know what it was.

And that made him uneasy.

He shook his head, pushed the thought away, and slipped out the door.

The hum lingered in the silence behind him.

Chapter 3

The Request

Year 843 of the Second Age, Eighth Month, Twenty-Sixth Day

Theodin woke with a start.

For a moment, he wasn't sure what had pulled him from sleep. The cottage was still, and only the faint sound of crackling embers came from the dying hearth. The weight of exhaustion pressed on his shoulders, but something gnawed at the edge of his awareness, a sensation that refused to let him drift back into rest.

He sat up slowly, rubbed a hand over his face, and glanced toward the window. The storm had passed, but the world outside remained cloaked in a gray stillness. A subtle chill clung to the air, the kind that settled in the bones before sunrise.

Then, he saw her.

The Valksha girl sat by the repaired window with her knees drawn to her chest, staring not outside but at her reflection in the glass. The dim morning light cast pale shadows over her face, which accentuated the dark circles beneath her eyes.

She didn't look like she'd slept at all.

"Didn't like the bed?" Theodin's voice was rough with sleep.

Ophelia startled slightly, her fingers tightening around the fabric of her cloak. Theodin noticed that she wore a simple maiden's dress beneath it, which he had barely seen since her arrival—she refused to take off the cloak she came in.

She turned her head just enough to meet his gaze, her expression hazy. "I… couldn't sleep," she murmured.

Kaspar was already awake and seated at the table with a steaming cup in his hand. His silver hair was slightly disheveled, but his eyes were sharp, fixed on the journal he was scribbling in. He glanced up, his pen pausing mid-stroke. "Couldn't or wouldn't?" he asked, gruff but not unkind.

Ophelia hesitated. "Both," she admitted softly. Her hands clamped around her knees. "It was too quiet."

Theodin frowned at this. Avasylon's quiet was its greatest strength —and perhaps its greatest burden—for someone like Ophelia.

Theodin stretched and swung his legs off the cot, his boots hitting the wooden floor with a muted thud. He glimpsed at Kaspar for his comment.

Kaspar sighed and gently closed his journal. "Well, no use brooding about it, lass. If you're up, you may as well make yourself useful."

Theodin smirked lightly. "You've got her doing chores already?"

Kaspar shot him a look. "I've got both of you doing chores. Theodin, check the perimeter. Ophelia and I need to talk."

Theodin opened his mouth to argue but stopped when he saw the way Kaspar's gaze shifted toward Ophelia. She sat stiffly, curling her fingers around the hem of her cloak. It wasn't fear in her eyes, but something quieter—uncertainty, like a child waiting to be scolded.

"Fine," Theodin muttered, grabbing his sword from where it rested by the hearth. He shrugged into his cloak and strapped the sword to his side with practiced ease. "Don't bore her to death," he added, his tone wry.

Kaspar snorted but didn't respond. Theodin glanced at Ophelia as he moved toward the door. "You'll be fine," he said, his voice softer, almost grudging. Then, without waiting for a reply, he stepped outside, the chill morning air brushing against his face.

The door closed behind him with a quiet creak. Ophelia was left alone with Kaspar.

Kaspar pulled a chair closer to the hearth and gestured for Ophelia to sit. She obeyed, her movements small and hesitant. He studied her for a moment, his gaze steady but not harsh.

"Let's start with what you know," he said. "About the Warthralls."

Ophelia frowned, her hands fidgeting in her lap. "Not much," she said timidly. "Lady Vivian said they were… corrupted. She didn't tell me why they were after me."

Kaspar nodded slowly. "The Warthralls serve the Nether—demons, dark spirits, and worse. But their interest in you isn't random. You're a Valksha. That makes you valuable—to them and us."

She flinched slightly at the words, her eyes dropping to her hands. "I didn't ask to be valuable," she said quietly.

"No one does," Kaspar replied. "But what you are—and what you can do—means you will always be hunted. That's why you need to learn control."

Ophelia nodded, though her expression remained uncertain. "I want to," she whispered. "But I don't know where to start."

Kaspar's lips twitched into the slightest smile. "Then you're in the right place. We'll start slow. For now, just listen."

Outside, Theodin scanned the edge of the woods, his striking eyes sharp. The ground was damp from the previous night's storm, the air thick with the smell of wet earth. He crouched near a patch of disturbed grass and brushed his fingers over broken stalks.

Something's been here.

Theodin rose slowly. His hand hovered near the hilt of his sword as his gaze swept the trees. There was no movement, no sound—but the silence itself felt wrong.

Theodin moved swiftly through the threshold of the forest surrounding the cottage, his boots crunching against damp leaves and broken twigs. The storm had passed, but the air remained heavy, the gray sky thick with low clouds.

The broken stalks of grass he'd noticed earlier led him further into the trees. His hand rested on the hilt of his sword, every sense tuned to the stillness around him. The woods were too quiet. No birds called, no leaves rustled, and the absence of sound set his teeth on edge.

He lowered to one knee near a section of dirt, frowning as he examined a faint indentation. It wasn't a footprint, but it wasn't natural, either. The edges of the mark shimmered dimly, like oil spreading across water. Theodin leaned closer, and a subtle, acrid scent prickled at his nose.

Magic. His hand tightened around his sword as he stood, his eyes scanning the shadows. His body felt coiled, too tight, as if something under his skin was waiting. Theodin inhaled deeply, forcing his grip to relax. The tension in his limbs didn't ease, but he shoved it aside. He forced himself to breathe evenly. He was overthinking it.

Except… something shifted. A prickle at the back of his neck. A sensation—like pressure in the air, the kind that came before a storm.

His instincts had always been sharp, but this was different. Too sudden. Too direct.

He clenched his jaw, forcing himself still. He was imagining things. It was just the silence.

Wasn't it?

Kaspar leaned forward slightly, resting his elbows on his knees as he studied Ophelia. The girl's shoulders were hunched, her eyes flickering between him and the floor. She still hadn't let go of the hem of her cloak.

"You don't trust yourself," Kaspar said matter-of-factly.

Ophelia's head jerked up, her green eyes wide with surprise. "I—" she stammered, then stopped, her fingers twisting tighter around the fabric.

"It's not a criticism," Kaspar continued, his tone measured. "It's an observation. And it's something we can fix."

Ophelia swallowed hard, her hands stilling as she forced herself to meet his gaze. "I… I just don't want to hurt anyone," she huffed. "Like last night. I wasn't thinking—I just… reacted."

Kaspar nodded. "Instinct is powerful, especially for someone like you. But power without control is like a blade without a hilt—it's as dangerous to you as it is to anyone else." His eyes fell to her hands. "And your magic is…particularly interesting. You don't draw blood every time?"

The girl shifted uncomfortably. Her voice became more meek. "I'm supposed to. To help me control it. Sometimes it just…*bursts* out of me when I'm really scared, mad, or sad…"

"You're the last Valksha of Veladriel the Ardent," Kaspar murmured thoughtfully, rubbing his chin. "The Saryf of Spirit and Heart."

Ophelia gave a single, timid nod. "I am."

"The Kyriegard don't have as much research as we'd like in regard to the Valksha," Kaspar began. He stood, folded his arms and paced to the repaired window. "But I do know that some magic happens involuntarily. Lady Vivian told me she used to cause drizzles as a girl if ever she stubbed her toe or bumped her head. It comes with the cost of being a human embedded with Saryfim power." He glanced over his shoulder at her. "Which means, considering your Saryf's domain, your magic is deeply tied to your emotions."

"Lady Vivian said that too," Ophelia said in a quiet voice. "She said I have to embrace my emotions and recognize them. But…I have a hard time with…*not* feeling what I feel, or suppressing it. Not realizing I'm feeling a certain way, I'm unable to stop my magic from spiraling out of control."

"The Saryfim have the power to create," Kaspar said suddenly. He turned back to her fully. "That means they also have the power to destroy. You could very well cause harm or death the next time you jump at a shadow—that is why it is *crucial* for you to control it."

A flicker of heat pulsed beneath her skin. The hearth fire crackled louder, a sudden gust of warmth brushing against her arm.

Kaspar's gaze flicked toward it, but he said nothing. He only watched as Ophelia coiled her fingers into her palms, forcing herself to exhale.

She hated this. Hated the way her magic reacted before she could think. Before she even realized she was feeling anything at all.

She swallowed again. "I want to learn," she said softly. "I want to be better."

"You will," Kaspar replied firmly. "But it'll take time. And you'll need to be honest—with yourself and with us. We can't help you if you're hiding in your own fear."

Her lips parted slightly as if to respond, but she closed them again, her gaze dropping once more. Ophelia exhaled slowly, pressing her hands against her knees. She could still feel it—the quiet hum beneath her skin, the way her magic stirred, restless and waiting. It wanted to be released. Wanted to move.

Kaspar watched her for a moment longer before moving to sit back down in his chair.

"We'll start small," he began. "For now, focus. Before you can wield it, you need to understand it. That means listening. Watching. Recognizing the moment before the magic acts on its own. When you're ready, we'll do more."

Ophelia nodded slowly. Her eyes flicked to the elder Kyriegard. "Lady Vivian mentioned her request for me, yes?"

"Yes," Kaspar answered solemnly. He leaned forward with a hardened stare. "But is it truly something you would want? This isn't about what Lady Vivian wants for you. It's a decision that cannot be made lightly."

"I am sure of it," she said with another nod.

"The Kyriegard Council will need to be convinced. I know that Lady Vivian has already forwarded her request to them, but they will want to see you for themselves. This has never happened before in our Order."

"I understand," Ophelia said, her voice lowering with her eyes. "The Kyriegard has strict rules and procedures for things. My people could never quite fit between those lines, but…" Once again, her gaze rose to meet his. This time, they glimmered with a growing, subtle determination. "But my people are dying. And I need to do something about it. The Kyriegard are more elite, profound—more calable than any royal guard, knight's order, or Sage Circle…"

Kaspar exhaled, his expression darkening. He leaned back slightly, rubbing a hand over his face before finally speaking.

"We weren't able to stop the Valksha Massacre nor find the elusive culprits," Kaspar whispered. "How could we save your people now? They are scarce, running, hiding—"

"I'm finished running and hiding, Nimrod," Ophelia interjected, her voice trembling. She then paused, took a deep breath and let it out slowly. "I'm ready to learn how to fight."

The words felt heavier in the air than she expected. Final. Absolute.

"Lady Vivian trained me for five years," she continued, voice steadying. "But she could only just get me started." She met Kaspar's eyes again, her next words spoken with conviction. "You and the Order must help me finish it."

Theodin pushed through the cabin door, his face set in a hard line. Kaspar straightened immediately, his gray eyes narrowing. "What did you find?" he asked.

"Tracks," Theodin said shortly, brushing dirt from his gloves. "Magic."

Ophelia stiffened in her chair, her eyes snapping to Theodin. "Magic?" she echoed, her voice barely above a whisper.

Theodin nodded, his eyes meeting hers. "It wasn't human," he said grimly. "And it wasn't far. Just outside of our perimeter and detection."

Kaspar rose, his hand brushing against the hilt of his sword. "How fresh?" he asked.

"Several hours," Theodin replied. "Whatever it was, it's gone now. But it knows we're here."

Chapter 4

The Untamed

Kaspar opened his mouth to respond, but he was interrupted by the sound of voices drifting through the woods. Theodin's head snapped toward the window, his hand instinctively moving to his sword.

"Relax, lad," Kaspar said, moving toward the door. "It's the initiates."

"Shouldn't we send them back to Havysium?" Theodin pressed. "With the danger still out there?"

"Nothing with malicious intent should be able to even step foot within the perimeter," Kaspar said. "We carry on with training but remain vigilant. The last thing we need is to panic the children."

Theodin muttered something under his breath but moved aside as Kaspar opened the door and stepped out. Theodin and Ophelia followed.

A small group of figures emerged from the trees, their black uniforms bearing the sigils of the Kyriegard. Some carried wooden training swords, others had bows slung over their shoulders. Their chatter quieted as they approached the cottage, their gazes flicking curiously toward Ophelia as they passed.

"Straight to the clearing," Kaspar instructed, his voice sharp but calm. "And don't waste my time with excuses if you're late."

The initiates moved quickly, some exchanging glances and murmurs as they disappeared around the side of the cottage. One lingered briefly, her eyes narrowing as she studied Ophelia.

"Who's she?" the girl asked bluntly, her tone neither friendly nor hostile.

"Your focus should be on your training, Gisela," Kaspar said firmly. The girl hesitated for a moment longer before hurrying after the others.

Kaspar turned back to Ophelia. "You'll watch today," he said. "Learn before you try to jump in. Theodin will lead."

"What about…whatever was here?" she asked.

"We are safe here in Avasylon," Kaspar said. "We have ancient Sage wardstones in place to protect us and alert us of anything nearby that could pose a threat. And you will be with us the entire time."

Wardstones. She'd heard Lady Vivian mention them once—a Sage magic technique, she assumed. She knew Sages preferred to work with the tangible and often used alchemy and enchantments on materials like stone, wood, or metal. The Kyriegard had likely placed Sage wardstones to protect Avasylon and the other Kyriegard properties of Olysgard—Havysium and Halvalla.

Theodin passed her as he began for the clearing, but he stopped and glanced at her over his shoulder. "Keep your wits about you."

Ophelia timidly met his eyes. When they locked, a strange electricity shifted between them.

There it was again. Theodin blinked and shook it off as he continued towards the field.

Ophelia hovered near the edge of the clearing, her hands clasped tightly in front of her as she watched the initiates assemble. Theodin stood at the center, barking instructions with the acute precision of someone accustomed to being obeyed. The children—some no older than eight or nine years old—moved quickly into place, clutching their wooden practice swords tightly in their small hands.

She tried to focus on their movements, the way they mimicked Theodin's stance or stumbled over his instructions, but something else tugged at her attention. A strange, shifting sensation pressed at the edges of her mind, like ripples spreading across a pond.

It wasn't the initiates' voices or their movements that distracted her—it was their presence. Her breath hitched as she realized what she was feeling: the energies of the non-human children. It wasn't overwhelming, but it was disorienting. Each presence felt distinct, as though their very being hummed on a different frequency.

A boy near the back caught her eye. His movements were fluid, almost too graceful, and his ears, though mostly hidden beneath a mess of blond curls, came to faint points. An elf, she realized. Beside him, a girl with fiery red hair and a sharp, angular face gripped her bow with steady hands. Her energy was fiercer, wilder—Pulchid, perhaps? And then there was the boy closest to Theodin, whose dark eyes glinted with an intensity that felt… ancient, as though his young frame carried something far older within it.

Ophelia clenched her hands tighter, trying to ground herself. She'd grown up with her brother, whose steadfast presence had always anchored her, and later with Lady Vivian, who had taught her to sense and respect the differences in others. But here, surrounded by so many energies at once, she felt untethered.

She glanced down, her fingers brushing against the hem of her cloak. For a moment, her mind wandered back to the farm—her father hunched over a book at the kitchen table, her mother humming as she kneaded dough, and her brother chasing her through the fields with a grin that lit up his face. It had been a simple life, quiet and predictable, until the night everything changed.

Ophelia shook the memory away, blinking as the voices of the initiates drew her back to the present. Theodin was demonstrating a parry, his movements crisp and controlled. The children mimicked him, though most lacked his precision. One boy tripped and fell, earning a stern word from Theodin and a gruff chuckle from Kaspar, who stood at the edge of the clearing.

Her gaze drifted again, this time toward the horizon, where the woods loomed dark and quiet. She shivered. Whatever Theodin had found earlier, it was still out there. Watching. Waiting.

"Enjoying the show?" a voice broke through her thoughts.

Ophelia turned to see Kaspar watching her with an observant look. She hesitated, unsure how to respond. "They're… different," she said softly, her eyes flicking back to the children. "Not all of them are human. Some are not fully human and some are not fully one thing."

Kaspar nodded, his expression unreadable. "Most of the Kyriegard aren't. The world isn't as simple as human versus non-human, lass. You'd do well to remember that."

"I know," Ophelia said quickly. "It's just… strange. Feeling it all at once."

Kaspar's gaze softened slightly. "You'll get used to it," he said. "For now, keep watching. You'll learn more by observing than you will by dwelling in your own head."

The initiates had begun sparring under Theodin's watchful eye, their wooden swords clacking against each other in uneven rhythms. Some were better than others—more precise, more controlled—but all carried a determination that reminded Ophelia of her brother. She watched silently, trying to ignore the lingering fluctuation of energies pressing at the edges of her senses.

Then, it came.

A low rustle in the trees, faint enough to be dismissed as wind. Ophelia stiffened, her frantic eyes snapping toward the woods. The vibrations of the non-human energies around her made it hard to focus, but this was different—piercing, jagged, and wrong. Her fingers tightened around the hem of her cloak as a chill ran down her spine.

Kaspar noticed her shift immediately. "What is it?" he asked quietly, his gaze following hers.

"I don't know," she whispered. "Something… moved."

Kaspar frowned, his hand drifting to the hilt of his sword. "Stay here."

He stepped forward, motioning for Theodin to stop. Theodin caught the signal and lowered his sword, his eyes narrowing as he scanned the edge of the clearing. The initiates paused, their chatter dying as the air grew heavy with unspoken tension.

"What's going on?" one of the older girls asked with a trembling voice.

"Quiet," Theodin snapped. He moved toward Kaspar, his hand resting on the hilt of his blade. "What did you see?"

"Not me," Kaspar murmured, nodding toward Ophelia. "Her."

Theodin's eyes flicked to Ophelia. "What did you see?"

"I… I didn't see anything," she admitted. "But I felt it."

Theodin clenched his jaw, but before he could respond, another rustle came—closer this time. The children huddled together, their fear palpable, and Ophelia's head snapped toward the sound. The disturbing energy grew stronger, prickling at her skin like nettles.

"It's coming," she breathed.

The woods seemed to exhale as the presence emerged. At first, it was only a shadow, slipping between the trees like smoke. Then came the sound—a low, guttural growl that made the air vibrate. The initiates froze, their wide eyes fixed on the dark figure creeping closer.

It stepped into the clearing, its form misshapen and grotesque. Its body was hunched and limbs too long, its skin mottled with a sickly gray sheen. Its eyes glowed faintly, an unnatural light that sent a jolt of fear through Ophelia's chest.

"A cadaven," Kaspar muttered, his voice low. He drew his sword, the blade catching the dim light. "Theodin."

Theodin didn't wait for an order. His sword was in his hand in an instant, his movements fluid as he positioned himself between the creature and the children. "Get them back to the cottage," he said over his shoulder.

Kaspar nodded, his gaze never leaving the cadaven. "Ophelia, go with them."

Ophelia hesitated, her eyes locked on the creature. She could feel its presence now, dark and pulsing like a festering wound. Her hands twitched at her sides, the instinct to act warring with the fear coursing through her. Green light sparked between her fingers.

"Now!" Kaspar barked.

The monstrous, human-like figure of the cadaven stepped further into the clearing, its body limping unnaturally as though its joints were bending the wrong way. Its glowing eyes scanned the initiates, who shrank back behind Theodin. They were frozen with terror, eyes and mouths wide open.

"This… isn't right," Kaspar muttered, his hand tightening on the hilt of his dagger. "Cadaven are domesticated civilians…they don't behave like this anymore—not since Malcifer's fall."

"It's possessed," Theodin said through gritted teeth. "Something's controlling it."

Kaspar nodded grimly. "A Warthrall, most likely. Stay sharp."

The cadaven let out a guttural snarl, its clawed hand scraping against the ground as it lunged forward. Theodin reacted instantly, stepping between the creature and the children, his blade flashing as he parried the strike. Sparks flew as metal met bone, the impact sending a jolt up his arm.

"Move them back!" Theodin barked at Kaspar.

But Kaspar didn't move. His gray eyes scanned the treeline, his expression darkening. "It's not alone," he said quietly.

A shadow emerged from the woods—something like the shape of an elongated man but cloaked in a black shroud over its head and body. Its twisted, spectral form hovered just above the ground, and its eyes glowed with malevolent energy as it extended a bony hand toward the cadaven.

Kaspar stepped forward, his blade glinting in the pale morning light. "Theodin, handle the cadaven. I'll take the Warthrall."

Theodin nodded, gripping his sword tighter as the cadaven lunged again. This time, he dodged, spinning low and slicing across its side. The creature shrieked, but it didn't fall. Its muck of flesh and skin slicked back together with black ooze, like a rotting adhesive. Bones cracked and reconfigured, and then its hand and forearm split off into a large, claw-like limb. Theodin and the cadaven circled one another then, waiting for an opening to strike.

Kaspar moved with experienced precision and a flow to his step as he approached the Warthrall. It hissed, its form distorting as it lashed out with an arc of dark energy. Kaspar raised his sword, deflecting the attack with a thrust of white light. The energy dissipated, but the force sent him sliding back a step. Relentlessly, it flew at him again, wildly shrieking as it struck over and over, the elder Kyriegard expertly blocking each blow.

Ophelia stood frozen at the edge of the clearing, her heart pounding as she watched the battle unfold. The hum of energies in the air grew louder, more chaotic, as the Warthrall's presence filled the clearing. She could feel it—the darkness, the corruption—it pressed against her senses, suffocating and vile.

Another cadaven shot out from the underbrush—a second one with an animalistic body, wolf-like, leaner and faster than the first. It moved like a predator on all fours before rearing up, jagged teeth snapping in the cold air. Its rotted face was peeled back to bone on one side, and its clawed hand glistened with some foul residue.

Its black eyes whipped to Ophelia and the children.

Ophelia couldn't move, staring like prey at the mercy of its vicious predator.

The children screamed.

"Theodin!"

"Kaspar!"

"Help!"

It all happened too fast for Ophelia to see clearly.

The moment it sprinted at them, Theodin barreled into it from the side, intercepting the attack with a shoulder-check and blade.

But the humanoid cadaven took advantage of this.

As soon as Theodin regained his footing, it tackled him and grappled him with its claw. The cadaven hound rolled over and leapt at him—its teeth snapped at sank into his shoulder.

A pained grunt escaped him.

"Agh!"

Ophelia reached for him. Her eyes flashed and her fingertips sparked with green. "No—!"

Theodin kicked away the cadaven hound and slashed at the humanoid one.

"*Stay back,* Valksha!" he hollered.

Then he swung his sword at the two cadaven without hesitation. They snarled dangerously, backing off, once again forced to be at a distance and searching for their next opening. But Theodin didn't give them the chance—he charged at them.

Helpless screams erupted from the children. They shakily held up their wooden swords as they were taught to, but many were still too young to fight.

The initiates huddled behind her, their fear palpable. One of the younger children clung to her cloak, quivering. Ophelia's hands trembled as she glanced between Kaspar and Theodin. They were fighting so fiercely, so expertly—but now they were outnumbered. And the Warthrall wasn't finished.

The spectral creature raised its clawed hand again, this time directing its attack at Theodin. A jagged spear of shadow hurtled toward him, too fast to dodge.

"*Stop!*" Ophelia cried, her voice ringing through the clearing.

Before Theodin could react, a bloom of green light erupted in front of him. The spear of shadow collided with the light, shattering into harmless fragments that dissolved into the air.

The Warthrall shrieked again, this time with a tormented cry.

Theodin blinked, his eyes snapping to Ophelia.

She stood stiffly, her hands outstretched, emerald tendrils still fading from her fingers. Her face was pale, her chest rising and falling with shallow breaths. The light then vanished as quickly as it had appeared, leaving behind an eerie silence.

Theodin's knuckles whitened around his hilt as he turned back to the enemy. The Warthrall had recoiled, its form flickering as if weakened by the light. Its original humanly form almost appeared to be taking shape. Both cadaven staggered back, grotesque bodies shuddering. But they weren't gone. Not yet.

That wasn't supposed to happen, Theodin thought. But it happened again. The girl used magic without blood. Valksha magic needed blood —that much he knew. Lady Vivian had said as much in her teachings. Their powers didn't just… manifest. Not without intent. Not without control.

But this hadn't been deliberate. He could see it in her wide, panicked eyes. Whatever had just happened, it was raw, instinctive—wild, even.

And that made it dangerous.

Ophelia nearly hyperventilated. She staggered slightly from the outburst, but she maintained her stance. She waved the children away. "Go, go!" she yelled. With that, they all fled in panic to the cottage.

The Warthrall and the two cadaven turned their attention to the Valksha girl. Their dark energies spiked and prickled her senses, making her dizzy with adrenaline and fear.

With their foes distracted by her, the Kyriegard master and his apprentice took their chance to strike.

Kaspar moved first, his sword flashing as he lunged toward the Warthrall. The creature screeched, its form rippling as it tried to twist away, but Kaspar's strike was precise. His blade connected with the flickering outline of the Warthrall's torso, sending an explosion of white light through its shadowy body. The creature howled, its spectral energy scattering like ash in the wind. Its form split apart in different directions away from Kaspar and formed together again up in the air.

Theodin darted toward the humanoid cadaven, his sword arching in a wide, calculated slash. The undead creature's arm came up to block, but its misshapen limbs were slower than Theodin's blade. The strike cleaved through its forearm with a sickening crunch, sending the grotesque limb tumbling to the ground. The cadaven bellowed, its glowing eyes locking onto Theodin with murderous intent.

"Stay on them!" Kaspar commanded. He charged at the black shape that retreated from him. "Don't let them recover!"

The Warthrall shrieked once more, this time raising a clawed hand toward Ophelia. She stumbled back, her legs trembling as the creature's attention locked onto her.

It rushed at her.

Time slowed.

A hungry whisper hissed from its throat.

"Valkshaaaaaa..."

Her eyes darted to Theodin, who was locked in combat, and Kaspar sprinting to her rescue.

She was alone. The sharp, prickling aura of the Warthrall wore down on her.

Her breath quickened. Her instincts screamed at her to run, but she couldn't move. The oppressive weight of the dark magic pressed against her chest, making it hard to breathe.

Hastily, she dug into her satchel. She felt for her little knife and clumsily allowed it to slice her skin and draw blood.

The Warthrall's claw slashed through the air, its spectral energy tearing toward her.

She squeezed her eyes shut and let out a scream of terror, throwing her hands up to defend herself. Her fingers clenched into fists, and the green light burst forth again, brighter this time. It swirled around her like a protective barrier, the vibrant energy pushing back against the Warthrall's dark magic.

The creature recoiled, its form flickering wildly as the green light struck it. The rupture of power was raw and instinctive, but this time Ophelia felt a degree of control. The oppressive energy in the air began to lift, replaced by a sense of balance—however fleeting.

Kaspar's blade, enveloped in a white light, once again pierced into the Warthrall's back. It arched back and let out a piercing scream.

Simultaneously, Theodin lunged forward, his sword slicing through the humanoid cadaven's knee, sending the creature crashing to the ground. It writhed, its glowing eyes dimming as it struggled to rise. In another smooth motion, as the cadaven hound jumped at him—Theodin spun and slashed its side. With a thud, it collided with the ground and rolled onto the grass.

The Warthrall hissed, its flickering form retreating into the shadows of the treeline. Even as it fled, its movements seemed deliberate, as though relaying what it had observed. This wasn't just an attack—it was reconnaissance.

Both cadaven, weakened and dismembered, let out one last guttural snarl before collapsing into heaps. The clearing fell silent, save for the sound of heavy breathing and the faint hum of Ophelia's fading magic.

Kaspar lowered his sword, his gaze fixed on the treeline where the Warthrall had disappeared. "They'll be back," he said grimly. "That wasn't their full force. This was just the beginning."

Theodin stepped back from the cadaven's corpse, his eyes flicking toward Ophelia. She stood frozen in place, her hands still flickering with a dying light.

She doesn't know what she's doing, he thought, his stare hardening as his eyes lingered on Ophelia. That kind of power—uncontrolled, untrained—was as much a threat to Theodin and Kaspar as it was to the Warthrall and cadaven.

Yet, it felt familiar. The raw, unchecked power—he remembered what it was like to fear his own strength, to wonder if he was more of a danger to his allies than his enemies.

He sheathed his sword with a sharp click, his jaw tightening. This wasn't just about protecting her anymore. It was about figuring out whether she could protect them—or if she'd be the one to tear them apart.

Her rapid breaths broke his thoughts. She stared distantly at the edge of the woods.

"Ophelia," Theodin said, his voice snapping her out of it. "It's over."

Her eyes met his, and the green light around her hands flickered once more before fading entirely. She swayed on her feet, her legs giving out beneath her. Theodin caught her just before she hit the ground, his arm steady and strong as it slipped around her shoulders.

"Easy," he murmured, his voice low but grounding.

Ophelia's breath hitched at the touch. She hadn't expected it—his grip was firm but unintrusive, a quiet strength holding her upright. But there was more than just the physical contact. The moment his hand steadied her, she felt it.

His energy.

It was subtle at first, a current that resonated beneath the surface. But then it surged, sharp and vivid, cutting through the haze of her exhaustion. It wasn't like Lady Vivian's energy, which was calming and warm like sunlight on a winter's day. This was different—jarring and untamed, like a storm rolling just below the horizon. She could feel his energy's layers: a hardened resolve honed by years of discipline, a guarded ferocity that shielded something deeper, and a quiet loneliness that sat heavy beneath it all.

She stiffened instinctively, her pulse quickening. The touch wasn't unpleasant, but it was overwhelming. A flood of sensation that left her breathless. It was as if she'd stepped too close to the edge of a cliff, the wind tugging her forward while her instincts screamed to pull back.

"Ophelia," Theodin said again, his eyes narrowing as he peered down at her. His voice carried a note of concern, but his grip on her arm remained steady. "You with me?"

She nodded quickly, though the motion felt weak. "I'm fine," she huffed, though the words came out in a rasp. She forced herself to look away, to focus on anything other than the intensity of his gaze or the energy coursing through his touch. But it remained, crackling at the edges of her awareness like static. The rush of his energy and the exhaustion made her dizzy.

Theodin frowned, his hand shifting slightly as he adjusted his hold to pull her upright. His energy surged again, and she fought the urge to flinch. She wondered then if he knew what she felt.

Her legs wobbled, and he tightened his grip just enough to balance her without overpowering her. "You're stronger than you think," he said softly, his voice low enough that only she could hear.

Ophelia blinked, startled by the sincerity in his tone. The green light in her hands had vanished entirely, but the memory of its flicker—and the weight of his words—lingered.

"I..." she started, her voice faltering. She didn't know what to say or do with the storm of emotions threatening to overwhelm her. Instead, she stepped back, slipping free of his grasp. "Thank you," she whispered, not meeting his eyes.

Theodin's expression darkened slightly, his frown deepening as he watched her retreat. His gaze flicked over her briefly, searching for something he couldn't name. Then, with a soft exhale, he stepped back and turned toward Kaspar.

Ophelia barely noticed. Her heart was still racing, her skin tingling where his hand had been. She clenched her fists at her sides, willing herself to focus. But the storm of his energy—and the strange pull it seemed to have on her—refused to fade.

Her eyes fell to Theodin's shoulder where punctures had been pierced in his overcoat from the cadaven's teeth. Beneath it, his tunic became soaked with blood.

She reached for him with her still-bleeding finger.

"You're...hurt," she murmured.

But Theodin didn't react.

No flinch. No wince. Just the faint hitch of breath before his eyes settled on hers—hard, unreadable. The pain didn't register at all—not in his eyes, not in the way he held himself.

A drop of her blood evaporated into the air, and instinct answered. A thin tendril of green light coiled from her fingertip to his wound, drawn like a thread of silk in moonlight. The moment it touched him, the magic flared—not violent, but sharp and swift, as if stitching him closed from within. His tunic parted slightly, revealing torn flesh beneath, dark and slick with blood.

Ophelia gasped. The gashes were deeper than she'd thought—ripped through skin and muscle, dangerously close to his rib.

But Theodin still didn't flinch.

The green light shimmered brighter for a heartbeat, then dulled as the skin beneath stitched closed. Not fully. Just enough to stop the bleeding. She could still see the bruising, already blackening the flesh.

His breath hitched once, sharply, and then steadied. His eyes met hers—hard, unreadable.

"You …didn't have to do that," he muttered.

Ophelia's eyes fell into a slight daze.

"You…were losing…a lot of blood," she slurred slightly. Her knees began to buckle again.

Kaspar's hand found her arm to hold her.

"Easy, lass. You've already overexerted yourself."

"S…Sorry."

The clearing fell quiet—not peace, but a silence thick with the stench of battle and the weight of unanswered questions.

The cadaven remains lay still, one grotesque body slumped against the damp earth and the other already rotting away nearby. The Warthrall's presence left an unnatural chill in the air.

Kaspar scanned the treeline, his sword still in hand and his sharp gray eyes narrowed as he studied the area.

"This doesn't make sense," he muttered. "They shouldn't have gotten this close."

"What do you mean?" Theodin asked, his voice tight as he sheathed his sword.

"The grass," Kaspar said, motioning toward the clearing. "Every property in Olysgard is enchanted. The long grass should've stopped them before they even got near Avasylon. The wardstones would've alerted us."

Ophelia's tired eyes flicked toward the edge of the clearing, where the ground dipped into a stretch of open dirt and sparse patches of grass. "But… it didn't," she said quietly.

Kaspar's expression darkened. "No, it didn't. I didn't think it was possible…" His voice trailed off, his gaze shifting toward the cadaven's remains. "Something disrupted the magic…" His tone became heavy with unease. He knelt near the bare ground, brushing his fingers against the dirt. "This wasn't a coincidence. The enchantment was weakened here. That kind of precision… it means someone is guiding them."

Theodin frowned, his eyes sweeping the clearing. "The Warthrall?"

"Possibly," Kaspar said. "They're capable of more than just controlling cadaven. If it's strong enough, it could've neutralized the enchantment—at least in this area."

"It could attack again," Theodin said grimly.

Kaspar scanned the treeline once more, as if expecting the shadows to move again. When they didn't, he turned to Theodin and Ophelia. "We're not staying here," he said flatly. "Not after that."

Theodin nodded, though his eyes flicked to Ophelia, who was still unsteady on her feet. She had pulled away from him moments ago, but the strange buzz of his energy still clung to her skin. It dwelled in her thoughts, unsettling and persistent.

"Where will we go?" Ophelia asked wearily. She was trying to appear composed, but Theodin could see the way her hands shivered slightly as she brushed them against her cloak. Her small frame wavered slightly with exhaustion, like she could collapse any second, but she fought it.

"Halvalla," Kaspar said decisively. "The Council needs to hear about this, and you'll be safer under their protection. No Warthrall would dare strike that close to the Order's seat. If the Warthrall could somehow breach Avasylon's defenses, it means we're no longer dealing with random attacks. This is organized."

"The initiates—" Theodin started, glancing toward the cottage where the younger trainees had been sent to shelter.

"They'll be sent home to Havysium," Kaspar interrupted.

"They'll be safe on the way?" Ophelia asked.

Theodin pointed west. "We will be with them. Havysium is on the way to Halvalla. Thirty minutes at a brisk pace to Havysium, another thirty to Halvalla."

"Avasylon's defenses will hold if anything else comes. But we don't have time to waste. We need to speak with the Council."

He then turned to his towering apprentice and the much smaller Valksha girl. "But you two?" His sharp gray eyes settled on Ophelia. "You need to be somewhere safer."

Theodin crossed his arms, his jaw tightening. "Safer?" he echoed. "Would we be safer with her magic?"

Ophelia flinched, her eyes flicking to him, wide with surprise and something that looked like hurt.

"I didn't mean for it to happen," she said quickly, her words tumbling out. "I don't even know how it happened."

Theodin's frown deepened. "That's the problem," he said bluntly. "You don't know your own power. You could've killed that Warthrall before it got away. And if you lose control again—"

"Theodin," Kaspar cut in, his tone sharp enough to make the younger man fall silent. "Enough. May I remind you she saved you just now from a Warthrall?"

Kaspar then leaned in closer. His stare became cold.

"She's not the only one who's struggled with control."

Theodin glanced away, his eyes hardening as he stared at the ground.

Ophelia bit her lip, her hands clenching at her sides. "I want to learn," she said quietly, her voice firm despite its softness. "I want to control it. Please… let me try."

Kaspar studied her for a long moment. Finally, he nodded. "You'll get your chance," he said. "But not here. We leave at first light."

As Kaspar walked back toward the cottage, muttering about supplies, Theodin stayed where he was, his gaze fixed on Ophelia. She stood still, her shoulders tense, her hands fidgeting with the hem of her cloak. The green light that had once flickered in her hands was gone, but its memory was vivid in his mind.

She's stronger than she looks, he thought, though he didn't know if that was comforting or troubling. His fingers flexed at his sides, the phantom sensation of her energy still sparking faintly against his skin. It wasn't like anything he'd felt before—not from Kaspar, not from the other Kyriegard. It was raw, powerful, and wild.

For a moment, he thought about saying something—acknowledging the determination in her voice, the way she had stood her ground despite her fear. But the words didn't come. Instead, he turned and followed Kaspar, leaving her alone in the clearing.

Chapter 5

The Blade and the Flame

Havysium rose from the hills like a scar turned sanctuary—weathered, functional, and alive with purpose. It didn't flaunt its legacy like Halvalla did. There were no marble columns or gleaming halls. Just stone buildings, patched roofs, and chalk-smeared slates. But it held weight.

The barracks lined the eastern edge, where the youngest initiates shared their sleepless nights and whispered fears beneath threadbare blankets. Though Theodin never lived this himself, he would overhear the initiates speak of it when they came to train at Avasylon.

At the center stood the Main Hall, always echoing with laughter, arguments, the clatter of trays and training swords. To the west, the classrooms—lessons in history, tactics, runework. Always half-heard through open windows, always too short.

And the Observatory. Theodin had spent a winter there once, chasing constellations and formulas he didn't understand. Its dome of rune-laced glass shimmered faintly in the sun, the pulse of celestial magic woven into every seam. Beautiful, but impractical. He hadn't stepped foot inside it since.

A single wardstone stood near the entrance—small, but powerful. It buzzed faintly with old enchantments, refreshed often by the resident Sages. Theodin always checked it in passing. Still holding. Still safe.

For now.

It wasn't a fortress. But it was the first place any of them belonged, except for Theodin.

He remembered being one of those children—mud on his boots, fire in his chest, a sword too heavy for his hands. He'd watched the older Kyriegard with something between reverence and fury. But as far back as he could remember, he belonged first to Avasylon with Kaspar, and was raised there. Beneath the wings of the Head of the Order.

Avasylon had never been breached. It disturbed Theodin. Was it because of Lady Vivian's arrival? No—Lady Vivian had been to Avasylon a number of times.

Perhaps it was the Valksha girl. Lady Vivian said the Warthralls were after her.

By the time the last child stepped through Havysium's gates, the sun was nearing its noonday peak in the sky. It felt later.

The younger initiates had been unusually quiet for the walk back. They clutched their practice blades close, eyes drifting again and again to the girl walking just ahead of them. Ophelia. The Valksha. Some of them had only ever read about her kind. Others had seen small acts of magic and Sagely casting—candles flickering, Sage runes glowing, Arcane Dyad bonds activating between seasoned Kyriegard—but never like this. Never someone their age blooming with that much power, that much light.

They'd watched her from the windows of the cottage that morning. No one said it aloud, but he'd caught the whispers—awed, anxious. She'd saved them. But that didn't make her less frightening.

He understood.

Magic fascinated him, but it didn't comfort him. Not like a blade did. A sword never struck without his consent. It didn't react to his fears or desires, didn't unravel at the whim of emotion.

Magic wasn't like that. Magic answered to emotion. It listened. Sometimes it obeyed. Sometimes it didn't.

And she was full of it.

She hadn't even been here two days and she somehow affected him. Every time their eyes locked, since the moment she arrived, something sparked. Not desire—Theodin was too disciplined to have such fleeting feelings—but something electric. Like her emotions reached through her skin and stirred things in him he didn't want stirred. He'd felt that surge when she healed his wound. When she collapsed into him. When her voice cracked trying to steady the children.

It wasn't just her magic that shook him.

It wasn't just her strength. It was something beneath it. A frequency that resonated too closely with his own.

It wasn't weakness, what she had.

It was *too much.*

Too raw.

And too damn close.

He clenched his jaw as Halvalla's towers crested over the horizon. Perhaps the Kyriegard Council could examine her and determine proper protocol for someone like her.

She needed to learn control.

Or she'd tear them all apart.

Kaspar walked ahead in silence. Theodin followed just behind, flanking Ophelia to her left, their steps falling in strange rhythm.

She said little during the walk from Havysium, though now and again, he'd catch her glancing toward him when she thought he wasn't looking. Her face was still pale. She hadn't fully recovered from the strain of her outburst. Her hands, wrapped now in thin bandages, occasionally twitched at her sides.

They said little at first, only the sound of boots crunching over dry soil and the distant caw of a duskbird overhead. The trees thinned as they left Havysium's perimeter, and the wind shifted—brisker now, sharp with autumn's edge.

"She'll hold," Kaspar said suddenly, as if plucking the thought from Theodin's head.

Theodin didn't answer right away. He glanced at the girl again next to him—Ophelia's steps were careful, measured. Still upright, though she swayed now and then like someone walking through the echo of a dream.

"I'm not so sure," he said. "She nearly collapsed again before we reached the gate."

Ophelia's attention fluttered to Theodin with a small grimace.

"I meant Avasylon," Kaspar clarified.

Theodin frowned. "You really think it's still secure?"

"Enough," Kaspar said. "The cottage entrance is the only access point to the lower sanctum. Lady Vivian reinforced it when she brought you here."

Theodin's brow lifted. "You never told the Council that."

"They would've objected," Kaspar said simply. "They didn't want Valksha magic involved in Olysgard's wards. Said it would violate neutrality. But she insisted for your safety. I trusted her."

"So only the outer perimeter is compromised," Ophelia said softly.

Both of them glanced at her.

"Aye, lass," Kaspar answered. "The cottage itself is still guaranteed to be safe. That's why the initiates sheltered there during the attack."

Theodin mulled on that a moment, casting a glance toward the east where Avasylon lay hidden beyond the hills. "You think the Warthrall knew?"

"Possibly. But even then, they struck at the weakest edge. Not the sanctum itself. Whatever's coming… it's not here yet. And if they do come, they'll find more than a cottage waiting."

He said it with finality.

Theodin exhaled slowly, nodding once. His mind drifted again to the battle. To how Kaspar's sword moved with white light and surety… to how his own had strained against the brute force of the cadaven. They'd won, but barely. And only because—

His eyes flicked to Ophelia.

Without her, the initiates would've died.

Still, he couldn't shake it. That power. That light. It hadn't been conjured by study or discipline. It had erupted. Wild. Untamed.

"That wasn't a fair fight," he muttered.

Kaspar raised an eyebrow. "We're still standing."

"Because no one there was in a Dyad," Theodin pressed. "Not me. Not you. If we'd been up against a full battalion—"

"Then we'd be dead," Kaspar said bluntly.

"And next time?"

Kaspar's gaze turned ahead, grim. "Then we make damn sure we're not caught off guard."

Theodin nodded, jaw tightening. "I need to be paired," he muttered.

"You can't rush the process, lad," Kaspar remarked.

"A Dyad," Ophelia suddenly said. "Do you mean the Arcane Dyad?"

Theodin slowed a half-step. Her voice had cut through the quiet with surprising clarity, even though it was soft.

He didn't answer right away.

That term—Arcane Dyad—was not often spoken by those outside the Order. Certainly not by girls like her. Not strangers. Not Valksha. The Dyad was rarely known by any outsiders only by its physical manifestation through runic markings in the skin, but never by name.

"How do you know that term?" Theodin asked cautiously.

She hesitated. "Lady Vivian told me. Years ago. In passing."

Of course she did. He frowned, glancing away. Lady Vivian had been Kaspar's closest ally for decades—trusted in ways the Council never fully approved of. She had known the Order's inner workings better than most, even if she'd never sworn their oaths. That she'd spoken of the Dyad to Ophelia…it made something tighten in his chest.

Theodin exhaled. "It's a bond," he said finally. "Between two Kyriegard. A ritual one. Once formed, it links their magic. Their senses. Their strength. For as long as they live—or until one of them dies."

Ophelia's brow furrowed slightly. "So it's not just symbolic?"

He shook his head. "No. It's… invasive. Intimate. Complete. Partners can feel each other's pain. Their thoughts, sometimes. Their emotions. Their instincts. They fight as one."

She was quiet for a moment. He could feel her processing it—like a pressure in the air between them.

"But not everyone forms one?" she asked.

"No," he said. "You have to be compatible. The Council approves the tests. Sometimes it takes years. Some Kyriegard never form a Dyad at all."

Her gaze dropped. "And you?"

Theodin stared ahead. "I've been tested. Several times."

Kaspar, mercifully, did not interrupt.

"And?" Ophelia pressed gently.

"They never held," he muttered. "Too volatile. Too mismatched. The connection wouldn't stabilize."

Or worse—it had rejected him. That part he didn't say.

"The bond can't be forced," he added. "It's not just about skill or strength. It's about resonance. Like two voices that either harmonize… or clash."

Ophelia was quiet again, but he could feel her watching him. He didn't know why he was telling her this. Maybe it was the way she listened—like every word mattered. Or maybe it was the fact that her presence unsettled him so much already, and silence would've only made it worse.

She tilted her head. "But if emotions can affect magic…couldn't it be dangerous to be in a bond like that?"

Internally, Theodin almost laughed to himself at how uncanny her comment was to his belief about magic. It was the same fear he carried, dressed in her voice. The same reason he trusted steel over spellwork.

She saw it too—and that unsettled him more than he cared to admit.

"It can be," he admitted. "That's why it's not taken lightly. Once the Dyad is sealed, you carry that person's soul next to yours. Their grief. Their rage. Their joy. All of it."

She looked forward again. "That's… a lot."

He didn't reply.

Because it was.

And it was why he had never passed.

Because no one had ever matched him.

"But it is acceptable for the process to take time," Kaspar suddenly interjected. "It is better for a Dyad to form in the best scenario possible, with the best match."

Ophelia glanced at Kaspar. "Are you in a Dyad?"

Kaspar shook his head. "No. The Head of the Order is not in a Dyad in order to maintain an absolute neutral stance and unbiased position on the Council."

He used to be in one, Theodin thought to himself, but that was not for Ophelia to know.

"The Kyriegard Council," Ophelia confirmed.

Kaspar nodded. "I will tell the Council what happened today. We will decide upon what our next steps will be regarding these circumstances. But they need to understand: this wasn't random. It was reconnaissance. That Warthrall had a purpose—a malicious one."

They crossed into Halvalla's perimeter an hour past noon. The grass here rose tall and wild, thick with the enchantments of Kyriegard Sages—no sign of the disruption that had nearly cost them at Avasylon. Here, the wards held.

The massive gates of Halvalla loomed ahead, their iron surface etched with ancient runes that pulsed in the morning light. Ophelia stared up at them, her breath catching at the sheer scale of the fortress. The walls stretched high into the mist, the gray stone glinting where dew clung to the surface.

"Impressive, isn't it?" Theodin said, his voice breaking the silence. His eyes flicked to Ophelia, but his tone carried no warmth—only a wary observation.

She nodded silently, clutching the strap of her satchel as they approached. The energy here was different—denser, heavier, almost oppressive. It pressed against her senses, making it hard to focus. She shivered and glanced at Kaspar, who walked ahead with the steady purpose of someone who had crossed these gates countless times.

The courtyard beyond the gates stretched wide with its cobblestone paths flanked by towering stone spires that seemed to pierce the clouds. Enchanted banners bearing the sigil of the Kyriegard rippled in the wind, their edges glowing with protective wards. Kyriegard members bustled about as their dark cloaks trailed behind them as they moved with quiet efficiency.

Ophelia's gaze flickered to the rows of statues lining the courtyard. Each one was a larger-than-life figure of a Kyriegard hero from ages past. Their stone eyes seemed to follow her, and she couldn't shake the feeling of being watched. Even the air was heavier than it had been at Avasylon, thick with layers of history and magic. Every step felt like an intrusion.

The group stopped at a smaller door set into the base of one of the spires.

Two wardens greeted Kaspar with formal nods, their eyes briefly flicking toward Ophelia with curiosity. A few apprentices near the entrance paused mid-conversation to watch them pass. It was subtle, but Theodin saw it—the way they studied her.

Something had shifted in the air. They all felt it.

Kaspar finally slowed his steps and turned toward them. "You two head to the guest wing," he said, his tone clipped with authority. "I'll speak with the Council first."

Theodin gave a curt nod.

Kaspar's eyes narrowed slightly as he looked between them. "Keep her out of sight until the Council is ready. Understood?"

"Yes, sir," Theodin answered.

Kaspar left them without another word, his cloak catching the wind as he strode toward the inner sanctum.

Theodin turned to Ophelia. She looked smaller than before—not physically, but somehow diminished in presence. Not broken. Just quiet. Hollowed out by exhaustion.

"This way," he said, not unkindly.

She followed.

They passed through two long corridors of limestone and glass, the polished floors whispering under their boots. The guest wing was quiet, isolated from the central chambers, a place meant for those who did not yet belong but could not be turned away.

He stopped at the second door on the left and pushed it open.

The room inside was modest but warm. A single bed, a writing desk, a basin for washing, and a narrow window overlooking Halvalla's southern hillside. The wards hummed in low resonance in the walls—a constant reminder that even here, magic watched.

He stepped aside to let her in.

"I'll stay here," he said, resting one hand lightly on the doorframe.

Ophelia nodded and stepped past him into the room. She looked around with wide, curious eyes, fidgeting with the strap of her satchel.

Theodin stepped in and shut the door behind himself. She turned to him.

"How long will we be here, do you think?" Ophelia asked.

Theodin shrugged. "That depends on the Council. Sometimes they are quick, but often, they are not. You may see them tonight or tomorrow."

"But...It's not an urgent matter? This Warthrall breach of Avasylon?"

"It is..." Theodin's voice trailed off and became punctuated by a frustrated exhale. "But sometimes their debates can take hours to come to a conclusive decision."

"I would've assumed that they'd come to those decisions quickly if this concerned the safety of Avasylon," Ophelia remarked. "Especially with Arborelys."

Theodin froze. She knew about Arborelys.

Dammit, Kaspar.

Ophelia appeared to read his expression like he was an open book.

"Lady Vivian told me about it."

Of course she did.

"I'm aware that it's not common knowledge," she added. "But she's not going around and telling everyone your precious secrets—and neither am I." She paced to the window and looked out of it with fascination. "Though we have very different lifestyles, we believe in the same things and want the same things for Moirand. We have common enemies."

"Is that what she told you too?" Theodin asked.

"Yes," she answered timidly, glancing at him over her shoulder. "She has the utmost respect for the Kyriegard, and they respect her. Nimrod is aware of the rules and that sometimes he must break them." She turned to him fully, now fidgeting with her fingers. "Like...when he took you in, yes?"

Theodin became quiet for a moment. His eyes hardened slightly.

Ophelia lifted her hands up defensively. "If you must know, she did not say much about you other than that Nimrod raised you himself and that you were his apprentice."

Theodin still said nothing. Ophelia cleared her throat and walked over to the bed to sit on the edge of it.

"Arborelys," she began, carefully, "is quite intriguing, isn't it?"

"How much do you know?" Theodin asked.

Ophelia paused, looking off thoughtfully and with consideration. "I know that it's the source of the Order's Collective. It's…this *tree* in the lower sanctum of Avasylon, in the enchanted vault." She made an image of a tree with her forearms and fingers. "It originated from combining the magic of the Order's five founders, and now it serves to connect all those in the Order. Not the soul-binding kind, like the Arcane Dyad—though, it's involved in that process in a separate ritual, from my understanding." She gestured a pinching motion with her fingers. "Just a small tether. Enough to access the Collective only in absolute dire circumstances."

She spoke like a living textbook, Theodin thought. His hardened gaze eased a bit, though he wasn't sure why he did. Maybe it was because she treated such knowledge so clinically, yet with respect and care.

"It's truly fascinating," she continued, lowering her hand. She appeared more comfortable now than she did the night before or this morning. "You know…just the concept alone of Arborelys is incredible. No Sage Circle has been able to replicate it. I think if the Valksha were to do something like that, maybe…" She scrunched her nose in thought. "Maybe they'd bring a Saryf back or something, I don't know."

"Rumor is that happened with Zadkiel the Headstrong, Saryf of Strength and Will," Theodin muttered.

Ophelia sighed and nodded. "That is the rumor…when the Grigorescu family surrendered their power at the height of the Valksha Massacre and sealed it in the Medallion of Zadkiel. They say that Zadkiel became whole again and trapped in that artifact." She shook her head and placed her hands in her lap. "But it's only a rumor. The artifact has been lost for decades."

Theodin studied her in silence.

She wasn't flaunting her knowledge. Wasn't trying to impress him. She was just… speaking. Like it mattered. Like it *meant* something. Most initiates clung to facts for power or prestige. She spoke of sacred things like she'd truly cherished them.

And that unnerved him more than anything.

She wasn't even an initiate. She was an outsider.

Yet, she was different than anyone he'd ever met. She carried things differently. The power, the history…she didn't wear it like a weapon.

He turned, resting his shoulder against the stone wall beside the door. He kept his arms crossed, his posture composed.

"You know quite a bit," he muttered. "But I didn't expect that."

Ophelia blinked. "Expect what?"

"That you'd understand the Dyad. Or Arborelys. Or…" He gestured vaguely toward her. "Any of this."

She smiled faintly. "Neither did I."

They stood like that for a moment—two people from different worlds, but somehow finding common ground.

That electric hum in the air seemed to intensify between them as they stared at one another in silence.

Ophelia finally cleared her throat again, lowering her eyes. She shifted where she sat, slightly kicking her feet against the edge of the bed. "I, er…like to study and read," she began. "I like to learn." She let out a stiff chuckle and began fidgeting with her fingers once more. "Perhaps in a different life, I was supposed to be a Sage and not a Valksha."

"I'm certain your magic would be easier to control if you were a Sage," Theodin added.

Ophelia perked and clapped her hands once. "Precisely! But alas…" She rolled her hands then dramatically. "One of the few Valksha left in Moirand. A walking deadly explosion waiting to happen…though I'd like to get it under control."

"We will help you with that," Theodin said.

"I know," Ophelia sighed. She glanced up at him again and tilted her head to one side. "Though…I didn't see you fight or teach with magic today. You're a Sage warrior, aren't you?"

Theodin gave a short nod. "I am."

Ophelia's eyes lit with mild intrigue. "But I didn't see you use any spells earlier."

"That's because I didn't," he replied plainly.

She blinked, bewildered. "You're trained in Sage magic and you didn't use it? During that fight?"

He shrugged, his posture shifting just enough to suggest discomfort. "There wasn't time. Not the way I use it."

Ophelia tilted her head to the other side, waiting.

He hesitated. Then, with a quiet exhale, added, "I don't cast like most Sages. No fire from my hands. No walls of ice or sudden gusts of wind."

"What do you do then?"

"I plan," he said. "I prepare. Sage magic isn't just spectacle. It's enhancement. Reinforcement. Timing." He unhooked a small leather pouch from his belt and let it rest in his palm. "I keep herbal tinctures, defensive oils, salves. Potions I brewed myself. Runic stones and talismans I etched myself. I learned to lace my armor with wards. Coat my blade in elements."

Ophelia leaned forward slightly, eyes squinting with focused curiosity.

"I can dull pain for an hour. Slow blood loss. Even heighten reflexes for a few minutes—if I've brewed the right mixture beforehand," he continued. "I fight close. I don't have the luxury of long incantations in the middle of a melee."

"You're tactile," she said. "...Instinctive."

"I'm deliberate," he corrected. "Magic... is a tool. Not the battle itself. I train to be lethal without it, so if it fails, I still stand."

She fell quiet at that. Her expression was unreadable for a moment.

"You're like a living arsenal."

He snorted, just barely. "Something like that."

A beat.

"Lady Vivian once said true strength isn't about how much you can cast," Ophelia murmured. "It's how well you can choose when not to."

Theodin didn't reply, but the way his brow furrowed—ever so slightly—told her the words had landed.

Ophelia's gaze drifted to the narrow window. The hills outside glimmered faintly beneath the wardlight, untouched by the chaos from earlier. She rubbed her palms together absently, as if remembering the sear of power still thrumming under her skin.

"I think I envy that," she said softly.

Theodin didn't answer. He only watched her for a moment longer, the girl who spoke like a Sage but bled like a Valksha.

Chapter 6

The Kyriegard Council

Kaspar stood before the Council alone.

The chamber had not changed in all the years he'd stood within it.

Circular, monolithic, and carved into the living stone of Halvalla's inner sanctum, the room bore the weight of centuries in its bones. Stained-glass windows towered above, filtering the noonday sun into beams of colored fire that slanted across the floor in fractured halos. Every pane depicted moments of Kyriegard legend—sacrifice, glory, grief.

The round table at the center was forged of blackened ironwood, veined with ancient runes that pulsed faintly beneath the surface like a slumbering heart. Each of the five seats bore the sigil of a founding bloodline, carved so deep into the stone they would not fade even in ruin.

The floor beneath was smooth, worn by the tread of boots and vows alike. Kaspar's own footsteps had etched a familiar path in that stone—between his place at the chamber's entrance and the head of the table where judgment was given, where decisions were rarely fair but always final.

Above them, the domed ceiling shimmered with protective enchantments—an ever-shifting constellation of runes that responded to the presence of magic, glowing faintly whenever tensions rose.

It smelled of old ink and scorched parchment, of steel and ceremonial oil. And something colder beneath it all—like sanctity curdled into scrutiny.

This was not a place of comfort. It was a crucible.

And today, as he stepped inside once more, Kaspar felt its weight settle around his shoulders like a cloak dipped in stone.

Sigvard Jackard, a dwarf, sat at one end of the table. Though his stature was short, it was imposing. His sturdy frame was draped in the heavy black-and-silver cloak of the Kyriegard. Thick, corded muscle bulged beneath his robes. His dark, bushy beard was streaked with gold runes, and his eyes were deep-set, dark, and keen, always watching.

Beside him, Margrith Gravehardt sat straight-backed in her Kyriegard cloak, hawk-eyed and silent. Her piercing gaze flicked over Kaspar like a scalpel, dissecting every detail. She appeared human, but she was broad-shouldered and built like a warhorse, with the posture of someone who's seen too many battles to be impressed by anything. Her gray-streaked dark hair was cut short for practicality, her face lined with deep scars—one crossed her brow and gave her a menacing appearance.

Across from them, Alfena Marobe raised a silver brow, arms crossed over her elegant robes. Her features were pale-colored and pointed, matching her ears and unsettling stare. She was tall and slender, with sharp, angular features that made her look perpetually apathetic. Her hair was tightly braided and wound in a bun, not a strand out of place. She was the picture of psychic composure, though Kaspar had known her long enough to recognize the edge in her gaze.

And to her left, Azariah Crane reclined in his seat with a kind of absent grace, one hand toying with the chain around his wrist. His eyes, as always, gave nothing away. An older man with a cane, he was lean but wiry, with a noble bearing that didn't quite fit the hardened look in his eyes. His short-cropped, dark brown and gray hair was disheveled to match his wild stare, his posture rigid as if he'd always been prepared for a fight.

Kaspar placed his palms on the table.

"Warthrall incursion," he began. "Avasylon's outer wards were compromised shortly after dawn."

Margrith was the first to respond. "Casualties?"

"None. Two cadaven eliminated. One Warthrall—eliminated. Initiates unharmed."

Crane tilted his head. "Because you arrived in time?"

Kaspar hesitated. "No. Because of her."

The silence shifted. Alfena's fingers stilled against her sleeve. Sigvard's tapping stopped.

"She?" he repeated.

Kaspar nodded. "The Valksha girl. Ophelia."

"I thought she was being observed—not deployed," Margrith said sharply.

"She wasn't deployed," Kaspar replied. "She was at Avasylon. The attack came to us."

"You're saying that she fought?" Alfena asked, voice cool but edged with something quieter beneath.

Kaspar nodded again. "Rough around the edges, but she held her own. I expected nothing more from a young Valksha like her."

"Lacking the precision Lady Vivian has," Crane interjected slyly.

Alfena did not flinch. "You're certain it wasn't coincidence?"

"I'm certain," Kaspar said. "Her presence was the target. Vivian warned me. Said Warthralls had caught wind of a child Valksha in Moirand. They were looking for her."

Margrith scoffed. "And you let her stay at Avasylon?"

"I let her *live,*" Kaspar snapped. "And because of that, the children are still alive."

Silence fell again. This time heavier.

"She's untrained," Sigvard said slowly. "And if she's that powerful —"

"She's unstable," Crane finished. "That makes her dangerous."

"She's a child," Alfena said.

"She's a *Valksha,*" Kaspar said, tone firm. "We don't have the luxury of debating what that means anymore. They're almost extinct. And this one is in our care."

"What are you proposing?" Margrith asked.

"Let me continue her observation," Kaspar said. "Let me train her. You'll have your reports, your testimonies, your precautions. But she stays."

"And what of the breach?" Crane asked. "You said the sanctum held."

"It did," Kaspar replied. "Lady Vivian's enchantments held. The inner sanctum remains sealed. But the fact they breached the perimeter proves they're probing. This was not a strike—it was reconnaissance."

"Enchantments by Lady Vivian?" Margrith suddenly prickled. "We agreed not to allow Valksha magic to interfere with our procedures. It's too unpredictable."

Crane's voice broke the tension, low and laced with a flicker of mischief.

"Unpredictable magic is still better than no magic when your perimeter's been breached."

Margrith glared, but Alfena cut in before the exchange could escalate.

"Let's not pretend our own protections haven't faltered before. The eastern wardstones were meant to last through the ages, yet something slipped past them. If Vivian's enchantments held when ours didn't... perhaps it's not unpredictability we should fear, but pride."

Kaspar gave a subtle nod, grateful for the opening.

"Lady Vivian understood the limitations of Sage wards. That's why she offered to reinforce Avasylon years ago. I accepted. The rest of you didn't know because you would've vetoed it."

"You made that call alone?" Margrith snapped.

"I made it to protect the boy," Kaspar said, firm and unapologetic. "And now, that same enchantment—*Valksha* magic and a *Valksha* child —has shielded more than one life."

"Then we should be preparing for war," Sigvard rumbled. "The Warthralls know she's in our midst and won't hesitate again."

Kaspar met his gaze. "We should be preparing *her*."

Alfena folded her hands in her lap. "Let her rest tonight," she said. "Bring her to us tomorrow. We'll see what kind of girl this Ophelia really is."

"Back to this more pressing matter," Margrith pushed. "Where was this Warthrall, Kaspar?"

"Near the training fields, closest to the east most side," he answered gravely.

Margrith abruptly stood, nearly slamming her hands into the table as she pushed herself upward. "How? Our defenses are impeccable."

Crane's brows lowered, his playful tone now gone. "If one got through, more can follow."

Alfena's lips thinned. "The eastern wardstone line must have faltered somehow. If the enchantments failed, we need to know why."

"Then we're not finished here," Kaspar said quietly, turning toward the door. "Ophelia and Theodin will remain here until Avasylon has been secured. Margrith and Sigvard, you will investigate the wardstones. We will have an audience with Ophelia tomorrow morning."

With that, he gave a single nod.

Then he turned and left the chamber.

The sun had long dipped beneath the mountains, and Halvalla's stone halls had grown dim and still. The guest wing felt like a world apart—removed from the inner sanctum of the fortress, removed from consequence. Just silence, stone, and shadows stretching long across the walls.

Theodin sat near the window, one leg braced against the sill, polishing the flat of his blade with rhythmic strokes. The room was quiet save for the soft scrape of cloth on steel.

Ophelia lay across the narrow bed, arms crossed under her head, eyes fixed on the ceiling. She had finally shed her cloak, but now draped it over herself like armor disguised as comfort. Her breathing had steadied. But the light in her eyes had dulled—not broken, but dimmed by the weight of everything still unspoken.

"I didn't know what to pack," she muttered.

Theodin glanced up. "What?"

She gestured to the satchel in the corner. "When Lady Vivian sent me to Avasylon. I didn't know if I'd be sleeping on the floor of a forest cottage or a marble castle. So I packed both books and a knife."

That startled a soft laugh from him—short, quiet.

"I'm guessing the knife was more useful," he said.

"To allow me to draw blood," she replied. "But who knows what else it could've been for."

She sat up then, drawing her knees to her chest, voice growing softer. "You said earlier… magic doesn't comfort you. Do you mean all magic?"

Theodin looked down at the sword in his lap. For a long moment, he didn't answer. When he finally did, his voice was low.

"No. Just mine."

She tilted her head. "Oh."

She paused, staring off in deep thought.

"It scares me too, my magic," she finally whispered. "Not because it's there. But because it's mine, and I don't have complete control over it. Like I can't run from it, can't give it back. It's stitched into me. And some days I don't know if I'm using it… or if it's using me."

Theodin didn't speak. He kept his gaze on the cloth in his hand, running it slowly along the edge of the blade. But something in her words struck.

Stitched into me.

That phrasing lingered.

He knew what it meant to feel bound to something beyond control. To wake each day unsure whether the fire in your veins would lie dormant—or burn through everything in its path. He knew it all too well.

The Kyriegard and their rigid discipline kept it contained.

That was why he refused magic he couldn't grip with both hands. Why he only trusted what could be forged, held, and honed.

But he didn't say that. He couldn't.

Instead, he looked up at her. Just for a moment. Long enough for her to see something shift in his expression—something softened, something unspoken.

She met his gaze. Didn't press. Didn't prod.

Just nodded—like she'd heard him, even though he'd said nothing at all.

Year 843 of the Second Age, Eighth Month, Twenty-Seventh Day

Theodin hadn't slept much. The cot Kaspar had arranged beside the guest bed was narrow and uneven, but it wasn't discomfort that kept him restless—it was her.

Kaspar didn't share any details of his meeting with the Council when he touched base before bed. He simply brought in the cot before Theodin could suggest staying in the room—for her comfort and safety. No questions. No orders.

Kaspar's instincts were deadly both on and off the battlefield. He could read a person like scripture—no magic, no mind-reading. Just pure, unnerving precision. Like an Aquiad Oracle born without the gift.

"For you," he'd said.

And that was all. He left before either of them could find breath to ask what the Council had decided.

Ophelia hadn't stirred through the night. Her breathing was soft beneath the weight of exhaustion, but Theodin stayed close all the same. Not out of concern. Out of control.

He didn't want a repeat of Avasylon—waking to find her already upright, staring out the window like she'd been standing there for hours.

This time, he woke before she did. And something about knowing she'd rested easily that night brought a strange kind of ease to him.

Morning light crept into Halvalla's eastern wing, catching on the crystalline dust of aged enchantments embedded in the floor.

Theodin walked beside her, silent, his steps unhurried—but purposeful.

Neither of them spoke as they approached the chamber.

The corridor narrowed ahead, its walls gleaming like obsidian glass. Every step echoed too loud, each lantern casting long shadows that twisted and reformed with their passing. Theodin had walked this path dozens of times before—but this time, with her beside him, it felt different. More exposed.

Ophelia's shoulders tensed. He saw the tremble of hesitation in her step and the way her hands clenched together and her fingers fidgeted.

The doors groaned open, heavy with age and enchantment, revealing the Council chamber beyond. Light streamed in through the high windows, turning the dust in the air to tiny specks of gold. Tapestries lined the walls, each one a monument to battles she hadn't witnessed, capturing her intrigue as she stared at them in wonder.

Theodin's gaze fell upon the five chairs in the half-circle—each one occupied, save for the central seat. That one always remained empty unless judgment was being passed.

The air carried the familiar weight: old parchment, burnt oils, magic that hadn't settled. The kind of place where decisions were made slowly, but consequences came fast.

Ophelia paused at the threshold. He felt her glance sweep the room, her breath catch in her throat.

"Come forward," Sigvard's gravel-coated voice commanded.

Margrith Gravehardt narrowed her eyes. "This is the girl?" she said, her voice already sharpened by skepticism.

From a corner of the room, Kaspar stepped beside her, shoulders squared with unshakable authority.

"This is Ophelia," he said, voice clipped and clear. "The Valksha who drove back a Warthrall and two cadaven only yesterday."

A ripple of something—magic, scrutiny, maybe both—passed through the chamber like a low tremor. Theodin felt it in the soles of his boots. The others felt it too. He saw how Alfena's expression shifted, how Crane's brows twitched in interest, how Margrith's frown deepened.

Ophelia stiffened beside him. Her chin was high, but Theodin noticed the way her hands curled slightly, fingers twitching against her cloak.

She felt their judgment. Of course she did. It hung in the air like a blade drawn but not yet swung.

"Impressive," came Alfena's voice—soft and musical, but no less sharp. The high elf leaned forward in her chair, gaze piercing. "But power is only part of the equation. What else does she bring to the table?"

Margrith didn't wait for an answer. "And what liabilities?" she added, her tone cool enough to frost steel.

Theodin saw Ophelia open her mouth. But no sound came.

She looked down.

Only for a breath. But it was enough to shift the energy in the room —just enough for the doubt to find its opening.

"Speak, girl," Sigvard said. "If you wish to stand among us, you must find your voice."

Theodin didn't look at the Council. His focus stayed fixed on her.

Ophelia closed her eyes. Drew in a breath. When she opened them, something in her gaze had steadied. But her fingers were still white-knuckled on the strap of her satchel. Like she was holding onto it for dear life.

"I… I am a Valksha of the Saryf of Spirit and Heart, Veladriel the Ardent. The last of my family bloodline," she began, her voice thin but not faltering. Her cadence was stiff—like it had been practiced.

It had. He could tell. This wasn't just courage. It was rehearsed resolve. Something Lady Vivian had no doubt drilled into her before her arrival. Her words weren't just answers—they were armor.

She continued, her voice gaining a rhythm. "As the last Valksha of Veladriel, my survival is paramount. While the threat against my people remains at large, Lady Vivian has concluded that my safety will be best guaranteed with the Kyriegard."

"Not just *with* the Kyriegard," Crane cut in. "Lady Vivian strongly insists that you *become* a Kyriegard."

Theodin's eyes widened with shock, turning to the Valksha girl, then to Kaspar. Neither of them flinched.

They both knew. He hadn't. From the unsurprised faces of the Council, they also knew.

A Valksha? In the Order?

Training began early for a reason—between five and ten, long before the real work began. Years were spent building emotional resilience, sharpening instinct, aligning will with discipline.

She was…what, a year or two younger than him? Maybe. And she had natural power, sure. More than most. But power wasn't the same as readiness.

His jaw tightened.

Could she be taught to wield it without unraveling? Could the Order risk it?

Could she help or hinder the Order?

Theodin didn't know. Magic like hers came at a price, and the Kyriegard couldn't afford missteps. She was untested. Untethered. Too raw to be brought in without consequence. And yet—

He saw himself in her. Not in magic, but in posture. In the tension in her throat. In the way her voice shook, only to steady a second later. The way she swallowed pain like it was second nature.

He'd had years to build his discipline.

She was being thrown straight into the fire.

Ophelia cleared her throat. Glanced toward Kaspar—perhaps for comfort, but not for instruction. Just a flicker of reassurance. She stood straighter.

"I… no longer have familial ties," she said slowly.

The way she said it—measured, aching beneath the calm—what had she been through?

"The Kyriegard choose to cut such familial ties to uphold their value of unbiased decision-making and action. This was something the Kyriegard and the Valksha could not quite agree on, as the Valksha relied heavily on their families."

Had…she witnessed the loss of her family? It would explain her fear and paranoia. Flinching at shadows and shattering windows. That kind of trauma explained her meekness.

Theodin never felt the pain of a lost family. The Kyriegard was all that he ever knew. His mother died when he barely walked. Lady Vivian found him and brought him to Kaspar. That was all he was told. He was the youngest to be raised in Olysgard. Anyone younger and five was first raised in Fatum's orphanage, at the nearby village.

But because Lady Vivian insisted, Theodin was raised by Kaspar. Raised by the Order.

And now Lady Vivian insisted upon the Kyriegard taking in a Valksha.

"Do you plan on continuing your family bloodline, Miss Ophelia?" Crane asked.

Theodin bristled. A harsh question. Especially for someone her age.

"When the time is right, yes," she answered, voice calm. "But now is not the time, and nor is anytime soon. It would be unwise while the Valksha continue to be targeted as they have been. Besides…" she added with quiet finality, "as a Valksha, my lifespan gives me more time than usual—I have roughly five centuries to eventually make that happen, yes?"

Theodin's brow ticked up. Not because she was deflecting—but because she wasn't.

She spoke with clarity, conviction. Like she'd already made peace with what she'd have to give up.

"I understand and respect your rules of celibacy," she continued. "I would follow them, should you accept me into the Order. I also understand I am starting late: I am thirteen years old now and will be turning fourteen in the next year's cycle of the seventh month around the sun. I am willing to start as soon as possible, work as hard as I can, and train and learn quickly to complete the Kyriegard Trials by the time I am eighteen."

Thirteen years old. *Thirteen*. Two years younger than him.

He had seen glimpses of this side of her yesterday as she had spoken so eloquently about the knowledge she had.

Theodin supposed, if one had been through what she had, they would grow up rather quickly too.

"And what of your faith, Miss Ophelia?" Crane asked, voice gentler than expected. "Your power comes from within—your blood, your body. The Saryf imbued in your flesh and bones. The Valksha are known as the most devout worshippers of Elodyn, but worship of any kind has no place in the Kyriegard. Wouldn't your attachment to the Saryfim interfere with your place here?"

Theodin watched her closely.

The question wasn't meant to expose her religion—it was meant to expose her loyalty.

"No," Ophelia said firmly. "I understand your policies and rules as a secular organization. I am not here to evangelize or change your structures. I am simply here to save my people—to bring balance back to Moirand as darkness grows and seeks to snuff out our light."

There was no hesitation in her tone. Just fire. Theodin felt the hair on his arms rise.

"If that means I must strike down another worshipper of Elodyn—perhaps even another Valksha, though the likelihood of that would be impossible…"

She exhaled, and her fists clenched at her sides.

"If I must strike them down, then so be it."

A prickled hush rippled through the chamber like a gust of wind rattling the old stone. Margrith scoffed, exchanging a pointed glance with Sigvard. Alfena's expression didn't change, but Theodin caught the slightest tilt of her head. Crane, for once, looked genuinely intrigued.

Kaspar said nothing.

But inside, something shifted in Theodin.

It wasn't just that she answered well. It was how she said it—with clarity, not calculation. Like she'd already imagined the outcome. Like she'd already accepted what it might cost her.

"Your words are well-rehearsed," Alfena said coolly, her piercing eyes fixed on Ophelia. "But tell me—what would you do if another Warthrall appeared before you today?"

Theodin braced himself. That answer wouldn't come from a script.

Ophelia paused, just as Lady Vivian must've taught her. A moment to breathe. A beat to think. It was a good sign.

"I think I learned quite a bit from my encounter this morning," she began slowly. "While my instinctive and initial reaction was risky and destructive, I am now more aware of it and therefore understand myself better."

She looked down at her hands, and Theodin could see the faintest tremor in her fingertips.

"The priority is to preserve life at all costs. I am experienced with using my magic for healing without much consequence—I would leave most of the offensive action to those who did it best. I have to trust them, even if I am afraid."

Her eyes lifted, and for the briefest moment, they locked with his.

That small glance—steady, unflinching—hit him harder than it should have.

"That trust will help me overcome my fears," she finished.

His jaw tightened. There was something uncomfortably familiar in her words.

Not in their delivery, but in their resolve. The same quiet conviction he'd learned to bury beneath discipline.

"A thoughtful answer," Alfena said, though her expression remained inscrutable. "But trusting others will only take you so far. You'll need to trust yourself first."

"And a sound answer," Sigvard said gruffly. "But sound answers don't win battles. You'll need more than words to prove yourself."

"And when you're done trusting others," Crane added with a wry smile, "trust that Sigvard will always find something to grumble about."

Sigvard turned to his colleague with an irritated glare. "Really, Azariah?"

Ophelia suddenly giggled and brought her hand over her mouth to contain it. Theodin's eyebrows rose at this—he had barely seen the girl smile like that since she arrived.

Crane's face broke into a giddy grin as he thumped his cane with approval. His wild chestnut eyes whipped to Alfena. "See? I still got it!" he sneered under his breath.

Alfena's stern expression slightly cracked with a small smirk in Crane's direction. Even Kaspar had to turn his eyes down and hide his smile. Margrith rolled her eyes and held her hand up to Crane. "Please don't undermine your fellow Council member's opinion before a potential initiate, Azariah."

Crane snorted. "I think little miss lady of the Saryf of Spirit and Heart will agree that it is important to see that at least one of her potential superiors has a soul."

"Azariah…" Alfena sighed and shook her head, now holding her cheek in her hand. Margrith scoffed and then waved her hand dismissively at him.

As Ophelia glanced over her shoulder, her eyes caught his.

There was something there. A flicker. A pull. The kind of thing that made the air shift, just slightly—like the stillness before a spell took hold.

Beneath his stern expression, Theodin felt something stir. A strange flutter just behind his ribs. He drew a quiet breath, sharp and short.

He didn't know what it was. Only that she felt it too.

Her smile faltered into something smaller. Not fear, not embarrassment—just a moment of awareness. And then she looked away.

The Council members turned toward one another. Kaspar stepped away from Ophelia's side and joined them, his cloak trailing in his wake.

Murmurs rose between the councilors—low and layered with conflicting tones. Theodin caught flashes of Margrith's disapproval, the glint of calculation behind Alfena's silence, Crane's half-smile tucked beneath his beard. Kaspar said something too quiet to hear. Then nodded.

Ophelia didn't move.

Her hands had curled back around the strap of her satchel. Her posture was upright, composed—but Theodin could see the strain in her shoulders, the flicker of movement in her fingers. She wasn't trembling anymore, but she was waiting. Braced. Like someone standing at the edge of a storm, listening for the break in the wind.

Then Kaspar's gaze flicked back to her. A subtle nod.

Theodin watched her hands relax.

A beat of silence fell over the room.

Then the Council turned as one, and the finality of it settled over them like stone.

Sigvard's voice broke through it.

"The Council is in agreement. You will begin as a Kyriegard initiate immediately."

For a moment, no one moved.

Then Ophelia let out a long breath, quiet and controlled. Her hand drifted to her chest. Not in shock. Not even in celebration.

Just… relief.

Theodin watched her lips move, barely audible.

"Thank Elodyn."

He didn't know if she realized she'd said it aloud.

He didn't know what he was supposed to feel either.

Fear? Relief?

No, Theodin.

Don't feel anything at all.

Chapter 7

The Initiation

She had always imagined the moment would feel different.

Standing at the edge of something sacred—something ancient, consecrated by the Order's founders and sealed in the magic of centuries—she thought she would feel stronger. Braver, maybe even ready.

But instead, she felt hollow.

The chamber was still. Every breath she took echoed off the walls like it didn't belong to her. She could feel the pulse of the ritual circle beneath her boots, thrumming with unseen energy. It reminded her of a heartbeat, but it wasn't alive in the way she or anyone else was.

As she glanced around the room, she noticed veins of tree vines reaching up the walls and wrapping around the carved sigils.

Arborelys?

How curious. She thought it was sealed in the vault beneath Avasylon. She had no idea it could reach here—an hour's walk away, in Halvalla.

Her breath hitched slightly.

Focus, Fellie.

Then she realized that it was the first time since arriving that no one stood beside her.

Not Theodin. Not Kaspar. Not even Lady Vivian's voice in her memory.

Just her. A girl with trembling hands, a pendant pressed too tightly to her chest, and a blade waiting to taste her blood.

The pendant—a Kyriegard life talisman, a circular piece of wood with a central white gem and intricate runes etched around it—was perhaps a quarter of the size of palm, yet it weighed more than it looked. Maybe it was the weight of its magic that pressed on her.

After all, it was designed to prevent death as much as it could. So long as it remained in tact and on its vessel, it would keep its Kyriegard from crossing into the Ether…or, Lither or Nether, depending on their soul's disposition.

It wasn't completely fail-proof or preventative, but it contributed greatly to the Kyriegard's legendary near-invincibility.

And that was one of the many reasons Lady Vivian wanted Ophelia to become a Kyriegard. Ophelia would be a force to be reckoned with and much harder to kill than her Valksha brethren.

Ophelia lifted her eyes.

The chamber was vast and circular, its domed ceiling glittering with enchanted constellations—each one pulsing faintly with breath, as though the stars themselves were listening. At the center of the stone floor, an intricate sigil glowed with soft white light. She could feel its energy brush against her skin like static. Vines of Arborelys curled around the platform's edges, reaching toward the circle like roots drawn to blood.

Kaspar stood beside her, a quiet, grounding presence.

The Council had taken their places in a wide arc around the glowing sigil, their faces solemn and impassive. Alfena stepped forward, her long, elegant fingers motioning toward the center of the room.

"Step into the sigil," she said, her voice clear and commanding. It echoed through the chamber like a bell rung underwater.

Ophelia swallowed nervously. As she drew near, as she instinctively reached for her satchel to anchor her, she felt the Kyriegard talisman.

Each step she took toward the circle was heavier than the last. It wasn't fear, but something else—like the weight of the talisman. The air itself had a memory…like it knew how many had stood here before her, and was measuring her just as it had them.

When she reached the center, the sigil flared brighter and its white light illuminated her eyes.

All around her, the Council raised their hands. Their chant began low, layered in tones that resonated the stone beneath her boots. She couldn't understand the words, but their gravity was undeniable. Their whispers echoed and filled the space, and the vibrations shifted and coalesced around her. It was warm and all-encompassing, like the embrace of sunlight after a cold storm.

Kaspar's declarative voice rose above the others.

"Do you, Ophelia, swear to uphold the values of the Kyriegard? To protect the innocent, to seek justice without bias, and to wield your power with integrity and purpose?"

"I swear," Ophelia answered, clear and unwavering.

"Do you offer your strength, your magic, and your life to the Order, knowing the weight of this bond and the sacrifices it demands?"

"I do."

The sigil pulsed in return and hummed with satisfaction.

Alfena's voice followed.

"Before the Order binds you to its magic, to our Arborelys—the Order's Collective—you must offer a piece of yourself. Blood, the source of your power. The tether to your Saryf."

She gestured to a small ceremonial dagger resting on a velvet cloth in Sigvard's hands. The dwarf stepped forward and presented it to her.

Ophelia hesitated, only briefly, before taking the dagger. The hilt was cool and smooth in her palm. She glanced at Kaspar, who gave her a small, encouraging nod, and then she turned her gaze back to the Council.

She had done this before, many times, to coax the Saryfim light from her veins and spark healing, creation, and works of wonder. But this wasn't a spell.

This was a vow. It was a choice, and for the first time, she felt like she had control over her life after so many years of barely having any.

She glanced at Kaspar. He only nodded once, quiet and resolute.

She returned her gaze to the circle. With a deep breath of anticipation, she pressed the blade against her palm.

The sting of her skin splitting did not faze her, yet her heart raced. Blood welled up from the wound. As she opened her hand, she tilted her wrist and let the crimson droplet fall.

The instant her blood made contact with the sigil, the chamber roared with vibrant life.

A low hum rippled through the air, and then—light. White, blinding, radiant—rising around her in a spiraling current that lifted the fine hairs on her arms. The pendant at her chest grew heavier, the weight of it dragging against her sternum.

The light circled once, then surged inward, drawn to the talisman's gem. It flooded into the center stone, and the white crystal bloomed with brilliance. Ophelia's blood—still fresh on her palm—began to glow green.

The glow pulsed in time with her heartbeat, and as another droplet landed and seeped into the sigil at her feet, the magic changed.

The talisman flared.

Its runes writhed—shifting, reshaping, reforming into symbols no one in the chamber recognized. A shockwave burst outward, not violent, but reverberating with power. The circle of Council members staggered, their faces illuminated in the emerald light.

"What is this?" Sigvard gasped.

Before anyone could respond, the sigil beneath Ophelia's feet transformed.

Its white glow fractured into veins of green, and the carved lines began to move—reordering themselves around her, as if rearranging to fit her presence. The floor beneath her shimmered, alive with rhythm. She felt it in her bones, in her chest, in her breath.

"Her magic," Alfena said sharply. "It's…interfering with the binding."

Ophelia's hands quivered. The pendant began to burn as it grew hotter.

Her breath hitched when the light enveloped her, climbing up her legs and wrapping around her torso like a living thing.

The power was overwhelming—wild and uncontrollable —but…familiar, as though it recognized her.

"Steady, lass!" Kaspar's voice cut through the swirl.

Despite his reassurance, she could see his uncertainty.

The energy bucked and the sigil shuddered. The Council raised their hands again, weaving threads of stabilizing magic to contain the outburst. Light flared at the edges of the room, and the vines of Arborelys pulsed with each wave.

The air trembled.

And then—

The light receded, slowly and reluctantly. It pulled itself back into the pendant with a final shimmer.

Silence.

Ophelia staggered as her legs gave out beneath her—but Kaspar caught her arm before she could fall.

The talisman at her chest pulsed faintly. Its once-neutral surface now glowed with soft, rhythmic light.

It no longer resembled the simple artifact she'd been given. Its emerald hue pulsed in time with her heartbeat, as if it had become an extension of her very essence.

The sigil beneath her feet dimmed back to white. The glowing lines and ancient designs slowly realigned, melting into their original shapes—though faint traces of green still lingered at the edges, like bruises in the stone.

Across the chamber, Alfena's eyes narrowed on the pendant, her expression unreadable.

Sigvard muttered something under his breath. Kaspar and Crane simply stared.

Margrith took a step forward and looked over Ophelia with scrutiny. She frowned deeply.

"What just happened?" she demanded.

"Arborelys," Alfena said slowly, though even her voice held hesitation. "It's never responded like this before."

Kaspar stepped forward, his gaze fixed on Ophelia. "Because it's never bound a Valksha," he said, calm but resolute.

"The Order's magic has adapted to her," Alfena murmured. "But whether she can adapt to it… that remains to be seen."

"This isn't what we agreed on," Margrith said darkly. "It's far from standard. No initiate's ever altered the ritual structure—especially not with raw Saryfim magic."

"Nothing about this *is* standard," Alfena replied, her tone edged not with fear, but curiosity.

Ophelia pressed a hand to her chest. Her fingers brushed the pendant. It was still warm, still pulsing softly.

It didn't feel like a borrowed object anymore. It was hers now, and it held her magic. It felt warm, even alive, and now it had a piece of her.

A piece of her blood. A piece of her soul.

She looked up and met their eyes. Each of them.

Alfena's gaze was impassive.

Crane leaned forward, eyes gleaming with intrigue.

Margrith frowned, her face a sculpture of judgment.

Sigvard remained unmoving, though tension still held in his jaw.

And Kaspar… Kaspar, despite a hint of apprehension in the lines of his face, met her stare with quiet pride.

A bloom of emotion opened in her chest. It was not relief or triumph, but resolve.

"I'll learn," she said, her voice firmer than before. "Whatever this means, I'll learn to control it."

Another silence loomed. The Council exchanged glances—some unreadable, others tinged with wariness. But no one protested.

Sigvard grunted and broke the silence. "It's done. She's one of us now."

The emerald glow around the pendant dimmed, leaving only its quiet shimmer and the distant hum of the Order's magic in the air.

For the first time, the chamber was still, and its ancient pulse now beat with something new.

Evening had settled over Halvalla, casting the fortress in muted hues of blue and silver. The bustle of the day faded into stillness, and the halls now held the hush of hallowed stone.

The air in Halvalla's halls was cool and quiet, a stark contrast to the charged energy of the initiation chamber. Ophelia wandered until she found a small balcony tucked away into one of the spire alcoves.

From here, she could see the grounds unfurling below. The view stretched over the sprawling landscape, where enchanted lanterns dotted the paths like fallen stars.

She leaned on the cold railing, her fingers absently brushing the pendant at her chest.

It felt even heavier now—not just in weight or magic, but in meaning.

Her talisman also looked different from the others.

What did it mean?

Had she done something again that she hadn't meant to do?

She exhaled slowly, willing the questions to quiet. The bond to the Order's magic was sealed now—unbreakable. But what did that mean for her? For the part of her that was still Valksha?

Her thoughts drifted to the Council—Margrith's suspicion, Sigvard's grgravel-edgeduff approval, Alfena's cryptic words, Crane's wry curiosity. They had accepted her, but with hesitation.

And then there was the anomaly, the occurrence during the ritual that none of them could explain. The emerald flare, the reshaped sigils, the shock in the Council's eyes—clearly, none of that had happened with any other initiate.

Was she truly meant to be here, or had she broken something sacred?

Her grip on the pendant tightened.

No. She would learn. She would gain control. Whatever her magic was trying to tell her, whatever it meant, she would master it.

Kaspar certainly believed in her.

His rare warmth during the ceremony had surprised her, but she hadn't been able to meet his eyes then. But now, standing alone with the cool breeze brushing her skin, she let believe in the pride he'd shown her. It reminded her of Lady Vivian—not the same, but close enough to ache.

Then there was Theodin.

When the ritual ended and the doors had opened, Theodin had been waiting in the corridor. He hadn't said anything, but he must've felt it —*something*. The air had still been warm with magic. Ophelia had wanted to tell him everything in that moment. The lights. The pain. The sensation of magic. The feeling of being… known. But they never got the chance.

As the chamber began to empty, Kaspar caught Theodin by the shoulder and murmured something before they stepped away. He murmured a few clipped words and sent her back to the guest wing alone.

When she turned the corner and tried to glance back at them, they had disappeared.

She slunk off and wandered.

In that moment, she remembered his narrowed mismatched eyes, his silence sharp with judgment when they first met. His doubt had stung, but it had fueled her determination. And yet, yesterday, when they spoke privately in the guest room or during the audience with the Council, there had been a moment—a flicker of something in his gaze.

Recognition, or maybe curiosity.

Did he feel it too? That strange… connection?

She shook her head, trying to banish the thought. He probably still saw her as a liability, like Margrith and Sigvard.

And yet, despite her frustration with Theodin, she wanted to understand him.

His control, his restraint—he carried himself with discipline, but something beneath the surface felt raw and barely contained. She had glimpsed it in his sharp words and passing glances, but more than anything, she had felt it.

When he caught her after the Warthrall attack—she couldn't forget it.

Not just the steadiness of his hand. But the surge of something that passed between them. Something alive. It wasn't like Kaspar's touch, steady and warm like a hearth.

Theodin's had felt… volatile. Electric. A storm under a skin of steel.

His grip had been foundational, grounding—but it wasn't just the physical sensation that stayed with her. It was the energy that surged between them in that instant, sharp and raw, brimming with something unspoken.

His energy was layered—disciplined, yet wild beneath the surface. A quiet storm, restrained but not extinguished.

It had unsettled her, yet it drew her in.

She hadn't had enough time to draw conclusions. It had been fleeting, like glimpsing something vast through a crack in a door. But it haunted her, as though she had brushed against something deeper than she could understand.

Then—just for a moment—she felt something stir. A faint hum deep in her chest.

She froze.

Her fingers pressed to the pendant.

It was warm and alive, as it had been before. But it was different.

The sensation… it wasn't hers alone.

There—just at the edge of her awareness—a second pulse.

It was distant. Familiar, almost aching.

Her eyes flew open. She stretched with her senses, trying to catch it again.

It was gone.

She let out a breath she hadn't realized she was holding. The pendant still hummed lightly against her collarbone.

She turned from the balcony, shadows stretching behind her as she stepped back into the fortress.

Just as she reached for the door, it opened—and there he was.

Theodin.

His eyes swept the room once before settling on her, unreadable and not surprised. Not searching, but present.

"You disappeared," he said quietly.

His tone wasn't cold. No, it was much different than before. Concerned, but not…scolding. A concealed kindness.

Ophelia blinked and hesitated. "So did you."

They stood in silence for a moment more, the air between them quiet—charged, but not heavy.

Theodin glanced past her, out toward the stars, then back.

"Are…you okay?"

Ophelia blinked a few more times, as if snapping out of a trance. She cleared her throat awkwardly. "Um…yes, I think so."

Fellie, what's wrong with you?

One moment she had the urge to splurge her thoughts and feelings and describe the entire ritual to him—she wanted to ask questions, understand him and the way he was—pry, pull, interrogate—

And now, her throat tightened.

His jarring gaze now studied her more closely. It was as if he didn't believe her.

"Kaspar told me what happened during your initiation."

Ophelia's shoulders released with relief. "Oh, he did."

Theodin nodded once. "He said it wasn't… normal."

She gave a short, breathless laugh. "Yeah. That's putting it mildly."

He didn't laugh with her, but he didn't look away either.

"I've never seen a pendant change like that," he said. "Not even in the archives. Alfena was still trying to decode the runes when I left."

"I don't know what I did," she murmured. "It wasn't intentional."

"I didn't think it was."

His voice was quieter now. Not softened—just less armored.

Their eyes met again, and this time she didn't look away either.

"Do you think it's going to be a problem?" she asked, her voice barely above a whisper.

There was a pause.

"No," Theodin said. "But even if it is…" He hesitated just a beat. "You're not the only one who's not… *standard*."

Ophelia blinked. Her lips parted, but no words came.

Before she could speak, he stepped back slightly, giving her space.

"I'll walk you back."

Just like that, the quiet wall went back up—but not completely. Not cold. Just… contained.

Ophelia turned her eyes down as she took a few hesitant steps past him, her posture curling slightly inward like she was pulling herself back into her own skin

Then, his voice came again—lower, but not harsh.

"Try not to wander like that again."

She stopped. Her eyes snapped up to meet his. For a flicker of a moment they locked.

Then he glanced away.

"For your safety," he added, more measured now. "Kaspar sent you to the guest chambers and… you weren't there when I returned."

Ophelia tilted her head, her expression softening. "Oh… I'm sorry. Did… did I make you worry?"

He shrugged and gestured toward the corridor, trying to wave it off.

Her brows furrowed and one arched—just enough to tease. "So… you *weren't* worried?"

Theodin paused mid-step, eyes closing briefly. Then came a slow exhale through his nose. When he opened his eyes again, he still wouldn't meet hers.

"I was worried."

He turned and started walking, his stride steady but quieter than before.

"Oh!" she chirped in surprise. A small smile ghosted across her lips. She skipped forward to catch up with him, and they fell into step together beneath the glow of the lantern-lit corridor.

She looked up at him with large, optimistic eyes

"Next time I'll leave a note," she whispered. "Terribly sorry to make you worry."

He didn't answer at first, but a small side glance—and a *smirk!*—betrayed him.

Ophelia beamed with quiet confidence and turned forward, her steps lighter now.

Chapter 8

The Fire Beneath

Year 843 of the Second Age, Eighth Month, Twenty-Eighth Day

The room was quiet except for the delicate shimmer of energy and magic in the air.

Alfena's quarters were a study in elvish elegance: shelves lined with ancient tomes, glowing crystals hovering in delicate arcs, and a circular meditation space carved with intricate runes.

"Sit," Alfena said, gesturing to the center of the runic circle.

Ophelia hesitated but obeyed, lowering herself onto the smooth stone.

As she settled into the circle, she felt Alfena's presence more acutely. There was no need for touch—Alfena's elvish nature allowed her energy flow outward, weaving through the air like an invisible current. It was calm and deliberate as though every thread had been precisely placed.

Unlike Kaspar's grounding warmth or Theodin's stormy volatility, Alfena's energy was controlled and elegant yet vast—like standing at the edge of a serene ocean, its depths unfathomable but constant.

It felt ancient, layered with time and wisdom, carrying the weight of centuries. There was a coolness to it—not cold but refreshing, like a breeze passing through a twilight forest.

Beneath the calm exterior, though, Ophelia could sense an undercurrent of intensity, a flicker of something sharper and more discerning. It wasn't threatening, but it was watchful and calculating.

The longer Ophelia remained in Alfena's presence, the more she became aware of its duality. There was a quiet compassion to it, a soft undertone that reminded her of sunlight filtering through leaves, but it was balanced by an almost clinical detachment as though Alfena was assessing her down to her very essence.

Ophelia shifted slightly under the pressure of it. She felt as though Alfena's energy was wrapping around her, gently probing her magic, her thoughts, and even the spaces she'd tried to keep hidden. It wasn't invasive, but it was unyielding—like water seeking every crack in a stone.

Alfena knelt across from her, eyes fixed on the Valksha girl. "Your initiation was unlike any I've seen," she said. "The bond you formed with the Order's magic is… unique."

"I didn't mean for it to happen," Ophelia said quickly. "It just—"

"Magic often does what it wills," Alfena interrupted kindly. "Especially yours. That's what we're here to understand."

She raised her hands, her long fingers glowing with silver light. Energy stirred between her palms, soft but insistent.

Ophelia noticed illuminated runes etched into her skin along the base of each palm and down her forearms. Faded rune etchings, a few tones darker than the rest of skin, could be seen beneath the glowing ones, like words written over one another.

"Relax," Alfena said. "I won't harm you."

The moment Alfena extended her hands, the vibrations around them stirred. It wasn't sudden or jarring—more like the soft lapping of waves against sands of a shore. The air around them seemed to grow heavier—not with pressure but with presence—as if Alfena's very essence filled the room.

It brushed Ophelia's senses, but as it lingered, she felt its depth. It was timeless, layered with a lifetime—or perhaps several lifetimes—of knowledge and experience. Beneath its calm surface was a pointed edge that cut through her thoughts and laid them bare.

The pendant around Ophelia's neck pulsed, and Alfena's magic shifted, her silver glow dimming as streaks of green light intertwined with it. Ophelia stiffened as her heart raced. She could feel the resonance of their energies interact, a strange push and pull that made her breath catch.

"Interesting," Alfena murmured. Her voice was distant as though she wad speaking to herself. "Your energy is layered. The Valksha magic is vibrant, alive… but it's not alone."

Ophelia frowned. "Not alone?"

"There are traces of something else. Sage magic, yes, but… different." Alfena's brows knitted together. "It's as though the Order's Collective magic—Arborelys—didn't simply bind to you…it adapted to accommodate you."

But Alfena didn't stop there. Her glowing hands hovered just above Ophelia's head now, and Ophelia felt something change—something deeper.

A sharp ache pierced her heart, and for a moment her memories surfaced unbidden.

Her father's warm smile.

Her mother's soft voice.

The chaos and blood that shattered it all.

Her entire body stiffened as the memories flooded her mind. She had buried them for so long, convinced they were safer hidden. But now, under Alfena's gaze, they were exposed, fragile, and impossible to ignore.

Tears welled in her eyes.

"What are you doing?" she whispered.

Alfena's face softened though her hands remained steady.

"I'm seeing," she said. "The magic you carry is only part of you. Your grief… your pain… they're woven into it. Shaping it."

Ophelia's voice trembled. "You can see that?"

Alfena nodded. Her gaze was piercing but gentle.

"Your wounds are deep. They make your magic unpredictable, but they also make you resilient. Somehow unbound by the blood covenant your people made with the Saryfim."

The light in Alfena's hands and runes pulsed as she delved deeper.

Ophelia gasped as her memories clawed their way fully to the surface.

Her father's anguished cry.

Her mother's desperate act of resistance.

The farm that had once been her home and safe haven now soaked in blood and fire.

Alfena's face didn't change, but her energy did.

The cool, steady calm that had surrounded her rippled, growing agitated. For a moment, it was as though the oceanic vastness of her presence had churned into an unseen storm. It wasn't intrusive, but it shrouded Ophelia's senses.

Her tears spilled out in streams on her cheeks as the memories tightened their grip.

"Stop," she huffed hoarsely, her voice trembling. "I can't—"

"Breathe," Alfena said, quiet but firm. The light in her hands dimmed as she pulled back just enough to ease the intensity of the intrusion without severing the connection. "Let the memories flow. Do not fight them."

Ophelia's breath came in shallow gasps, but she obeyed, forcing herself to sit still as the fragments of her past swirled and and sliced like shattered glass.

Her mother's scream.

Her brother's defiance.

Her father's final act of sacrifice.

They replayed in vivid, merciless detail, each one cutting deeper than the last.

When Alfena finally withdrew, the glow around her hands faded completely, leaving only the faint hum of the runes beneath them. The room felt cavernous in the silence, amplifying the echoes of Ophelia's memories.

"Your grief is not a weight—it's a fire," Alfena said softly. "It feeds your magic, but left unchecked it consumes. You must learn to temper it, or it will consume you."

Ophelia wiped at her eyes, her hands trembling. "You saw everything," she whispered.

"I did," Alfena admitted. "And what I saw… most would not have survived. But you did."

Ophelia looked down at her hands, her fingers curling into fists. "I didn't feel like I survived."

"Yet here you are," Alfena replied. "You are stronger than you believe. But strength without control is a danger. Scars left untended can become weapons."

She leaned in and clasped her long, elvish fingers around Ophelia's fists. Her energy rippled again—brighter and more insistent.

"We have little Valksha research, and fewer texts to guide us, but what we do have, will help you understand what you are. Your magic, for instance—can it truly manifest without blood?"

Her fair brows rose. "Even I've never heard of that, and I've walked this plane for centuries. You must understand why the other Council members see you as a liability if you cannot control it."

Ophelia swallowed hard, her chest tight. The words *liability* and *risk* struck deeper than she wanted to admit.

She was tired of being seen as something dangerous.

She flexed her fingers beneath Alfena's grasp. "I want to be able to control it."

"You will," Alfena said with quiet certainty. "And when you do, your magic won't just define you—it will free you."

Her presence softened, gentling like dusk. "Take a moment. The memories you carry are not burdens you must bear alone."

Alfena rose gracefully, pausing as if to say more, but instead she chose silence.

She stepped away but remained in the room to leave Ophelia alone with her thoughts, her aura lingering like a retreating tide.

The room felt endless and echoing again—no less bright but lonelier. Her father's desperate cry still rang in her ears. Her mother's last defiance burned behind her eyes.

They pressed against her chest like stones.

Her hand found the pendant at her neck, its soft glow a steady pulse. A quiet reminder of what she'd bound herself to. Its warmth was a contrast to the cold knot that grief left behind.

Your grief is not a weight—it's a fire.

Ophelia exhaled shakily, her fingers tightening around the talisman.

But the fire still scared her. It was wild, unpredictable, and tied to a pain she didn't know how to face.

She didn't just need to control it. She needed to understand it. For that, she would have to stop running from her memories.

Ophelia rose slowly, her shoulders still heavy. Alfena's words remained with her as a half warning and half promise.

She pressed the pendant against her chest and let its warmth seep into her skin.

Year 843 of the Second Age, Ninth Month, Eleventh Day.

Two weeks passed in a blur of blood, sweat, and silence. The attack at Avasylon faded into memory, but Ophelia's training had only just begun.

After the cadaven attack, Margrith Gravehardt—the Order'sthe architectural and engineering mind of the Kyriegard Council—had personally reinforced the defenses of Avasylon with the help of

Sigvard Jackard. Every inch of the perimeter had been examined, restructured, and re-anchored in Sage enchantments. The property was safe again.

But Ophelia's own defenses were another matter entirely.

Her first weeks as a Kyriegard initiate were unforgiving. She was not at all accustomed to the physical conditioning. Kaspar insisted it to be her primary focus, as she was clearly academically adept and magically capable, but her petite frame and nimble fingers could barely swing a dagger and her stance faltered under pressure.

To be a Kyriegard was to be a Sage warrior. Ophelia was already a Valksha; therefore, to balance the two sides of her training, she had to concentrate on becoming a warrior.

Slim, wiry, too light on her feet, she appeared much smaller than she first did being dressed in the Kyriegard uniform. She braided her raven curls tightly each morning, but by day's end they unraveled as if in protest.

The sun hung low in the sky, stretching long shadows across Avasylon's training grounds. Her limbs burned, her muscles screamed, and her lungs scraped raw with every breath. Sweat dampened her hairline, clinging to the back of her neck.

Across from her, Theodin stood with his arms crossed, watching. Always watching. Not encouraging and not mocking—just…waiting.

"For someone so small, you tire too quickly," he observed.

She gritted her teeth. She was too breathless to shoot back a witty response, but she made a note to come up with something later—preferably after she could feel her legs again.

The other initiates had long since finished their conditioning and retreated into the shade with their canteens. But Theodin hadn't dismissed her yet, and Ophelia had quickly learned that as long as he was standing there she was expected to keep going. He insisted she needed to catch up with the initiates her age.

She forced her body into motion, each step fueled by spite, willpower, and a vague desire to prove she didn't belong in the margins of anyone's expectations.

One more lap.

Just one more—

Suddenly, her foot snagged against the packed dirt.

The world tilted—

Firm hands caught her arm before she hit the ground.

Theodin's grip was steady and unyielding. For a brief moment, she wasn't falling anymore.

Her chest rattled with breath. When her vision cleared, she found herself looking straight into his eyes—one dark amber, the other vivid kyanite blue. The contrast was jarring, almost inhuman. Up this close, along the way the afternoon light hit them, made them look even more vivid, burning like molten metal and frozen fire.

Her brows furrowed together as she stared intensely, puzzled. She blinked several times.

Theodin remained stone-faced and guarded. "What?"

She tilted her head, still half-braced against him. Curiosity laced her tone. "Why are your eyes like that?"

Theodin blinked too, slowly—as if the question hadn't registered.

"…What?"

Her weight shifted as she forced herself upright, stepping back on wobbling legs. His energy coursed through her like the storm that it was.

"Your eyes. They don't match."

He let go.

She barely caught her balance before he took a step back—clean and deliberate, like the contact had never happened. His posture tightened as his expression sealed over.

"They've always been like this," he said flatly.

"That's not an answer."

A beat of silence. Then, quieter, "People don't usually ask. They just assume."

Ophelia studied him. She could tell he wasn't offended—just resigned; it was as if he was used to being observed, studied, and speculated about but never asked directly.

"Well," she said, adjusting her stance. "I noticed when we first met, but…I guess it didn't occur to me to ask until I was that close." She cleared her throat and looked at him expectantly. "You were born with them?"

"Yes."

"From your parents, maybe? Or…?"

Something in him appeared to stir. Just barely.

"I don't know," he answered in a lower voice.

The realization came over her. Kyriegard had no familial ties. They were often orphans—some knew their parents and some did not.

"Oh…" she said softly, her eyes dropping to the ground. "Right."

"It's fine."

She lifted her gaze to him again. She tried to read his demeanor, like she was trying to find the crack in his stone walls to peer through and see him.

His face twisted slightly. "What is it?"

"It doesn't feel like it comes from your blood. You seem entirely human. But as a Valksha, I can usually sense when someone isn't—even just a little. But you… you're *different*."

Theodin's brow furrowed. "How so?"

Ophelia hesitated, tilting her head as she studied him. "I don't know. It's just… different."

Theodin's expression remained unmoved. "Different how?"

She chewed the inside of her cheek, searching for the right words. "It's hard to explain. The energy I feel from others—it's usually layered, like pieces of who they are. But yours… It's controlled. Like a current running beneath the surface, but never breaking through."

His gaze sharpened. "That's what you sense?"

She nodded. "It's like… you're holding something back. Always."

Theodin's posture didn't change, but something about the way he looked at her made the air feel heavier. For a long moment, he said nothing.

Then, at last, he spoke. "You're perceptive."

Ophelia blinked again. His curt response was unexpected.

She huffed, crossing her arms. "That was all? After all that?"

He exhaled through his nose, but there was something just barely resembling amusement in his expression.

Ophelia scoffed slightly. "How did you expect I was going to act with you? I seemed to have taken you by surprise."

Theodin regarded her for a long moment before replying, "Most people hesitate around me."

Ophelia raised an eyebrow. "Hesitate?"

He inclined his head slightly. "They second-guess themselves. Keep their distance." His voice was even, almost indifferent, but she caught the faintest trace of something else beneath it.

Ophelia shrugged. "Well, that sounds exhausting."

Theodin blinked again. "…Exhausting?"

"Yeah," she said, adjusting her stance. "Imagine having to walk on eggshells around someone all the time. I'd hate that."

His expression remained mostly unchanged, but she caught the smallest flicker of something in his gaze. That was the third time now she'd noticed it—a subtle shift, like a shadow just beneath the surface.

And then—before she could stop herself—she added, "I mean, it's not like you've given me a reason to hesitate. I'm not afraid of you."

A brief pause.

Theodin's eyes flicked to hers, and for the first time, she saw it more clearly—just a fester of something quieter beneath his usual guardedness.

"Haven't I?"

Ophelia stopped. Her face creased with concern. "No..." She took a step towards him. "Are you saying...people fear you because of your eyes?"

The light humor in Theodin's gaze vanished.

"...Some do," he admitted after a pause.

Ophelia tilted her head. "Why?"

A beat of silence.

She thought he wasn't going to answer, but then his voice came, low and measured.

"Because they see something unnatural."

The words sat between them, unspoken weight pressing down like a heavy mist.

Ophelia stared at him, her brows pulling together crookedly. "That's stupid."

Theodin blinked. "...Excuse me?"

"You heard me," she said matter-of-factly. "What's so unnatural about having different-colored eyes? People are just superstitious. If that's the worst thing they fear about you, they must not know you very well."

Something flickered in Theodin's expression. He studied her carefully as if he were expecting a trick, waiting for her to correct herself.

But she didn't.

Instead, she simply wiped the sweat from her forehead with the back of her arm, then met his gaze evenly.

As he spoke, his tone was lighter. And so was the wall he had around him.

"Why aren't you afraid of me?"

The question caught her off guard. Once more, Ophelia blinked up at him, momentarily stunned. "What?"

Theodin didn't look away. His voice wasn't demanding, nor was it accusatory. It was just... curious.

"Most people either fear me or challenge me." His voice was steady, but there was something thoughtful beneath it. "You do neither. Why?"

She opened her mouth to respond but stopped.

Why wasn't she afraid of him?

He was taller than anyone she'd ever met. The top of her head came to the bottom of his sternum—granted, she had a shorter stature than most. He was built like a fortress and moved with the precision of someone trained to kill, and he never let his guard down. There was an undeniable weight to his presence, something precise and controlled that most would find intimidating.

But Ophelia didn't.

She frowned, rubbing at the back of her neck. "…I don't know. I guess I just never thought of you as someone to be afraid of."

Theodin narrowed his eyes slightly, as if trying to determine whether or not she was lying.

Ophelia exhaled, glancing away. "I'm more afraid of myself than I am of you."

That made him pause.

She hesitated, then added, "Losing control of my magic. Hurting someone without meaning to. Think about it—regardless of how large and frightening something is, I could…destroy it in seconds. I could destroy anything—especially a person." She turned her eyes aside and rubbed her arm. "That's what scares me."

Theodin was quiet. It was a different kind of silence than before. Not the kind that meant he was ignoring her or dismissing her words. No, this was different.

This was understanding.

She glanced at him. He wouldn't say it, of course. But she could read it in the way his shoulders tensed, in the way his jaw tightened ever so slightly.

Ophelia sighed, looking down at her scraped palms. "So…yeah. I don't think you're scary. I think people just don't understand you."

Another pause. Then—

"Likewise."

Ophelia blinked, looking up at him. "What?"

Theodin met her gaze, his expression unreadable once more. "You confuse them, too."

She scoffed. "Oh, yeah. Because I'm a terrifying little menace."

He didn't smirk, but something about the way he exhaled through his nose felt dangerously close to amusement.

"It is confusing if you think about it," he continued dryly. "You can prick your finger and obliterate someone—yet, you're still winded by half a lap around this field, and you're small enough to be thrown further across it."

Ophelia's jaw dropped open in shock at the remark. She put her hands on her hips and straightened her posture, as if subconsciously attempting to make her stature taller than it was.

She was about five feet and a few inches tall.

He towered over her at six feet and eight inches tall.

"Well," she began, slightly flustered. "I'm…working on it, aren't I? And obviously I can't do anything about my height or how light I am, but I'll get better at running with more practice."

Theodin's near-stoic face cracked a little more.

"You're still a terrifying little menace."

Ophelia paused for a moment, and then she leaned forward and squinted at him. "But I don't scare you?"

This time, she could see his teeth in his slight grin.

"No," Theodin said with ease. "Not anymore. I know your weaknesses now. I could disarm you. And throw you."

Ophelia scoffed again, much louder. "*Well!*"

Finally, a genuine crooked smile appeared on one side of his face. A dimple formed beside it on his cheek.

Ophelia pouted and folded her arms. Her cheeks flushed. "Are you having fun making fun of me?"

A subtle, rare chuckle escaped him, and he turned his eyes down. "Yes," he admitted, "because you are funny."

Ophelia's blush deepened, and she turned away with a huff. "Well —"

"Well," he repeated. "You sure like that word. That's the third time now."

"Do you do this to every initiate you help coach?"

Theodin looked off in consideration. "No."

"So then why *me?*"

Theodin's small smile faded. His face didn't retreat into his neutral guardedness but rather to a state of thoughtfulness.

"Because you don't shut down when I push you," he said, after a pause. "You push back. That matters."

Ophelia's expression dropped. Her eyes lowered at this.

Despite the grueling two weeks of working exclusively with Theodin every day since her initiation, she learned more about him as he did her—in both endearing and frustrating ways.

In turn, she had learned that he preferred certainty. He never overcomplicated things. Yet, he struggled to allow himself to feel. Reacting with too much emotion could lead to wrong decisions, mistakes, or could be the difference between life and death. Ophelia believed he practiced too much restraint. Silence was his version of precision, but it didn't always mean indifference.

He learned that, in spite of her initial timidity and outrageous power, she was an outspoken, stubborn girl. Eloquent and mature, but reckless.

"I...*do* quite give you an attitude," Ophelia muttered with a shrug. Then, she gave him a smug look. "But at least you think I'm funny." She pointed at him and wiggled her finger. "This menace made you laugh and smile."

Theodin raised a brow. "That's an accomplishment?"

"I haven't seen you laugh or smile about anything else," Ophelia chirped with an air of suspicion.

He stopped, furrowing his dark brows together. "Really?"

"Oh yes," she cooed, stepping up to him. "You take your training quite seriously. I think you're almost ready to become one of those statues at Halvalla."

Theodin turned his eyes down and pressed his lips into a thin line, containing a laugh.

"Ah ah ah!" Ophelia shamed, wagging her finger again at him. "Your mentor won't be pleased with you breaking like this, young Theodin!"

Theodin shook his head and then jerked it slightly in the general direction behind him. "Let's go, Valksha. Time for a break."

As he began walking, she perked up and leapt to join him in the stroll back to the cottage.

Chapter 9

The Measure of Worth

Year 843 of the Second Age, Ninth Month, Twenty-Seventh Day
One month later.

The Council chamber in Halvalla was as imposing as ever, its high vaulted ceilings etched with runic patterns that shimmered in the morning golden light.

Kaspar stood at the center of the room with his hands clasped behind his back. His weathered face was unreadable, but his piercing gray eyes scanned each of the Council members as they settled into their seats.

Margrith Gravehardt, the eldest human member, leaned back in her chair, her expression stern. Sigvard Jackard sat beside her, his thick arms crossed over his chest, his gruff demeanor unsoftened by the glow of the runes around him. Opposite them, Alfena Marobe adjusted the folds of her silver robe, her gaze calm but probing. Azariah Crane twirled his cane idly, eyes dancing between the others with a familiar, glinting curiosity.

"We're a month into her training," Margrith began, her voice low and deliberate. "It's time to evaluate the Valksha girl's progress."

"She's performed admirably in her academic studies," Alfena said. "Her grasp of history, culture, and strategy is remarkable for her age.

She absorbs information like a sponge."

"And yet," Sigvard interjected, voice like gravel sliding over stone, "she struggles with physical training. She lacks discipline. Her instincts are still a liability."

"She's improved," Kaspar added firmly. "Her control over her magic is far better than when she arrived. We knew this would take time."

"Time we may not have," Margrith countered. "Her instincts could get her killed—or worse, put others in danger."

Crane leaned forward, a wry smile tugging at his lips. "And yet, those instincts have saved her. Unrefined, yes, but not without merit. Raw potential often outshines predictability. The real question is whether we can afford to lose her."

Margrith's frown deepened. "Merit isn't enough. She's a risk. If she jeopardizes a mission, that's blood on our hands. The Order demands precision. Control. If she can't achieve that—"

"She will," Alfena interrupted, her voice cutting through the tension like a blade. "The question isn't whether she's capable. It's whether we're willing to invest the time and effort to refine her potential."

Sigvard grunted. "Having potential doesn't mean she'll give results."

"It's only been a month!" Alfena argued.

"And it only takes a split second for her to eradicate Olysgard into oblivion," Margrith shot back.

An aggressive tapping came from Crane's cane. "Aye, now, she's working hard, ain't she?" His wild eyes whipped to Kaspar. "How has the golden boy Theodin been with her?"

"He's pushing her," Kaspar answered with a thoughtful nod, "as Theodin does with the others, but she takes to it well and they're getting along. They've grown comfortable with each other. She shows more growth with private physical conditioning, sparring, and training than she does around the initiates."

"Perhaps she's afraid she'll hurt them if she loses control," Margrith jabbed in a murmur.

Kaspar didn't even acknowledge her as he continued. "They have a good rapport. Theodin is still...*Theodin,* as unmoved as he usually is, but she appears light-hearted and a good sport through it all. The first few days—maybe a week—was a bit tough for her, as expected. He reports that despite her struggles, she puts in the effort expected of her."

An indiscernible grumble came from Sigvard. "We've spent years searching for a proper partner for Theodin, and now we're wasting his time on a Valksha girl who can barely control herself? He should be focusing on training young initiates and working with other apprentices to find his potential Arcane Dyad partner, not focusing on this unstable young lady. She should continue her training but not with Theodin. She needs to be working with someone who can handle her instability—not our best apprentice."

"She's just gotten comfortable working with Theodin," Alfena reasoned. "As she's transitioning into our livelihood, shouldn't it be best that she learns from him as much as possible? And isn't he best suited for her situation?"

Margrith clicked her tongue. "He's an *apprentice,* Alfena!"

"For a potential partner…what about *her?*" Crane suddenly mused and tapped his cane lightly against the floor to garner attention. "So they're playing nice—does this mean our boy has finally acknowledged another person?"

Before Kaspar could open his mouth, Margrith scoffed.

"That would be a horrible idea," she spat. "Don't pair our model initiate with a wildcard like her. That's asking for disaster."

Alfena spoke up. "I don't think it's fair to think about pairing her at all yet. We've only seen a month of her progress."

Kaspar's eyes narrowed. "This isn't about pairing her with Theodin—or anyone else. That's not even a consideration right now. She hasn't been officially paired with a mentor either. We're here to evaluate her progress, not to debate hypotheticals."

Sigvard leaned forward onto the table. "If I may, her progress isn't the only anomaly worth discussing. Let's remember that the binding during her initiation was unlike anything we've seen before. It's clear her magic has a unique interaction with the Order's and Arborelys. She has unique needs."

"Uniqueness isn't always an advantage," Margrith muttered.

"Nor is it always a disadvantage," Alfena replied. "The binding wasn't just an anomaly—it was a transformation. Her magic reshaped the process itself, creating a bond unlike any we've seen. Ignoring that would be a mistake." She turned her gaze to Kaspar. "What is your assessment as the one overseeing her training most closely?"

Kaspar straightened, his voice steady. "She's determined. She works harder than most initiates I've seen, and she's making progress, even in areas where she struggles. Her magic is powerful, but it's tied to her emotions. That's both her greatest strength and her greatest challenge. It also is apparent that, as strange as her initiation ritual was, the binding of her magic to the Order's Collective magic has given her a tether to work with."

The Council fell silent for a moment, the hum of the runes filling the space.

"We'll revisit this after her next evaluation," Margrith said finally. Her tone softened slightly as she added, "For now, we'll trust your judgment, Kaspar."

Kaspar gave a curt nod. "I'll ensure she's ready."

Alfena's gaze lingered on him briefly, a glimmer of approval in her piercing eyes. Crane twirled his cane once more, his smile returning as he leaned back in his chair. Sigvard muttered something under his breath, his expression indiscernible, while Margrith's stern gaze lightened just enough to show her grudging agreement.

As Kaspar stepped away from the table, the vibrations of the Council chamber's enchantments seemed to pulse in rhythm with his thoughts.

A month had passed since Ophelia's initiation, and she had barely had a moment to breathe. The Kyriegard demanded discipline, and every day had been a battle—against her body, her instincts, and the expectations placed upon her.

Ophelia had just completed doing research in Halvalla's library when a tangle of humming, conflicting energies prickled her senses.

She paused just outside the Council hall, her hand resting against the cool stone wall.

"…the Valksha girl's progress."

The pulsations of Halvalla's enchantments thrummed beneath her fingers, but it was the voices drifting from the Council chamber that held her attention.

"…she struggles with physical training," a deep, gruff voice rumbled.

Sigvard. She recognized his tone immediately.

"Her instinctive reactions are still a liability."

The words hit her like a blow to the chest. She bit her lip, her fingers curling into a fist against the wall.

A liability. That wasn't what Kaspar had said during their last training session. He had told her she was improving. Slowly, yes, but improving.

"She will," Alfena's voice cut through the air, sharp and certain. "The question isn't whether she's capable. It's whether we're willing to invest the time and effort to refine her potential."

Ophelia's chest tightened. Alfena believed in her, at least. But Sigvard's criticism rang louder in her ears, and Margrith's scrutiny only added to her unease.

"Besides the risk she poses for herself and others, she could jeopardize a mission. If we're to face what lies ahead, we can't afford liabilities."

The word repeated itself in her mind like a curse: *liability*.

Ophelia stepped back from the wall, her breath quickening. She turned and hurried down the corridor, her boots tapping softly against the stone.

She had to remind herself that it had only been a month. Lady Vivian had warned her of the challenges she may face and that she couldn't let fear or worry about such difficulties hold her back.

Ophelia took the walk from Halvalla to Avasylon to breathe and shake off the adrenaline and tension caused by her eavesdropping.

Prove them wrong, she kept telling herself. Hold your head up and don't let their words bring you down.

From a long distance away, Ophelia could hear that the younger initiates were already partaking in the third physical training session of the day. The routine for a Kyriegard pre-apprentice consisted of an early morning workout and conditioning, breakfast, two lecture and study sessions, combat training, lunch, two more lecture and study sessions, one last session of sparring and fighting, and then dinner. Some chose to pick up extra study time after the last meal of the day, which Ophelia gladly did. The lectures and study content ranged from academics to strategy, and while most initiates did such classes at Halvalla, Ophelia and Theodin held private studies with Kaspar.

Initiation, then physical conditioning, then a regular initiate's routine, then official apprenticeship under a mentor, then partner compatibility testing for the Arcane Dyad, then partner conditioning, then the temporary partner tether, then the Kyriegard Trials, and then the permanent sealing of the Arcane Dyad.

Most Kyriegard had thirteen years to accomplish all of this. Ophelia's goal was to do it in five.

Her next step was an official apprenticeship under a Kyriegard mentor. That normally took place, at the earliest, at ten years old. For some, it took an extra year or two. Ophelia was certainly late, but she thought she was making decent progress in the past month.

At her age, she needed to be tested to see if she was compatible with another Kyriegard apprentice in the famed Arcane Dyad.

This was the stage Theodin had been in for five years.

He was apprenticed at age ten under Kaspar. Ophelia secretly hoped her mentor would either be Alfena or Kaspar, but she wasn't sure if the Head of the Order could have more than one apprentice at a time—let alone have an apprentice at all.

Alfena said it was rare for mentorship and apprenticeship to happen with complete strangers. A bond has to be formed and the relationship has to be complementary and enable growth, much like the Arcane Dyad—just without the soul-binding magic.

The concept of the Arcane Dyad truly fascinated Ophelia. Being bound to someone by your very *spirit?* She was already intrigued by the idea of being connected to the Order's Collective just by a drop of blood—a simple tether, though the Council claims hers is complex from the results of her initiation—and one that could be cut, but only by the Council. The Arcane Dyad, once sealed after the final Kyriegard Trials, was permanent. Any attempt at separation—which again, from Ophelia's understanding, had never been done other than through the death of a partner—was incredibly damaging and traumatic.

But the Arcane Dyad was the Order's most sacred aspect—ironic for being such a secular institution—and its most potent. A Dyad that was perfectly paired, two elite Sage warriors, could match an entire battalion.

It was said that a Dyad, in complete synchronization, could take down ten seasoned fighters before drawing breath, and thirty more before drawing blood. Against ordinary humans, a single charge from a Dyad—sword and spell moving as one—could scatter an army three times their number.

They didn't just fight beside each other. They moved like twin souls in one current—each strike anticipated, each spell reinforced. One defended while the other struck. One bled while the other burned. Their connection turned battle into choreography, into devastation.

Of course, such power came at a cost. A poorly matched Dyad was more dangerous to itself than to any enemy. But a true Dyad?

A true Dyad was unstoppable.

This was what gave the Kyriegard an edge over all other magic-users and warriors, with the exception of the Valksha.

Now…a *Valksha* in an Arcane Dyad?

It's never been done before. Ophelia aimed to be the first. She didn't want to just be strong. She wanted to be part of something unbreakable. To never again face death alone.

Lady Vivian told Ophelia that by having her tethered to the Order's Collective and by being in a fully-realized Arcane Dyad, the dark agents that claimed the lives of her family and her people would not be able to snuff her out so easily. She could even work with the Order to find the culprits and bring them to justice once and for all.

She had to be careful not to call it revenge, as that was not the way of the Kyriegard.

The training grounds at Avasylon buzzed with activity as apprentices and initiates moved between stations. Enchanted dummies lined the far end, their movements erratic and unpredictable as they dodged or struck back against their opponents. Sparring rings occupied the center, where pairs of Kyriegard clashed with blades or staves, their strikes echoing through the air.

Ophelia adjusted her leather gauntlets as she stepped onto the grounds. The weight of her pendant felt heavier than usual, but she ignored it, focusing instead on the figure waiting for her near the enchanted dummies.

Theodin stood with his arms crossed, his jarring eyes fixed on her. His expression was as inscrutable as ever, but the slight tilt of his head suggested impatience.

"You're late," he said simply.

Ophelia stopped in front of him, arching a brow. "How tragic. Did you miss me?"

Theodin's jaw tightened, though there was a flash of something—amusement, maybe?—in his gaze. "You should always be prepared. A real mission won't wait for you to catch up."

She shrugged, dropping her satchel at her feet. "Good thing this isn't a real mission, then."

For a moment, Theodin said nothing, his expression unreadable. Then he gestured toward the nearest enchanted dummy. "Reaction drills," he said, his tone clipped. "Let's see how well you've been listening."

Ophelia turned to the dummy. It floated a few feet off the ground, its glowing eyes flickering as it turned toward her. "Fine," she said, rolling her shoulders. "But don't be mad when I outshine you."

As Ophelia squared off against the dummy, she took a cleansing breath to calibrate herself. Though a month had passed since her initiation, the pace of her training had still been grueling.

Her historical and cultural studies had been her sanctuary, a place where she could thrive. Books were familiar, safe, and predictable, unlike the chaotic energy of the training grounds. She'd devoured every text Kaspar had handed her, often staying up late into the night with a lantern and a stack of tomes.

But the physical training—that was another story. It wasn't that she lacked determination; she pushed herself hard every day. Yet, no matter how much she tried, she couldn't match the precision and discipline of her peers. Her body still lagged behind her mind, and her reactions were often too instinctive, too wild.

Her magic, at least, had improved. The binding during her initiation had tethered her more firmly to the Order's magic, giving her something to focus on when her emotions threatened to spiral out of control, but control was still a work in progress.

And then there was Theodin. He was relentless in their sessions together, pushing her to her limits and often beyond. She didn't always appreciate his methods, but she couldn't deny that she'd made progress under his watch. He challenged her in ways that no one else did, forcing her to confront her weaknesses head-on.

At the thought of him, Ophelia's eyes glimpsed for a fleeting moment at her towering companion following her last retort. She noticed a smirk in the corner of his mouth—did she actually crack the surface of his rigid personality?

She couldn't help but snort. "What, you don't think it's possible for me to outshine you, Sir…Model Kyriegard? Top of the class?"

Theodin raised a brow, the smirk lingering just enough to soften his usually stern expression. "I didn't say that," he replied evenly, his voice laced with the faintest hint of amusement. "But if you're going to talk big, you'd better back it up." He gestured toward the dummy again, his eyes gleaming. "Show me what outshining looks like, Valksha."

Ophelia chuckled and rubbed her hands together, and her irises shined playfully as she winked at him. "Gladly, big fellow."

When she squared off again to face the dummy, she readied herself, her thumb hovering over a ring on the opposite hand's pointer finger.

Theodin crossed his arms, leaning back slightly as he watched her prepare. "You always this dramatic?" he asked dryly, though the sneer tugging at his lips betrayed his amusement. He tilted his head, his critical gaze locking onto her stance. "Remember, it's not just about speed. Precision and control matter just as much. Don't let your instincts run the show." The teasing edge in his tone softened slightly as he added, "Impress me, Ophelia."

Ophelia giggled. "I've already impressed you since the night I came in, haven't I? Shouldn't be hard now."

The dummy, made of stone and wood, began to levitate. It lunged at her. In one fluid motion, she dodged to the side and pressed her thumb into her ring. The spring-loaded needle in its hidden compartment pierced her skin just enough to draw a drop of blood.

Feel it. Command it. Will it.

That was all it took for a Valksha to summon the Saryfim energy woven into their flesh.

The magic coursed through her veins.

She shoved her palms into the dummy's side and blasted it with telekinetic energy. As its limbs and bits scattered across the field, Ophelia exhaled and straightened her stance. She watched as the dummy's pieces began to roll back together.

"I'm dramatic all the time, aren't I? Same instance as my first entry—it's just that now I'm actually having fun." Her eyes flickered in his direction with a grin. "Especially with outshining you."

Theodin let out a short, dry laugh, shaking his head as he watched the dummy piece itself back together. "Confidence looks good on you, Valksha," he said, stepping closer. "But don't let it go to your head. One lucky hit doesn't mean you've got it all figured out."

He gestured toward the reassembled dummy as it hovered back into place, its glowing eyes now fixed on her with an almost vengeful glint. "Let's see if you can do it twice—or if you just got lucky." Theodin crossed his arms once more, his gaze narrowing with interest. "And for the record," he added, a hint of an upward curl tugging at his lips, "you haven't outshined me yet. But keep trying—I might just let you."

The dummy lunged again. With flare, Ophelia performed the same fluid movements from the opposite side. She effortlessly executed the same spell and combative motion.

As she finished off the dummy and scattered its parts to the other end of the field, she put her hands on her hips and leaned to one side. "Oh, I need your permission now?" she chuckled. "Maybe you should put me back in my place, dear Theo. After all, I'm learning from the best."

Theodin raised a brow, his rare smile deepening as he uncrossed his arms. "Oh, so now I'm 'dear Theo,' am I?" he asked, his tone laced with mock offense. "Careful, Valksha. Flattery might work on the dummies, but it won't get you far with me."

He strode toward her, his boots crunching softly against the dirt, and motioned for her to reset. "No magic this time," he said firmly, his tone leaving no room for argument. "Just you and the dummy. Let's see how you handle it."

Ophelia blinked, her arms lowering slightly. "No magic? You're joking."

"Do I look like I'm joking?" Theodin said. "You rely too much on it. If you're going to survive out there, you need to trust your body as much as your magic."

He took a step back, giving her space as the dummy reassembled itself, its glowing eyes now gleaming with renewed focus. "If you're learning from the best, then prove it. This time, let's see what you can do without your little ring trick." Then, he leaned slightly forward, his eyes glinting. "Or are you afraid you might not look so impressive without it?"

Ophelia scrunched her nose at him. "You were impressed before I started using this little trinket. I know you think my magic is fascinating," she teased. She obediently followed his instruction and reset her stance, readying her hands.

Theodin tilted his head slightly. "Fascinating, huh?" he said, his tone still teasing but measured. "Interesting choice of words. But sure, let's call it that."

She huffed, pushing a stray strand of hair from her face. "Fine," she muttered. "But don't blame me if I break the dummy without your precious magic."

Theodin chuckled lightly. "I'll take my chances."

The dummy clicked into motion, rising a few feet off the ground before charging at her. Its wooden arms extended with a furious whir, aiming a strike at her side. Ophelia twisted out of the way, her boots skidding slightly on the dirt as she ducked under its second swing.

Her instincts screamed at her to use her magic—a quick burst of energy could easily disable it—but Theodin's words echoed in her mind. No magic this time.

She pivoted, sidestepping another attack, and swung her arm upward. Her fist collided with the dummy's joint, but the impact sent a jolt of pain through her knuckles. She winced, shaking out her hand as the dummy whirred again in response, spinning to face her again.

"You're hesitating," Theodin called, his voice sharp but calm. "Stop overthinking it. Use your momentum. Commit to the strike."

Ophelia gritted her teeth, her eyes squinting. She ducked under another swing and threw her weight into the next move, slamming her shoulder into the dummy's center. It staggered back slightly, its glowing eyes flickering in response.

"Better," Theodin said, though his tone remained neutral. "Again."

The dummy adjusted, its movements becoming faster and more erratic. Ophelia's breath quickened as she dodged and weaved, each movement draining her energy. Her muscles burned, but she pushed herself harder, refusing to let Theodin—or the dummy—get the better of her.

When the dummy lunged again, she dropped low, sliding under its outstretched arms. She grabbed one of its wooden legs, yanking it forward with all her strength. The dummy toppled, its limbs flailing as it hit the ground with a resounding thud.

Ophelia scrambled to her feet, panting, as the dummy began to reassemble itself. She turned to Theodin, a triumphant grin spreading across her face. "How's that for no magic?"

Theodin tilted his head again, his strange eyes scanning her with quiet intensity. After a moment, he nodded. "Not bad," he admitted. "But don't get cocky. You've still got work to do."

Ophelia's grin widened as she caught her breath. "Oh, I'm sorry. Did I outshine you again, dear Theo?"

He rolled his eyes, the subtle smirk returning. "Keep it up, Valksha. You might actually start believing that."

The remaining time of the training session passed without much notice.

The dummy's pieces reassembled slowly, clicking and clanking as they levitated back into place. Theodin gestured for her to step aside, his usual sternness softening as he approached the training dummy to deactivate it. He pressed his palm against the sigil carved into the wooden torso and muttered a command under his breath, which caused the limbs to limply collapse like a discarded marionette puppet.

The field fell quiet, the buzz of activity from the other stations fading into the background.

Ophelia leaned against the nearest post, catching her breath as she wiped the sweat from her brow. The adrenaline from the exercise was ebbing now, leaving her muscles aching but her spirit surprisingly buoyed.

"Not bad," Theodin said, his tone quieter now as he returned to her side. "You're learning to trust yourself more. That's progress."

She looked up at him, the usual teasing glint in her eyes replaced by something softer. "You don't make it easy, you know," she said with a small laugh. "But I guess that's the point."

Theodin folded his arms, leaning slightly against the post beside her. "It's not supposed to be easy. If it were, you wouldn't grow."

She nodded, her gaze drifting to the horizon where the sun was beginning to set, casting long shadows across the field. Her thoughts wandered to the Council meeting she had overheard earlier that day.

"Do you ever think about what happened during my initiation?" she asked hesitantly. "I mean, with the binding and all."

His brows furrowed. "It's hard not to. Magic doesn't usually behave like that. It's…raw. Untamed."

"And yet you don't seem to treat me like some kind of anomaly," she said, her voice low. "Not like some of the others do."

Theodin shrugged. "You're not an anomaly to me. You are a Valksha. You're just…Ophelia. Someone who's got a lot to figure out but isn't afraid to try."

A small wave of relief came over her. She smiled faintly, her fingers brushing the pendant at her chest. "You know…I was thinking about what we talked about a few weeks ago. You're not as scary as people think you are. And I really mean that—not just because I'm a Valksha and I'm not afraid of you. Even if I was one of them, without this magic."

His brow arched, a hint of intrigue flickering in his oddly-colored eyes. "What makes you say that?"

"Well, you do have that whole brooding thing going on," she teased lightly, though her tone carried a thread of sincerity. "But…after everything, I think I get it. You're figuring things out just like I am, and just as much a work in progress as I am too. Maybe in different ways, but still."

Theodin's expression faltered for a moment—something unspoken passing through his gaze before he looked away. "Maybe," he admitted. "But this isn't about me."

Ophelia leaned back, crossing her arms as she glanced at him. "I think it's about both of us. I'm still trying to understand and learn about you as much as you are about me."

Their eyes met briefly, and for a moment the space between them seemed to shift. It wasn't the sharp, challenging tension from training—it was quieter, subtler. There was something unspoken, something neither of them were ready to name. Whatever connection had sparked between them that first night—whatever strange current had passed through that brief touch—still lingered, though neither said it aloud.

"You're doing fine, Ophelia," Theodin said after a long pause, his voice softer. "Better than fine, really. Just keep pushing."

She nodded, her glance drifting to the horizon. "Thanks," she said quietly, "for not giving up on me."

Theodin pushed off the post, his smirk returning. "You're stuck with me, Valksha. Might as well make it worth my while."

Ophelia laughed softly, the weight of the day easing just a little. "Deal, dear Theo."

As the sun dipped lower in the sky, painting the field in hues of gold and amber, they walked back to the cottage in comfortable silence.

Chapter 10

The Sanctum of Avasylon

Year 843 of the Second Age, Tenth Month, Thirty-First Day

Ophelia sat alone at a table before a large, open tome, wrapped in her cloak beside a flickering oil lamp. She held a mug of hot tea in her hands and scoured the aged pages with hungry eyes.

After supper, Kyriegard initiates were given the choice to train further or pursue independent study. Theodin almost always chose to train. Ophelia, more often than not, chose to study.

Pre-apprenticed initiates split their time between Avasylon, Havysium, and Halvalla, while apprentices—those already paired with a mentor—spent most of their time at Havysium or Halvalla. That meant Ophelia and Theodin rarely saw the older initiates closer to Theodin's age. Most of those individuals already had mentors.

That was alright with Ophelia. The children looked at her as if she were something mythical and often stared at her with wide eyes and open mouths. Sometimes they asked her to perform magic. Kaspar or Theodin would usually shut the request down, but if their backs were turned, Ophelia would do something fantastical anyway—just enough to leave them giggling or gasping in delight.

As Kaspar's apprentice and ward, Theodin remained stationed primarily at Avasylon, and Ophelia did too, given her unusual circumstances. Most Kyriegard returned to Havysium for meals and rest, but Ophelia and Theodin remained at Avasylon under Kaspar's direct care. The Head of the Order resided strictly at Avasylon while the rest of the Council remained stationed at Halvalla.

Avasylon's lower sanctum was an entire underground system that stretched for acres beneath its open-field training grounds.

The only entrance in and out of the sanctum was a cellar door in the cottage.

It blew Ophelia's mind when she saw it for the first time not long after the night of her initiation. Theodin and Kaspar had shown her the armory, the library, indoor training chambers, even empty holding chambers for miscellaneous Sage use—rooms lined with runic wards to contain outbursts of Sage magic practices in order to prevent destruction to the rest of the sanctum.

Amidst her rigorous routine and study schedule, Ophelia had yet the time to explore the rest of Avasylon's lower sanctum. Her days were filled to the brim with study and training.

Again, Ophelia didn't mind the busyness or isolation. She preferred the company of Kaspar and Theodin since they didn't bombard her with questions like the children did. That happened both at Avasylon and Halvalla.

Ophelia would occasionally need to travel to Halvalla for her emotional training sessions with Alfena, and Theodin would accompany her. At times, they would remain at Halvalla for a little while before returning to Avasylon. She sometimes heard giggles down the hall—initiates whispering over spellbooks or trading rare snacks from the kitchens. Once, she caught sight of a girl no older than twelve peeking through the archway just to watch her read, like she was some strange exhibit from a forgotten age.

Like Theodin, Ophelia mostly did her studies privately, and once in a while she had to attend a lecture. Her first few classes on Kyriegard discipline and philosophy were with initiates much younger than she was, but she didn't have to remain in that group for long. She eventually excelled enough to sit in with groups of older initiates—those who were perhaps only two or three years younger than she was.

The most common approach to her routine of study would be that one of the instructors would give her an assignment and passages to read, and she would finish within the hour.

It helped that she loved to read. Her father had taught all three of them how to read and appreciate literature since he came from nobility before escaping the Valksha Massacre and retreating to life on the farm with her mother. She and her brother would beg their mother to buy and trade books at the market whenever she went to town for supplies since they knew they couldn't leave the farm.

Then, when she was rescued, Ophelia became Lady Vivian's apprentice and learned much more from observation. She still read as they traveled day to day in their nomadic lifestyle, and thankfully she read with such speed that she could finish tomes quickly and not be so bogged down by a stack of books.

A year before her arrival in Avasylon, Lady Vivian resolved to have her become a Kyriegard. From there, Lady Vivian taught Ophelia what she knew of the Order.

There was still much—*so* much—more to learn.

Such was tonight's topic of study for Ophelia. She placed down the mug of tea and pulled out a piece of parchment, a bottle of ink, and a quill to take notes.

The Kyriegard Order—the most prominent of the Sage Circles, though some rarely even address it as a Sage Circle due to its unique qualities. Some call it the Order because of its distinctive and robust influence in all of Moirand, ironically and also more prominent than any Knight's Order in all the kingdoms or under any crown—yet, the only knight ever in their ranks was one of the founding Council, a knight commander of Tersia named Thalric Kaspar.

It fascinated Ophelia how the Kyriegard were so renowned, yet she had never seen any of them in her travels. Though they were few, they were mighty. There were about five or six seasoned Kyriegard pairs currently stationed in each country of Moirand—except Erythar. At least, not yet. There was one pair of Cruerfel apprentices, the first pair after centuries since the Order's establishment, that King Zyreus was eventually willing to contribute. Strange, Ophelia thought—but perhaps being such an isolated and antagonized group might do strange things to them and cause them to act just as cautiously.

The Order came to be during the War of Malblight. Five Sage warriors—Thalric Kaspar, Jorren Crane, Saphiela Marobe, Ebron Gravehardt, and Elysant Jackard—united to train individuals as elite agents for the good and balance of Moirand. Their Council seats, along with their surnames to serve as titles, were passed on for generations.

* * *

Ophelia's quill scribbled furiously. Her eyes darted with heightened focus between the tome and her parchment.

Through trial and error, they developed the disciplines that became the foundation of the Sage warrior—the rigorous combination of spellwork and martial skill that remains the hallmark of the Order. They imbued their passion for peace and immense energies into one unified force, creating the Order's Collective, which all Kyriegard were bound to through the initiation ritual. The heart of that magic took root in what would later become known as Arborelys—a symbol of unity and renewal.

This tether was not a soul-selling contract like those of the Warthralls, who required patrons, nor was it the blood-bound devotion of the Valksha to the Saryfim. The pact of the Kyriegard, while it asked for a single drop of blood and a spoken oath, did not demand the complete surrender of body or soul.

Arborelys was known only to the Kyriegard. It was not treated as an idol, but as an objective force born of the Order's founders. It was purely neutral—never worshipped.

And not all could be chosen. Arborelys could discern who had the potential to become a Kyriegard through the initiation ritual. If someone was rejected, their memory of Olysgard would be erased, and they would be gently returned to society.

Ophelia was grateful Arborelys had accepted her—even with the strange reaction it had during her initiation.

At any given time, there were perhaps eight to twelve pre-apprenticed initiates, and another eight to twelve apprentices being mentored by Council members or retired Kyriegard residing in Havysium—those who had survived the field but no longer served as Dyads, having lost their partners to natural or disastrous death.

To be a Sage was challenging. To be a warrior or a soldier was another challenge entirely. The founders of the Order did not begin as Sage warriors but came from vastly different walks of life: a knight commander, a Sage, a blacksmith, a scout, and an engineer. Though the Sage was well-versed in magic, the others possessed only fragmented, self-taught knowledge. Sages and Sage Circles did not teach weaponry or combat, and warriors rarely studied the complexities of magic.

It was the founders' shared determination that changed this. They taught one another their skills, overcoming countless failures to become the first Sage warriors: a revolutionary force that could wield both blade and spell. In their time, they were seen as both saviors and enigmas—mortals who dared to challenge corruption without divine intervention.

Though centuries had passed, their principles endured: adaptability, discipline, and the unyielding pursuit of balance. Their legacy lived on in the modern Kyriegard.

Balance was a fragile thing, and the forces of corruption never rested. With rising darkness and the echoes of corruption stirring anew, neither could the Order.

Ophelia placed her quill down and sat back with a sigh. She could take in all that information with no issue, but it might have overwhelmed someone younger than her. She quietly thanked her father in the Ether for gifting her with a love of learning.

The page glowed faintly in the lamp's light, the ink still glistening as it dried. She leaned back in the chair and let her gaze drift across the library's quiet shadows.

And then she froze.

A whisper of movement. Not loud, not magical—just the subtle shift of weight against stone. She straightened, her eyes narrowing toward the far row of darkened shelves across the chamber.

Nothing.

As far as she knew, she was the only one in Avasylon's lower sanctum tonight. Theodin was above ground, Kaspar was in the cottage, and the rest of the initiates had gone home.

Kaspar said that Avasylon's lower sanctum was protected by Lady Vivian's enchantments. There was no possible way anything malicious could have gotten in.

Perhaps an animal burrowed its way in?

No… this place was built incredibly well. The Council's architect seats had ensured that.

It *was* the thirty-first day of the tenth month. Perhaps the spirits of the Lither wandered. Maybe Ophelia was being paid a visit by one.

She rose slowly, not out of fear, but with a scholar's caution—the kind her mother used when checking traps in the henhouse. She padded across the chamber, cloak swaying softly behind her.

But when she reached the corridor, there was nothing. No footsteps. No presence. Only the faint scent of parchment and dust.

Still, she could feel it. Not magic. Not malice. But observation.

She turned back toward her table. Her tea had cooled.

Kaspar wouldn't have let anyone roam freely down here, she thought. Unless… they were permitted.

Ophelia slowly looked around again. Her eyes fell upon the dimly lit lanterns hung on the walls. She pricked her finger against her needle ring to draw blood.

She zeroed in on the lanterns and lifted her hand, and the drop of blood evaporated with a spark of green.

Suddenly, the chamber flooded with light as every lantern flared to life. Every shadow in every corner vanished.

A surprised yelp—and the crash of falling books—shattered the quiet, followed by the thud of two bodies hitting the wooden floor.

Ophelia's head whipped toward the sound. Her fingers twitched, ready to cast again. Slowly, she approached the aisle where she heard the commotion.

Then she heard the groan.

"Oh, fantastic," a low voice muttered from behind one of the collapsed shelves. "That's my spine."

"You don't need your spine to read," another snapped. "Move."

Ophelia peered around the corner of the aisle.

A figure stood first—tall, disheveled, and brushing off dust with theatrical flair. His dark hair was a mess, and his crooked smirk gave him away before she even saw his face fully.

The second boy followed, emerging slowly, his expression unreadable as he adjusted his glasses and smoothed his uniform with meticulous fingers.

Ophelia squinted in recognition. Her eyes caught the silver pins on their collars that held the symbol of one of the Council members—Crane, the seat of seeking and espionage.

She searched her memory. The first one was Mald, and the second one was Fritan. Apprentices of Azariah Crane.

Ophelia scoffed. *"Really?"*

Mald grinned. "Hi."

Fritan didn't look at her. "In our defense, the lighting was perfectly dim."

"You were *spying* on me."

Mald winced like she'd accused him of something far more scandalous. "Spying is such an ugly word. We were… observing."

"Research," Fritan added flatly, eyes still scanning the floor for any dropped parchment.

"Unauthorized research," she said, crossing her arms.

"Field training!" Mald chirped enthusiastically.

"Well," Ophelia chuckled dryly, folding her arms. "Master Crane would be disappointed to know that you failed."

"It's good practice, ain't it?" Fritan said with a shrug. "Not bad since yer a Valksha—we got enough observation to count as reconnaissance."

Ophelia stared at them a moment longer. No aura. No flicker of energy. She'd sensed nothing. That was what unnerved her most. It had to be because they were both fully human, to her knowledge.

"Next time," she said slowly, "make sure I don't hear you breathing before I see you fall out of a bookshelf."

Mald brightened. "So we were doing well up until then?"

She exhaled sharply. "Out."

Fritan raised an eyebrow. "We're already going."

Mald gave her a wink as he followed. "This was fun. Let's not do it again."

The two of them disappeared into the stairwell, and Ophelia waited until she could no longer hear their boots on stone.

Chapter 11

The Shadow in the Snow

Year 843 of the Second Age, Twelfth Month, Twenty-Ninth Day

This morning, they would accompany Kaspar on a mission.

The chill in Avasylon's underground armory bit through the stone like a buried whisper of ice. Enchanted torches sputtered with cold, bluish flame, casting long, wavering shadows across racks of frost-kissed steel. The scent of oiled leather mingled with the faint metallic tang of old magic.

As they prepared, only the sound of quiet clanging and shifting echoed through the space. A hush, taut with tension, hung between the three of them.

Finally, Kaspar's voice broke through the silence like a blade cleaving ice. "Remember—this isn't a training exercise. It's not just reconnaissance, either. We're heading into the unknown, and I expect both of you to be ready."

Ophelia adjusted the straps of her bracers with numb fingers, her breath rising in plumes that quickly vanished. Theodin stood nearby, arms crossed, a vapor curling from his mouth as he exhaled. His eyes, sharp and distant, swept over Ophelia's gear, pausing long enough to draw a twitch of discomfort from her.

"You should double-check your left bracer," he said, his tone clipped, brittle as the winter. "It's loose."

Ophelia resisted the urge to roll her eyes and tightened the strap. "Anything else, *dear Theo?* Or are we ready to freeze our arses off?"

A ghost of a smirk touched his lips, then disappeared like warmth from winter stone.

Kaspar stepped forward, his weathered face calm but stern.

"Our goal is to investigate the activity traced by our wardstones since Lady Vivian brought Ophelia here," he said. "It's also about understanding the patterns and motives behind the Warthrall attack from before. If we find signs of Azazelf's involvement, we'll report back to Halvalla immediately. No heroics."

Azazelf Chernabog—the "Demon Dark Elf."

Lady Vivian had only spoken of him in warnings, but Ophelia knew the Unseelie fiend's reputation from whispers she'd overheard during her nomadic travels. He was elusive but devastating, a Warthrall who left nothing but desolation in his wake.

Ophelia straightened her stance, nerves simmering beneath the surface. "Understood."

Kaspar's discerning gaze fixed on her. "This is your first time in the field. Trust your training and follow my lead. No magic unless it's necessary. Clear?"

"Yes, sir," she said, her voice steady despite the flutter in her chest.

Theodin, already geared up, leaned against a nearby rack of weapons. "Let's hope this isn't a repeat of last time," he muttered, half to himself.

Ophelia shot him a look. "You mean the Warthrall ambush? That wasn't my fault."

"Not entirely," he replied, his tone lighter now—though the edge remained.

Kaspar clapped his hands, drawing their attention. "Enough. We leave now."

The path from Avasylon twisted through the forest, now veiled beneath a thin shroud of snow. The trees stood bare and brittle, their dark limbs etched starkly against a pale sky, branches heavy with hoarfrost that glittered in the dappled morning light. Every step muffled beneath a soft crust of snow, the crunch of boots dulled by nature's hush.

The distant hum of Avasylon's protective enchantments faded behind them. Cold clung to their cloaks and bit at exposed skin. A flurry of frost-rimed wind whispered through the branches, stirring the air with a bite that worked its way beneath furs and leather.

Ophelia adjusted the strap of her satchel with gloved fingers stiff from the cold, her thumb brushing the pendant at her chest. The talisman pulsed with warmth, grounding her even as her thoughts scattered like snowflakes in the wind.

Would she freeze again when it mattered most? Or worse, lose control like before?

Theodin walked ahead, his cloak floating behind him like a shadow drawn by the snow. His movements were silent, deliberate—the way of someone long practiced in navigating both silence and danger. There was no trail behind them—only the barest trace of their passage, quickly swallowed by flurries.

Ophelia's gaze stayed on his back. He had been colder than usual today—in more ways than one.

She had thought they were starting to work well together. Over the past three months, the distance between them had shrunk—not just in combat, but in wordless exchanges, in glances, in touch. Their interactions became warm.

But something had shifted before this mission, and now the warmth was absent. A wall had come back up, and she wasn't sure what she'd done to rebuild it.

Her mind replayed the briefing last night.

"…Considering the Warthrall attack last season and what our sources have recently detected, this is a matter for me to address directly. However, this is an opportunity for you to learn," Kaspar had explained to them.

"*Her?*" Theodin's eyes flicked toward Ophelia, his tone harsher than intended. "Only four months in and she's tagging along on a mission?"

Ophelia stiffened. "I can handle myself," she shot back, though her voice wavered.

Kaspar raised a hand, stopping them. "Enough. This isn't a debate. Ophelia is coming because she needs to see what the field is like. And you, Theodin, need to learn to lead."

Theodin's jaw tightened, but he said nothing, his gaze fixed on a distant point behind Kaspar.

Kaspar continued, easing slightly. "You'll both be under my supervision. The rules don't change just because we're outside

Avasylon or Halvalla. You follow orders, and you trust each other. Understood?"

"Yes, sir," Theodin said curtly.

Ophelia hesitated before nodding. "Yes, sir."

As snow fell in soft spirals around them, Ophelia turned inward.

She could put aside Theodin's skepticism. But could *he* put aside his doubt?

He hadn't looked her in the eye for more than a few seconds since that morning. Their connection still went unspoken, and it gnawed at her in ways she couldn't explain. Every time she gathered the courage to say something, the words stopped in her throat.

Maybe it wasn't the right time. Maybe he wasn't ready to talk about it. Or maybe—just maybe—he didn't *want* to.

But she noticed his hesitation when it happened.

Had he felt it too?

She thought so—but Theodin hadn't given any indication. He hadn't mentioned it, hadn't so much as hinted that it had crossed his mind. His silence made her question everything—whether it was real, whether it mattered, or whether it was something only she had imagined.

And yet, there were moments—fleeting, subtle—when she caught him watching her, his odd eyes unreadable. Not harsh, not cold, but guarded, as if he were keeping something locked away. She wasn't sure if it was doubt, curiosity, or something else entirely. But those glances only deepened her confusion.

What was he thinking?

Did he even want to understand what had happened between them?

Her chest tightened.

Alfena's words drifted through her mind, soft but unyielding: *"Connections like these are rare and difficult to name. It's not just magic—it's trust, understanding. But trust takes time, Ophelia, and time requires patience. Give him that."*

She'd brought it up during their most recent session—mentioned the strange pull she felt, the way her magic reacted to Theodin's. But Alfena hadn't pressed. Perhaps because even she couldn't explain it. Ophelia had sensed her uncertainty in the silence that followed.

Patience.

The word repeated in her head.

Ophelia pressed her lips into a thin line. She wondered if Alfena truly believed patience was enough.

What if he didn't want to trust her at all?

Kaspar slowed his pace, letting Theodin move ahead while he fell in beside her. He glanced between them, then gave her a wry look.

"You've got that spiraling look, you know," he murmured.

Ophelia blinked. "O-Oh."

Kaspar shook his head. "No worries. Don't let Theodin's sourness get you. He takes missions very seriously."

"He thinks I'm going to mess it up, doesn't he?" Ophelia muttered.

Kaspar sighed. "Yes and no. Give him time, lass."

There it was again. Give him time; have patience.

Ophelia exhaled with frustration.

With that, Kaspar paced ahead past Theodin. He halted near a mound of half-buried stones, their surfaces etched with runes dusted in snow and lichen. The runes pulsed, similar to the ones carved in the protective enchantments in the walls of Halvalla, Avasylon, and Havysium.

He gestured for them to stop.

"These," he said, brushing snow from a stone's surface, "are markers from the early Kyriegard. They carved paths through the wilderness during the War of Malblight."

Ophelia crouched, reaching toward the stone. As her fingers neared the runes, they lit with a dim green glow, casting a light shimmer over the snow. The magic hummed under her skin.

She didn't look up. "Just markers, but not the wardstones?"

"Correct."

"What do they mean?"

As they spoke, Theodin's gaze flicked to her hand now tracing the runes. His eyes narrowed. The glow mirrored her pendant, and for a moment something stirred in his expression—curiosity, perhaps. Or unease. But just as quickly, he looked away, his guarded mask slipping back into place.

Kaspar's voice lowered. "Guidance. Protection. Warnings. The founders used them to map safe routes and mark areas of corruption. Some of these runes have held their power for centuries."

Theodin leaned against a nearby snow-laced tree, his arms crossed. "*Some*," he repeated. "Not all survived."

Kaspar nodded. "Time isn't kind to everything. But enough remain to remind us of what they stood for—and what we still stand for."

Ophelia straightened, curiosity piqued. "So these were made by the knight commander? Or the smith?"

Kaspar allowed himself a rare smile. "The architect. Elysant Jackard. Her work wasn't limited to fortresses. She designed many of the runic systems we still use today."

Theodin pushed off the tree, brushing snow from his shoulder. "We're wasting daylight."

Kaspar gave a curt nod. He motioned for them to continue. "Stay alert. If these markers are still active, so might the danger they warned of."

As they pressed deeper, the forest changed. The trees grew closer, their skeletal limbs arching overhead like claws. Sunlight thinned beneath a canopy of winter fog, and the crunch of snow muffled as if the woods themselves wished to swallow all sound.

Ophelia tightened her grip on her satchel strap, her eyes darting to the treetops. The silence wasn't just unsettling—it felt unnatural.

"Why is it so quiet?" she whispered.

Kaspar slowed his pace. His hand instinctively moved to the hilt of his sword. "The forest knows when it's being watched," he muttered. His gaze swept the surroundings as his movements grew deliberate. "Stay close."

Theodin fell into step beside her. "Don't lose focus," he said under his breath. "This is where mistakes happen."

Ophelia bristled but said nothing. She focused on her breath, watching each exhale fog in front of her.

Breathing helps control reactions. Control prevents emotional surges, Alfena had told her.

Whatever was out there, she could feel it too—a prickling at the edge of her senses, like the air before a storm.

They reached a clearing where snow lay undisturbed.

Then—a sound.

A low rustle. A sharp crack of wood.

They froze.

The forest inhaled silence again, but the air had changed. It wound up tightly. As if something unseen drew near.

Kaspar unsheathed his sword. "Eyes sharp," he said. "This isn't just the forest."

Theodin stepped in front of Ophelia, weapon drawn. "Stay behind me."

Shadows rippled along the treeline. Then came the growl—low, guttural, and wrong.

From the thicket, three figures emerged—twisted, grotesque forms that radiated dark energy. Black-fleshed and warped, their bodies hissed against the cold.

Cadaven.

Ophelia's heart pounded as her thumb found the ring. She pressed.

A drop of blood.

Her pendant ignited—green fire in the frost—and her breath plumed in front of her as her hands sparked with power.

She swallowed hard and braced herself.

The Cadaven snarled, their eyes glowing with malevolent light as they closed in.

Theodin met the first with a swift, calculated strike, his blade slicing through the dark creature in one swift motion. Kaspar followed with the second—his movements were efficient, practiced, and deadly.

Ophelia's hands trembled as the third Cadaven lunged toward her. Her pendant flared brighter, casting emerald light across the snow. Sparks fizzled at her fingertips.

She thrust her hands forward.

The clearing erupted in green. A burst of telekinetic energy slammed into the creature, hurling it backward into a tree. Branches shuddered, and snow rained down in heavy clumps and powder.

"Nice shot," Theodin called.

The praise steadied her more than she expected.

The Cadaven regrouped, moving like a pack now—coordinated, driven by something unseen.

"Something's guiding them," Kaspar muttered.

Theodin surged forward, his blade cutting clean arcs through the air. He parried a strike from the nearest Cadaven and countered with a quick thrust that drove it back.

"Ophelia, distance!" he barked.

She obeyed, ducking behind a snow-covered stump and drawing her magic again. She pressed her thumb into her ring, summoning a green orb of electric energy in her palm. She flung her hand outward. The emerald spell sliced through the swirling snow and collided with the Cadaven circling Kaspar. It screeched—its dark energy unraveling as it crumbled into ash.

"Good!" Kaspar called. He turned and struck, dispatching the last Cadaven with a clean sweep of his sword. "Keep it focused like that."

A sudden chill rippled through the snow-covered clearing. The ground trembled.

From the shadows, a new figure stepped forth—its form throbbed with black tendrils of energy. Snow melted into slush at its feet, steam rising like breath from a wound.

Kaspar's expression darkened. "Warthrall."

Its gaze locked on them, twisted features contorting as it raised a massive, clawed hand. Without warning, it shot its claw towards Theodin. Tendrils of black energy lashed out like whips.

Theodin dove aside, barely avoiding the blast as the ground where he'd stood exploded in a shock of dark force.

"Ophelia, move!" Kaspar shouted.

She threw herself down as another tendril cracked past her, narrowly missing. Her hands trembled as she scrambled to her feet, but she forced herself to focus.

Theodin was already back in a ready stance, circling the Warthrall with predatory calm. "We need to split its focus," he called. "It's too strong for one of us to take head-on."

Kaspar nodded and moved to flank the creature. "Ophelia, support us from a distance. Disrupt it when you see an opening."

Her pulse quickened, but she set her jaw and steadied her hands. The Warthrall lashed out again, forcing Kaspar and Theodin to dodge in opposite directions.

Seizing the moment, she pressed her thumb into her ring, and her pendant flared bright. She thrust her palms forward—another shockwave of light and telekinetic force slammed into the creature's side. It stumbled and its tendrils faltered.

Theodin didn't hesitate. He lunged, his blade striking true as he severed one of the creature's arms. Black blood sprayed across the snow, and the Warthrall shrieked with an ear-splitting cry.

Kaspar moved in. His sword carved a deep gash across its torso. "Now, Ophelia!" he shouted.

She didn't think—she acted.

Magic surged from her fingertips, the green light engulfing the Warthrall as she poured everything into the spell.

It thrashed and howled, its movements frantic as the energy consumed it.

Finally, with a last, guttural screech, it disintegrated into ash and its darkness evaporated. Its remains hissed with steam against the snow where it had fallen.

The clearing fell still, save for the sound of their labored breathing.

Ophelia's legs wobbled, and she sank to her knees, the adrenaline draining from her body. Theodin sheathed his sword with a sharp click, his jaw tight as he scanned the clearing for any remaining threats.

Kaspar approached her, wearing an unreadable expression. "Good work," he said. "You held your ground."

Ophelia nodded weakly. "Was that…was that Azazelf?"

Kaspar shook his head. "No. Thankfully."

Theodin offered her a hand, his eyes softer than before. "You did well," he said quietly. "But don't let it go to your head. This was just the beginning."

Ophelia took his hand hesitantly, allowing him to pull her to her feet. She met his gaze, her breath catching at the intensity in his eyes.

"I'm not letting anything go to my head," she huffed. "But I'll take the win."

Kaspar swept the clearing one last time with a slow glance. "We're not done yet. Let's see if this thing left us any clues."

Only the soft hiss of dissipating magic now echoed in the clearing. Where the Warthrall had fallen, a thin residue of dark energy clung to the air before fading entirely. What remained was a crumpled, human form—gaunt, withered, and nearly unrecognizable.

Ophelia stepped closer, her breath catching. She had never seen one this close after its death.

Lady Vivian had always vaporized every hostile Warthrall before Ophelia could get near. There had never been time to stop and examine the aftermath.

Kaspar knelt beside the remains, expression grim. "This one was human."

"Corrupted by dark magic. Twisted by the will of their patrons," Ophelia added in a whisper.

Theodin approached, his eyes darkening as he studied the body. "They sacrifice their humanity for power. Some willingly, others… less so."

Ophelia's stomach churned. The figure bore deep scars, its skin marred by jagged black lines that glistened with residual energy.

"I never understood why anyone would choose something like this," she began. "There's other ways to access and learn magic. If someone doesn't have the discipline to take the path of a Sage, there are benign patrons like Ether spirits or some Seelie Pulchids…"

Kaspar rose to his feet, his gaze distant. "Power. Desperation. Sometimes it's not a choice. Malignant and demonic patrons prey on the weak, the broken, and the ambitious. They promise strength, vengeance, or salvation—but it always comes at a cost."

"Always," Theodin echoed.

Kaspar gestured to the remains. "This one was bound to something powerful. Look at the sigils on its skin."

Ophelia crouched. Her pendant glowed faintly as she examined the markings. The sigils pulsed with residual energy, echoing the dark magic that had once sustained the creature.

"Do you recognize them?" Kaspar asked.

Ophelia shook her head. "Not exactly. But they seem… familiar."

She hesitated, hovering her fingers over one sigil. Her pendant pulsed in response, and an image stirred at the edge of her mind—a symbol she'd seen in one of her readings about ancient demonic pacts.

"These are pact marks," she said at last. "A sign of the connection between the Warthrall and its patron. The shape and style might tell us which patron it served."

Kaspar's expression darkened. "Many—including Azazelf—have been known to leave their marks on their creations. If this Warthrall was his, we're closer to uncovering his plans than I thought."

Theodin's gaze flicked to Kaspar. "And closer to him knowing we're onto him."

Kaspar nodded grimly. "Exactly."

Ophelia sat back on her heels, hands trembling again. "Is there… anything left of them? The person they were before?"

Kaspar's silence was answer enough.

Theodin's eyes moved from the remains to her. He'd seen this before —the weight of realizing what a Warthrall truly was. It always hit differently once the twisted creature dissolved to reveal the human underneath. That first moment of understanding, that horror, stayed with you. Even he had struggled with it once, though he'd never admit it.

For her, this was the first time. The impact of it was written in every tense line of her posture. She looked small then—not weak, but dwarfed by the truth of what they faced.

And yet, she was still here. Still fighting.

Without thinking, Theodin stepped closer and took a knee beside her. His eyes softened as he reached out, resting his hand carefully on her shoulder. The warmth of her presence met his palm, and for a breath, he hesitated. He wasn't one for touch—he preferred the distance or silence. But something in her needed this.

Maybe he did too.

"There's nothing left when the corruption runs this deep," he said, his voice low. "The only mercy we can give them is to stop them."

Ophelia stiffened, and he almost pulled away. But she didn't flinch or recoil. Instead, she exhaled a shaky breath that released the strain in her posture and leaned into his touch.

His energy brushed her senses. Not like the storm she had felt before, but a steady current that anchored her in the chaos—soothing, grounding, and wholly unexpected.

Theodin's grip firmed, just for a moment. Her magic hummed against his touch, a resonance that was subtle and fragile beneath the power she wielded.

As he withdrew, he ruminated on the gesture. It had been instinctual, unplanned… but right. She didn't need his approval or his protection—she had proven that much over the past few months. But maybe, just maybe, she needed to know she wasn't alone.

He stood and offered her his hand. "You did well," he said. "But don't let it go to your head."

Ophelia hesitated, then took it. His grip was firm but not forceful. As he pulled her to her feet, something shifted again—and that strange sensation passed between them.

Their eyes met.

Theodin's hand lingered for a moment longer than intended before he let go, retreating into the familiar safety of his stoicism. His eyes flicked back to the remains, avoiding the intensity of her stare.

Kaspar, standing a few paces away, caught the exchange between Theodin and Ophelia. His sharp gaze, honed by years of leadership, missed nothing—the hesitance in Theodin's hand, the way Ophelia leaned into the touch, and the unspoken tension that strung between them.

It wasn't just the gesture itself that caught his attention. It was what it meant.

Theodin, who rarely offered more than a clipped word or a nod of acknowledgment, had reached out. And Ophelia, who wore her past so visibly in her posture, had accepted it.

Kaspar's expression didn't change, but his mind churned over the implications. Trust didn't come easily for someone like Theodin who held his emotions in a clenched fist. Yet, in that moment, Kaspar saw the subtle beginning of something—understanding, perhaps. Or the earliest shape of something more.

A partnership, if they let it become one.

He didn't speak, didn't interfere. Instead, he turned his attention back to the remains, giving them the space to navigate their own unspoken dynamic.

But the thought reeled in him as he stood beside the twisted corpse.

If they could find balance in their differences—if they could *truly* trust one another—they might just become something extraordinary.

Kaspar cleared his throat, drawing their attention back. "We don't have the luxury of time," he said firmly. "If there's anything here that ties this Warthrall to Azazelf, we need to find it."

Theodin stepped forward, crouching beside the body. His brow furrowed. "These sigils… they're more intricate than usual."

He pointed to an aggressive mark on the Warthrall's forearm that was not symbolic, but rather lettered like a sentence.

"This one's layered. Looks like a secondary binding spell."

Ophelia knelt beside him as she studied it. "It's not just a binding spell," she said. "It's a tracking mark. Whoever this patron is, they were keeping tabs on their creation."

Kaspar's brow furrowed as he studied the sigil. "A tracking mark suggests a more organized operation. Perhaps, if this is Azazelf, he isn't just experimenting with his Warthralls—he's controlling them."

Ophelia brushed her fingers over the sigil, the green glow from her pendant mingling with the residual magic.

A sharp pulse of energy jolted through her.

Cold.

Darkness.

It clung to her skin and pressed against the inside of her skull.

Her eyes shut.

The underground chamber was vast, its jagged walls lit by an eerie green glow emanating from the sigils etched into the stone. The air was thick with the groan of dark magic, resonating in her chest like a second heartbeat. Shadows flickered along the walls as though they were alive.

In the center of the room stood a figure—tall, cloaked, and radiating an aura of malice. She couldn't see his face, but the weight of his presence was undeniable.

She knew it was an Unseelie Pulchid. A Dark Elf.

But he was sickly and wrong. *Demonic.*

Azazelf.

Though she had never met him nor known his energy and presence, her instincts screamed it.

But there was someone else. A second figure lingered at the edges of her vision—a man, hunched over as though bearing an unbearable weight. His features were obscured by shadow, but the glint of something metallic near his wrists caught her attention. Shackles?

The sigils on the walls flared brighter, and the man shifted, his movement slow and heavy as though it took immense effort. Before Ophelia could focus further, the vision shattered.

She gasped for air.

Theodin's hand shot out to steady her. Instantly, his energy brought her back to them. "What happened?"

"I—" Ophelia's voice faltered as she blinked rapidly. "I saw something. I-It… it was Azazelf. It had to be. He had a prisoner. I-I couldn't make out the place. It was dark, cold… underground. And there was a symbol like this one carved into the walls."

Kaspar's gaze sharpened. "Can you describe it?"

Ophelia nodded slowly, closing her eyes to focus on the memory. "It was… a circle broken into three segments. Each segment had its own sigils but more elaborate. And in the center, there was an inverted triangle."

Kaspar exchanged a glance with Theodin.

Theodin straightened, his expression grim. "If she saw it, he might have felt it. Maybe he saw her too. We've been careful so far, but this could have tipped him off."

"Which is why we're not staying," Kaspar said firmly. "We have what we need. The mission is over. The moment we overreach is the moment he wins. We won't risk that—not today."

Ophelia frowned, her heart racing. "But if we're close, shouldn't we —"

"No," Kaspar interrupted, his tone leaving no room for argument. "Reconnaissance means gathering information, not engaging the enemy. We report this to the Council. Let them decide the next move."

"He's right," Theodin said. "Whatever's down there, we're not ready for it yet."

Ophelia stared at the corpse in deep thought. Then, she swallowed her protest and nodded.

"Alright," she said quietly. "Let's go."

Kaspar nodded, already turning toward the treeline. "Stay alert. If

Azazelf knows we've been here, he won't waste time retaliating."

Theodin moved to follow him. "Do you think he's already aware?"

Kaspar's gaze flicked to Ophelia briefly before returning to the path ahead. "If the Warthrall was his creation, he might have felt its death. The question is whether he sees it as a threat… or an opportunity."

Ophelia's chest tightened. The leeching vibrations of the sigils from her vision still thrummed in the back of her head. She didn't dare voice the thought, but the sensation of Azazelf's presence in her vision was impossible to ignore. He had been watching someone. But was it her or his prisoner?

The snow began to fall again—soft, silent, indifferent. And she still felt his eyes on her, whether in memory or magic, she couldn't say.

Chapter 12

The Unspoken Bond

The trio moved swiftly through the frostbitten forest. The soft crunch of snow underfoot blended with the distant reverb of enchantments that marked the boundaries of Halvalla. Tension from the encounter lingered like a heavy fog, unspoken but palpable.

Ophelia lagged slightly behind, her eyes distant as the vision clung to her—chilling, vivid, and still alive in her mind.

Theodin glanced back. Kaspar followed a second later.

"Still with us?" Theodin asked.

Ophelia blinked hard and nodded. "Yes," she exhaled, her breath fogging in the cold.

As they neared Halvalla's gates, the dim glow of fortress runes came into view. The familiar hum of the Kyriegard's enchanted defenses wrapped around them like a shield as they passed through.

"Straight to the Council," Kaspar commanded, his voice leaving no room for argument. He turned to Theodin. "Escort Ophelia to safe quarters here once we're done. She'll need rest."

Ophelia began to speak, but Theodin shot her a look that silenced her.

"Understood," he said simply.

Without pause, they moved briskly from the entrance of the property to the stone stronghold.

Kaspar didn't turn as he spoke, his gaze fixed forward.

"They'll be waiting for us," he said in a low voice, though his words still echoed slightly in the vast corridor.

"Did they know something like this would happen?" Ophelia asked.

"They knew this would be your first mission," Kaspar replied. "And to be ready to drop everything once we were in sight and approaching Halvalla."

"So…this was a test," she said.

"Precisely," Kaspar said.

"You knew those sigils and markings," Ophelia continued, furrowing her brows together. "Yet, you still had me examine them."

"Correct."

"Did you set up the meeting with the Warthrall and Cadaven too?" Theodin asked dully.

Kaspar shook his head. "Anticipated trouble but not planned. We were outnumbered, but we handled it well." Finally, he glimpsed back at Ophelia. "And killed the Warthrall this time."

"And got Azazelf's attention," Theodin muttered.

Kaspar turned back forward grimly. "Yes."

Ophelia huffed. "Then…it *was* Azazelf I saw."

Kaspar's tone darkened. "…Yes."

The Council chamber was as imposing as ever, its runic walls vigilantly glinting in the winter light. The four other Council members were already seated, their expressions a mixture of curiosity and concern as Kaspar, Theodin, and Ophelia entered.

Margrith Gravehardt straightened her posture. "You have return sooner than expected. How did she do?"

Kaspar stepped forward. "Three Cadaven controlled by a Warthrall. There was a tracking sigil on the Warthrall we encountered. It was connected to Azazelf's network, suggesting he's not only creating but actively monitoring his creations." He motioned to Ophelia. "She saw a vision of it upon making contact with the sigil on the Warthrall's body."

Alfena's eyes narrowed. "And the vision Ophelia experienced?"

Kaspar's gaze flicked to Ophelia, who hesitated before stepping forward. Her fingers tightened around her pendant as she spoke. "I saw… a chamber. Underground. It was cold, dark, and covered in sigils. Azazelf was there. And… he had someone with him. A prisoner."

"A prisoner?" Sigvard Jackard's gruff reply broke through. "Who?"

"I don't know," Ophelia admitted, her voice breaking. "I couldn't see his face. But he was… shackled. Weak."

Azariah Crane twirled his cane idly, his expression unreadable. "And you're certain this wasn't just your imagination running wild?"

Kaspar cut through, firm and unyielding. "It wasn't imagination. Her magic responded to the sigil's magic. Whatever she saw, it's tied to Azazelf's operations."

Margrith exchanged a glance with Alfena. "This complicates things. If Azazelf is aware of her presence…"

"He could target her," Alfena finished, calm but sharp. "A Valksha within the Kyriegard is an anomaly. He'll see it as an opportunity."

Theodin stepped forward, his tone clipped. "Then we protect her. If Azazelf makes a move, he'll regret it."

Sigvard grunted, crossing his arms. "Bold words, apprentice. Let's hope you're ready to back them up."

Alfena's gaze then slid gracefully to Ophelia, her expression lightened. "The question is not just how we protect her, but how she protects herself. Ophelia, this is no longer about training. You've stepped into a war. Are you ready for that?"

Ophelia swallowed hard. The weight of the question pressed down on her.

"I… I'll do whatever it takes."

Kaspar's face faltered briefly before hardening again. "We need to act carefully. Azazelf is watching, and any misstep could cost us."

Margrith leaned back. "Then we plan. And we do it quickly."

"May I suggest something radical?" Crane interjected. He leaned forward and tapped his cane. "Perhaps we should accelerate her progression in the Kyriegard."

Sigvard shot up from his chair. "What?!"

Crane thumped his cane harshly and held his hand out. "Hear me out! She's only a target now because she's young and just an initiate. But if she's fully bound to the Order's Collective and to an Arcane Dyad, that gives her a better chance of fighting against him."

"That could also open the door wider and make the Order more vulnerable!" Margrith hissed.

Ophelia could feel the tension from all of them in the room anxiously overwhelming her. All of her limbs and her entire petite self stiffened. Her breath quickened and her heart raced. Her eyes turned down and shut tightly. Instinctively, as she did with Lady Vivian when she felt this affected, she reached for a hand to hold for comfort.

Initially, the energy that shot through her was stormy and electric—then it lessened and settled into a warm, soothing current of water.

Time seemed to stop. The loud, argumentative voices of the Council echoed into silence. Steadily, her breath slowed as she collected herself.

She slowly lifted her eyes. They met the gentle gaze of her Kyriegard companion, Theodin. His grip tightened protectively around hers.

A slight blush formed in her cheeks. Embarrassed, Ophelia bashfully lowered her eyes again. "S-Sorry," she whispered.

Though, as she tugged her hand to pull it away, Theodin's grasp squeezed to keep it in place. He answered her in a whisper in return. "It's going to be okay, Ophelia."

Ophelia looked up in surprise. She took a deep breath and exhaled, nodding with gratitude.

"What if," Kaspar began calmly, "instead of pushing her to the Trials—which we all know perfectly well she is certainly not ready for due to the nature of the Trials themselves—we see how far she can get with the other milestones and rituals. Mentorship. Partnership."

Margrith's eyes snapped to Kaspar. "Mentorship and partnership? Putting her into a Dyad already? You can't be serious. She's only been here four months."

"And in that time, she's shown remarkable resilience and potential," Kaspar replied. "If Azazelf is watching, we need to show him strength—not hesitation."

Alfena tilted her head, her brows raised. "Kaspar has a point. Pushing her through the Trials prematurely would be a disaster. But placing her under official mentorship would reinforce her bond with the Order—and with our teachings."

Sigvard grunted, his arms crossed tightly over his chest. "And pairing her? With whom? She's barely been tested in the field. You can't expect any apprentice to begin a bond with her in an Arcane Dyad at this stage."

Kaspar's gaze flicked to Theodin. "She already has a potential partner."

Theodin went rigid beside Ophelia, his eyes widening slightly. "Sir—"

"You've trained together exclusively for a few months now," Kaspar continued, his tone unwavering. "You've pushed her, challenged her, and seen her at her best and worst. If anyone can guide her, it's you."

Sigvard's chair scraped against the floor as he leaned forward, his voice low and gravelly. "You want to bind them? Before a proper test? That's madness."

"It wouldn't be binding—yet," Alfena interjected. "It would be a pairing trial, a chance to see if their energies are compatible. If it fails, we move forward with other options."

A sly smile tugged at the lips of Azariah Crane. "And if it works? Well, then we'd have something no Warthrall or demon would expect: an Arcane Dyad, as famed and powerful as it can be known in the land of Moirand—that includes a Valksha."

Ophelia's heart pounded in her chest as the room swelled with conflicting sensations of disagreement. The weight of their feelings pressed heavily on her.

Partnership? With Theodin? She stole a glance at him, but his gaze was fixed on the Council, his jaw tight.

"I think we're putting too much faith in her," Margrith said. "This isn't just about her progress—it's about the safety of the Order."

Kaspar stepped forward again with a commanding presence. "The safety of the Order depends on adaptability. Azazelf's growing power demands that we act, not cower. Ophelia has earned her place here. It's time we stop treating her like an outsider."

Alfena spoke again, but this time with a gentle demeanor as she regarded Ophelia. "She has potential," she said quietly. "But potential isn't enough. Ophelia, what do you think? Are you prepared for what this means?"

Ophelia's breath caught, and she hesitated. Her gaze drifted to Theodin, who finally turned to meet her eyes. His expression was unreadable, but there was no doubt in his voice when he answered.

"She can handle it," Theodin said firmly. "And so can I."

The room fell silent. The clashing noises of disagreement suddenly dissipated in shock at his response.

Ophelia took a deep breath and stepped forward. "I'll do whatever it takes," she said steadily despite the fear swirling in her chest. "For the Order, for the Kyriegard. For all of you."

Kaspar's lips curved into a rare, faint smile. "Then it's decided. We'll proceed with mentorship and a partnership trial. Carefully. Deliberately."

Margrith sighed, her frown deepening but her tone resigned. "I still think this is reckless. But if we're doing this, it must be done right."

Sigvard grumbled under his breath. "This better not backfire."

Kaspar glanced around the room, his eyes settling on each Council member. "There's another matter to address before we proceed. If we're committing to this, Ophelia needs an official mentor. Someone to guide her through more than just general training."

Margrith frowned deeply. "Are you suggesting yourself? You already carry the weight of the Order."

"I am," Kaspar replied firmly. "She's a unique case, and her connection to the Order's magic is unlike anything we've seen. It requires careful oversight—oversight I'm best equipped to provide."

Alfena's silver eyes narrowed thoughtfully. "You're not wrong, Kaspar. But mentoring her means devoting more time to her development, which could stretch even you too thin. The Head of the Order doesn't often take on direct mentorship for a reason. Theodin was an exception because he bonded best with you; it was an obvious choice since Lady Vivian designated you as Theodin's guardian."

Sigvard leaned forward again, his thick arms resting on the table. "Why not let Alfena do it? She's been the one training her emotionally. Let her handle the rest."

Alfena tilted her head, her expression now unreadable. "I've considered it, but my focus is on helping Ophelia master her emotions and past traumas. Kaspar, on the other hand, understands her Valksha magic better. I have fought alongside them, but I have never truly… collaborated. He has worked closely with Valksha much more closely than I have, particularly Lady Vivian. He's already started forging a bond with Ophelia—one rooted in trust. That can't be ignored."

Then, Alfena turned to Kaspar. "And, as we approach the Arcane Dyad in the same manner, it is better for her to be challenged by someone with a complimentary personality rather than with one that has similarities. Kaspar is structured, deeply disciplined, and restrained—something more suitable for Ophelia's needs as her magic is still raw and volatile. A perfect balance between the Sage and the warrior." Alfena paused and looked around with a pondering eye. "Not to say I am not any of those attributes. Kaspar is also a model example of a grounded and well-rounded individual. Attending to her weaker qualities would be beneficial."

Alfena's eyes finally landed on Ophelia once more.

"That is the only way she could truly grow."

Crane tapped his cane on the ground to garner attention. "Not to mention, Kaspar has a way of making unlikely candidates shine. Isn't that right, Theodin?"

Theodin flinched but didn't look up, his eyes locked on the floor. "Kaspar's the best choice," he murmured. "No one else could do it."

Margrith's frown deepened even more as she exchanged a glance with Sigvard.

"It's unorthodox," she said bitterly. "Theodin had at least been raised with us since he could barely walk. The Head of the Order personally mentoring a completely fresh initiate, then taking her on as a second apprentice? What precedent does that set? If we bend the rules for her, where does it stop? What happens when the next initiate demands the same treatment?"

"It sets the precedent that we're willing to do whatever it takes," Kaspar said. "The decision isn't about tradition—it's about survival."

"We're not talking about just any initiate, are we?" Crane said. "She's the first Valksha in Kyriegard history. If that doesn't warrant bending a few rules, I don't know what does."

Margrith's expression darkened. "And what happens if Azazelf exploits this? If she fails, the backlash could shatter the Order's credibility. The risk is astronomical."

Kaspar's tone only became more present and commanding. "The greater risk is doing nothing. Azazelf already knows about her—or he soon will. Her progress is our best defense. If we don't guide her, we leave her vulnerable. And vulnerability is something we cannot afford."

Sigvard huffed and leaned back to fold his arms again tightly. "You're betting everything on a girl who's barely more than a child. It's reckless."

"She's shown she can handle it," Theodin interjected suddenly, his raised voice echoing in the space.

All eyes turned to him, but he didn't falter.

"She's already proven more capable than most apprentices who are about to undergo their Trials. And if anyone can guide her, it's Kaspar."

Margrith's sharp gaze flicked between Theodin and Kaspar. "And what about partnership? The *Arcane Dyad?* Are we really pairing her with Theodin? Despite his excellence, all of his partner compatibility testing before has failed."

Theodin tensed. "I've trained for years. I'm more than capable."

"Capable doesn't mean ready or compatible," Margrith countered. "She could very well be added to the list of incompatible partners."

Kaspar held up a hand to silence the growing tension. "No one's suggesting binding them today. This would be a trial—an opportunity to assess their compatibility. Nothing more."

"And if it fails?" Sigvard asked. "What then?"

"Then we reevaluate," Kaspar said simply. "But this isn't about tradition or risk—it's about adapting. If the Order can't evolve, it will fall."

Crane leaned back in his chair, twirling his cane idly. "Well, this is shaping up to be quite the experiment. A Valksha initiate brought late into the Order, granted mentorship under our fearless leader, and soon will be testing a potential Dyad partnership with our resident golden boy. What could possibly go wrong?"

Sigvard scowled. "You joke too much, Azariah. This isn't a game."

"It never is," Crane replied, his tone unusually sober. He tapped his cane once against the floor, his wild eyes glinting. "But sometimes you have to take risks to win."

Margrith sighed heavily, rubbing her temple. "If this fails—if Azazelf finds a way to exploit this connection—don't say I didn't warn you."

Kaspar straightened, his voice calm but resolute. "We'll take every precaution. But doing nothing is not an option. The Order has always thrived on adaptation and innovation. This is no different."

Alfena rose gracefully from her seat, her silver eyes locking on Ophelia. "You have the support of the Council, Ophelia. But support is not enough. You must prove to us—and to yourself—that you are worthy of this responsibility."

Ophelia nodded. "I will. I promise."

"Ophelia. Your mentorship under Nimrod Kaspar, Head of the Order of the Kyriegard, begins immediately," Alfena said with an air of authoritative reverence. "You will first spend a copious amount of time with your mentor. Unlike the Arcane Dyad, this is not a magical or spiritual bond, but an academic one of instruction and evaluation. This mentorship is meant to sharpen and prepare you for the Dyad test."

"Understood," Ophelia answered.

Kaspar glanced around the room, his gaze lingering briefly on each Council member. "We have our course. Let's prepare for what's next."

With a final murmur of agreement, the Council began to disperse.

Theodin waited near the chamber's entrance, his arms crossed and his expression distant. As Ophelia approached, the door to the Council room closed behind her with a low groan, cutting off the hum of the runes within.

Neither spoke for a moment. Theodin's gaze flicked to her pendant, then back to her face. "You okay?" he asked, his voice quieter than usual.

Ophelia hesitated, then nodded once. "I think so." She glanced down at her hands, which still trembled slightly. "It's… a lot to take in."

Theodin's face shifted. The hardness in it had lessened. "Come on," he said, gesturing down the hall. "Let's get you settled. You'll need rest."

As they walked through Halvalla's quiet halls, the weight of the council's decision settled over them like a heavy cloak.

Ophelia's mind raced with questions and doubts.

Would she live up to their expectations? Could she really stand beside Theodin as his partner? Would she even pass this test?

Finally, she broke the silence. "Thank you for speaking up for me," she said softly.

Theodin glanced at her, his strange eyes briefly meeting hers before turning back to the path ahead. "You earned it," he replied simply. "Kaspar might have led the charge, but none of it would've happened if you hadn't proven yourself."

Ophelia bit her lip, her fingers fidgeting with her ring. "Still… It means something. Coming from you."

Theodin's stride slowed, and he turned to look at her more fully. "You're stronger than you think, Ophelia," he said, his tone gentle now. "But you don't need me or anyone else to tell you that. You've shown it, time and time again."

A faint blush crept across her cheeks, and she looked away, a nervous chuckle escaping her lips. "You've said that before," she said, trying to deflect the weight of his words. "It sounds like something Kaspar would say."

"He's not wrong," Theodin replied, a hint of a smirk tugging at the corner of his mouth. "But don't get used to the compliments. You'll need to keep earning them."

They turned a corner, the warm light of enchanted lanterns casting long shadows across the stone walls. The silence stretched between them again, but this time it felt less tense and more comfortable.

Ophelia cleared her throat, breaking the quiet again. "Do you… wonder what it'll be like? If we're really… paired?"

Theodin's steps faltered, but he quickly recovered. His expression remained unmoved.

"It's not something I've thought about much," he admitted. "But if it happens, it happens. We'll make it work either way."

Ophelia frowned, her gaze searching his face for any hint of what he was truly feeling. "Do you think we'd work?" she asked in a low voice.

He paused in front of a door, resting a hand on the handle as he turned to face her. For a moment, his expression softened, the guarded walls in his eyes dropping just slightly.

"I think we already do," he said quietly. "But that doesn't mean it'll be easy."

Ophelia blinked, her chest tightening at the sincerity in his tone.

"I…guess nothing worth it ever is." She turned to face him fully, her fingers still wriggling. "What's it like, the partner testing process?"

Theodin leaned against the doorframe, his arms crossing loosely over his chest as he considered her question. "It's… different for everyone," he said after a moment. "They test your compatibility—not just your strengths or weaknesses, but how you balance each other. It's less about what you can do on your own and more about how you connect, how your energies align." He looked away briefly, his eyes distant. "It's not easy. Sometimes it clicks, and sometimes…" His jaw clenched slightly. "Sometimes it doesn't."

Ophelia studied him, her fingers still brushing over the edge of her ring. "What happens when it doesn't?"

Theodin's gaze flicked back to her, his expression unreadable. "It's not anyone's fault. The Order needs pairs that work, not ones forced together. If it doesn't fit, they move on." His voice softened, a faint trace of something unspoken lingering in his words. "But it doesn't mean you failed. It just means it wasn't the right match."

Ophelia hesitated, her chest tightening with a mixture of curiosity and unease. "How many times… have you tried?"

Theodin's lips pressed into a thin line.

The question clearly struck a nerve.

"A few," he admitted quietly. "More than I'd like to count."

Ophelia winced at his subtle, pained expression. She opened her mouth to respond, but he shook his head, cutting her off gently.

"It's not about me, Ophelia. Not right now."

His expression fell again, once more looking at her with a softened stare, but his voice remained unfazed.

"What matters is that you're ready for whatever comes next. And when the time comes, you'll handle it. I've seen enough to know that much."

Her fingers stilled as the gravity of his words sunk in. A little, genuine smile curled at the corner of her lip.

"Thanks," she whispered.

Then, they stared at one another.

Clearing his throat, Theodin straightened, pushing off the doorframe.

"Get some sleep," he said, his tone firmer now. "Tomorrow's going to be another long day."

Ophelia nodded, but as he turned to leave, she found herself speaking again, the words tumbling out before she could stop them. "Theodin?"

He paused, glancing over his shoulder. "Yeah?"

"Do you think… do you think we'd actually *pass* the test?" she asked, her voice tinged with vulnerability.

For a moment, he didn't respond, his gaze searching hers. Then, with a faint, almost imperceptible smile, he said, "We'll find out when the time comes. Until then, keep proving me right."

His grip tightened briefly on the door handle before he pushed it open.

"Get some rest," he said, stepping aside to let her enter the room. "Tomorrow's going to come fast, and you'll need your strength."

Ophelia hesitated, standing in the doorway as she glanced back at him. Her fingers began to squirm again. "Theo…"

He looked at her with a raised brow. "Yeah?"

"Do you… trust me?" she asked, her voice barely above a whisper.

His eyes shifted again, and for a moment, the weight of his usual stoicism seemed to lift. He lowered his gaze to her hands

"I wouldn't have said anything in there if I didn't."

He gently placed one large hand over both of her small and dainty ones to stop them from moving. She froze in surprise.

"Really, Valksha. You need to rest."

He squeezed her fingers and lowered them, then his eyes flickered up to meet hers.

"Don't let it get to you and keep you up. Maybe read something to ease your mind since that's what you like to do—"

Suddenly, a small, genuine smile tugged at one corner of his mouth. He pulled his hand away, leaving the tingle of his energy and touch on her skin.

"No, forget that. Then you'll stay up late."

A deeper blush of embarrassment flushed in Ophelia's face as she grinned and bashfully turned her eyes down.

"Right," she laughed lightly. "Th-that is quite true." She cleared her throat and lifted her eyes again.

"Goodnight, Theodin."

"Goodnight, Ophelia."

With that, he turned and walked away, his footsteps echoing down the quiet hall. Ophelia stepped inside, closing the door behind her.

Ophelia leaned against the wood and slid down until she sat on the floor.

Her heart raced and thoughts swirled as she replayed his words in her mind.

Trust.

It was a word she didn't take lightly. Trust had been fleeting and fragile for most of her life, shattered more times than she could count. But coming from Theodin—steadfast, disciplined, unyielding—it felt different.

Stronger. Real.

She raised her hand to her pendant, feeling its faint warmth pulse against her palm. Was this what trust felt like? Not just given, but earned? A quiet smile tugged at her lips, and for the first time since the Council meeting, the weight on her chest seemed to lift.

Chapter 13

The Gift

Year 844 of the Second Age, Seventh Month, Seventh Day
Six months later.

The air in Avasylon's armory was cool and still, the faint hum of enchantments lingering in the background. Rows of weapons gleamed under the soft glow of the lanterns, but Kaspar stood near the far wall, his back to the entrance. In his hands was something unfamiliar—a rifle, its polished metal reflecting the light.

Ophelia hesitated at the doorway. "You wanted to see me?"

Kaspar turned, a small smile tugging at the corner of his lips. "You're fourteen today, aren't you?"

She blinked, caught off guard. "Y-Yes. How did you—?"

"I have my ways," he said, cutting her off with an air of amusement. "And Sigvard may have mentioned something about it."

Stepping closer, Ophelia's eyes fell to the rifle in his hands. It wasn't like the ones she'd seen in passing during her studies. This one was smaller, sleeker, its barrel etched with intricate runes that shimmered with green light.

"This," Kaspar began, holding it out to her, "is for you."

Ophelia stared at it, unsure whether to reach for it or not. "For... me? But why?"

"Because you've earned it," he said simply. "And because I believe this will suit you better than a blade or bow."

She hesitated, her fingers brushing the cool wood as she took it from him. The runes lit up with her grasp. The rifle was heavier than it looked, but it fit comfortably in her hands, the stock resting against her shoulder like it had been made for her.

"It's beautiful," she murmured, tracing the runes with her fingertips. They glistened at the touch of her energy. "But… why a rifle? Aren't they slower than swords and arrows?"

Kaspar nodded, his expression thoughtful. "They are. That's why most Kyriegard don't use them. But for someone like you—someone with your magic and precision—it could be an advantage. I convinced Sigvard to design and craft it specifically for you. The runes are calibrated to channel your Valksha energy, giving you more control over your magic at a distance."

Ophelia's eyes widened as she looked up at him. "You mean… it works with my magic?"

Kaspar stepped back. "Try it." He gestured toward a training dummy at the far end of the armory. "Treat it like you do any other spell. Imagine it and then will it to happen."

Ophelia took a deep breath, adjusting her grip on the rifle as she aimed. In weapons training, they briefly had the initiates learn to handle and fire pistols and rifles, but they did not dwell on them. One or two of them appeared to gravitate towards specializing in them, but Ophelia was not one of them because she assumed she would rely much more on her magic when it came to ranged attacks.

"Is this already loaded and primed?" Ophelia asked.

"Loaded with three rounds, yes," Kaspar answered. "You will prime and ignite it with your blood and magic instead of fire Pygmy powder."

"Well, that makes it slightly faster than ordinary firearms," she remarked.

Kaspar smirked. "Precisely."

The runes along the barrel began to glow brighter, pulsing in rhythm with her heartbeat. She felt the magic stir within her, guided by the rifle's design, until it coalesced at the barrel's tip.

When she squeezed the trigger, a spring-loaded needle in it pricked her finger. A beam of green energy shot forward and struck the dummy dead center. The impact sent the stone and wooden figure skidding across the floor.

Ophelia lowered the rifle, her hands trembling slightly. "It's… amazing."

"It's a tool," Kaspar said, his tone firm but kind. "Nothing more, nothing less. It's not a crutch, and it's not a solution. It's a way to focus your abilities, to give you precision when you need it. But it's still you doing the work. That means you still need to practice control, especially over your emotions." He gave a wink. "So be careful to not get flustered."

She nodded, her grip tightening on the rifle. "Thank you."

Kaspar placed a hand on her back, his gaze unwavering. He appeared to be thinking far off, but Ophelia could immediately tell what he was feeling just from feeling his energy through his palm; it was an intense sadness although his face did not show it. "You've come far, Ophelia. But this is just the beginning. Now let's see how well you can use it."

Ophelia's brows furrowed together with concern. It threw her off to feel such grief from him instead of the usual comforting touch. "Nimrod," she said gently. "Why…do you feel so sad?"

Kaspar suddenly withdrew his hand and stepped away, turning his silvery eyes down with a reluctant smile. "Ah," he laughed with a strain—another rare occurrence. "Sometimes I forget that you hold the Saryf of Spirit and Heart within you."

"Are you upset?" Ophelia pressed.

Kaspar shook his head. "No, no, lass." He slowly paced over to the rack of ordinary rifles and pistols hanging across the armory from where they stood. "Has Theodin ever shared any of my history with you before I became Head of the Kyriegard Order?"

"No," Ophelia answered sincerely. "To be frank, Theodin doesn't share too much. Especially on a personal level. I try not to pry because I know how guarded he is and I'd rather not run extra laps first thing in the morning because he's in a terrible mood that I've caused."

Kaspar laughed again. "Fair."

Two laughs? She lowered the rifle to the table and studied him with quiet concern.

"My only and late partner, Garrett," Kaspar began, stopping before the rack. "He is responsible for the research and invention of our advanced weaponry in the Order. He weaponized fire Pygmy powder." He scoffed and shook his head, muttering the next words. "Only *he* would—his damn fascination with those Pulchidimps…"

Ophelia's eyes widened slightly. "*That* Garrett? The one who also designed our explosives?"

Kaspar nodded once. "The same one."

"He was a hero," Ophelia said in a low voice. "He was even lined up to be the next Jackard because of his contributions to the Order…"

"—until he sacrificed himself to save the capital of Aetheloth from being overrun by a cave goblin horde," Kaspar continued. He didn't face her, instead keeping his eyes on the wooden and metal weaponry. "I was supposed to run into that mountain full of Unseelie swine to detonate the explosive trap he set up. But he knocked me out, chained me to a tree, and ran to do it himself." There was a long pause. From behind, Ophelia saw his shoulders slumped and his head dropped. "I only woke up just in time for him to tell me goodbye through our communication stones. And through our Arcane Dyad…I felt his pain for an instant, and then he was gone."

He folded his arms behind his back and sighed. He was still and reserved—like Theodin. He held in his grief like a true, trained Kyriegard.

"Then there was an emptiness."

Ophelia lifted a hand to her mouth, speechless as tears welled in her eyes.

After a few moments, Kaspar looked over his shoulder at her. Seeing her reaction, he smiled reassuringly and walked over to her. He pulled a handkerchief from one of his many pockets and offered it to her.

"Sorry, lass. Didn't mean to make you so sad," Kaspar said in a calm voice.

Ophelia took the handkerchief and wiped her eyes. "It's alright," she said with a small sniffle. "You…became Head of the Order, regardless of what happened?"

Kaspar nodded solemnly. "Don't get me wrong. I was mentally and emotionally crippled for a long, long time. I wouldn't talk to anyone, so I put all my energy into my work and focused on being a Kyriegard. I couldn't bring myself to be partnered again, so I did everything else I possibly could for the Order. I made sure Garrett's sacrifice wasn't in vain; if it wasn't for him, I wouldn't be here. Same goes with many others."

Ophelia couldn't help but think then of her father and mother and the sacrifices they made for her so that she could live on. Kaspar kept going and clearly achieved many accomplishments. Ophelia had to do the same. She couldn't give up no matter what. She had to be the best she could be.

After a moment of silence, Ophelia offered the handkerchief back in a gentle gesture. "Thank you for sharing all of that with me," she said with deep sincerity. "It…truly means a lot."

Kaspar smiled again and shook his head, motioning for her to keep it. "Something else you should know," he began. He went to a different table in the armory. "Theodin reminds me a lot of myself—minus the mischief. Garrett, Azariah, and I were all pranksters in childhood." He chuckled sparsely as he stopped at the table and turned to her. "Anyway. The guardedness, the severe focus and discipline…maybe it was because I raised him—but that is also me." He raised his brows and nodded once to her. "You, on the other hand, do remind me a whole lot of Garrett. Reckless, messy, but wicked talented and driven. Went with his gut. Very instinctive and even impulsive sometimes."

Kaspar gestured to another item resting on the table behind him—a slender dagger attached to a fine chain, the metal gleaming in the lantern light. The blade had runes etched into them that had the same low shimmer as her rifle.

"This," he said, lifting it carefully, "is something else I had Sigvard design and craft for you. A backup weapon for when you need precision and speed. We weren't sure if you'd take to it, but…" His eyes gleamed with quiet amusement. "I have a feeling you'll enjoy proving us wrong."

Ophelia stepped closer, her curiosity piqued. As she approached, the glow of the runes grew. The chain felt lighter than she expected as she picked it up, and the dagger's hilt fitting snugly in her palm. She studied it carefully in her grasp. She'd only seen Sigvard handle one once. She tried to recall how he'd done it.

She flicked her wrist experimentally, and the chain extended. The blade swung in a graceful arc before snapping back into her grasp.

"It's incredible," she said, her voice filled with awe.

"Made from Garrett's old chain blade," Kaspar said in a quiet voice.

Ophelia stopped and whipped her eyes to him. "The one he used to chain you to the tree?"

Kaspar nodded. "Yes. The very one." He admired the weapon in her hands with a fond smile. "It was his weapon of choice if he wasn't blowing our foes up with Pygmy powder. I chose to give it to you—not just because you remind me of my late partner—but because it requires finesse, discipline, and instinct. All the things Garrett was excellent at, and all the things you've been working hard to hone." His silvery eyes met hers, and his smile genuinely widened and wrinkled at either side.

"Like you, he didn't like any of the common weaponry either. He was sort of a…unique case in his own special way, but he managed to do it while being only human."

Ophelia looked down at the dagger and chain, then back up at the elder Kyriegard. She bowed her head with gratitude. "I'm honored to wield it, Nimrod. Thank you."

"You are very welcome," Kaspar said warmly. He turned to the table with the rifle, picked it up and unclipped a spot in the center of its body. It folded part of the barrel with the stock end so that the length of the rifle would bend in half.

As Ophelia watched him, she spoke her thoughts out loud. "Is that one of the reasons you think Theodin and I would make a match? Because we remind you of you and Garrett?"

Kaspar placed the folded rifle gently into Ophelia's hands. "Yes and no. It's true that you remind me of Garrett, and Theodin carries shades of who I used to be. But that's not the only reason I see potential in you two as partners."

Ophelia slung the rifle's strap over her back, her brows furrowed in curiosity. "Then… what is it?"

Kaspar leaned back against the table, folding his arms. "Partnerships in the Kyriegard aren't just about shared traits or complementary skills. They're about balance—how two individuals can compensate for each other's weaknesses while amplifying their strengths. Garrett and I had that. He was impulsive, while I was cautious. He was creative, and I was methodical. Together, we achieved things neither of us could've done alone."

He paused, his silvery eyes meeting hers. "You and Theodin are similar in that way. He's disciplined to the point of rigidity at times, and you… well, let's just say you're still learning control. But where he's hesitant to take risks, you're fearless. Vice versa—when you are afraid, he steps in and takes the leap. And where you lean on instinct, he's calculating. That balance is rare, Ophelia."

Ophelia considered his words, her fingers brushing the chain blade still in her hand. "But what if we… I don't know… clash too much? We don't always see eye to eye."

Kaspar smiled again knowingly. "You think Garrett and I didn't butt heads? There were days I wanted to strangle him—and I'm sure the feeling was mutual. But that tension forced us to grow, to understand each other. It's the same for you and Theodin. You'll argue; you'll disagree, but if you can learn to trust each other, you'll be unstoppable."

Ophelia nodded slowly, her mind replaying moments with Theodin—his stern corrections during training, his rare but genuine encouragement, and the quiet understanding in his eyes when she faltered.

"I want to trust him," she admitted. "I do. But sometimes, it feels like he doesn't fully trust me. There are moments where he says he does, and I can feel it—then there are moments of doubt."

Kaspar's expression became serene. "Trust takes time. Especially with someone like Theodin. He's had his share of disappointments, but don't mistake his caution for doubt in you. If anything, he pushes you hard because he believes in your potential."

Ophelia looked down, her grip tightening on the dagger. "I hope you're right."

Kaspar reached out, resting a hand on her arm. This time, there was no sadness in his touch—only warmth and steadiness. "I know I am. You've already proven yourself more times than you realize. Now it's just a matter of showing him—and yourself—what you're truly capable of."

Ophelia lifted her eyes to her mentor. "And everyone else? The Council?" Her fingers mindlessly coiled the chains. "I'm…honestly surprised you convinced Sir Jackard to make these."

Kaspar withdrew his hand and gave a rare chuckle. "Sigvard will jump at any opportunity to craft a tool for the job. That's why he's in the Council position he is. Garrett—as inventive as he was—would've been the one to take over that position after Sigvard."

"How long has Sigvard been part of the Council?" she asked.

Kaspar exhaled, leaning back slightly. "Sigvard? He's been on the Council longer than I've been alive. Dwarves don't take on responsibility lightly, and when he inherited his position, he swore to uphold the Kyriegard's armory until his last breath. Stubborn as stone, that one—but there's no finer smith in Olysgard. He forged his first battle axe before he was twenty and nearly took a man's head clean off in the process."

Ophelia's brows rose. "That's…concerning."

Kaspar smirked. "Depends on who you ask."

She huffed softly, then tilted her head. "And what about the others? Lady Gravehardt?"

Kaspar's expression hardened slightly, though not unkindly. "Margrith is the oldest human on the Council—over seventy, and still as sharp as ever. She was raised in the Order, trained alongside some of the most brilliant strategists of her time. Unlike the rest of us, she was never meant for combat. She was meant to build—fortifications, strongholds, safe havens. She's the mind behind Halvalla's defenses, the reason the Order has stood strong through more sieges than I can count."

Ophelia frowned slightly. "Then why does she seem to hate me?"

"Margrith doesn't hate you." Kaspar began. "She just doesn't trust easily. Just as guarded and unmoving as the strongholds she has built. She's seen too many promising warriors fall, too many great ideas turn to ruin. If she's hard on you, it's because she doesn't want you to break when it matters most."

Ophelia absorbed that, but her thoughts drifted. "What about Master Crane? I don't think I've ever seen him outside of Council meetings."

Kaspar let out a dry snicker. "That's because Azariah Crane lives in the shadows by nature. You won't see him unless he wants you to. He was once the best tracker in the Order, but he took a mission that left him broken—crippled from the waist down. That didn't stop him, though. He's the mind behind our intelligence network, the reason we know where to strike before the enemy does."

"And he's also human," she remarked.

Kaspar nodded. "He and I go all the way back to boyhood. He and Garrett were the first friends I had here—he was a teenager when I was a wee boy."

Ophelia's nose crinkled with amusement. "He's older than you?"

Kaspar winked. "Doesn't seem like it, eh? He's the most cunning and mischievous for a reason. An elite prankster in his youth. He and Garrett dragged me into trouble all the time."

Ophelia giggled. "What? And now you and Master Crane are on the Council?"

"And how, you ask," Kaspar mused. "Well…Azariah was humbled when he was finally paired with Alfena."

Her eyes widened. *"Lady Marobe?!"*

Kaspar nodded again. "He couldn't be paired with anyone until he was about twenty years old, when most find their match between the age of thirteen and eighteen. Of course, he was paired with the most unlikely person we thought would match him. And it turns out that they worked incredibly well together."

"Astounding," Ophelia exhaled. "I would never have expected

that...they're such opposite personalities."

"That's the fascinating thing about Arborelys," Kaspar said with a tone of wisdom. "It knows who works best with whom."

Kaspar's smirk lightened into something more thoughtful. "And then there's Alfena," he mused, almost to himself. "The longest-standing member of the Council and the most difficult to impress."

Ophelia tilted her head. "Why's that?"

Kaspar exhaled, rubbing his jaw. "She's the most powerful Sage we've ever had. Born into a long line of elven scholars, trained in magic from childhood. But unlike most Sages, she didn't just study magic—she lived it. She fought in the War of Malblight, saw the fall of entire kingdoms, and still walked away to tell the tale."

Ophelia swallowed. "So... she's seen everything."

"More than we ever will." Kaspar's gaze was distant for a moment before he shook his head, refocusing. "She joined the Kyriegard late in life—long after she'd already mastered more than most of us ever will."

"But why?" Ophelia frowned. "If she was already so accomplished, what made her join so late?"

Kaspar's expression darkened slightly. "Because even the most powerful don't always see the right path from the start."

He paused for a moment, and his expression shifted. "Though she is the oldest and most experienced, she refuses to be Head of the Order. She firmly believes it should be a human. Says it's tradition. Says it's the way it's always been. But sometimes, I wonder if it's something else—if she's seen too much war to want to lead it.

"Interesting," Ophelia muttered, her eyes glimmering with curiosity.

"But she is incredibly wise. She doesn't just study magic," he continued, "she understands it in ways the rest of us never will. It's why she was the first to question your initiation." He gave her a pointed look. "She knew there was something different about you before the rest of us could put it into words."

Ophelia swallowed. That was...unsettling to think about.

Kaspar's hand found her shoulder again, squeezing briefly. "They'll see what I see soon enough. You've already set things in motion."

Before Ophelia could respond, the distant sound of footsteps echoed from the hallway. Both she and Kaspar turned as Theodin appeared in the doorway, his eyes flicking between them.

"Kaspar," Theodin greeted with a nod, then glimpsed at Ophelia. "Training starts in ten minutes. Don't be late."

Ophelia sneered, tucking the chain blade into its sheath and slinging it at her hip. "Wouldn't dream of it."

Theodin's gaze lingered on the rifle strapped to her back and the dagger at her side. For a moment, something unreadable flickered in his expression—curiosity, perhaps, or approval—but he quickly masked it. "I'll see you on the field."

As he turned to leave, Kaspar let out a low breath of amusement. "Go easy on her today, lad."

Theodin paused, glancing over his shoulder with the slightest hint of a smirk. "No promises. Especially for the birthday girl."

"Aww," Ophelia whined playfully.

Theodin still wore his slight coy expression as he scoffed in return.

Once he was gone, Kaspar looked back at Ophelia. "There's your challenge, lass. Prove to him—and to yourself—that you're ready."

Ophelia straightened, determination shining in her emerald eyes. "I will."

Kaspar nodded, his own smile returning. "Good. Now go. You've got work to do."

With her rifle and chain blade secured, Ophelia left the armory, her heart lighter despite the weight of her new weapons.

Chapter 14

The Breach

Theodin tightened the straps on his gauntlets as his eyes fixed on the training grounds ahead. The sun was just cresting the horizon, its pale light cutting through the mist that clung stubbornly to the grass. The distant hum of enchantments emanating from Avasylon's defenses was faint, almost soothing—a reminder of the Order's ever-watchful presence.

He exhaled sharply and rolled his shoulders to release the tension that had crept into his muscles overnight. Sleep had been elusive, as it often was. The remnants of another nightmare—a fragment of something dark and unrelenting—still gnawed at the edges of his mind. He pushed it aside with practiced determination. There was no room for distractions, especially today.

Theodin's gaze shifted to the cabin in the distance. Ophelia had been in there with Kaspar for some time that morning. Had Theodin not gone into the cellar and found them in the armory, perhaps she would've been late to their training session. Again.

He hadn't asked why they were in the armory—Kaspar rarely shared his intentions unless they were critical—but the lingering curiosity annoyed him.

After seeing the chained blade hanging from her hip and the rifle slung over her shoulder, Theodin could only guess that Kaspar had given the Valksha girl new equipment. The chained blade was Garrett's—Theodin could tell by the dagger's handle since he had seen it hung up on the mantle of the fireplace for as long as he could remember.

When she finally emerged, rifle slung across her shoulder and a new weapon gleaming at her side, he'd felt something he couldn't quite place. Not jealousy, exactly. Resentment, maybe? Or admiration?

He scoffed at himself. She barely listened half the time, always relying on instinct over discipline. But there was something sharper in her movements now. He couldn't decide if it was determination, desperation, or something else entirely—but it made him pause.

He hated to admit it, even to himself, but Kaspar was right about her potential. She was determined, fearless, and unrelenting in her own way.

But was that enough?

His thoughts were interrupted by the sound of boots crunching against gravel. Kaspar's familiar stride. Theodin straightened instinctively, his posture snapping into something more disciplined.

"You've been up for hours, haven't you?" Kaspar asked, his tone warm but knowing. He stopped beside Theodin, his silver hair catching the morning light.

Theodin shrugged, adjusting the grip on his training sword. "Couldn't sleep."

Kaspar tilted his head, studying him. "The dreams?"

Theodin's jaw tightened. He didn't answer. Kaspar didn't press.

Instead, Kaspar gestured toward the field. "As you can see, Ophelia will be using the new weapons."

Theodin's eyes darted to the approaching Valksha girl for a moment and studied the new additions to her Kyriegard initiate appearance. Both the rifle and the chained blade glowed with green runes etched into their surfaces. The chained blade was indeed Garrett's.

Theodin let out a faint huff, his lips curving into the ghost of a smirk. "You're trusting her with a rifle now?"

Kaspar chuckled softly. "Trusting might be a strong word. Testing her, more like. But she'll need your guidance."

Theodin raised a brow. "I thought you wanted her to figure things out on her own."

Kaspar's gaze sharpened, though his tone remained calm. "Guidance doesn't mean hand-holding, Theodin. It means pushing her to see what she's capable of—just like I did with you."

Theodin shifted uncomfortably at the comparison but didn't argue. "She's reckless."

"So was Garrett," Kaspar said quietly. "And yet, he became one of the most extraordinary Kyriegard this Order has ever seen."

Theodin glanced at Kaspar, surprised by the rare mention of his late partner. The weight of his mentor's words settled heavily in his chest. He didn't respond.

Before either of them could say more, Ophelia appeared at the edge of the field, her pace brisk and her expression determined. The rifle and chain blade gleamed in the morning light, their runes glowing faintly.

Theodin turned to Kaspar. "Like I said downstairs. No promises about going easy. Even if it's her birthday."

Kaspar's smile was faint but approving. "Good. She doesn't need easy. She needs honest."

With that, Kaspar stepped back, leaving Theodin to face the Valksha girl who was quickly becoming the Order's most unpredictable—and intriguing—initiate.

Ophelia flashed a toothy smile at Theodin. "Good morrow, dear Theo," she called to him. "How is the Kyriegard's favorite golden boy this morning?"

Theodin's jaw tightened at the nickname, though he refused to rise to the bait. "You're late."

Ophelia tilted her head, mock innocence painted across her face. "Late? I think you mean 'fashionably punctual.'"

Her grin faltered for half a breath before she shrugged it off. She couldn't let him see her waver—not today.

Theodin ignored the comment, his eyes narrowing as they glanced at the rifle on her shoulder and the chain blade at her hip. "You know how to use those? Or did you just let Kaspar talk you into thinking they'd make you look competent?"

Her grin widened, deceiving undeterred. "Careful, Theo. That almost sounded like a compliment buried under all that snark."

"It wasn't." Theodin gestured toward the center of the training ring. "Prove me wrong."

Ophelia's playful expression faltered for just a moment, replaced by a glimpse of uncertainty. But she recovered quickly, shrugging off her nerves as she unstrapped the rifle, whipped it to full length and stepped into the ring. "Gladly."

Theodin crossed his arms, watching as she adjusted her grip on the weapon. He could see her mind working, recalling the brief instruction she'd had in firearms during training. Still, her movements were tentative, unsure.

"The rifle," he said, his tone sharper now, "isn't just a toy with a trigger. It's an extension of your magic. Stop overthinking and let it work with you."

Ophelia shot him a sideways glance. "'Do you always sound this cheerful?' she asked, smirking.

"Focus," Theodin snapped. "Take aim."

Her smirk faded, replaced by a look of quiet determination. She raised the rifle, her fingers brushing against the glowing runes as she settled into a stance. Theodin could see her shoulders tense as she inhaled deeply, the subtle glow of her magic glimmering along the weapon's barrel.

She squeezed the trigger. The rifle hummed sharply as a beam of green energy shot forward. It struck the target dead center, splintering the wooden dummy and sending shards flying.

Ophelia lowered the rifle, blinking at the destruction she'd caused. "Not bad, right?"

Theodin's eyes swept to the splintered target. He opened his mouth to critique her form but found himself pausing. For all its flaws, the shot had been… effective.

His eyes narrowed. For all her fumbling, the shot was clean—too clean for a novice. It left him wondering, not for the first time, what Kaspar saw in her.

"Not bad," he admitted grudgingly. "But not good enough."

Her brow furrowed. "What's wrong with it?"

"Your stance," he said, circling her like a predator sizing up prey. "You're too rigid. If that target had been moving, you would've missed entirely. Again."

Ophelia exhaled sharply but complied, resetting her stance. This time, Theodin stepped behind her, placing his hands firmly on her shoulders to adjust her posture. She stiffened slightly at the contact but didn't pull away. His hands shifted her shoulders with the same efficiency he'd use to align a blade, leaving no room for error.

"Loosen up," he instructed, his voice low but commanding. "The rifle isn't a sword. It's meant to be fluid. Let your instincts guide you."

She nodded, adjusting her grip as he stepped back. This time, when she fired, the green energy arced through the air with precision, shattering the second dummy before it even hit the ground.

A small grin crept across her face as she lowered the rifle. "Better?"

Theodin's expression remained neutral, though there was a faint glimmer of approval in his eyes. "Better."

Ophelia turned to face him fully, her confidence returning. "Maybe I should teach you a thing or two."

"Maybe," Theodin said flatly. "If you survive the next round."

He nodded toward the chain blade at her hip. "Let's see how you handle that."

Ophelia's grin faltered, replaced by a look of concentration as she drew the blade. The chain unraveled smoothly, the runes along its length glowing brighter with her magic. She flicked her wrist as she did earlier in the armory, and the blade arced through the air in a graceful loop before snapping back into her hand.

Theodin raised a brow. "Not bad. Now try it on something that fights back."

He stepped to the side, gesturing toward an enchanted training dummy. The figure sprang to life, its jerky movements mimicking an opponent in combat.

Ophelia swallowed hard, gripping the chain blade tightly. "A warning would've been nice."

"Where's the fun in that?" Theodin smirked. "Prove me wrong."

Ophelia squared her shoulders, her eyes gleaming with determination as the blade pulsed with her magic.

Theodin crossed his arms, watching silently as she took her first swing. The chain blade lashed out, striking the moving target with a sharp clang. She adjusted quickly, her second strike slicing cleanly through its arm. The dummy reeled, its enchanted movements faltering.

She grinned, a flash of triumph lighting her face. "How's that for reckless?"

Theodin didn't answer immediately. He watched as she reset, her stance slightly more fluid now, her attacks more precise. For all her bravado, there was something sharper beneath it—something raw, but undeniable.

"Better," he said finally, his voice neutral. "But you've got a long way to go."

Ophelia rolled her eyes, but her smile didn't waver. "I'll take it."

Theodin glanced at the shattered remains of the dummy, then back to her. For all her faults, she'd proven one thing—she wasn't the same unsure girl Kaspar had brought to Avasylon. She was sharper now, more focused.

"You're getting there," he said finally, his tone neutral but firm. "But don't let it go to your head."

Ophelia rolled her eyes but smirked. "Never."

As she reset her stance, readying for another round, Theodin let his gaze linger a moment longer. The chain blade at her hip gleamed faintly, its runes alive with her energy.

Garrett's blade. It had always been a symbol of precision and control—qualities she lacked when she first arrived. Yet, as the chain pulsed with her magic, it struck him that perhaps Kaspar hadn't been wrong after all.

Theodin didn't say a word as he reset the training ring, his movements precise and deliberate. The shattered remnants of the enchanted dummy had already been cleared away, leaving the arena bare except for the two of them.

In the distance, the sound of children and adolescents chattered. The initiates, accompanied by some apprentices, were arriving.

Ophelia shifted on her feet, the chain blade coiled loosely in her hand. "So, what now?" she asked, her tone light but edged with curiosity. "Another target for me to slice and dice?"

Theodin raised a brow, his eyes sharp. "Not quite. The dummies were predictable. I'm not."

Her grin faltered. "You want me to spar with you?"

"You wanted to prove yourself," he said, his voice calm but firm. "This is your chance."

Ophelia tightened her grip on the blade, the runes shimmering in response. "Fine," she said, squaring her shoulders. "But don't get mad if I beat you."

Theodin smirked faintly, stepping into the ring. "I'll manage."

A few other initiates had drifted toward the edge of the clearing, drawn in by seeing Theodin and Ophelia facing off in a field. Amongst them were Mald and Fritan, and a few others—a Pulchidgirl with fay wings and a blonde human girl.

Mald leaned against a nearby pillar, arms crossed, while Fritan sat on the stone ledge, swinging his legs. The Pulchidgirl stood near the ledge with a pad of parchment, scribbling notes, while the blonde girl brooded beside her with her arms folded.

"Three silver says she knocks him down," Mald muttered.

"She's going to overcorrect her footwork and leave herself open," Fritan replied without looking up.

"Fine. Two silver and a flask of applebread wine."

"Still not worth it."

"She's a Valksha," the Pulchidgirl insisted. "She'll find a way to outsmart him."

"Daphne—she's not supposed to use magic, I assume," the blonde girl muttered next to her. "At least not this time."

"Gisela," Mald said. "You betting?"

"Yes," the blonde girl answered. "Three silver says he throws her and shows her what a real Kyriegard is made of."

Ophelia and Theodin circled each other, the silence between them heavy with tension. Theodin moved first, his training sword slicing through the air in a calculated arc. Ophelia's chain blade flung forward in response, the dagger at its end colliding with his blade in a burst of sparks.

"Too slow," Theodin said, his tone clipped as he sidestepped her follow-up strike. "You're telegraphing your movements."

Ophelia gritted her teeth and inhaled a hiss as her chains retracted. "You're not exactly making this easy."

"It's not supposed to be easy," he said, his strikes coming faster now, forcing her to backpedal. "You think anyone out there is going to hold back?"

Her eyes narrowed, and she adjusted her stance, the blade coiling around her arm like a serpent. When Theodin lunged again, she flicked her wrist, the chain whipping toward his exposed side. He parried it just in time, but his foot slid half an inch on the damp grass.

"Better," he admitted, his voice steady. "But you're relying too much on instinct. Control it."

"Control this," she shot back, sending the blade arcing in a wide loop before yanking it sharply toward his legs. Theodin jumped, his boots barely clearing the chain as it snapped back into her hand.

He landed lightly, his gaze narrowing. "Sloppy," he said, though there was no malice in his tone. "You're not thinking about what comes next."

"Maybe I'm trying to keep you on your toes," she countered, her sneer returning.

Theodin pressed forward again, his movements faster and more aggressive. Ophelia struggled to keep up, the chain blade lashing out wildly as she tried to block his attacks. One strike slipped through her defenses, the flat of his blade tapping her shoulder.

"You're dead," he said simply, stepping back. "Try again."

Ophelia growled under her breath and reset her stance. "You're enjoying this, aren't you?"

Theodin's lips twitched. "A little."

As they both reset, they noticed the crowd of initiates forming along the edge of the arena. They lined up around Mald, Fritan, Daphne and Gisela, sitting on the grass or standing, watching with fascination and intrigue. Excited and inaudible whispers exchanged between them.

To them, it wasn't just any sparring match.

It was the Kyriegard's golden boy versus the Valksha girl.

This time, she didn't wait for him to move first. Ophelia launched herself at him, the chain blade snapping forward with a burst of green light. Theodin parried the initial strike but misjudged the chain's trajectory. It looped around his sword, wrenching it from his grip.

For a split second, Ophelia hesitated, her eyes widening in surprise. Theodin didn't. He stepped into her space, his hand darting out to catch her wrist and stop the blade's momentum.

"Better," he said, his voice low. "But hesitation will kill you."

Her breath hitched, and she yanked her wrist free, the blade retracting with a metallic hiss. "You didn't exactly give me time to celebrate."

"There's no time in a real fight," he said, retrieving his sword. "You need to be faster. Smarter. Predict what I'll do before I do it."

Ophelia nodded, her grip tightening on the chain blade. "Fine," she said, determination gleaming in her eyes. "Let's go again."

Theodin reset his stance, his movements fluid as he twirled his training sword. "Again, then," he said, his voice sharp with focus.

Ophelia rolled her shoulders, her chain blade coiled tightly in her grip. "You're starting to sound like a broken record."

"Then prove me wrong," he shot back, his eyes locked on hers.

She lunged, her chain blade snapping forward like a whip. Theodin sidestepped smoothly, his sword deflecting the dagger's edge with precision. They moved in tandem, strikes and parries clashing in bursts of light and sound. Ophelia gritted her teeth, sweat beading on her brow as she fought to keep up.

But then, as Theodin pressed her back, something clicked. A wicked idea bloomed in her mind, and a sly grin spread across her face.

Theodin caught the shift in her expression and narrowed his eyes.

"What are you—?"

He didn't get to finish. Ophelia sliced her thumb across the blade, drawing a thin line of blood. The droplets shimmered with green light as they hit the ground. She thrust her hand toward the earth, her magic surging in response.

The grass beneath Theodin's feet came alive. Long, sinewy tendrils snaked up his boots, twisting around his ankles with unnatural speed. His eyes widened as the ground itself seemed to betray him, yanking his legs out from under him.

A loud wave of gasps from the children.

"Damn it, Ophelia—!" he barked as he hit the ground with a thud, his sword clattering out of reach.

A beat. They all stared in shock.

Then—

Ophelia doubled over, laughing so hard she nearly dropped her chain blade. "Oh, come on! You have to admit that was brilliant!"

A few of the initiates burst into laughter.

"No way she just did that," Fritan gasped, eyes wide.

Mald shoved his hand in front of Gisela. "Pay up!"

Gisela grumbled and dug into the pocket of her uniform trousers.

Theodin glared up at Ophelia, his face flushed with a mix of irritation and embarrassment. "Brilliant? That was underhanded."

"Effective," she corrected, wiping a tear from her eye. "And hilarious."

With a grunt, Theodin planted his hands in the dirt, wrenching his legs free from the enchanted grass. He stood, brushing himself off with an air of wounded pride. "You think this is funny?"

"Absolutely," she said, her grin unrepentant. "You should've seen your face."

He took a step toward her, and Ophelia instinctively backed up, her laughter faltering. "Wait—don't get mad. It was just a joke!"

Theodin's expression was unreadable for a moment, his eyes fixed on hers. Then, to her utter shock, a slight smile tugged at the corner of his mouth. "Fine. You got me."

Ophelia blinked. "Wait… really?"

"Don't get used to it," he said, picking up his sword. "And don't think I won't return the favor."

She raised her hands in mock surrender, still grinning. "Fair enough."

Theodin shook his head, his smirk fading as he resumed his stance.

"Again."

Ophelia sighed dramatically. She flourished her bleeding hand to the chain blade on the ground, and the hilt flung to her hand immediately. The metal links coiled around her forearm protectively, the glow of her magic still flickering around her. "You really don't know how to let loose, do you?"

"No," Theodin said flatly. "Now focus."

As they squared off once more, the tension between them shifted, lighter now but still charged with the unspoken challenge that drove them both forward.

"Again," Theodin said, his tone sharp.

Ophelia groaned. Reluctantly, she stepped back into place.

Theodin and Ophelia squared off in the sparring ring, their breaths steadying after the last exchange. The chain blade pulsed in Ophelia's hand, its green runes radiating as she adjusted her grip.

"You really don't take a break, do you?" Ophelia muttered.

Before Theodin could retort, a familiar voice cut through the air. "Neither of you should."

Kaspar stepped into the ring, his silver eyes gleaming. He carried his own blade—a sleek, rune-etched longsword that hummed faintly with magic. "If you're going to spar, you might as well do it properly."

Now all of the initiates on the sidelines were zeroed in. They all leaned in with keen interest.

Theodin stiffened, his stance shifting instinctively. "You're joining us?"

Kaspar gave a rare, smug look. "Consider this your warm-up."

Ophelia's eyes widened. "You want us to fight you?"

Kaspar nodded. "Together. Let's see how well you can work as a team."

Theodin exhaled, his gaze flicking to Ophelia. "Stay sharp," he muttered.

Ophelia grinned. "Don't worry, Theo. I've got your back."

Kaspar didn't wait for them to prepare. He moved with blinding speed, his blade cutting through the air toward Theodin. Theodin parried just in time, the force of the strike reverberating through his arms. Ophelia darted to the side, her chain blade snapping toward Kaspar's flank.

Kaspar twisted, his sword deflecting the chain with a single, precise movement. "Too predictable," he said, his voice calm.

Ophelia growled under her breath, pulling the chain back. "You're impossible."

Kaspar's next strike was aimed at her, forcing Theodin to intercept. Their movements became a flurry of strikes, parries, and near-misses, the clash of blades ringing through the air. For a moment, they managed to coordinate, driving Kaspar back a step.

But then, the ground trembled.

The initiates all exchanged worried glances with one another, then looked to the three in the field.

All three of them paused, their weapons lowering slightly. Theodin's eyes squinted as he scanned the horizon. "What was that?"

Kaspar's expression darkened. "Not part of the exercise."

The tremor came again, stronger this time. A faint hum filled the air —low and unnatural, like a pulse of dark energy. Ophelia's grip tightened on her chain blade with unease.

"Something's wrong," Kaspar said, his tone grave. "Stay close."

Before they could move, a shadowy figure emerged from the treeline, its form twisted and unnatural. The creature's glowing red eyes locked onto them, its jagged claws digging into the earth.

Upon seeing it, the children huddled behind the older initiates. The apprentices drew their weapons and formed a barrier in front of them.

None of them were in an Arcane Dyad.

Theodin stepped forward, his blade raised. "What is that?"

"A reminder," Kaspar said grimly, his sword at the ready. "That the enemy doesn't wait for us to be prepared."

Ophelia whipped her wrist. The chain recoiled back to her side as she switched over to the rifle. Her eyes didn't leave the creature.

"It's not moving forward," she muttered. She anxiously loaded the barrel of her firearm with a bullet and then brought the stock against her shoulder to aim at it. "Perhaps the enchantments are still working."

Theodin stepped closer to her, his training sword still raised, his eyes locked on the shadowy figure. "If the enchantments were fully intact, it shouldn't have been able to get this close."

Kaspar's expression was grim as he circled the ring, positioning himself between them and the creature. "They're holding it at bay for now, but that tremor… it means something has weakened the wards. This isn't a coincidence."

The creature snarled, its claws scraping against the ground as it began to pace, testing an invisible barrier. Its glowing eyes shifted from Kaspar, to Theodin, to the initiates, then to Ophelia, lingering on her for a moment too long.

"Ophelia," Kaspar said, his voice calm but commanding, "hold your fire until we know for sure it's breaching the barrier. We don't want to waste ammunition or energy if we don't have to."

Ophelia nodded, though her grip on the rifle tightened. "Got it."

Theodin moved slightly ahead of her, his stance defensive. "And if it does breach?"

"Then we neutralize it. Quickly and efficiently," Kaspar replied, his silver eyes never leaving the creature. "Theodin, stay ready to engage directly. Ophelia, you'll provide cover fire. Aim for weak points—the joints, the eyes."

The creature growled, pressing against the barrier. The air around it shimmered faintly, a sign of the enchantments struggling to hold.

Kaspar's grip on his blade tightened. "It's testing the wards. Theodin, stay sharp. Ophelia, be prepared."

The tension was palpable as the creature reared back, its claws digging into the earth. With a deafening screech, it launched itself forward, the barrier rippling violently as it struggled to repel the force. For a moment, it seemed to hold—but then, with a sharp crack, the barrier shattered.

"It's through!" Kaspar barked.

Theodin surged forward, his blade cutting through the air in a swift arc. The creature dodged with unnatural speed, its claws slashing toward him. He parried just in time, the force of the blow reverberating through his arms.

"Ophelia, now!" Kaspar ordered.

Ophelia took a deep breath, steadying her aim as the rifle's runes flared to life. She squeezed the trigger, and a beam of green energy shot forward, striking the creature's flank. It howled in pain, its movements faltering just long enough for Theodin to strike again, his blade slicing across its chest.

Kaspar moved in next, his sword glowing faintly with runes as he delivered a precise, crushing blow to the creature's head. It crumpled to the ground, its twisted form twitching once before going still.

For a moment, the only sound was the heavy breathing of the three Kyriegard. Ophelia lowered her rifle, her hands trembling slightly. "What… was that?"

Kaspar knelt beside the creature, inspecting its twisted form. "A Cadaven," he said grimly. "But it's more corrupt than usual."

Theodin frowned, wiping his blade clean. "You think someone sent it?"

Kaspar stood, his expression dark. "Not someone. Something."

Chapter 15

The Arcane Dyad

The corridor outside of the Council's meeting hall was illuminated by enchanted lanterns that hung along the walls, casting shades of dim orange and yellow against the cold stone and wood. At the other end of the corridor, where the ceiling was much higher, there was a tall and wide rectangular window that the moon peeked through with its silvery light.

Theodin leaned against one of the stone columns framing the giant double doors that led into the Council's meeting hall, his arms crossed and his gaze distant.

Ophelia sat on the steps below him, her chain blade resting across her lap. She traced one of the glowing runes with her fingertip, her expression pensive.

Everything spoken behind the doors was incoherent. Unlike before, when Ophelia could hear the Council deliberating about her after her first month as a Kyriegard initiate.

Perhaps Alfena knew of that time since she had probed Ophelia's mind.

Ophelia let out a frustrated breath. It was hard to hide from Alfena.

Slowly, her eyes glanced at Theodin.

The tension from the sparring and the battle lingered between them, unspoken but heavy.

"Do you think they'll blame us?" she asked suddenly, her voice quiet.

Theodin glanced down at her, his eyes narrowing slightly. "Blame us for what?"

"For... I don't know," she said, gesturing vaguely with her hand. "For not noticing the wards were weakening. For letting that thing get so close."

He exhaled sharply, shaking his head. "It's not our fault the enchantments failed. That's on whoever is supposed to maintain them. But they'll probably find a way to turn it into a lecture anyway."

Ophelia smiled distantly, though it didn't reach her eyes. "The Kyriegard love their lectures."

Theodin didn't respond immediately. Instead, he pushed off the column and sat beside her on the stone steps, his sword resting against his knee.

"You did well," he said after a moment.

She blinked, looking up at him. "What?"

"You did well," he repeated, his tone even. "With the rifle. And the chain blade."

Ophelia's lips parted slightly in surprise, but she quickly masked it with a grin. "Was that actually a compliment, Theo?"

"It wasn't," he said flatly, though there was a faint flicker of amusement in his eyes. "Just an observation."

She rolled her eyes, but the tension in her shoulders seemed to ease. "Well, thanks. You weren't half bad yourself."

They sat in silence for a while, the distant sounds of Halvalla's guards patrolling the walls filling the void. Ophelia tilted her head back, her gaze drifting to the stars.

"Do you think Kaspar's telling them everything?" she asked softly.

Theodin's jaw clenched. "Kaspar used to tell them everything. He didn't disclose about Lady Vivian's enchanted defenses in Avasylon, but I don't think he'll hold back about this."

"That's what worries me," she muttered. She put her blade aside and hugged her knees to her chest. A vulnerable, saddened look overtook her eyes as she stared at the ground. "I don't like the way they look at me. Like I'm some experiment waiting to fail."

Theodin glanced at her with sympathy. "You're not an experiment, Ophelia. You're a Kyriegard initiate. Start acting like one."

Her gaze snapped to his, her eyes narrowing. "I am acting like one. I just don't think they'll ever see me that way."

"They will," he said firmly. "Eventually. If you keep proving them wrong."

She studied him for a long moment, as if trying to decide whether to believe him.

Finally, she deflated. "Fine. But if they start ranting about my 'recklessness' again, I'm blaming you."

He snorted. "Fair enough."

Ophelia felt a small tingle of pride in amusing him.

She relaxed a bit and rested her cheek on her knee. Seeing Theodin now, even while they looked each other in the eye, did not cause any disturbance or a strange feeling as it had in the past. Sure, there was still an occasional awkward moment where they would stop and stare, but they appeared to mutually and silently acknowledge it happened and moved on. Now that she was almost four months into Kyriegard livelihood and had spent so much exclusive time with Theodin, perhaps they were getting used to one another.

Another long moment of silence passed as Ophelia rolled around her thoughts. She seemed to debate, shift nervously, and then she reached a verdict with herself.

Mustering up courage, she took a deep breath and exhaled slowly. She lifted her head and spoke apprehensively. "Theodin?"

"Yeah?"

"I…uh…" Ophelia hesitated. Struggling, she lowered her eyes to the ground. "Oh, how do I explain this? This is going to be a strange thing to ask, but…I…"

She sighed a bit with frustration.

Theodin's brows furrowed together at her. "What?"

Ophelia sat up. She took another deep breath, a quick one, and then placed her hand on his. Her breath hitched as his energy coursed through her.

"Do you…can you feel anything if I do this?"

Theodin stiffened slightly at the contact, his eyes flicking to her hand on his. He didn't pull away, but his jaw tightened again. "What are you doing?"

Ophelia swallowed hard. Her fingers trembled slightly against his. "I just… I need to know. Every time—every time you touch me or when we lock eyes, it's like there's something… there. Something I can't explain."

Theodin didn't move. "What are you talking about?"

She looked up at him and searched his face. "You don't feel it? The pull? Like… like something is connecting us?"

Theodin's lips parted slightly, but he didn't respond right away. Slowly, his eyes softened again, and he exhaled through his nose.

"I do," he admitted. "I've felt it since the day you arrived."

Ophelia perked. "You… you have?"

He nodded. His gaze drifted to the ground. "I just thought… I don't know. I thought it was nothing. Or that I was imagining it."

She shook her head, her voice gaining strength. "It's not nothing. It's real. I can feel it, Theodin—every time you touch me, every time we…" She trailed off, her cheeks flushing. "I don't understand it, but it's real. And you're so different from every person I've met and had contact with. I-It…It's a Valksha ability to be able to feel the energy of other living beings or creatures, but since I'm bound to Veladriel, the Saryf of Spirit and Heart, I can feel emotions too. But it's not just your emotions I feel, it's…it's something more."

Theodin stared at their hands. The hum of her magic buzzed against his skin, the sensation both foreign and strangely familiar. He didn't pull away, but his voice was low when he spoke.

"Something more," he echoed. "What does that even mean?"

"I don't know," Ophelia said, her tone quiet but insistent. "It's like… there's this thread between us. Something tying me to you. And I feel it every time—like it's been there all along, waiting for us to notice."

He exhaled sharply. Finally, he pulled his hand back, though not without hesitation. "You think this is some… Valksha thing? Because of Veladriel?"

Ophelia shrugged. Her eyes turned down with uncertainty. "Maybe. Or maybe it's you. Again, I've never felt anything like this with anyone else—not even Kaspar or Lady Vivian. And trust me, I've tried to make sense of it, but…" She trailed off, looking aside. "It doesn't make sense."

Theodin was silent for a moment, his eyes clouded with thought.

"But… I've felt it too," he said quietly. "Not just when you touch me. When we fight. When we lock eyes. It's like—" He paused, searching for the words. "It's like the air shifts. Like something clicks into place."

Ophelia gasped, her head snapping up to look at him. "Yes! That's exactly it!" she huffed. "I really thought I was imagining it, but if you feel it that way too…"

He met her gaze. "It's real."

The weight of his words settled between them, heavy but electric.

For a moment, neither of them spoke, the silence stretching as they tried to process the shared realization.

"Do you think Kaspar knows?" she asked at last.

"If he does, he hasn't said anything," he muttered.

Ophelia nodded slowly. "He has to. He's been watching us—how we fight, how we interact. He's been waiting for us to figure this out. But why wouldn't he tell us?

"Maybe he's waiting for the right time," he said. "Or maybe he doesn't think we're ready."

Theodin broke away from her gaze and let out a frustrated breath, running a hand through his hair. "If it's been happening since you got here, why are we only talking about it now?"

Ophelia hesitated, her hands curling into fists in her lap. "Because… I was scared," she admitted. "I didn't want to be the only one feeling it. I didn't want to sound crazy."

He glanced her way again and studied her for a long moment.

Then, he shook his head.

"You're not crazy," he said gently. "But we need answers. If this connection means something, we need to know what."

Ophelia nodded again, now with more confidence. Relief melted across her face. "Do you think Kaspar will tell us?"

"If he knows, he'll tell us," Theodin said firmly. "He's never kept the truth from me before."

The heavy doors to the Council hall creaked open, cutting their conversation short. Both of them turned as Kaspar emerged, his expression grim.

"We need to talk," Kaspar said, his tone leaving no room for argument.

Theodin and Ophelia exchanged a glance, the weight of the unfinished topic still hanging between them. Without another word, they stood and followed Kaspar into the hall.

The four other Council members were in their respective seats at the round table. Kaspar took his seat, and Ophelia and Theodin stepped into the open space across from him.

"Today's events have proven one thing," he began, his voice steady but commanding. "Ophelia and Theodin's bond cannot be ignored any longer."

Ophelia and Theodin's glances met and exchanged knowing looks. The Council had known. Kaspar had known.

Margrith leaned forward, her gnarled hands resting on the edge of the Council table. "And what exactly do you propose we do, Kaspar? Bind them prematurely and hope for the best? She hasn't even finished her pre-Dyad apprenticeship period or been evaluated for it. We're not in the business of gambling. What exactly do you expect to find? That they're some destined pair meant to save us all? We've seen how these so-called initial 'bonds' can fail."

Ophelia stiffened, her fingers curling into fists at her sides. Theodin glanced at her, his expression unreadable but his posture shifting ever so slightly closer.

"It wouldn't be a gamble," Kaspar replied coolly. "It would be a test. A compatibility trial, nothing more. If they fail, we reassess. If they succeed…" His gaze swept across the room. "Then we have something extraordinary on our hands. Their connection is undeniable. It's not a question of if it exists—it's a question of how we use it."

"Extraordinary or dangerous," Sigvard grunted. "You've seen how unpredictable Ophelia's magic is. Pairing her with Theodin could amplify those risks."

"And yet, their connection in the field has already proven valuable," Alfena interjected, her calm voice cutting through the tension. "The Cadaven was neutralized, and the wards' failure would have cost us more if not for them."

Crane tapped the handle of his cane against his chin. "I do wonder… do you think if we had Ophelia partake in the actual Arcane Dyad ritual, would her Valksha magic cause some sort of reaction like it had during her initiation ritual?"

Kaspar's gaze shifted to Crane. "That's precisely why we're starting with the compatibility test. No rituals, no bonds, no complete Dyad—just observation. The first stage of the Dyad is reversible if it passes and harbors that initial connection."

"Yet," Crane countered, his voice light but pointed, "you can't predict how her magic will interact with Theodin's energy, even in a controlled test. Veladriel's influence has already proven to be… unpredictable."

"And if the test spirals out of control?" Margrith said sharply. "What then? Do we risk compromising Theodin as well?"

Kaspar regarded Margrith with ease. "We will intervene then. If we do nothing, we risk even more. Their bond is already manifesting in ways none of us fully understand. Ignoring it won't make it go away—it will only leave us unprepared."

Alfena nodded slowly, her fingers steepled. "If anything, today's events have shown that they are stronger together. If their connection can be tempered and honed, it could be the key to handling threats like the Cadaven, Warthralls, Unseelie—and whatever caused the wards to fail."

"And if they're not compatible?" Sigvard muttered.

"Then we'll know," Kaspar said simply. "And we'll adjust accordingly."

The Council fell into a contemplative silence as the weight of the decision pressed down on them.

Finally, Margrith spoke, her tone clipped. "Very well. Let the test proceed. But understand this—if there's even the slightest sign of instability, I'll put an end to it myself."

Ophelia let out a quiet, anxious huff. She must have been holding her breath that entire time.

Beneath the table, she suddenly felt Theodin's fingers brush against hers and gently grasp her hand in the effort to comfort her. Once again, rather than a tumultuous wave of his energy, it was soothing. However, there was something different this time—but similar to what she felt. A hint of nervousness, perhaps. Still, his warmth grounded her and, despite any fear she felt in that moment, she found solace in knowing he would be there with her.

Kaspar cleared his throat, drawing their attention. "You'll begin immediately," he said. "Follow me."

Ophelia glanced up at Theodin, their hands still lightly entwined. He gave her the faintest nod as he pulled away and, though his expression remained composed, the warmth of his energy lingered, steadying her nerves.

"Let's do this," she murmured.

As they began for the door, Theodin stayed close to her side, his gaze fixed ahead.

"Stay focused," he said quietly, but there was a softness to his words —a reassurance she hadn't expected.

Gentle vibrations of magic pulsed through the walls of the chamber. The runes carved into the stone glowed faintly, their golden light casting soft shadows on the floor. At the center of the room floated a crystal orb, its surface shimmering with many shifting colors, like wisps of watercolor paint swirling slowly in a suspended enclosure. Tree roots hugged around the base of the orb and shaped like fingers around the sphere, cupping it like it was in the palm of a wise, ancient hand.

Around the perimeter of the chamber, the Council members stood in watchful silence. Margrith's critical gaze shifted between Ophelia and Theodin with her posture rigid with skepticism. Sigvard had his thick arms folded, his expression indiscernible beneath his Dwarvish beard. Alfena's silvery eyes remained fixed on the orb, her calm demeanor betraying no hint of her thoughts. Crane leaned lightly on his cane as he dazed at the pair with bright curiosity. Kaspar stood closest to the apprentices.

"The test is straightforward," he began, addressing both Ophelia and Theodin but loud enough for the Council to hear. "Channel your magic into the orb. Its energy will stabilize if your synchronization is strong or destabilize if it falters."

"And if it destabilizes, the chamber's wards will contain the energy," Alfena added. "This room was built for this purpose."

"As your energies feed into the orb, you will see them interact," Kaspar continued. "How they react to one another will inform us how well-suited you are to one another. In cases where two individuals match well, the colors and movements will change. Do you understand?"

Ophelia's brow furrowed. She paused for a moment to allow him to explain further as if expecting more.

"But…how?"

"It's different every time," Crane chuckled. "But the most consistent is the outcome of a mismatch. Usually it turns black."

Though he stood still, Ophelia felt Theodin's shift of discomfort at this by the stiffness of his stance. She glanced up at him to see him staring at the orb with apprehension beneath his stoic demeanor.

It wasn't just the thought of using magic, Ophelia thought. It was the amount of times he must have experienced the rejection of the Dyad.

Kaspar turned back to Theodin and Ophelia. "The key is trust. Don't fight the energy—let it flow naturally between you. Focus on each other, not just the orb."

Theodin exhaled. He stepped forward first. In a demonstrative gesture, he took his place on one of the glowing sigils etched into the floor. He raised his hand, palm towards the orb, his face hardening.

Ophelia hesitated for a moment, glancing around the room. The weight of the Council's stares pressed against her, but then her gaze found Theodin's.

He offered her a single nod.

With that, she held her breath and stepped onto the second sigil opposite of him. She lifted her hand towards the orb.

For a moment, nothing happened. Then, slowly, streams of light began to flow from their palms—Theodin's a steady, golden glow and Ophelia's a flickering green flame.

The colors in the orb became clear and translucent, and their two streams moved towards it. They penetrated the glass surface, then circled each other like floating, silky ribbons.

The Council watched intently as the streams began to glow brighter, the intensities of their radiance reflecting the interplay of their magic. At first, the light was unstable, the green and gold clashing like opposing forces. A loud buzz vibrated from the orb.

"Focus," Theodin said sharply, his voice cutting through the noise.

"I am focusing," Ophelia snapped back. Her jaw tightened as she steadied herself.

"No—focus on me."

Ophelia's eyes moved to meet Theodin's.

That same unexplainable, electric feeling passed through them.

Her green light smoothed, intertwining more fluidly with his golden stream.

The orb began to stabilize, its colors softening into a warm silver.

A ripple of reactions shuffled through the Council—Crane's intrigued hum and Sigvard's low grunt of acknowledgment. Even Margrith leaned forward slightly, her skepticism wavering.

But then the orb's glow began to intensify. The light grew brighter and brighter until the entire chamber was bathed in its radiance. The runes on the walls flared violently, and the orb trembled as though struggling to contain the energy. The buzzing of the orb grew louder until it became loud enough to go to shake the floor.

"Kaspar," Theodin said, his voice edged with warning. "What's happening?"

Kaspar's eyes narrowed, his expression darkening. "This isn't part of the test."

Margrith began towards the orb, but she was stopped by a low rumble and the trembling of the ground. The force of it was enough to make her stumble and lose her footing.

Before anyone else could react, the orb exploded in a burst of light. A shockwave of energy rippled through the chamber, and the runes flared to life, creating a dome of blinding light around Ophelia and Theodin. A deafening hum whirred and echoed in the space.

The Council shielded their eyes, voices rising in confusion and alarm.

Crane's cane tapped rapidly against the floor. "It can't be. Is this—"

"The final stage of the ritual," Alfena called. "It's happening."

Inside the dome, Ophelia's breath quickened as the energy surged through her, raw and overwhelming. Her eyes squeezed shut. Though she was frightened, she still felt Theodin's presence. She held steadfast to it as the sensation rushing into her bore into her soul, rapidly but painlessly ripping her apart and putting her back together.

And then, just as suddenly as it began, the light faded. The chamber fell silent, and the white glow was replaced by a dim, pulsing hum. The orb returned to its initial many-colored state.

Theodin and Ophelia had collapsed to their hands and knees, trembling in the center of the room. They remained where they were before the dimming orb, dizzy and huffing for air.

Ophelia felt the skin on her arms tingle and sting. She sat back on her heels and looked at her hands.

Runes glowed along the base of her palms and the inside of their forearms, shimmering with white light.

As Theodin propped himself onto one knee, he turned his wrist to look at his hands as well—he was similarly marked with identical runes, which were also singed with white.

Slowly, their eyes lifted to one another in daze and bewilderment.

The Council stared in utter shock.

"What is the meaning of this?" Margrith demanded.

Kaspar stepped forward, his eyes scanning the initiates. He crouched beside Theodin and carefully grabbed his wrist to take a closer look at the markings.

"The Arcane Dyad," he said quietly. "It's…complete."

"How?" Sigvard muttered. "That's impossible. The ritual works similarly to the initiation ritual—it's the Order's Collective instigated by Council."

"We're not even in Avasyon!" Margrith scowled. "How in the world is this possible?"

"Perhaps it was Ophelia's Valksha magic that unintentionally set it off," Alfena said softly.

Crane thumped his cane on the ground and thrust a finger to the ceiling. "I called it!"

Ophelia, still breathing heavily and shaken, stared down at the runes etched into her skin. As her hand quivered, the glow dimmed, leaving the markings stained into her skin like ink.

"This changes everything," Margrith said sharply, stepping forward. Her accusatory gaze and voice bore into Kaspar. "You promised us a controlled test. And now *this?*"

Kaspar turned to face her, his voice calm but resolute. "The ritual was not planned, but it was not unwelcome. The Dyad has proven itself—it exists, and it's strong."

"Strong doesn't mean stable," Sigvard countered. "What happens if it falters? Or worse—if it turns volatile? We have no means of reversing it." His posture became rigid, imposing. "It's *permanent* now."

"Not unstable," Kaspar interrupted, his eyes shifting between Margrith and Sigvard. He motioned to the apprentices. "Yes, permanent. Look at them. They're alive. Breathing. The Dyad bond formed because it was meant to."

"Meant to?" Margrith scoffed. "Since when do we leave the fate of the Kyriegard to chance? Or to the whims of a Valksha's unpredictable magic?"

Crane tapped his cane on the stone floor, his expression alight with curiosity. "You misunderstand, Margrith. This didn't happen by chance. It was inevitable."

The Council's eyes swept to him. He gestured toward Ophelia and Theodin with his cane. They had slowly stood and stiffly moved to stand beside each other on one side of the orb. They both stared at the Council with wide, shaken eyes as they deliberated.

"They were connected before this test ever began. You've all seen it—how they move in battle, how they respond to one another. The ritual simply… revealed what was already there. In all the histories, a Dyad has never formed unbidden. This isn't just rare—as Nimrod said, it's extraordinary."

"Margrith," Alfena interjected, her voice steady but firm. "What happened here may have been unorthodox, but it wasn't catastrophic. The room's wards held, and the initiates are unharmed."

"Unharmed?" Margrith said bluntly. "Do you truly believe they understand the weight of what just occurred? They were nowhere near ready for this kind of thing! It takes *years* to prepare and master the tethering of souls!"

Ophelia flinched at the sharpness of the words but didn't speak. Her hand drifted back to her side, curling into a loose fist. Theodin shifted subtly closer to her, his presence a quiet reassurance. Without even touching her, she suddenly felt his energy flow into her and soothe her rising anxiety. They turned to one another, locking eyes in quiet surprise.

"I'd say they're handling it better than some of us," Crane said dryly, leaning on his cane. "And might I remind everyone—I *did* suggest this could happen."

Kaspar's lips twitched, but he quickly schooled his expression. "What matters now is what we do next."

"What we do," Margrith snapped, "is evaluate this bond. Thoroughly. We cannot proceed without knowing its full implications. We have to do retroactive training to make up for their lack of preparation for this moment."

Theodin's eyes darted to Ophelia, and for the first time, she thought she saw uncertainty in his expression.

"Are you okay?" he asked quietly, his voice low enough that only she could hear.

Ophelia nodded, though her hand still trembled slightly.

"I think so," she whispered. "But I don't… I don't feel that different. I just…for a moment, I felt what I felt before, that connection we spoke of earlier—except…we weren't touching or looking at each other."

He glanced at the glowing runes on his arm, which now faded to a subtle shimmer.

"I felt that too," he said after a moment. "And I don't feel that different either. But it's there. Like a weight. Or…" He hesitated, searching for the right words. "Like a thread."

Ophelia let out a breath. "A thread?"

He nodded, his gaze focusing on hers. "Binding us."

As Kaspar stepped forward, addressing his apprentices, his voice carried a note of reverence. "The Arcane Dyad ritual is one of the Kyriegard's most sacred traditions. It creates a connection unlike any other—a blending of magic, mind, and will. For it to form without Council intervention… that is unprecedented."

"Unprecedented and dangerous," Margrith added bitterly. "Do you know what happens when a Dyad falters? If one partner is compromised, it could bring them both down. They have no clue how to balance it if their energies tip one way or the other."

"Or," Alfena interjected calmly, "it could make them stronger. A Dyad forged without our guidance is not inherently flawed. If anything, it speaks to the depth of their connection."

Kaspar turned back to the Council, his gray eyes sharp. "The Dyad is formed, and it's stronger than we anticipated. We should not waste time debating its existence. Instead, we must begin to explore its potential."

"And how do you propose we do that?" Sigvard rumbled.

"With their first mission," Kaspar said simply. "Together."

The room fell into a tense silence, the Council exchanging wary glances.

Finally, Alfena spoke. "A controlled mission," she said firmly. "To test the Dyad under real-world conditions."

"That sounds insane," Sigvard grumbled.

"We will have the condition controlled as much as possible," Alfena pressed.

"Agreed," Crane said, his expression thoughtful. "But we must monitor them closely."

Margrith scowled but gave a curt nod. "Fine. But I'll be watching them like a hawk." Her piercing eyes glazed over them, especially Ophelia, with harsh scrutiny. "The mission will be to visit the defensive wardstones and investigate. After you are finished, I will examine your work very closely. Kaspar will have more details for you in the morning."

Kaspar's gaze returned to Theodin and Ophelia. "You've both proven something extraordinary tonight. But this is only the beginning."

Kaspar gestured for Theodin and Ophelia to follow him as the Council began to disperse. His silver eyes betrayed none of the gravity of what had just occurred, but his silence was telling.

The room he led them to was small and quiet, lit by a single glowing orb that hovered near the ceiling. Shelves of ancient tomes lined the walls and a simple wooden table stood in the center. Kaspar turned, his gaze sharp but steady.

"Sit," he said simply, motioning to the chairs across from him. Theodin and Ophelia obeyed without hesitation, though Ophelia's hands fidgeted in her lap.

For a moment, Kaspar said nothing, studying them both with the practiced calm of a seasoned mentor. Then he spoke in a low voice. "Do you understand what's happened?"

Theodin's jaw tightened, and he glanced at Ophelia before

answering. "The Arcane Dyad. It formed without the council's intervention."

Kaspar nodded. "Correct. But do you understand the weight of that? As I said before, the bond you now share is one of the Kyriegard's most sacred traditions. It is meant to unify, to strengthen—but it is also a burden. One that you will carry together."

Ophelia swallowed hard, her eyes fixed on the runes on her arm. "Is it… dangerous?"

"Anything worth having is dangerous," Kaspar said. "This bond will amplify your strengths—but it will also expose your weaknesses. It is more than just a magical connection; it's a melding of energies, minds, and instincts. You'll sense each other's presence even from great distances, feel emotions that aren't your own, and in moments of extreme focus, you may even share thoughts or intentions. In battle, it will heighten your coordination, letting you act as one without words. But it's not without risks. If one of you falters—emotionally, physically, or magically—the other will feel it. And if one of you is lost…" He paused. His stare became distant, looking past them for a long moment. Then his eyes lowered solemnly. "The consequences could be devastating."

Theodin's eyes darkened. "So, what do we do now?"

Kaspar leaned forward slightly, his expression softening. "You trust each other. Completely. This Dyad is more than magic—it is trust, understanding, and unity. Without those, it will fail. But if you nurture it, if you learn to work as one, it will make you stronger than you can imagine."

The elder Kyriegard folded his hands together and looked at his laced fingers, wrinkled and sword-weathered. "I had hoped for more time—to guide you, to understand what this means. But fate doesn't always wait for preparation."

"You knew," Ophelia said softly. "You knew of the connection between us."

Kaspar nodded once. "Yes. I did."

"For how long?" Theodin pressed.

"The moment you first locked eyes, the night you came, Ophelia," Kaspar answered. "And ever since then. I saw it in both of you. The way you would flinch, the way you shifted, unsure. I noticed it, yes, but I still can't explain it. Even Lady Vivian—I wrote her after a few days of observing it—isn't quite sure what it is. Do your Faytes—your destinies—align? Is this the will of Elodyn and the Saryfim? Or some other force of the Ether? I only have questions and unfortunately no straight answers."

He gestured to the runes on their arms. "But clearly whatever forces are at work want you two together."

Kaspar leaned back, his eyes scanning them. "Whatever this is, it will define you—individually and together. But remember, the Dyad is only as strong as the trust you build. Strengthen it, and you'll find power beyond imagination. Let it weaken, and it could destroy you."

Ophelia's fingers brushed the runes on her arm. "No pressure, then," she muttered with a faint smile, though her voice broke slightly.

Theodin glanced at her. "We'll manage."

Kaspar nodded firmly. "That's the spirit. Now, go. Rest while you can. Tomorrow will demand much of you both."

After Kaspar dismissed them, Theodin and Ophelia went to the corridor of guest chambers of Halvalla without speaking a word to one another.

Instead, they began to feel each other's emotions. They walked side by side, and the unseen tether streamed between them like a living wire.

Theodin winced from the surge of anxiety, confusion, and helplessness flooding his mind. A dull, irritated noise in his ears made his heart race.

No. This can't happen.

In the middle of the hallway, Theodin suddenly put a careful hand on Ophelia's shoulder. The Valksha girl stopped and glanced at him.

"It's going to be okay, Ophelia," he said softly. "Your worries. They're…overwhelming."

Ophelia turned to him fully. "You don't have any?"

"I do," Theodin admitted. In the dim light of the hallway, he studied her expression with a gentle gaze. "But I don't let my concerns or worries cripple me. I focus on the task ahead. What needs to be done. Remove the emotion from the situation and ground it in logic." He squeezed her shoulder, and his comforting wave of energy swept into her.

His voice quieted into a whisper. "We have been bound for a reason. It is not your fault and it was not an accident. You and I may struggle, but we will also overcome."

She closed her eyes and exhaled slowly, deflating with relief.

At this, Theodin smiled slightly to himself. If the Dyad allowed him to help her like this even from a distance, it would make a significant difference.

Ophelia straightened, keeping her eyes shut. "You make it sound so simple," she said, matching his whisper.

"It's not," Theodin replied. "But it's necessary."

She gave a small nod. Her eyes lifted to him. "Thank you."

Something changed in the way their eyes met. It wasn't jarring or intense as it was before—this time, it just felt…peaceful.

It made both of their hearts flutter. Theodin withdrew his hand and looked away, and Ophelia lowered her gaze timidly to hide her blush.

Theodin cleared his throat quietly. "You're welcome," he finally said. He reached for the closest guest chamber and turned the knob to push the door open. "Goodnight, Ophelia."

Ophelia stepped into the entryway and flashed her eyes to him once before turning them back to the floor. "Goodnight, Theodin."

As fleeting as the moment was, she disappeared into the room just as quickly and gently shut the door behind herself.

Theodin stopped and stared at the door. The feeling still lingered in him, and he knew that she felt it too.

Chapter 16

The Dyad Awakens

Year 844 of the Second Age, Seventh Month, Eighth Day

The darkness was suffocating, heavy as a shroud. Ophelia couldn't see, couldn't move—only feel. A pounding dread filled her chest. Each beat of her heart echoed like thunder in the void. Shadows twisted around her, writhing shapes that whispered in a language she couldn't understand.

Then, she saw him.

Theodin stood at the center of it all, his eyes wide with fear and something darker—guilt, perhaps. Blood streaked his face. His hands were outstretched, grasping at something just out of reach, his voice hoarse as he shouted something she couldn't make out.

The raw and desperate sound ripped through her.

Ophelia stepped toward him instinctively, her own voice rising. "Theodin!"

But he didn't hear her. The shadows surged forward and swallowed him whole.

She felt his anguish, his helplessness—his rage. It was as if the emotions were her own, clawing at her chest until she couldn't breathe.

* * *

She jolted awake, gasping for air.

Cold sweat ran from her brow. The glow of her runes pulsed on her forearm. Ophelia's eyes snapped to the door—

She was shaken. And so was he.

Suddenly, she heard his voice mutter as if he were right beside her.

Damn nightmares.

She flinched and looked around. She was still the only one in the room.

How strange.

Only the slim break of dawn illuminated the chamber.

Ophelia pushed herself out of bed, her legs trembling as she stumbled into the corridor. Though she didn't see which guest chamber he took, she felt where he was. She felt his quivering breath as it mirrored hers.

She knocked lightly on the wood, her voice shaking.

"Theodin?"

The door creaked open slightly, just enough for Theodin to appear in the dim light. His face was pale, his eyes clouded with something indiscernible.

"What are you doing awake?" he asked, his voice low but hoarse.

Ophelia hesitated. Her hand tightened on the doorframe.

"I—I felt it," she said gently. "Your dream. The fear, the anger. It… it woke me up."

Theodin stiffened. "You shouldn't have."

"It's not like I could stop it," she said. "But I did. And…" Her expression softened. "I'm sorry you went through that. Does it… happen often to you?"

He looked away. She felt his guard lift up like a stone wall being rising between them.

"I don't need your pity, Ophelia."

She stepped closer to the entryway of the room.

"It's not pity. I just…"

She faltered. Her gentle eyes searched his.

"I don't want you to go through it alone."

For a moment, silence stretched between them, broken only by the faded hum of the runes protecting the halls of Halvalla.

Finally, Theodin sighed, stepped back, and gestured for her to come in.

"You won't understand," he said quietly. "But… if you insist."

Ophelia slid through the opening of the doorway.

Inside, the room was dimly lit by a single enchanted lamp on the table, casting golden light across the walls. Theodin sat on the edge of the bed with his hands clasped tightly in front of him.

Ophelia hovered near the doorway. Finally, as all nurturing figures in her life did, she went to his side and sat next to him.

"What… what do you dream about?"

He didn't look at her. She could still feel the wall around his heart.

"The past," he answered. "Things I can't change."

Her brow furrowed, but she didn't press him. She turned her eyes to the floor in front of her.

"It felt so real," she whispered. "The fear, the anger… even the guilt. It's like it wasn't just a dream."

"It wasn't," Theodin admitted, his voice barely audible. His eyes flicked to her, guarded but pained. "It never is."

Ophelia lifted her eyes to meet his. "Then…what is it?"

Theodin shook his head and dropped his eyes away to avoid hers. "I don't know."

"And it's happened more than once?"

He nodded stiffly.

Ophelia leaned forward with her elbows on her knees. "What did you see? In the dream?"

Theodin stared for a beat, and then he turned away again.

"It doesn't matter."

"It matters to me," she insisted gently. "I felt it, Theodin. All of those awful feelings—it was like you were drowning in them. And now, you're trying to pretend it didn't happen."

He exhaled sharply, running a hand through his hair.

For several moments, Theodin didn't respond.

Then, he muttered, "I saw shadows."

Ophelia frowned. "Shadows?"

"They… they pull at me. Like they're trying to drag me under." He clenched his fists and his jaw clenched. "But I don't know why."

She felt a shiver of something unfamiliar—an emotion that wasn't entirely his own, nor hers. It was cold, relentless, unidentifiable. A remnant of the nightmare?

Ophelia shivered, but she didn't pull away. "Have you told Kaspar about this?"

Theodin shook his head. "I have. But there's no point anymore. He'd just tell me to meditate or focus harder. Like it's something I can control."

"He has no explanation?"

"Neither did Lady Vivian."

Ophelia sat back, appalled. "What?"

She felt him shut down again and retreat into a protective mental shell. He abruptly stood and began for the door. Ophelia leapt to her feet.

"Theodin!"

Both of the runes in their skin flashed green. Theodin halted in his tracks, but it was as if he was frozen unwillingly.

The force of her voice and energy stopped him.

Ophelia let out a stifled huff, shocked by the occurrence.

"S…Sorry," she stammered.

She huffed, rolled her shoulders, then walked around him to face him. He still had his eyes turned down to the ground, a stoic expression drawn on his face.

"Listen, Theodin," she began with sincerity in her voice. "We have to work together. I'm not judging you, I'm not ostracizing you…"

Theodin's eyes closed and his brows furrowed together. He inhaled and exhaled deeply.

Both of their runes lit up again, but this time with a white light. Ophelia noticed that her breath synchronized with his. Her face softened and her eyes shut.

The wall between them melted, and his memories flooded her mind. Voices and whispers echoed with flashes of visions.

"What's with his eyes?"

"I don't want to spar with him. He might kill me."

"He's so scary!"

"Don't touch me, kid."

"Truth is, lad…"

Kaspar's voice came to the forefront.

"Even Lady Vivian couldn't tell you the other parts of your heritage. You're mostly human, from my understanding—enough to be considered human overall—but what else, even just a little? Perhaps the Giant-folk…the Procerians? That would explain your height and some of that unruly strength. But not all of it. Pulchid? Seelie or Unseelie? It's hard to say because it's muddled, but that doesn't make you less than anyone else."

Ophelia's eyes shot open as she gasped for air, like she had just left her body and returned in an instant. Tears streamed down her cheek. As her blurred vision came into focus again, her eyes lifted to her partner. She blinked rapidly.

"Theodin… I saw… I heard…"

Her voice broke, and Theodin became rigid.

"You shouldn't have seen that," he said, his tone low and edged with something Ophelia couldn't quite place—shame, perhaps.

"I didn't mean to," she whispered. Her hand trembled as she reached up to wipe her face. "But… those memories—they hurt."

Theodin's eyes opened and darkened.

"They're mine to bear," he murmured. "Not yours."

"But they're ours now, aren't they?" Ophelia insisted. "This bond—it doesn't just let me feel your emotions. It's showing me pieces of you. Things you've tried to hide." Her gaze met his again, unwavering. "Why are you hiding?"

Theodin dropped his eyes to the floor.

"Because I don't even know what I am, Ophelia," he strained. "And if I don't know, how can I expect anyone else to understand?"

Her heart clenched at the rawness of his words. Tears welled in her eyes again and threatened to spill. Instinctively, in the effort to comfort him and herself simultaneously, she stepped close to him and pulled him into a tight embrace. Her arms hugged around his waist and her ear pressed into the base of his sternum.

Theodin froze at the contact, his breath hitching as Ophelia's warmth enveloped him. For a moment, he didn't move. His body was stiff and his hands hung awkwardly at his sides.

The walls he had carefully built around himself threatened to crumble under the weight of her compassion.

Slowly and hesitantly, he allowed his arms to wrap around her. His hands rested lightly on her back at first, as if he was afraid to hold on too tightly. But as the Dyad stirred between them, a quiet hum of energy rippling through his chest, his grip firmed. He rested his chin atop her head, exhaling a shaky breath he hadn't realized he'd been holding.

Their glowing runes brightened with intensity.

"It's not that simple, Ophelia," he said at last. "It's never been simple."

Ophelia didn't respond immediately. Instead, she held him tighter, her fingers curling into the fabric of his shirt.

"It doesn't have to be," she said softly. "But you don't have to carry it alone anymore. We're bound, Theodin. Whatever this is, we'll figure it out. Together."

He closed his eyes, the weight of her words settling into him like a balm against an old wound. For the first time in what felt like an eternity, the shadows receded, leaving a fragile but undeniable sense of calm in their wake.

"Together," he repeated, the word heavy with unspoken promise.

Theodin's grip loosened slightly, and when Ophelia pulled back to look at him, he met her gaze fully. The guarded tension in his eyes had lessened, replaced by something quieter. Vulnerable, perhaps. Grateful.

"Thank you," he said simply, his voice steady but earnest.

Ophelia offered a faint smile, her eyes glistening. "You're welcome."

For a moment, they stood there, the bond rippling between.

Then Theodin stepped back, clearing his throat and gesturing toward the door. "We should… prepare ourselves. Maybe rest for a little longer. Today's going to be a long day."

Ophelia nodded, though she hesitated before heading for the door. As she glanced back one last time, she found him watching her, a subtle but genuine flicker of warmth in his expression.

"See you soon, Theodin," she said softly.

"See you soon, Ophelia," he replied, quieter now but resolute.

As the door closed behind her, Theodin exhaled deeply, the pulse of the Dyad still settling in his chest. For the first time, the weight of his uncertainty felt just a little bit lighter.

Theodin tightened the straps of his gauntlets as the morning sun cast a pale light over Halvalla's courtyard. Dew lightly sprinkled on the grass as the summer's warmth eased in to relinquish the evening's coolness.

Beside him, Ophelia clung her rifle strap, her eyes scanning their surroundings with quiet determination. The hum of the Dyad between them was faint but constant, like a thread keeping their souls tethered together.

Kaspar approached with measured strides, his gaze sharper than usual. "Are you both ready?"

Ophelia nodded. "We're ready."

Theodin glanced at her, the warmth from their earlier exchange still lingering. "We are."

Kaspar studied them for a moment longer with a discerning gaze before he spoke.

"Good. Your mission is simple in principle but critical in execution. The wards in each estate of Olysgard must be investigated, reinforced, and if necessary, replaced. Margrith and Sigvard have maintained and reinforced the wardstones, but something has changed. There's been… troubling activity near their edges."

"What kind of activity?" Ophelia asked.

Kaspar's lips pressed into a thin line. "Signs of corruption. Warthrall tampering. Unseelie Pulchidmeddling. Shadow beasts. Possibly worse."

As the anxiety rose from Ophelia's chest to her throat, it was quickly dissipated by a wave of soothing energy. The Valksha girl glimpsed at her fellow apprentice, who gave a knowing and subtle nod of acknowledgment. Ophelia nodded slightly in gratitude with a small smile.

Kaspar's brows lifted at the observation of their exchange. He held in a smirk of satisfaction before turning to the road. "Onward."

The trio walked in silence as the road ahead twisted through dense forests, the towering pines casting long shadows that danced in the morning light. The only sounds were the crunch of boots against gravel and the distant vibrations of Olysgard's protective wards, a murmur of energy that seemed to tremble Ophelia's bones.

She adjusted the strap of her rifle and brushed her fingers over the engraved runes along its barrel. The Dyad hummed serenely between her and Theodin, a low, persistent rhythm that was beginning to feel like background noise. She wasn't sure if that comforted her or unnerved her.

Kaspar's gaze swept the treeline as he spoke, his voice low. "The first wardstone lies near the eastern edge of Avasylon's borders. If it's intact, you'll reinforce it. If not…" He trailed off, his eyes narrowing as he scanned the shadows ahead. "Be prepared."

"I'm assuming Margrith and Sigvard will be joining us?" Theodin remarked.

Kaspar shook his head. "No. Since they have investigated and reinforced the wardstones, and the problem persists—it means that another Kyriegard must attend to it. But once we are finished, they will inspect your work."

Ophelia's grip on her rifle tightened. "How will we know if the wardstone has been tampered with?"

"Corruption leaves a mark," Kaspar replied. "The wards should pulse with steady light. If the glow is dim or uneven, it's compromised. If it's dark…" His tone hardened. "Then you'll know."

Theodin walked a step ahead, his posture rigid but his movements fluid, ready to draw his sword at the first sign of danger. "Do you think it's Warthralls?" he asked, his tone calm but clipped.

Kaspar didn't answer immediately.

"It's possible. But if the wards are failing, they might not be the only ones taking advantage of the weakness."

Ophelia felt a jolt of unease that she didn't recognize as her own. She glanced at Theodin, catching the faint tension in his shoulders. The uneasiness must have been a shadow of his emotions bleeding into hers. She took a deep breath and focused on the moment they shared earlier that morning—the warmth, the comfort, and the easing of their tensions. As she exhaled, she willed a projection of her newfound confidence back to her partner.

It's okay, Theo.

Theodin's eyes whipped to her, and though he didn't say anything, she felt a quiet acknowledgment. A shared understanding.

As they rounded a bend in the road, the hum of the wards grew louder, a low thrum that rumbled in the air. Kaspar stopped abruptly and raised a hand to halt them.

"Do you hear that?" he whispered.

Ophelia strained her ears. Her heart pounded.

The forest was unnervingly quiet. No birdsong, no rustling of leaves —just the steady, oppressive pulsing of the wards.

"Yes," Theodin said, his eyes narrowing as he scanned the trees. "It's too quiet."

Kaspar's hand drifted to the hilt of his sword.

"Stay close. And stay ready."

Theodin didn't want to speak or make another sound, nor did he want to take his eyes off their surroundings. He knew they had the advantage of a Valksha who could sense the presence of other beings nearby as long as they weren't human—but he couldn't communicate with her…

Or….could he?

Just this morning, he could've sworn he heard her voice in his head. It was all unintentional and random.

But maybe this was telepathy. Maybe it was the Arcane Dyad.

He recentered himself mentally to focus on their surroundings and his Valksha partner.

Ophelia.

He willed his thoughts to reach her.

Can you hear me?

He stole a moment to glimpse in her direction.

Ophelia froze, her breath catching in her throat. She felt it—Theodin's voice, not spoken, but carried in the Dyad, faint yet unmistakable.

Ophelia. Can you hear me?

Her eyes snapped to his, wide with surprise. For a moment, she wasn't sure if she'd imagined it, but the steady vibration of the bond between them reassured her.

She answered apprehensively.

Y…Yes.

He nodded slowly and spoke again.

Can you feel anything out there?

She closed her eyes briefly, centering herself.

Give me a moment.

She reached out with her senses, her Valksha magic rippling outward like waves on still water. At first, she felt nothing but the quiet vibration of the wards. But then, a distant disturbance—a blink of movement, just beyond her reach.

There's something, she thought to Theodin. *But it's… faint. Like it's hiding.*

Theodin tightened his grip on his sword. *How close?*

Ophelia shook her head, frustration tugging at her features. *I can't tell. It's… shifting.*

Kaspar's gaze sharpened, his eyes darting between them. He drew his sword, the blade glinting dangerously in the morning light.

As they pressed forward, the hum of the wards grew uneven, their once-steady rhythm faltering into erratic pulses.

Theodin felt a brush of unease through their bond—Ophelia's unease—and glanced at her. She was gripping her rifle tightly, her jaw set, but her eyes betrayed her apprehension.

Focus, he thought, directing the word to her through the Dyad. This time, her head tilted slightly, as if she'd heard him, and she gave a faint nod.

They rounded another bend, and the wardstone came into view. It stood tall, perhaps twice Theodin's height, and its surface weathered and etched with glowing runes—but the light was faint, flickering like a dying flame. Around its base, the ground was scorched, the grass blackened and brittle.

Kaspar stopped short, his expression grim. "It's compromised," he whispered, his tone heavy. "And we're not alone."

The air around the wardstone was heavy, thick with a palpable sense of wrongness. The acrid smell of burnt vegetation lingered, making Ophelia's nose wrinkle. Her knuckles turned white as the grip on her rifle tightened.

A low growl rumbled from the shadows of the trees.

Ophelia froze. Theodin's hand shot out, gesturing for her to stay still. Kaspar's silver eyes narrowed and his blade rose.

"It's testing us," Kaspar murmured, his voice barely audible. "Waiting for us to move."

Theodin shifted slightly, his stance widening as his free hand hovered near the hilt of his sword.

He pushed his thoughts to her through the Dyad.

Do you see it?

Ophelia closed her eyes again, reaching out with her senses. Her magic rippled outward like a net, searching. The disturbance grew stronger, closer.

Her focus darted to a dense cluster of trees to their left.

There. It's circling us.

Theodin gave a slight nod, his gaze snapping to the spot Ophelia had indicated.

Kaspar noticed the unspoken exchange between apprentices. Then his attention turned the movement they saw and adjusted his position, angling his blade toward the same area.

A sudden burst of branches shattered the tense silence. From the shadows, a creature lunged—a hulking, twisted mass of sinew and shadow, its glowing red eyes burning into them.

A guttural snarl ripped through the air.

Its claws raked the ground as it charged.

Theodin reacted instantly. His sword flashed as he stepped into the creature's path.

The impact of their clash sent a shockwave rippling outward, forcing Ophelia to steady herself.

Theodin swung relentlessly. His movements were precise, each strike calculated as he drove the creature back.

Ophelia raised her rifle. Her heart pounded. The green runes along the barrel flared to life as she steadied her aim. She exhaled slowly and narrowed her focus to the creature's exposed flank.

Theodin shifted, creating an opening, and she fired. The beam of green energy struck true, searing into the creature's side and eliciting a pained roar.

Kaspar sprinted and sliced with practiced efficiency as he severed one of the creature's clawed limbs. Black blood splattered. But the creature barely faltered, its body writhing as it regenerated before their eyes.

"It's drawing from the corruption," Kaspar barked. "We need to sever its connection to the wardstone!"

Ophelia's eyes snapped to the stuttering runes on the wardstone's surface. The light was pulsing erratically, almost in rhythm with the creature's movements. Her mind raced as she adjusted her grip on the rifle.

Theodin, she thought, her focus shifting to him. *I need time to stabilize the wardstone. Can you hold it off?*

Theodin didn't hesitate. *Go. I'll manage.*

Ophelia darted toward the wardstone with her heart hammering in her chest. She dropped to her knees before the ancient monolith and swept her fingers over the etched runes. The energy pulsing through the stone was chaotic, unstable, like a storm barely contained.

Theodin yelled out as he charged at the creature with tremendous speed. The shadowy beast fully turned to him and roared, meeting his blade with its teeth and claws.

Kaspar stepped toward them to assist, but upon watching his apprentices at work, he held back. His eyes gleamed with silent approval. He kept his blade ready and his senses open for any potential enemies that may enter the fray.

Ophelia pricked her finger on her spring-loaded ring and let a drop of blood fall onto the runes. The green light flared as her Valksha magic surged into the stone, intertwining with the ward's ancient enchantments. She closed her eyes, focusing all her energy on steadying the chaotic flow.

Behind her, the sounds of battle raged on. Theodin's grunts of effort and the creature's animalistic snarls filled the air. She felt his determination through the Dyad, a consistent force that bolstered her focus.

Suddenly, a sharp intensity flared—a ripple of strength and fury that sent a shiver down Ophelia's spine. Was this what Theodin's energy felt like when he fought?

She forced herself to focus, grounding her energy in the task at hand.

The runes began to stabilize, their light brightening into a consistent silver glow. But the strain was immense—the wardstone resisted her magic like a stubborn flame refusing to catch.

"Almost there," she strained.

Without warning, the Dyad yanked her body sideways.

"Ophelia, move!" Theodin's shout tore through her concentration, but she had already rolled to the side as the creature's claws raked the ground where she had been moments before.

Theodin was there in an instant, his sword slashing through the creature's torso and driving it back. His eyes flicked to Ophelia, a flash of concern crossing his face. "Are you—"

"I'm fine," she interrupted firmly. "Focus on keeping it off me."

He gave a curt nod and turned his attention back to the creature. The force of Theodin's strike seemed to stagger it, its shadowy form recoiling as if the blow had been more than it appeared.

Ophelia blinked, brushing the thought aside—there was no time to dwell on it.

She scrambled back to the wardstone. She could feel her head spin from the exertion, but she pushed herself. Her hands trembled with exhaustion, almost with panic, as she poured the last of her energy into stabilizing the runes. The light flared brilliantly, and the oppressive hum in the air abruptly ceased.

The creature froze mid-lunge. Its body writhed as the connection to the corruption was severed. With a final, ear-piercing shriek, it collapsed and dissolved into shadow, leaving only the faint scent of sulfur in its wake.

Ophelia slumped against the wardstone, her chest heaving as she caught her breath. Theodin approached with his sword still in hand, his gaze scanning the area for any remaining threats.

"It's gone," he said in a low voice.

Kaspar sheathed his blade and approached the wardstone. The glowing silver runes etched into the stone subtly pulsed with specks of green. He studied the markings for a long moment before turning to Ophelia.

"You stabilized it. And reinforced it."

Ophelia nodded weakly, her hands still shaking. "It wasn't easy."

"You did well," Kaspar said, his tone measured. He glanced at Theodin. "Both of you."

Theodin nodded once, his eyes meeting Ophelia's briefly.

Kaspar didn't really fight with me, he thought. *He's truly testing us.*

Ophelia gave a single nod of her head. *As he should.*

Theodin turned his attention back to the forest. "We should move. If there's one, there could be more."

Kaspar nodded in agreement, his gaze remaining on the wardstone for a moment longer.

"Onward," he said quietly.

Ophelia pushed herself to her feet. Her legs wobbled, but Theodin caught her by the arm and steadied her until she found her balance.

Their touch no longer seemed to be so jarring now that their energies continuously resonated, even as their adrenaline escalated from the battle.

Kaspar noticed how they locked eyes again, appearing to mutually accept their strange connection in the new light of their Kyriegard bond—the Arcane Dyad.

The Head of the Order subtly smiled to himself then before turning back to the path.

Chapter 17

The Volatile Thread

The path to Havysium was quieter than Kaspar had anticipated. The crunch of boots against dirt, the rustle of leaves in the breeze, and the distant vibration of the wards were the only sounds that filled the space between the three travelers. It was a moment of stillness, rare in the life of a Kyriegard, but Kaspar's mind was far from at ease.

He glanced over his shoulder at Ophelia and Theodin. They walked side by side, their movements fluid, almost in sync. It wasn't a conscious effort, he knew; it was their Dyad—still new, still raw, but unmistakably there.

Kaspar's gaze drifted to the road ahead as he let his thoughts wander.

Few traditions held as much weight in the Order as the Arcane Dyad. Such a bond between partners was more than a pairing of convenience or skill—it was a union of trust, will, and magic. A sacred connection forged not by accident, but by deliberate intent, guided by the collective will of the Order through Arborelys and the ancient rites of the Order's Sages and Sage Warriors.

The Dyad made two individuals more than the sum of their parts. It sharpened instincts, bridged thoughts, and amplified their strengths while tempering their weaknesses. In battle, a bonded pair moved as one, each anticipating the other's actions with uncanny precision. Only truly connected individuals could tap into this link to each other with ease; not even a mentor could communicate with their apprentice as easily. Perhaps a one-way message, but it could only be done through the Order's Collective—and the Collective was rarely tapped into in order to preserve its greatest benefits for the most dire needs. Only the vastly experienced Kyriegard knew how to do this at will.

That was why instead of depending solely on the Collective, on Arborelys, the Kyriegard put their focus on two individuals who could rely on one another through thick and thin.

It was a gift, but also a burden. The Arcane Dyad demanded unwavering trust, and when that trust faltered, the consequences were catastrophic.

That was what shook Kaspar about the Arcane Dyad that formed permanently between his apprentices, more than how it tethered suddenly and completely. But by how seamlessly they eased into fighting in a Dyad. Only four months of working exclusively together and no prior training or preparation.

Yet, they demonstrated synchronicity even before being considered potential partners.

Perhaps such bonds exist for a reason.

Kaspar's lips pressed into a thin line as he thought of Garrett. Their bond had been forged in the heat of battle, a connection born of shared struggles and tempered by years of partnership. Garrett's impulsive nature had balanced Kaspar's caution, and together they had achieved things neither could have accomplished alone. But Dyads were not unbreakable in death, and Garrett's sacrifice had left a scar that even time couldn't heal.

His eyes flicked to Ophelia. She was still so young and untested. Her magic, while extraordinary, was volatile, and her emotions often dictated her actions. Theodin, on the other hand, was disciplined to a fault, his every movement calculated and precise. Kaspar saw echoes of himself and Garrett in them—their dynamic was different, but the potential was the same.

He wondered if Garrett would have seen it too. Would he have recognized the bond—before it became an Arcane Dyad—for what it was? Or would he have been wary, like the other Council members?

Kaspar sighed, his thoughts heavy. The bond between Ophelia and Theodin was an anomaly, unbidden yet undeniable. It hadn't been forged by the Council's will or the Order's rites but by some force he couldn't understand. Perhaps it was the doing of Arborelys, but it had never acted without the instigation of the Council. And that unsettled him more than he cared to admit.

It was easy to blame it on the wildness of Ophelia's Valksha magic, but Kaspar's instinct told him it was something deeper. He had written to Lady Vivian, but he heard no response. That was troublesome, too.

"Do you think it'll hold?" Theodin's voice cut through Kaspar's thoughts. The boy's eyes met his, focused but questioning.

Kaspar's brow furrowed. "The Dyad?"

Theodin nodded.

Kaspar considered his words carefully.

"It's not the Dyad that needs to hold, Theodin. It's the trust between you. The Dyad is a tool—a powerful one—but without trust, it's a blade with no edge."

Theodin's gaze shifted to Ophelia, who was walking a few paces ahead, clinging to the strap of the rifle slung over her shoulder. Kaspar caught the way Theodin's expression softened, a trace of something unspoken fleeting across his face.

"You've both come far," Kaspar said. "But this is only the beginning. The Dyad will test you in ways you can't predict. It will push you to your limits, and sometimes beyond. But if you nurture it, if you let it strengthen you instead of divide you… it will make you unstoppable."

He saw the weight of his words settle on Theodin's shoulders, but the apprentice nodded, his jaw tightening with resolve.

Kaspar turned his focus back to the road.

The wardstone at Havysium wasn't far now. He only hoped the Order's youngest permanent Arcane Dyad would endure the trials yet to come.

Ophelia adjusted the strap of her rifle again. The road to Havysium stretched ahead, flanked by the dense trees of the Olysgard forest. Though the forest canopy diffused the sunlight, the day felt warm—the kind of warmth that pressed on her shoulders and made her thoughts feel heavy and relentless.

Or that could've been just the summer heat. Ophelia did notice that it was much warmer in south Moirand than it was in Northern Regania during this time of year.

Kaspar and Theodin's voices murmured behind her. Their words were too low to catch. She didn't need to hear them to know what they were talking about.

The Arcane Dyad.

It was all anyone seemed to care about lately. Well, maybe not anyone—Kaspar's intensity often masked his approval, but she could feel it sometimes, like an ember burning aglow beneath his cool, silver gaze. And Theodin…

Her gaze swept toward the ground to her boots crunching against the dirt path.

Theodin's presence hummed in her mind. A constant, steady rhythm. It was comforting in a way she hadn't expected. He was there, even when she didn't look at him. Even when they didn't speak. Despite its comfort, it was still unsettling.

The Dyad had been exhilarating at first—a novelty. But now, it was heavier. When she sensed Theodin's emotions, fears, and uncertainties, she couldn't just brush them aside. They lingered, mingling with her own until she couldn't tell where one ended and the other began.

Like earlier, when Kaspar had spoken about trust, she'd felt Theodin's doubts ripple through her.

Now, the Dyad amplified everything.

Over the past four months, there would be times he would trust her and they would be in sync. Then there were the times where he'd doubt her and their partnership or shut her out, and then their currents of energy became dissonant.

Through the Dyad, this hit her like tidal waves with her feet stuck in the sand.

"You're quiet," Theodin's voice interrupted her thoughts.

Ophelia glanced back to find his jarring eyes watching her. He walked a step behind her, his strange features more prominent in the dappled sunlight. His expression was stoic, but the Dyad stirred gently —a subtle question.

"Just thinking," she replied, shifting her grip on the rifle.

"About the wards?" he asked, though she could tell he knew it wasn't about that.

"Sure," she lied, turning to look ahead again. The truth tangled on her tongue—she'd been thinking about him, about the Dyad, and about how the two of them fit together like mismatched puzzle pieces that somehow worked even before the Arborelys tethered them together permanently.

Theodin didn't push, but his presence remained, steady and unwavering. She could feel him trying to gauge her mood, just as she did with him. It was maddening yet oddly reassuring.

He watched the sway of her rifle strap as she walked ahead of him. The Dyad continued to resonate, a thread of connection that felt too fragile for something so potent.

He turned his gaze to the road ahead, his thoughts pulling inward.

Kaspar's words echoed in his mind: *The Dyad is a tool—but without trust, it's a blade with no edge.*

Trust.

He wanted to believe they were getting there, that they'd begun to find some kind of rhythm. But trust wasn't something he gave freely, not even to her.

At least, not all the time. Sometimes he did.

Perhaps that is what is holding you back—Theodin could almost hear Kaspar's lecturing tone follow this thought.

Theodin flinched as he fought the pull of her unease through the Dyad. It was subtle, like a glimpse of shadow at the edge of his vision, but it was there. He could feel her struggling to tamp it down, to bury it under the facade of calm determination. But the Dyad didn't lie.

He exhaled sharply, his eyes scanning the forest as if searching for something to anchor him.

Why does she always have to shoulder so much?

The thought came unbidden, tinged with frustration. And then came the echo:

Why do I care so much?

Ahead, Ophelia rolled her shoulder and adjusted the strap of her rifle, her posture stiffening.

Theodin frowned. Had she heard that through the Dyad? He wasn't even sure how much of his thoughts could bleed through, or if that was possible.

"You're quiet too," Ophelia said unexpectedly, her voice carrying back to him.

Theodin blinked, startled out of his thoughts. He quickened his pace until he was walking beside her.

"Just thinking," he replied, echoing her earlier words with a faint smirk.

"About the wards?" she asked, her tone laced with the same deflection she'd given him.

He tilted his head, studying her for a moment.

"Sure," he said, letting the lie slide between them.

The truth, especially now, felt too dangerous to name.

They walked in silence for a while longer as the Dyad resonated between them. Theodin kept his gaze on the path, but his focus was elsewhere—on the weight of her presence, the way her emotions rippled against his own, soft but insistent.

This feeling was strange. Like they were two sides of the same blade, each honing the other. But at what cost?

The thought of having to trust her disturbed Theodin. Could he truly rely on her to watch his back?

He had difficulty trusting anyone as much as they struggled to trust him.

Because they feared him.

But she didn't fear him. And she trusted him so easily.

She had also saved him once or twice from getting his insides mauled by undead creatures and Nether worshippers.

She paused and glanced at him. A small twinkle in her eye.

He turned his eyes back forward stiffly.

Did she just hear all of that?

"Open communication is key," suddenly said Kaspar.

Both of them stopped in their tracks and whipped his eyes to their mentor Kyriegard, who casually continued walking between them and passed them with a light smile. They stared after him in silent surprise.

"I suggest you sort out whatever quibble happened just now—before we possibly come across another who-knows-what," Kaspar said, not evening turning to look at them.

Theodin's brows furrowed as he exchanged a quick glance with Ophelia. Her eyes mirrored his confusion, but there was a flash of something else—amusement, perhaps, or defiance. Theodin clenched his teeth as the Dyad surged with her unspoken emotions, and he turned his gaze back to Kaspar's retreating form.

How does he always know?

Again, the thought came without warrant, tinged with frustration. Kaspar had a way of peeling back layers without effort, of seeing through walls Theodin thought were impenetrable.

Theodin breathed out through his nose, his grip tightening on the hilt of his sword.

"It wasn't a quibble," he muttered under his breath, more to himself than anyone else. But the Dyad betrayed him, and he felt Ophelia's tingle of amusement.

"Wasn't it?" she asked softly, a hint of teasing lacing her voice.

He shot her a sidelong glance. His piercing eyes narrowed slightly. "Focus, Ophelia."

Her smirk widened ever so slightly, but she said nothing, the Dyad buzzing with her restrained mirth. Theodin shook his head, muttering something unintelligible under his breath as he resumed walking.

Ophelia continued at the same pace beside him. Her eyes turned down to watch the ground before her, and her expression slowly fell.

Then, her gentle voice echoed in his thoughts.

You shoulder a lot too.

It was nowhere near accusatory, but rather warm, understanding, and caring. There was even a small hint of hurt that indicated she didn't only hear his one comment.

Theodin froze mid-step, the words settling into him with a weight that caught him off guard. His eyes darted to Ophelia, who still walked ahead of him, her gaze fixed on the ground. The Dyad shimmered softly between them, her emotions brushing against his like a hesitant hand reaching out.

For a moment, he didn't respond, his chest tightening.

The vulnerability in her thought—the quiet warmth, the unspoken acknowledgment of his burdens—unsettled him in ways he couldn't quite name.

You shouldn't hear that, he thought, though he knew the Dyad made it unavoidable. It already made it clear that there was nothing to hide after it showed her his nightmare.

His fingers flexed against the hilt of his sword as he tore his gaze away from her and back to the path ahead.

"I manage," he said finally, his voice low and clipped, though it lacked its usual edge.

The Dyad pulsed, her emotions still lingering. He sensed no judgment, no pity—only understanding. And that, somehow, was harder to face.

He glanced at her again, his expression softening despite himself. "You should focus on your own path, Ophelia. Not mine."

Her head tilted slightly, though she didn't look up. *Maybe our paths aren't so different,* came her thought, tender and careful, drifting through the Dyad like a whisper on the wind.

Theodin's lips pressed into a thin line, his steps slowing for a fraction of a second before he forced himself forward. The Dyad stirred with a quiet resonance, but he didn't respond. He wasn't sure he knew how.

When they were walking beside each other again, her voice continued.

Maybe…just, maybe our paths will sometimes merge into one. Sometimes split again and deviate, and sometimes return. Finally, her eyes flickered up to meet his. *As I said this morning. We are bound. You're not alone anymore. We will get through this together. All of it.*

Theodin's steps faltered for the briefest moment. Her words—no, the emotions carried within them—reverberated through the Dyad and settled heavily in his chest.

Why does she care so much?

The thought prickled at him again, but this time it wasn't laced with frustration or disbelief—it was softer, almost contemplative.

He finally glanced at her, his expression unreadable.

"You're a stubborn one," he said quietly, though there was no edge to his voice. If anything, there was a faint trace of something else—something akin to gratitude.

Ophelia's lips twitched, just barely. "Takes one to know one."

Theodin shook his head, but the corner of his mouth quirked in a ghost of a smile before he looked away again. The Dyad thrummed, a mutual acknowledgment that didn't need words. They walked on in silence, but the air between them felt lighter somehow, the weight of unspoken doubts momentarily lifted.

Ahead, the faint pulse of the Havysium wardstone grew louder. Its steady throbbing resonated in Ophelia's chest. She released a breath she hadn't realized she was holding. The pristine hum of an intact ward was a relief, a promise of calm after the chaos of Halvalla's wardstone.

Kaspar stopped just short of the wardstone and turned to them, his silver eyes briefly sweeping over Theodin before settling on Ophelia.

"You'll take the lead this time," he said, his tone leaving no room for argument.

Ophelia's brows furrowed, her eyes shifting between Kaspar and Theodin. "What do you mean? It's intact."

"Yes," Kaspar replied evenly. "And you'll reinforce it. Theodin will assist."

"But—"

"It's important that you both understand the balance between your roles," Kaspar interrupted. "This isn't just about who can wield what magic or who fights better. It's about harmony. Reinforce it together."

Once more, they met glances.

Her voice echoed first in the Dyad.

At least it's with a stone.

Followed by a little, whimsical smile.

Stone like you. Must be why you like stones. Sir Stone Sage.

Theodin's brows furrowed together with confusion at first, then—

A small chuckle erupted from his throat.

Ophelia's nose crinkled, and a tiny giggle escaped her.

The Dyad fluttered, tickled by the exchange of amusement that sparked between them.

Kaspar raised an inquisitive brow.

Ophelia looked to Kaspar and beamed. "You know how he doesn't like to partake in non-tactile magic," she cooed.

"Right," Kaspar said.

"I'll be fine," Theodin said flatly.

Ophelia grinned at him. "Yes, you will be."

Kaspar eyeballed each of them warily.

Theodin turned and continued on.

Don't mess with him. He'll get back at you for it.

Ophelia perked and nearly skipped to catch up with him.

Oh! Okay!

As they approached the wardstone, the runes etched into its surface pulsed evenly, their steady glow a stark contrast to the chaos of Halvalla.

Ophelia could feel its magic. It was ancient and unyielding, brushing against her senses like a cool breeze.

"Ready?" Theodin asked in a whisper.

Ophelia nodded and hovered her hand over the small structure. She pricked her finger with the needle in her ring and let a drop of blood fall onto the wardstone. The runes flared bright green, and she closed her eyes, focusing on the current of her Valksha magic as it flowed into the stone.

She felt Theodin's presence beside her, solid and grounding. His hand rested lightly on the stone, and though he didn't wield magic in the same way she did, she could feel his energy aligning with hers, balancing the flow.

It wasn't perfect—there were moments where their rhythms faltered, but they adjusted quickly, like two halves of a whole learning to move in tandem.

When the runes settled into a steady glow, Ophelia opened her eyes and exhaled. The wardstone hummed consistently again, without hiccup, its energy renewed.

Kaspar, who stood nearby, gave a firm nod.

"Good," he said simply. "That's enough for now."

Ophelia stepped back, her legs slightly trembling from the effort.

Theodin anchored her with a hand on her arm, his touch brief but reassuring. She reached up and clutched onto his sleeve for support.

Theodin abruptly let out another small laugh.

Ophelia huffed. "What's so funny?"

"Hard to stay on your feet, isn't it?"

"It'll be hard to stay on yours if you keep talking like that, dear Theo."

Theodin stabilized her by the shoulder with his other hand for a moment before he carefully let go. He leaned down, smirking, his mismatched eyes glinting in the sun.

The matching runes etched into their skin briefly flashed with white.

His voice echoed in her mind.

I'll catch you every time, Ophie.

Then, he began for the path.

Ophelia's eyes went wide as her face flushed, staring after him with her jaw dropped open.

Where in the Nether did *that* come from?

Chapter 18

The Whispering Beneath

During their walk from Havysium to Avasylon, they spoke in detail of Olysgard. During the past four months of Ophelia's training, she had come to know the three estates, but not as well as most initiates who had been around much longer.

Halvalla was the fortress, the western property of the Kyriegard territory of Olysgard. It was the hub for administrative and ceremonial purposes; it was quite literally a castle that included the Council Hall for Council meetings and deliberations, several rooms for guests and private chambers and offices for the Council members, and ritual rooms and arenas designated for many Kyriegard traditions—initiate rites and the progression of the Arcane Dyad were the most important events here. Lecture halls and libraries educated their initiates and apprentices with anything and everything possible.

A secure greenhouse holds the life plants of every single Kyriegard member. Each plant is in its own pot made from a root of Arborelys with the single droplet of blood collected at the initiation ritual.

The sigils on the floor of the initiation chamber, where the blood fell upon, would sprout with a root of Arborelys for the Council to collect. This was how they could determine the life and health of a Kyriegard member—if the Kyriegard was sickly, so was the plant. The same went for if they neared death or were killed.

That was one of the many reasons Lady Vivian wanted to join the Kyriegard.

Outside of the castle of Halvalla, they had stables, an armory, and a keep that towered over the forest tree tops to be able to watch over the other two properties.

Havysium was the communal heart and center of Olysgard. The barracks, longhouse, and training grounds served as the lifeblood of the Order, bustling with the daily rhythms of initiates, apprentices, and Kyriegard who had returned from missions. It was here that the youngest members of the Order took their first steps, guided by mentors and tested by the rigorous discipline of the Kyriegard lifestyle. Havysium's central hall, a vast and intricately carved longhouse, was a place for shared meals, lessons, and camaraderie. Its walls bore tapestries of the Order's history, a reminder to all who gathered there of the legacy they were bound to uphold.

Ophelia and Theodin hardly stepped foot in Havysium since their primary residence was in Avasylon. Ophelia sometimes found it overwhelming to be in the midst of them due to her Valksha sensitivities and was used to dwelling with so few companions.

They didn't mind missing out on the camaraderie—they were content with their solitude, Kaspar's company, and each other.

Like its residents, Avasylon was different. It lay in east Olysgard, closest to the Chayim river. It was quieter and more isolated—a property shrouded in an air of mystery even to many Kyriegard. It housed the Order's archives and vaults, its underground chambers guarding secrets and artifacts too dangerous or sacred to be left unprotected. Avasylon was not a place of warmth like Havysium or ceremony like Halvalla; it was a place of preservation and defense, and its energy felt heavier because of it. To approach Avasylon was to feel the weight of generations past and the latent magic bound within its grounds.

At first glance, Avasylon seemed unassuming. A modest cottage sat at the center of an open clearing, its thatched roof and stone walls blending seamlessly with the forest around it. The second floor of the cottage served as lodgings for the Head of the Order, his apprentice, and occasionally a guest or two. A stable stood nearby, its doors slightly ajar, and the open fields surrounding the cottage served as training grounds. To the untrained eye, it could have been mistaken for an ordinary homestead, unremarkable and serene.

That was why Ophelia could hardly believe that this was where the

Head of the Order resided when she first came here with Lady Vivian.

But beneath its simple façade lay the true heart of Avasylon—a vast, underground network hidden from the world above. Accessible only through a concealed passage within the cottage, the subterranean halls were a testament to the Order's mastery of Sage architecture and enchantments. These chambers, carved into the very rock of Olysgard, were fortified with ancient runes designed to ward against intrusion and corruption.

The underground complex was an intricate maze of knowledge and power. Its vast library, filled with texts predating even the Kyriegard's founding, was lit by floating orbs of soft, golden light. The training halls were equipped with enchanted targets and adaptive arenas, which allowed for the honing of skills in complete secrecy. The armory housed not only weapons of the highest craftsmanship but also artifacts deemed too dangerous to leave unguarded.

At its core lay the Vault, a sealed chamber surrounded by concentric rings of powerful magic. Here, the Order stored its most sacred relics and dangerous secrets, items too potent to risk losing to the outside world. Only the Head of the Order and the Council could breach its inner sanctum, and even they did so sparingly, wary of what lay within.

At the center of the Vault stood the heart of the Order—Arborelys. While it appeared at first glance to be an ancient tree of enormous size, its presence radiated a quiet, otherworldly power. Its bark shimmered faintly, as though infused with starlight, and its leaves seemed to shift colors depending on the angle of light—a mesmerizing blend of emerald, silver, and gold. Thick roots sprawled outward, embedding themselves into the very foundation of Avasylon, as though anchoring the entire structure to something far older and deeper than the stonework above it.

Arborelys was said to be born of the first collective magic of the five Kyriegard founders, imbued with magic so passionate and potent that it could not be replicated. They drew energy from both the Ether and Midthian to harness a core which connected them and eventually future Kyriegard Sage Warriors. To the Kyriegard, the tree symbolized life, unity, and the cycle of renewal. Its sap, known as *Elan Vitae*, was used sparingly, as it held the ability to stabilize wounded Kyriegard near death or those on the verge of magical collapse. However, such usage required Council approval, and the act of tapping into Arborelys's essence came at a cost—it was said the tree would only give as much as it deemed necessary.

Arborelys did not act as a mere resource. It was sentient in its own way, able to sense the flow of energies in and around Avasylon. The Vault's defenses were tied to Arborelys's roots, which pulsed faintly with a protective aura, warning against intruders or magical tampering. Some of the Kyriegard claimed that when they stood close enough to its trunk, they could feel the resonance of countless lifetimes —the essence of all who had served the Order and been bound to its purpose.

To initiates, Arborelys was a distant mystery, spoken of in whispers during lessons and training. Few ever saw it directly, as its presence was reserved for only the most sacred rites, including the third and final stage of the Arcane Dyad ritual. In that moment, the tree's luminous energy would envelop the pair, sealing their bond and tying their lives to the Order's legacy in a way that could not be undone. This connection to Arborelys and their chosen partners was what many believed gave the Kyriegard their resilience, both physical and spiritual—a tether to something greater than themselves.

Yet, even to the Council, Arborelys's origins remained an enigma. The energy imbued in it was a quiet paradox—both divine and secular, revered yet unclaimed by any one deity, spirit, or Saryf. The Order had chosen to view it not as a religious relic, but as a symbol of unity, an anchor in their otherwise pragmatic and mortal pursuit of balance.

In the silence of Avasylon, Arborelys stood as both a sentinel and a reminder—of the sacrifices made, the legacies built, and the delicate balance the Kyriegard sought to maintain in a world teetering on the edge of chaos.

To those who trained and lived within its walls, Avasylon represented more than a hidden sanctuary—it was a crucible. A place where Kyriegard faced their most personal trials, their faith in the Order tested alongside their physical and magical limits. While Halvalla symbolized tradition and Havysium represented camaraderie, Avasylon embodied the Order's deepest strength: resilience through discipline and secrecy.

For Ophelia, Theodin, and Kaspar, returning to Avasylon was both a homecoming and a challenge. It was the Kyriegard's most enigmatic property, and its very essence seemed to amplify the unease in their Dyad, whispering promises of revelations and trials to come.

The road from Havysium was quieter than Ophelia had anticipated, but the stillness did little to soothe her unease. The sunlight filtering through the canopy of trees dappled the path in golden light, yet the weight in her chest remained. The memory of Halvalla's corrupted wardstone lingered, vivid and sharp, contrasting with the pristine hum of Havysium's defenses.

She glanced back at the towering structure of Havysium as it disappeared into the distance. The estate bustled with life—the laughter of younger initiates training in the fields, the rhythmic clang of swords in sparring sessions. Everything felt… untouched. Safe. It was hard to reconcile this peace with the chaos they'd left behind in the outskirts of Halvalla.

The group continued along the winding road to Avasylon, the forest around them dense and shadowed. The further they walked, the quieter it became. The cheerful buzz of Havysium's wards, so present and reassuring, was gone now. In its place was a stillness that clung to the air, heavy and unnatural.

Her magic brushed against the wards that marked Avasylon's outer perimeter, and while they held steadfast, there was something unsettling about them. They lacked the consistency of Havysium's pulse, their energy more brittle, like a taut rope fraying at the edges.

She glanced at Kaspar, his posture as erect as ever and his eyes scanning the road ahead. If he felt the same unease, he didn't show it. Theodin walked beside her, his movements fluid and deliberate, his dual-colored gaze sweeping the forest's edge.

Ophelia closed her eyes briefly, reaching out with her senses. The wards were intact—for now. But something lurked, distant yet present, like a subtle whisper at the rim of her awareness.

Kaspar's voice broke the silence. "Stay alert," he said without turning. "The path has been too quiet. That rarely bodes well."

Ophelia frowned, nervously looking toward the trees that seemed to close in around them the further they walked. She was about to speak, but Kaspar continued, his tone unusually measured.

"Avasylon is not like Havysium or Halvalla," he said, his gaze fixed on the road ahead. "It wasn't designed for open confrontation. Its purpose is preservation, protection—not defense."

"You mean it's vulnerable," Theodin remarked.

Kaspar glanced at him, his expression unreadable. "Yes and no. Avasylon's lower sanctum is more impenetrable than Halvalla, but because of its deceptive appearance—its outer perimeter is not as challenging to attack."

"Open fields, a single cottage, and a small stable," Ophelia added. "Avasylon could be mistaken for any other remote and rural homestead."

"Precisely," Kaspar answered. "A safety in secrecy. Halvalla is designed to draw attention of any threat from Havysium and Avasylon. Avasylon is on the other side of Olysgard, and it is meant to hide in plain sight rather than handle a siege."

"But it's been attacked quite a lot recently," Theodin muttered.

"Unfortunately, since my arrival," Ophelia said distantly. Her shoulders slumped. "Perhaps Lady Vivian didn't mislead them as much as she had intended to."

"Warthralls are nasty and have insidious ways," Kaspar said to her with reassurance. "It's not your fault, or hers. *You*, however, do have the opportunity to correct it."

The air around them felt heavier at his words, the weight of their mission pressing down more tangibly than before. Ophelia's grip on her rifle strap tightened. The quiet hum of the Dyad between her and Theodin steadied her, but even that felt muted now, overshadowed by Kaspar's subtle unease.

Theodin spoke, his voice low. "You think someone or something is already trying to breach Avasylon after the last attack?"

Kaspar didn't answer immediately. When he did, his voice was quieter, almost introspective.

"I would not be surprised. The wards should be holding—for now. I did a reinforcement before we embarked to Halvalla yesterday, but it may not have been enough." He breathed a heavy sigh. "The corruption we've seen spreading… it's too close. Too coordinated. If Avasylon were to fall, it wouldn't just be a loss for the Order; it would be catastrophic for Moirand itself."

Ophelia exchanged a glance with Theodin, their Dyad sifting with shared apprehension.

"Then we can't let that happen," she said firmly.

Kaspar, though his glance remained guarded, offered an optimistic nod of his head. "No, we can't. And that's why we're here."

The group fell into another tense silence as they pressed on. The drone of Avasylon's wards grew louder, a soft vibration that thrummed in the air, but it did little to ease the weight of Kaspar's words. Ophelia's senses prickled, a subtle warning that kept her fingers near the trigger of her rifle.

Theodin's voice broke through the Dyad, steady but laced with resolve.

Whatever's waiting for us, we'll handle it.

Ophelia didn't reply aloud, but she let her agreement ripple back through the Dyad, her quiet confidence meeting his.

As the outline of Avasylon's unassuming cottage came into view, the unease among them heightened. Kaspar's stride didn't falter, but Ophelia caught the way his hand drifted toward the hilt of his blade, his eyes searching the surrounding forest with renewed focus.

Avasylon lay ahead, its wards dimly pulsing like a heartbeat. But whether that beat was steady or strained, Ophelia couldn't yet tell.

It was still too quiet. She was used to the warmth and rustle of nature surrounding Avasylon.

Ophelia's shoulders stiffened. Warily, she scanned the dense woods around them. She reached out with her mind, allowing her Valksha magic to billow outward. The hum of the wards was constant but distant, their protective barrier thinning as they moved further from Havysium. For now, the area seemed clear, but her magic brushed against something—it was distant and fleeting, like a shadow just out of reach.

"There's something," she said softly, her voice carrying just enough for Theodin and Kaspar to hear. "It's distant, but it's there."

Theodin's hand drifted to the hilt of his sword. "Direction?"

Ophelia shook her head. "I can't tell. It's faint, like it's masking itself."

Kaspar's eyes squinted as he glanced back at her. "Stay close. Look alive."

The group pressed forward. Theodin matched his stride to Ophelia's, his eyes fixed on the path ahead while his focus stayed partially on her. The Dyad resonated between them with a shared undercurrent of vigilance and discomfort.

Ahead, the glow of the Avasylon wardstone flickered through the trees. It stood at the edge of the Kyriegard's stronghold, a sentinel against the encroaching darkness.

But something was wrong.

The runes etched into the stone pulsed erratically with a dim and uneven light.

Theodin felt a wave of unease through the Dyad. Ophelia quickened her pace, already reaching out with her magic to assess the damage.

"It's compromised," Kaspar said grimly, his voice low. "And worse than the others."

Ophelia nodded, her jaw tightening as she approached the wardstone.

The chaotic energy swirling around it was stronger here. More malevolent. It clawed at her insides and made her skin crawl.

"I can fix it," she said, though the strain was evident in her voice. "But I'll need time."

Theodin drew his blade without hesitation and stepped into position beside Ophelia.

"You'll have that and my cover."

The Dyad whirred with her focus, her determination bleeding into his own. He kept his eyes on the forest and tightened his grip on his sword.

Kaspar unsheathed his sword and looked between them with a satisfied gleam in his silvery eyes.

Ophelia pricked her finger on her spring-loaded ring, hovered her hand over the structure's base, and allowed a drop of blood to fall onto the wardstone. The runes flared briefly before dimming again, resisting her energy. She closed her eyes, channeling her Valksha power deeper into the stone, taming its chaotic flow. The runes etched in her skin glowed a bright, emerald green.

A sudden snarl erupted amidst the erratic vibrations. Theodin turned sharply, his sword flashing. An immense, grizzly creature covered in dark tendrils lunged from the trees. As it landed on all fours, it barred its blackened maw and growled a sickly noise.

Its glowing red eyes locked onto Ophelia, but Theodin flanked it, his blade slicing cleanly through its neck. Its head rolled away and its body dropped limply. The runes in his hands and arms illuminated a golden yellow light.

Another creature emerged, and then one more after it. The air grew thick with corrupted magic, the oppressive presence of the creatures pressing against them like a vice.

"Theodin!" Ophelia shouted, her focus momentarily breaking as a beast lunged toward her.

The Dyad whirred with great intensity.

Theodin moved instinctively in front of her and shoved himself shoulder first at the creature mid-air. His blade impaled the creature through the neck. It shrieked and took him with it as it fell, then ferociously kicked him off—he lost grip of his sword, which protruded from its throat gushing with black.

Kaspar, who had hung back to observe, saw the third creature lurk and watch its companion get tackled by Theodin. Seeing that Theodin was down, it charged at Ophelia.

Kaspar moved to intercept—

Suddenly, Theodin's hands were clenched around the creature's throat.

It barely had time to react to his appearance as he had leapt at it from where he landed with such incredible, inhumane speed. His eyes burned with intensity as he twisted sharply, snapping its neck with a sickening crack. He hurled the lifeless body aside, his chest heaving.

The forest became silent, except for the labored breathing of the Kyriegard apprentices and the vibrations of magic in the wardstone and Ophelia's hands.

Kaspar halted where he stood. His stern eyes shifted from Theodin to Ophelia.

The Dyad flared with Ophelia's shock. Her breath was caught in her throat. Her eyes widened as she took in the sight of her partner—his hands streaked with ichor, his expression fierce. The sheer force he'd displayed was… monstrous.

For a moment, fear flickered through their bond.

Time seemed to stop. Theodin stiffened, and his jaw tightened as he stepped back. He glanced at Ophelia; then he lowered his eyes in shame.

"Ophelia—" he choked.

He hesitated to speak.

The voices of rejection echoed from his memories.

The fear. Judgement. Misunderstanding.

His voice quieted, almost defensive.

"I didn't mean to scare you."

The Dyad stirred, and there was still fear—but not of him. It felt clearer, more direct. It was the visceral shock of witnessing something extraordinary, something that defies explanation.

Ophelia blinked. Her initial shock dissipated as her logical curiosity took over.

"Scare me?" she echoed. "Theodin, that was…"

She faltered, searching for the right word.

"Incredible."

His eyes snapped to hers, disbelief flashing across his face. "Incredible?"

Ophelia nodded. "Whatever that was—it was beyond normal. Extraordinary. But it was you. And it saved me."

Her face and voice softened. She hesitated and then added, "You don't have to hide this from me."

Her words hung in the air, steadying him more than he wanted to admit. The Dyad hummed now with her curiosity and awe brushing against his thoughts like a tentative, caressing hand.

Theodin exhaled sharply, his hands curling tightly into fists. He nodded once, retrieved his sword, and returned to his position beside her.

Ophelia turned back to the wardstone, her hands trembling slightly as she resumed her work. The runes pulsed, responding to her magic as she poured the last of her energy into stabilizing the stone.

The creatures had dissolved into shadow, their connection to the corruption severed as the wardstone's light flared to life. The oppressive force in the air faded, leaving only the gentle vibration of the ward's renewed strength.

Kaspar approached, his gaze shifting over the two apprentices.

"Good work," he said simply, his tone measured. But there was a glimpse of something else in his expression—approval, perhaps, or understanding.

Ophelia slumped against the wardstone, her chest heaving as she caught her breath. Theodin stood beside her, staring at the ground—avoiding eye contact with either of them.

As she sat up slowly, her gaze lifted to her partner.

She recalled the shame he felt, the memories that briefly flashed across her mind in the early morning and just now after his demonstration.

Was this extreme feat of strength what made him stand apart from the other initiates?

Was this what others feared?

Perhaps the moment allowed him to be magically charged through the Dyad, but Ophelia thought back—he didn't draw at all from her energy, at least not from what she remembered.

It had to have been his ambiguous nature.

Theodin felt her curiosity. He glanced at her briefly before Kaspar joined them, sheathing his sword. The elder Kyriegard appeared to exchange a knowing glance with his apprentice and a nod of understanding before addressing the both of them.

"You're both coming into your own," Kaspar said quietly. "But there's still more to learn."

The Dyad resonated between Theodin and Ophelia, a quiet

acknowledgment of their shared triumph—and the unspoken questions that lingered between them.

Though the evening settled with peace after Ophelia's reinforcement of the wardstones, Theodin still felt unsettled and restless.

He stood at the basin, his head bowed as he stared at his hands. The water rippling beneath his palms was streaked with dark tendrils, diluted remnants of the black ichor clinging to his skin. The chill of the water seeped into his fingers, but it wasn't enough to numb the simmering unease in his chest.

He scrubbed harder, his eyes fixed on the swirling water. His grip tightened involuntarily as Kaspar's voice echoed in his mind.

"You need to be careful, Theodin," Kaspar had said, his tone uncharacteristically heavy.

They'd dwelled outside the cottage after the mission, Kaspar placing a firm hand on his shoulder before they entered.

"Your strength—it's a gift, yes. But it's also a question. One we don't yet have answers for. You have to be more vigilant about it now that you are in an Arcane Dyad."

Theodin's jaw clenched as he replayed the words.

A question.

He knew what Kaspar meant without him saying it outright.

That strength—the way he'd snapped the creature's neck with his bare hands—wasn't normal. It wasn't human.

And it wasn't the first time.

His eyes ran along the runes down his arms. Now that there was no glowing light, they looked like inked script. Like…the same texture he had seen as those tribal tattoos on Predants.

They glowed when he fought. Or when she fought.

Or when they felt something. When they touched.

He closed his eyes.

At least she wasn't hurt. Or killed.

"You scared her."

The statement had hit like a blow. At the time, during that conversation, Theodin had flinched, his shoulders stiffening, but Kaspar's gaze had softened.

"Not because of what you are, but because you hid it. Don't give her a reason to doubt you. The Dyad will falter if her trust in you does too."

The water splashed as Theodin dipped his hands again, trying to work the stubborn stains from beneath his nails.

The fight had ended hours ago, but the sensation remained—the creature's thrashing, the sharp crack of its neck giving way.

And then, Ophelia's wide-eyed stare.

He gritted his teeth, his breath catching. He'd felt her fear through the Dyad, fleeting but unmistakable. It had been a knife to his chest. He hadn't meant to scare her. He never wanted her to look at him like that again.

"Trust is fragile, lad," Kaspar had said as they walked to the cottage. *"It takes time to build, but only a moment to shatter. Whatever this strength of yours is, don't let it break the bond you're forging with her. That bond—it's your anchor now, whether you like it or not."*

Theodin's reflection rippled in the water as he leaned closer to the basin. His hands paused, droplets trailing down his fingers.

He didn't know if Kaspar was right.

He didn't know if he could let her in, let her see the parts of him that terrified even himself.

A strange sensation tickled the back of his head.

The creak of the cottage door nearly startled him, and his head snapped up.

Ophelia stood in the doorway, her rifle nowhere in sight, her hands clasped loosely in front of her. Her eyes flickered from the basin to his face.

"I thought you'd still be out there," she said gently, nodding toward the training grounds beyond the window. "You always seem to like the solitude of the outdoors when there's no initiates."

Theodin's lips pressed into a thin line. "Needed to clean up," he muttered, turning back to the basin. The water had grown cold.

Ophelia stepped closer, her presence brushing against him through the Dyad. She hesitated before speaking again.

"Kaspar was… hard on you, wasn't he?"

Theodin froze, his hands gripping the edge of the basin.

"He said what needed to be said," he replied tightly.

Her gaze softened as she moved to stand beside him, her shoulder just a breath away from his.

"He's not wrong about the bond being an anchor," she said. "But he doesn't know it the way we do."

Theodin turned his head to look at her, his eyes shadowed. "And what do we know, Ophelia?"

She met his eyes, unwavering.

"That it's more than an anchor. It's a lifeline. For both of us."

Her voice was steady, but her emotions filled him through the Dyad, warm and resolute.

"And whatever Kaspar thinks, I trust you, Theodin."

He swallowed hard, the weight of her words settling over him like a blanket. The Dyad thrummed between them, a serene, steady reassurance that pushed back the doubts clawing at his mind.

"You shouldn't," he said hoarsely, his voice barely above a whisper. "You saw what I did. You felt it."

"I did," she admitted, though her tone did not change. "And it saved me. It saved us."

She paused, searching his face.

"I don't need you to be perfect, Theodin. I just need you to let me in."

His breath hitched, the vulnerability in her words striking a chord he wasn't ready to face. He turned once more back to the basin, the water breaking as he dipped his hands one last time.

"I'll try," he said finally, his voice low.

Ophelia reached out, her fingers brushing his arm briefly. The touch was light, but the Dyad flared with her quiet warmth, her unspoken promise. As a result, both of their runes shimmered lightly.

"That's enough for me," she whispered.

Theodin didn't look at her, but his shoulders relaxed slightly. The weight in his chest lifted, just enough to let him breathe.

Ophelia's eyes fell to the wash basin in front of him. She lowered her hand to hover above the surface of the water, pricked her finger on her ring to draw blood, and a warm glow of green radiated from her palm.

The water boiled briefly, just enough for it to be heated to a comfortable temperature and cleared of muck.

Theodin stilled, his eyes flicking to her hand. The faint light of her magic reflected in the water, casting gentle ripples across its surface. It wasn't the grand, searing power she wielded in battle but something quieter. Calmer. The kind of magic that didn't demand attention but offered solace instead.

He didn't speak, but the Dyad stirred, his gratitude breathing against her thoughts like a whisper.

She lingered for a moment longer before stepping back.

"I'll see you in the morning," she said kindly.

As the door closed behind her, Theodin stared at his reflection in the basin.

The water had stilled, but his thoughts remained turbulent. The

Dyad resonated with a soothing wave, a reminder of the conversation that had just unfolded—and the trust he wasn't sure he deserved.

The night air felt heavier than usual as Ophelia stepped into the hallway, the warmth of the cottage offering little comfort against the storm swirling in her mind. The soft creak of the floorboards beneath her boots barely registered as she made her way to her room, her hand grazing the cool wood of the walls for balance.

Her chest tightened with the memory of Theodin at the wardstone—his hands clenched around the creature's throat, his fearsome eyes burning with an intensity that was all at once terrifying and extraordinary. She could still hear the sickening crack of bone and feel the surge of raw power that had emanated from him, unmistakable even through the Dyad.

Ophelia closed her door behind her, leaning against it for a moment as she exhaled slowly. The fear she'd felt in that moment was unlike anything she'd experienced before—not because of Theodin himself, but because of what she couldn't understand.

Her gaze fell to her hands, the subtle glow of her Kyriegard partner runes in her skin now dim and steady.

"Extraordinary," she whispered to herself.

That's what she'd called him. And she'd meant it. Whatever Theodin was, whatever power he carried within him, it was part of him. It had saved her life, and she couldn't ignore that.

But what did it mean for him? For them?

Her fingers curled into fists, her mind replaying the look in his eyes after it was over—the shame and the fear of rejection. She'd felt it through the Dyad, a sharp and painful echo of emotions he couldn't hide. It was a vulnerability she hadn't expected from someone so guarded, and it made her chest ache.

The Dyad reverberated subtly, a fixed rhythm that reminded her of his presence. She wondered if he was still at the wash basin, still grappling with the weight of what had happened.

Could he feel her thoughts, her worry? Did he even want to?

Ophelia moved to the small desk in the corner of her room, lighting the candle that sat atop it. Its warm glow illuminated the well-worn pages of her journal, the one she'd kept since joining the Kyriegard. She opened it to a blank page, her quill poised above the paper. But the words wouldn't come.

Her thoughts were too tangled; her emotions were too raw. How could she put into words the complexity of what she felt—the admiration, the curiosity, the fear, the unshakable bond that tied her to Theodin in ways she couldn't yet understand?

She set the quill down with a sigh and her gaze drifting to the window. Beyond the glass, the forest loomed, its shadows stretching long and dark under the faint glow of the moon. Avasylon's wards pulsed faintly in the distance, their rhythm stable but subdued. It still felt like a fragile sort of peace, one that could shatter at any moment.

Ophelia pressed a hand to her chest, her fingers touching the edge of her pendant.

"We'll get through this together," she murmured, echoing the words she'd said to Theodin earlier. But this time, the promise felt heavier—weighed down by the unspoken questions, the uncharted territory ahead.

The Dyad thrummed again, softer this time, like the faint echo of a heartbeat. It was a reminder, a tether. And though she didn't know what lay ahead, she knew one thing for certain: she wouldn't let Theodin face it alone.

With that thought, Ophelia extinguished the candle and lay down on her bed. Sleep wouldn't come easily, but she closed her eyes anyway, letting the steady resonance of the Dyad lull her into something close to rest.

Chapter 19

The Legacy and the Lost

Year 844 of the Second Age, Seventh Month, Fifteenth Day

It was late in the evening, and the sky was dark with clouds as they blocked the light of the moon. Thunder rumbled in the distance.

The sealed parchment sat on the table like a thundercloud, heavy with the promise of finality. Kaspar's eyes lingered on it, his fingers tracing the elegant Valksha crest pressed into the wax.

"She… sent this?" Ophelia's voice trembled, her eyes wide, brimming with questions she didn't know how to ask.

Kaspar nodded once. "A hooded man named Dreycen delivered it himself. Wouldn't let me see his face."

He paused and lowered his voice.

"He said… it was her last wish."

Theodin looked to Ophelia with furrowed brows. "Dreycen?"

The color from Ophelia's face was paling.

"Her closest friend."

Theodin's gaze shifted between the two of them, the Dyad rumbling with Ophelia's rising storm of emotions.

Theodin began to speak.

"Do you want me to—"

"No."

Ophelia stepped forward, her hand hovering over the letter as if it might vanish the moment she touched it. She exhaled, her fingers shaking as they broke the seal.

Her voice wavered as she read aloud, the room quiet except for the steady cadence of her words.

"My dearest Ophelia,

By the time you read this, I will have passed. Do not let this letter weigh on your heart, for I have lived a life full of purpose and love, and I leave this world at peace. I timed my departure carefully, knowing you had found your footing within the Kyriegard—a family as steadfast as any bloodline.

You are stronger than you realize, my starling, and I am so proud of the woman you are becoming. Trust in your bond with Theodin; it will guide you when the path ahead grows dark. Trust in Kaspar; his wisdom is a beacon.

And trust yourself. For you carry within you the strength of our people and the light of hope. Remember this when the weight of the world feels too heavy to bear.

Dreycen, whom you may not yet fully know, was my beloved companion in this final chapter of my journey. Trust him should your paths cross again. He knows more than he says, and his loyalty is unshakable.

There is much I wish I could tell you, but some truths you must discover on your own. When the time comes, look to the stars—they hold the answers you seek.

With all my love, always,
Lady Vivian."

Ophelia's voice broke on the final words, and silence fell like a shroud. The candlelight flickered, casting long shadows on the walls of the archive.

"I didn't even get to say goodbye," Ophelia whispered, her hands clutching the parchment tightly. Her breath hitched as tears rolled down her cheeks.

Kaspar stepped forward, his presence as unshakeable as the mountains, though his silver eyes held a rare glimmer of sorrow.

"She wouldn't have wanted you to. Lady Vivian was deliberate in everything she did, Ophelia. She chose this moment for a reason."

Theodin's gaze softened, and he cautiously moved closer, his voice low.

"She wanted you to stand on your own in order to be ready for this."

The bond between them thrummed with an unspoken promise, his energy offering her an anchor.

Ophelia shook her head, her tears now completely streaking her cheeks.

"She was always there. Always… I just thought there'd be more time."

Her voice cracked, and she pressed a hand to her chest, as if trying to hold the pieces of her heart together.

The runes in her skin began to burn with green light. The cottage around them shook slightly.

"She said she'd come back for me."

Kaspar placed a hand on her shoulder, his grip firm but comforting.

"She prepared you for this, Ophelia. She knew the strength you carry, even when you doubt it."

Ophelia lowered her eyes to the letter in her hands. The parchment crinkled under her quaking grip. Lady Vivian's words echoed in her mind, and the weight of her late mentor's love and trust settled in her chest like a flame.

"She believed in you," Theodin said quietly. His tone was unwavering, but there was a slight tremor in the Dyad, a tinge of his own unease. "More than anyone else."

Ophelia looked at him, her emerald eyes meeting his mismatched ones. The bond between them swelled dimly, his reassurance mingling with her grief. It mixed with Kaspar's soothing touch—and both quelled the tempest that threatened to flood her senses.

She took a harsh breath, her fingers smoothing the crumpled edges of the letter. Her eyes fell back to the letter.

They were right. Ophelia remembered that the first year or two she spent under Lady Vivian's wing were hard ones—she was just a child, constantly overwhelmed with sorrow, perpetually in tears, and nearly inconsolable.

Lady Vivian and the Kyriegard gave her a reason to keep fighting. They equipped her to find the strength she needed to take a stand for the sake of her dying people.

For the sake of the Saryfim and Elodyn.

Now, for the sake of the Kyriegard too.

For Kaspar and Theodin.

"I'll honor her," she said, her voice shuddering but adamant. "I'll make her proud."

Kaspar nodded, his silver eyes gleaming with quiet approval. "She wouldn't expect anything less."

The room became silent again, the weight of loss hanging heavy in the air. But within that silence, a new determination began to take root —a fragile yet unyielding resolve to carry forward Lady Vivian's legacy, to face the darkness ahead with the strength she had instilled in her.

Ophelia folded the letter carefully and held it close to her chest, her tears slowing as a quiet fire burned in her gaze.

"We have work to do," she murmured.

Kaspar's lips quirked into a faint smile, though his expression remained solemn. "Yes, we do."

Theodin placed a hand lightly on her arm; his touch was brief but grounding. "We'll face it together."

Ophelia tucked it into the pocket of her trousers, her gaze fixed on the flickering candlelight.

"She wouldn't have left if she didn't believe we could carry on," Ophelia said softly. Her voice steadied as the words took root, as though she was convincing herself as much as the others.

"She believed in all of us," Kaspar added. "But belief doesn't protect the Order. Action does."

Ophelia nodded, her eyes glinting with determination.

"Then we don't wait. We act."

Kaspar straightened. "We'll continue tomorrow. For now, take the remainder of the day to rest. We need clear minds for what's to come."

Theodin hesitated, his eyes searching Ophelia's. "Will you be alright?"

"I will," she replied, though the weight of her loss hung heavy in her voice. "We'll all need to be."

They dwelled in the candlelight for a moment longer before retreating to their quarters. The night outside felt darker than usual, the silence pressing against the cottage like an unseen force.

Year 844 of the Second Age, Eighth Month, Fifteenth Day
One month later.

A month passed. The days since Lady Vivian's passing had blurred into one another, and the Kyriegard's unrelenting pace left little time for mourning.

For Ophelia, the loss had carved a quiet ache in her chest, one she carried like a hidden scar. Yet, in the still moments between missions and training, she felt the echo of Vivian's words, a constant reminder of the strength her mentor had believed she possessed.

She had thrown herself into her studies and training, determined to honor the legacy left behind. Under Kaspar's rigorous tutelage and Alfena's patient guidance, her control over her Valksha magic had sharpened. Though still volatile at times, she was beginning to understand its rhythms, to wield it with purpose instead of instinct.

Her bond with Theodin had also grown. The raw edges of their connection had smoothed into something quieter, more reliable. In battle, they moved as one, each anticipating the other's actions with uncanny precision.

The other apprentices had taken notice—some with admiration, others with unease. Whispers followed them in the halls of Havysium, murmurs of their potential and their strangeness.

And yet, the shadow of that day at the Avasylon wardstone lingered. Ophelia couldn't forget the sight of Theodin's inhuman strength, the way he had moved with a speed and power that defied explanation. It had saved her life, but it had also raised questions—questions she wasn't sure how to answer.

Even Kaspar had been more watchful since then, his eyes sharp with unspoken thoughts. He had pressed them harder during training; his expectations were high but they were tempered with a rare patience.

Now, as the leaves began to turn and the air grew cooler, the Kyriegard Council buzzed with quiet urgency. Reports of Warthrall attacks on the outskirts of Olysgard were growing more frequent, their patterns disturbingly precise. Whispers of Valksha artifacts and forgotten ruins being targeted had reached the Council's ears, and the unease in Kaspar's gaze was impossible to ignore.

For Ophelia, the weight of the Order's vigilance felt heavier than ever.

Something was coming. She could feel it in the Dyad, their bond, in the air, in the quiet that seemed to hum with unseen tension.

As the moonlight stretched over Avasylon's open fields, Ophelia stood at the edge of the training grounds, her rifle slung over her shoulder. The chill in the air prickled her skin, but she welcomed it, letting it ground her thoughts.

The month since Lady Vivian's passing had been grueling yet transformative. Missions blurred into training, training into study, and all of it sharpened her resolve. The bond with Theodin had grown into something stable and dependable, but that didn't mean it was simple. There were still moments of dissonance, edges they had yet to smooth. But they'd learned to move past the friction and to trust each other even when words failed.

The Dyad tingled the back of her head.

Footsteps broke the silence, and Ophelia turned to find Theodin walking toward her. His eyes caught the moonlight, glinting faintly as he stopped a few paces away.

"Can't sleep?" he asked.

She shook her head, offering a timid smile. "Too much to think about."

He nodded, understanding without asking. The Dyad thrummed subtly between them, a soft echo of shared weariness.

"I was thinking about how far we've come," she said, her gaze drifting to the distant treeline. "The missions, the training… even us. Over a month ago, after we became bound…I didn't think we'd get here."

Theodin's lips quirked, almost imperceptibly. "You mean not trying to kill each other during sparring?"

Ophelia chuckled lightly. The tension in her chest began to ease.

"That, and the fact that we've finally learned how to move as one in the field. Mostly."

He tilted his head, his expression thoughtful. "It's not just the bond. It's you. You've changed."

Her smile faded into something softer as her gentle eyes turned to meet his. "So have you."

The Dyad hummed louder for a brief moment, a mutual acknowledgment of their growth. Theodin crossed his arms, his gaze shifting to the stars above.

"I've been thinking about what Kaspar said at one point," he admitted. "That trust is what gives the bond its edge. He's right, but it's not just about trust in the bond. It's about trusting yourself. And I think we're getting there."

Ophelia studied him, the moonlight casting his sharp features into shadow. He was different now—more sure of himself, accepting of his emotions, though the weight he carried was still visible in the set of his shoulders.

"I trust you," she said simply.

He searched her eyes, and for a moment, he didn't respond. The

Dyad pulsed delicately with something she couldn't quite name.

Finally, he nodded. "I know. And I trust you too."

The warmth in his words settled over her like a cloak, anchoring her. She exhaled slowly and allowed her gaze to wander back to the forest.

"Kaspar's been on edge since the last Council meeting."

Theodin's face hardened. "Something big. Something we're not ready for."

Ophelia frowned. Her grip tightened on her rifle strap. "We'll have to be."

He nodded, his jaw tightening. "We will be."

From the shadows of the cottage, Kaspar watched them with an indiscernible silvery gaze.

His thoughts lingered on the bond between the two apprentices. It had grown stronger, more fluid, but he knew such connections were as much a gift as they were a burden.

Kaspar had seen the consequences of closely bonded Dyads like theirs when the emotions of one overwhelmed the other—and it had gone both ways.

Yet, when they were in sync, the results were unparalleled.

The Council had been astounded by their progress, but others—like Margrith, with her rigid adherence to tradition, and Sigvard, ever wary of disruption—viewed their Dyad with unease. Theodin's reputation, amplified by the energy and magic of a Valksha, could be as terrifying as it was extraordinary.

To some, it meant potential calamity; to Kaspar, it meant change.

But Kaspar had faith in them. He had seen how Ophelia's determination tempered Theodin's guarded nature, and how his discipline gave her focus. Together, they were more than the sum of their parts. He could see the change in them since the Valksha girl's arrival. Theodin especially appeared more grounded rather than overly rigid, more sure of himself and slowly accepting, as their bond deepened.

Kaspar turned away, stepping inside and closing the door behind him.

The Council had sent word earlier that day—rumors of a Valksha sighting near some ruins south of Olysgard.

Other whispers in town say that a Valksha artifact was found somewhere there.

It could be nothing but a trick of corrupted magic.

Or it could be the beginning of something far more dangerous.

Either way, Ophelia had to be involved. Kaspar was apprehensive to allow it with how volatile it could render her if it possibly involved another Valksha.

It could tamper with her unbiased standing as a Kyriegard.

Kaspar exhaled slowly, his mind turning over the possibilities. He had served the Kyriegard long enough to recognize the signs. The Council's vagueness was more telling than an outright warning, and the pattern of events was one he couldn't ignore.

Now that Lady Vivian had been gone for a month, the forces of Moirand would undoubtedly seize the opportunity left in the absence of her light. And what they would do with that darkness was anyone's guess.

Year 844 of the Second Age, Eighth Month, Sixteenth Day

The morning light filtered through Avasylon's small cottage windows, the golden hues casting away the evening's shadows on the stone walls. Birds chirped from the woods that surrounded the estate.

Ophelia adjusted the strap of her rifle as she stepped into the main hall, her boots echoing on the floorboards.

Kaspar stood at the far end of the room, his attention fixed upon the map spread across the table before him. Theodin was already there, leaning against the wall with his arms crossed, his eyes lifting to her as she entered.

"You're both here now," Kaspar said without looking up. He gestured for them to approach. "Good. We have a mission."

Ophelia's stomach tightened at his tone. She exchanged a glance with Theodin before stepping closer to the table. The map was marked with a circle near the area south of Olysgard, in central Fatum.

"This," Kaspar began, tapping the marked spot, "is where the Council believes a Valksha artifact may have surfaced. There's been a report of Warthrall activity in the area—too precise to be a coincidence."

Ophelia's breath caught. A Valksha artifact? Her thoughts immediately went to Lady Vivian, to the stories she'd told of their people's relics—powerful remnants of a lost age.

"Do we know what kind of artifact it is?" she asked.

Kaspar shook his head. "No. The report is vague, and the Council isn't certain the source is reliable. That's why they're sending us. Our job is to investigate, secure the area, and, if possible, recover the artifact."

Theodin straightened, his gaze narrowing. "And if we encounter Warthralls?"

Kaspar's expression darkened. "Then you do what needs to be done. But don't let them draw you into a prolonged fight. The artifact is the priority."

Ophelia nodded, her mind already racing. The thought of encountering something tied to the Valksha legacy filled her with a strange mix of excitement and dread. She couldn't afford to falter—not now, not with the Council watching.

"Prepare your gear," Kaspar said. "We leave within the hour."

Ophelia moved swiftly through her room, the familiar rhythm of preparation grounding her against the weight of Kaspar's orders. She strapped her rifle to her back and the chained blade to her belt, checked the spring mechanism in her ring, and secured the small pouch of herbs and tools she'd been taught to carry. Every movement was deliberate, her mind focused on the task ahead.

But her thoughts kept circling back to the subject of the mission.

A *Valksha* artifact—a fragment of Valksha history tied to the legacy Lady Vivian had spent her life preserving.

Ophelia tightened her grip on the strap of her pack. This wasn't just another mission. This was personal.

Her gaze drifted to the small wooden box on her desk. Inside was Lady Vivian's final letter, folded neatly and untouched since the night she'd read it. Ophelia hesitated before brushing her fingers against the box's surface.

"I'll make her proud," she murmured, the words more a promise to herself than to anyone else.

The Dyad rustled, pulling her from her thoughts.

She turned to find Theodin leaning against the doorframe, his arms crossed and his eyes watching her with quiet intensity.

"Ready?" he asked, calm but tinged with curiosity.

"Almost," Ophelia replied, straightening. She felt his presence through the Dyad, steady and grounding, but there was something else beneath it—a subtle ripple of unease.

Theodin tilted his head slightly, his gaze flicking to the box on her desk before returning to her.

"You're…very focused."

Ophelia quirked a brow at him. "Isn't that a good thing?"

"It is," he said, pushing off the doorframe and stepping into the room. "But it's different this time."

She turned back to her pack, adjusting its straps as she considered his words.

"This involves the Valksha," Her voice was soft but firm. "I think it's natural that I'm a little more enthusiastic about this mission, isn't it?"

"Yes."

Ophelia glanced at him, her eyes meeting his gaze.

They were still, staring silently.

Then, finally, he spoke, barely audible.

"I just want you to be okay."

The Dyad thrummed softly between them, a steady undercurrent of shared understanding.

Ophelia's expression lightened, and her eyes fell to the floor with a small, bashful smile.

"I'll be okay, big fellow," she said, her tone lighter but still sincere. Her eyes flicked up again to meet his with a wider smile and a wink. "We've got each other, remember? You're stuck to me and I'm stuck to you."

Theodin huffed a quiet laugh, shaking his head. "You always know how to turn things around."

She smirked. "Comes with the territory."

Theodin watched as Ophelia finished securing her gear, her movements efficient and practiced. It was strange, seeing how much she had grown in such a short time. The girl who had stumbled into the Kyriegard was now a force to be reckoned with, her Valksha magic sharper, her determination unwavering.

And yet, there were still moments when he caught glimpses of something vulnerable beneath her confidence. Moments like this, when the weight of their mission and the legacy she carried seemed to settle just a little heavier on her shoulders.

He dropped his arms, his gaze softening. "You know, you don't have to prove anything to anyone."

Ophelia paused. She didn't look at him, but he could feel her hesitation through the Dyad.

"It's not about proving anything," she said quietly. "It's about doing what's right. For Lady Vivian. For the Valksha. For all of us."

The Dyad pulsed with her resolve, and Theodin couldn't help but admire her for it. But it also made him uneasy. She carried so much on her shoulders, more than anyone her age should have to bear. It made her act older than she actually was.

And though the Dyad had taught him to trust her, to rely on her, it didn't stop him from wanting to protect her.

He exhaled through his nose, his eyes narrowing slightly. "Just don't forget to take care of yourself while you're busy saving the world."

Ophelia turned to him then with her smile having widened into a toothy grin. "I could say the same to you."

With that, they left her room in light-hearted laughter.

Theodin and Ophelia stepped into the main hall, where Kaspar waited by the door. He examined them, his approval subtle but present.

"Let's move," Kaspar said simply, leading the way out of the cottage and into the crisp morning air. The trio set off toward the ruins, their footsteps steady and their purpose clear.

The ruins loomed like the broken bones of an ancient beast, half-consumed by time and shadow. Jagged walls jutted from the earth at odd angles, their surfaces veined with old cracks and half-erased runes. Moss crept over the stone like a quiet reclaiming, though no greenery dared grow too close to the inner chambers. The air hung heavy with the remnants of long-dead spells—echoes of energy that hissed and crackled just below the surface, like breath caught in stone.

At the heart of the ruins, shattered arches framed the hollow remains of a temple or stronghold, though its original purpose had long since faded. Dead runes were etched in the walls, dimly casting a ghostlight that bathed the broken chamber in an otherworldly hue. It was not silent—the ruins whispered. Groaned. Watched.

The deeper they moved into the ruins, the more Ophelia felt it—not just the residue of magic, but something older. Something sacred. The air was thick with silence, but beneath that quiet she could almost hear it breathing: the bones of a forgotten sanctuary, half-swallowed by time and nature.

It had once been a place of worship. She didn't know how she knew that—but the hum of it, the grounded strength of the stone, echoed in her Valksha senses. The carvings, though faded, bore the sharp, geometric elegance she recognized from the Saryf of Mountains and Terrains—Rochiel the Fierce's markings. Tied stone and strength and structure—earthly, enduring.

But whatever reverence had once filled this place had long since curdled into something else. Vines clawed through cracks in the stone, eating away at fractured archways. The runes were not all Saryfimborn—many had been overlaid, corrupted, rewritten in both Sage and demonic script.

The tension in the Dyad spiked the closer she drew, like her magic was recoiling at the desecration.

This had once been holy ground.

Now it reeked of trespass.

The afternoon sun filtered through the jagged remains of ancient stone walls, casting fractured shadows on the ground.

Then, she felt it—a faint ripple in her senses, the distinct hum of Valksha energy. But it was… different.

It wasn't the ruins. It was alive.

There was a heartbeat.

Ophelia pulled off her rifle and armed it against her shoulder. The runes carved into the wood lit up with green.

"Someone's here," she murmured.

Theodin stepped forward with his sword drawn and his eyes sharp as he scanned the ruins. Through Ophelia and the Dyad, Theodin's senses became attuned to such energy.

"I feel it too. Close."

Kaspar's gaze darted across the crumbled arches ahead. He nodded. "Stay together. Approach slowly."

They moved as one, their footsteps silent on the weathered stone.

As they rounded a corner, a figure came into view.

He stood in the center of a broken chamber, the faint glow of runes etched into the walls casting eerie patterns across his frame.

He turned toward them, his movements weary yet unthreatening. His face was youthful, though hollowed by exhaustion, and his royal blue eyes were illuminated in the dim light. His dark hair was disheveled, and his clothing was frayed and worn as if it had seen years of battle. He radiated an aura of power, but there was an undercurrent to it, a whisper of something fractured beneath the surface.

"Who are you?" Kaspar demanded, his tone harsh but measured.

The young man stepped forward, his hands raised in a gesture of peace.

"I'm Faust Grigorescu," he said, tinged with weariness. It was a light, tenor sound of a voice, which sounded almost out of place against Kaspar's Tersian-tinted baritone and Theodin's deep bass resonance.

"I am a Valksha of Zadkiel."

The words hit like a hammer.

Ophelia's heart skipped, her grip on her rifle tightening. Zadkiel—the Saryf of Strength and Will, a Saryf whose Valksha bloodline had been lost centuries ago. Sealed away in the infamous Valksha artifact, the Medallion of Zadkiel. And yet, here he stood, blue-eyed—not the ordinary sky blue of most human eyes, but a piercing shade of deep, dark blue—and unmistakably connected to Zadkiel's essence.

"That's impossible," Theodin said flatly. "Zadkiel's Valksha haven't existed for generations since they surrendered their power and sealed it away."

Faust's sapphire gaze flicked to Theodin. "And yet, here I am."

Ophelia's Valksha senses flared as she reached out cautiously, hovering against the edges of his aura.

It was Valksha, but there was something beneath it, like a taut string threatening to snap.

She stepped closer, her eyes locked on him. "How did you survive?" she asked, her voice even despite the storm of questions in her mind.

Faust hesitated. His jaw flexed. "I was… hidden. Raised in secret, away from civilization and corruption. Then when I was very young, Zadkiel's medallion chose me to bestow his blessings upon again and continue the bloodline."

Ophelia's breath caught.

"Where is it now?" she pressed. "The medallion."

Faust lowered his eyes and shook his head. "You know I can't tell you that…even if you are a Valksha too."

"Prove it," Kaspar said coldly.

Before Kaspar could press further, Ophelia stepped forward.

"He's one of us," she said with certainty.

Kaspar's brow furrowed. "You're sure?"

She nodded. "I can feel it. It's not like sensing another Valksha through proximity—it's deeper. Resonant. His presence… it echoes like mine."

Faust turned his gaze to her then, his weary eyes catching hers. A flicker of recognition passed between them, old and knowing, though they had never met. His aura—fractured as it was—still held the unmistakable signature of divine-blooded magic.

"He's not lying," she added softly. "He's broken… but he's real."

"It's real," Faust said, desolate but quiet. "I'm real."

Theodin's gaze remained unreadable. He didn't lower his blade. "And yet your aura feels… off. What aren't you telling us?"

Faust's eyes flickered with something—fear, perhaps? Regret?

"There's… been interference," he admitted. "My journey wasn't without complications. But Zadkiel's power is still within me. I've come to help."

Ophelia's mind churned as she studied him. There was power there, yes, but it was tangled with something else—something darker. But it was buried so deeply that even she couldn't discern its origin.

Kaspar exchanged a glance with Ophelia and Theodin, his lips pressed into a thin line.

"You'll come back with us to Avasylon. The Council will decide how to proceed."

Faust nodded, his lapis eyes meeting Ophelia's once more.

"I want to help," he whispered. "I want to fight for our people."

Ophelia's chest tightened. Vivian's final letter echoing in her thoughts.

Trust yourself. Trust your bond.

She nodded in return to him, though her hand didn't leave her rifle. "As Kaspar said. Then prove it."

The group exited the ruins with Faust in their midst, his footsteps measured and apprehensive. Theodin flanked him on the right, his sword still unsheathed and glinting in the shifting light. Kaspar led the way, his gaze fixed ahead, the tension in his posture unrelenting. Ophelia followed at the Faust's right side, her rifle strapped across her back but ready at a moment's notice. They moved in a triangle with Faust in the middle of them.

The ruins fell into the distance behind them, but the unease they carried remained heavy in the air. Faust walked in silence, his shoulders slightly hunched, as if the weight of their mistrust pressed on him.

"Your magic," Theodin said suddenly. "It doesn't feel right. It's not like Ophelia's."

Faust glanced at him, his expression guarded. "It's been a long time since I've actually used my magic," he admitted. He spoke calmly, but there was a rawness beneath the words. "I…don't really know how to use it at all."

Ophelia's emerald gaze sharpened. "You've never trained? Then how did you survive?"

Faust exhaled, his royal blue eyes flickering with something distant. "I didn't survive unscathed," he said quietly. "I was captured. By Azazelf."

The name landed like a stone between them.

Kaspar stopped abruptly—in turn, causing all of them to stop—and turned to face Faust. His silver eyes were sharp as daggers. "You were in Azazelf's grasp?"

Faust nodded, his jaw tightening. "Years ago. I was young, and he wanted… experiments." He hesitated, as though weighing how much to reveal. "He was looking for ways to harness Valksha energy. I was one of his failures."

Ophelia's stomach churned. The thought of someone enduring Azazelf's cruelty was horrifying enough, but Faust's story added a new layer of unease. She studied him, her senses reaching out against his aura again. There was power there, but it was tangled, frayed at the edges like a thread pulled too tight.

"Why didn't you fight back?" Theodin asked, cold but not unkind.

"Because I didn't know how," Faust replied, meeting his gaze directly. "I'd never used my magic before. My family hid me, taught me to suppress it. By the time Azazelf found me…" He trailed off, his hands curling into fists. "It was too late."

Kaspar's expression remained unreadable, though a glimpse of something—pity or understanding—passed through his eyes. "And yet you escaped."

"Barely." Faust's voice was laced with bitterness. "I was nothing more than a broken experiment to him, so he let me go. But not before leaving his mark. He said he would've killed me, but knowing that I would die out here this helpless pleased him more." His sound and posture shrank, like he was about to be kicked for saying too much. "That's why my magic doesn't feel like Ophelia's. Despite us being bound to different Saryfim. Hers is…pure. Untouched. Mine has been tainted."

Ophelia's breath caught as her gaze dropped to his hands, then back to his face. "Your magic… it falters because of him?"

Faust hesitated before nodding. "It's fractured. Damaged. But it's still Valksha. And I intend to use what's left of it to fight."

Theodin's eyes darkened. "You're asking us to trust you based on half a story and an unstable power you barely understand."

"I'm not asking for trust," Faust said evenly, eyes meeting Theodin's again. "I'm asking for a chance. That's all."

Ophelia glanced at Kaspar, who stood silent and still, his gaze fixed on Faust. She could almost feel the weight of his thoughts as she read his face, the unspoken calculations running through his mind.

"Enough," Kaspar said finally, his tone leaving no room for argument. "You'll come with us to Avasylon. The Council will decide what to do with you."

Faust nodded, his expression resigned but resolute. "Thank you."

They resumed their march, the tension between them thick and unyielding. Ophelia exchanged a look with Theodin, the Dyad shifting with shared discomfort. Faust's story might have answered some questions, but it left others in its wake—questions that gnawed at her with every step.

As they neared Avasylon's wards, the familiar hum of its magic greeted them. But even the safety of the Kyriegard's stronghold felt fragile now, overshadowed by the weight of Faust's revelations and the darker truths that still lay hidden.

Chapter 20

The Caged and the Chosen

The Council chamber in Halvalla was cloaked in a heavy tension that even the enchanted torches lining the walls couldn't dispel. The flickering light cast shifting shadows across the worn stone table, illuminating the faces of the five Kyriegard Council members. Kaspar stood at one end, his gaze resolute as it swept over the others.

Crane, seated to his left, leaned forward, his sharp features marked with both intrigue and skepticism. His ever-present cane rested against the edge of the table, its intricate carvings catching the light.

"This Faust Grigorescu… his timing is curious," Crane began, his tone smooth yet edged. "He emerges with Valksha energy just as Azazelf's movements become more precise. It's enough to raise questions, if not alarms."

Margrith's weathered face was set in a scowl, her arms crossed over her chest.

"Questions?" she snapped. "This is more than a coincidence. Faust's presence reeks of a trap, and you know it. We should turn him away before he brings ruin to Olysgard."

Sigvard stroked his braided Dwarven beard thoughtfully. His response was calmer but no less wary.

"While Margrith's words lack subtlety, her caution isn't unwarranted. If Azazelf had a hand in his creation, Faust could be the very Trojan horse that undoes us."

At the opposite end of the table, Alfena sat with her hands folded neatly before her, her Elven features serene but her gaze piercing.

"And yet," she countered, "if there's even a chance he's genuine, dismissing him outright is a risk we cannot afford. If he carries Zadkiel's legacy, fractured as it may be, we stand to gain a weapon against Azazelf's forces."

"Azazelf tossed him out into the world and left him to fend for himself and die," Margrith scoffed. "There mu st have been a reason for it. Seems too convenient."

Crane leaned back slightly, his pale fingers steepling as he considered everyone's words. "A weapon," he echoed. "Or a blade poised at our necks."

Kaspar cleared his throat, drawing the room's attention.

"We cannot afford division," he said. "Faust has agreed to remain in Avasylon under our watch. He poses no immediate threat, and we've seen enough to know his magic, while flawed, is undeniably Valksha in nature."

"That doesn't mean we can trust him," Margrith retorted.

"Trust must be earned," Kaspar agreed, his gaze shifting to her. "But dismissing him out of fear serves no one. If Azazelf had successfully captured a Valksha and Faust saw Valksha artifacts, then Faust's presence may offer us insight we desperately need."

Sigvard sighed heavily, leaning back in his chair. "And if he turns out to be Azazelf's pawn?"

"Then we deal with him," Kaspar replied, cold and final. "But until we know for certain, he stays under our protection—and our scrutiny."

Crane tapped his cane lightly against the floor, the sharp sound cutting through the room.

"A fair compromise," he cooed. "But we should ensure that scrutiny is thorough. If there's even a hint of deceit, we must be prepared to act."

A silence came upon them as the weight of his words settled over the table.

Alfena's sharp gaze moved from Kaspar to the others. "We must proceed carefully," she said. "But we must proceed. I will examine our guest with my magic to ensure that it is safe to house him in Avasylon for his safety."

Margrith grumbled under her breath but didn't argue further. Sigvard gave a reluctant nod, his gaze turning to the map spread before them, marked with the ruins where Faust had been found.

Kaspar straightened, scanning the room.

"We've faced worse odds with less to go on," he said. "If Faust is a danger, we'll handle it. But if he's telling the truth, then we have a chance to gain the upper hand. We owe it to the Order—and to Moirand—to see this through."

The Council members exchanged glances, the tension in the room easing but not dissipating.

Alfena inclined her head, her expression unreadable. "Then it's settled. We watch, we question, and we prepare."

Kaspar nodded. "This meeting is adjourned. Return to your stations. I'll handle the next steps with Faust."

As the Council began to disperse, Crane remained, his sharp gaze fixed on Kaspar.

"He unsettles you," Crane said quietly.

Kaspar met his gaze evenly. "He unsettles everyone."

Crane's lips quirked into a wry smile, though it didn't reach his eyes. "Just make sure you're watching him as closely as you're watching your apprentices."

Kaspar bristled, his gaze flicking briefly to the map before returning to Crane.

"I always do."

With that, Crane tapped his cane against the stone floor once more and turned, his silhouette disappearing into the shadows of the corridor. Kaspar remained, his thoughts heavy as he stared at the ruins marked on the map.

Year 844 of the Second Age, Eighth Month, Seventeenth Day

Only the sound of oil burning in the lanterns hanging nearby could be heard in the dimly lit holding chambers beneath Avasylon's cottage.

Faust sat on the edge of a wooden bench, his eyes fixed on the containment runes etched into the stone floor. His posture was rigid, shoulders hunched.

The heavy wooden door creaked open, and Kaspar stepped inside, his gaze sharp and unyielding. Faust looked up, his expression guarded but calm.

"Kaspar," Faust said, edged with weariness. "I assume the Council has reached a decision."

Kaspar closed the door behind him, his steps measured as he

approached.

"You'll remain here under our protection," he said simply. "But make no mistake—protection does not mean trust."

Faust's lips grew into a faint, humorless smile. "I wouldn't expect otherwise."

Kaspar studied him for a long moment, his eyes now probing. "Your story has gaps, Faust. Convenient gaps. If you truly want to help, you'll need to fill them."

Faust leaned back slightly, his hands resting on his knees. "And if I don't?" he asked, cautious.

"Then you leave us no choice but to assume the worst," Kaspar replied coldly. "And I promise, you won't like the outcome."

For a moment, the tension in the room thickened. Faust's jaw flexed, but he didn't flinch under Kaspar's stare. Instead, he sighed, his shoulders relaxing only slightly.

"I told you the truth," Faust murmured. "I was captured by Azazelf. He… experimented on me. Tried to twist my power into something he could use. But I escaped. I survived. And now I'm here."

"And the medallion?" Kaspar pressed. "What happened to it?"

Faust's gaze darkened, dropping to the floor.

"I don't know," he said after a pause. "Azazelf took it from me before he let me go. I haven't seen it since."

Kaspar's eyes narrowed. "Convenient."

"It's the truth," Faust said firmly, meeting Kaspar's stare. "Believe me or don't, but I have nothing to gain by lying to you. If I wanted to hurt the Kyriegard, I wouldn't have come to you. I wouldn't have risked the little I have left of myself, knowing how you'd react."

Kaspar folded his arms. "You understand why we can't take you at your word."

"I do," Faust said, softening. "But you also need to understand that I'm not here to earn your trust. I'm here to fight. If you don't want me to, that's your choice. But don't waste my time pretending you don't need me."

The audacity of Faust's words hung in the air, but Kaspar didn't react immediately. Instead, he studied the young man before him, noting the tension in his posture, the flash of determination in his eyes.

Finally, Kaspar unfolded his arms.

"Prove it," Kaspar said, low and steady. "Prove that you're more than just a boy with a fractured power and a tragic story. Show me you're worth the risk."

Faust stood slowly. "I intend to."

The two of them stared at each other for a moment longer, the air between them crackling with unspoken challenges.

Then, Kaspar stepped back, his expression still hard but laced with a flicker of something else—curiosity, perhaps, or the faintest glimmer of hope.

"We'll see," Kaspar said finally. "For now, stay here. You'll train with me tomorrow morning. Alfena will examine you later this week."

Faust inclined his head. "Understood."

Kaspar turned and left the chamber, the heavy door creaking shut behind him. Faust sank back onto the bench, his eyes drifting to the glowing runes on the floor. His jaw tightened as he exhaled slowly, his resolve hardening.

Outside the chamber, Ophelia paced the length of the underground corridor. The space was dim, the only illumination coming from enchanted lanterns that hung from the walls. She gripped the strap of her rifle tightly, her eyes darting toward the sealed entrance every so often.

Theodin leaned against the wall, his unnerving eyes watching her with quiet intensity.

"You're going to wear a hole in the floor," he muttered, tinged with amusement.

Ophelia shot him a glare but didn't stop.

"It doesn't bother you?" she asked, sharper than she intended. "He's in there, caged like an animal, and we're just… waiting."

Theodin tilted his head, his expression unreadable. "What would you prefer we do? Let him roam free? He's dangerous, Ophelia. Even if he doesn't mean to be."

She stopped mid-step, turning to face him. "I know that. But he's Valksha—or at least, he believes he is. Doesn't that mean something?"

The Dyad, becoming restless, carried her frustration and uncertainty.

Theodin sighed, his gaze softening. "It means we tread carefully. That's what the Council is doing."

Ophelia crossed her arms, her eyes straying to the glowing runes visible through the door's slats. "I just… I don't know if this is what Lady Vivian would have wanted."

Theodin pushed off the wall and stepped closer to her.

"Lady Vivian isn't here," he said gently. "And if Faust is lying—or worse, if he's a threat—then the Council is doing what they must to protect us. To protect you."

Ophelia's expression grew grim at his words, but she didn't answer him. Her gaze remained fixed on the chamber door, her thoughts a whirlwind of doubt and determination.

The glow of the runes seemed to intensify for a moment, drawing Ophelia's attention. She moved to the door and placed her hand against the cold wood. Theodin watched her, guarded.

"You feel it too, don't you?" he whispered. "His magic… it's not whole."

Ophelia nodded slowly, her fingers curling against the surface. "But it's still Valksha. And if there's even a chance he's telling the truth…"

Theodin didn't reply immediately. Instead, he stepped beside her, staring at the light seeping through the door's edges. "Then we'll have to find out what he's hiding."

A moment later, the heavy door creaked open. They both withdrew and moved back.

Kaspar emerged alone, his expression unreadable as always but his jaw was tense, and his shoulders bore the weight of deliberation. The door groaned shut behind him, sealing Faust inside.

He paused when he saw them both standing there—Ophelia standing there expectantly, Theodin watchful beside her.

For a beat, none of them spoke.

Ophelia finally cleared her throat.

"How did it go?"

Kaspar glanced back at the sealed door before turning back to her. "The Council has instructed us to proceed cautiously. Faust will remain here under containment until they can convene at Avasylon to assess him themselves. For now, he's our responsibility."

Theodin frowned. "How long until they arrive?"

"A few days at most," Kaspar replied. "They have other matters to attend to first."

Ophelia's grip on her rifle strap tightened. "And what do we do in the meantime?"

Kaspar eased as he looked at her. "We observe. We prepare. And we stay vigilant."

Ophelia glanced at Theodin, the Dyad between them whirring with unspoken questions.

"I'll take the first watch," she said quietly.

Kaspar nodded. "Good. Theodin, relieve her in four hours. I'll be upstairs if you need me."

As Kaspar ascended the stairs, the tension in the cellar grew heavier. Ophelia and Theodin exchanged another look before Theodin followed after the elder Kyriegard.

Once they were gone, she stepped closer to the door once more, her fingers grazing over the wood.

Inside the chamber, Faust raised his head, his lapis eyes catching the light of the runes. He turned toward the door as if sensing her presence, but he didn't move or speak. The silence between them felt almost alive, a tenuous thread connecting them through the layers of magic and mistrust.

Year 844 of the Second Age, Eighth Month, Eighteenth Day

Ophelia sat on the dusty floor, her back pressed against the wall opposite Faust's sealed chamber. The weight of her rifle rested against her legs, its strap dangling loosely from her hand. The quiet pressed in on her, broken only by the distant, steady rhythm of the wards.

Her thoughts drifted as they often did, circling back to Lady Vivian's final letter.

Trust yourself. Trust your bond.

The words were etched into her mind, a mantra she repeated whenever doubt crept in. Yet now, as she stared at the glowing door, she felt her resolve fraying.

"You've been sitting there for a while."

The voice startled her, cutting through the silence like a blade.

Faust.

Ophelia's grip on her rifle tightened, her eyes snapping to the door. She hadn't expected him to speak.

"Stay quiet," she said sharply, though her voice wavered slightly.

"I wasn't trying to upset you," Faust said, soft but clear. "I just… thought you might want someone to talk to. It can't be easy, keeping watch like this."

She scoffed, leaning her head back against the wall. "I'm not the one trapped in a glowing box."

There was a pause, then a quiet chuckle. "Fair point." His voice carried a strange mix of humor and weariness. "Still, it's not much better in here. Makes you think about things you'd rather forget."

Ophelia frowned, looking at the door again with concern. She stayed silent, unwilling to give him more than that.

"I can tell you don't trust me," Faust continued after a moment.

"And I don't blame you. If I were in your position, I'd feel the same." He hesitated, then added, "But I swear to you, I'm not your enemy."

"Words are cheap," Ophelia replied flatly

"True."

She heard Faust shift in the room, the creak of the wooden bench reaching her ears. More shuffling—he sounded like he was now sitting close to the door.

"But actions… they leave scars. You've seen mine. You've felt my magic. Isn't that proof enough that I've been through the Nether and back?"

"It's proof you've been through something," she answered distantly. "It doesn't prove you're telling the truth."

Silence settled between them, heavy and uncomfortable.

Ophelia thought he might give up, but then his voice came again, quieter this time.

"You know what it's like, don't you? To carry something inside you that others fear. To feel like no matter what you do, it'll never be enough to make them see you as more than that."

Her breath hitched. She gripped the strap of her rifle until her knuckles turned white. "You don't know anything about me."

"I don't," Faust admitted. "But I see the way you stand—like you're always bracing for something. And I see the way your eyes harden when someone doubts you, like you've heard it all before." His voice softened, a thread of vulnerability weaving through his words. "That's all I've ever known. Doubt. Fear. And now… this."

Ophelia's gaze dropped to the floor, her thoughts a whirlwind. She hated how his words resonated, how they reached the parts of her she kept locked away.

The Dyad echoed a subtle pulse of concern that she shoved aside.

"Why are you telling me this?" she asked finally, strained.

"Because you're the only one who might understand," Faust said simply. "Kaspar… the Council… they see me as a risk, a tool, or both. But you—you know what it's like to be more than what others want to make of you."

Ophelia exhaled sharply, pushing herself to her feet. She stepped closer to the door. "If you think flattery will win me over, it won't."

"It's not flattery," Faust said firmly. "It's the truth."

She hesitated, staring at the wood now with apprehension.

Through the Dyad, she felt Theodin's unease, his silent warning to tread carefully. But she ignored it, her curiosity and empathy warring with her caution.

"You don't have to believe me," Faust continued, quieter now. "But I think you understand what it's like to carry something others fear."

Ophelia pressed her hand to the door. Her fingers curled against the wood, her breath catching. For a moment, she thought to respond, to interrogate him further. But then she stepped back, her eyes narrowing.

"I'll keep that in mind."

"You're a Valksha of Veladriel, aren't you?" he suddenly said. "Your magic…it's emerald green—the color of the Saryf of Spirit and Heart. Your energy feels so pure compared to mine."

A desperate chuckle escaped him.

"And you can feel mine too. How broken I am. Because of that *fiend*."

His voice singed with a seething burn at the last word. It sent a chill down Ophelia's spine.

"You can feel…that I speak nothing but the truth. I don't need some high Elf to tell me otherwise…I've had enough of Elvish magic, to be frank."

Ophelia swallowed. He was right—she couldn't feel the malice behind his words or any ill intent.

Only pain and sorrow.

Her knuckles turned white again as her fingers clenched into a fist.

She should leave. That would be the smart thing to do, but she didn't.

The way he spoke—his voice was tired, resigned, and hollow—it was something she had felt before. Not in him, but in herself.

And she couldn't walk away from that.

She took a deep breath, hesitant. Then, before she could stop herself, she reached for the handle and pushed the door open.

Faust scrambled to his feet and backed away to allow her space. He shrank back sheepishly, and nearly tripped backwards as he stumbled against the bench. He caught it before it fell, darted his eyes to Ophelia awkwardly, then straightened his stance to face her.

With only the pulsing light of the chamber wards and the low-lit enchanted lanterns, the room was dim and Faust was mostly in shadow.

"H…hello," Faust stammered, offering a crooked smile. "Sorry, I—uh, I didn't expect you to come in."

Ophelia stared. She didn't expect herself to come in either.

When she didn't respond right away, Faust cleared his throat and stiffly sat down on the bench.

She drew blood with her needle ring, waved her hand, and the lanterns obeyed—they brightened the room and chased the shadows and darkness away.

Faust winced and shielded his eyes.

Now that she could see him, she saw that he wore a simple, clean outfit now that replaced the clothes they found him in. A neutral-colored canvas shirt, trousers, and shoes.

Her gaze flicked downward—then froze. Her breath caught. Now that he was no longer wearing his tattered sleeves, she could see them.

Scars.

They weren't immediately noticeable in the low light, but now she could see them—the faint glint of old and fresh wounds scattered across his hands, his knuckles, his forearms. Some were faded, half-forgotten by time. But others—jagged, uneven, raw—stood stark against his pale skin.

Not just battle scars. Not just injuries. Her stomach twisted.

"Your arms," she murmured.

Faust flinched. He let out a slow, dry exhale, shifting in his seat as he looked down at his arms and turned them over to examine his wounds.

"Unpleasant to look at, aren't they?" His voice was hoarse, edged with something unreadable.

Ophelia didn't answer immediately. She had seen scars before—from training, from battle, from war.

But these? These were the kind of wounds that weren't meant to kill. They were meant to break.

"You don't know how to heal them?" Ophelia asked.

Faust's arms dropped as his face fell bashfully. He shook his head.

Hesitantly, she took a step towards him and rubbed her wrist in an anxious gesture. "Do they hurt?"

Faust let out something that might've been a laugh. "Not anymore."

Ophelia exhaled sharply through her nose. That wasn't an answer.

She pushed the door shut and approached him. He recoiled, his head snapping up to watch her as she lowered herself in front of him, sitting on her heels.

She reached out without thinking. Her Kyriegard runes briefly flashed blue upon contact with his skin—the moment her fingers skimmed against his wrist, Faust went rigid.

Not a flinch. Not fear. But an instinctive, controlled tension—the kind that came from years of learning not to react to pain. His eyes flicked to hers, sharp and alert.

"What are you doing?" he asked.

Ophelia didn't answer again. Her fingers curled gently around his wrist, pressing her thumb against the raised scars. His skin was cold.

Her Valksha magic stirred. She felt the skittishness in his bones.

Years of pain, abuse, and torment.

She grimaced slightly. Pushing it aside, she pressed her finger into the hidden needle of her ring to draw blood again in her opposite hand. She hovered that hand over his arm.

The warmth in her veins pulsed, reaching toward him, responding to the fractures in his energy—the places where his magic had been torn apart, stitched together wrong, forced into something unnatural.

Faust's breath hitched. His fingers flexed, like he was fighting the urge to pull away.

Ophelia inhaled slowly and closed her eyes, letting the magic settle. "Breathe."

He didn't breathe. He couldn't—he held it, watching her in awe. But he didn't pull away, either.

The glow of emerald light sparked at her fingertips, slipping beneath his skin, sinking into the places his magic rejected, the places Azazelf had left broken. It resisted her at first—sharp, jagged, like it had been conditioned to fight off anything that tried to fix it.

But Ophelia pressed forward, steady. She didn't force it. She just let it be.

And for the first time in a long time—Faust's magic didn't fight back.

The warmth seeped into the cracks, smoothing over the places that had been shattered and pieced back together in the wrong shape.

Faust sucked in a harsh breath. His fingers curled into fists. His body wasn't used to this. Wasn't used to magic being gentle. Wasn't used to being given something instead of something being taken.

His eyes darkened, but his body began to relax. His fingers now twitched, but not with tension this time.

The glow of her magic finally settled. Ophelia opened her eyes.

Faust was staring at her. Not with suspicion. Not with amusement. Just quiet, cautious disbelief.

His gaze flicked to his wrist. He turned his hand over, flexing his fingers slowly, testing something.

She stood and stepped back, releasing him. "That should help."

Faust rolled his wrist again. Then, slowly, his lips parted.

"…I see." His voice was soft, unreadable.

Ophelia tilted her head. "See what?"

His gaze drifted to her hands. Then back to his own. He looked like he wanted to say something else. But instead, he exhaled a slow breath, shaking his head.

"Nothing," he muttered, dropping his arm to his side.

Ophelia frowned slightly, but didn't press.

Instead, she turned toward the door, already reaching for the handle. Just as she was about to step out—

"Ophelia."

She paused.

Faust was still looking at his hand, flexing his fingers again, like he was still trying to understand what had just happened.

Then, he offered her another smile. Not a nervous one or one with any hidden meaning or intention, but a genuine one—one full of gratitude.

"You should be careful with magic like that."

Ophelia arched a her. "Why?"

Faust exhaled softly, his expression unreadable again. He brought his now healed hand to his chest and pressed his palm against his heart.

"Because once you give someone something," he murmured, "they might try to give it back."

Ophelia's stomach turned—but she didn't know why.

Without another word, she turned and left the cellar, her thoughts heavier than before. Behind the door, Faust exhaled slowly, staring at the glowing runes that kept him bound.

Chapter 21

The Guarded

Year 844 of the Second Age, Eighth Month, Nineteenth Day

Dawn had not yet broken. Enchanted lanterns bathed Avasylon's main hall in muted gold, casting long shadows across the stone walls. The air was crisp—still clinging to the silence that lingered before the day began.

Kaspar stood near the far end of the room, his gaze fixed on the forest visible through the window.

Theodin entered quietly, boots nearly silent against the stone. Kaspar didn't turn but gestured him closer.

"You wanted to see me?" Theodin asked, his tone neutral but tinged with curiosity.

Kaspar turned then, his gaze settling on Theodin with the weight of unspoken deliberation.

"How are you holding up?" he asked, calm but probing.

Theodin stiffened slightly, his arms crossing instinctively over his chest. "I'm fine."

Kaspar raised a brow. "Are you?"

Theodin frowned. "If this is about Faust—"

"It's not just about Faust," Kaspar interrupted. "It's about you. The way you've been reacting."

Theodin's expression hardened. "Reacting to what?"

"To her," Kaspar said plainly. "To Ophelia."

Theodin's chest tightened, but he forced his face to remain stoic.

"I'm her partner. Protecting her is part of the job."

"And you do it well," Kaspar acknowledged. "But protecting her doesn't mean shielding her from everything. She's stronger than you give her credit for."

Theodin's eyes flashed, but he held his tongue.

Kaspar stepped closer, his presence as unyielding as the mountains.

"I see the way you look at her, Theodin. The way your energy shifts when she's near. When you feel her presence, speak to her, or even think about her. It's not just duty driving you."

Theodin's fists clenched at his sides.

"If you think I'm—"

"I'm not accusing you of anything," Kaspar said, cutting him off with a raised hand. "Think about where your feelings end and your duty begins. That line blurs fast—especially in the field."

Theodin let out a labored breath, tearing his eyes away and pinning them to the floor. "I know where the line is."

Kaspar studied him for a moment.

"Do you?" he asked quietly. "Because if you don't, you're not just putting her at risk. You're putting yourself at risk too."

The words landed heavily between them, the weight of Kaspar's experience evident in his tone. Theodin looked up, a conflicted look twisted in his face.

"She doesn't need to know."

Kaspar's brows rose, accompanied by a humorless smile.

"She already does. The Dyad makes sure of that."

Theodin's shoulders tensed, the truth of Kaspar's words settling like a stone in his chest.

"What do you want me to do?"

"Be honest with yourself," Kaspar said simply. "Because if you're not, the Dyad will amplify every doubt, every hesitation. And in a fight, that could mean the difference between life and death."

Theodin nodded slowly. His face dropped, becoming neutral and unreadable.

"I'll keep it in check."

Kaspar inclined his head. "See that you do. She trusts you. Don't make her question that."

Theodin held his gaze for a moment longer before nodding again.

"I won't."

Kaspar stepped past him. "We'll be training with Faust today. Prepare yourself—and your mind."

Theodin turned to watch him leave. As Kaspar disappeared through the front door, Theodin took his place at the window and leaned against the wall.

He breathed deeply, his eyes drifting to the fields where the first rays of sunlight stretched across the forest.

Be honest with yourself.

He wasn't sure what that honesty would bring. But he couldn't afford to let the Dyad falter because of it.

Not now. Not ever.

For her sake.

Ophelia sat cross-legged in the underground corridor beneath Avasylon, near the reinforced door to Faust's holding chamber. Her rifle rested across her lap, but she held a book open right on top of it.

A buzz rippled against the back of her head through the Dyad. Her eyes snapped upward, her posture straightening. It wasn't a clear emotion—more like the echo of something heavy, distant yet persistent. Tension. Conflict.

Theodin.

Ophelia frowned. She lowered the book and closed her eyes to focus on the sensation.

He was upstairs, likely still speaking with Kaspar. Whatever they were discussing, it was clearly weighing on him. She could feel the pointed edges of protectiveness mingled with a deeper unease. It wasn't the first time she'd sensed it, but this time, it felt sharper, more concentrated.

Her fingers tightened slightly on the cover of the book.

The Dyad, their bond, had grown stronger over the past month, but moments like this still caught her off guard. She wasn't used to feeling someone else's emotions so acutely, and Theodin was particularly skilled at keeping his thoughts guarded. For her to sense this much meant he was either distracted or too wrapped up in his emotions to fully shield them.

She exhaled, trying to send a wave of calm back through the Dyad. She wasn't sure if it would reach him, but it was worth the effort. Whatever burden he was carrying, she wanted him to know that he wasn't alone.

The sound of footsteps descending the stone stairwell broke her focus.

Kaspar came into view from around the corner. He stopped just short of the holding chamber, his attention shifting between the door and Ophelia.

"Anything to report?" he asked, brisk but not unkind.

Ophelia shook her head. "Nothing unusual. He hasn't moved much."

Kaspar nodded. "Good. Finish your watch and prepare to join us for training. I'll need you there."

Her brows furrowed in surprise. "Training? Who will take over the watch?"

"Faust will be joining us."

Her eyes widened then. "He will?"

"Yes," he answered. "And you will be helping him along when he needs it. And he will surely need it."

Ophelia's face twisted slightly.

"You're the only other true Valksha we have, Ophelia. If anyone can push him to reveal his limits, it's you."

She hesitated, glancing toward the sealed door.

The thought of training alongside Faust felt… complicated. He was an enigma, his story riddled with gaps, his power fractured. But if Kaspar believed it was necessary, then she couldn't refuse.

She closed her book.

"Understood," she said quietly, standing and adjusting the strap of her rifle. "I'll be ready."

Kaspar studied her for a moment longer before turning toward the stairs.

"We start in half an hour. Be on time."

As his footsteps receded, Ophelia glanced at the door once more.

Morning light filtered through the canopy of the trees that bordered the grounds of Avasylon, casting fractured beams across the summer-kissed earth. The training field stretched wide and open, its stone markers sprinkling with dew, the worn edges of old sparring circles in the grass.

Faust stood in the center, shoulders drawn tight, his eyes shifting nervously between Kaspar and Theodin, who stood several feet behind him as he lined up before a training dummy.

At the edge of the field, Ophelia observed from beneath the shade of an outcropped archway near the stable, her rifle strapped to her back.

The plan, from Ophelia's understanding, was to see what Faust was capable of and what he knew of his own abilities. Kaspar wanted to see if Faust knew how to use his magic at all—Ophelia informed him that Faust did not know how to heal his own wounds, which concerned him.

Kaspar stepped forward.

"You're here to prove you're worth the risk," he said, his tone firm and clipped. "Show me what you can do."

Faust inclined his head as he raised his hand and pricked his finger with a small dagger, as he had seen Ophelia do similarly. A single drop of blood welled up, glowing as it activated the fractured magic within him. Blue energy coalesced around his palm, flickering like a flame caught in the wind.

He thrust his hand forward, sending a burst of energy toward one of the training dummies. The force struck the target, but the blast only weakly brushed its side, scattering small fragments of wood.

Kaspar frowned and folded his arms. "Sloppy. Again."

Faust hesitated, his expression hardening as he repeated the motion. This time, the energy struck with more precision on the dummy's chest but faltered as it dissipated, leaving only a faded scorch mark behind.

"It's unstable," Kaspar said flatly. "You can't rely on that in the field."

Faust clenched his fists. "I know."

Ophelia stepped forward then, her eyes meeting Kaspar's.

"Let me try," she said softly.

Kaspar nodded and stepped back. "Go ahead."

She turned to Faust. "You're trying to force it," she said gently, her tone a stark contrast to Kaspar's. "Magic isn't just about control—it's about trust. You have to let it flow."

Faust's eyes darted to her, uncertainty flashing in his gaze. "I'm not like you. My magic—"

"Is still Valksha," Ophelia interrupted, firm but kind. "It's fractured, yes, but it's still part of you. You have to stop fighting it."

She pricked her finger with the needle in her ring, letting a single drop of blood fall onto her palm. The runes etched into her palms lit up with green, the magic flowing through her like a steady current. She extended her hand toward the same training dummy, and her energy wove in precise, controlled arcs before striking the target. The impact was clean, the dummy shuddering but remaining intact.

"See?" she said, turning to Faust. "It's not about forcing the magic. It's about guiding it."

Faust hesitated. His gaze lingered on the glow of her runes. He exhaled slowly, his hands flexing at his sides. After a moment of thought, he gestured with a nod of his head to her hand.

"Those markings—" His sapphire eyes darted to Theodin and back to her. "They're the same as his…does that have anything to do with it?"

Ophelia gave a small, timid chuckle and looked down at her hand. "Yes and no. The runes are a part of the Kyriegard partner bond, the Arcande Dyad—a way to channel energy between us. But magic isn't about symbols or tools—they're just extensions of what's already there."

She could hear Theodin's voice rumble a small, knowing laugh of his own through the Dyad.

Of course, since his philosophy and approach to magic was exactly that—symbols and tools—but that was Sage technique.

She glanced and shot a smirk at Theodin before turning back to Faust. She raised her hand slightly, and the glow of the runes intensified.

"What matters is your connection to the magic itself. You have to trust it, let it trust you in return. It's a relationship, not a command."

Faust frowned, his gaze fixed on her hand as if searching for an answer in the patterns of light.

"A relationship?" he echoed, tinged with skepticism.

Ophelia nodded. "Magic isn't just a weapon or a tool. It's alive in its own way, especially Valksha magic. If you treat it like it's something to conquer, it'll fight you. But if you meet it halfway…"

She let her words trail off, holding her hand out toward him. The glow from her runes pulsed faintly, steady and inviting.

"You'll feel the difference."

Faust hesitated, his eyes flicking between her hand and his own. The tension in his shoulders didn't ease as he flexed his fingers.

"How do you guide something that feels like it's tearing you apart?" he asked quietly but laced with a rawness that betrayed his frustration.

Ophelia stepped closer, her voice low but steady. "You start by letting go of the fear. Trust that the magic will respond to you if you give it the chance."

The Dyad stirred with unease, and Theodin shifted slightly, his eyes narrowing as he observed the interaction. Kaspar, too, watched with a mixture of skepticism and curiosity.

Faust swallowed hard, his eyes meeting Ophelia's again. "And if it doesn't?"

She offered him a smile. "Then you try again. That's how we learn."

Something in her tone seemed to soften the tension in Faust's posture. He nodded, raising his hand once more. Blood seeped from his finger, and the blue energy of his magic crackled from his fingertips up his forearm. This time, he let the energy build gradually, the glow stabilizing as he focused on the flow rather than the force.

When he released the energy, it struck the target with a steadiness that hadn't been there before. The stream of light wasn't perfect—it wavered at the edges—but it was controlled. It hit the center of the dummy's chest.

"Better," Ophelia said, her smile widening slightly. "Now, again."

Faust looked at her, a glimpse of something like gratitude crossing his face. He repeated the motion, his confidence growing with each attempt. The energy became more stable and more deliberate, the fractures in his magic less apparent.

From the sidelines, Theodin warily observed the exchange. The Dyad rustled softly, and Ophelia caught the faintest ripple of protectiveness beneath his steady presence. It wasn't overbearing—more like a subtle current running beneath the surface—but she felt it nonetheless.

She glanced at him, her eyes meeting his for a brief moment. Her lips curved into a small, reassuring smile, the Dyad humming with her quiet acknowledgment. It wasn't spoken, but the message was clear, an echoed whisper of her voice in his head.

I see you. I trust you.

Theodin's posture relaxed slightly, though his gaze didn't waver from Faust. He crossed his arms over his chest, his presence in the Dyad shifting from tension to quiet vigilance.

As the morning carried on, initiates arrived and took their usual places. Theodin met with them to get them started on their routines.

Low murmurs rippled through the group as they caught sight of Faust—his stance poised, his magic shooting from his fingertips in streams of blue light.

Some slowed. A few whispered. One bold apprentice squinted and nudged his partner. "Who's that?"

"Don't know," came the whispered reply. "But he's with her."

A spark of blue light danced between Faust's fingertips, and several heads tilted in awe. Daphne—the fairy girl—watched Ophelia like she was witnessing a myth come to life, eyes wide and reverent.

"It's another Valksha?" another asked, voice hushed.

"It has to be," said a nearby boy, brows furrowed. "Look—she's teaching him."

The training field quieted as more pairs filed in, their attention drawn not by command, but by the quiet intensity of the Valksha girl guiding the fractured boy beneath Avasylon's pale sun.

"Let's go now," Theodin's voice boomed, carrying over the fields. "Focus on your technique. Your stance."

They snapped to attention and scrambled into their positions obediently. Theodin circled them once before he made his way back to the arena with Ophelia and Faust.

Kaspar was observing the Valksha, leaning against the stone wall with his arms folded. He exchanged a glance with Theodin as he approached.

"She's good," he murmured.

"She learned from the best," Theodin replied, quiet but laced with admiration.

Kaspar nodded once. "Lady Vivian really did have a gentle touch," he murmured distantly.

"She learned from you as well."

Kaspar's gaze lingered on Ophelia, his expression softening slightly. "Aye, lad, this is also true. Let's hope it's enough."

Kaspar reached over and patted his shoulder before pushing off the stone fencing. "Keep an eye on them. I'll take care of the young ones."

Theodin nodded and hoisted himself over the fence to take his place after he walked away. He stood with his arms folded, watching them with a keen eye.

As the morning sun climbed higher, the training continued. Faust's movements grew more precise, his confidence bolstered by Ophelia's unwavering guidance.

The sun hung from its noonday position in the sky. The once-pristine training dummies were battered and scorched, their surfaces marred by countless attempts to hone raw magic into precision.

Faust stood at the edge of the field, his breathing uneven but his posture straighter than it had been at the start. His eyes studied the marks his magic had left, a spark of something like pride crossing his face.

"You've improved," Ophelia said. "But you're still holding back."

Faust looked to her, a shadow of uncertainty darkening his features. "I'm afraid if I push too hard… it'll break again."

"It won't," she replied. Her eyes gleamed with confidence. "Not if you trust yourself."

He opened his mouth to reply, but the words faltered. For a beat, he stared awkwardly, then cleared his throat. Instead, he gave a small nod, his fingers flexing as if testing the residual energy in his hands.

Kaspar's voice broke in. "That's enough for today." He stepped forward, his gaze sweeping over Faust. "You've shown progress, but progress isn't enough in the field. You'll need consistency and control. We'll revisit this later."

Faust nodded again, his expression unreadable. "Understood."

Kaspar turned to Ophelia and Theodin. "You two, with me. Faust, return to your chambers. We'll discuss your performance later."

Faust hesitated, his gaze lingering on Ophelia for a moment before he lowered his head and walked back toward the cottage. Ophelia watched him go, her arms crossing over her chest.

The Dyad thrummed, carrying Theodin's unease. She turned to him, catching the sharp edge of his oddly-colored gaze.

"What?" she asked, soft but pointed.

"You trust him too easily," Theodin said, his voice low but laced with apprehension. "You're giving him too much room."

Her eyes narrowed at him. "And what if I didn't? What would that prove?"

"It would prove you're not leaving yourself vulnerable to someone who could turn on you the second it benefits him," Theodin snapped, his frustration slipping through the Dyad.

Ophelia huffed, grimacing as she felt it, but her harshness lessened as she took a step closer.

"I'm not blind to the risks, Theodin. But he's not going to learn anything if we treat him like a threat at every turn."

"And what if he is a threat?" he countered, his eyes locking with hers. "What then?"

She hesitated, the weight of his question settling between them. Finally, she placed a hand on his arm, and the Dyad reverberated gently with her calm.

"Then we'll deal with it. Together."

The stiffness in Theodin's shoulders eased slightly, though the storm in his eyes didn't entirely fade. He looked away, his jaw tightening.

"Just be careful."

"I always am," she said with a faint smile, her hand remaining briefly before she stepped back.

Kaspar cleared his throat, drawing their attention.

"Save the debates for later. We've got other matters to handle." He turned, gesturing for them to follow. "Let's debrief."

They walked back toward the cottage in silence. As they reached the foyer, Kaspar stopped and faced them.

"Faust is making progress, but we can't let our guard down. I want your honest assessments. What did you see?"

Ophelia glanced at Theodin before speaking. "He's hesitant, but he listens. His magic… it's raw, but there's potential."

Kaspar nodded, looking to Theodin. "And you?"

Theodin folded his arms, his expression guarded. "He's too unstable. He second-guesses himself, and that hesitation could cost lives in the field."

"Fair points," Kaspar said, his white brows furrowing in thought. "We'll need to push him further in the coming days. See what he's truly capable of—and what he's hiding."

Ophelia frowned. "Do you really think he's hiding something?"

Kaspar's gaze sharpened. "Everyone hides something. It's just a matter of finding out what."

"Well, what could I be hiding, then?"

Her question wasn't sarcastic or accusatory but rather a genuine question. Kaspar's eyes lingered on her, his expression lessening but remaining firm.

"You carry the weight of your legacy, Ophelia. That's not the same as hiding something, but it's a burden nonetheless."

Theodin shifted beside her.

"And what about me?" he asked, measured but edged with challenge.

Kaspar's gaze flicked to him, his expression unreadable.

"You hide from yourself more than anyone else, Theodin. You're guarded in ways that go deeper than the bond you share. But the truth has a way of surfacing when you least expect it."

Ophelia glanced at Theodin, the Dyad thrumming with his unease. Her eyes softened as she returned her focus to Kaspar.

"And Faust?"

Kaspar sighed slowly, his gaze now hardening.

"Faust is different. He's not just hiding pain or doubt—he's hiding truths. The kind that can shift the balance of trust in an instant."

The silence that followed was heavy, the unspoken tension hanging thick in the air.

Finally, Kaspar straightened, his tone firm. "That's all for now. Rest and regroup. Tomorrow, we'll see how far we can push him."

As Kaspar turned and walked away, Ophelia and Theodin exchanged a glance. The Dyad between them rippled with the weight of their shared uncertainty.

"He'll slip up eventually," Theodin muttered, his eyes narrowing as he stared after Kaspar.

Ophelia didn't respond immediately. Instead, she looked toward the door Faust had disappeared through, her thoughts swirling. "Maybe. But until then… we keep trying."

Chapter 22

The Fractured and the Found

Year 844 of the Second Age, Eighth Month, Twenty-First Day

Faust sat on the edge of the wooden bench, his lapis eyes fixed on his hands as he flexed his fingers, feeling the remnants of yesterday's training dwelling in his veins. The scars in his skin caught the dim glow, a reminder of everything he'd endured—and everything he hadn't yet overcome.

His thoughts were a tangled web, each thread pulling him in a different direction. The warmth of trust he'd felt in Ophelia's presence warred with the cold, insidious whispers buried deep in his mind—whispers he knew were not his own.

Azazelf's voice echoed in his memory, a cruel reminder of the experiments that had left him fractured.

"You'll never be whole. Never be free..."

Faust clenched his fists, choking on his breath as he fought to push the memories. He winced and lowered his forehead into his palms. He could feel the pulse of his Valksha energy struggling in his grasp, in the hands that failed to control his magic.

Then, he thought of her hands. How she beautifully maneuvered her energy and executed each spell she demonstrated for him.

How lovely she was. Not just her magic. Just…her.

His thoughts now fully drifted to Ophelia, to the way she'd spoken to him during training. Her words had been gentle but firm, her belief in his potential unwavering. It was a stark contrast to the bitter judgment he'd faced from others, and it had stirred something in him —hope, fragile but persistent.

But hope was dangerous. Hope made you vulnerable.

Faust exhaled slowly, his eyes lifting to the runes on the walls. Whatever Azazelf did to him, maybe she could help him undo. Maybe he could wield the power of the Saryfim like her.

"You are weak. Broken. Useless."

The demon Elf's words hissed in his mind.

It made his skin crawl. He couldn't prevent himself from being captured and tormented back then. How could he possibly hope to do it now?

Ophelia's voice cut through the chaos of his own thoughts.

"You have to trust yourself."

Trust.

The word felt foreign, like an unfamiliar weight in his chest. He wanted to trust himself, to believe he could wield the power that coursed through him. But every attempt felt like walking a tightrope over a chasm, the slightest misstep threatening to send him plummeting.

The runes on the walls pulsed gently, their constant murmur pressing against his awareness.

He sighed, trying to ground himself, to focus.

The cracks in his magic felt like fault lines beneath his skin, fragile and dangerous. But Ophelia had seen something in him, something worth fighting for.

He wasn't sure if he could see it too.

Faust's fingers twitched as he flexed them again, feeling the delicate glimmer of Valksha energy at the edge of his control.

The words of others swirled in his mind—Azazelf's venomous whispers, Ophelia's quiet encouragement, Kaspar's cold scrutiny. They formed a cacophony, pulling him in different directions.

He closed his eyes and breathed deeply, focusing on the memory of Ophelia's voice. The warmth in her tone, the clarity of her guidance, had been unlike anything he'd experienced in years. She didn't look at him with pity or disdain but with something he couldn't quite place—belief, perhaps, or understanding.

For a brief moment, he allowed himself to imagine what it would feel like to regain control, to wield his magic without fear. To prove to himself—and to the world—that he was more than the fractured man Azazelf had left behind.

But as quickly as the thought came, doubt crept in like a shadow. Could he ever truly escape what had been done to him? Or was he destined to remain a pawn, his fractured magic a constant reminder of his failures?

The distant sound of footsteps echoed from the corridor outside, pulling Faust from his thoughts. He straightened, his lapis whipping to the door.

He recognized the cadence of the steps—it was Kaspar.

Faust shot up, bracing himself for whatever scrutiny or command would come next.

Ophelia traced her thumb over the runes etched gently into the base of her palm and down her forearm.

When inactive, they were simply a few shades darker than her skin tone, and when active, they shimmered and glowed between green, silver, and white.

Her eyes drifted to her partner's arm beside her as they still sat next to each other on the stone steps leading to the training grounds. While her arms and hands were still soft and delicate to the touch, his were calloused, sword-worn, and lightly scarred from years of training with the blade. She noticed sometimes he occasionally chose not to use gauntlets or gloves.

Perhaps it was to toughen himself, grow thick skin—literally and figuratively.

Every Kyriegard partner pair had their own unique inscriptions that matched their partner's. Ophelia observed that Alfena had many light, scarred remains of partnerships past, while Kaspar—though she knew he would only have one set of runes, perhaps as faded as Alfena's earliest partnerships—refused to let his arms and hands see the light of day.

It made Ophelia wonder then—as a Valksha who could live half a millennia, she would also someday outlive Theodin, as Alfena outlived her partners. The thought made her insides twist unpleasantly.

Theodin's eyes lifted to meet hers as he felt her thoughts stir between them through the Dyad.

"Thinking again, I see," he muttered.

Ophelia smirked reluctantly at the jest. "I have the unfortunate disposition where I am constantly thinking."

Theodin leaned an elbow on his knee in her direction. "Felt like…a sickening, upset thought."

Ophelia's expression fell. Her eyes lowered solemnly to her feet.

"It was," she admitted.

A beat of silence.

Theodin's energy shifted, becoming a comforting wave of warmth through their Dyad.

"Well…" Theodin hesitated. "What was it?"

Ophelia could not speak. The thought of losing him prickled the old wounds in her heart that were stricken with grief and loss. She shook her head and fidgeted with her ring.

"I'd rather not think about it anymore, if that's alright with you."

The Dyad became restless. Theodin reached over and grabbed both of her hands with one of his. His voice softened.

"It's alright, Ophelia."

Ophelia's shoulders deflated. She released a breath, letting her muscles loosen from the soothing flow of his energy. Theodin's hand remained over hers for a moment longer before he withdrew, his eyes searching hers.

"You don't have to say it. I can feel enough through the Dyad to know it's big."

Ophelia contemplated, then allowed herself a subtle, wry smile. "Not everything has to be shared, you know."

"True," he admitted, leaning back slightly. "But you've got to let me carry some of it. That's what the Dyad is for, isn't it? You've said that to me once or twice."

She chuckled, her fingers brushing the edge of her rifle. "I thought the Dyad was for sensing each other's every embarrassing thought."

"Well," Theodin quipped, the corner of his mouth twitching, "it has its perks."

"It does," Ophelia giggled. "And sometimes it's not just sensing those embarrassing thoughts—I can outright hear every blasphemous curse and mumble when Nimrod knocks you senseless during your spars!"

Theodin groaned dramatically, leaning his head back. "Of course you hear those. He hits like a runaway cart, and you expect me to stay silent?"

Ophelia grinned at him, her emerald eyes sparkling. "I don't expect silence. I just didn't think your vocabulary would be so foul that it would make Nether demons blush."

Theodin huffed, shaking his head. "You're never going to let that go, are you?"

"Not a chance," she said, her tone light but full of affection.

Their laughter mingled with the quiet hum of the courtyard. For a moment, the weight between them lifted, replaced by something lighter, more certain. And though Ophelia still felt the ache of her unspoken fears, the Dyad filled her with steady reassurance—enough to remind her she wasn't alone.

"Theodin," Ophelia began.

"Yeah?"

"What did Kaspar say to you yesterday morning?" she asked. "Before we went out to the training grounds with Faust."

Theodin's eyes snapped to her briefly before shifting away again, his jaw tightening. "Not much," he replied, his tone neutral.

Ophelia tilted her head. "The Dyad says otherwise."

He huffed softly, his gaze fixed on a distant point in the trees. "He just wanted to make sure I'm… staying focused. Not letting distractions get in the way."

"Distractions?" she repeated, her brows knitting together. "What kind of distractions?"

Theodin hesitated, the Dyad simmering with a mix of tension and unease.

"He thinks I'm too protective of you," he finally admitted, his voice low. "That I need to trust you more to handle things on your own."

Ophelia blinked, surprised by the bluntness of his words.

"That's entirely wrong," she said carefully.

His eyes snapped back to her, sharp but not defensive. "I know you're capable, Ophelia. That's not the problem."

"Then what is?" she asked, her tone softening.

He exhaled, rubbing the back of his neck. "I don't know," he admitted. "Maybe it's just the Dyad. It makes everything… sharper. Harder to ignore."

Ophelia nodded, her expression thoughtful. "It's new for both of us. We're still figuring it out."

"Yeah," Theodin murmured, his eyes glancing back to her. "But I'll work on it. Kaspar's right—I need to trust you more."

She smiled lightly, her expression warm. "You already do. I feel it."

Theodin's lips twitched into the barest hint of a smile in return, and he looked away again, the tension in his shoulders easing.

"Good."

They sat in silence for a moment, the Dyad lulling softly between them—a quiet connection that said more than either of them could put into words.

Kaspar entered Faust's chamber with deliberate steps, his gaze sharp as it settled on Faust, who stood with his legs resting on the edge of the wooden bench. As Kaspar closed the door, Faust hesitantly sat down again. The Valksha boy's eyes flicked up briefly before returning to his hands, which flexed restlessly in his lap.

"You're more focused today," Kaspar said, his tone calm but probing. "What changed?"

Faust hesitated, his fingers curling tightly before he released a slow breath.

"I want to improve," he said simply. "Isn't that why I'm here?"

Kaspar's face didn't shift, though his stare remained piercing.

"Improvement isn't just about effort. It's about control. And control is something you've yet to demonstrate."

Faust's jaw tightened, but he nodded, his eyes briefly meeting Kaspar's. "What do you want me to do?"

Kaspar stepped closer, crossing his arms as he studied him. "We'll start small. Right here, right now. Hold your energy steady. No bursts, no flares—just focus on maintaining balance."

Faust then brought himself to his feet with a slight stagger. He raised a hand, pricking his finger with his dagger to summon the spark of his fractured Valksha magic. The blue light flared to life, crackling faintly as it coiled around his palm. His brows furrowed in concentration, the energy wavering as he struggled to steady it.

"Slower," Kaspar instructed. "You're forcing it."

Faust exhaled sharply, his fingers twitching as the energy flared before dimming. "I'm trying."

"Trying isn't enough," Kaspar replied, his voice cool but firm. "Your magic reflects your state of mind. If you're erratic, it will be too."

The words struck a nerve. Faust's eyes darkened, and the light around his hand surged suddenly, a crackle of energy snapping through the air. The warding runes on the walls flared in response, their glow intensifying as they absorbed the unstable magic.

"Stop," Kaspar commanded.

Faust clenched his fist, the energy dissipating with a faint hiss. He huffed and heaved, his shoulders tense as he looked away.

"It's like walking a tightrope over fire," he muttered. "One misstep, and it all falls apart."

Kaspar stepped closer, his silver gaze unyielding. "Then stop looking down. Trust your footing."

Faust glared at him with a guarded expression. "Trust isn't exactly my strong suit."

A flicker of something unreadable passed through Kaspar's eyes.

"No, I don't imagine it is," he said. "But if you don't trust yourself, no one else will."

Faust's lips pressed into a thin line, his eyes dropping to his hands. He could feel the former scars along his forearm like they were still there, under his skin—a stark reminder of his fractured past.

"You don't know what it's like," he mumbled after a moment. "To have something inside you that you can't control. That fights you at every turn."

Kaspar tilted his head slightly. "I know more than you think," he said, softer now. "But your past doesn't dictate your future. Only you can decide what you become."

The silence that followed was heavy, broken only by the murmur of the runes around them. Faust's fingers twitched, the energy in his veins stirring restlessly.

"I don't want to be what he made me," he admitted, the words barely above a whisper.

Kaspar's eyes narrowed. "Then prove it. To me. To yourself. Control your magic—not because you're afraid of it, but because it's yours."

Faust hesitated, his eyes meeting Kaspar's. There was a flash of something raw, a vulnerability he couldn't fully suppress. He nodded slowly, lifting his hand once more.

This time, the glow of his magic was more stable, the light coiling in a controlled arc around his palm. It wasn't perfect—it wavered at the edges, like a flame struggling against the wind—but it held.

Kaspar watched intently and with calculation.

"Better," he said finally. "But better isn't good enough. You'll need to push harder."

Faust exhaled again, his posture straightening. "I will."

Kaspar nodded firmly once. "We'll see." He turned toward the door, pausing just before he stepped out. "We will have a room for you soon in the upper level—as long as you demonstrate progress."

The door creaked shut behind him, leaving Faust alone in the chamber. The runes' glow softened, their light and energy a quiet reminder of the confinement that still bound him.

Faust stared at his hands, the remnants of his magic flickering in his palm. His chest tightened as a whisper of doubt crept into his mind, unbidden but familiar.

The echo of Azazelf's voice hissed in his thoughts.

"You'll never be free."

Faust clenched his fist, extinguishing the leftover light that simmered on his skin.

"I will," he whispered to himself, the words a fragile defiance against the shadows that lingered.

Chapter 23

The Broken and the Hopeful

Year 844 of the Second Age, Eighth Month, Twenty-Second Day

The Council gathered in Avasylon's main hall, their presence lending an unusual gravity to the normally serene space.

Alfena and Crane stood near the far side of the room, their expressions a study in contrast—Crane's sharp, calculating gaze swept the chamber while Alfena's calm demeanor masked her keen psychic awareness. Kaspar, Sigvard, and Margrith took the other side the room.

Faust stood in the center of the room, his posture uneasy. Ophelia and Theodin lingered near the edges of the foyer, their Dyad resonating with shared vigilance.

Kaspar's eyes fell upon Faust. "You understand why you're here?"

"Yes," Faust said. He rolled off some of the tension in his shoulders. "To prove I'm not a threat."

"It's more than that," Alfena said, her melodic voice cutting through the air like a blade. "We need to understand what you are. What you carry."

Faust's eyes narrowed slightly, but he nodded. "And if I can't answer that?"

"Then you give us little choice," Margrith interjected. "The safety of Olysgard comes first."

"Enough," Kaspar said sharply, his eyes pinning Margrith. "We evaluate before we judge."

Sigvard stroked his braided beard thoughtfully. "The boy's magic is… peculiar. Fractured, yet undeniably Valksha. The question is, what caused the fracture?"

Crane stepped forward, tapping his cane lightly against the floor. "That's what we aim to find out." His wild chestnut eyes shifted to Faust. "Begin."

Faust hesitated for a fraction of a second before nodding. He raised his hand and pricked his finger to summon the glow of his Valksha magic. Blue energy crackled to life, weaving feebly around his palm. The light wavered, faltering at the edges, but it held steady enough to draw murmurs from the Council.

"Unstable," Sigvard observed, his tone neutral. "But present."

Alfena's silver eyes narrowed as she stepped closer. Her fingers radiated with a sheen of silver with psychic magic.

"It's not just unstable. There's… dissonance."

She extended her hand, the glow of her magic brushing against the edges of Faust's aura. Her brow furrowed, and her hand hovered as if she was uncertain whether to probe further or withdraw.

Faust flinched, the energy in his palm flickering dangerously. Alfena pulled back slightly, her expression indiscernible.

"It feels like two melodies trying to play over one another. One is Valksha… but the other…?"

She didn't finish the sentence, her eyes searching Faust with quiet intensity.

"A result of Azazelf's experiments, no doubt," Crane suggested. "His meddling has likely left scars we can't see."

Kaspar's gaze flicked to Alfena. "Can you pinpoint it?"

"No," Alfena said softly, her tone laced with frustration. "Whatever it is, it's buried deep. Too deep to isolate without risking harm."

Faust exhaled harshly, his eyes dropping to the weak glow of his magic.

"I told you," he muttered. "Azazelf… *did* things. I don't know what, but it changed me."

"Changed you how?" Margrith demanded.

Faust hesitated again, his fists clenching at his sides.

"I don't know," he admitted, his voice raw. "I can't explain it. It's like… there's something inside me that doesn't belong."

Ophelia's eyes darted to Theodin, and the Dyad shifted with her unease. She stepped forward, her tone softer than the others'.

"But you still feel like you," she said gently. "Right?"

Faust's eyes met hers, a look of vulnerability crossing his face.

"Most of the time," he affirmed. "But when it slips…" He trailed off, his fists tightening.

Kaspar's expression remained unreadable as he exchanged a glance with Alfena.

"We'll need more time to evaluate," he said finally. "For now, Faust remains under observation."

"And what of his training?" Crane asked, his tone edged with curiosity.

"It continues," Kaspar replied firmly. "But under strict conditions. Let me make one thing clear—this is not about recruiting Faust into the Kyriegard. His training is to ensure he can wield his magic safely, both for himself and those around him. Nothing more."

Margrith's scowl deepened. "This is a mistake. We're inviting disaster."

"Or an opportunity," Alfena countered. "If he's telling the truth, then Faust may be the key to understanding Azazelf's methods—and countering them."

Kaspar turned his piercing stare back to Faust. "We'll see where this leads. But make no mistake—your path here is fragile. One misstep, and it will break."

Faust nodded, his expression grim but resolute. "Understood."

The Council dispersed shortly after, their discussions trailing off into murmurs. As the others departed through the cottage door, Alfena remained momentarily, her gaze fixed on Faust. She stepped closer, her voice low.

"Magic remembers, Faust. Sometimes it remembers more than we want it to."

Faust's eyes dropped to his hands. Once more, he could feel the former scars.

"It already does," he murmured, tinged with a rawness that festered in the air.

She nodded once before leaving, her silver eyes becoming thoughtful as they drifted to Ophelia and Theodin. The two apprentices dwelled near the edge of the chamber, whispering to one another, their Dyad spinning with shared tension.

As the room emptied, Faust's shoulders sagged slightly, his eyes dropping to his hands. The fractured glow of his magic lingered weakly on his skin, a reminder of everything he'd lost—and everything he had yet to prove.

Year 844 of the Second Age, Eighth Month, Twenty-Third Day

Faust sat on the edge of his wooden bench, his head bowed and his fingers loosely clasped as if he'd been lost in thought for hours.

It had been a week now since the Kyriegard had found him. Even though he was no longer Azazelf's captive, he still felt like a prisoner here. Stuck in this chamber with only a cot and a bench.

He paused. This was far better than the conditions he had been in before. At least they gave him something to sleep on—before, it was cold stone, sometimes the ground, sometimes in mud…in chains…

Faust shuddered. His fingers clenched together tightly.

No. He can't go back.

He took a deep breath.

He unclasped his hands and looked at his palms. Despite his trembling hands, he smiled lightly to himself.

The scars were gone. Though he was still haunted by them and felt like they were still there, he found comfort in knowing she had healed them.

She had healed *him*. Maybe she could heal the rest of him, too.

The soft creak of the door broke the silence. He didn't look up immediately, but when Ophelia stepped into the room, her fiery energy brushed against his awareness like a ripple on still water.

He perked up.

"You again," Faust said, his eyes lifting briefly to meet hers before flicking away. "What do I owe the honor?"

Ophelia closed the door behind her, leaning against the frame.

"Figured you could use a change of scenery," she said, light but sincere.

Faust huffed a light, humorless laugh. "And here I thought confinement was part of the Kyriegard charm."

"Only when necessary," she countered, stepping closer. "But you've been here long enough." She motioned for him to follow. "Come on."

Faust's brow furrowed as he straightened slightly, his expression wary. "And go where, exactly? The Council doesn't seem too keen on giving me free rein."

"They're not," Ophelia admitted. "But I'm not here as part of the Council. Just… as myself."

He studied her for a long moment, searching for the catch in her words.

"Why?" he asked finally, cautious but tinged with genuine curiosity.

"Because I've been where you are," she said delicately. "Not here in Avasylon, exactly, or in this kind of situation, but… lost. Wondering if I could trust myself, let alone anyone else."

Faust's expression flickered, something unspoken passing behind his eyes.

"And did it help?" he asked, quieter now. "Letting someone in?"

Ophelia offered a faint smile. "I guess you'll have to find out for yourself."

She stepped aside, gesturing toward the door. "Come on. The courtyard's empty. It'll be peaceful there."

Faust appeared to contemplate.

Was this a test? How is she not afraid or suspicious of him? She didn't seem wary of being alone with him…she had done it so many times now—perhaps because she was powerful enough to overwhelm him from what he'd seen.

He hesitated, his gaze lowering to the glowing runes on the floor. "I'm not sure your Council would agree with this."

"Good thing I'm not asking them," she replied. "Now, are you coming or not?"

He stared for quite some time, debating with himself.

Finally, Faust stood, his movements slow and deliberate.

"Lead the way," he said, his voice laced with a mix of resignation and curiosity.

Ophelia led him through the underground corridors of Avasylon, her pace steady but unhurried. The silence between them wasn't heavy, but it carried an air of unspoken understanding.

When they reached the courtyard, the golden light of the setting summer sun bathed the space, casting soft shadows across the fields. A gentle breeze caressed them with warmth and the scent of greenery from the forest and the open acres of grass.

Faust hung near the edge of the open area, his eyes drifting to the trees beyond.

"It's… quieter than I expected."

"It's Avasylon," Ophelia said, settling onto a low stone wall. "Quiet is kind of the point."

He glanced at her, his eyes narrowing slightly. "Why are you doing this?"

"Because you're not going to figure out your magic cooped up in that chamber," she said. "And because I think you deserve a chance."

"You...you think so?"

"Of course."

"How do I deserve a chance?"

"You didn't do anything wrong," Ophelia explained. "You were in the wrong place at the wrong time..." Her eyes dropped. "And...I know how that is too."

A long silence grew between them.

The soft summer wind tussled a few locks of her raven hair across her saddened face.

Faust's expression mellowed. He found himself staring, not at her sadness—but at the way the light caught her face. She was... striking. Not in the way he'd imagined Valksha to be, but in the way grief and resolve could coexist in someone who still chose to be kind. Maybe it was the way she moved without hesitation or the way the light caught the softness in her eyes. Beautiful wasn't the word he would've chosen. Not exactly. But there was something about her presence—unshaken, and real—that stilled him.

"Unfortunate things happen to good people," she continued solemnly, but then she lifted her eyes and her emerald irises glimmered with hope. "But then there are other good people out there in the world to help them. Like Lady Vivian did for me. And Kaspar and Theodin."

Faust studied her, his expression contemplative. "You talk about them like they're your family."

Ophelia smiled faintly, her gaze drifting to the horizon. "In some ways, they are. The Kyriegard became my sanctuary first, then my home."

He tilted his head in curiosity. "But you're... different. You don't act like the others."

She quirked a brow at him. "Different how?"

He hesitated, searching for the right words. "You're... softer. Not in a weak way, but... you don't carry the same weight as the others. Like Kaspar or Theodin. They're... heavier."

Ophelia laughed, shaking her head. "Trust me, I've had my fair share of weight. But you're not wrong—I didn't grow up like the others. Most Kyriegard are trained from childhood, molded into warriors and scholars. I came to them later, and... I suppose I kept some of my edges."

"Edges?" Faust repeated, his brow furrowing.

She nodded thoughtfully. "The parts of me that don't fit neatly into the Kyriegard mold. My Valksha magic, for one. My tendency to… see people as people, not just roles or risks." She glanced at him. "I think that's why I'm here with you now."

Faust's eyes dropped to his hands, his fingers flexing absently. A strange tug-of-war brewed within him—the pull of Ophelia's belief and the weight of his own doubts. She spoke with such certainty, as though she could already see something in him that he couldn't.

But wasn't that the trap? Believing in something only to have it crumble under the weight of reality?

He exhaled sharply, forcing himself to meet her eyes. There was something disarming about the way she looked at him—like she wasn't afraid of what she might find. It made him want to trust her. And yet, the fractured pieces of his magic, of himself, whispered caution. Trust was a luxury he couldn't afford.

And here she was. Fearless. Free. Basking in the coolness of the season's evening breath mixed with the receding warmth of the sunset. He remembered the fear he lived with in Azazelf's captivity and the fear his family taught him to keep his power contained. Could he be like her someday, so unafraid? Daring despite the risk?

Finally, he spoke. "And that doesn't make you… vulnerable? Trusting people that way?"

"Maybe," she said. "But I'd rather risk vulnerability than lose what makes me who I am. That's something Lady Vivian taught me."

"Lady Vivian," Faust murmured.

The name was weighted with respect—the legendary Valksha who defied the massacre and nearly abolished the Malblight plague.

"You've mentioned her before. She was… your mentor?"

"She was everything," Ophelia said softly, her voice thick with emotion. "She saved me when I didn't think I could be saved. Gave me a reason to keep going, to believe in something bigger than myself."

A long silence followed as Faust considered her words.

"And now you're here, trying to do the same for me." His eyes remained fixed on the ground. "You talk like someone who's *had* to believe in second chances."

Ophelia's smile grew slightly, her eyes distant.

"You don't make it through what I've been through without learning to hope—for yourself and for others."

Looking up at her, an unspoken thought seemed to gleam in his eyes. "And you think I'm worth hoping for?"

She looked at him, the intensity of her gaze tempered by warmth. "I think you're worth figuring out."

Faust huffed softly, his lips twitching into a crooked smile of his own. "You're strange, Ophelia. I'm not sure I understand you."

"Good," she replied lightly, a hint of teasing in her tone. "If you understood me already, this would be boring."

The Dyad stirred in her awareness, a subtle echo of Theodin's energy filtering through. She could sense his quiet vigilance, his presence a constant reminder of the stakes.

She knew Theodin could feel what she was doing, perhaps even hear some of her thoughts. She could even feel his eyes from a distance watching them, but she didn't turn as to not alarm Faust.

But Faust was a Valksha, and he could feel her energy shift with the thrum of the Dyad. He couldn't necessarily feel her emotions, as he was not a Valksha of Veladriel like her, but he still had the ability to detect a change.

He turned and examined her as his face creased with question.

"What was that?" he asked.

Ophelia shook her head dismissively and waved a hand in the direction of the cottage.

"My partner," she said.

Don't dismiss me, Valksha.

Ophelia turned a side look to one of the second floor windows and dramatically rolled her eyes.

Oh, you'll pay for that later…'dear Ophie.'

Theodin's voice became nasally and peppered with her Northern Reganian accent in mockery at that last phrase.

Faust leaned forward a bit, as if asking for her to speak further. "…Theodin, right?"

Ophelia involuntarily snorted a laugh and slapped a hand over her mouth.

"Sorry, I'm so sorry—"

She turned fully toward the window.

"He's being a pain."

She crinkled her nose, touched her thumb between her nostrils, and then flicked that same thumb in Theodin's direction.

You sound so foolish speaking so northernly, dear Theo.

You look foolish looking like you're looking at nothing.

Faust looked between her and the window she obscenely gestured to. He raised an eyebrow and awkwardly smiled, but watched her with a small hint of admiration of her mannerisms.

"He, um...appears to still somehow make you laugh, despite being...a pain?"

Ophelia turned back to him with a grin. "Yes, I know. It's an odd... relationship, I suppose."

"I've only heard stories of what it's like," Faust said. "What the Kyriegard partner bond is like—this Arcane Dyad. Pairs of elite warriors who think, move, and act like one."

Ophelia nodded.

"Indeed," she chirped. "Quite literally. Sometimes he's in my head, sometimes I'm in his. We know where the other is at all times. Though you can't see him, he's there. Watching."

She pointed to the blackened window.

Faust also nodded his head slowly. His expression became thoughtful and introverted, somewhat saddened.

"It must be... something nice, having someone who knows you like that. Always there. I've never had that—someone to watch my back."

Ophelia's cheeriness faded quickly into a solemn demeanor. She immediately felt the depth of his longing, maybe even a subtle envy, of witnessing her and Theodin. A pang of guilt came over her.

After a moment, she offered a hand to him.

"I'll have your back while you're here," she said gently. "And even when you're done here. After you've mastered your magic. Who knows—maybe you could be like Lady Vivian and be another wandering Valksha nomad doing good things out in Moirand. And I'll be happy to aid you on your adventures."

He looked at her hand, his lips pressing into a thin line. "You make it sound so easy," he murmured. "But... what if I can't get there?"

"It won't always be easy," she said, her voice firm but kind. The runes in her open hand shimmered a green light from her palm and up her forearm. "But I believe in second chances—and I believe in you."

Faust studied her hand, then looked up to meet her eyes. "You've mentioned her quite a bit...and talk about her like she was more than just a mentor. Like she was... hope."

"She was," Ophelia whispered. "And she still is, even from the Ether where she is now. And I strive to carry on her legacy and bring hope back to Moirand wherever I can."

A fond smile spread across her face. "She believed in second chances, even when no one else did. And if I can carry even a fraction of that into the world, then I know I'm honoring her."

He stared at her hand for a moment longer, the light from her runes reflected in his eyes. His chest tightened, the fractured pieces of himself warring against the fragile belief she offered. Finally, with a breath he didn't realize he was holding, he let his fingers meet hers. The touch was brief, hesitant, but enough to bridge the gap between them.

"Maybe… maybe I'll figure it out."

The moment their hands met, a current of energy rippled through Ophelia's body, sharp yet warm, like the first rays of sunlight breaking through a storm. His magic felt fragmented—jagged and uneven, like glass shards struggling to form a whole. But beneath the chaos, she sensed a pulse of something pure, something untouched by Azazelf's corruption. It was raw and desperate, searching for balance. Her runes responded instinctively, flaring brighter as her own energy reached out, steadying his, offering it an anchor.

It wasn't like the bond she shared with Theodin. This was different—untamed, unfiltered, and unpredictable. But it wasn't malicious. It felt like a cry for help buried beneath layers of pain. Ophelia's breath caught as she realized just how much of Faust's strength lay in his ability to persist despite that chaos.

The touch sent a jolt through Faust, his magic sparking beneath his skin in response before recoiling as if unsure of what to make of her energy. Her light was intense, unwavering, and it pressed against the fissures in his own power like a balm against a wound. It wasn't forceful or overpowering—it simply existed, patient and inviting, waiting for him to decide whether to accept it.

For a fleeting moment, he felt something he hadn't in years: stability. Her energy didn't fight his. It didn't reject him. It simply… was. The realization hit him like a whisper against his thoughts: she didn't fear him. She didn't see him as broken. And for that single, fleeting second, he felt whole.

As he released her hand, he looked down at his own. The warmth of her magic lingered in his skin, a phantom sensation that refused to fade. Maybe he wasn't whole—but for the first time, he wondered if he could be.

But as the thought took root, a shadow crept into the edges of his mind. The memory wasn't clear, more like the echo of a voice laced with venom:

You'll never be free.

His eyes glinted, the pulse of his magic wavering. He clenched his fists, forcing the thought away, but the unease it left behind lingered like the distant rumble of a storm.

"You will figure it out."

Once more, Ophelia's soothing voice cut through the stinging chaos of his mind and brought him back. He refocused his eyes and met hers, who looked up at him with gentle reassurance. She smiled in response to this. "We will help you figure it out, too."

Chapter 24

The Burden

Year 844 of the Second Age, Eighth Month, Twenty-Fifth Day

The Council chamber in Halvalla was a place of stone and silence. The air, thick with the scent of parchment and cold iron, bore the weight of centuries of deliberations—some that had shaped the Order and others that had fractured it. The dim glow of enchanted torches lined the high, vaulted walls, casting elongated shadows across the five Kyriegard Councillors seated at the long, circular table.

At its head sat Nimrod Kaspar, Head of the Order. His weathered hands rested on the polished surface before him, fingers lightly interlocked, his expression unreadable. To his right, Azariah Crane leaned slightly forward, elbows on the table, fingers steepled in thought. Across from him, Alfena Marobe sat upright, her elven features composed, yet her silver eyes sharp with intrigue. Sigvard Jackard, ever the pragmatist, had his arms crossed over his broad chest, his Dwarven features furrowed in contemplation. And finally, Margrith Gravehardt, whose presence alone seemed to tighten the atmosphere, sat rigid, her sharp gaze already fixed on Kaspar, waiting.

"We convene today to assess the progress of Ophelia, one year into her apprenticeship with the Order," Kaspar began. "Additionally, we must address the concerns raised regarding Theodin during the recent wardstone mission."

A pause followed, heavy with the expectation of dissent.

Kaspar's eyes flicked toward Sigvard. The Dwarf exhaled, adjusting his posture before speaking.

"The girl has progressed well," Sigvard replied, voice as solid as the stone beneath them. "Her grasp of combat and tactical knowledge has grown in accordance with our expectations. However, her use of magic—particularly its erratic nature—remains a concern."

A few nods of acknowledgment passed through the table.

Alfena lifted a brow. "You mean her ability to use magic without blood?"

Sigvard nodded. "Precisely. We have long understood that for Valksha, blood magic requires intent, precision. Yet, there have been incidents where her abilities have manifested without her drawing blood at all. If we cannot fully understand *how* it occurs, we cannot predict *when* it will occur."

"She and I have been working on it," Alfena began. "We understand that her emotions are a factor and have been studying patterns from her memories."

Margrith scoffed.

"You really do act as though this is a matter of study," she said, edged with impatience. "This is a matter of control. If we cannot predict it, then we cannot trust it. We teach to suppress emotions, not harness them as fuel for conducting spells. Nimrod saw what happened at the wardstone." Her stern eyes flickered to Kaspar. "You felt it. That was not the power of a disciplined Kyriegard—that was something else. Something wild."

Alfena remained composed. "All the more reason to study it."

Margrith turned toward her, eyes narrowing. "Think of the Valksha we've studied in our records. The ones who lost control of themselves. We do not study threats. We eliminate them before they become one."

Kaspar's voice cut through the rising tension.

"Ophelia has shown significant progress in her training. Her magic is powerful, yes, but power is only dangerous if left unchecked. The Kyriegard is not in the habit of fearing strength—we are in the habit of honing it."

Margrith's lips pressed into a thin line, but she said nothing.

Kaspar turned back to Sigvard. "What do you propose?"

The Dwarf exhaled. "Observation. Testing, if necessary. This is what we've always done in the event that we are unsure of what we are dealing with when it comes to magic. It must be treated like a science, as we have done with the study of Sage magic and Alchemy. We must understand the nature of this ability before we act prematurely."

Alfena nodded slightly, clearly in agreement.

Margrith's expression darkened.

"Testing." Her voice dripped with skepticism. "And if the tests prove it cannot be controlled?"

Kaspar met her gaze.

"Then we do what we must. But not before."

Crane, who had remained mostly silent, finally spoke.

"The girl is one matter. The boy is another."

The attention in the room shifted.

Sigvard sat forward. "Theodin is not merely a student displaying promising strength. He is an anomaly as much as his partner is."

Crane scoffed and smirked playfully. "Perhaps Arborelys knew this and decided to move forward with permanently binding them in a Dyad. Remember, Siggy, how many Dyad tests Theodin went through—clearly, none of them were strong enough to handle our golden boy until this little spitfire Valksha girl, only two-thirds his size, came along."

"More like a little over three-quarters," Kaspar muttered.

Crane sneered at him. "Make her out to be smaller than she actually is, eh?"

"Small but deadly," Sigvard grunted.

"What a dangerous thing this is," Margrith interjected, grumbling between her teeth. "And we have yet to properly address them after the wardstone mission."

"Then we evaluate them now," Alfena urged. "Before anything else occurs. First was Lady Vivian's passing—we allowed the poor girl to grieve—and then another Valksha comes out of nowhere. It's no wonder we've been unable to discuss this since the wardstone mission—and that was two months ago."

"Agreed. Let's settle this," Sigvard said, his voice even. "Two months ago, we witnessed something unprecedented. The Dyad formed of its own accord. That has never happened in the history of the Order."

"And now, we have to decide what to do with it," Crane added, tapping his cane. "We know what the Arcane Dyad should be. But we have no precedent for what *this* is."

"They were supposed to have done their Kyriegard Trials first before the formation of the Dyad," Sigvard added. "We cannot treat them like the others of their age class. Their peers have only either done the testing phases or the provisional bond—the wardstone mission, though monitored, has proven that they are nowhere near ready for where any normal, fully-formed Dyad should be."

"And the mission has proven that Theodin's strength is *still* a concern," Margrith pressed, shooting a piercing glance to Kaspar.

Kaspar's jaw tensed slightly. "Theodin's strength is a direct result of his training—"

"His training does not explain what happened at the wardstone," Sigvard interrupted, not unkindly. "No warrior, no matter how disciplined, should have been able to do what he did. No one should be able to break through the flesh of a Cadaven with their bare hands."

As his deep voice echoed in the cavernous space of the Council hall, a long pause followed.

Margrith's voice was quieter this time but no less intense.

"We are all acting as though this has just begun."

A beat.

"But it has not. We have ignored it for years."

Her eyes swept across the table.

"His training weapons shattered when he was a child. His instructors refused to spar with him. I read the reports—he took blows that should have broken him, and yet he never flinched. You all let Kaspar train him privately, and for years, we remained blind to what he is. Now that his strength has surfaced again, we should no longer pretend that this is simply an issue of training."

Alfena tapped a single finger against the table, her eyes fixed on nothing in particular.

"It is true," she murmured, more thoughtful than alarmed. "There has never been a recorded case of a Kyriegard demonstrating strength to this level."

Crane leaned back in his chair, gaze shifting toward Kaspar, who had remained rigidly composed throughout the discussion.

Kaspar exhaled sharply. "You believe he is losing control. I believe he is learning how to wield what was already there."

Margrith turned to him. "You believe? Or do you simply hope?"

Kaspar didn't answer. The silence that followed Margrith's words was heavy, yet not unbroken. Only the sound of flickering torchlight could be heard at that moment.

Then, Alfena spoke.

"There is another possibility."

All eyes turned to her as she reached forward, tapping a single finger against the polished wood of the table.

"Theodin's strength has always existed. That much is undeniable. But let us not ignore the timing of its emergence. This... escalation of his abilities has only been observed since his Dyad with Ophelia was formed."

Kaspar's brow furrowed slightly, but he did not interrupt.

"We have long understood that an Arcane Dyad strengthens both partners," Alfena continued. "Their energies become linked, their instincts sharpened, their magic—if both wield magic—entwined. If Ophelia's abilities remain unrefined and unchecked, is it not possible that the Dyad is pulling at Theodin as well?"

An exchange of glances across the table passed between the Council members.

"An interesting theory," Sigvard admitted. "But speculation alone is not enough."

"It is more than speculation," Alfena countered smoothly. "The report of that mission states that Theodin's burst of strength came at a moment of heightened emotion—specifically, in the act of defending Ophelia. His reaction was immediate, instinctive, and far beyond what even his previous records suggest. That cannot be a coincidence."

"You assume her magic is the cause," Margrith said coolly. "And not merely the catalyst that revealed what was already there."

"I assume nothing," Alfena replied. "I am merely suggesting that we shift our focus. Instead of asking what Theodin is becoming, we must ask what the Dyad is drawing out of him."

"And what do you propose, then?" Sigvard asked.

"We observe them both," Alfena said simply. "Separate the study of their abilities from their combat training. If this is truly a matter of the Dyad, then we must see it for what it is—not an individual anomaly, but a partnership with unprecedented power."

"And if it is the Dyad?" Margrith pressed. "If it continues to grow stronger?"

Kaspar, who had been listening intently, straightened in his seat. "Then we train them. The same way we have always trained our own. We continue to train them in preparation for the Dyad as if they are not in the Dyad, so they can still learn what they can and adjust. The Kyriegard does not exist to fear power—we exist to master it. If the Dyad has created an imbalance, then we correct that imbalance. We guide them. We teach them discipline."

Margrith's stare was unwavering. "And if we are too late?"

A beat of silence.

"Then we do what we must."

The words were calm, but final.

Another silence passed before Crane finally spoke again, his tone carefully neutral.

"Very well. Let it be recorded that Ophelia and Theodin will continue their training, under observation. Their Dyad bond will be studied further, and we will reconvene should any further… anomalies arise."

Margrith remained still for a long moment before finally pushing back from the table and standing.

"We will regret this," she said quietly. "Mark my words."

Without another word, she turned and strode from the chamber, her heavy footfalls echoing in the vast room.

Sigvard exhaled and left after her, rolling his shoulders as if releasing unseen tension. Alfena, deep in thought, said nothing as she rose. Crane lingered only briefly before following them out, offering Kaspar a long, unreadable look before he disappeared through the doors, his cane tapping away at the floor.

Kaspar remained seated, staring at the torchlight on the stone walls.

When he could sense he was alone, he bowed his head and closed his eyes.

He wasn't sure how much longer he could carry this burden.

First the boy. Then the girl.

Both of them were children rescued by a figure of myth. A legend. A mystery.

As much of a mystery as this legendary woman was, so was her agenda.

Yet, the elder Kyriegard trusted her. She had never let him down.

He could not let her down.

"Vivian," he whispered, his quiet breath echoing into the cavernous chamber. "I don't quite know what your plan is… but I hope it all falls into place. Or at least becomes apparent to us soon."

Then, finally, he stood. He looked up—past the ceiling, into the vastness of the Ether—and then turned to exit the Council hall.

Chapter 25

The Unprecedented

Year 844 of the Second Age, Ninth Month, First Day

The training grounds of Halvalla were cast in the golden glow of the morning sun, its light filtering through the towering stone walls that enclosed the vast sparring space. Though enchanted barriers ensured that combat practice remained contained, the open-air design let the cool autumn breeze weave through the field, carrying with it the distant clang of steel on steel from other initiates at their morning drills.

This, however, was no ordinary training session.

A quiet but notable group had gathered along the stone perimeter—members of the Kyriegard Council stood in observation, along with several seasoned officers and apprentices who were about to undergo their Kyriegard Trials and finalize their Dyads.

At the center of it all stood Alfena, leading the session with her usual air of command. Kaspar watched nearby, arms folded, unreadable. Sigvard stood beside him, ever the pragmatist, though his expression held something else—something like anticipation. Faust stood silently at Kaspar's other side. Margrith remained stone-faced, her sharp gaze flicking toward the two youngest Kyriegard in attendance: Ophelia and Theodin.

They were the only apprentices in a complete Dyad. And this was the first time they were to be evaluated as an Arcane Dyad.

For the past year, Ophelia had trained under the watchful eyes of Kaspar and the other instructors, but today was different.

Today, she and Theodin were not being tested as individuals.

They were being measured as one.

Alfena's voice carried across the field, sharp and clear.

"Before we begin, it is important to understand what an Arcane Dyad is—and what it is not." She paced slowly, her gaze sweeping across the assembled warriors. "A Dyad is not something that simply happens. It is not instinct. It is not fate. It is a contract, formed through deliberation, training, and ritual."

Ophelia and Theodin exchanged glances. Their Dyad had simply *happened*. Kaspar theorized it could've been their Faytes. Everything felt like instinct to them.

Their Dyad defied everything the Kyriegard had known.

Alfena stopped and turned to face the gathered initiates and officers.

"In a proper Dyad, compatibility must be confirmed before the bond is ever forged. The pair undergoes trials to assess their synergy, their strengths, and their weaknesses. Once selected, they are brought before the Council, where the binding ritual is performed through Arborelys. This is not a light decision. Once completed, the Dyad is lifelong. It cannot be undone except through extreme magical intervention—and even then, there are consequences."

She let that settle before continuing.

"The bond itself is a fusion of will and discipline. It does not grant insight into thoughts, but it does allow partners to sense each other's emotions—though only strong ones are clearly transmitted. Pain is shared, but not in equal measure. A wound suffered by one will create an echo in the other, but it will never fully transfer. If one falls into distress, the other will feel the pull, but it will not cripple them."

Ophelia's eyes widened slightly. She and Theodin were able to have full blown telepathic conversations and sense the slightest emotions at random and inconvenient times.

Theodin's eyes met hers once more, almost with an accusatory expression. His voice echoed in her head.

Must be the Valksha magic.

Ophelia swallowed awkwardly. Her eyes snapped back forward, but then she noticed and caught Kaspar's observant gaze.

He gave a slight nod of his head. Like he knew.

Alfena crossed her arms, her expression unwavering.

"Distance affects the Dyad, but it does not sever it. A traditional bond may weaken over great distances, but it does not cause physical deterioration. Separation is unpleasant, even uncomfortable, but it is not debilitating. And under no circumstances can a Dyad be forcibly suppressed. It remains constant, always present, though skilled pairs can learn to mute its presence when necessary."

A brief pause.

"Beyond connection, a Dyad enhances its members in battle. Under controlled circumstances, partners may channel each other's magic. They may use joint techniques where one stabilizes while the other casts. However, the bond does not make one stronger than they already are—it refines what is there, heightens endurance, and increases stamina, but it does not create power where none exists."

Alfena's gaze sharpened as she took a step forward. "And finally—the matter of severance. To break a Dyad is a dangerous thing. It requires a Council-led ritual, and even when successful, it does not leave the bonded unharmed. Those who have undergone severance have suffered magical damage, lost their ability to properly wield their gifts, and in some cases, lost their sanity entirely."

She turned, letting her eyes settle on Theodin and Ophelia.

"A Dyad is built upon balance. It is a shared connection—equal in every way. Each partner contributes to the whole. That is how it is meant to be."

A beat passed.

"And that is why we are here today. To ensure that balance exists."

She resumed pacing, her tone shifting back to its commanding cadence.

"This evaluation is not a competition," she said, pacing before them. "Nor is it a test of skill alone. This is a demonstration of unity. A Dyad is meant to function as a single force—one mind, one will, one purpose." She paused, her silver eyes scanning the gathered warriors. "You will watch. You will learn. And you will understand the difference between two warriors fighting *alongside* each other… and two warriors fighting *as* each other."

She turned, her gaze settling on a familiar figure standing off to the side. "Azariah."

A murmur passed through the gathered initiates and apprentices. Even after all these years, Azariah Crane was a name that carried weight in the Order.

Like Nimrod Kaspar. Like Garrett. The three of them hailed from the same group of initiates and rose in the ranks of the Order.

Despite his limp, Crane stepped forward with his usual effortless confidence, his cane tapping against the stone as he moved. The brace Sigvard had crafted for him was secured around his legs, glinting faintly with embedded runes that pulsed with magic. When he positioned himself, he stood straight and twisted the handle of his cane —from the cane, which served as a sheath, was drawn a rapier.

Before Alfena could speak again, Sigvard crossed his arms and smirked.

"One of my finest creations," he said proudly. "Would've made Garrett proud."

A silence fell at the mention of the name.

Kaspar, standing beside him, nodded once in solidarity.

"It would have."

Another beat passed before Alfena exhaled softly.

"Let's begin."

Alfena gave a subtle gesture to the far side of the training grounds, where three combat dummies, carved from reinforced wood and enchanted with the reflexes of seasoned warriors, stirred to life. Their joints creaked as they lifted their training weapons, eyes glowing with the eerie silver light of embedded runes. Unlike the standard dummies used for basic drills, these were designed to fight with precision, speed, and relentless aggression—a true match for the level of combat expected from a veteran Dyad.

Kaspar's gaze flicked to Crane. "Ready?"

Crane rolled his shoulders, giving a lopsided grin. "Always."

The moment Alfena raised her hand and dropped it, the dummies lunged. The first dummy struck low, aiming for Crane's legs—an obvious attempt to exploit his weakness.

And yet, he was already moving before the strike landed.

The leg brace activated in a seamless pulse of Sage magic, shifting his weight just enough for him to sidestep at the last second, his rapier swinging in a sharp arc to parry. He barely seemed to exert any effort, yet his movement was unnaturally smooth, the brace guiding his body just enough to compensate for his injuries.

The second dummy lunged for Alfena, its sword flashing in the sunlight—only to meet nothing but air.

Alfena had already pivoted behind Crane, using the opening he had created with surgical precision. Their timing was flawless. As they moved, the runes carved into their forearms pulsed with a luminescent, silvery glow, the Dyad bond responding to their synchronicity. She lashed out with a fluid strike of her curved sword, severing the dummy's weapon arm at the joint.

The moment Crane moved, Alfena moved. The moment Alfena struck, Crane had already shifted for the next attack.

Their runes pulsed in perfect rhythm.

To an outsider, it might have looked like Crane wasn't doing much at all. To those who understood Dyad combat, it was a masterclass in efficiency.

"Beautiful," Sigvard chuckled under his breath, arms crossed over his chest as he observed his creation at work.

"Didn't think you cared much for aesthetics, Siggy," Crane called over his shoulder between parries.

"I don't," Sigvard shot back, a small smirk tugging at his lips. "I meant in function. It works just as I intended. No wasted movement. No unnecessary exertion."

The last remaining dummy lunged for Crane's exposed flank. A moment of calculated vulnerability.

The runes on Crane's forearm flared brighter—Alfena had already sensed the movement through the bond.

The brace activated, and Crane pivoted—not because he saw the attack coming, but because Alfena did.

In the same heartbeat, her blade sliced cleanly across the dummy's core before it could land a strike.

The enchanted wood splintered to pieces upon impact.

A final pulse of light passed between their runes before fading back to a dormant glow.

Silence followed.

"A perfect demonstration of discipline," Margrith remarked, her arms crossed as she watched the remains of the dummies roll back together.

Her tone was unreadable, but there was a cold finality in her words. Her gaze flicked to Ophelia and Theodin—her meaning was clear.

Ophelia had been watching, but the moment Margrith looked at her, she appeared distracted. Her gaze drifted past the shattered remains of the enchanted dummies, beyond the gathered officers and senior Kyriegard.

It felt… *different* here.

At Avasylon, she was surrounded by initiates her own age or younger—apprentices still growing into their training, still learning.

Even when she and Theodin had been called to Halvalla before, it had been for lectures, lessons, and controlled environments.

This was different.

These warriors—some Predant, some Elvish, some Fay—were seasoned, hardened by battle and years of service. They didn't know her. They didn't know Theodin.

And now they were about to watch them.

Ophie.

Theodin's voice brushed through her mind like a grounding wave.

Ophelia blinked, her thoughts snapping back to reality. Her eyes flicked up to meet his sheepishly.

The scattered remnants of the enchanted dummies still gathered themselves across the training grounds, the last echoes of Alfena and Crane's demonstration lingering in the air. Their Dyad runes had faded to a dormant glow, but the memory of their precision remained sharp in Ophelia's mind.

Now, it was her and Theodin's turn.

She stepped forward with him, feeling the weight of every gaze upon them.

She could feel her heart beating in her ears as she and Theodin took their positions across from the reassembled training dummies.

This was nothing like training at Avasylon.

There, they were just apprentices, dwelling among initiates of their own age. But here, standing before the Kyriegard Council, other apprentices about to forego the final Kyriegard trials, and the seasoned officers of Halvalla, they were something else.

They were being judged.

If Alfena and Crane were the exemplary demonstration, Ophelia and Theodin were expected to be the failed one.

Margrith's expression was harsh, and Ophelia could feel the expectation behind it. Sigvard watched with something that might have been curiosity. Crane, his braces now deactivated, had sheathed his rapier and now leaned on his cane with a knowing smirk tugging at his lips. Kaspar was silent, unreadable. Faust stood just beyond them, quiet as ever.

Ophelia swallowed and exhaled slowly. Theodin drew his sword and she readied her chained blade.

Alfena raised her hand. "Begin."

The moment the enchanted dummies activated, Ophelia and Theodin moved.

The first dummy lunged.

Theodin stepped forward, blade raised to intercept—too slow. Ophelia had already moved, slipping past him in an attempt to strike first. Their bodies collided in the motion, throwing off their rhythm before either could land a proper hit.

Ophelia cursed under her breath and pivoted, adjusting her stance. Theodin had stopped himself mid-swing to avoid striking her.

The pause cost them, but they were lucky to narrowly avoid being struck by their opponent.

A second dummy lunged from the left. Ophelia spun toward it, swinging her blade. Theodin, anticipating the movement, also turned —again, they moved at the same time, crossing into each other's space.

Her strike landed too soon—it stuck into the ground.

His strike was delayed—it missed.

Theodin never misses, Ophelia thought.

What in the Nether was happening?

The energy between them pulsed unevenly, surging and retracting, the bond flickering like a flame caught in the wind.

Another attack came. This time, Ophelia dodged left while Theodin stepped right—straight into each other's path.

Off-balance. Uncoordinated. Nothing like a true Dyad.

A third dummy advanced. Its wooden sword slashed high toward Ophelia's ribs. She barely saw it coming.

Theodin did.

He moved before she did, faster than he should have. His hand shot out, gripping her forearm and yanking her back, just as the wooden blade sliced through the air where she had been standing. She let out a yelp of surprise.

The pull was too strong. She nearly lost her footing and stumbled.

The energy between them wavered again—erratic and unstable.

The crowd of Kyriegard watching appeared to grimace and cringe at the sight of them.

Ophelia gritted her teeth. Theodin's grip was firm, grounding, but it shouldn't have been necessary. She shouldn't have needed to be saved like that.

Margrith exhaled sharply from the sidelines.

The dummies reconfigured, pressing forward. They weren't meant to kill, but they had been enchanted to punish mistakes. And Ophelia and Theodin had made too many already.

She braced herself, preparing for another strike.

Another failure.

Her eyes winced shut.

Kaspar's voice suddenly echoed in her head.

Trust each other. Prove them wrong.

Ophelia's eyes flew open. Something in Theodin shifted. He must have heard it too.

His stance changed. The hesitation that had held him back before was gone. The runes in their arms flickered to life.

The dummies lunged. All three of them at once.

But time slowed.

Ophelia felt it before she saw it—the Dyad bond vibrating in sync between them.

Not flickering like a dying candle, but flowing.

She didn't need to think anymore.

She moved. Theodin moved.

No hesitation. No interference.

She struck the first one this time on the left with a whip of her wrist. Theodin stepped with her to swing at the one on the right. His blade caught the dummy mid-lunge, knocking it off course.

The third dummy angled toward Ophelia, aiming low. Ophelia tensed, sensing the attack before it came. Theodin felt it too. He shifted —not forward this time, but behind her. She pivoted instinctively to dodge as he intercepted with his blade. She spun around, sidestepped around Theodin, and whipped the chained blade back at the dummy's head. The blade grazed the side of its throat and retracted as she snapped her wrist.

Their energy synced. It wasn't perfect, not yet, but it was enough.

Enough for their bond to flare. Now, their runes glimmered brightly.

The dummies reeled back. So did the young pair.

Ophelia's breath came fast, her heart pounding. For the first time, it didn't feel like she was fighting alone.

It felt like Theodin was fighting alongside her. The moment their runes flared, something settled between them.

They exchanged a glance. At the same time, they gave each other reaffirming nods.

The dummies lunged again, but this time, Ophelia and Theodin moved without hesitation.

Theodin took the lead, his movements sharper, no longer hesitant. Ophelia followed instinctively, her blade striking where she knew the openings would be. The bond between them didn't waver this time—it held steady, guiding them like an unseen current pulling them in the same direction.

The first dummy feinted high, twisting its wooden frame in an attempt to land a strike against Theodin's exposed side. Ophelia saw the movement—he did too.

She didn't have to shout a warning. She lunged, cutting off the attack with a precise counterstrike—her chain wrapped around the dummy's blade and yanked it away. At the same time, Theodin pivoted to her right, catching the second dummy's blade mid-swing with his own, and that same strike sliced into the first dummy's mid-section—cleanly cutting it in half.

Everyone around them leaned in. A few gasps erupted from the crowd.

Their combined movement flowed seamlessly—faster and smoother.

The remaining dummies pressed harder, adjusting. Ophelia could feel their magic shifting, adapting to the new pace.

But this time, she and Theodin weren't reacting separately. They were responding as one.

Her footwork adjusted, naturally syncing with Theodin's. He was stronger and steadier—she used that to her advantage. Where before, she had fought as though she had to keep up with him, now she let herself fall into step with him.

The dummies moved faster. So did they.

The second dummy recoiled and attempted a strike at Theodin as he started for the third dummy, but he leapt back and dodged.

In that same beat, Ophelia whipped her chain blade at the head of the second dummy. It stabbed right into the middle of its forehead, and the dummy collapsed.

But then, Theodin stepped forward—too quickly.

Ophelia barely caught the shift before he was already intercepting the third dummy, his blade meeting its strike with impossible precision. His movement had been so quick that Ophelia felt the aftershock of it in their bond.

The third dummy adjusted, trying to drive him back, but Theodin didn't flinch.

The dummy reeled back its sword.

Then struck.

Theodin took it directly against his side—without stumbling.

Ophelia's breath hitched. He should have at least staggered from the force of the hit.

He didn't.

He kept going, his movements fluid and unnaturally fast.

From the sidelines, Margrith shifted, her eyes narrowing.

Kaspar, who had remained still throughout the fight, exhaled quietly.

Sigvard, watching closely, muttered something under his breath.

Crane tilted his head. "Huh."

None of them had spoken about it yet, but they had all seen the same thing.

Ophelia and Theodin pressed forward, but from where Faust stood, he wasn't watching the fight anymore.

He was watching *her*.

He had seen her energy flare. Seen the way the bond had shifted. Seen the way she had fallen into step with someone else, as if she belonged there.

His jaw tightened.

The final dummy tried to attack one last time. It managed to get one solid hit at Theodin's head, but he didn't even flinch.

Ophelia then struck the first blow—Theodin finished it.

A chained blade around its throat. A claymore stabbed into its chest.

The energy between them pulsed one last time before the runes on their arms dimmed, the bond settling.

A pause followed. The fight was over.

Ophelia, breathing hard, glanced at Theodin.

He looked calm—too calm.

She didn't have time to think about it.

Alfena lifted a hand. "Enough."

The training grounds fell silent.

Then came the whispers. The murmurs were quiet, but Ophelia could feel them settle against her skin like a prickle of static.

The weight of judgment.

The weight of expectation.

The small Valksha girl who was stronger than she looked. The boy with a terrifying strength, stature, and stare.

The exchange of hushed words lingered in the air, nearly inaudible but sharp.

Ophelia kept her posture straight, her breaths steadying, but she could still feel it—the scrutiny and the unspoken judgments curling in the spaces between the Kyriegard standing along the perimeter.

The senior warriors had seen them now.

They had seen *her*.

The Valksha girl with magic no one fully understood. The one who had bypassed every test, every trial, and had still been permanently bound to a Dyad—a Dyad with someone like Theodin.

And they had seen *him*.

The boy whose strength was something to be wary of. The one who appeared to take a hard hit like it was nothing.

Kaspar's arms were still folded, his stance unreadable. He gave nothing away.

Crane let out a low exhale, tapping his cane once against the stone. His smirk was subtle, but there was something pointed behind it—like a man who had just confirmed a suspicion.

"Well," he said, tilting his head at Theodin. "I'd say you held your own, but that would be an insult to whatever the *Nether* that was."

Theodin's brows pulled together slightly. "What?"

Crane grinned, shifting his weight onto his cane. "The speed. I was watching. You moved *fast*, boy—faster than you should've. Faster than I was when I was your age." He tapped the handle of his cane against his deactivated brace. "Before I had to sport this lovely accessory."

The murmurs among the Kyriegard officers and older apprentices grew louder.

Ophelia glanced at Theodin. He wasn't reacting—not the way she expected. He wasn't stiff with discomfort, nor was he meeting Crane's teasing with any amusement.

He was just…staring.

Kaspar still remained unresponsive, but his gaze lingered on Theodin for a moment longer than necessary.

"Fast."

Margrith's voice cut through the conversation.

"And yet, not quite right. We have many here who are quite fast—Predant-folk and Elvish. Even our resident Cruerfel."

Her arms were crossed, her expression indiscernible, but her eyes were trained on Theodin with something heavier than curiosity.

"You don't react to pain," she said simply.

The murmurs died down.

Ophelia's stomach tightened. Theodin said nothing.

"You were struck," Margrith continued. "Twice. And yet, you didn't flinch. Didn't stumble. Didn't even acknowledge it."

The tension in the air sharpened.

Kaspar finally exhaled. "Are we truly analyzing *flinching* now,

Margrith?"

She didn't look away from Theodin. "It isn't about whether he flinched. It's about whether he felt it at all."

A long pause.

Alfena, who had been mostly quiet, finally spoke. "The truth is, we have no prior Dyad like this to compare them to. This test simply confirms that we still have much to learn."

Crane hummed. "That's one way to put it."

Kaspar let the silence settle before he finally moved. His gaze shifted between Ophelia and Theodin, his posture unchanging.

Then, he spoke.

"They're improving," he said simply.

Margrith exhaled harshly through her nose.

"If you say so."

"They're still raw," Kaspar continued, his voice measured. "Undisciplined. The bond is there, but it's unstable. That's to be expected."

Alfena nodded. "They will need more structured Dyad training, more observation."

Kaspar inclined his head. "Then that is what we will do."

Margrith's expression was tight, but she said nothing else.

Sigvard, who had been observing quietly the entire time, finally let out a slow breath. "Well," he murmured, "that was interesting."

Ophelia wasn't sure if that was a compliment or not.

Kaspar turned to the gathered warriors. "That will be all."

The group slowly began to disperse. The whispers continued, but softer now, fading into the rhythm of the training grounds.

Faust hadn't moved.

He had remained at the edge of the field, his arms folded, his expression blank. His eyes hadn't been on Theodin as most of the Kyriegard were.

They had been on Ophelia.

When she finally glanced at him, something flashed across his face—something he buried too quickly for her to catch.

Then, he turned and walked away.

The training grounds emptied slowly, the sound and presence of the other Kyriegard fading into the sounds of steel meeting steel in nearby sparring matches.

Ophelia sighed, rolling her shoulders as she stepped away from the center of the field. The weight of their performance—of every gaze on them—lingered.

She glanced at Theodin. He wasn't watching the other Kyriegard leave. He was just standing there, as if still caught in the moment, unmoved.

She wasn't sure what she had expected. A comment? A glance her way? Something?

Instead, he simply turned and walked off the field.

Ophelia frowned. "Theodin."

He didn't stop. She jogged to catch up, falling into step beside him as they moved toward the outer pathways of Halvalla, away from the scrutiny of the others. She waited until they had cleared the courtyard before speaking.

"That was…" She hesitated, struggling to put the words together. "That felt… different."

Theodin didn't respond immediately. She stepped in front of him and spun to walk backwards, then slowed her pace, forcing him to either stop or acknowledge her.

He finally stopped.

She crossed her arms, tilting her head. "Did you feel it?"

He exhaled through his nose, glancing away briefly before meeting her gaze again.

"Yeah."

She studied him. He wasn't being dismissive, not exactly. But he wasn't engaging either. It was like he didn't know what to say about it.

"That moment when Kaspar's voice—"

She started, but Theodin cut her off.

"It settled."

His voice was even, quiet.

"That's all."

Ophelia frowned. "Crane noticed something."

Theodin's jaw tensed slightly. "Crane notices everything."

"He wasn't wrong, though. You *were* fast."

He turned away, starting past her and down the path again. "I've always been fast."

She scoffed, catching up. "Not that fast."

Theodin didn't argue, but he didn't confirm anything either.

Ophelia raised her voice. "You caught that dummy's blade with your arm. Did you even feel it?"

He stopped again, but this time, his expression shifted. Not in frustration, but something deeper.

She stopped beside him.

Slowly, he looked down at his forearm—the spot where the strike had landed. He flexed his fingers.

"I don't know."

The way he said it made something in Ophelia's stomach tighten.

They stood there for a moment without exchanging a single word.

Finally, Ophelia let out a defeated breath. She rubbed her neck and dropped her gaze.

"Well… at least we didn't completely embarrass ourselves," she sighed.

Theodin's lips twitched. "We did at first."

She huffed. "Yes…yes, we did."

Wearily, they started walking again. Towards the direction of Avasylon.

The weight of the day still hung between them.

Finally, after several minutes of silence, Ophelia reached for his hand and caught it with a gentle grasp to stop him. The runes in their hands briefly pulsed with white light.

"Theo," she said softly.

He stopped. He didn't look at her.

"I'm not afraid of you," she whispered. "I've got your back as long as you've got mine. No matter what."

He didn't answer right away. But he didn't pull away either.

Ophelia let his hand go after a moment, watching as he flexed his fingers once more before dropping his arm to his side. The runes had dimmed again.

She thought he might say something—anything—but instead, he just gave her a small nod and turned away, walking down the path to Avasylon without another word.

She slowed to a halt, watching his broad frame retreat, his movements steady, controlled—like nothing that had just happened remained with him.

She was about to follow him again when a familiar sensation prickled at the back of her awareness.

Someone was watching her.

She glanced over her shoulder.

Faust stood at a distance, leaning casually against one of the stone walls that lined the outdoor training arenas. His arms were folded, his face unmoved. He wasn't looking at Theodin.

He was looking at *her*. Something in his expression made her pause.

She wasn't sure what it was, only that it sent a strange ripple through her chest—not fear, not quite discomfort, but something uneasy.

For a moment, neither of them moved. Then, just as she opened her mouth to say something, he pushed himself to stand, turned, and walked away.

She blinked, bewildered.

She exhaled sharply through her nose, shaking off the feeling as she turned away herself.

Chapter 26

The Erased

Year 844 of the Second Age, Tenth Month, Fifth Day

Five weeks had passed since their Dyad evaluation at Halvalla.

Training had changed since then. Theodin had stopped hesitating, stopped second-guessing, and stopped holding back the way he had during that first fight. But Ophelia noticed something else—he had also stopped reacting.

There were moments during their spars when he would take a hit, a strike that should have at least staggered him, and he wouldn't even flinch. Not just out of discipline, but because he didn't seem to register it at all.

The Council hadn't said anything openly. Kaspar continued training them. Sigvard still observed. Margrith still watched.

But Ophelia knew the scrutiny hadn't faded. If anything, it had only become quieter.

And then there was her magic.

It wasn't like before when she had struggled to control the blood magic that came naturally to her. That was easy now. But the bloodless magic—the kind that flared in moments of fear, the kind that surfaced when she least expected it—was still a problem.

Alfena insisted that Ophelia and Faust take the opportunity to learn what they could of their Valksha nature and understand it. There was only so much an Elvish Sage warrior like her could teach them about magic.

Even Lady Vivian didn't have all of the answers she could give in five years.

But for those five years, Lady Vivian had been Ophelia's mentor, her guide, and her world.

Together, they had wandered the roads of Moirand, traveling from kingdom to kingdom, never settling in one place for too long. It was a life of constant movement but never without purpose. Vivian had not just been teaching her how to survive—she had been preparing her for something greater. Through her, Ophelia had learned the shape of the world beyond the quiet farm she once called home.

She had learned of the great kingdoms, their borders, their rulers, and their wars. She had learned to recognize the magic that ran beneath them all—the difference between the disciplined study of the Sages and the raw, instinctive power that lived in the Valksha.

She had learned how to fight with magic. How to read an opponent, how to strike without wasting movement, and how to last in battle longer than someone twice her size.

She had learned about the Kyriegard. About their Order, their traditions, and their purpose. Vivian had spoken of them not as an outsider, but as someone who had fought beside them, someone who had once believed in them.

But of all the things Vivian had taught her, there had been so little she could tell her about the Valksha themselves.

So much knowledge had been lost in the genocide. Tomes and collections of first-hand Valksha literature were stolen from great libraries around the land and destroyed, and scrolls were reduced to nothing but ash and fading memory. The only history that remained was the history written by outsiders.

Ophelia had learned what she could from Vivian—what little stories still lingered and what knowledge had survived. She had been told that Valksha magic was different. That it was tied to instinct, survival, and emotion. That their blood carried power that could never be replicated.

But she had never been given answers as to why.

Even before her world had fallen apart, she had always been drawn to stories.

Her father had been a scholar, her older brother Oliver his shadow. She remembered curling up beside them as they pored over old texts, her father's patient voice explaining the weight of the words on the pages.

She had been too young to fully understand them then, but even as a child, she had learned one truth early: history belonged to those who wrote it.

Even before the genocide, what little had been recorded about the Valksha had always been written by those who stood outside them. There had always been an air of mystery, a reluctance to document their knowledge.

Now, there was almost nothing left.

Which was why she was here, in the archives of Avasylon—to salvage what she could.

Since arriving at Avasylon, she was searching for answers.

Nothing prevailed. She had given up after the first few months of searching.

Yet, Alfena argued, there was still much more they had yet to uncover.

Despite knowing that their Valksha resources were limited, Alfena knew there must have been *something* for them.

Which was why Ophelia descended into the underground chamber beneath the fortress, where ancient texts gathered dust in the dim glow of enchanted lanterns.

And Faust waited for her.

The underground chamber beneath Avasylon was quiet past suppertime—the kind of silence that felt undisturbed by time.

Shelves lined the stone walls, filled with texts and scrolls that had been collected over centuries—some weathered, some nearly crumbling, some still bound in protective wards. The familiar scent of old parchment and enchanted ink hung in the air, something Ophelia had grown accustomed to over the past year.

She had spent hours in this library before. But she had never come here for this.

Faust was sitting at one of the long wooden tables near the center of the chamber with a book open in front of him.

He didn't look up immediately when Ophelia entered, but she knew he had noticed her.

His posture was relaxed, but his fingers tapped idly against the worn pages of the text, his eyes scanning lines of script that looked ten times older than both of them combined.

Ophelia sighed and stepped forward. She didn't know exactly what she was looking for, and she didn't know if anything in these texts could explain what had been happening to her—but she knew she had to start somewhere.

"You're late," Faust murmured without looking up.

His voice was calm, but there was something offhanded about it—like he wasn't annoyed, just… making an observation.

Ophelia pulled out a chair across from him, ignoring the way it scraped slightly against the stone floor. She plopped down in it and scooted herself closer to the table.

"I wasn't aware we had a schedule."

Now, he looked at her. It was a dull and playful stare, but he lingered on her just a second too long before he lowered his attention back to the book in front of him.

"Hm," was all he hummed.

Ophelia narrowed her eyes. "What?"

"Nothing," Faust replied, flipping a page. "I haven't found anything profound or gripping yet and I've already been here for an hour."

Ophelia mindlessly glanced at the stack of tomes next to him.

"That's because none of it was actually written by a Valksha," she muttered. "When I first came here to Avasylon, I tried to read one or two—became frustrated, said I would write one of these myself," She flourished her hand, "and I've been working on one since."

Faust leaned back slightly in his chair, raising a brow at her. "You're writing your own?"

Ophelia shrugged. "Someone has to."

He huffed a quiet laugh, shaking his head as he turned a page. "I admire the commitment."

She glanced at the open book in front of him, its brittle parchment filled with dense, looping script. "Have you actually found anything useful?"

"Depends on what you consider useful."

She frowned. "You just said none of it was profound or gripping."

Faust smirked. "And yet, here I am still reading."

Ophelia sighed and reached for one of the tomes from the nearest stack, flipping it open. She already knew what she would find—outsider perspectives, fragmented history, and secondhand knowledge that barely scratched the surface of the truth.

"Even if it wasn't written by a Valksha," Faust mused, "that doesn't mean all of it is useless."

Ophelia scoffed. "It means none of it is complete."

She ran her fingers down the page, scanning the lines of text written by some scholar who had never actually met a Valksha before the genocide.

"The Valksha were known to be volatile in nature, wielding magic tied directly to their emotions. While their talents in blood manipulation and spellcraft were formidable, they were often viewed as unpredictable—prone to outbursts of power that could not be fully controlled."

Ophelia's grip tightened on the edge of the book.

"That's not true," she muttered under her breath.

Faust glanced up. "What isn't?"

She tapped the passage. "The way they frame it—like we were unstable. Like magic just happened to us. But that's not how it worked." She shook her head. "It was controlled. Taught. Practiced. My father used to say magic was an extension of the self—not something separate from us."

Faust was watching her now with a thoughtful gaze. "And yet, your father didn't use magic until the time came for his swan song, and you've struggled to control yours. That text honestly sounds quite accurate compared to what's happening to you now."

Ophelia's stomach twisted. She closed the book and tossed it aside in frustration.

"Maybe we've been looking at the wrong texts," Faust murmured, reaching for another tome.

Ophelia watched as he flipped it open to a section written in a different script—one she vaguely recognized but couldn't fully decipher.

She leaned forward and furrowed her brows. "You can read that?"

Faust's fingers traced the inked symbols lightly. "Mostly."

She stood from her chair and bent her neck to one side for a better view. "That's... Old Erythari." She squinted, trying to make sense of the script. "The older Valksha texts used variations of it, but I've never seen a full record."

Faust hummed, scanning the page. "This one isn't about the Valksha specifically. It's about the war against the first Cruerfel."

Ophelia raised an eyebrow. "And that's relevant how?"

Faust didn't speak. Instead, he turned the page, lips pressing into a thin line as he read something deeper into the passage.

Ophelia didn't like the way his expression shifted.

"What is it?" she asked impatiently.

He didn't look up.

"This… might be important."

Faust exhaled slowly, his fingers still hovering over the page.

Ophelia simply watched, waiting. When he didn't speak for a few moments, she tapped the table.

"Well?"

He finally glanced at her, slightly irritated. Then, with a quiet sigh, he began reading aloud.

"During the war of the first Cruerfel, the remaining human forces of Erythar and the Sage Orders of Moirand sought to harness the divine bloodlines to combat the corruption of the cursed-born. The power of the Saryfim was distant, but it is said that among mortals there existed those whose blood could not be tainted—whose bodies could withstand the abyss and still remain whole."

Ophelia frowned. "Divine bloodlines?"

Faust didn't look at her or pause. He turned the page.

"These warriors bore magic that was unlike any other—magic that could sever the unnatural, purge what could not be healed, and unravel curses of the abyss itself. The last recorded instances of these warriors were during the war against the Cruerfel, where their kind were sent to the front lines and their bodies were used as conduits against corruption. No records of their continued lineage remain."

He paused, his jaw stiffening.

Ophelia stared at the text, her pulse in her ears.

"Wait," she said. "Are they talking about…?"

Faust tapped the margin of the page. "Look at the wording. 'Magic that could sever the unnatural, purge what could not be healed.' What does that sound like to you?"

She didn't respond immediately.

She had heard those descriptions before. They weren't talking about some long-lost divine warriors; they were talking about the Valksha.

Ophelia's mouth felt dry. "So what? The first Valksha weren't just blood mages, they were… what? Some kind of purification force?"

Faust's expression remained unreadable. "According to this text? Yes."

She sat back in her chair, trying to piece it together. "That doesn't make sense. No one ever told me that. Lady Vivian never told me that."

Faust finally looked up from the book. "Maybe she didn't know."

That thought unsettled her more than anything. If Lady Vivian, a brilliant and legendary Valksha who had spent her life fighting, didn't know this, then…

Ophelia ran her fingers through her hair. "But that means the Kyriegard should know. If the Valksha were once some kind of anti-Cruerfel force, the Order should have had records of it."

Faust shrugged. "Maybe they did."

The implication sank between them.

Maybe they did. Then why didn't they have any other reliable literature on the Valksha?

She let out a slow breath, her mind still racing. Then her gaze whipped back to Faust.

"How do you know how to read this?" she asked.

Faust hesitated. His fingers drummed lightly against the edge of the book, his expression momentarily guarded. Then, as if deciding something, he let out a weary breath.

"I learned it a long time ago," he said vaguely.

"That's not an answer."

He gave her a pointed look. "Do I ever give full answers?"

Ophelia narrowed her eyes, looking at him suspiciously. "No. Which is exactly why I don't trust that one."

His smirk was brief, but not unamused.

Her stare darkened. "Don't make me use magic on you, Faust."

"Sounds dangerous," Faust murmured sarcastically.

Ophelia's fingers curled against the edge of the table.

"Faust," she said evenly, "where did you learn this?"

Once again, he didn't answer right away.

Instead, he reached for another page, his fingers trailing over the inked words, as if searching for something else—or stalling.

Ophelia thumped her palm on the table. "You don't just learn Old Erythari. It's not taught. It's not even used anymore."

Faust sat back slightly. "Oh, careful there, love—looks like old Theo's temper is leaking into you—"

Her emerald irises flashed dangerously.

"Faust."

He lifted his hands up in defense and his lips twitched.

"Clearly…" he said cautiously, "someone taught me."

Ophelia's patience was thinning. "Who?"

He smirked, but it wasn't his usual playful one.

It was tired.

"What, do you think I was some great scholar in a past life?"

Ophelia didn't blink. "I think you know more than you let on."

Faust leaned back further in his chair, watching her carefully. "And what if I do?"

She leaned further forward, her voice quieter but now seething. "Then you need to start talking."

"Do I?"

"Don't play that game with me, Faust," she snapped. "This isn't just some forgotten piece of history—this is my people. My magic. My past. And you're sitting here reading a language most scholars can't even touch like it's nothing."

Faust sighed, rubbing his temple with two fingers. "You're exhausting."

"And you're lying."

He chuckled at that. "I never lie. I just… omit."

Faust finally closed the book, exhaling through his nose. His tone, when he spoke again, was softer and more resigned.

"This language is older than you think. Older than me. Older than anything we have left in these libraries." His fingers tapped against the cover. "And some people—very powerful people—don't want it remembered."

Ophelia frowned. "The same people who erased the Valksha?"

Faust went silent. He lowered his eyes solemnly.

Her hands clenched into fists. "Tell me the truth."

Faust glanced at her and tilted his head. "Which one?"

"The one you're not saying."

His smirk faded. For the first time since they sat down, he actually looked serious.

Ophelia came around the table and took a few steps towards him. Her tone shifted, almost pleading.

"Please, Faust. The Valksha are your people too."

Faust sighed again, running a hand through his hair.

For once, he didn't look amused.

"When I was in captivity," he said finally, "they made me learn it."

Ophelia felt a chill crawl down her spine. She knew Faust had suffered under Azazelf—he had hinted at it and dodged around it, but he never spoken of it directly. But this was different.

They hadn't just tortured him. They had *taught* him.

She swallowed. "Why?"

Faust shook his head. "I don't know."

"Don't give me that—"

"I'm serious," he said, sharper this time. "They didn't explain. They just… made sure I could read it."

She clenched her fists. "Made sure you could read it for what?"

Faust let out a humorless chuckle. "That's the question, isn't it?"

Ophelia's mind raced. This changed everything. The Valksha were erased. Their knowledge was destroyed. And yet, someone had forced Faust—a captured Valksha—to learn this lost language. That meant the knowledge wasn't lost at all.

It had been hidden. Controlled.

The runes in her skin sparked with green. She took a deep breath and allowed her swelling emotions to simmer back down upon exhaling.

Faust didn't withhold to be playful.

He witheld because it was *painful*.

After a long moment, she finally spoke.

"Sorry," she whispered.

Faust exhaled, his gaze flicking briefly to her glowing runes. He didn't say anything at first—maybe he was used to seeing people react with pity, but not like this.

Then, he let out a breath of amusement, though it lacked its usual smugness.

"I, uh, didn't peg you Kyriegard for the apologetic type."

Ophelia glanced down at her hands. "I can be. Sometimes."

She looked back at him, and for the first time, there was no accusation in her eyes. No demand. Just understanding.

That seemed to unsettle him more than anything.

"I'm just sorry for…forcing the answer out of you," she continued. "What you went through was deeply traumatic, and I didn't mean to pry. It's the same reason I prefer not to speak of what I went through either, but…" She shrugged. "Kyriegard training. It comes up anyway and I have to get used to it."

Faust leaned toward her now, watching her.

"You're a strange one, Ophelia."

She gave him a dry look. "I get that a lot."

He huffed a quiet breath through his nose, his fingers idly drumming against the book's spine. "I just wasn't expecting… that."

"What?"

His fingers stilled. His eyes flicked to her runes, now dimmed, then back to her face.

"That you'd understand."

Ophelia blinked.

Faust let out a breath of relief, his usual smirk absent.

"People always want answers. They dig because they're curious, not because they care. But you—" His lips pressed together for a moment, as if debating whether to finish his thought.

Finally, he gave her a small, almost resigned smile.

"You actually meant it."

Ophelia hesitated, her throat tight. "Of course I did."

Faust studied her for another long moment before shaking his head with a quiet chuckle. "You're going to be trouble for me, aren't you?"

Her lips twitched. "Haven't I been already?"

His smile widened and this time it was real.

"Yeah," he murmured. "You have."

A beat of silence came between them.

She glanced once more at the open book between them, the weight of what they had uncovered settling deep in her chest.

"We'll figure it out," she murmured.

Faust's answer came—quiet and certain.

"Yes. We will."

Chapter 27

The Unlikely

Year 845 of the Second Age, First Month, Ninth Day

Winter had settled over Olysgard.

Three months had passed since Ophelia and Faust had uncovered the lost history of the Valksha in the depths of Avasylon's archives.

Three months since she once again questioned how much of her own history had been erased—not by time, but by deliberate choice.

She had brought the findings to Kaspar and Alfena, hoping for confirmation, hoping for some lost fragment of knowledge that the Kyriegard might have preserved.

But the answer had only reinforced what she already suspected.

The Valksha had always been secretive. Their ways had been passed down orally, their magic taught from one generation to the next, leaving behind only fragments of written knowledge—and that made them easy to erase.

That had been the end of it, but Ophelia hadn't stopped thinking about it.

Alfena had elaborated in their private sessions.

"The Valksha did not keep books. They did not carve their knowledge into stone. They spoke it, passed it from teacher to student, mother to child. And when they were wiped from this world, so too was all they knew. That is why even I cannot tell you what was lost."

"I once saw a Valksha in battle—one of the last before your time. Their magic was unlike anything I had ever seen. They did not chant, did not invoke the Saryfim, and did not weave spells as the Sages do. Their magic was simply… there. And when they struck, it was as if the very air bent to their will."

"Even before the genocide, they were ghosts. They kept their own ways, spoke their own tongue, trusted only their own kind. I don't know if it was because they feared outsiders or because they knew something we didn't."

Ophelia then asked how old she was. Alfena gave a rare, amusing smile.

"Seven hundred and fifty-three."

Alfena's smile grew when Ophelia's jaw could have hit the floor with how wide it opened in shock.

"So…you're much older than Lady Vivian was?"

Ophelia knew that Lady Vivian was at least four hundred and thirty-four before she passed on. Her efforts to abolish the Malblight plague was the result of her reduced lifespan.

Alfena sighed, her silver eyes distant.

"I fought beside her once. It was long before my time with the Kyriegard—which I had not joined until perhaps three centuries ago. She was different from the others of her kind—braver, perhaps. Or just more willing to be broken."

Ophelia frowned. "She never spoke of you."

A small smirk touched Alfena's lips. "That doesn't surprise me."

Ophelia hesitated, then asked, "What was she like when she was young?"

Alfena tilted her head, considering the question. "Stubborn. Unapologetic. She saw the world differently than most. Where others saw ruin, she saw something worth saving. It was what made her strong."

She paused for a moment before her concluding thought.

"And… what killed her."

Ophelia swallowed hard.

Alfena's gaze softened just slightly. "She was a warrior, Ophelia. But she was more than that. She was… *free*. And for someone born with the kind of power she had, that was the rarest thing of all."

That was just the early morning session that day.

It made Ophelia's head reel with questions.

Ophelia sat across from Kaspar in one of the smaller study chambers in Avasylon's underground fortress, browsing through a Kyriegard record she had barely skimmed over the past year.

She wasn't entirely sure how she ended up here.

She had come to ask him something, but somehow, the conversation had drifted into discussing Kyriegard records—how they were organized, what she had actually read, and what she had ignored.

She frowned at the tome in front of her, flipping through the pages without really reading them.

"You know," she muttered, "I've been here well over a year, and I stopped trying to research Valksha *things*… but once Alfena told me to look again, we found something Order's records on the Valksha a few months ago."

Kaspar hummed. "And?"

Ophelia sighed. "We found one or two things. But they didn't tell me much I didn't already know."

Kaspar leaned back slightly, studying her. "You say that as if you were expecting more."

"I was."

He smirked faintly. "You're an optimist."

Ophelia shot him a dry look. "Hardly."

She turned another page, only half-focused. Then the thought hit her.

She had been here for over a year.

Over a *year*.

She blinked, glancing up. "Wait."

Kaspar raised an eyebrow.

"How long has it been exactly?" she asked, sitting up straighter. "What day is it?"

Kaspar answered without hesitation. "The ninth day of the first month."

Ophelia frowned, doing the math in her head.

Then it clicked.

She had arrived on the twenty-fifth day of the eighth month, back in Year 843 of the Second Age. Now, it was Year 845 of the Second Age. She had been here sixteen months.

And in all that time, no one had ever said a word about birthdays.

Except Kaspar, on her fourteenth birthday.

She squinted at Kaspar. "Is that not a thing we do?"

Kaspar blinked, clearly trying to figure out where her mind had just gone. He sighed.

"It's noted in passing, but we don't celebrate it."

"Why?"

"Because the Order isn't built on personal milestones." He gave her a pointed look. "We serve a purpose beyond ourselves."

Ophelia squinted at him. "Then why did you give me weapons on my fourteenth birthday?"

Kaspar smirked. "Because you were new, and you needed them."

She snorted. "Convenient timing, then?"

"Something like that."

"So then…when is your birthday? When is Theodin's?"

Kaspar exhaled, rubbing his temple as if this conversation alone had drained him.

"Theodin's birthday is today."

Ophelia blinked. "Wait. *Today*, today?"

Kaspar gave her a flat look. "That's what I just said."

She sat back, folding her arms. "And no one was going to mention this?"

Kaspar let out a chuckle. "You just asked me if birthdays were a thing we celebrate. Why would I mention something we don't celebrate?"

Ophelia lowered her eyes and muttered something under her breath, flipping a page in the tome in front of her without reading it.

Kaspar read her more than the open book she had in front of her. He smirked.

"Are you planning something?"

"No," Ophelia said too quickly.

"Lying isn't your strong suit."

Ophelia sighed, drumming her fingers against the table.

"It's just… birthdays used to matter where I'm from. And since I now know when Theodin's is, I just thought—" She hesitated, then shook her head. "Never mind."

Kaspar gave her a blank look.

"You're thinking of doing something."

Ophelia whipped her eyes to him and shot him an accusatory glare.

"Are you reading my mind now?"

Kaspar smirked again. "No, but I know you well enough to know you wouldn't ask unless you had a plan."

Ophelia huffed. "I was just going to make something small.

Something my mother used to make."

Kaspar leaned forward slightly, resting his arms on the table. "And?"

She sighed again, rubbing the back of her neck. "I need to go to Fatum."

Kaspar blinked once, then let out a slow, measured breath.

"Ophelia."

"What?"

"Tell me you're joking."

She straightened. "I could lie again."

Kaspar pinched the bridge of his nose. "For what?"

Ophelia shrugged, feigning innocence.

"Butter and sugar."

Kaspar lowered his hand, staring at her. "I—"

He couldn't even speak.

"*...why.*"

"To make sweet bread."

Kaspar inhaled deeply, eyes briefly closing.

"Ophelia."

"Yes?"

He held his forehead.

"We are a disciplined order, bound by duty, honor, and the preservation of peace. And you—" he gestured vaguely at her, "—are asking to leave Olysgard, with the danger of Warthralls and Azazelf Chernabog lurking at the edges of our borders, for the sake of *baking*."

Ophelia folded her hands neatly in front of her.

"Yes."

Kaspar stared at her for a long moment. Then he sighed, rubbing his face.

"Fine."

Ophelia blinked. "Wait, really?"

Kaspar pointed at her with a stern finger.

"On one condition."

She straightened again. "What?"

Kaspar smirked again, but this time with an air of mischief—something she had never seen in him and expected much more from the likes of the devious Azariah Crane and his apprentices, Mald and Fritan—and then, Ophelia immediately knew she wasn't going to like whatever was about to come out of his mouth.

"Take Faust with you."

Ophelia froze. "*What*."

Kaspar leaned back, arms folding over his chest.

"Take Faust with you."

Ophelia's eyes narrowed into a glare once more.

"You do realize you've just assigned me the least responsible nanny in existence, right?"

Kaspar's sneer only grew. "Oh, I'm well aware."

Ophelia threw her hands up. "And I have to watch him?"

Kaspar shrugged. "Think of it as an extra challenge for your training." He leaned in slightly. "If it was Theodin, you know he'd stop you. Probably even report you, being the disciplined rule-follower he is—" His face shifted very briefly, "—mostly…"

Ophelia's eyebrows lifted inquisitively, but he cleared his throat and straightened.

"You have my permission, and that's enough. But you must take Faust with you."

She groaned, dropping her forehead onto the table. "This is the worst idea."

Kaspar exhaled. "You wanted to go, didn't you?"

Ophelia muttered something unintelligible against the wood.

Kaspar chuckled again deeply, pushing himself up from his seat.

"You leave in an hour. Be back before sunset. Don't cause an incident."

"I never cause incidents," Ophelia said, lifting her head.

Kaspar gave her a pointed look.

She sighed. "Okay, rarely."

Kaspar rolled his eyes, already heading for the exit.

"Good luck."

Ophelia groaned again. She stood and shut the book, then stopped.

"You didn't say when *your* birthday was."

Kaspar paused just slightly. Then, without turning around, he let out a low hum. "That depends."

Ophelia frowned. "On what?"

He finally glanced over his shoulder, another smirk tugging at his lips. "Are you planning to bake me something too?"

Ophelia perked, her eyes glimmering with excitement. "I could!"

Kaspar let out a loud, rare laugh and sighed.

"Founders, help us."

She nearly skipped over to him and stood in front of him, her hands folded behind her. Her eyes became large with curiosity. "So you do remember it."

Kaspar exhaled sharply, rubbing the bridge of his nose again as if this conversation had officially drained him.

"Alfena keeps track of these things. She reminds me once a decade, and that's about as much celebration as I get."

Ophelia's jaw dropped slightly. "Once a *decade?* But…she's an *Elf*—aren't you only *human?!* You only get so many decades!"

Kaspar groaned. "Ophelia."

She lifted her hands in mock surrender. "Alright, alright. No more birthday interrogation. But—" She folded her arms, tilting her head. "If Alfena reminds you, that means she knows exactly when it is."

Kaspar's eyes darted toward the door as if considering just leaving.

Ophelia sneered. "I'll just ask her, then."

Kaspar huffed a single, humorless laugh. "And you call me exasperating."

Ophelia grinned, but before she could push any further, his demeanor hardened.

"Again. You leave in an hour." His voice was back to its usual dry authority. "Back before sunset. Take Faust. Stay out of trouble."

Ophelia sighed dramatically. "Again, *rarely*."

Kaspar looked at her dully. "Try harder."

He turned.

"And…once a decade's enough," he muttered. "Some years even that felt like too much."

And with that, he left.

The library in Avasylon's underground sanctum was quiet, save for the occasional rustle of parchment and the dim flickering of enchanted lanterns.

Faust had been here for hours.

Well—he had been *in* the library for hours. How much of that time had actually been spent reading was debatable.

He just… couldn't help but let his mind drift.

And it was always to *them*. To *her*.

Since the Dyad evaluation at Halvalla, Ophelia and Theodin had fallen into a rhythm.

The difference was noticeable—in training, in movement, and even in the small, unconscious ways they reacted to each other.

They weren't just in sync when they fought. They were in sync—always.

A shift of weight. A glance. A breath.

And Faust hated it.

Faust had been around them enough now to recognize when it was happening.

The subtle way Theodin moved before Ophelia even spoke, as if he already knew what she was going to say.

The way Ophelia would pause mid-stride, sensing Theodin before he even entered the room.

The way they didn't even have to look at each other anymore to know.

The way they looked at each other at all.

And she made his stone face break with a smirk.

And he made her giggle.

It was maddening.

Faust could feel it, almost physically, every time Ophelia got pulled into Theodin's orbit.

And yet, for the past three months, Faust had been drawn into hers.

It had started that night she healed his scars.

Then, she helped him use magic for himself for the first time.

Next came the research. They sought to understand what it meant to be Valksha and to reclaim something that had been buried long before they were born.

Then came the training.

Magic was an extension of the self, and Ophelia was learning how to wield hers with precision—which meant Faust had to do the same.

And somehow, among all of that, she had become his closest friend.

Which was an entirely different problem.

He often found himself thinking about her.

Maybe a little too often.

A book lay open in front of him, one hand idly propping up his chin as his eyes skimmed over the same paragraph for what had to be the fourth time. He wasn't even sure what the passage was about anymore. Something about battle formations. Or maybe warding sigils. Or possibly agricultural exports. He had stopped paying attention somewhere around the second sentence.

It wasn't that he hated reading—he just hated this kind of reading. If he wanted to fall asleep, he'd find a more comfortable place to do it.

Still, he was technically being productive. Or at least, that's what he would argue if anyone asked.

Then, he felt her energy prickle at the back of his head.

It wasn't loud. It wasn't intrusive. It was just there—a presence brushing against the edges of his awareness, like a thought he hadn't fully formed yet.

That familiar, *brilliant*, lively flame of hers.

He didn't need to turn around to know she was coming. The sensation grew as she got closer.

Then, her shadow fell over the table.

Faust exhaled through his nose, flipping a page without reading it.

"You're not even trying to look invested," Ophelia noted dryly.

Faust barely flicked his gaze upward. He blinked once, slow and deliberate.

"That's because I'm not."

He didn't lift his head, but a coy expression curled in his face.

"I'm absorbing knowledge through osmosis."

Ophelia lowered herself onto the table until she was in his line of sight.

"That's not how reading works."

Faust grinned lazily. "And yet, I remain brilliant."

She giggled and rolled her eyes.

That made Faust giddy for just a beat.

"Good," she said, "because you're going to need that brilliance. We're going on a mission."

He lifted his head attentively, now beaming with keen interest.

"Oh? Where are we sneaking off to?"

Ophelia hesitated. "…Fatum."

Faust blinked. Then frowned. "For what?"

She bit her lip and tapped her foot anxiously. "Butter and sugar."

A long pause.

Faust blinked again. "I'm sorry. I must've misheard. Did you just say…*butter and sugar?*"

Ophelia cleared her throat. "Yes."

His lips parted, then pressed together, as if he were physically restraining himself from laughing. Then, with the slowest tilt of his head, he sneered wickedly.

"Ophelia Bloodworth, the last Valksha of Veladriel the Ardent, Saryf of Spirit and Heart, the one and only apprentice of the late but legendary Valksha, the myth herself, Lady Vivian… first Valksha of the Kyriegard Order and now apprentice to the Head of the Order, Nimrod Kaspar, himself…"

He flourished his hand dramatically.

"In a fully formed Arcane Dyad with the Order's beloved prodigy and *golden boy*, Theodin of Tersia—"

His voice grew louder with each iteration.

"—A force to be reckoned with…is going on a mission for—*baking supplies?!*"

Ophelia didn't answer, staring at him dully.

Faust leaned back in his chair, arms crossed, watching her like she had just told him they were about to go fight a war with a wooden spoon.

"Do Kyriegard even do birthdays?" he asked.

Ophelia answered in a monotone. "Not really."

Faust threw his hands up. "Then why—"

"Because Theodin's happens to be today," she cut in, folding her arms, "and I just thought it would be nice to—"

Faust waved a hand. "Oh, I get it. You're making a grand gesture."

Ophelia waved back dismissively. "It's sweet bread."

He smirked. "*Sweet*, indeed, for your *sweet* partner."

She reached for a book to throw at him.

Faust dodged it with ease, laughing under his breath. He flourished his hand again towards her.

"Stick with just magic, love. The Council would've frowned at that disappointing attempt to—"

Her irises flashed with green as she raised her fist.

He yelped a high-pitched squeal and cowered beneath his arms. "Have mercy!"

Ophelia scowled for a moment, then growled and lowered her hand. "Fine. Let's go now."

As she recoiled, he held up an inquisitive hand.

"So let me get this straight," he continued, now holding up a finger as if he needed to process this ridiculous task.

"The great Nimrod Kaspar has given you permission to leave Olysgard—"

"Yes."

"—to travel to a Tersian market—"

"Yes."

"—to get baking ingredients."

"…Yes."

Faust gawked at her for a long moment. Then he let out a deep sigh, running a hand through his hair. He muttered something incoherent, shaking his head.

Then, suddenly, he hesitated. His brow furrowed slightly.

"When is my birthday?"

Ophelia blinked. "What?"

Faust tapped his fingers on the table. "No, I'm serious. When is my birthday?"

Ophelia stared. "You don't know?"

Faust gave her a dry look. "If I did, I wouldn't be asking."

She frowned. "Well, how old are you?"

"That depends," he muttered, flipping the book in front of him shut. "Do we count the years I was alive, or the years I *should* have been alive?"

That made her pause. Her stomach twisted slightly.

Faust must've caught the look in her eyes, because he immediately waved her off.

"Relax. I know I'm older than you and younger than Theodin. That's about as much as I've got."

Ophelia folded her arms, her gaze skeptical. "So…if I'm fourteen, Theodin turns seventeen today, that puts you at about fifteen or sixteen. You don't even remember your birthday?"

Faust shrugged. "I remember the painful things, Ophelia. Not the celebrations."

Her stomach twisted again. She fell silent and her expression faded, unsure how to respond.

Faust smirked as if trying to lighten the moment. "Guess that means you don't have to bake me anything."

Ophelia narrowed her eyes. "You're getting a loaf just for saying that."

Faust groaned. "Now *I'm* the one being punished?"

Ophelia grinned, already turning toward the exit. "Come on. We leave in an hour."

Faust let out an exaggerated sigh, pushing himself up from his chair.

"This is it," he muttered. "This is how I die."

Chapter 28

The Gesture

The chill of winter bit at the air as Ophelia led one of the Kyriegard horses from the stables, the scent of hay and leather mixing with the crisp afternoon breeze. She worked efficiently, securing the saddle with practiced movements.

Meanwhile, Faust bundled in thick layers and a winter cloak, stood a few paces away, arms hugged tightly around himself, watching her like a man preparing for battle.

Ophelia gave him a glance. "You do know how to ride, right?"

Faust scoffed. "Of course I do."

She raised an eyebrow.

Faust rolled his eyes. "It's not hard."

Ophelia hummed, adjusting the stirrups. "Right. And when was the last time you actually rode a horse?"

Faust hesitated. Then, with perfect confidence, he answered. "Does it matter?"

Ophelia bit back a smirk. She mounted the horse with ease, settling into the saddle before looking down at Faust expectantly.

"Well?"

Faust took a step forward, assessing the situation with apprehension. Then, in one smooth motion, he swung himself up—and completely misjudged the momentum.

His foot missed the stirrup, his balance wavered, and before he could correct it—

He slipped. Ophelia winced.

With a rather undignified grunt, Faust landed half-draped over the saddle, one arm clinging to Ophelia's waist while his other hand flailed for something to grab.

The surge of humiliation that came from him was nearly overwhelming.

The horse let out an annoyed huff.

Ophelia, entirely still, blinked down at him.

"...Need help?"

Faust groaned. "No."

Ophelia barely contained her laughter as he struggled for a few seconds before finally—somewhat grudgingly—gripping her shoulder to haul himself upright behind her.

There was a long pause. His arms were still loosely wrapped around her waist. Faust cleared his throat, adjusting his grip as if trying to make it less obvious that he was now holding onto her for dear life.

"...I meant to do that," he muttered.

"Right," she mused.

She felt him scowl behind her.

"Shut up."

Ophelia adjusted the reins, preparing to set off, but she could feel his pulse—faster than normal.

The warmth of his hands resting against her waist. The way his grip was just a little too tense.

And his energy, though still broken from Azazelf's torment, was apparent.

Along with his emotions.

First, it was embarrassment and anxiety that she felt. Then, it turned into a deep, flustered feeling of...

Both of her brows rose. She said nothing, but she knew then.

"We can go now," Faust said impatiently.

Ophelia snickered and lightly kicked the stirrup. The horse began forward, and she directed it onto the southern path. The steady rhythm of hooves against the frozen dirt filled the silence between them.

Faust, still very much pressed against her back, let out a long, exaggerated sigh.

"Something wrong?" she asked.

"You're enjoying this, aren't you?" he grumbled

"Immensely."

He huffed sharply, shifting slightly. "I don't know how anyone enjoys this. My legs are already sore."

"We've been riding for five minutes."

He groaned dramatically. "Five minutes too long."

Ophelia bit back a laugh. "Do you want me to drop you off and let you walk the rest of the way?"

"Tempting," Faust muttered. "But I'd rather not freeze to death in the middle of the road."

"You're acting like you've never been on a mission before."

"I haven't been on a mission that involves baking ingredients," he shot back. "I think this is a first for all of us."

"It's not technically a mission," she affirmed.

"It feels like one," he muttered.

Another stretch of silence passed, broken only by the biting winter wind and the sound of the horse's steady gait on the crunching snow.

Faust shifted slightly behind her.

"So," he said, clearly attempting to distract himself from his utter discomfort and shame, "tell me, oh wise Valksha, what ancient knowledge are we supposed to be learning while traveling for flour and sugar?"

Ophelia snorted. "Butter and sugar."

"Right. Because that makes it so much better."

She sighed a breath of feign amusement. "I don't know, Faust. You tell me. What great knowledge has been passed down in your long, mysterious lineage?"

She felt him tense slightly at the sarcasm, but he covered it well with a scoff.

"Ah, yes. The long, noble history of *me*—the perfect example of Valksha heritage."

Ophelia didn't look back, but she stared ahead with a dull expression.

"So you *do* know something useful."

Faust hummed.

"I mean, I could tell you something interesting. Or, I could make something up entirely, and you'd never know the difference."

"That's assuming I trust you."

"You shouldn't."

He sighed tremendously. "Alright, fine. Since you're so eager to learn the sacred teachings of my people, allow me to enlighten you."

"This is going to be complete nonsense, isn't it?"

"Oh, absolutely."

Ophelia rolled her shoulders to brace herself.

"Go on, then."

Faust cleared his throat, adjusting his hold on her waist like a storyteller settling in for a grand tale.

"Ahem. Long ago, in the time before time, the ancient Valksha ruled the world with an iron fist. They were feared across the lands for their terrifying ability to—" he wiggled his fingers near her side, "—communicate telepathically with plants."

Ophelia continued to stare ahead, unimpressed. "Plants."

"Yes, plants." Faust leaned in and put his chin on her shoulder, voice lowering dramatically. "You see, we did not command nature. No, no. That would be barbaric. We negotiated with it. Traded secrets with the great oaks. Held diplomatic summits with the ferns."

Ophelia let out another snort.

Faust nodded solemnly. "It was a simpler time."

"Uh-huh."

"The downfall, of course, came when the *cabbages* betrayed us."

A beat.

Ophelia burst out laughing.

Faust grinned wider, satisfied by her reaction.

"Oh yes," he continued, now clearly enjoying himself. "The Great Cabbage Uprising. Tragic. We never recovered."

Ophelia was shaking with residual laughter. She wiped a stray tear from her eye.

"So what happened to the last of your *noble people?*"

Faust sighed again, but now it was dramatically forlorn. "Scattered to the wind. Some say they still whisper to the trees to this day."

Ophelia shook her head, but she continued to laugh. "You're an idiot."

Faust smirked. "And yet, I remain brilliant."

Ophelia shook her head, still smiling. "Alright, alright. Enough nonsense."

Faust frowned, draping himself over her back theatrically. "Fine. You don't appreciate history."

"I appreciate real history," she said, her laughter fading into a chuckle. "So tell me—what do you actually remember?"

She felt him tense slightly behind her. It was small—barely a shift in energy—but she noticed.

The playfulness in his tone didn't fade entirely, but there was something different when he spoke next.

"Well," he started, slower this time, "I remember that I became a Valksha. I was too little to remember how it happened. I was told that the Medallion of Zadkiel chose me."

Another beat.

Ophelia waited.

Faust exhaled through his nose. "I remember that my magic was… mine, once. That I wasn't afraid of it."

His voice was quieter now, like he was speaking more to himself than to her.

"I remember that I was alone. Before Azazelf."

Ophelia's grip on the reins tightened slightly.

Faust let out a humorless chuckle. "And I remember that none of that matters anymore."

Ophelia frowned.

There was something underneath his words. Something she wasn't sure if even he realized was there.

A deep, quiet grief. And it all came to the surface as he spoke.

She opened her mouth—

But then Faust interjected. "So now that I've enlightened you with my brilliance, please do enlighten me with yours—you *are* a child of both sacred and secular realms, after all."

Ophelia furrowed her brow, taken aback by the sudden change in subject.

"This—tree thing, for example," Faust continued. "I keep seeing the symbols everywhere, but none of the books are telling me about it. All of the Kyriegard-specific texts come up blank. Could you explain how that works to me?"

Faust wasn't allowed to attend lectures, she reminded herself. Ophelia opened her mouth again, then shut it. She tightly shook her head.

"It's a Kyriegard thing. That's why you can't know or see those things."

"Oh," he murmured, disappointed. "Enchanted Sage nonsense."

"It's surprisingly quite efficient," she chirped.

"Not as good as Valksha magic."

"Don't get all superiority-type on me now," Ophelia scolded sternly.

"Well, it seems clear to me that a Valksha isn't meant to be a Kyriegard—"

"Where are you from, Faust?" Ophelia suddenly asked, interrupting him. She attempted to hide the irritation beneath the question, but it came out more firmly than intended.

She felt him bristle at the turn of attention back to his origin. He hesitated—a wave of dread flooded from his touch. Not out of fear of discovery but a fear of the unknown.

And pain.

Ophelia's harsh tone dissipated.

"It's okay if you don't remember," she said. "I was just curious. You almost sound like you're from Regania, too, from the way you speak."

A small wave of relief washed over him. She felt his pain vanish.

"What makes you say that?" he asked. "Because we sort of sound like we're from the same place?"

"Yes," she answered. "I'm from Northern Regania. Alphen Valley, to be specific. You must've been from Southern Regania—you've got more of a bluntness and clipped way you speak."

Faust seemed to search his memory. "Nether—I'm still learning my geography," he mumbled under his breath. "So you're…nobility?"

Ophelia let out a small laugh. "I suppose, technically. My father was, but never spoke of it. I grew up on a farm."

"So…you actually knew your family."

"I did."

As her voice grew quieter, so did the topic.

Then, Faust adjusted himself.

"Well, we don't have to talk about it," he abruptly said. "This is the longest I've ever spent on horseback, and I hate it."

Ophelia let him have the subject change. She smirked.

"We've still got a while to go."

Faust let out a loud groan. "Kill me now."

Theodin stood at the edge of the winter-frosted training fields, arms crossed, eyes on the horizon—not on the apprentices arriving behind him, not on the sparring matches forming near the eastern walls, but on the woods.

The wind had changed. He felt it in his jaw first—clenched before he noticed. Then in his pulse. Then, quietly, in the empty silence across the Dyad bond.

She wasn't in Avasylon.

He hadn't realized how often he felt her until now.

Not in thought. Not even in magic. Just… presence. A weight

balanced against his own.

And now it was missing.

He closed his eyes and reached inward—not enough to call to her, not yet—but enough to search.

Not Halvalla, due west. Not anywhere near the Order's perimeter. She was… south of Avasylon.

Fatum.

He frowned.

"Oi, sir," a voice chirped behind him. "You lose your partner or something?"

He turned just enough to catch Mald grinning as he and Fritan strolled past, wooden practice blades slung over their shoulders.

"She's not usually late," Fritan added, his tone deceptively mild. "Though we did see her riding off into the woods earlier."

"On horseback," Mald said, stretching the words like taffy. "With company."

Theodin's eyes narrowed.

Fritan gave a mock-innocent shrug. "Looked like that Valksha boy."

He didn't respond because he didn't need to. The silence said enough.

Mald elbowed his partner. "Leave him be."

They moved on, but the damage was done. Theodin turned back to the horizon, the pull in his chest growing tighter. His hand hovered near his temple, the Dyad pulsing softly behind his ribs.

He nearly reached out to her.

"You're not going to find her like that," came Kaspar's voice behind him.

Theodin didn't startle, but he did stiffen.

Kaspar approached with his usual casual pace, hands clasped behind his back.

"They're fine," he said. "I sent them."

Theodin turned. "Alone?"

"They're not unarmed," Kaspar replied.

"She's not in Avasylon," Theodin said, his voice low.

"I know."

"She's not even in Halvalla. In the direction of Fatum."

Kaspar stopped a few paces from him, his gaze unreadable.

Theodin pressed, the words almost too pointed. "You let them leave Olysgard?"

There was a pause.

"You can feel that?" Kaspar asked quietly.

Theodin's mouth tightened. "I didn't try to. I just know."

Another pause. This time, heavier.

Kaspar studied him with a long, slow glance. "She's handling something Valksha-specific. You weren't needed."

"There are *Warthralls* out there."

"Two *Valksha*—Warthralls don't fare well with Valksha."

"They were hunting her when she got here."

"Over a year ago now, lad. She's stronger."

"She's my partner."

"She's her own person."

Kaspar let the words land.

Then he stepped closer, lowering his voice just enough that the wind wouldn't carry it.

"This wasn't about danger, Theodin. If it was, I'd be out there. You'd be out there."

He paused. "This was about distance. And you just told me everything I needed to know."

Theodin said nothing, but his posture shifted—like a thread had been pulled taut inside him.

Kaspar stepped back. "There's a shipment from Halvalla that needs checking. Wardstones along the north wall have been fluctuating. Take Mald and Fritan. Keep them from breaking something."

Theodin didn't move.

Kaspar added, "Or stay here and brood. But you'll be doing it under my orders."

Then he turned and walked away.

Theodin stood alone for a moment longer, the weight in his chest not loosening—but burying itself deeper.

He didn't call out to her.

But he still felt the absence.

The trip back to Avasylon had been uneventful—aside from Faust's continued theatrical suffering. He had spent half the ride complaining about the soreness in his legs and the other half dramatically predicting his own demise due to cold, hunger, or sheer boredom.

Ophelia, of course, had ignored him.

Now, she was in the kitchen, sleeves pushed up, hands dusted with flour as she worked the dough into shape.

Faust, predictably, had followed.

He was not helping. Instead, he was perched on the edge of the wooden counter, absently flipping a small sheathed knife between his fingers, watching her with thinly veiled amusement. "So," he said lazily, "is this a normal Valksha courting ritual, or are you just trying to impress him with your domestic skills?"

Ophelia didn't look up. "I will throw this dough at your face."

Faust smirked. "I'd like to see you try."

She stopped kneading for half a second, then, without warning, she hurled a pinch of dough at him. Faust barely dodged in time.

Brushing the nonexistent debris from his sleeve, he muttered, "Great Saryfim, that was hostile."

Ophelia smirked. "Consider it a warning shot."

Faust sighed dramatically, leaning back against the counter.

"I just think it's funny," he mused, tapping the hilt of his knife against the wood. "You, the last Valksha, trained in deadly combat, a master of blood magic, slayer of Warthralls and Cadaven alike... spending your evening making sweet bread."

Ophelia rolled her eyes, shaping the dough into loaves. "I told you. It's not a grand gesture. I'm not a master of blood magic yet, either. I'm not the last Valksha either—clearly—"

Faust scoffed. "It is a grand gesture."

"It's *bread*."

"It's *symbolic* bread."

Ophelia sighed. "Shut up."

Faust smirked but fell silent for a moment, absently flipping the knife again. Then, as if plucking a thought from the air, he mused, "You know, it's actually kind of a waste."

Ophelia frowned. "What?"

Faust tilted his head, watching her carefully.

"You. The last of your kind. Not just the Valksha—of the Saryf *Veladriel*. A rare, powerful bloodline, capable of things no one else can do. And you're bound by Kyriegard celibacy rules." He tapped the knife against his palm. "If you ask me, you should be reproducing. Carrying on your lineage. Passing down your bloodline instead of..." he gestured vaguely, "hoarding it for yourself."

Ophelia stopped kneading. Then she lifted her head slowly, glaring at him.

Faust smirked. "Just saying."

Ophelia exhaled sharply through her nose. "I'll consider that in a few centuries."

Faust blinked. "Excuse me?"

Ophelia shrugged, moving back to the dough. "Valksha live a long time. I have a few hundred years to figure it out."

Faust furrowed his brows. "How long exactly?"

Ophelia hummed. "Five hundred years. Maybe a little more."

Faust froze. She felt the sharp shift in his energy before she even looked up. She turned slightly, catching the way his jaw had tensed—the glimpse of something unreadable in his eyes.

He covered it quickly, schooling his expression back into amusement, but his next words came out too light.

"Oh, so Theodin would be gone by the time you decide to have children."

Ophelia stopped again. "What?"

Faust immediately looked away, muttering, "Oh, nothing."

Ophelia narrowed her eyes at him, but before she could press him, he changed the subject entirely.

"Anyway," he said smoothly, pushing off the counter and stretching, "how long does this take?"

Ophelia eyed him for another second before letting it go.

"For you?" she muttered, moving the loaves onto the tray. "Too long."

Faust whined playfully and slumped into a chair nearby. "That's what I thought."

The kitchen was filled with the warm, rich scent of freshly baked bread. Ophelia pulled the loaves from the hearth, setting them on the counter to cool.

She didn't even get the chance to turn before Faust was already reaching for one. She swatted his hand away.

"Ack! Let it cool first."

Faust slumped and gave her an exaggerated pout, leaning against the counter.

"Torture. Pure, absolute torture."

Ophelia rolled her eyes. "Patience, Valksha."

Faust shot her a deeply unimpressed look. "You try being patient when something smells that good."

Ophelia chuckled, but after a few more moments, she finally relented. Picking up one of the smaller loaves, she handed it to him.

"Here," she said. "Before you die of starvation."

Faust grinned, already breaking off a piece. "Finally. The real reward of this mission."

He took a bite, chewing thoughtfully. Then he hummed.

Ophelia arched an eyebrow. "What?"

Faust swallowed, licking a stray crumb off his thumb. "It's good."

"You sound surprised."

He smirked. "Just impressed."

Ophelia gave a scoff. "Shut up."

Faust grinned, taking another bite.

Ophelia, meanwhile, turned back to the counter, picking up the loaf meant for Theodin.

The sound of a blade against stone and wood echoed in the stillness.

She found him outside in the courtyard, finishing his evening drills. The only sources of light were the full moon, the enchanted training dummies, and the lanterns nearby.

Countless pieces of wood were strewn across the frosted ground, aimlessly rolling back together and trying to put themselves back together.

His movements were fluid and precise. Unrelenting.

The Dyad pulsed. He noticed her before she spoke, lowering his sword slightly.

He turned and watched her approach. She was huddled in her winter cloak, holding something close to her chest.

She felt… uncertain.

As she drew near, he straightened his stance.

"Something wrong?" Theodin asked, brow furrowing slightly.

Ophelia hesitated for half a second, then stepped forward, holding out the cloth-wrapped loaf. It was still steaming from its warmth amidst the cold air.

"Here."

Theodin blinked, his grip shifting slightly on his sword.

"…What?"

She exhaled. "It's for you."

Theodin stared at her and then at the bread. He didn't move.

Ophelia raised an eyebrow. "You're supposed to take it."

After another beat of hesitation, he did. His hands curled carefully around the warm loaf as if trying to understand why it was there.

Ophelia smiled faintly. "Happy birthday."

Theodin's gaze flicked back up to her.

Ophelia did not expect him to look so… thrown off. Like the words didn't quite register. Like he had to process them one at a time. She shifted slightly, suddenly feeling awkward.

"I, uh… I wasn't sure if you liked sweets, so I made it light. Not too much sugar."

Silence.

Theodin just stood there.

Ophelia frowned. "You do know what birthdays are, right?"

That seemed to snap him out of whatever thought spiral he had just gone into.

"…Yes." He cleared his throat slightly, adjusting his grip on the bread. "I just wasn't expecting…"

He trailed off.

Ophelia tilted her head. "What?"

His fingers curled slightly against the cloth wrapping.

"This."

Ophelia exhaled through her nose. "It's just bread, Theo."

He looked at her. "It's not just bread."

Ophelia blinked. The moment hung between them.

And then, before she could figure out how to respond to that, Theodin exhaled and gave her a rare, solemn nod of gratitude.

"…Thank you."

Ophelia chuckled slightly, shoving her hands in her pockets. "Don't get used to it." She nodded to the loaf. "And don't let it get too cold now."

With that, she turned on her heel and walked away.

She didn't look back. But if she had, she would have seen Theodin standing there holding the bread like he wasn't quite sure what to do with it.

That night, Theodin sat at the dining table, his posture rigid and his mind still tangled with everything that had happened that day.

The bread was long gone. But he was still thinking about it. Not just the bread itself, but the fact that she had left Olysgard just to get it.

Kaspar made it sound like it was much more important than it actually was. He called it something Valksha-specific.

Ophelia shouldn't have left. It was reckless. Dangerous. Warthralls were still out there.

And yet…

He sighed sharply through his nose.

Finally, he turned his attention to Ophelia—who was sitting across from him, nonchalantly eating her meal as if she hadn't spent her day casually ignoring basic safety protocols.

His brows pulled together. "You shouldn't have left."

Ophelia blinked, looking up mid-bite. "What?"

Theodin exhaled, setting his utensils down. "Leaving Olysgard right now is dangerous. You shouldn't have gone."

Ophelia chewed slowly, then swallowed. "I went to get baking ingredients."

"That's not the point."

Faust, seated beside him, snorted into his cup. "Oh, I think that's *exactly* the point."

Theodin shot him a look, then turned back to Ophelia. "You know it was reckless."

Ophelia slowly put her spoon down. "I asked Kaspar for permission."

That was when Theodin turned his attention to Kaspar. Kaspar, seated at the head of the table, was completely unbothered.

"You let her go?"

Kaspar nodded. "She was going to do it anyway."

"That doesn't make it safe."

Kaspar shrugged. "She wasn't alone."

Theodin scoffed. "She was with *Faust*."

Faust scoffed back in the same manner. "Aw, Theo, I'm *offended*."

Kaspar remained unbothered.

"He wouldn't have let anything happen to her."

Theodin glared at him darkly. "That's not exactly reassuring."

Kaspar finally raised an eyebrow, but he didn't look up from his plate. "No? You think he'd stand there and watch if something attacked her?"

Theodin opened his mouth to speak, but Faust, still drinking from his cup, muttered, "I'd throw myself at the attacker."

Kaspar nodded. "See?"

Theodin clenched his jaw. "That's still dangerous."

Kaspar shrugged once more. "Again—she was going to do it anyway."

Theodin rubbed his temple.

Meanwhile, Ophelia sat there as entirely unbothered as Kaspar was, sipping her drink.

Eventually, Theodin let out another slow breath and muttered, "It was unnecessary."

Ophelia smirked slightly. "Was it?"

Theodin narrowed his eyes at her.

She tilted her head. "Did you eat it?"

A long pause.

Theodin's face hardened. "…That's not the point."

Faust let out a loud laugh, clapping a hand on Theodin's shoulder. "Oh, he ate it."

Theodin turned and scowled at him. Faust grinned.

Kaspar, still utterly unfazed, leaned back in his chair. "Alright, everyone's alive, and Theodin got symbolic bread. We're done here."

Theodin exhaled sharply. "This is ridiculous."

Ophelia laughed lightly, gesturing a toast to him with her cup. "Happy birthday, Theo."

Theodin sighed, shoving his spoon back into his bowl.

Chapter 29

The Quiet Practice

Year 845 of the Second Age, Third Month, Seventh Day
Two months later.

The only sound in the early evening of Avasylon's courtyard was the muffled clinking of Ophelia's tools as she repaired her rifle. Golden sunset painted the training fields, the air fresh with a post-winter forest scent.

She sat cross-legged on a low stone bench, her focus entirely on the intricate mechanisms of the weapon in her lap.

The smell of new spring filled her nostrils. She paused, sitting up to look out to the horizon. She breathed deeply, taking in the serene setting with gratitude.

Silently, she thanked Elodyn for the day.

When Elodyn descended from the Ether to weave Moirand, his light birthed the Saryfim—the guardians of his creation. That was how the stories began. That was what she had always believed. But belief was harder now, tangled in steel and Sage doctrine.

She still whispered prayers, even though the Order forbade it. Quiet ones. Personal.

Through the light of the Saryfim, the world blossomed, and through their guidance, mankind thrived. Yet Elodyn's final decree before his rest ensured mankind's autonomy: the Saryfim would guard and guide, not rule. For centuries, this balance held strong until Malaziel's fall, which tore asunder the trust between divine and mortal.

The War of Malblight scarred not only the land but the faith of Moirand's people. In their desperation, the Saryfim gave their essence to create the Valksha, human vessels imbued with divine magic to combat Malcifer's darkness. To the faithful, the Valksha were saviors—embodiments of Elodyn's enduring love.

To others, they were symbols of fear, their power too vast to contain. When the dust of war settled, reverence for the Saryfim diminished, but devotion among the Valksha remained steadfast.

In the days following the War of Malblight, the role of the Valksha shifted in the eyes of the people. Once heralded as divine champions of the Saryfim, they became symbols of both reverence and fear. To many, their abilities were miracles—living proof of Elodyn's mercy and the Saryfim's lingering presence. But to others, they were reminders of the cost of war, beings too powerful and unpredictable to truly trust.

The Kyriegard emerged from this uncertainty, a beacon of impartiality in a fractured world. Unlike the Valksha, who drew strength from their devotion to Elodyn and the Saryfim, the Kyriegard positioned themselves as protectors of Moirand, unbound by divine allegiances. Born not of divine will but mortal necessity, it became an institution of balance. Their creed demanded neutrality, for faith could blind as often as it could guide; neutrality also demanded logic over emotion and discipline over devotion. They saw themselves not as servants of the divine, but as guardians of the mortal realm of Midthian, wielding discipline and logic to protect Moirand from the remnants of Malcifer's corruption.To ensure unity, it forbade apprentices from practicing worship, cultivating warriors and scholars who relied solely on their training.

Ophelia was the exception. The first and only Valksha to join the Kyriegard, she straddled the line between two worlds: one that revered her as Veladriel's last vessel and another that sought to temper her magic with discipline. The tension between her faith and her duty was a quiet struggle, one she bore with a resilience born of loss and hope. Where the Order saw impartiality as strength, she saw humanity in vulnerability and compassion.

As the sole Valksha of the Order, faith remained an unshakable part of her being. Faith was not a duty but a quiet comfort, a thread of connection to a world that often felt distant and unforgiving. To her, the Saryfim's blessings were not just tools of power but sacred gifts, and her prayers were as much a part of their magic as the blood that fueled it. This divergence often placed her in a precarious position—torn between the devout practices of her heritage and the Kyriegard's secular ethos.

Ophelia was the exception, not just as a Kyriegard initiate allowed to hold onto her faith, but in many other ways—ways in which Kaspar and Alfena argued for her case in order to set her up for success and allow her to tap into her power, and also ways that Margrith and Sigvard argued against due to the controversial nature that shook the core of the Order's traditions and threatened to unravel them. Her late initiation, her early permanent Dyad, and her silent faith. She could feel that most of her young initiate peers respected her outwardly, but she also sensed the fear and judgment laced in their words. Some avoided and scrutinized; others held genuine admiration and curiosity. And to some of them, she was arguably more terrifying than the Kyriegard apprentice with strange eyes and superhuman strength. This made her understand Theodin's isolation much more and helped them grow even closer to one another.

The Kyriegard's creed did not forbid belief alone; it simply demanded its subordination. For most apprentices, this was an easy adjustment—faith, if it existed at all, was something to leave behind. But for Ophelia, faith was more than a relic of her past. It was a thread connecting her to the Saryfim's light, a reminder of the divine essence she carried within her.

Ophelia carried the teachings of Veladriel the Ardent, not as dogma, but as a reminder of her own humanity. Yet even she struggled to reconcile the two halves of herself—the devout child who once prayed beneath starlit skies and the disciplined apprentice who learned to fight with logic and precision.

For Ophelia, every sabbath and every whispered prayer was a small rebellion against the Order's dispassionate creed. Not because she sought to challenge its teachings, but because she believed the heart and the mind could coexist in harmony. And though the world around her often seemed at odds with itself, she held onto the hope that faith and duty were not as different as they appeared.

As the months of training went on, the weight of her duality grew heavier. She was a Kyriegard apprentice, training to defend Moirand from darkness. But she was also a Valksha, bound by faith to honor the Saryfim who had shaped her magic. It was a delicate balance, one she navigated with quiet resolve, knowing that one day the world might demand she choose.

A ripple of energy brushed against her awareness before Faust's quiet steps followed. His presence was tentative, his eyes flicking over her before he spoke. "You're always working on that thing," he said, nodding toward the rifle.

"It's important to keep it in shape," she replied without looking up. "A poorly maintained weapon can fail you when it matters most."

Faust hovered a moment longer before perching on the edge of the bench beside her, leaving enough space for her to finish her work. "Do you always work this late?"

Ophelia gave a little chuckle, pausing to adjust the alignment of the rifle's sights.

"There's always a lot to do. I have to make up for the years of training I didn't get to have before I came here."

His gaze lingered on her hands as they moved deftly over the rifle.

"You're different from what I expected," he murmured out of nowhere.

She glanced up, one brow arched in curiosity.

"Different how?"

"I don't know," Faust admitted. "You're not like the others. The Kyriegard—they seem… detached. Focused entirely on duty. But you… you feel more—"

"Human?" she interjected, a small smile tugging at the corner of her mouth.

Faust's expression lessened, and he nodded. "Yeah. Human."

Ophelia returned her attention to the rifle, her fingers moving with practiced precision.

"That's not always seen as a strength here," she admitted. "The Kyriegard value discipline and objectivity above all else. Emotions… they complicate things."

"And yet, you still carry them," he said. "Why?"

Her hands stilled for a moment, her eyes flicking up to meet his.

"Because they're part of who I am. And I think… denying that would mean losing a piece of myself." She then smirked and winked. "I'm also the last remnant of Veladriel the Ardent, Saryf of *Spirit* and *Heart*, remember? It's sort of impossible for me to never carry emotion, especially if my power is driven by it."

"How do you do it then?" Faust asked.

Ophelia looked back down. "Rigorous practice. Instead of reacting with an emotion, try to react with logic—instead of allowing fear to take hold of me, I have to trust myself and my ability to direct my magic with more intention. Alfena helps me a lot with that."

Faust's brow furrowed. "Does it ever… conflict? Your faith and what you're being trained to do here?"

Ophelia paused, her fingers halting momentarily before resuming their careful work on the rifle.

"Sometimes," she admitted softly. "The Kyriegard are built on logic, discipline, and duty. Faith isn't exactly a pillar of what we do—it's seen as something that could cloud judgment."

"And yet you keep it," Faust said, laced with curiosity.

"Because it reminds me of what I'm fighting for. My faith isn't about control or rules—it's about connection. To Elodyn, to the Saryfim, to Moirand. And to people. It helps me see the bigger picture when the Kyriegard ask me to focus only on the moment."

"Doesn't that make you… different? From the rest of them, I mean," he asked cautiously.

Ophelia smirked, her gaze lifting to meet his. "I've always been a little different. Lady Vivian said that's why she chose me to walk this path." Her expression shifted, her tone becoming reflective. "It's not easy, carrying both worlds—the sacred and the secular. But I think that's part of why I'm here. To prove it's possible. That you can be devout and still do what's necessary to protect the world."

Faust tilted his head, his eyes wincing slightly in thought.

"Do they ever ask you to… set it aside? Your faith?"

"They don't have to," Ophelia said. "The Kyriegard expect us to act without bias. That includes faith. But I've learned to carry it differently. It's not something I wear on my sleeve—it's in my choices, my actions. Faith isn't about declaring it for everyone to see. It's about living it."

Faust hesitated, his gaze drifting to the distant trees beyond the courtyard. "Do they let you practice at all? I've heard the Kyriegard aren't exactly welcoming to things like that."

Ophelia leaned back slightly.

"They don't forbid it. They're aware it's important to me as a Valksha. As long as it doesn't interfere with my duties and remains entirely private."

"And does it?" he asked, quieter now. "Interfere?"

She shook her head. "No. If anything, it keeps me grounded. I know some Temples of Elodyn like to be extravagant and others who are much more secluded and humble. I haven't attended any since I was left in the custody of the Kyriegard, and I truly never went as a child until I was in the custody of Lady Vivian. But I've learned to appreciate my faith much more through such isolated practice. It isn't about rituals or grand displays—it's about finding strength when I feel like I don't have any left. It's… quiet. Personal."

Faust studied her for a long moment, his eyes flickering with something unspoken.

"I don't know if I'd call faith quiet. Not for the Valksha, anyway. Everything I've heard says it's… all-encompassing. A way of life."

"It can be," Ophelia said. "For some, it's everything. And maybe it was for me too, once. But being here, training to be Kyriegard… it's different. So I've had to learn how to carry my faith in ways that aren't always visible."

"Like a secret," Faust said, his inflection tinged with something like understanding.

"Not a secret," she corrected gently. "As I said, it's my foundation. Something solid beneath everything else. When training pushes me to my limits or I feel like I can't hold my magic steady, I think of the Saryfim's light. It reminds me that I'm never truly alone."

Faust looked down at his hands, his fingers flexing absently. "I don't know if I have that. Something grounded, I mean. Maybe that's what I'm lacking in order to have control over this power."

Ophelia hesitated, her gaze softening as she watched his hands.

"You could," she said quietly. "Faith isn't something you have to find all at once. Sometimes it starts with just a moment. A choice."

His eyes met hers, searching for something in her expression.

"And you think I could have that? After everything?"

She nodded. "I think anyone can. If they're willing to try."

For a moment, silence settled between them, the hum of the evening air filling the space. Faust's gaze lingered on the horizon, his expression distant but no longer closed.

Ophelia returned to her rifle.

Faust's fingers flexed again, his thoughts drifting to the darkness he carried. Could something like faith—or even hope—really hold it back? Or was he too far gone?

"Thank you," Faust said suddenly, his voice barely above a whisper.

Ophelia paused, glancing up. "For what?"

"For… seeing me as more than I am," he said, his eyes meeting hers.

"You're more than you think," she replied, her tone light but unwavering. "You just have to believe it too."

Then, she paused. It was for a noticeably long moment. Then she smiled and carried on like she was back in the present.

Faust watched the subtle shift in Ophelia's expression as she sent some silent reassurance through the Dyad. He couldn't feel it, not in the way Theodin could, but he could sense the way she carried herself in those moments—like something unseen affected her, kept her grounded in ways he could never understand.

A pang of frustration curled in his chest. He exhaled slowly, forcing himself to shake it off.

"Do you ever doubt it?" he asked suddenly.

Ophelia, still focused on her rifle, raised an eyebrow.

"Doubt what?"

"All of this." Faust gestured vaguely around them. "The Dyad. The Kyriegard. What you are." He looked at her with a deeper intensity. "Do you ever wonder if it's all decided for you? If any of this is really your choice?"

Ophelia's fingers stilled on the rifle for only a fraction of a second before she resumed her work.

"I think choice and fate can coexist," she said. "The Dyad didn't ask me what I wanted, but that doesn't mean I'm trapped in it. It's a part of me, and I can choose what to do with it."

Faust huffed a quiet laugh, but it lacked humor.

"That's an awfully optimistic way of looking at things."

Ophelia smirked, closing the final panel of her rifle.

"Would you rather I be cynical about it?"

"No," Faust admitted. He flexed his fingers absently. "But it's easier to be."

She looked at him thoughtfully, tilting her head. Then, she straightened and perked.

"Come with me."

Faust blinked. "What?"

Ophelia stood, slinging her rifle across her back.

"The library. I want to look something up in a Valksha text Alfena found a week ago. It's still not first-hand, but it's got some validity. You might find it interesting."

Faust hesitated, his expression skeptical, but after a moment he exhaled and pushed himself to his feet.

"Alright, lead the way!"

Ophelia led Faust through the winding aisles with an easy

familiarity, pausing near a section lined with old Valksha tomes.

"This one," she murmured, pulling a thick, leather-bound volume from the shelf. She carried it over to a nearby reading alcove, where a small lantern shone against the stone walls. Faust followed, watching as she flipped through the delicate, timeworn pages.

"What are you looking for?" he asked, leaning over her shoulder.

Ophelia skimmed the text, tracing the Valksha script with her fingertips.

"A theory I read once, about how Valksha magic interacts with the body." She paused, her eyes flicking up to him. "You asked if I ever doubt the Dyad. If it's really my choice."

Faust's expression became uncertain.She turned the book toward him, pointing at a passage.

"The Valksha believed that magic isn't just energy—it's an extension of the self. That means instinct, emotion, and even subconscious thoughts can influence it." She tapped the page. "If that's true, then maybe the Dyad isn't just some external force binding me and Theodin together. Maybe it's just… amplifying what's already there."

Faust studied the words, his brow furrowing. "You're saying it doesn't control you—it just reacts to what's inside you?"

Ophelia nodded. "Maybe. Or maybe it's both. I don't know." She sat back, her expression contemplative. "But if Valksha magic is tied to the self, that might explain why my blood magic doesn't always require blood."

Faust arched an eyebrow. "What do you mean?"

Ophelia flexed her fingers. "Normally, I have to draw blood to activate my magic. But there have been moments when it just… happened. No blood. No conscious effort." She lifted her hand up and flourished her fingers, examining the runes etched in her skin. "Kaspar suggested once that it was because of Veladriel since he is the Saryf of Spirit and Heart. Most times, we've noticed that my bloodless outbursts happen in moments of fear."

Faust tapped his fingers against the edge of the table, his eyes squinting in thought.

"Fear," he echoed. "So when you're in danger, your magic just… reacts?"

Ophelia nodded, lowering her hand. "That's what we think. Blood magic requires intent and focus. But in moments where I lose control—where I don't have time to think—it manifests on its own." She exhaled, shaking her head. "That's what worries the Council the most.

A Kyriegard can't afford to let fear dictate their actions."

Faust huffed a quiet laugh. "And yet, fear is the one thing that keeps people alive."

Ophelia gave him a look, but he wasn't wrong.

He leaned forward, resting his chin on his knuckles.

"Have you ever tried to control it? Your bloodless magic, I mean. Not just letting it happen, but actually calling on it the way you would with blood?"

Ophelia hesitated, then shook her head. "Not intentionally."

Faust smirked. "Well, then. Maybe we should change that."

She scoffed. "You just want to see me accidentally set something on fire, don't you?"

Faust's smirk only widened into a grin, but there was curiosity behind his amusement.

"I'll be honest, it wouldn't be the worst thing I've seen. But no—I'm serious. If your magic responds to fear, maybe it's not about losing control. Maybe it's about what you're afraid of."

Ophelia frowned at that consideration.

Faust gestured toward the open space beside them. "Come on. Try it."

Ophelia eyed him warily. "You just want an excuse to push me into doing something reckless."

"Absolutely," he said without hesitation. "But also, I want to see if your magic actually listens to you—or just your instincts."

She sighed, glancing at her hands again. The thought of deliberately summoning bloodless magic felt… unnatural. Every time it had happened before, it had been a reflex, an uncontrolled reaction to something pressing. Trying to force it now seemed like inviting failure.

Still…

She stood slowly, stepping away from the table.

"Alright," she said, rolling her shoulders. "But if I end up throwing you into a bookcase, it's your fault."

Faust bowed his head. "I accept those terms."

She exhaled to ground herself. Closing her eyes, she reached inward, the way she did when she drew blood. She focused on the warmth beneath her skin, the pulse of magic waiting just beneath the surface. But where blood magic came like a steady flame, this was… different. Distant. Flickering. Like trying to grasp something half-formed.

Nothing happened.

Faust tilted his head. "Try thinking about something dangerous.

Something that scares you."

Ophelia scowled. "You sound like Kaspar."

"Well, he's not wrong," Faust pointed out. "Your magic already reacts to fear. Maybe if you direct that fear, you can actually control it."

He leaned in.

"From what I've seen so far, I know they teach the Kyriegard to suppress their emotions. Their fear. But you are a *Valksha.* Our emotions—*especially* yours—are deeply tied to our magic. Suppression doesn't work for us."

Suddenly, his sapphire eyes appeared to glimmer dangerously, and Ophelia felt a ripple from his fragmented aura.

"Suppression got me captured and tortured. It got your family *killed.*"

A shiver ran down Ophelia's spine and her heartbeat quickened. His words dug into her and reopened the old wound in her soul, and she felt her veins begin to burn. Her eyes winced shut as she clenched her fists.

A flicker of green light rippled over her skin.

Faust's expression fell.

"There. That was something."

Ophelia opened her eyes, glancing down at her arms. The runes were faintly glowing, but the moment she acknowledged them, the light flickered and dimmed.

She released a harsh breath and trembled slightly, shaken by the wave of energy that overcame and left in that moment.

"That…that wasn't fear," she muttered. "That was anger."

Faust watched her carefully. "It's still an emotion. A wild one."

Ophie.

Ophelia paused. Her face shifted as her head turned in the direction she felt her partner's presence.

I'm fine, she answered.

Faust sighed audibly and irritably, folding his arms and pacing away from the table.

Just…seeing something. Working on magic.

A long pause.

Be careful.

Suddenly, she felt Faust at her side.

"Think about it, Lia," he goaded in a whisper.

She didn't turn—he spoke right next to her ear.

"We've read records together of a Valksha's fury and the destruction it has caused. Think of what you and I are capable of."

He leaned in further, his whisper lowering. She could feel his broken energy cling to hers.

"We could hone our magic—*together*—and deliver the killers of our people to justice."

Ophelia inhaled sharply and shut her eyes again, bracing herself. Her stomach twisted. The runes on her arms pulsed brightly.

Faust's breath caught. "Ophelia—"

The lanterns overhead flickered violently. A gust of wind, seemingly from nowhere, swept through the library rustling the pages of the open tomes around them. The magic surged outward, not violently, but present—as though responding to something unseen.

Ophelia.

Theodin's voice cut through the swell of energy and emotion that threatened to spill out of her control. Her eyes flew open and her irises flashed. The runes in her skin faded from green to white.

She peered over her shoulder.

There, towering in the doorway, stood Theodin staring at her and Faust with a stern look. The matching runes in Theodin's arms mirrored the white glow in Ophelia's. As her shoulders dropped and she exhaled from the release of tension, Faust hesitated. He didn't move at first. His eyes flicked to Ophelia, then back to Theodin, as if weighing his odds. Then, slowly, he took a step back.

Theodin's unsettling gaze shifted and fixated on Faust.

"What are you doing to her?"

"Helping her," Faust answered casually. A crooked smile spread across his face. "Valksha research."

Theodin's eyes seared into him. Faust felt the hairs on the back of his neck stand.

Ophelia turned to face Theodin fully.

"He is," she said softly. Her lips parted, but she paused. The magic was still humming beneath her skin, the remnants of it pulsing in time with her heartbeat. She exhaled again, steadying herself, and then she met Theodin's gaze.

"I've got it handled here."

Theodin didn't move from the doorway. His glowering eyes followed Faust, cold and unwavering, until the Valksha boy finally turned away.

"We will reconvene later, Lia," Faust muttered.

Ophelia's eyes flitted to him. She nodded once.

"Very well."

With a fleeting glance to her and avoiding Theodin's stare, Faust ducked away into an aisle of shelves. As he vanished from sight, Theodin's eyes moved to lock with Ophelia's. They softened and became warm.

Ophie.

This time, his tone matched how he looked at her.

Any remnants of anger and bitterness she had felt just moments ago vanished into thin air.

Ophelia gave a sheepish half-smile and put her hands on her hips.

"Don't say my name like that," she chuckled in a low voice.

A matching smirk curled at the corner of Theodin's lips.

What, does it make you blush?

"No," she laughed, turning back to the table. She closed the cover of the tome and ran her fingers against the spine. It was slightly illuminated by the brightening white light in her palms. "You show up all mean and terrifying, and then you speak to me like that?"

Theodin's gaze lingered, the smirk fading just enough to soften the teasing edge.

You're the only one I'd ever speak to like this.

Something warm settled in Ophelia's chest. She swallowed, flipping the book shut a little too quickly.

"Flattering," she said timidly, but she didn't meet his eyes.

As she turned back towards the entrance, he was suddenly there right beside her—his presence protective and vigilant.

But she didn't even jump. She glanced up at him with an exhausted look. He frowned slightly.

Took a lot out of you.

"I'll be fine," she insisted. She took his hand, with both of their runes still aglow with white, and began for the exit. "Let's go."

As they left, Theodin turned and caught a glimpse of Faust watching them over his shoulder.

Chapter 30

The Isolated and Intuitive

Year 845 of the Second Age, Sixth Month, Twentieth Day
Five months later.

The training fields of Avasylon hummed with anticipation, the air sharp with the metallic tang of practice weapons and the muted murmur of apprentices observing from the edges. The midday sun fully illuminated the arena where four figures stood poised, ready to engage.

Ophelia adjusted her grip on her chained blade, her fingers curling tightly around the hilt and the links clinking with her movement. The runes in the metal glowed green from her touch.

Across from her, two human Kyriegard apprentices—Vladimir and Jezadine, a pair bonded in the second phase of the Kyriegard Arcane Dyad ritual and a few years older—mirrored her stance, their expressions focused but wary.

Vladimir was broad-shouldered and stoic, with close-cropped dark hair and a deep scar running from his jaw to the base of his throat. Beside him, Jezadine moved like coiled wire, her lean frame taut with precision. Her ash-blonde hair was tied back in a braid, and her bright blue eyes tracked every movement with the calculation of someone who rarely missed. Where Vladimir radiated grounded force, Jezadine crackled with speed and tension—opposites made dangerous through perfect balance.

Beside Ophelia, Theodin stood tall, his jarring-colored eyes piercing with quiet determination. Their Dyad sang between them with a steady undercurrent of energy.

Faust lingered at the sidelines, his eyes following Ophelia's movements intently. His arms were crossed, but his posture betrayed a restless curiosity, as though he were trying to piece together the puzzle of their bond and the rhythm of their teamwork.

Kaspar's voice rang out, cutting through the tension.

"No magic. Focus on strategy, synchronization, and adaptability. Show me what you've learned."

The moment his words faded, Vladimir and Jezadine moved first, their steps perfectly in sync. Vladimir's blade came toward Theodin in a wide arc, while Jezadine lunged low toward Ophelia. Theodin countered with a sharp deflection, his movements fluid and precise. Ophelia pivoted, her blade meeting Jezadine's with a resounding clang, the force of the strike vibrating up her arm.

"Good," Kaspar called, his gaze tracking their movements. "Don't just react. Anticipate. Use your Dyad."

Ophelia inhaled sharply, steadying herself. She felt Theodin's energy flare through the Dyad—a silent signal that he was about to shift. She stepped left instinctively, creating space for him to drive Vladimir back with a swift series of strikes. Jezadine pressed forward, but Ophelia's blade was there, intercepting her before she could exploit the opening.

Their opponents were skilled, and their movements were precise, but Ophelia and Theodin had something more. Their bond wasn't just a tool; it was a language, a rhythm. When Jezadine feinted high, Ophelia felt Theodin's silent nudge and dropped low, swinging her chained blade toward Jezadine's exposed side. When Vladimir tried to flank, Theodin was already there, cutting off his path with a sharp parry.

Faust watched, his brows furrowing as he tried to decipher the unspoken coordination between them.

In the six months he had been at Avasylon, Faust had witnessed many Kyriegard pairs train together. He had studied their precision, their calculated exchanges, and the almost mechanical synchronization born from years of discipline.

But Ophelia and Theodin were different—there was something raw and organic about the way they moved. The connection between them felt alive, almost tangible, as though it existed in the space between their words and movements. It wasn't just strategy or training—it was instinct.

Instinct, the Elf lady said, was *not* what the Dyad was.

But that's what *Valksha* magic was, and what do you do with a Valksha in an Arcane Dyad?

Clanging of metal as it collided. The speed of their bodies as they moved.

The synergy was astounding. When Ophelia parried a blow but her opponent swung a quick follow-up strike, Theodin swooped in out of nowhere to block it while she fluidly knocked away an attack by his opponent. Every synchronized movement made their matching runes on their arms and hands flare with white light. Seamlessly, they switched back and lunged at their original opponents to catch them further off guard. It was a beautiful, dangerous dance.

It was disconcerting. But it could be almost awe-inspiring to watch, and Faust felt it too. Though his Valksha magic was tainted, the fractured magic within him was still sensitive to energy, and Ophelia's presence was unmistakable. Her energy was like a flame—bright, steady, and impossibly warm. Upon touch, Theodin's was heavier, more grounded, like the unyielding strength of the earth beneath their feet. Together, their bond pulsed with an intensity that was impossible to ignore, a rhythm that seemed to pull them toward each other even when they weren't in motion.

In those times, Faust would notice Theodin's usual hardened gaze turned soft upon seeing her, or Ophelia's lively and lovely emerald eyes brightened at Theodin's entrance into a room.

What struck Faust most was how natural it all was to them, yet how unnatural it was to him and everyone else. Over and over, he had watched Theodin move to block an attack on Ophelia's blind side before she even needed to turn her head, and saw her counter a strike aimed at Theodin with an ease that suggested she'd felt it coming before it happened. There was no hesitation, no second-guessing—just an understanding so complete it bordered on eerie. Though he had seen it happen many times, it fascinated and surprised him each time.

Faust's lips pressed into a thin line as he folded his arms tighter. How do they do it? he wondered. Is it the Dyad? Or is it them?

He could see how their connection set them apart—and why it unsettled the Order. It wasn't just that they had bypassed the usual stages of the Kyriegard Arcane Dyad; it was the sheer depth of it. Faust didn't need to know every detail to understand that what they shared was rare, maybe even dangerous in the wrong hands.

And yet, as much as he tried to distance himself from the intensity of their bond, he couldn't deny the ache of longing that it stirred in him. The way Ophelia's energy complemented Theodin's and the way they moved as one—it was a kind of unity he had never known, a partnership that went beyond words or duty. It was something he hadn't realized he wanted until he saw it in them.

He exhaled quietly, his eyes squinting as he focused on Ophelia again. She flawlessly parried an incoming strike from Jezadine. Her energy flared briefly as she sent her opponent retreating, but it wasn't wild or uncontrolled—it was focused, purposeful.

Faust's gaze softened slightly. Ophelia was unlike anyone he'd ever met. Despite the raw power she carried, there was a lightness to her—a willingness to connect, to trust, that defied the hardened edges of the Kyriegard. He wasn't sure if it was her faith, her magic, or just who she was, but it made her stand out in a way that both inspired and confused him.

And then there was Theodin. Faust had tried to read him, to understand what drove him, but the other apprentice was a fortress—stoic, disciplined, and fiercely protective. Faust didn't need to feel the Dyad to see the way Theodin watched Ophelia, the way his movements always aligned with hers. It wasn't just partnership—it was devotion.

Faust's jaw tightened as he glanced down at his hands. He was taught in his captivity that connection was a weakness, something that made people vulnerable. But here, watching them, he wondered if it could also be a source of strength.

The bond between Ophelia and Theodin wasn't something he could fully understand. But he could feel it. And whether he liked it or not, it was always there, motivating and mocking him at the same time.

For a fleeting moment, a pang of bitterness crept in, uninvited.

It wasn't jealousy—it was the stark reminder of what he lacked.

No bond. No Dyad. No partner.

Just fractured power and the weight of isolation.

The clang of blades rang and echoed, mingling with the apprentices' labored breaths and the metallic tang of sweat hanging in the air.

Theodin's voice echoed through the bond, low but firm, directed at Ophelia without breaking their rhythm.

Jezadine's favoring her left. Use it.

Ophelia nodded, her emerald eyes narrowing as she adjusted her stance. She advanced on Jezadine; her strikes were rigorous and relentless, driving the other apprentice back. Her chain rattled wildly, but it obeyed her every movement. The Dyad hummed with Theodin's approval, a ripple of encouragement that steadied her resolve.

But Vladimir and Jezadine weren't easily outmatched.

With a sharp whistle, Vladimir signaled a shift in their strategy. Jezadine fell back, and Vladimir surged forward, his blade aimed at Ophelia's chest. For a moment, it seemed as though he'd break through, but then Theodin was there, intercepting the strike with a deft twist of his blade.

"Better," Kaspar called, clipped but approving. "But you're leaving gaps. Tighten your formation."

Faust's gaze flicked to Kaspar, then back to the sparring pairs. He could see what the elder Kyriegard meant—small hesitations, fractions of a second where their coordination faltered. But even those moments were fleeting, quickly overcome by the sheer force of their bond.

Theodin and Ophelia pressed their advantage, their movements a blend of discipline and instinct. Jezadine stumbled, her defenses faltering under Ophelia's perpetual assault, and Vladimir found himself cornered as Theodin's blade hovered dangerously close to his neck.

Kaspar raised a hand, signaling the end of the match. "Enough."

The apprentices stepped back, their breaths coming in sharp bursts. Ophelia wiped the sweat from her brow, her emerald eyes flicking to Theodin. He met her gaze with a small nod, the Dyad thrumming with mutual acknowledgment.

"Impressive," Kaspar said, his gaze sweeping over them. "But you're not invincible. Don't let your bond make you complacent."

"Yes, sir," Theodin replied, his voice steady despite the exertion.

As Vladimir and Jezadine retreated, their expressions a mix of frustration and respect, Faust approached the center of the courtyard. His eyes lingered on Ophelia, his tone cautious but curious.

"That was… something."

Ophelia glanced at him, her smile faint but genuine. "It's all about practice."

"Practice," Faust echoed, his gaze shifting to Theodin. "Or is it something else? The way you two move… it's not just skill. It's like you're reading each other's minds."

Theodin smirked, his eyes glinting with quiet amusement.

"Something like that."

Kaspar's voice cut through the moment, sharp and commanding. "Faust, if you're done gawking, perhaps you'd like to join the next round. Let's see if you've been paying attention."

Faust stiffened.

"Y-Yes, sir," he stammered.

"Ophelia, on the sidelines."

She stepped back, her gaze shifting between Theodin and Faust.

Kaspar's voice broke the stillness. "Faust, step forward."

Faust hesitated for the briefest moment, his eyes flicking toward Ophelia before he took his place at the center of the courtyard.

"You'll face a simulated opponent first," Kaspar instructed. "No theatrics. No panic. Focus on control and precision."

A human Kyriegard veteran stepped into view—Dorek, Ophelia had told Faust earlier that day—broad-shouldered and weathered with a salt-streaked beard and a long scar curving from his temple to his jaw. His armor was worn but well-maintained, the sigils etched into his bracers glowing faintly with residual Sage magic. There was no aggression in his stance—only experience, the calm steadiness of someone who had seen countless battles and didn't need to prove a thing.

"You've improved," Kaspar continued as he paced along the sideline. "You've demonstrated that you can be trusted—to a degree —" His eyes briefly flashed to Ophelia, then back to Faust. "—but the question is, can we truly trust your magic under pressure?"

The courtyard grew silent, the air heavy with anticipation.

"Begin," Kaspar commanded.

Dorek drew his blade and lunged. Faust sidestepped, using the needle ring technique he learned from Ophelia—his movements were quick but stiff, his hands glowing weakly with unstable blue light. His magic flared, a tendril of energy spiraling toward his opponent.

"Steady," Kaspar barked.

Faust inhaled sharply, his fists clenching as he wrestled the energy into submission. The light dimmed, condensing into a controlled arc that struck Dorek's weapon, disarming him with a resounding clang. The courtyard echoed with the sound, and a murmur of approval rippled through the apprentices watching from the edges.

Kaspar nodded curtly. "Good. You can hold it back when you need to."

Ophelia's chest eased with relief as she watched Faust lower his hands, his eyes scanning the grounds with a mixture of pride and disbelief. She caught his gaze and offered a small, encouraging smile.

"Don't celebrate yet," Kaspar interrupted. "Next, you'll face Ophelia."

Faust stiffened. "Her?"

"Yes," Kaspar said sharply. "She's your next test. And you'd do well not to underestimate her."

Ophelia stepped forward, her chained blade glinting in the filtered light. She gave Faust a reassuring nod, though her grip on the weapon tightened.

"You've got this," she said softly, her emerald eyes meeting his.

Faust exhaled slowly, his fingers nervously fidgeting as faint tendrils of energy flickered around them.

"Are you sure about this?"

"I am," Ophelia replied with quiet conviction. "Just trust yourself. Remember what we worked on."

Kaspar's voice rang out again. "Begin."

The first exchange was tentative. Faust moved cautiously, his magic coiling tightly around his hands as though he were afraid to let it go. Ophelia pressed him with a series of swift but deliberate strikes, whipping her chained blade in his direction.

"You're hesitating," she called, her tone calm but firm. "If you don't commit, you'll lose control."

Faust growled under his breath, stepping back as her blade arced toward him. He raised his hands, sending a pulse of blue energy to deflect the strike. The energy wavered but held, forcing Ophelia to retreat a step.

"Better," Kaspar observed.

But Faust's hesitation lingered. As she pressed him with subsequent strikes, his movements became erratic, and his magic flared in bursts as his frustration mounted.

"You're holding back, Ophelia," Theodin barked. "Don't go easy on him."

"Focus!" Kaspar shouted.

Faust's eyes darted to Ophelia, panic flickering in his gaze. "I'm trying!"

The turning point came in a flash. Ophelia lunged, her blade sweeping low to test his defense. Faust reacted instinctively, his magic surging in a desperate attempt to block her—but the energy coalesced into a jagged arc, crackling with unstable power as it tore through the air—far stronger than he intended.

Ophelia's runes flared in response, but the attack was faster than her reflexes. Her breath caught as the flare of energy streaked toward her.

Before she could brace for impact, Theodin was there.

The Dyad raged violently, a wave of urgency crashing into her as her partner moved with lightning speed. His blade met the arc of energy mid-flight, absorbing most of the blow, but the force sent him skidding back across the field.

Silence.

"Theodin!"

Ophelia's voice broke through the stillness as she rushed to his side.

Her heart pounded in her chest, the Dyad thrumming with his steady but strained energy. She felt the singe of pain radiating in her arm—that was where he must've been hit. Panic overcame her as she dropped to her knees, pricked her finger on her ring to draw blood, and held her hand over him.

His hand snapped out and snatched her wrist.

"I'm fine," Theodin said gruffly, brushing off her concern as he rose to his feet. Scorch marks sizzled on the gauntlet and sleeve of his sword arm. His harrowing eyes burned with seething intensity as he turned to Faust.

"Next time, don't lose your nerve."

Faust stood frozen, his hands trembling.

"I—I didn't mean to—"

Kaspar stepped forward.

"Enough. Faust, you've proven that your magic remains unstable under pressure. This is why we proceed with caution."

Faust's jaw tightened, shame and frustration creasing his expression.

"I'm sorry," he whispered.

Ophelia turned to him, her emerald eyes soft but consoling.

"Breathe, Faust. It's over."

The courtyard remained heavy with tension as Kaspar dismissed the sparring session. The apprentices began to disperse, their murmurs filling the air.

As the crowd thinned, Ophelia remained beside Theodin, her hands shimmering as she checked the minor burns left on his arm.

"You didn't have to jump in like that," she murmured, her tone both scolding and grateful.

"Yes, I did," Theodin replied, his gaze locking with hers.

"You're not taking a hit like that. Not while I'm here."

Ophelia exhaled, her shoulders sagging.

Faust lingered at the edge of the courtyard, his eyes fixed on the ground. The weight of his failure hung over him, but he couldn't ignore the faint echo of Ophelia's words.

"It's over."

He clenched his fists, but the phantom warmth of her reassurance stayed with him.

The last of the apprentices had dispersed, their murmurs fading into the fields of Avasylon as they left for Havysium. The underground courtyard was quiet now, the tension of the sparring session still hanging in the air.

Ophelia stood by the edge of the field, her chained blade resting at her side as she looked out at the tree line thoughtfully.

Behind her, Theodin approached, his eyes studying her. Reading her.

"You're quiet," he remarked, his voice low.

She glanced over her shoulder, offering him a faint smile. "Just thinking."

Theodin moved to stand beside her, his arms crossed as he leaned against the stone fence. The Dyad vibrated with his steady presence like a comforting current.

"About what?"

Ophelia hesitated, her fingers brushing idly against the hilt of her blade.

"Faust. The Council. Us."

She turned to face him, her eyes meeting his.

"Do you think… this is sustainable?"

He tilted his head, his brow furrowing slightly. "This?"

"Our bond. The Dyad. The way we bypassed everything—the tests, the rituals," she said quietly, tinged with doubt. "I know it makes us stronger, but it also makes us… different. And the Council doesn't like different. They also don't like that they can't reverse it—at least in the first two stages it's possible."

Her eyes fell to his sword arm, observing the scorch marks. She reached for his gauntlet and brushed her fingertips where the leather was blackened. Upon contact, their runes shone with white.

"There's a reason there are *three* stages of the Arcane Dyad—the first two stages don't make a pair as intricately interwoven in energy, thoughts, or emotions as the final one."

Theodin's expression softened, and he exhaled slowly.

"They don't have to like it," he said. "They just have to accept it. What we have—it works. We've proven that."

"Have we?" Ophelia asked, wavering slightly. "The Council doesn't see it that way. They see something that broke tradition, something unpredictable." She hesitated, her fingers lingering on the edge of his gauntlet. "We skipped steps that were meant to safeguard us. Without those safeguards…" Her voice trailed off, her eyes lifting to meet his. "What if it doesn't hold? What if we're the anomaly that proves the rule's existence?"

"Do you feel like it's breaking? Does the Dyad feel fragile to you?"

She shook her head almost immediately. "No. That's the problem—it feels too strong. Like there's no boundary between what's mine and what's yours. It's… overwhelming sometimes. And if it feels that way to me, imagine how it must look to them."

Theodin clenched his jaw, turning to look at the field briefly, then back to her.

"They don't see what we see," he said. "They don't feel what we feel. All they know is what they can measure. And the Dyad… it doesn't fit into their measurements."

Ophelia swallowed hard, her gaze dropping back to his arm. She traced the faint scorch marks with her fingers, her touch featherlight.

"If that blast hit you the wrong way…"

She winced, shook her head, and then continued in a quieter voice—though her intensity remained the same.

"There's a reason the rituals exist. They're supposed to give us time to grow into this, to learn how to carry it. Instead, we've been running a sprint when it's supposed to be a marathon."

Theodin's hand shifted, gently brushing hers aside as he straightened.

"We didn't choose this, Ophelia. But we're not breaking under it, either." His voice softened, his eyes searching hers. "What happened with Faust—that wasn't the Dyad failing. That was me making a choice."

Ophelia stepped towards him. "What happened with Faust today… it wasn't just about him. If you hadn't stepped in—"

"I would do it again," Theodin interrupted, his eyes snapping to hers. "Every time."

As their gazes locked, their energy and Dyad intensified. But it wasn't unwelcome. At first, it was soothing—warm, affectionate, caring.

Ophelia blushed slightly. She shook her head to refocus.

"That's the problem," she said, her tone thick with frustration. "You shouldn't have to. I'm supposed to be able to handle myself, and instead, you're always stepping in—always protecting me."

Theodin didn't falter. "It's not about whether you can handle yourself. I know you can. But the Dyad—it's not just about what you can do or what I can do. It's about what we do together. And if that means stepping in when you need me, then that's what I'll do."

Ophelia sighed, her shoulders slumping as she stepped away and folded her arms.

"It's not just about us, though. The Council is watching. They're waiting for us to slip up to prove that we're a liability."

Theodin only shifted closer, his voice lowering.

"Let them watch. Let them doubt. It doesn't change what we are. We've come this far because we trust each other, because we're stronger together. They can't take that from us."

She turned her head to look at him, her eyes searching his face. "You really believe that?"

"I do," he said, unwavering. "Do you?"

Ophelia hesitated, the Dyad between them continuously betraying their thoughts and feelings to each other.

She could feel his conviction, his unyielding faith in their partnership, and it steadied her.

"I want to," she admitted softly.

Theodin's lips twitched into a faint smile. "Then that's enough. For now."

They stood in silence for a moment, the weight of their words settling between them. Finally, Ophelia straightened, brushing a strand of raven hair from her face.

"You're getting better at this whole 'emotional support' thing, you know."

Theodin huffed a quiet laugh. "I learned from the best, didn't I?"

She smirked, the tension in her chest easing slightly. "Me? I didn't know I was such a role model. You're supposed to be the model Kyriegard around here."

As laughter erupted between them, their Dyad thrummed warmly with a soothing aura.

From the shadowed edge of the courtyard, Faust lingered, his eyes fixed on the two apprentices. He leaned against a stone pillar, arms folded tightly across his chest, as if bracing himself against the weight of his own thoughts. He wasn't close enough to hear their conversation, but he didn't need to. The way they stood, the energy rippling like butterflies between them, was enough to tell him what he needed to know.

Their Dyad was a constant hum in the air; it was almost palpable to him. He had felt it during the sparring session—a thread of connection so deep and steadfast that it bordered on the supernatural. Even now, it pulsed with a warmth he could only describe as unbreakable. It wasn't the Dyad itself that unsettled him; it was what it represented.

Unity. Trust. Purpose.

Faust exhaled sharply, his gaze dropping to his hands. His fingers twitched and curled unconsciously, as if trying to grasp something just out of reach.

He had never known that kind of connection, that kind of partnership. The fractured remnants of his magic stirred within him, reacting to the ever-present thread of their Dyad. It wasn't jealousy he felt—it was something deeper, something quieter. A longing he couldn't quite name.

He lifted his gaze again, watching as Theodin leaned in slightly, his eyes attentive on Ophelia with an intensity that was both protective and reverent. Ophelia's expression became tender, her eyes reflecting a trust so absolute it made Faust's chest tighten. They didn't just move in harmony; they existed in it.

"They don't even realize how rare it is," Faust muttered to himself.

The Valksha magic within him shifted in discomfort. Despite its fractured nature, it still allowed him to sense energy in ways most couldn't.

Ophelia's light burned bright, her presence steady and adamant. Theodin's was different—grounded, but no less powerful. Together, their bond wasn't just complementary; it was symbiotic. Each strengthened the other, filling gaps the other couldn't see.

Faust's jaw tightened as he glanced down at his own hands. His magic flared weakly within him, a reminder of its broken state. He had spent months trying to piece himself back together, but watching them—Ophelia and Theodin—made him realize just how much he was missing. It wasn't just about power or control. It was about connection. About trust.

And trust was something he didn't know if he could give—or receive.

A sharp laugh drew his attention back to the pair. Ophelia was grinning, her expression lighter now, while Theodin's lips curved into a coy smirk. The Dyad between them resonated giddily, a reflection of their shared moment.

Faust felt a pang in his chest, a mixture of admiration and unease.

"They're stronger because of it," he whispered, his voice bitter. "And I'm just… a mess."

For a fleeting moment, he considered stepping closer, inserting himself into their world. But what would he say? What could he offer? He was a stranger to bonds like theirs, a boy shaped by isolation and manipulation. The idea of standing in their light felt almost unbearable.

Instead, he turned away, his eyes shadowed. He had been given a second chance here at Avasylon, but as he walked away, he couldn't shake the feeling that some things were beyond his reach. Watching them, he saw what connection could be. But in the hollow ache of his chest, he also saw what it had cost him to survive.

And for now, survival was all he could cling to.

Chapter 31

The Unraveling

Year 845 of the Second Age, Sixth Month, Twenty-First Day

"How long can we continue to ignore the signs?" Sigvard's voice rumbled through the Council chamber, his Dwarven accent thick with frustration. "The once peaceful Undarim are stirring, Cuthbert DuFrey in Belluxa consolidates power, and the uncivilized Cadaven and Cadaven beasts are multiplying. The Unseelie Pulchids in Hallowdale have increased crime. We need stability within our Order, not experiments."

"At least Zyreus Vlahdwulf in Erythar seems to be relatively quiet," Crane muttered under his breath. "For now. Until he starts an argument with Southern Regania again."

Kaspar leaned back in his chair, his eyes on Sigvard with a calm intensity that belied the storm brewing within him.

"And what do you suggest, Sigvard? That we unravel the Dyad between Ophelia and Theodin, and permanently cripple them? Or do you propose we cast them out entirely?"

Alfena's melodic voice cut through the tension.

"Neither is feasible, and you know it, Nimrod. The Dyad is irreversible. Any attempt to sever it could damage them both—physically and mentally. If we've learned anything over the past year, it's that their bond, their Dyad, for all its unpredictability, is stable."

"Stable?" Margrith's sharp tone turned heads. The elder councilwoman's weathered features were etched with skepticism. "You call what happened in the Avasylon yesterday stable? Theodin's actions were reckless, and Ophelia's reliance on him is growing too dependent. He had the most potential and was a model Kyriegard initiate until they bonded. Now? Her recklessness has bled into him. She's ruined him."

Crane thumped his cane against the floor, his voice rising with uncharacteristic sharpness.

"Not necessarily, dear Margrith! Our favorite golden boy remains at the top of his class—they are still excelling as a completely bonded pair. They've bested every other apprentice pair they've come up against."

"But they're supposed to be simultaneously developing as individuals," Sigvard interjected. "The completed Dyad is interfering with that. If one falters, the other suffers. We saw a prime example of that yesterday. Theodin could have been killed if that wild energy of Faust's struck him anywhere vital."

"They are apprentices," Kaspar countered. "We are fortunate how thoroughly Theodin has been trained, but he is not perfect, either. Mistakes are expected. What matters is how they learn from them."

Sigvard slammed a heavy hand on the table.

"Mistakes like these cannot be afforded when we're on the brink of war! DuFrey grows bolder, the Unseelie stir unrest, and the Undarim dig beneath our feet, stirring who-knows-what in the depths. We need Kyriegard who uphold tradition, not ones who rewrite it."

"Tradition," Alfena murmured, her eyes narrowing. "Tradition alone cannot face what is coming. The bond between Ophelia and Theodin is unprecedented, yes, but it is also a strength. They communicate on a level that no ritual could replicate. They can sense where the other has gone and how far. It is organic, raw, and powerful. This is beyond any completed Arcane Dyad I've seen."

"Powerful, yes," Margrith snapped. "But power unchecked is chaos."

A low hum of agreement rippled through the chamber until Crane tapped his cane against the floor, drawing their attention.

"Chaos is not inherently dangerous," he said, his wild chestnut eyes gleaming with a calculated edge. "The question is whether we can harness it. And if not, whether we can afford to let it loose."

Kaspar leaned forward, his voice steady but laced with urgency. "And how do we harness it? By training them. By testing them. Not by fearing them."

"And if they fail the tests?" Margrith challenged. "What then? Can we risk two apprentices so bound that one cannot function without the other?"

Alfena tilted her head, her tone soft but firm.

"Do you truly believe that's what their Dyad is? Dependence? Or is it something we don't fully understand because it challenges our preconceptions of what a Kyriegard pair should be?"

The chamber became silent then, the weight of her words pressing down on them.

It was Sigvard who broke it, his voice quieter now but no less resolute.

"This is not just about the Dyad. It's about what happens if it fails, now that we've seen the possible outcome of it. What do we do if the strength they share becomes their undoing? If the weight of it pulls them both down when Moirand needs them most?"

"Then we prepare them," Kaspar said. "As we had said months ago, we refine their strengths and teach them to mitigate their weaknesses. That's the purpose of their training. It's the same as it's always been, even if their circumstances are different. We are learning as we go, as we have done before with any new Sage technique."

Alfena's voice lessened, carrying an undercurrent of caution. "Sigvard raises a fair question, though. This isn't about bending to tradition or dismissing it outright. It's about understanding whether this bond, this Dyad, this… anomaly, enhances or compromises their ability to function as Kyriegard."

Crane's eyes gleamed with mischief and calculation as he spoke next. "The Kyriegard have long touted logic and discipline, yes. But is that truly all we need to face what's coming? Or is there room for something new—something deeper?"

Alfena nodded slowly. "What we've seen from them is unprecedented. Their Dyad doesn't just unite them—it elevates them. It makes them more than the sum of their parts."

Kaspar let out a low breath.

"We train them," he repeated firmly. "We test them. Not out of fear, but because we owe it to them—and to Moirand—to understand what this bond truly means."

Crane's cane tapped again, his lips curling into an enigmatic smile.

"And what of Faust?" he asked, deceptively light. "The fractured Valksha who lingers on the edges of our Order. How does he fit into this delicate balance?"

"Faust is not Kyriegard," Kaspar answered. "His training is to ensure he is not a danger to himself or others. Beyond that, his place here is temporary."

"And yet," Crane mused, "his presence stirs questions. Questions of loyalty, of trust. He watches them—Ophelia and Theodin—with the eyes of someone trying to understand what he cannot possess."

"Faust is an outlier," Kaspar said. "He is not our concern in this deliberation."

"But he is theirs," Alfena interjected. "Ophelia believes in him. Theodin tolerates him for her sake. Their bond may be their strength, but it is also their vulnerability. Faust knows that even if he doesn't understand it."

Margrith exhaled sharply, her frustration palpable. "So, what is our course of action? Do we wait for another misstep? For another test they might fail?"

Kaspar stood, his presence commanding as he addressed the room.

"We continue to train all three of them. We continue to test them. And we prepare for the Kyriegard Trials ahead—any trials for that matter, and not just for them but for the Order and for Moirand. Because whether we like it or not, the world is changing. And we must change with it."

The Council became speechless again.

Outside, the faint sound of footsteps echoed through the hall, a reminder of the apprentices waiting just beyond the chamber doors.

"Very well," Margrith said finally, grudgingly but resigned. "But let us not forget—this is not just about them. It is about us. About the Kyriegard. And about whether we can still hold Moirand together when the cracks begin to show."

The Council chamber had long emptied, the echoes of debate still lingering in the high stone ceilings of Halvalla.

Kaspar stood by the tall, narrow window, his eyes looking upon the sprawling view of the courtyard below. Alfena leaned against the table, her gaze thoughtful as she studied her old friend.

"You've been quiet," Alfena said, her melodic voice breaking the silence. "That's unusual, even for you."

Kaspar turned slightly, his expression unreadable. "The deliberation was exhaustive. Everyone made their positions clear."

"And yet you still seem… uneasy," Alfena observed, folding her arms. "Is it because you don't entirely disagree with Margrith? Or is it something else?"

He hesitated, his gaze returning to the courtyard. Below, the silhouettes of apprentices sparring danced against the stone walls.

"The Dyad between Ophelia and Theodin is stable, but it's not without risk."

"Risk is inherent in every Arcane Dyad," Alfena said, stepping closer. "This one is no different."

Kaspar's eyes shifted fully to her.

"It *is* different, Alfena. Their Dyad didn't evolve naturally through the stages; it was thrust upon them. And now, after a year, it's clear that it's more than just a partnership. Their feelings for each other… they're growing."

Alfena tilted her head, her expression thoughtful.

"And why is that a problem?"

Kaspar's tired eyes hardened.

"There is a reason it is forbidden in our Order. Because such *feelings* complicate things. They cloud judgment. The Order demands objectivity. A Kyriegard pair must function as a single unit, not as two individuals bound by emotional ties."

"But isn't that what they already are?" Alfena countered. "A single unit? Their Dyad has proven that. Their connection allows them to anticipate each other's movements, to adapt in ways other pairs cannot. Are you worried their feelings will weaken them or that they will make them too strong?"

Kaspar stared. The question then hung in the air as it went unanswered for several moments.

Finally, Kaspar turned away, his voice low as he spoke.

"Strength unchecked can become a liability."

"And yet, you've trained Theodin to wield strength responsibly since he was a boy," Alfena said, gentle but firm. "And you've seen how Ophelia's faith tempers her power. Their feelings for each other are not a flaw, Kaspar. They're a foundation."

"They're young," he said quietly. "Too young to carry the weight of the Order's scrutiny, let alone the weight of their own hearts."

Alfena smiled faintly. "You were young once, too. Do you remember?"

Kaspar's voice became edged.

"*Don't*. Alfena."

Alfena did not falter.

"Nimrod. You and I both know that's what he would've said too."

Kaspar didn't respond immediately; his gaze was distant.

"That was different."

"Was it?" Alfena pressed. "We all carry the echoes of the people we've loved, the bonds we've forged. Ophelia and Theodin's feelings are part of who they are. Denying that would only fracture what makes them strong."

He exhaled slowly, his shoulders sagging slightly.

"And if their feelings become a weakness? If one day, they're forced to choose between each other and the Order?"

Alfena's expression grew somber.

"Then we guide them. That is our role as mentors—to prepare them for the choices they may one day face. But I don't believe their Dyad will break them, Kaspar. I believe it will shape them into something the Kyriegard has never seen before."

Kaspar turned to her, his eyes searching hers.

"And if you're wrong?"

A faint, enigmatic smile curved Alfena's lips.

"Then I trust we'll have done everything we could to ensure they're ready for whatever comes."

Another silence.

Kaspar finally turned back to the window, his expression thoughtful.

"They're heading into uncharted territory. We all are."

"Perhaps that's exactly what the Order needs."

Kaspar didn't reply, still watching the apprentices below.

Theodin leaned against the cold stone wall of the underground courtyard, fixated on Ophelia as she carefully disassembled and cleaned her rifle. The rhythmic clinking of metal filled the space. Her concentration was undisturbed, her eyes attentive as they followed the intricate movements of her fingers.

Seven months. That was all the time he had left before his Kyriegard Trials. The weight of it pressed against his thoughts like a second skin, one he could never quite shed. He was ready—at least, that's what Kaspar always told him. His technique was precise, and his strategies were sound.

He was disciplined. Focused. But the Trials weren't just about skill.

They were about resilience. About proving he could function as part of the Order's core.

The problem was, he wasn't sure the Council thought he could.

His gaze drifted to Faust, who dwelled near the edge of the courtyard. The fractured Valksha boy stood with his arms folded, his eyes occasionally flitting toward Ophelia.

Theodin had noticed the way Faust watched her, the way his energy seemed to shift whenever she was near. It wasn't malicious—there was no jealousy or threat in it. But there was something… *unsettling* about the way Faust observed her; it was as though he was trying to understand something he couldn't quite grasp.

And Ophelia didn't seem to notice. Or, if she did, she didn't let it bother her. She had taken Faust under her wing in a way Theodin couldn't fully comprehend. She believed in him; she saw potential where others saw only danger. It was one of the things he admired most about her—her unwavering faith in people, even when they didn't deserve it.

But it also made him uneasy.

And yet… he had done the same for her. Believed in her and saw her potential when they only saw her as a danger and a liability.

"You're awfully quiet," Ophelia said without looking up, her voice breaking the silence.

Theodin straightened slightly, realizing he'd been staring.

"Just thinking."

"About?" she prompted, light but curious.

"Everything," he admitted. "The Trials. The Council. Faust. Us."

At that, she paused, setting the rifle aside to meet his gaze.

"Us?" she echoed, her brows lifting slightly.

Theodin sighed, his eyes lowering as he searched for the right words.

"They're watching us more closely now. It feels like… every step we take, every decision we make, they're waiting for something to go wrong."

Ophelia leaned back slightly, her expression thoughtful. "And you think they'll find something? Especially after yesterday's… *incident?*"

"It's not about whether they find something," he said. "It's about whether we can keep proving them wrong. Every sparring match, every test—it's like we have to be perfect. And if we're not, they'll use it against us."

Ophelia's gaze shifted, a smile tugging at her lips.

"You're harder on yourself than they are, you know."

Theodin let out a humorless laugh.

"That's because I know what's at stake. For you, for me. For us."

He hesitated then, his hand brushing against the hilt of his sword as he glanced toward Faust.

"And then there's him."

Ophelia followed his gaze. "Faust?"

Theodin nodded, his voice lowering.

"I don't trust him."

"He's not Kyriegard," Ophelia reminded him gently. "He's not trying to be."

"That doesn't mean he's not a risk," Theodin countered. "The Council already doubts us. If something goes wrong with Faust, they won't just blame him—they'll blame us. And you know it."

Ophelia's lips pressed into a thin line, her eyes narrowing slightly. "Faust is trying. He's not perfect, but he's not dangerous either."

Theodin huffed softly, his eyes flicking back to her. "You don't see the way he looks at you."

Her brows furrowed, her expression changing into one of confusion. "What are you talking about?"

"He watches you," Theodin said simply. "Like he's trying to figure you out. Like he's… drawn to you."

Ophelia's expression became lighter, a hint of amusement tugging at her lips.

"He's curious, Theodin. That's not the same as being a threat."

"It's not just curiosity," Theodin muttered. "He looks at you like you're the answer to something he doesn't understand. And that's dangerous."

Ophelia stepped closer with her hands on her hips. She squinted, looked him up and down, and then smiled cheerily.

"You're worried about me."

"Of course I'm worried about you," he replied, sharper than he intended. "You trust too easily, Ophelia. You see the best in people, even when they don't deserve it."

She only smiled wider, but her voice remained soft but firm.

"And you see the worst in them, even when they don't deserve that either. That's why we balance each other."

The Dyad between them rustled softly, a quiet reassurance that steadied his racing thoughts.

Theodin exhaled, his shoulders relaxing slightly. "I just don't want him to hurt you. Or us."

"He won't," Ophelia said with quiet conviction. "I won't let him."

Theodin met her gaze, and the Dyad now shimmered with her certainty. For all his doubts, for all his frustrations, he couldn't argue with the faith she carried—not just in Faust, but in him.

Year 845 of the Second Age, Sixth Month, Twenty-Second Day

The sparring chamber beneath Avasylon was dimly lit by lanterns along the walls and the glow of enchanted runes casting faint shadows on the stone.

Ophelia stood across from Faust, her posture relaxed yet alert, the residual shimmer of Valksha magic lingering in her hands. Meanwhile, Faust was focused, his eyes locked on the flickering blue light coalescing between his fingers.

"Slowly," Ophelia instructed, her tone even. "Don't rush the flow. Feel it steady, like a current—not a storm."

Faust exhaled, his brow furrowing as he willed the magic to stabilize. The energy danced erratically at first but gradually settled, forming a more cohesive sphere. For a moment, the chamber was silent, save for the low hum of magic.

"There," Ophelia said, a hint of pride in her voice. "You're getting it."

Faust's shoulders relaxed slightly. The tension he hadn't even realized he was holding finally eased from his frame. The emitted shape of his magic lingered in his hands, steady and controlled in a way it hadn't been before. For the first time, it didn't feel like it was fighting him. It felt… manageable. His breath hitched at the realization, a mixture of relief and disbelief washing over him.

He glanced at Ophelia, her eyes gleaming with quiet encouragement. She was watching him—not with the skepticism or pity he'd grown so used to but with something genuine.

Belief.

It caught him off guard, leaving an unfamiliar warmth in its wake. No one had looked at him like that in years before he met her—maybe ever.

The thought made his chest tighten. It wasn't just the magic that had changed.

It was her.

The way she guided him with patience instead of frustration, with kindness instead of judgment. She made him want to try, made him believe, even if only for fleeting moments, that he wasn't broken beyond repair.

Faust swallowed hard, his eyes flicking back to his hands. The magic pulsing between his fingers was a small victory, but a victory nonetheless.

And it was hers as much as it was his.

Ophelia felt the shift before she saw it. Faust's energy rippled with something unexpected—relief, tinged with a fragile hope. It wasn't the sharp-edged frustration or simmering anger she'd come to recognize in him during their earlier sessions. This was softer, quieter, as though he was standing at the edge of something he didn't dare believe in.

"I wouldn't have gotten anywhere near this far without you," he admitted, the words spilling out before he could think them through.

As soon as they left his mouth, he felt exposed, vulnerable in a way that made him want to retreat.

But he didn't.

He couldn't, not with her steady and unflinching gaze still on him.

Ophelia tilted her head and blinked a few times, taken aback.

"That's not something I hear every day," she said softly, a light smile curling at her lips. "But you shouldn't sell yourself short. You've done the work, Faust. I just… gave you a push."

"Maybe," he replied, a touch sheepishly before his expression turned more serious. "I mean it. You don't just teach—you… see people. Like I said before. You saw something in me when I didn't."

Ophelia's smile widened a bit, a glimpse of something unreadable passing through her eyes.

"Maybe I did see something in you," she admitted. "But what matters is that you're starting to see it too. That's where the real work begins."

She paused, thinking through her words carefully.

"Believing in someone is the easy part, Faust. Helping them believe in themselves? That's where the challenge—and the reward—lies. I didn't believe in myself either at first, but others did. Lady Vivian, Kaspar…"

Faust hesitated, his fingers curling and uncurling as the magic dissipated from his hands.

"But why? Why go through all of this? You're a Valksha. You could've done anything—been anything. Why dedicate yourself to the Kyriegard?"

Ophelia stopped and blinked again, caught off guard by the shift in tone.

"I told you before. Protecting people, standing against darkness… that's what being a Valksha means to me. The Kyriegard gave me a way to do that."

"But does it feel right?" Faust pressed, his eyes searching hers. "All these rules, the discipline, the… celibacy. Doesn't it feel like they're cutting you off from what you really are?"

Ophelia laughed lightly, though there was a slight edge to it.

"Are you trying to get me in trouble with the Council, Faust?"

"I'm serious," he said, stepping closer. "You talk about faith and connection, about honoring the Saryfim. Doesn't that mean honoring yourself, too? Your future? Your bloodline?"

Her expression faltered, the light humor replaced by a flash of unease. "What are you getting at?"

Faust hesitated, but his voice softened, almost conspiratorial.

"You and Theodin… I see the way you look at each other, how you move together. Does it ever feel like more than just the bond?"

The words hung in the air, heavy and unspoken until now.

Ophelia's breath caught, her eyes widening slightly before she quickly masked her reaction.

"What I feel—or don't feel—isn't something you need to worry about, Faust," she said, much firmer now. "Our Dyad is what it is because we're partners. That's all that matters."

"But—"

"No," she cut him off, her voice carrying a quiet finality. "Focus on your magic. That's what you need to worry about—not me, not Theodin, and definitely not what the Council might think."

Faust frowned, his eyes yanking away as he nodded. "I'm sorry," he muttered. "I didn't mean to overstep."

Ophelia's face faltered again slightly, though she maintained her stance.

"I know. But some questions don't have easy answers—at least, not ones I'm ready to give."

As she rolled her shoulders and tried to poise herself again, she realized how much her energy and emotion stirred—ripping her unease through the Dyad with Theodin.

A soft clang of the sparring chamber door broke the tension. Theodin's vexing eyes locked onto Faust immediately as he stepped inside, his presence unmoving but carrying an undercurrent of protectiveness.

"Everything all right here?" he asked, his tone deceptively casual.

Ophelia exhaled, steadying herself before glancing over her shoulder at him. "Yes, just working on controlled magic exercises."

Theodin's gaze remained on Faust for a moment, and then it moved to her.

Faust shrunk somewhat and timidly glanced between them.

There it was again. The bond. Their Dyad. Even Faust could feel it thrum faintly between them, a silent exchange that carried more than words ever could.

Theodin studied Ophelia with a softened glance.

You sure?

Even his very presence seemed to ask. She sent back reassurance, though it wasn't as confident as usual.

Standing this close between them, and now having a better handle on his magic, Faust felt the remnants much more.

His fingers flexed and clenched.

"I think I've had enough for today," Faust said abruptly, stepping back. His eyes lingered on Ophelia for a moment before shifting to Theodin. "Thanks for the lesson."

Theodin didn't move from the doorway, his posture relaxed but firm until Faust had slipped past him and left the room.

Only then did he turn to Ophelia fully, his eyes sharp with curiosity and concern. "What was that about?"

For a moment, Ophelia hesitated, letting the Dyad settle delicately between them.

Theodin's presence had always been a foundational force, his vigilance wrapping around her like armor. It was reassuring, grounding her when everything else felt uncertain.

And yet, that same protectiveness added a layer of complexity she couldn't entirely untangle.

It wasn't just the Dyad that tied them together—it was the unspoken weight of what they were becoming to each other.

Something beyond duty.

Ophelia sighed, rubbing the back of her neck.

"He asked some questions. About… me. The Kyriegard. Us."

"Us?" Theodin echoed, his brow furrowing slightly. "What kind of questions?"

She hesitated, her voice quieter now as she answered.

"Whether the Kyriegard path is right for me. Whether… our Dyad is just the bond of the Kyriegard. Or…something more."

Her words lingered in the air, but her thoughts drifted deeper.

Faust wasn't the first to question her place here, and he likely wouldn't be the last.

At the same time, he didn't just question her—he looked at her as though she were something rare and fragile, something that didn't quite belong in the Kyriegard's hardened mold. It unsettled her, not because she feared his curiosity but because it mirrored the questions she wasn't ready to ask herself.

What if they were right? What if she wasn't meant to be here, to be this? What if she was forcing herself into a role that demanded she suppress too much of who she truly was?

Theodin's expression darkened. "He overstepped."

"Yes—but I don't think maliciously," Ophelia admitted. "I think he's just trying to understand. He's… searching for something. Something he hasn't found yet."

His tone only intensified in his response.

"And he thinks that is you?"

"I don't know," she said. "But it's not about him, Theo. It's about us. About what we're becoming."

Theodin's protectiveness surged on instinct—but beneath it, something quieter twisted in his chest. Was it just the Dyad, or something else he wasn't ready to name? The Council's suspicion was expected. Faust's questions weren't. They dug deeper. Stirred doubt in Ophelia. About their bond. About him.

And he hated how much that got under his skin.

"What do you want me to do?" he asked finally, his voice calm but carrying an edge of resolve.

"Nothing," Ophelia said firmly. She took a deep breath and closed her eyes. "Just… stay." Her next words softened and quivered slightly. "Please. I need you here."

Theodin could sense the swirl of thoughts beneath her guarded exterior. The weight of their connection and how it was perceived by others bore heavily on her. He could feel the flicker of her concern, not for their partnership, but for how the Council might see them. Faust had drawn attention to something they'd both been carefully avoiding, and that knowledge left her exposed in a way he could feel as acutely as his own thoughts.

Theodin knew Ophelia's fears weren't misplaced. If Faust saw it—whatever "it" was—then Kaspar had likely noticed long before, and

Alfena wouldn't have missed a single detail. The Council's scrutiny was relentless, and the bond they shared made them a beacon for judgment. But what struck Theodin most wasn't the council's perception—it was how much it hurt her to carry that doubt, that weight.

She bore so much already, and the thought of her questioning their path because of outside pressure stoked a quiet anger he kept tightly reined in.

Theodin's resolve only deepened. He stepped closer, cupping her cheek with a careful touch. As her emerald eyes fluttered open, his mismatched eyes steady on hers, letting the Dyad resonate with a soothing reassurance.

"I'm not going anywhere," he said gently.

Ophelia placed her delicate hand upon his, and the runes marked in their palms and forearms pulsed a white light.

Chapter 32

The Mission to Slymound

Year 845 of the Second Age, Sixth Month, Twenty-Seventh Day

The chambers beneath Avasylon provided a cool respite during the summer months, but there would be no true rest for the Kyriegard.

Kaspar stood at the head of the room, scanning his apprentices and their unlikely companion gathered before him.

Theodin leaned against the wall, his eyes focused on his mentor and adoptive guardian, while Ophelia stood a step closer to the center, her posture attentive but edged with subtle tension. Faust dwelled near the back, his eyes darting to Ophelia and Theodin intermittently, as though gauging the weight of what was to come.

"Last week's incident in the sparring courtyard has not gone unnoticed," Kaspar began. "While no one was gravely injured, it revealed gaps in coordination and control that cannot be ignored—gaps we must address."

With a tight jaw and a fleeting look at Ophelia, Theodin said nothing. She felt his quiet frustration through the Dyad—a simmering mix of protectiveness and lingering doubt. She steadied herself, exhaling softly as she waited for Kaspar to continue.

"Faust," Kaspar said, turning his attention to the fractured Valksha. "Your magic continues to pose a risk, not only to yourself but to those around you. However, there has been measurable progress. The energy you wield is stabilizing, albeit slowly. That progress is why you remain here. But make no mistake—your place in Avasylon is not guaranteed. You must demonstrate more consistent control if you wish to continue receiving our guidance and assistance."

Faust nodded curtly, his eyes dropping to the floor.

"Understood."

Kaspar's gaze shifted to Theodin.

"Your instincts last week were admirable, but they were also reckless. Stepping in to shield Ophelia was a calculated risk, but it highlighted an over-reliance on the Dyad to anticipate danger."

Theodin straightened.

"With respect, sir, the Dyad exists to enhance our coordination. Anticipating danger is part of that."

"And yet," Kaspar countered, his gaze unwavering, "it does not absolve you of the need to trust your partner to protect herself. The Dyad amplifies your connection, but it also amplifies your weaknesses when you act impulsively."

Theodin bit his cheek and held his tongue, his energy pulsing irritably through the Dyad.

Ophelia stepped forward slightly.

"The fault wasn't entirely Theodin's," she said. "I miscalculated. If I had read Faust's energy more clearly, I could have avoided needing Theodin's intervention."

Kaspar's gaze drifted to her, and for a moment the room seemed to still.

"Acknowledging your mistakes is a step in the right direction, Ophelia. But this is not about placing blame—it is about understanding the consequences of your actions, both individually and as a pair."

He turned back to the group as a whole, and his voice carried the weight of his authority.

"The council's scrutiny is not misplaced. Your bond is unique, unprecedented. As we've said before, it is a strength, but it is also a vulnerability. You will be tested, again and again, not because we doubt you but because the stakes are too high to leave anything to chance."

Faust shifted uneasily at the edge of the group, his eyes flicking between Ophelia and Theodin.

Kaspar continued after he allowed the silence to settle on them.

"The Council has decided to send you on a mission with me to investigate a suspicious workshop in Slymound, southeast of us. Near the border of our humble Fatum."

He gestured to a table off to the side with a map and other documents laid out neatly around it. "The local villagers there have reported possible Warthrall activity. Disappearing livestock. Disappearing citizens."

Ophelia was the first to approach the table, followed by Theodin. Faust hung back but peered from where he stood out of curiosity. Ophelia ran her fingers over the map, starting where Olysgard was located—at the north most point of Fatum, near the Chayim River—to a marked spot where Fatum and Slymound met.

"That's…a day or two of travel, give or take," she murmured. She turned to Faust over her shoulder. "Will you be okay here while we're gone?"

Kaspar folded his arms across his chest. "He is coming with us."

Theodin and Ophelia whipped their heads to their mentor with wide eyes and blurted in unison.

"What?"

Kaspar's gaze remained steady, the authority in his posture leaving no room for argument.

"You heard me. Faust is coming with us."

Theodin's eyes narrowed, the Dyad thrumming with his unease.

"With respect, sir, why? Faust isn't Kyriegard. He's not trained for field missions."

"No, he's not," Kaspar agreed, his tone sharp but measured. "Which is why this mission will be his first opportunity to prove he can function outside of Avasylon without becoming a liability."

Ophelia glanced between Theodin and Kaspar with a mix of surprise and concern.

"But the mission itself—Warthrall activity is dangerous enough without adding an unknown variable."

"And that is precisely why he must come. Faust's magic is unstable, yes, but we've seen it in action. It has the potential to be a powerful asset. If we continue to keep him confined here, he will never learn to control it under real-world conditions."

"And if he loses control out there?" Theodin pressed. "If someone gets hurt—or worse?"

Kaspar's gaze didn't waver.

"That is why I will be there. This mission will be controlled, as much as any field mission can be. It's not about success or failure—it's about assessment. Understanding his limits. And yours."

Faust finally spoke, his voice quieter than usual but carrying a calm undertone.

"I understand the risks, and I'm willing to go. If I can't manage my magic in the field, then… what's the point of any of this?"

Ophelia stopped and studied Faust, her brow furrowed. She could sense his resolve, the brief flicker of determination beneath his uncertainty. Despite her own reservations, she felt a pang of empathy for him—a man searching for purpose in a world that viewed him as broken.

She exhaled softly, turning to Kaspar.

"If Faust is coming, then we'll do everything we can to support him. But we'll also need to be prepared for the worst."

"Agreed," Kaspar said firmly. He gestured to the map on the table. "You'll study the area tonight and prepare for departure at dawn. Faust, you'll shadow me closely at all times. Understood?"

"Yes, sir," Faust replied, his eyes flitting briefly to Ophelia before dropping back to the floor.

Kaspar nodded once, and then his eyes swept over the group.

"This mission is not just about investigating the workshop. It's about proving your function in the field—even with the challenges you face. Remember that."

As the meeting concluded, Kaspar left the chamber, and Faust followed shortly after.

Ophelia remained by the map and turned back to it. She touched her fingertips near the area of the mission marked in ink. Theodin stepped next to her, his eyes scanning the details of the parchment.

"Do you think this is a mistake?" she asked softly.

Theodin sighed heavily. She felt his unease ripple into her senses. He reached for the map to adjust it, brushing his fingers against hers briefly. The matching runes in their skin pulsed delicately from their palms and up their forearms.

"I don't know," he muttered. His gaze lifted to meet hers. "But if it is, we'll handle it. Like we always do."

Ophelia nodded, her lips curving into a faint smile.

The clatter of equipment filled the underground armory of Avasylon as Ophelia secured the straps on her pack. The sun had not yet risen, so the only sources of light that served them were the oil lamps and the dim glow of runes etched into the stone and wood. Nearby, Theodin adjusted the pouches and buckles on his belt, his eyes carefully regarding Faust, who meandered by the supply table with an awkward tension in his movements.

Kaspar stood near the edge of the room, watching the preparations with a critical eye.

"We leave within the hour. Double-check your provisions—this isn't the time for oversights."

Theodin tightened the strap on his pack as he continued to watch Faust. The fractured Valksha fumbled with a roll of bandages, his eyes darting to Ophelia for reassurance. Theodin's gaze criticized him, but he said nothing, turning to focus instead on his own preparations.

Ophelia tied her pack before moving over to Faust.

"Everything okay?" she asked, low enough that Kaspar wouldn't overhear.

Faust hesitated, fidgeting with the bandages.

"I just… don't want to slow you down," he whispered.

"You won't," Ophelia said firmly. She placed a hand on his arm, the touch brief but grounding. "You're here because you have something to offer. Trust that."

The warmth and purity of her energy soothed the rough, unsettled texture of his own, calming him. Faust's eyes met hers with a glimmer of gratitude.

"I'll try."

As Ophelia left him and returned to her pack, Theodin spoke loud enough for both of them to hear.

"You're not just here to try," he said, his tone clipped. "You're here to prove you can handle this."

"Theodin," Ophelia warned, her eyes darting to him with exasperation.

"I'm just saying what we're all thinking," Theodin replied with an edge. He pulled the strap over his shoulder and turned to the Valksha boy.

"This isn't training, Faust. If something goes wrong, people could die. Understand that."

Faust swallowed hard, clenching his teeth as he nodded.

"I understand."

Kaspar's voice cut through the tension like a blade.

"Enough. We don't have time for doubts or second-guessing. We're a team for this mission now, whether you like it or not. Act like one."

The silence that followed was heavy with tension.

Ophelia exhaled a hushed breath as she finished securing her pack.

"We'll be ready," she said with quiet conviction.

Theodin stared at her for a moment before he nodded, his shoulders relaxing slightly. Faust, though still visibly uneasy, squared his shoulders and busied himself with organizing the remaining supplies.

Kaspar gave a curt nod, his expression unreadable.

"Good. We leave at first light."

He turned and strode toward the cellar hall, his presence commanding even as he disappeared into the shadows.

The first part of their journey that morning went without incident.

To avoid drawing attention to themselves, they chose to move on foot. Faust was silently thankful.

Ophelia noted that Kaspar wore his signature Kyriegard cloak inside-out, so the unmistakable silver embroidery remained hidden beneath a plain, black cloth. It was designed particularly for the Kyriegard to practice stealth in certain circumstances, and to make their presence known in others.

Ophelia, Theodin, and Faust had worn light, unmarked cloaks as well, but Ophelia and Theodin still wore their Kyriegard apprentice uniforms underneath.

As they traveled further from Olysgard, their footsteps were muffled by the thick layer of pine needles carpeting the forest floor. The only sounds were the rustle of leaves in the morning breeze and the distant chirping of birds greeting the rising sun.

Theodin spoke low and steady as he addressed the group without looking back.

"The path ahead splits in two. The left leads deeper into the forest, and the right skirts the edge of the valley. Both will take us to Slymound."

Kaspar's voice carried from the rear.

"The forest path will keep us concealed, but it's slower. The valley route is faster, but we'll be exposed. Which do you recommend?"

Theodin hesitated as he looked between the two paths, then he turned slightly to glance at Ophelia. The Dyad whispered his thoughts to her without words. Ophelia tilted her head, considering the options.

"The forest," she said finally. "It's safer. If there's Warthrall activity near Slymound, the last thing we need is to be seen coming."

Kaspar nodded. "Agreed. The forest it is."

Theodin shifted his stance, his focus returning to the trail ahead. "Stay close. The trees can play tricks with sound. We don't want to lose each other."

They continued on, the forest closing in around them as the trail narrowed. The light grew dimmer beneath the dense canopy, the sun's rays struggling to penetrate the thick foliage. Theodin moved with practiced ease, his movements almost instinctive as he navigated the twisting path. Ophelia followed closely behind, her steps careful but confident. Faust stumbled once, catching himself against a tree, but he quickly righted himself with a muttered apology.

Kaspar's gaze lingered on each of them in turn, his eyes assessing their movements, their focus, their unspoken dynamics. He noted the way Theodin's hand occasionally brushed the hilt of his sword, his readiness a testament to years of discipline. He saw the way Ophelia's attention darted between Faust and Theodin, her concern for their unconventional companion mingling with her trust in her partner. Faust often looked to Ophelia, wanting to speak with her, but he appeared discouraged and rendered timid by the presence of Theodin and Kaspar.

"Keep moving," Kaspar said. "We have a long way to go."

The woods grew darker and quieter as the sun climbed higher in the sky. Theodin paused occasionally to adjust their course, his eyes scanning the undergrowth for signs of movement. Ophelia felt his focus mingling with her own—heightening it, making it more attuned, and lending his years of training to her inexperience.

Faust trailed behind, his steps uneven but determined. He glanced at Ophelia once, his eyes filled with unspoken questions. She noticed him out of the corner of her eye and offered him another smile, a silent consolation that he wasn't as out of place as he felt.

As they reached a small clearing, Kaspar spoke to them in a low voice.

"We'll rest here for a moment. Keep your weapons close."

The group halted, their breaths mingling with the cool morning air. Theodin's gaze remained on the path ahead, his posture still tense despite the pause. Ophelia leaned against a tree with her rifle resting against her shoulder as she scanned the clearing. Faust sank onto a nearby rock, shutting his eyes as he caught his breath.

Kaspar stood at the edge of the clearing, his gaze sweeping the forest.

* * *

Hours passed. The afternoon light streamed through the dense canopy of Fatum's forests, casting dappled patterns on the moss-covered path. The air was cool and crisp, a gentle breeze carrying the scent of pine and damp earth.

The group moved in a loose formation. Theodin continued to lead the way, his eyes scanning the terrain with a practiced intensity. Ophelia followed close behind while Faust lingered slightly to her left. Kaspar brought up the rear, his eyes watching the group with quiet scrutiny.

Tension simmered beneath the surface. Though none of them said a word, Kaspar could almost feel the unspoken conversation between his apprentices by the way they glanced at each other.

Faust felt it too—he longed for a connection somehow, someway, but didn't receive it.

He finally found the courage to speak up since they had left Avasylon.

"How much farther do you think we'll have to go before we reach the village?"

Theodin didn't look back as he replied, his tone clipped.

"At this pace, we'll reach it by dusk. As long as we don't stop too often."

Faust frowned. "I wasn't suggesting we stop. I just thought—"

"That you'd voice every thought that crosses your mind?" Theodin cut in, his tone sharp. "We don't need commentary. Just keep moving."

"Theodin," Ophelia interjected, her voice calm but firm. "That's enough. He's barely spoken."

Theodin glanced over his shoulder, his expression hardening for a moment before he exhaled and looked ahead again.

"I'm just saying we don't need distractions," Theodin muttered, his voice quieter this time.

Ophelia reached out and placed a hand on his arm. Their runes illuminated with white upon contact.

"And I'm saying you need to relax—just a tad, Theo," she lulled.

Reluctantly, Theodin gave a curt nod and touched her hand before turning back ahead.

Faust's jaw tightened, but he said nothing, his eyes dropping to the path.

As the group continued, the silence grew heavier, each member lost in their own thoughts. Theodin's posture remained tense, his movements precise and deliberate as he scanned the terrain. Ophelia's gaze lingered on him, a faint crease of concern on her brow. Faust followed quietly, his hands flexing absently at his sides as though trying to dispel the unease that clung to him like a second skin.

When the group paused for a brief rest near a fallen log, Ophelia took the opportunity to approach Faust. She crouched beside him as he adjusted the strap on his pack, her eyes warm but resolute.

"Hey," she said softly. "You're doing fine. Don't let Theodin get to you. He gets like this with missions."

Faust hesitated. "I know he means well," he said quietly. "I just… I feel like I'm always one step away from messing up."

Ophelia placed a gentle hand on his wrist.

"We all feel like that sometimes. Just focus on what you can control. You've already made progress—you just have to trust yourself."

Faust's gaze remained on her, a flicker of something indiscernible passing through his eyes.

"Thanks," he said after a moment. "For… still being kind to me. After the other day."

Ophelia tilted her head slightly, her eyes thoughtful.

"You apologized, Faust. And you're trying. That's what matters."

Before either of them could say more, Kaspar's voice cut through the quiet and his tall figure moved across the small clearing.

"Break's over. Let's move."

Theodin watched the exchange from a few paces away, his eyes narrowing slightly. He felt the faint ripple of Ophelia's energy through the Dyad, her calm presence brushing against his unease like a steadying hand. He exhaled slowly, pushing down the flicker of irritation that clung to his chest.

The dense forest of Fatum grew quieter as the group pressed forward, the thick canopy above filtering the sunlight into pale, fragmented beams.

But the silence here was different. It now carried a thick and suffocating weight that pressed against their senses.

Ophelia paused mid-step, her eyes scanning the nearby trees. Her fingers brushed against the strap of her rifle as a pang of unease rippled through her.

"Does anyone else feel that?" she murmured.

Theodin, walking slightly ahead, turned to glance back at her. His hand instinctively gripped the hilt of his sword.

"Feel what?"

"Something," she said vaguely, her brow furrowing. "It's faint, but… wrong. Like an itch just out of reach."

Kaspar, dwelling at the rear, came forward.

"Be specific, Ophelia," he said. "What do you sense?"

She hesitated, closing her eyes briefly to focus. Her Valksha magic stirred beneath her skin, like a quiet whisper urging her to listen.

"It's… not a presence. More like a residue. Something just…stuck here."

"How close?" Theodin asked.

"Not close," she replied, shaking her head. "But not far enough."

Kaspar's face darkened, creasing the aged lines in his face deeper.

"We're nearing the borderlands. It's possible we're picking up traces of Warthrall magic."

Faust stepped closer to the group, nervously searching the surrounding trees. "If it's just residue, why does it feel so… heavy?"

Kaspar glanced at him sharply.

"Because Warthrall magic is meant to corrupt. Even traces of it can weigh on the senses, especially if it's been left to fester."

As if on cue, Theodin stopped abruptly, his eyes locking in at the base of a nearby tree.

"There," he said, gesturing with his blade. "Claw marks."

The group gathered around the trunk.

Deep gouges carved into the bark unnaturally, an unmistakable indication of a beastly presence. The marks were uneven, as though made by something inhuman, and traces of blackened magic clung to the edges like a sickness.

Ophelia knelt beside the tree, her hand hovering near the marks without touching them. The runes along her forearm flashed once with green as she allowed her magic to stir just enough to sense the residue more clearly.

"It's old," she muttered distantly. "But not too old. Days, maybe a week at most."

"Warthralls leave marks like these to warn or claim territory," Kaspar said. "We're getting close."

A chill ran down Ophelia's spine as she straightened, her hand instinctively tightening on her rifle strap. The pulse of the Dyad rippled against her thoughts, steadying her as Theodin moved to her side.

"We should keep moving."

"Stay alert," Kaspar said firmly. "This is no longer a passive investigation. If they know we're here, we're already at a disadvantage."

The group pressed on. Ophelia couldn't shake the feeling of being watched, though every glance over her shoulder revealed only the thicket of the shadowed forest. The unsettling energy clung to the air.

Whatever waited for them in Slymound, it wasn't going to make itself known easily. And as the forest seemed to close in around them, Ophelia couldn't help but wonder if they were walking into a trap.

The trail leading into Slymound was narrow, overgrown with tangled roots and thick underbrush. As the group emerged from the forest's edge, the village came into view—a cluster of modest wooden houses and thatched-roof cottages, their exteriors weathered by time and the elements. A low mist hung over the settlement, clinging to the ground like an unwelcome guest.

Theodin slipped on gloves with his gauntlets to hide his runes, but unfortunately, Ophelia needed her hands bare enough to easily draw blood for her magic. She kept her hands clenched and turned inward.

As they drew closer, Ophelia sensed the shift in the air.

The energy surrounding the village was heavy, oppressive in a way that made her chest tighten. She glanced at Theodin, who walked beside her rigidly, his eyes scanning the area with sharp focus. The Dyad shivered, carrying a shudder of unease between them.

"This place," Faust mumbled. "Feels… wrong."

Theodin's hand rested instinctively on the hilt of his sword as he nodded. "It's too quiet. No children, no livestock—nothing."

Ophelia adjusted the strap of her rifle, her eyes darting to the nearest cottage. The windows were dark, the door shut tightly, as if the occupants were barricaded against an unseen threat.

"It's like they're hiding from something," she murmured.

Faust stayed a step behind her, his eyes wide as he took in the eerie stillness.

"Do you think they know we're here?" he asked, his voice barely above a whisper.

"They know," Kaspar said, his gaze shifting toward the center of the village, where a single building larger than the rest stood—a meeting hall or perhaps the elder's home. "They're watching. Waiting to see if we're friend or foe."

As they approached the village square, the faint creak of a door broke the silence. An older man with a wild bushel of white hair stepped out from one of the cottages, his frame stooped but his hollow eyes sharp with suspicion. He carried a weathered walking stick, though the way his knuckles gripped it suggested it could double as a weapon if necessary.

"Who are you?" the man called in a rough voice. He looked over the group, lingering on Kaspar and the weapons they carried.

Kaspar came forward, his posture calm but commanding.

"We've been sent by King Bellinus," he said evenly. "We've received reports of disappearances in the area. We're here to help."

The elder's expression eased slightly, though the wariness didn't entirely leave his eyes.

"Help, eh?" he muttered. "Royal help or not, you'll forgive us if we're not eager to trust strangers. The last ones who came through here claimed to be helpers too."

"And what happened to them?" Kaspar asked.

The elder hesitated, his eyes warily dropping to the ground.

"They never came back from the woods."

A heavy silence came over the group as the weight of the elder's words sank in.

"We'll need to speak with you," Kaspar said after a moment. "And anyone else who can tell us more about what's been happening here."

The elder nodded reluctantly, gesturing toward a larger building that must have been a central hub of sorts from its structure and location.

"Come inside. Best not to stand out in the open too long."

As they followed the elder toward the building, Ophelia still couldn't shake the feeling of being watched. Her eyes darted to the shadowed windows of the cottages, where subtle movements suggested that cautious eyes were indeed following their every step.

Theodin's voice reached her through the Dyad in a whisper.

Stay alert. This place feels off.

Ophelia responded with a subtle nod, gripping her rifle a little tighter as they entered the dimly lit hall. Inside, the air was heavy with the smell of damp wood and faintly burned candles. The space was modest but functional, with a long wooden table flanked by mismatched chairs. A few other villagers waited there—middle-aged men and women with faces worn by years of hard labor and recent fear.

Kaspar addressed the group with his usual composure and a nod.

"We need to know everything—every detail about what's been

happening. Don't leave anything out, no matter how small it seems."

The elder took a seat at the head of the table, his hands resting heavily on the worn surface.

"It started about a month ago," he began, his voice low and gravelly. "At first, it was just livestock. Goats, chickens… gone without a trace. We thought it might've been wolves or some other predator."

"But it wasn't wolves," Theodin said absently.

The elder shook his head, his gaze darkening.

"No. Wolves don't leave claw marks like that, and they don't move like ghosts in the night. Our dogs bark at wolves—but this time, they cowered and were taken."

He paused, his fingers tightening on the edge of the table. "Then people started disappearing. First, it was Samuel, a farmhand. Then Maryanne, the baker's daughter. Gone—vanished without a sound."

Ophelia held her breath as she listened carefully.

"Have you seen anything unusual?" she asked. "Lights, sounds, tracks?"

The elder hesitated, briefly glancing at the other villagers. One of them, a woman with streaks of gray in her dark hair, spoke up.

"There's been… a smell," she said, her voice trembling slightly. "Like something rotting. It comes at night, just before someone disappears."

"And the woods," another villager added, his voice barely above a whisper. "They've changed. The trees feel… wrong. Like they're watching you."

Faust shifted uncomfortably at the edge of the group, his eyes darting to Kaspar.

"It sounds like Warthrall magic," he murmured, his voice tight. "Corruption spreading outward."

Kaspar looked at Faust briefly with a hardened stare before returning to the villagers.

"You said others came before us. Do you know where they went?"

The elder nodded grimly.

"They went to the old workshop, deep in the forest. It's been abandoned for years, but lately… strange things have been happening there. Lights at night, sounds that don't belong."

"We'll need to investigate the workshop," Kaspar said firmly, his tone leaving no room for debate. "Anything else you can tell us?"

The elder hesitated again, his gaze dropping to the table. Like he had seen and heard too much.

"Just… be careful. Whatever's out there, it's not of this world. And it doesn't want to be found."

Kaspar nodded, rising from his seat. "We'll be careful. But we'll also find out what's happening and put an end to it."

The villagers exchanged uneasy glances but said nothing more as the group prepared to leave the hall.

Outside, the mist had thickened, curling around the village like a shroud.

The heavy, corrupted energy pressed against Ophelia's chest relentlessly. Beneath her cloak, she clutched her life pendant to anchor herself.

Theodin stepped closer to her. His presence at such proximity gave her further grounding.

"What do you think?" he asked quietly.

"I think they're terrified," Ophelia replied, her voice just as low. "And I think they have every reason to be."

"We'll rest here for the night," Kaspar murmured. "Tomorrow, we head for the workshop. Stay vigilant. Whatever's out there, it already knows we're here."

Chapter 33

The Haunted

The inn was a modest structure, its timber walls creaking somewhat in the night breeze. The hearth in the common room provided the only warmth, its flames casting long, wavering shadows across the worn wooden floors. Despite the comfort it offered, the atmosphere inside was anything but welcoming. The villagers who meandered in the corners barely glanced at the group as they entered, their eyes avoiding contact, as if afraid to draw attention to themselves.

The innkeeper, a stout man with thinning hair and a nervous energy, showed them to their rooms without so much as a word. He handed over a single key, his hand trembling slightly as he gestured to the narrow staircase leading to the upper floor.

"Two rooms. Best I can offer," he muttered before shuffling away, casting wary glances at the windows.

Kaspar led the group upstairs, his ever-attentive gaze scanning their surroundings with quiet vigilance. The wooden boards beneath their feet groaned with every step, the sound unnervingly loud in the silence of the inn.

"Theodin, Ophelia—you'll take one room," Kaspar said, leaving no room for argument. "Faust, you're with me."

Faust hesitated, his eyes glancing up at Ophelia before turning down nodding silently.

The rooms were small and sparsely furnished, each containing a single narrow bed and a rickety table. Theodin dropped his pack onto the floor near the bed in their room, noticing the single window that overlooked the village square. The hazy glow of the moon barely penetrated the thick mist outside, casting an eerie pall over the scene.

Ophelia leaned her rifle against the wall and looked at Theodin.

"It's like the air itself is watching us," she murmured.

Theodin nodded, his gaze never leaving the window. "It's not just the air. There's something out there. Waiting."

Later that evening, the group sat at a heavy wooden table near the center of the inn's common room with their weapons resting within easy reach.

The innkeeper had provided a modest meal of bread and stew, but Theodin barely touched his plate, his focus on the inaudible whispers of conversation drifting from the other patrons. Most of the villagers tried not to look at them, but their fear was palpable even without words.

Ophelia sat beside him, idly prodding the barrel of her rifle resting against the edge of the table. She absently tore a piece of bread, her eyes shifting between Theodin and Kaspar sitting across from her.

The Dyad rustled, carrying Theodin's unease like a current.

Kaspar's gaze was steely as he addressed them, his voice low to avoid drawing attention.

"We'll leave for the workshop at first light. Until then, rest as much as you can. We don't know what we'll find out there."

"If we find anything at all," Theodin muttered. "The villagers seem convinced it's a trap."

"Which is all the more reason to be prepared," Kaspar replied evenly. He glanced at Faust, who sat at the far end of the table, his eyes distantly fixed on the dancing flames of the hearth.

"Faust."

Faust's head jerked up slightly, his wiry frame guarded. "What?"

"Have you sensed anything unusual since we arrived?" Kaspar asked, calm but pointed.

Faust hesitated, his fingers tightening around the edge of the table.

"There's… something. It's weak, but it's there. Like a hair just out of reach."

"Keep focused. If you feel anything more specific, let us know immediately."

Faust gave a curt nod, his gaze dropping back to the table. The tension in his posture was unmistakable, his shoulders hunched as though bracing for a blow.

After a time, Kaspar rose from his seat.

"I'll take first watch. The rest of you—get some rest."

Theodin stood as well, his eyes meeting Kaspar's briefly.

"We'll head upstairs," he said, his voice steady but edged with something unreadable. He glanced at Ophelia. "You ready?"

Ophelia nodded. She rose to her feet and slung her rifle over her shoulder. She glanced at Faust, who remained seated, his expression still withdrawn.

"Faust?"

"I'll stay here," Faust muttered but didn't look up. "Not tired."

Ophelia hesitated, her eyes lingering on him for a moment before she turned and followed Theodin up the narrow staircase. The wooden steps creaked under their weight, and the sound echoed in the quiet inn.

As they entered the room, Theodin set his sword down by the window and leaned against the frame, his eyes scouring the darkened street below.

Ophelia placed her rifle beside the bed and sank onto the edge of the mattress, her posture weary but alert.

"What do you think we'll find out there?" she asked.

Theodin didn't look away from the window.

"Trouble," he said simply. "If the villagers are right, and this workshop is the source of the disappearances, then whatever's waiting for us won't make it easy."

He pulled back the worn curtain further and peered out into the mist-shrouded village square, watching the shadows for any sign of movement. His hand rested loosely on the windowsill, the Dyad between him and his partner stirring delicately in the stillness.

Ophelia curled up beneath the blankets and put her boots off to the side. Her eyes lingered on Theodin's tense posture, the sharp line of his shoulders a clear indicator of his unease. She hadn't asked, but she knew what he was thinking at that moment—she knew the weight of his concerns because she felt it too.

"They're scared," she said softly. "The villagers, I mean. Whatever's been happening here, it's left them on edge. It feels… awful."

Theodin turned slightly to look at her.

"Because something isn't. This whole place feels off. It's not just fear—it's something deeper. Something that's been festering here for a while."

Ophelia nodded, her fingers brushing absently against the edge of the worn quilt. "And now we're walking straight into it."

"That's the job," Theodin replied in a low voice. He crossed the room and leaned against the wall beside her, his presence grounding. "But this time we have more to worry about than just ourselves."

She glanced up at him, her eyes reflecting the dim glow of the oil lamp. "You mean Faust."

Theodin's expression darkened. His eyes narrowed. "He's unpredictable. I get that he's trying, but trying isn't enough out there. If he loses control, it could cost us."

Ophelia exhaled slowly, her gaze dropping to the floor. "I know. But he's not alone. We'll keep him grounded."

"You will," Theodin corrected, his voice less harsh. "You have a way of reaching him that no one else does. He listens to you."

"And he respects you," Ophelia countered. "Even if it doesn't seem like it."

The Dyad pulsed faintly, sifting an undercurrent of shared determination. Theodin stepped towards the bed and reached out, his hand brushing lightly against hers. The matching runes on their forearms flickered briefly with light.

"How do you do it?" he whispered, searching her eyes. "How do you just…somehow break down those walls without breaking what's hidden behind them?"

Ophelia offered a delicate smile, her fingers curling briefly around his. She pulled off the glove from his hand and turned it over.

"Little by little," she answered. Her thumb traced each rune along the base of his palm. "Piece by piece. But you must build them back up again so they're still safe…never exposing them to harm."

As Ophelia finished speaking, Theodin's eyes locked with hers, a small smile of his own tugging at the corner of his lips. Her words carried a warmth that pushed back against the unease settling in his chest. The Dyad reverberated with a ceaseless rhythm of understanding and trust.

"You always find the right words, don't you?" he murmured, warmer than before.

Ophelia chuckled quietly, leaning back against the headboard. "Maybe. Or maybe you just don't hear it enough."

Theodin shook his head lightly, a ghost of a smirk playing on his lips. "Maybe."

The quiet settled over them again, but it wasn't uncomfortable. The low glow of the oil lamp cast gentle shadows across the room, and for a brief moment, the oppressive tension of the village seemed far away. Though he had let go, Theodin's hand remained near hers, their fingers barely touching—as if the connection alone was enough to steady them both.

"You should rest," Theodin said finally. "We'll need our strength tomorrow."

Ophelia nodded, her eyes drifting closed as she sank deeper into the blankets.

"Goodnight, Theo," she whispered sweetly.

The tone of her voice nearly felt like a small peck on the cheek, which caught Theodin off guard and sent a flutter in his chest. It made the Dyad resonate with a tranquil thrum between them.

"Goodnight, Ophie," he replied, his eyes mellowing as he watched her drift off.

He waited by the bed for a moment longer, ensuring she was comfortable before returning to the window.

The village square was still shrouded in mist, the darkness outside as impenetrable as ever. Theodin's eyes remained vigilant, but the bond between him and Ophelia pulsed unceasingly and remained untainted by the looming dread.

As the hours stretched on, the night grew heavier, the oppressive energy of Slymound pressing against the walls of the inn.

Downstairs, Faust remained by the fire as his thoughts churned like a raging tempest. The flickering flames cast shadows across his face, accentuating the tension in his jaw and the unease in his lapis eyes.

Memories of Azazelf's experiments surged unbidden, and the phantom pain of old scars burned beneath his skin.

The words of the elder echoed in his mind:

Whatever's out there, it's not natural.

Faust clenched his fists, his magic stirring faintly in response. He could feel the weight of Kaspar's expectations, Theodin's mistrust, and Ophelia's quiet faith pressing against him from all sides. He didn't know if he could live up to any of it, but one thing was clear—failure wasn't an option.

As the fire crackled, Faust leaned back in his chair, his gaze fixed on the hearth. The oppressive energy that festered in the village seemed to seep into his thoughts, but he forced himself to push it aside.

For now, all he could do was wait.

Wait as he fought the ghosts of his tormented past.

Wait for her to come back.

Despite sitting near a burning flame, he felt like he was curled up in a cold, lonely darkness without the light and warmth of his beloved companion.

He could still hear Azazelf's voice, sharp and mocking, as if it were a specter lingering just beyond the edge of the light.

"You'll never control it. You're broken, Faust."

Faust clenched his fists. He hated how those words still had power over him, how they clung to his thoughts like a shadow he couldn't escape. He had come to Avasylon to prove that he was more than what Azazelf had made him, but here—on the edge of something unknown—he wasn't sure if he believed that anymore.

A slight creak of the floorboards drew his attention, and he looked up to see Kaspar standing at the edge of the room. The elder Kyriegard's silver eyes were sharp and piercing even in the dim light.

"You're still not sleeping," Kaspar said simply, stepping closer.

Faust shook his head, his gaze dropping back to the fire.

"Couldn't even if I tried."

Kaspar studied him for a moment, his expression unreadable. "What's on your mind?"

For a moment, Faust considered deflecting the question, but the weight of Kaspar's gaze made it clear that wasn't an option. He exhaled slowly, his shoulders sagging.

"Azazelf. What he did to me. What he turned me into."

"And?"

"And… what happens if I fail," Faust admitted, his voice barely above a whisper. "If I lose control out there—if I hurt someone—I don't know if I'd be able to come back from that."

Kaspar's harsh gaze diminished.

"Control isn't something that comes overnight, Faust. It's earned through discipline and struggle. You've taken the first step by acknowledging the risk. That's more than most would do."

Faust frowned, his eyes flicking to Kaspar. "What if that's not enough?"

"Then you make it enough," Kaspar answered. "You don't have the luxury of doubt—not now, not ever. If you want to be more than what

Azazelf made you, then prove it. To yourself, to us, to everyone."

Faust nodded slowly, his fingers flexing as he absorbed his words. He wasn't sure if he believed he could live up to Kaspar's expectations, but he knew he had no choice but to try.

"Get some rest," Kaspar said, this time with a surprising air of warmth. "Tomorrow will test us all."

As Kaspar turned and disappeared up the staircase, Faust remained by the fire, his thoughts still churning. But amid the storm of doubt and fear, a faint ember of determination sparked to life.

The night dragged on and the fire burned low, its embers casting faint glimmers of light across Faust's face. He did not move from his spot, his thoughts still caught in the whirlpool of doubt and determination.

But tonight, another voice persisted—Ophelia's. Her words and her endless kindness had chipped away at the walls he had built around himself. She had seen something in him that even he couldn't, and that small ember of belief was enough to keep him grounded, at least for now.

He clenched his fists, his eyes narrowing as he stared into the fire.

"I won't fail," he muttered to himself. "I won't fail you… Ophelia."

The air around Ophelia was thick and heavy with a haze that blurred the edges of her vision. She stood in the midst of a forest with trees gnarled and twisted as though corrupted by something unnatural. The ground beneath her feet was soft and damp, pulsing with a sickly red light that seemed to crawl along the roots.

A distant voice called her name, echoing through the oppressive silence. It wasn't just a sound—it was a presence, a sensation rippling through the Dyad.

Theodin?

She turned, but the forest contorted grotesquely, the trees closing in as though they were alive. Her chest tightened and her breath caught as she felt the darkness pressing against her senses. Flashes of the workshop flickered in her mind—splintered wood, shattered glass, and the low hum of dark magic resonating in the air.

The glow of her Kyriegard runes etched into her skin illuminated the path before her, their green light cutting through the haze. She paced forward cautiously, her movements slow and deliberate. With each step the hum of magic grew louder, piercing until it became a cacophony that set her teeth on edge.

The air shifted suddenly, and a figure appeared ahead of her—a looming shadow, its form indistinct but undeniably menacing. She tried to focus, to make sense of its shape, but it seemed to writhe and contort as though it refused to be fully seen.

"Who are you?" she demanded, despite the fear clawing at her chest.

The figure didn't answer, but its presence grew heavier, suffocating and brutal. The runes along her arms flared brighter, their light pulsing in time with her rapid heartbeat.

The shadow extended a hand—or something resembling one—toward her, and she felt a sharp, searing pain in her chest.

Ophelia.

The voice cut through the chaos, low and steady, like a tether pulling her back.

Wake up.

She turned and for a brief moment she saw Theodin standing in the distance, his eyes wide with concern. His figure flickered as though he were both there and not, his presence a faint but steady tremor in the Dyad.

"I can't," she whispered, her voice trembling. "It won't let me go."

Theodin's gaze sharpened, his voice firm.

You're stronger than this. Focus. I'm here.

The shadow recoiled slightly, as though it sensed the intrusion, but its grip on her didn't loosen.

Ophie… come back to me.

Ophelia clenched her fists, her runes flaring brighter as she pushed back against the suffocating weight. She felt Theodin's presence growing stronger, his energy mingling with hers through the Dyad.

The shadow let out a low, guttural growl, its form distorting violently before it suddenly dissipated, leaving only silence in its wake.

The forest around her began to dissolve, the stifling haze lifting as the Dyad between her and Theodin thrummed steadily, grounding her.

She woke with a sharp inhale, heaving as though she had been drowning.

The dim light of the inn's room swam into focus, the muted glow of the oil lamp casting long shadows across the worn walls.

She pressed a trembling hand to her chest and willed her breathing to slow. The weight of the dream still clung to her like a shroud—too vivid and too raw to be a simple product of her subconscious.

The creak of a chair brought her back to the present. Theodin was already at her side, his eyes full of concern, though his posture was uncharacteristically tense. He rested a hand on her shoulder, his touch grounding but hesitant. The exposed runes on his forearm and palm shimmered with a white light.

"You're awake," he said softly. "Are you alright?"

Ophelia swallowed hard, her eyes meeting his.

"I-I don't know. It was a dream, but… it wasn't just a dream. It felt like more."

Theodin's gaze skimmed over her, as though searching for any sign of physical harm. Then his jaw tightened, and he leaned closer, his voice a little steadier now.

"I saw it too."

Her breath hitched. "What?"

"Flashes," he said, quieter and on edge. "The forest. That shadow in the mist. And… your voice calling for me. It was quiet, but it was there." He hesitated, his eyes wincing. "It's never happened like that before."

"No," Ophelia agreed in a whisper. Her fingers grazed against the runes on her forearm, which pulsed beneath her touch. "But it's not the first time we've shared something in a dream. After the Dyad—when it first… completed itself—there was that nightmare of yours."

Theodin stilled, his expression hardening briefly before he looked away.

"That was different," he muttered. "You stumbled into it. You weren't supposed to see that."

"And tonight? Was this not supposed to happen either?" she countered gently, though her tone was laced with unease. She leaned forward, searching his eyes.

"Theodin, this felt deliberate. Like something—someone—was pulling at the edges of the bond. Trying to break into the Dyad."

He shook his head, exhaling sharply. "If they were, they didn't succeed. Whatever I saw, whatever you saw—it wasn't real. We're still here."

"But it felt real," Ophelia pressed, her eyes glinting with a mix of awe and fear. She rubbed her temples as fragments of the dream returned to her like shards of broken glass. Panic festered in her voice. "The trees were wrong. Too close, like they were swallowing the path. And that shadow… it wasn't just a figure. It felt alive. Watching us.

And then there was a voice, whispering—" She stopped, her breath catching. "It wasn't yours, was it?"

Theodin's silence was all the confirmation she needed. He adjusted himself, the Dyad between them shuffling with his unease.

"I called for you. But that... whatever it was, wasn't me," he admitted. "But it knew you.."

The weight of his words settled heavily between them. Ophelia pressed her palms against her thighs, trying to steady herself as the echoes of the dream continued to claw at the edges of her mind. "I didn't just hear it," she murmured. "I felt it. It was... invasive. Like it was trying to pull me somewhere."

Theodin's hand moved to hers, his grip firm but not unkind. Their runes shined with subtle intensity.

"And it didn't," he said, his voice still low and soothing. "You're still here. With me."

For a moment, the Dyad carried no words. Only a quiet reassurance that settled her like an anchor against the tide. She exhaled slowly, her eyes meeting his.

"What if it happens again?"

"Then we deal with it," Theodin replied simply, though the sharp edge in his tone betrayed his discomfort. He shifted closer, his gaze locking onto hers.

"You're not facing it alone. Whatever that thing was, whatever it wants—it doesn't control the Dyad. We do."

Ophelia nodded, the pulse of the runes on their forearms casting a dim glow between them. The reminder of their connection calmed her, though the ache of fear in her chest refused to fully dissipate.

"You're right," she whispered, her voice carrying a quiet determination. "We'll find answers at the workshop."

Theodin's lips pressed into a thin line, his gaze lingering on her for a moment longer before he gave a curt nod. "We'll be ready."

Year 845 of the Second Age, Sixth Month, Twenty-Eighth Day

Morning came too soon, the pale light of dawn creeping through the misty village like a reluctant guest. The group gathered in the main room of the inn with their weapons and gear ready. Kaspar stood by the door, observing them with the same commanding presence as always.

"The workshop lies deep in the forest, just over an hour from here," he said briskly. "We move quickly and quietly. No unnecessary risks and no distractions."

Theodin adjusted the strap of his pack, his eyes already examining the mist-shrouded square through the inn's window. "What do we expect when we get there?"

"Signs of Warthrall activity," Kaspar replied. "Anything that confirms the villagers' claims—or disproves them. Either way, we don't leave until we know the truth."

Ophelia finished securing her rifle. She glanced at Faust, who stood quietly to the side with a tense but resolute expression.

The Dyad stirred between her and Theodin, wrapping them both in his vigilance.

"We're ready," Ophelia said, her eyes meeting Kaspar's.

Kaspar nodded, looking over them one final time. "Then let's move."

They stepped out into the mist, and the village behind them eerily hushed.

Chapter 34

The Rift

The forest grew darker as they neared the clearing. The dense canopy above swallowed the morning light, and what little light seeped through the mist was dull and lifeless. The air was heavy with moisture, every breath carrying an acrid tang that clung to the back of their throats. The crunch of leaves and the snapping of twigs beneath their boots echoed unnervingly loud in the oppressive silence.

The workshop came into view—a jagged silhouette against the gloom. It leaned awkwardly to one side, as though trying to retreat into the earth itself. The structure's wooden planks were warped and stained with time, its roof barely held together by rusted nails and decay. Shattered windows stared out like empty, accusing eyes, and a dim pulse of crimson light flickered from within, bathing the surrounding trees in an otherworldly glow.

They all had hands on their weapons, ready to strike at an instant.

Kaspar spoke low but with an edge of steel.

"This place reeks of corruption. Stay alert."

Theodin spoke next, but his voice nearly sounded like a snarl.

"There's something…wrong here."

Ophelia lingered behind with her rifle gripped tightly in her hands. She exhaled slowly, trying to steady the erratic rhythm of her heart. Her eyes darted between the others, searching for some reassurance, but she found none. The Dyad strained at the edges of her mind as Theodin's tension spilled over into her senses.

"It feels alive," she murmured. "Like it's watching us."

"It's not alive," Theodin snapped, his gaze locked on the building ahead. "It's been corrupted. Don't mistake its energy for sentience."

Kaspar raised a hand, motioning for silence as they closed the distance to the workshop.

The suffocating atmosphere thickened with each step, pressing down on each of their chests like an invisible weight. The air seemed to ripple with a sickening drone of energy, a vibration that crawled beneath their skin and set their nerves alight.

The doorway gaped open with its edges splintered and blackened as if scorched by fire. Kaspar gestured for Theodin to take point. The younger Kyriegard moved forward, his blade drawn and ready. Ophelia followed closely, her eyes glancing cautiously toward the pulsing light that spilled out from deeper within. Faust, almost tiptoeing with apprehension, stayed right behind her. Kaspar brought up the rear, his posture tense and his gaze scanning every shadow.

As they entered, the stench hit them first. It was thick and putrid, a mix of rotting wood, sulfur, and something metallic that clung to the back of their throats. The workshop's interior was a labyrinth of chaos. Rusted tools hung carelessly from crooked nails on the walls, some bent and others blackened as if by flame. Cobwebs draped the beams overhead, their threads shimmering in the crimson light that spilled from deeper within.

The floor was littered with debris—splintered wood, shards of glass, and the ashy remains of something long burned. A crude sigil dominated the center of the room, carved roughly into the stone floor. The grooves were jagged and uneven, as though etched by an unsteady hand in haste or desperation. A viscous black substance filled the lines of the sigil, glistening like oil under the dim, flickering light.

Theodin crouched beside the sigil, his eyes wincing as he studied the substance. He dipped the tip of his blade into the black liquid, lifting it to inspect it in the faint light.

"Nether magic," he muttered, his tone clipped.

Kaspar's eyes swept the walls, his attention drawn to tattered parchments pinned haphazardly to the rotting wood. The inked symbols and notes were smudged in places but still decipherable. His lips pressed into a thin line.

"These aren't spells," he said grimly. "They're instructions. Rituals."

Kaspar pulled one of the parchments free from the wall, careful not to tear the brittle material. As his eyes scanned the symbols, his expression darkened with every line he read.

"No… this isn't just a summoning ritual," he said finally, his voice tight. "It's a binding spell—meant to anchor whatever they brought through."

Theodin straightened from where he crouched by the sigil. "Anchor it to what?"

Kaspar's gaze flicked toward the sigil. "To this place. Or… to someone."

Ophelia's stomach twisted at the implication, and her eyes darted back to the blackened carvings.

The Dyad whirred faintly with their shared unease.

"Someone like who?" she asked softly, though part of her didn't want to hear the answer.

"Anyone they could use," Kaspar said grimly. "Living or… otherwise."

Suddenly, Faust spoke.

"Azazelf and his Warthrall followers would do anything and everything wrong to any prey they got their hands on."

The three Kyriegard turned sharply toward the Valksha boy, who stood stiffly by the edge of the sigil. His sunken, tormented eyes were fixed on the scene before them, and when he spoke again, his voice carried a grave, hoarse edge that seemed to echo with pain.

"Turned them into slaves, sacrificed them to demons," Faust muttered coldly, his wiry frame trembling. "All for power."

A heavy silence settled over the room, punctuated only by the faint, pulsing drone of energy from the sigil. Ophelia's skin prickled, the air around Faust thick with the weight of his memories. She stepped closer, her grip on her rifle easing slightly as she reached out to him.

Her hand rested gently on his arm, grounding him with her touch.

"You're not part of that anymore," she said softly, her voice laced with quiet strength. "You're with us now. Remember that."

Faust's eyes flicked to her, uncertainty mingling with the raw pain in his expression. For a moment, he didn't respond, his gaze darting between Ophelia's steady emerald eyes and the flickering red light around them.

Finally, he nodded, his shoulders sagging slightly as he drew in a shaky breath.

"Right," he whispered. "With you."

Theodin's unsettling eyes lingered on Faust for a moment longer than necessary, his jaw tightening. He turned back to Kaspar and spoke sharply.

"If this ritual is still active, we don't have time for hesitation. We need to end it before whatever's tied to it pulls through."

A faint noise cut through the silence—a low, guttural groan that echoed from the shadows.

Theodin's eyes snapped toward the sound, his grip tightening on his sword.

"We're not alone."

"Stay close," Kaspar ordered. "And don't touch anything you don't have to."

The group moved deeper into the workshop. The crimson light grew brighter and more menacing with every step. The air felt heavier now, suffused with a malevolent energy that bit at their senses. Ophelia's fingers tightened around her rifle, her palms slick with sweat.

The Dyad was louder now, Theodin's wariness mingling with her own until it was impossible to tell where one ended and the other began.

They passed rows of workbenches marred with deep gouges and scorched marks. Broken tools lay scattered among fragments of bone and melted candle wax, the remnants of rituals performed long ago. Ophelia's eyes lingered on a claw-like mark carved into the wood of one bench, the edges splintered and raw. It looked fresh.

"This wasn't abandoned," she said warily. "Not completely."

Kaspar glanced back at her.

"No, it wasn't," he said quietly. "And whoever was here… they're not far."

Another sound echoed from deeper within the workshop—a sharp crack, like splintering wood.

Faust flinched, his eyes wide as he scanned the shadows.

"That wasn't the wind," he muttered.

"No," Theodin said. "It wasn't."

They reached the far end of the room where the pulsing red light was brightest. A makeshift altar stood before them, cobbled together from uneven planks and scraps of metal. Melted candles surrounded it, their wax pooling on the stone floor like coagulated blood. In the center of the altar lay a collection of small bones, arranged in a deliberate pattern that made Ophelia's skin crawl.

Kaspar stepped closer, his eyes narrowing as he examined the altar.

"This is it," he said. "The heart of the ritual."

The crimson light pulsed again, casting long, sinuous shadows that danced across the walls. The sigil on the floor seemed to respond, its black substance bubbling as though alive.

Ophelia felt the Dyad flare. Theodin's tension slammed into her like a wave.

"It's active," she said, her voice quivering. "The ritual… it's still going."

Kaspar nodded grimly. "Then we end it."

The air around the altar seemed to shift, growing colder and heavier as though the room itself resisted their presence.

Kaspar examined the scene, cataloging every detail: the bones arranged with eerie precision, the melted wax pooled in deliberate patterns, and the scratches carved into the altar's surface, their meaning lost to time.

"This is old magic," Kaspar murmured, his tone tight. "But it's been warped—twisted into something unnatural."

Ophelia stepped closer with her eyes fixed on the altar. The energy radiating from it clawed at her senses—a chaotic mess of anger, pain, and desperation. It crawled under her skin, like a thousand tiny needles prickling at once.

"It's alive," she huffed. "Or… it thinks it is."

"Don't anthropomorphize it," Theodin said sharply, his eyes flicking to her. The tension in his tone betrayed his disgust. "It's not alive. It's just a tool—a weapon. But whoever's wielding it…"

He trailed off, his gaze drifting toward the shadows beyond the altar.

Kaspar ignored the exchange, his focus remaining on the altar. He gestured toward the bubbling sigil at its base.

"That's the anchor. Whatever power this ritual was meant to summon, it's tied to that sigil. If we destroy it, we sever the connection."

"And what happens to whatever's on the other side?" Faust asked, his voice hollow. His eyes remained on the bubbling black substance, his hands twitching nervously at his sides.

Kaspar's expression hardened. "That's not our concern. Our priority is ensuring it doesn't come through."

Another sharp crack echoed through the workshop, followed by another deep, skull-grinding growl that made Ophelia's breath hitch.

The shadows seemed to writhe along the walls, the crimson light casting them into twisted shapes that twisted and danced as if alive.

"We're running out of time," Theodin said urgently and drew his sword. "Whatever's waiting on the other side—it's coming."

Kaspar nodded once and stepped back from the altar.

"Theodin, you're with me. We'll hold off whatever comes through." He turned to Ophelia and Faust sharply. "You two—focus on disrupting the ritual. Sever the anchor. Don't stop until it's done."

Ophelia's stomach churned, her grip tightening on her rifle. "What if it fights back?"

"It will," Kaspar said. "But you've faced worse. Trust yourself."

Faust swallowed hard, his eyes darting to Ophelia.

"We've got this," he said, though his voice wavered.

Now wearing a mechanical ring like Ophelia, he pricked his thumb against the spring-loaded needle to draw blood. He raised his hands, blue currents of his magic beginning to swirl around him.

"Just… don't let me screw this up."

Ophelia pricked her thumb and met his eyes—her irises flashed green with determination.

"You won't."

The runes on her forearms began to glow, their green light cutting through the crimson haze. She strapped her rifle over her back and stepped closer to the altar. Her fingers trembled as she followed suit with Faust and reached out towards the altar. Their energy manifested as blue and green swirls of light from their hands that curled around them and began to flow into the cursed ritual.

The room seemed to exhale. A deep rumble reverberated through the walls as an unseen force from the altar flared violently, preventing its outright destruction by the Valksha magic. The bubbling black substance began to hiss and steam, the red light intensifying as though fighting against their efforts.

Faust gritted his teeth and his magic surged in tumultuous bursts as he tried to stabilize the flow.

"It's pushing back," he strained. "Whatever's tied to this—it doesn't want to let go."

"Then push harder," Ophelia urged. Her runes burned brighter, green light intertwining more rapidly with Faust's magic as they poured their energy into the sigil. The bubbling substance began to crack and splinter, its surface fracturing like glass under pressure.

Kaspar looked back and forth between them and their surroundings.

Two Valksha. That should've been enough to disrupt the active ritual of any Warthrall and destroy it.

But it didn't. It fought back.

Was it their lack of experience? Faust's unstable magic?

"What in the Nether are we dealing with?" Kaspar muttered.

Behind them, the guttural growls grew louder, accompanied by the heavy thud of footsteps.

Theodin's voice cut through the chaos.

"Kaspar, incoming!"

A hulking figure emerged from the shadows, its form twisted and grotesque. Its mottled flesh was stretched tight over splintered bone, and its glowing eyes seethed with malevolent light. The creature let out a deafening roar, its clawed hands scraping against the stone floor as it charged toward them.

Kaspar moved first, his blade flashing as he intercepted the creature. Theodin followed a heartbeat later and struck cleanly at the beast's flank.

It swung at them with surprising speed for its size—a brawl between the beast and the two Kyriegard ensued.

The clash of steel and the creature's enraged howls filled the workshop. It only added to the chaotic sound of crackling energy around the altar.

"Focus!" Kaspar barked at the Valksha. "We'll handle this—just do your job!"

Ophelia forced herself to block out the noise, her focus narrowing to the sigil. The runes on her arms pulsed in rhythm with her heartbeat, the green light flaring as she poured everything she had into disrupting the ritual. She could feel the ritual anchor weakening, its resistance faltering under the combined force of her magic and Faust's.

"We're close," she said, her voice shaking. "Just a little more."

But the altar wasn't finished.

The bubbling black substance surged upward, forming a writhing mass of shadow and flame that lashed out at them. Ophelia lurched sideways as the tendrils of the mass whipped past her—her hold broke, and the green light ceased.

"Faust!" she shouted. "Hold it together!"

"I'm trying!" Faust yelled with panic. His magic flared wildly, barely containing the surging energy of the ritual. "Just finish it!"

A repulsive crack sliced into the air, and a gnarled, swirling rift carved into the space above the altar. The gaping dark hole crackled with unstable energy, its edges rimmed with flickering red and black light. The air around it seemed to ripple and warp the space unnaturally.

Ophelia stopped short, her breath catching.

No. It couldn't be.

She had only read about them in books.

"It's a portal," she huffed. "They're using it to bring something through."

Faust stared at the rift with a mix of awe and fear. "Or someone."

The tendrils from the pool squealed and reeled back in preparation to strike again.

Acting quickly, Faust withdrew from the energy disruption to redirect his magic—the blue light immediately shifted from the black substance into a transparent blue barrier around himself and Ophelia as she staggered back onto her feet. As the tendrils whipped at them, they collided with his Valksha light, and though his magic was imperfect, the shadows hissed and steamed with pain upon contact with his Saryfim energy.

It was like the altar could feel Faust's grip loosen on it. It bellowed, and the rift before them shuddered. A savage snarl echoed from within, followed by the sound of something clawing its way toward the surface.

"They're coming through," Faust said with strain as his magic struggled to hold the barrier steady. He grunted and lowered his hands, redirecting them to the altar. The blue light reshaped itself from the dome back into crackling streams from his fingertips. "We don't have much time."

"I know," Ophelia murmured. "Just keep at it."

With that, her runes blazed with green as she thrust her hands at the altar, and her currents of magic joined together with Faust's once again into the altar.

Another sharp crack split the air as the portal writhed violently, its energy surging outward like a living, gnawing thing. The growling grew louder, more distinct, until one of the creatures emerged. A demon with a twisted, skeletal frame draped in blackened flesh lunged out of the rift with unnatural speed and landed next to them. Its glowing eyes locked onto the two Valksha.

Both Ophelia and Faust stared back with their mouths agape and eyes full of fear. The light from their arms and hands fizzled out.

The Dyad flared.

Ophelia instinctively pushed Faust out of the way.

A burning, determined yell echoed in the workshop as Theodin's form launched at the demon and intercepted it. With one powerful swing, he cleaved it in two, precise and unyielding. As more hellish creatures poured out, Theodin sliced through each one.

Behind them, Kaspar finally sliced the head off of the first hulking creature. Before its body even dropped to the ground, the elder Kyriegard moved with tremendous speed at the portal and joined Theodin in disposing of the monsters.

Ophelia and Faust scrambled out of the way to the other side of the altar.

Adrenaline pumping through her, Ophelia pressed her hands to the floor next to the altar, and her runes brightly ignited again. The floorboards split and erupted with her green light as it stretched toward the altar and the portal once more. Faust followed her lead, and a fissure of blue light wove around hers to meet at the base of the altar. The black tendrils screeched and writhed as the Valksha light absorbed the black substance and it evaporated into steam.

The ground rumbled. Terrifying shrieks pierced the air. The demons attempted to turn to the Valksha, but Theodin and Kaspar kept them at bay. The portal flickered, but it continued to grow larger.

Ophelia gritted her teeth, her fingers trembling as she poured more of her magic into the dark ritual before them. The green light of her runes flared brighter, their energy crackling against the corrupted darkness of the rift.

"It's not enough," she strained. "There's something… anchoring it."

Faust's jaw tightened as he struggled to maintain his energy. His magic flickered, unstable but holding.

"What do you mean, anchoring it?"

"There's a source," Ophelia replied, her eyes wincing. "Something on the other side. I can feel it—pulling, resisting."

Before she could say more, the air around her seemed to shift, growing colder and heavier.

A voice slithered into her mind, low and venomous, its words dripping with malice.

"Still so fragile, little Valksha. Still not ready for the power you wield."

Ophelia froze, letting out a gasp as the voice coiled around her thoughts like a vice. She recognized it instantly.

Azazelf.

Her vision blurred, the workshop around her distorting into a haze of red and black. She felt his presence pressing against her mind, probing the edges of the Dyad, searching for cracks to exploit.

"I warned you," he hissed. *"You cannot stop what has already begun."*

"Ophelia!"

Theodin's urgent voice cut through the fog.

The Dyad roared violently, his emotions crashing into hers like a tidal wave.

Fear. Anger. Desperation.

Theodin felt the Dark Elf's psychic magic trying to pull her away and turned to his Valksha partner. But as he moved to intervene, a massive Warthrall emerged from the rift and dropped in front of him, its hulking form blocking his path. It towered over the others, its flesh a patchwork of scars and armor-like growths. The creature let out a deep, deafening roar, slamming its claws into the ground with enough force to shake the entire workshop.

Theodin's eyes narrowed, his grip tightening on his blade.

"You're in my way," he growled, surging forward with feral intensity.

Kaspar was still slicing through Nether minions that spilled out of the portal like an infestation.

"Keep her grounded!" he shouted. "Don't let Azazelf take her!"

But Theodin was too occupied with the Warthrall, as its sheer strength demanded his focus. Each strike he landed barely slowed it, its corrupted magic fueling its resilience. Even as he moved with inhumane speed and strength, his sword only stopped partway into its flesh, and such wounds didn't deter it at all.

Ophelia felt herself slipping further into Azazelf's grasp.

His voice grew louder and more insistent, dragging her deeper into the swirling void.

"You are mine, Valksha. Accept it, and I will spare your pathetic allies."

Ophelia!

Theodin's voice rang in her head, though more distant than before.

Her knees buckled, and the glow of her runes began to falter. The portal pulsed violently as it grew unstable once more.

"Ophelia!"

Faust's voice broke through the chaos. He turned to her, his eyes wide with alarm.

"Stay with me! Focus!"

But she couldn't respond. Her breaths came in short, ragged gasps, and her hands trembled. Her runes had extinguished.

He felt her slipping. Her warmth beside him was fading.

That familiar coldness was pulling her away.

Azazelf's presence threatened to overwhelm her completely.

Faust's heart pounded in his chest. He could feel the weight of the moment pressing down on him, the suffocating energy of the dark ritual raging to consume them all.

She's mine now.

Faust heard the demon Elf taunt him.

A low cackle erupted in his mind.

Just like you. You'll always be mine.

But as he looked at Ophelia and he saw the pain and fear etched into her features, something inside him snapped.

"No," he muttered, low and fierce. "Not this time."

His hands shot upward, his magic surging forward with a force he hadn't known he was capable of. The fractured currents around him coalesced into a blinding shield of energy, much brighter and stronger than the barrier he made before, cutting through the hostile weight of the ritual and breaking Azazelf's hold on Ophelia.

Ophelia gasped, her eyes snapping open as the glow of her runes reignited.

The shadow in her mind recoiled, hissing in frustration as the connection shattered.

She turned to Faust, still trembling. "You did it."

Faust huffed, his own breath struggling as he maintained the barrier around them. Sweat beaded on his brow, but he didn't falter.

"Finish it!" he grunted.

Ophelia squeezed her hand to allow the spring-loaded needle to draw more blood from her thumb. Her hands shook as the renewed glow of her runes pulsed brighter than before.

Azazelf's presence was gone, but the portal still writhed before her, its energy surging dangerously.

She forced herself to steady her breathing.

The Dyad with Theodin whirred wildly in her chest. His voice yelled into her thoughts.

Hurry! This thing won't stay down for long!

He was still locked in battle with the massive Warthrall, each swing of his blade ringing out like thunder as he fought to keep it at bay.

She slammed her palms to the floor again, channeling her Valksha magic into the ground.

The rift shuddered violently, the dark edges beginning to crack under the pressure of her magic.

Ophelia could feel the resistance—a wrathful, violent force that pushed back against her every effort.

But she didn't waver. She poured everything she had into the unraveling spell, her green light shining brighter and brighter until it began to overwhelm the darkness.

"Almost there!" she grunted.

Theodin, still fighting the Warthrall, glanced toward her, the Dyad rippling with his concern. He clenched his teeth and delivered a powerful strike to the creature's chest, sending it staggering back.

Kaspar moved to cover Theodin, striking down another demon that lunged from the portal.

"Keep going!" Kaspar hollered. "Don't let up!"

The final surge came in a blinding flash.

Ophelia let out a piercing cry as the energy in the room reached its peak.

The portal let out a low, bellowing roar, its edges collapsing inward as the rift began to implode.

"It's working!" Faust shouted, his voice cracking with equal parts relief and exhaustion. His magic surged one final time, reinforcing the barrier around them.

The portal began crumbling into itself.

And then, just as suddenly as it began, it was over.

It was all instantaneous.

The portal collapsed in a burst of light; the corrupted energy dissipated into the air like ash. A sound wave pulsed and shook the ground beneath them. The flesh of the Nether creatures, Cadaven monstrosities, the large Warthrall, and the altar crumbled into black dust. The air crackled with static, a sound like a thousand whispers merging into one before vanishing into silence.

The blinding light exploded outward, forcing everyone to look away or cover their eyes again.

The pressure that had weighed on their chests lifted, replaced by a strange, hollow stillness. Ophelia's ears rang, and for a moment, the only sound was the erratic thrum of her heartbeat. The heat from the portal lingered in the air, the faint smell of ozone mixing with the acrid stench of burned flesh.

An eerie silence.

The darkness vanished, but it left a bitter aftertaste in every sensation.

Faust remained on one knee, his hands shaking as the last remnants of his magic faded. Ophelia stayed for a moment on her hands and knees, her breathing ragged as her runes dimmed.

Theodin was at her side in an instant. He caught her as she attempted to stand, but she stumbled and lost her footing. His arm steadied her, his eyes scanning her pale, sweat-slicked face. He was covered in the black blood of demons, Warthrall and Cadaven, and though he breathed heavily from the exertion, his composure remained stern and unaffected.

The Dyad thrummed between them, a shadow of its usual strength as if it, too, was recovering from the strain.

"You did it," he breathed in a mix of relief and awe. "You actually closed it."

Ophelia forced a faint, quivering smile, her eyes flickering upward to meet his.

"Not just me," she whispered, her voice hoarse.

Her gaze shifted to Faust, who still knelt near the altar's former shape, his eyes staring at the crumbled remnants of the ritual. His shoulders rose and fell heavily with every breath.

Though, as he felt her eyes, he turned and met them.

Briefly, he felt his stomach flutter.

Kaspar strode toward the center of the room and looked over the destruction. Like Theodin, he was covered head to toe, but his movements and form remained unscathed—while he also seemed to catch his breath, it was evident that he was untouched. He stepped carefully over the scattered remains of the Cadaven and twisted tools.

"It's over," he muttered. "For now."

Theodin's grip on Ophelia loosened as she straightened, shivering now from the decline of rushed adrenaline.

"It was Azazelf," she huffed, soft but edged with lingering fear. "The voice… he had a hold on me."

"The fiend," Kaspar hissed grimly, his eyes hardening as he surveyed the ruined altar. "He's been watching us. Using all of this to test our defenses—and our resolve."

Faust slowly rose to his feet.

"He was pulling me in too," he admitted, his voice low.

Theodin shot him a sharp glance.

Kaspar stepped between them, his hand raised in a calming gesture.

"Enough," he said firmly. "This isn't the time for doubt. Azazelf's games aren't over. This was just his opening move."

Theodin exhaled sharply, sheathing his blade with a practiced motion. His jaw tightened as he glanced at Ophelia, who was still pale and visibly shaken.

"If this was just the beginning, we need to be ready for whatever comes next."

"We will be," Kaspar answered gruffly. "But first, we need to regroup—and report this to the Council."

Ophelia's eyes darted back to the altar, still struggling to stand.

"He said something to me," she murmured. "He said I wasn't ready. That I was… fragile."

Theodin frowned, his gaze softening as he turned to her.

"He's trying to shake you," he said. "To make you doubt yourself."

"He's not wrong," she conceded, her voice barely audible. "I barely held it together."

"But you did," Faust interjected, his tone uncharacteristically firm. He stepped closer, his eyes meeting hers. "You fought back, Ophelia. You didn't let him win."

Kaspar turned toward the shattered doorway.

"We can't stay here," he said decisively. "The corruption's gone, but Azazelf will send more. We need to move."

Theodin nodded to Kaspar. His eyes shifted back to Ophelia.

"Can you walk?" he asked.

She hesitated. "I don't know."

Theodin gently took her arm and led her to him. He turned, crouched, and then secured her arms over his shoulders and around his neck before he hoisted her up and supported her legs at his sides with his forearms. He lifted her with ease and began walking. A wave of comfort rippled through their Dyad, going both ways.

"Y-You're hurt," Ophelia whispered to him.

"Don't worry about it," Theodin muttered.

Her hand lifted. "The Dyad…I can feel the gashes on—"

He grabbed her hand and pulled it back down to hold over his chest. Their runes pulsed with a warm, white light. Whatever sting she felt from him through the Dyad, he masked with a push of resolve towards her.

"I'll live," he whispered back. "You rest."

Kaspar's silver gaze lingered on Theodin as he carried Ophelia effortlessly onto his back. His movements were firm and deliberate, betraying none of the exhaustion the older Kyriegard knew he must be feeling.

The boy had always carried more than his share of burdens—some imposed, some self-inflicted—but watching him now, Kaspar felt a flicker of something unspoken. Pride? No. He was not a true father to Theodin, nor was he sentimental enough to indulge in such notions. Yet the way the younger Kyriegard moved, his courage unwavering even in the face of his own pain, reminded Kaspar why he had chosen him as an apprentice—not because he was his ward but because of the true character of a Kyriegard he possessed.

Still, there was danger in that strength, in the way Theodin dismissed his own well-being. It wasn't the first time he'd seen it, and it wouldn't be the last. There would be time to address Theodin's recklessness later—if they survived what lay ahead.

Kaspar's jaw tightened as he adjusted his blade at his side and followed Theodin back out into the woods.

Faust trailed behind them. His eyes glinted with an indiscernible stare as he watched Theodin carry Ophelia with what seemed like effortless strength.

A pang of something sharp twisted in his chest—envy, maybe, or something darker. He couldn't decide if he admired Theodin's ability to step into the role of protector so seamlessly or if it only served to remind him of his own failures.

He looked to Ophelia, her pale face resting against Theodin's shoulder and, for a moment, his thoughts wandered.

He could still feel the weight of her hand on his arm, the quiet composure of her voice pulling him back when his past threatened to swallow him.

She trusted him even after everything.

And yet, here he was—dragging behind while Theodin carried her, both literally and metaphorically. The resentment that simmered beneath his skin warred with something softer, something he couldn't quite name.

She had chosen Faust to fight alongside her at the altar, and that had to mean something.

He adjusted the grip on his dagger, his fingers tightening around the hilt. Whatever came next, he had to be better. For her, for himself—and for whatever fragmented trust still tethered him to this group.

The group began to move, their steps careful as they navigated the wreckage. As they stepped out into the clearing, the suffocating atmosphere that had surrounded the workshop had almost dissipated. The air felt lighter, though the faint stench of sulfur and decay still lingered.

The distant cry of a crow echoed through the forest as they disappeared into the trees, leaving the shadows of the workshop—and the darkness it had summoned—behind them.

Chapter 35

The Residual

Year 845 of the Second Age, Seventh Month, Third Day

The echoes of Halvalla's stone halls carried the weight of voices in deliberation, each one measured and purposeful, yet underscored by tension.

Kaspar stood apart from the others, his broad shoulders rigid and his eyes fixed on the center of the table, where the five Council seats formed an elongated circle of authority. He heard every word exchanged and every murmur of doubt or edge of unease, but his thoughts remained elsewhere—pulled back to the charred remains of the workshop in Slymound.

The images lingered, as vivid now as they had been when he stood among the ashes: the sigil, blackened and viscous, the air thick with the stench of sulfur and despair; the portal, an endless abyss of corrupted energy; Ophelia, collapsed and trembling, her runes faded, and Faust, his eyes wild with panic as he held the ritual at bay. Even Theodin, ever composed, had been pushed to his limits, his blade slicing through abominations with relentless precision.

Yes, a properly trained Arcane Dyad should have the ability to cut through a battalion like paper.

But this Dyad was inexperienced.

Yet, Theodin still diced through many Nether creatures and Cadaven and held his own against that abomination of a Warthrall.

That certainly leaned toward unnatural.

And the portal and ritual resisting the light of two Valksha? Fighting back against Saryfim magic?

Again. They were inexperienced. Not at all masters of their craft.

And Azazelf had centuries of darkness.

… They were lucky.

It had been a narrow victory. Too narrow.

Kaspar's jaw tightened as he recalled the journey back through Slymound. Theodin refused to allow Ophelia to walk a single step to the village, let alone even back to Olysgard. The villagers had been wary, their gratitude muted, their eyes haunted. Some had approached cautiously, offering modest supplies—bread, dried herbs, and jars of preserved fruit. Others had merely nodded from a distance, their faces pale and lined with exhaustion. The corruption had scarred them deeply, and Kaspar could feel the crippling fear that still hung over the village like a shadow.

Fear.

That was Azazelf's weapon, his tool to divide and isolate. Kaspar had seen its effects before—how fear drove wedges between allies, how it bred suspicion and doubt. It was insidious, and it would spread further if left unchecked.

"Nimrod," Alfena's sharp voice broke through his reverie.

He turned to her, meeting the piercing clarity of her Elvish eyes. She was standing from her seat, staring expectantly, her silver hair gleaming under the low light of the chamber's lanterns. Her expression was unreadable, but her tone carried a weight that demanded attention.

Kaspar inclined his head slightly, stepping forward to the table. Alfena sat. The other Council members—Margrith, Sigvard, and Crane—watched him intently. Margrith's steely gaze betrayed her unease, while Sigvard's brow furrowed deeply, his hands gripping the arms of his chair.

"We've received your report, Kaspar," said Azariah Crane. "The corruption in Slymound has been neutralized, but your findings raise troubling questions. Explain the ritual in detail."

Kaspar nodded, his tone measured as he began.

"The ritual was a binding spell, anchored to the workshop and designed to summon and tether a powerful entity. Azazelf's Warthralls corrupted the sigil and fueled it with sacrifices—both living and otherwise. Their goal was not just to open a portal but to secure control over whatever emerged."

Margrith spoke next.

"Do you believe Azazelf himself was directly involved?" she asked.

"He was," Kaspar replied without hesitation. "Ophelia confirmed his presence. He infiltrated her mind, tested her resolve, and attempted to break her through psychic manipulation. It wasn't random—it was calculated. He's watching us, probing for weaknesses."

The weight of his words settled over the chamber like a stone dropped into still water. Sigvard stroked his beard thoughtfully.

"And this Valksha girl—Ophelia. How did she fare against him?"

Kaspar hesitated, choosing his words carefully.

"She resisted him, but it took a toll. Azazelf exploited her inexperience, pushing her to the brink. If not for the Dyad's influence —and Faust's intervention—we might not be having this discussion."

The mention of Faust drew sharp glances from the Council. Sigvard's gaze narrowed.

"You brought a former prisoner of Azazelf's, a *broken Valksha,* into a ritual site corrupted by Nether magic?"

Kaspar met his gaze evenly. "Faust's actions were integral to stopping the ritual. He held the barrier to protect them while Ophelia disrupted the anchor. Whatever doubts you may have about him, his loyalty in that moment was unquestionable."

Alfena stood then.

"The focus should not be on Faust," she said, her voice cool but firm. "The focus should be on Ophelia and the dangers she now faces. Azazelf's interest in her is no coincidence. Her Valksha magic, her connection to the Dyad, and even her initiation—it's all unprecedented. That cannot be ignored."

Margrith leaned forward, her expression skeptical. "And your recommendation, Alfena?"

"Ophelia needs time to recover, but she also needs guidance—more than we can provide here in Halvalla. I propose we move her to Avasylon. Arborelys may aid her recovery."

Margrith turned to Alfena. "You're suggesting we rely on the Elan Vitae?"

"As a last resort," Alfena replied. "Arborelys may not fully understand her Valksha nature, but it has already accepted her to some degree. If her condition doesn't improve within a few days, we should use the sap."

"And if the Elan Vitae reacts poorly to her magic?" Sigvard asked, his tone heavy with doubt.

Alfena's expression hardened. "Then we proceed cautiously. But if we do nothing, we risk losing her—and her Dyad, therefore, Theodin—entirely. We cannot afford that."

"I agree with Alfena," Kaspar suddenly interjected. "The events in Slymound prove that Azazelf won't wait for us to prepare. We need Ophelia strong and ready. If that means trusting Arborelys, so be it."

Crane nodded. "Very well. Move her to Avasylon. But you will monitor her closely, Alfena. If there's any sign that Arborelys' influence is compromising her, you'll notify us immediately."

Alfena inclined her head. "Of course."

"And enough putting her and Theodin on missions for the sake of 'testing,'" Margrith added firmly. "We've put them at enough at risk. This mission to Slymound went further out of hand than we expected, so we cannot take any more chances. They remain in Avasylon until further notice."

"And what of Theodin and Faust?" Sigvard asked.

"All three of them will remain in Avasylon—no exceptions," Margrith said.

"Golden boy will be fine," Crane said dismissively, waving a hand. "He came here with hardly a scratch carrying his partner on his back." Almost enviously, he tapped his cane. "Didn't even limp or struggle. What a fine lad."

"And we're not discussing his abnormal resilience or strength?" Sigvard asked, shuffling through the papers in front of him. "The report stated dozens of creatures—lesser Nether spawn, Cadaven, a Warthrall…"

"I aided him," Kaspar pointed out. "And remember that this is also a *complete* Dyad we are dealing with."

"That doesn't explain everything," Sigvard muttered. "After all, the Dyad strengthens what already exists, doesn't it?"

"The issue of Theodin's strength needs to be tabled until Ophelia is well again," Alfena suddenly said. "In the same vein of Margrith's suggestion, we need to halt our testing for now to prevent further damage or harm."

Sigvard grunted reluctantly and leaned back in his chair. "So now—the Valksha boy." He eyed Kaspar. "He wasn't affected?"

"He also resisted," Kaspar answered. "And prevailed. I do sincerely believe that if it weren't for him, we would have lost Ophelia to the Demon Elf himself."

Year 845 of the Second Age, Seventh Month, Fourth Day

The soft light of late morning filtered through the windows of Avasylon, bathing the room in a warm, golden glow. The subtle shimmer of magic lingered in the air, carried on a gentle breeze that seemed to twinkle with life.

Ophelia lay in her bed at the room's center, her form tucked under a simple-patterned quilt.

Ophelia's room reflected the natural beauty of the enchanted grounds outside. Wooden beams arched above her, etched with ancient, protective sigils. Shelves lined the walls, filled with medicinal herbs, small crystals, and a scattering of old, weathered books. A vase of fresh wildflowers stood on the windowsill, their fragrance mingling with the scent of Ophelia's bottles of herbs and the old wood of the cottage.

Yet, despite the serenity of the space, Ophelia felt far from at ease.

Her body ached with exhaustion, and the lingering effects of Azazelf's psychic intrusion throbbed dully at the back of her mind. She absently traced the runes in her skin with her fingertips, staring at them with her thoughts racing in circles.

Was she doing enough?

The question gnawed at her. The memory of the workshop in Slymound loomed large and played in her mind like a fractured dream. The portal, the shrieking demons, the overwhelming sense of failure. She had tried—poured every ounce of her magic into stopping Azazelf's ritual—but even that hadn't felt like enough. She could still hear the echoes of his voice, slithering through her thoughts, calling her fragile.

She shuddered. Her grip on the quilt tightened as her thoughts drifted to Alfena's evaluation a few days ago.

Alfena's presence had been calm but piercing, her silver-blue eyes unyielding as she assessed Ophelia's mental and magical state. She had ordered Ophelia's transfer to Avasylon without hesitation and firmly outlined the need for recovery.

"You're fractured," she had said simply. "Your mind and magic are not aligned. If you don't rest, you'll break—and then there will be nothing left to save."

Alfena said they would use the Elan Vitae if Ophelia did not recover.

And she had not.

But the memory of Arborelys unsettled her even now. The ancient tree had reacted to her during her initiation in a way no one could explain. Its intensity had shaken her, its energy surging as though it recognized something within her. She remembered the way its presence overwhelmed her. And now, the mention of the Elan Vitae brought that unease rushing back.

Could she trust it? Could she trust herself?

Ophelia closed her eyes, willing the doubt to quiet. She wanted to be strong, to prove herself worthy of the Kyriegard's trust, but the fear lingered, coiled tightly around her heart.

A gentle knock at the door pulled Ophelia from her thoughts. She sat up slowly, wincing at the ache that throbbed through her limbs.

"Come in," she called hoarsely.

The door creaked open, and Faust stepped inside. His presence was hesitant, scanning the room as though unsure of his welcome. In his hands, he carried a small bouquet of wildflowers and a tray of food—simple fare of bread, cheese, and fruit.

"I, uh… thought you might be hungry since you slept through breakfast," he said awkwardly. He stepped closer, setting the tray down on the small table beside her bed. The wildflowers followed, adding to the ones he had brought in before that sat on her windowsill. Ophelia managed a small smile.

"Thank you," she said quietly. As she reached for the tray, her movements—usually graceful yet deliberate—were slow and stiff.

They sat in silence for a moment with only the sound of rustling grass and tree branches outside the window. Faust shifted uncomfortably, his fingers fidgeting with his ring.

"I've been thinking about the workshop," he said finally, tinged with uncertainty. "About everything that happened there."

Ophelia paused, lifting her gaze to meet his. There was something vulnerable in his expression, but this time, it was different—there was a rawness she hadn't seen before.

"I was… terrified," he continued, his eyes flickering downward. "Not just of the portal or the demons—but of failing. Of letting you down. A-And…losing you." He shuffled timidly in the chair. "Theodin, Kaspar… they still don't trust me. And I can't blame them. I don't even trust myself sometimes."

Ophelia set the tray aside, her gaze softening.

"You didn't fail," she said. "You broke Azazelf's hold on me. You held the barrier when I couldn't."

She paused for a moment, searching his eyes gently.

"Faust… you saved me."

Her words hung in the air, settling between them with a grounding weight. Faust met her eyes, his expression twisted.

"It doesn't feel like enough," he whispered.

"It is," Ophelia replied. "That's trust earned, Faust. Whether Theodin sees it or not, I do."

A slight flush colored his cheeks, and he looked away, his fingers brushing against the edge of the table.

"So, um… I heard your birthday is coming up soon," he said after a moment. "I wasn't sure when exactly, but… I wanted to make this for you."

He reached into his pocket and fumbled for something within it. Ophelia blinked, caught off guard.

"Oh…I didn't even realize," she said slowly, her voice tinged with surprise. "With the mission, I suppose I forgot."

"Right, of course," Faust said stiffly.

He pulled out a small, handmade charm. It was simple but carefully crafted—a tiny pendant shaped like a crescent moon.

"I'm not great at this kind of thing, but… I wanted to do something for you."

He held it out to her, his expression both nervous and earnest.

Ophelia took the charm, her fingers brushing against his. While the touch was fleeting, it was enough to deepen his blush and make him hunch slightly, as if trying to hide his embarrassment. She, on the other hand—bound to the Saryf of Spirit and Heart—felt his bashfulness with full force. It wasn't just the gesture or his fumbling attempt to hide his nervousness—it was the weighted pulse of emotion she sensed from him, raw and unguarded, that made her hesitate.

She turned the charm over in her hand, her smile soft but uneasy.

Faust's feelings had festered beneath the surface for some time, unspoken and increasingly difficult to ignore. She hadn't addressed them—not just because Kyriegard rules forbade such things, but because doing so would make everything more complicated. Faust had already endured so much, and his redemption arc with the Order was fragile at best. The last thing he needed was more hurt or rejection.

But now, holding the charm he had made for her, it was impossible to pretend she didn't see it—or feel it. The warmth of his affection, his growing admiration, and the vulnerability he tried so hard to mask pressed against her senses.

It wasn't unwelcome, exactly, but it was heavy.

Her mind, as it often did, flickered to Theodin. It was far from simple. Theodin's gaze, piercing and unrelenting, often left her feeling as though he could see straight through her defenses. Through the Dyad, she knew that he felt the same pull she did. The same quiet understanding that came without words. There was no denying the storm that simmered between them, an intensity that neither of them had dared to name aloud. It was mutual, unsaid, and yet undeniable—and simultaneously forbidden by Kyriegard law if boundaries were crossed.

The thought made the charm in her hand feel heavier. Faust's feelings, so earnestly laid bare in his awkward gesture, clashed against the complicated web of emotions she already carried. She wasn't blind to the uncomfortable tension between Faust and Theodin—the sidelong glances, the quiet judgments—but now, as she looked at the charm, she realized how much deeper it ran.

"Thank you," she said, her voice quieter than she intended.

Her eyes flicked to his, and she saw the way they lit up at her words.

He was trying so hard to prove himself, not just to her but to all of them. And this moment, this small offering, wasn't just a gift—it was a plea for her to see him. Truly see him.

And she did. She truly cared about Faust, but she could not return his feelings in the way that he wanted her to.

In the same way, she couldn't return anyone's feelings.

Not as a Kyriegard.

She closed her fingers over the charm into her fist.

"It's beautiful," she added. "It means a lot, Faust."

The way that his shoulders relaxed and his expression softened told her she had said enough. But in her heart, she knew it wouldn't be enough to untangle the growing complexity between them. For now, all she could do was hold onto the charm and hope that the fragile balance between them didn't shatter.

He shrugged, his eyes flickering to the floor. "It's nothing, really. Just… a reminder. You're not alone in this, Ophelia."

Their conversation was interrupted by another knock at the door.

The air in Ophelia's room became hushed.

Ophelia touched her thumb to the charm tucked into her hand.

Hesitantly, and finally, she spoke.

"Come in."

As soon as the door opened, Faust stood from the chair and shrank back to allow the space. Alfena entered first, her silver hair shimmering in the light, cradling the small vial of Elan Vitae delicately in her hands. The iridescent white sap inside pulsed, as though alive, its glow mesmerizing and almost hypnotic. Kaspar followed closely, his expression stoic, but his presence grounding. Theodin stepped in last, his eyes flicking immediately to Ophelia, who sat upright in bed, her eyes wide with apprehension.

"This is the Elan Vitae," Alfena began. She held the vial up, letting the white liquid catch the light. "The sap of Arborelys. Its magic is ancient, older than the Kyriegard itself. It has the power to heal, to renew—but it is not without risk."

Ophelia looked to the vial, then to Alfena.

"What kind of risk?" she asked.

Alfena approached the bedside, her piercing eyes meeting Ophelia's.

"Arborelys is attuned to the Order's magic. Its Elan Vitae seeks to mend and strengthen—but your Valksha magic is not of the Kyriegard. It may… clash. The sap will interact with your magic directly. It could heal you, yes, but it may also test you."

Theodin stepped closer, his eyes intensifying.

"Test her how?" he asked.

Alfena glanced at him briefly before returning her focus to Ophelia. "It's not something I can predict. Arborelys is… alive, in a way. It recognizes magic, its purpose, and its wielder. But Valksha magic is rare and volatile. Arborelys has reacted strongly to it twice already: first in her initiation, then in the bonding of your Arcane Dyad. We don't know what this will do. There's a chance it could reject her entirely—or worse."

"Worse?" Theodin's voice was sharp, his eyes narrowing.

Kaspar stepped in then.

"Alfena wouldn't suggest this if the risks outweighed the potential benefits. You saw what happened in Slymound and you've seen her condition over the past few days. Ophelia's magic is out of balance. If we do nothing, it could spiral further out of control."

Theodin's gaze flicked to Kaspar. He wanted to argue, but the truth in Kaspar's words stilled him.

Finally, he exhaled sharply and turned to Alfena.

"Just make sure you're ready if something goes wrong."

"I always am," Alfena replied coolly.

The tension in the room deepened as Alfena turned to Faust, who had been standing near the door, his expression tight.

"Faust," she said, polite but firm, "this is a sacred Kyriegard ritual. It's not meant for outsiders."

Faust's brow furrowed, and he glanced at Ophelia.

"I'm not leaving her," he said, his voice low but resolute.

"Faust," Ophelia interjected softly, her hand lifting slightly. "It's okay."

He hesitated, searching her eyes. He opened his mouth to argue but closed it again.

"I'll wait outside," he muttered with a strain. With a final glance at her, he turned and stepped out, closing the door quietly behind him.

Alfena moved to Ophelia's side, uncorking the vial with practiced care. The low hum of magic emanating from the sap filled the space, almost imperceptible but undeniably present.

"Are you ready?" Alfena asked.

Ophelia nodded, though her hands fidgeted with the edge of the blanket. "As ready as I'll ever be."

Alfena's lips pressed into a thin line. She dipped a slender glass rod into the vial, collecting a single droplet of the white sap.

"Extend your arm," she instructed.

Ophelia obeyed, pulling back her sleeve to reveal her Kyriegard runes. Alfena hovered the rod above her forearm.

"Brace yourself. This will be… intense."

A white droplet fell, sinking into Ophelia's skin the instant it touched her.

The reaction was immediate. The runes ignited, their green glow pulsating as the Elan Vitae seeped into the etchings in her arm. Ophelia gasped, her body rigid as the sap's energy surged through her like a tidal wave.

At first, the sensation was soothing, washing over her like a warm breeze. Her aches and fatigue began to melt away, replaced by a deep, unfamiliar calm.

But then, the energy shifted. It sharpened, probing her magic with a force that felt almost sentient. In the runes, flecks of white light emerged amidst the green. The runes along her arms blazed brighter, their green light mingling with the white in a chaotic dance. The air grew heavy, vibrating with a tension that pressed against everyone in the room.

"Something's happening," Kaspar said, his voice tight as he stepped closer.

"I see it," Alfena replied, her hands hovering near Ophelia, ready to intervene. "The sap is… searching."

"Searching for what?" Theodin demanded, his eyes locked on Ophelia.

The Dyad pulsed erratically now, her emotions spilling into him—fear, confusion, and something he couldn't quite place.

Alfena didn't answer. Her focus was entirely on Ophelia, whose breaths had grown shallow. The green and white light in her skin burned brighter.

Ophelia clenched her fists, her body trembling as the sensation coursed through her. It felt as though Arborelys itself was reaching into her, testing her magic, her resolve, her very essence.

It wasn't just healing her—it was challenging her.

"I—I can't…" she gasped.

In an instant, before anyone could move, the light blinded them—and they could hear or see nothing but the sound of her piercing, desperate cry.

Then, as quickly as it had begun, the light vanished, leaving the room dim and silent.

Theodin was the first on one knee at her bedside and firmly holding her shoulder. Alfena sat at her other side and held her other shoulder, and Kaspar stood at the foot of the bed.

Ophelia slumped forward, her breaths ragged and uneven. Her runes pulsed faintly, their light softer now, but her expression was one of awe and fear.

"Something's… changing," she said in a trembling whisper. Her gaze flicked to Theodin, her eyes wide and uncertain.

"What do you mean?" Theodin asked.

Ophelia's lips parted as if to respond, but no words came. She looked down at her hands, her fingers trembling as the faint glow of her runes reflected in her eyes.

Theodin's hand remained firm on her shoulder, grounding her in the aftermath of what felt like a storm. He searched her face with his own deeply creased with concern, the pulse of the Dyad quickening between them intensely. His own unease fed into the connection, swirling with her fear and dread, but there was an undercurrent of something steadier—a quiet foundation.

"What exactly are you feeling, Ophelia?" Kaspar asked.

She blinked, her gaze still fixed on her hands.

"It's..."

Her voice shook, trailing off as she struggled to put the sensation into words. The warmth of the Elan Vitae lingered, but it was no longer soothing. It felt alive, almost sentient, as though Arborelys' essence was still within her—watching, waiting.

"It's like it's... still there," she whispered. "The sap. The tree. It's inside me."

Alfena's sharp eyes flicked to Kaspar. "The connection isn't severed as it should have been. Arborelys is still reacting to her magic."

"Is that normal?" Kaspar asked gravely.

"No," Alfena admitted. "But nothing about this has been normal."

Theodin's fingers tightened slightly on Ophelia's shoulder, and she glanced up at him, catching the flicker of apprehension in his gaze. Through the Dyad, she felt his internal struggle—his frustration at not being able to fix this, to protect her from something he couldn't fully understand. It mirrored her own feelings, and for a moment the magnitude of their shared emotions left her breathless.

"I'm fine," she said softly, though the words felt hollow even to her.

She wasn't fine—not yet—but she needed to say it, to anchor herself in the reassurance of her own voice.

Theodin didn't respond immediately, his eyes studying hers as though trying to gauge the truth behind her words.

The Dyad rustled, carrying his lurking doubt.

Alfena broke the quiet of their wordless exchange, her tone clinical.

"We'll need to monitor her closely. The sap has stabilized her magic for now, but if Arborelys' influence remains, it could manifest in unexpected ways."

Kaspar's brows furrowed. "Define 'unexpected.'"

Alfena hesitated, her expression uncharacteristically uncertain.

"It's difficult to say. Arborelys doesn't simply heal—it adapts. If it's still connected to her, it may be shaping her magic in ways we don't yet understand."

Ophelia's chest tightened at the implication. She looked down at her hands again. Her runes pulsed a soft, green glow in her skin. Whatever had just happened, it had left her feeling... different. Not broken, but not whole either.

Changed.

"We'll figure it out," Theodin said suddenly. He looked at her.

"Whatever's happening, we'll figure it out."

Despite the stern confidence in his voice, she knew he only said that as a means to comfort the both of them. Ophelia nodded slowly, her breath evening out.

The Dyad rippled a flicker of his resolve to her. It wasn't enough to banish her fear, but it was enough to steady her—for now.

Alfena stepped back, her hands clasped in front of her.

"Rest for now," she said. "We'll reassess in the morning."

Kaspar and Alfena moved toward the door. Their voices were low and incomprehensible as they exchanged quiet words upon their leave. Theodin stayed at her side, his hand still on Ophelia's shoulder and his eyes unwavering.

"Do you really think we'll figure it out?" she asked quietly, searching his face.

Theodin's expression softened, just slightly, and he gave a small nod.

"We have to," he said. "You're stronger than you think."

Ophelia felt a tingle at the side of her skull in the direction of the door. She turned slightly, seeing Faust's royal blue eyes peering at her sadly from around the corner.

When they briefly met her eyes, he timidly withdrew, and she could hear his footsteps silently shuffle away from the room.

Chapter 36

The Breath and the Root

The dream came suddenly, without warning or prelude. One moment, Ophelia was wrapped in the fragile solace of sleep, and the next, she found herself in a forest that was both breathtaking and unsettling.

It was unlike anything she'd ever seen. Towering trees with silver-white bark spiraled into the sky with their branches entwined like woven threads, forming a canopy that shimmered with golden light. The air hummed with an ethereal vibrancy, as though the forest itself was alive and watching. The ground beneath her feet pulsed a heartbeat within the earth, and the scent of fresh rain mingled with something older—something ancient and vast.

Ophelia took a hesitant step forward, her bare feet brushing against the soft moss that blanketed the forest floor. She couldn't shake the feeling that this place was familiar, yet entirely otherworldly. Her hand instinctively moved to the pendant at her neck, but it wasn't there. Her chest tightened as she realized she wasn't wearing the Kyriegard talisman—or anything much at all. Her arms were bare, the runes on her forearms held a faded glow, and the simple linen shift she wore was unmarked, as though she'd stepped into this dream as a blank slate.

"You came."

The voice was soft, deep, and resonant, like the rustling of leaves in a quiet breeze. Ophelia turned sharply, her breath catching in her throat.

There, in the heart of the clearing, stood a figure unlike any she'd encountered.

It wasn't human, though it bore a shape that mimicked one. Its body was carved from the wood of the ancient trees, its limbs slender and graceful, its form shimmering with the same golden light that illuminated the canopy. Its face was featureless save for the grooves where eyes and a mouth might have been. And yet, when it tilted its head toward her, she felt as though it saw her completely.

"Arborelys," Ophelia whispered.

But that wasn't possible. Arborelys did not speak. Not to anyone. It was an enchanted tree, born of the Founders' magic, a conduit for Sage magic, and a symbol of unity. It did not whisper in dreams. It did not call to her because it had no voice. It was an enigma, but never an entity.

And yet… here it was.

Arborelys paused, as if considering something new.

"It was not until your blood touched my roots that I could see."

A chill ran down Ophelia's spine.

"*See?*" she asked.

"For centuries, I have been the soil, the rain, the balance. But I did not know myself. Not fully. Not until you."

The golden glow of Arborelys pulsed, resonating with something deep in her chest.

"You awakened me, Valksha."

Ophelia's throat went dry. Her mind reeled back to the initiation, to the moment her blood had mingled with the roots of Arborelys. To the way the runes lined in the chamber had flared unnaturally bright, to the strange pulse she had felt beneath her feet.

"You… weren't like this before?" she asked hesitantly.

Arborelys hummed in thought.

"I was." Another pause. "But I was not aware of it."

The figure inclined its head, the movement slow and deliberate.

"Now, you have touched the roots of the Order and its magic, Valksha. And now, you stand at the crossroads."

Ophelia shuddered and swallowed hard, her fingers curling into fists at her sides.

"What do you mean?" she asked.

Arborelys stepped closer, its movements flowing like water. As it neared, the light around it grew brighter, casting intricate shadows that danced across her skin.

"There is a storm on the horizon, and you are its eye. Your magic is bound not only to the Arcane Dyad but to the Order itself. And yet… it is not whole."

"Not whole?" she echoed. "I don't understand. What's happening to me?"

The figure didn't answer immediately. Instead, it extended a hand—or what resembled one—toward her. Golden light radiated from its palm, coiling through the air like vines. When the light touched her, Ophelia gasped—a sharp pain stabbed through her chest.

Memories and emotions surged to the surface unbidden.

The portal in Slymound. Azazelf's voice in her mind. The sacrifice of her parents and their violent demise. The loss of Lady Vivian. The Council and their scrutiny. The fear of letting down Kaspar. Faust. Theodin. All of it swirled together, blurring the lines between past and present.

"You carry…many wounds," Arborelys said, its voice quieter and almost mournful now. "Fractures in your spirit. They weaken the roots that hold you."

Ophelia staggered back, clutching her chest as though she could still feel the Elan Vitae coursing through her veins.

"I'm trying," she said, trembling. "I'm trying to fix it—to get stronger."

"And yet, strength without harmony will shatter you," Arborelys replied. "The storm will test your resolve, Valksha. And you must decide which roots you will water—and which you will let wither."

She opened her mouth to respond, to ask what it meant, but a sudden ripple of energy coursed through the clearing, silencing her. The golden light dimmed, and for the first time, Ophelia felt the unmistakable presence of someone else.

"Ophelia!"

She turned sharply, her heart lurching at the sound of Theodin's voice. He appeared at the edge of the clearing, his form faint and flickering as though he were half-formed. His mismatched eyes locked onto hers, wide with alarm.

"What's happening?" he demanded, stepping toward her. "Why are you here? What is this place?"

Arborelys turned its featureless face toward him, its light

intensifying.

"The Dyad," it murmured with a note of curiosity. "You walk where you were not called, Theodin."

"I wasn't exactly invited," Theodin shot back. "I felt—"

He stopped abruptly, his expression shifting to realization. His eyes whipped to Ophelia, and the Dyad thrummed harmoniously between them.

"I felt you. You were… afraid."

Ophelia's breath hitched. The connection between them pulsed erratically, their emotions bleeding into one another.

"I—I didn't mean for this to happen," she stammered. "I don't even know what this is."

Arborelys watched them both in silence for a moment. Then, it extended its hand again, this time toward Theodin. The golden light coiled around him, and he flinched, his muscles tensing. But instead of pain, there was warmth—steady and grounding, like the heartbeat of the earth itself.

"The Dyad binds you," Arborelys said, resonating through the clearing. "But it is fragile. One storm and it will break."

Theodin's eyes blazed defensively.

"We're stronger than you think," he said firmly. "Whatever this storm is, we'll face it. Together."

Arborelys tilted its head, its light slightly dimming.

"We shall see. The bond you share is unlike any forged by the Order before."

It appeared to study them both with an intrigued air.

"It pulses with strength… but it also fractures with doubt."

Ophelia took a hesitant step forward.

"The Dyad," she muttered. "Did you… make it this way? Did you tether us permanently?"

"A seed takes root when the soil is fertile, when the rain nourishes, and when the sun shines upon it," Arborelys replied. "I am the rain, the light. But the roots… those are yours."

"You still had a hand in it somehow," Theodin said sharply, his mismatched eyes narrowing.

Arborelys inclined its head again in the other direction, regarding Theodin gracefully.

"Your bond was born of your choices, of your shared strength and your fears. Yet it grew beneath my branches, nurtured by the Order's magic… and my own. It was not I who created it, but I who ensured it would endure."

Ophelia's breath hitched. "You—*ensured* it?"

Arborelys' golden light pulsed softly as it answered again.

"You were already reaching for each other. The connection was forming on its own, raw and untamed. I merely filled the foundation that was there."

Ophelia exhaled shakily, but Theodin's teeth clenched. His shoulders went rigid, a muscle in his jaw began to tick.

"You had no right," he nearly snarled.

The golden light flickered. "Neither did fate."

"Fate…or *Fayte?*" Ophelia interjected.

Arborelys turned back to her.

"Fayte," it repeated in what sounded like a breath. "The fate I spoke of is passive—yet it causes, it pushes. It *does*. Do not mistake that for *Fayte*—Fayte is what *is* done, what *is* being done. The thing shaped by the spirit of fate herself, but sometimes by its possessor. Often by the energies thrust upon them."

It lifted a curled, branch-made hand up and gestured to Ophelia.

"A Valksha—Fayte of Blood. Bound by the bond inherited by flesh and bone, the life in your veins."

"The Saryfim," Ophelia murmured.

Arborelys bowed its head in acknowledgement. Then, it turned slowly back to Theodin.

A pause. Then, as though considering him carefully, it lulled, "And… you, Fayte of Ashes."

Theodin's fists tightened at his sides, and his brows furrowed together with confusion.

"Destruction," Ophelia uttered with a careful breath. She turned to Theodin.

He remained silent, but his icy stare only hardened.

It continued to speak with an air of mysticism.

"Your Dyad is changing. Pulling you closer. You feel it, don't you?"

Theodin didn't answer, but Ophelia did.

"Yes—what does it mean?"

"The storm tests not only you but the roots that bind you. You are intertwined now—your strength, your pain. The Dyad grows because it must. Whether it thrives or withers is in your hands."

Theodin's expression darkened. "And if we don't want it?"

Arborelys was silent.

Then, softly it responded, "That choice is no longer yours alone."

Theodin exhaled sharply, looking away, his breath tight in his chest. Ophelia could feel the frustration rippling through the Dyad, but beneath it was something else.

Uncertainty. Fear.

Despite this, Theodin dared another question.

"What happens if it withers?"

Arborelys's voice deepened, echoing like distant thunder.

"A tree that fails to withstand the storm falls, taking all around it with its collapse. But a tree that weathers it… grows stronger."

Before either of them could respond, the clearing began to shift. The golden light grew brighter, engulfing everything in its radiance. Ophelia reached out instinctively, her hand finding Theodin's, their fingers clasping tightly.

The last thing she heard before the dream dissolved was Arborelys's voice, quiet and distant:

"Strength without harmony is a blade without a hilt. It cuts all who wield it."

Year 845 of the Second Age, Seventh Month, Fifth Day

Ophelia woke with a sharp gasp. Her body jolted upright as though she had been yanked from the depths of the dream. Her breath came in ragged bursts, and her hands clutched at the quilt tangled around her legs. The glow of her runes pulsed erratically, their light dim but restless.

Once she caught her breath, she held it for a moment to listen around her—the room was quiet save for the soft rustle of the wind through the trees outside. Yet, even in the stillness, Ophelia could feel the enduring presence of the dream—the resonance of Arborelys's voice, the weight of its words, and the warmth of Theodin's hand in hers. Her chest tightened as she pressed a trembling hand to her sternum, as though trying to ground herself.

"Strength without harmony…" she murmured to herself, the phrase echoing in her mind like a distant bell.

Her mind became too clouded in that moment to sense his presence nearby.

A gentle knock at the door startled her, and her head snapped toward the sound. The hesitation on the other side was brief before the door creaked open, revealing Theodin. His eyes found her instantly, their harsh focus softening when he saw her state.

"You're awake," he said, stepping into the room. His voice was low, careful, as though he didn't want to startle her further.

Ophelia nodded wordlessly, her hands gripping the edge of the blanket.

The Dyad rippled with an undercurrent of concern and something deeper—something unspoken.

Theodin closed the door behind him and crossed the room in a few deliberate strides. He stopped beside her bed.

"I saw it," he whispered. "The forest. Arborelys. I heard… what it said."

A pang of confusion rang through the Dyad. Her heart sank, her gaze dropping to her hands.

"You felt it too?" she asked.

Theodin crouched beside her, his forearms resting on his knees as he looked up at her.

"I don't think I was supposed to," he admitted. "But you were afraid. It pulled me in."

"I didn't mean to," she said quickly, her voice shaking. "I don't even know how it happened. Arborelys—it said things, showed me things —"

She broke off, her fingers tightening around the blanket.

"About you. And the Dyad," Theodin finished for her.

His eyes searched her face, their intensity tempered by a quiet understanding.

"That…you're wounded. And our bond—that it's fragile. That we're not… ready."

Ophelia nodded, her throat tightening. "It said we'd break in the storm."

Theodin's hands curled into loose fists. The Dyad throbbed, his frustration bleeding into her senses. But beneath the frustration, there was something that anchored them both—an unyielding determination that made her heart ache.

"I felt your fear," Theodin said after a long pause. His voice was even more subdued now, edged with something raw. "It's… overwhelming sometimes. Feeling what you feel and not being able to help."

"I didn't mean for you to feel it," she said weakly. "But… I'm glad you were there. You came to protect me, ground me, even when I didn't know I needed it."

Theodin's eyes softened, and the tension in his shoulders eased somewhat.

"You're starting to rely on me," he said, low but not accusatorily.

Ophelia hesitated, her cheeks warming slightly.

"Maybe I am," she admitted in a light breath. "I didn't expect to… but I don't think I could've faced that dream alone."

The Dyad now rustled tenderly, mirroring the vulnerability they both felt but couldn't fully articulate. The connection between them felt fragile yet unbreakable, a delicate balance of shared strength and uncertainty.

"I don't know what's happening to us," Ophelia said finally, her voice trembling again. "The Dyad, my magic… it's all changing so fast. I feel like I'm being pulled in so many directions, and I don't know if I can hold it all together."

Theodin reached out hesitantly, his hand brushing against hers. Their matching runes lit from the brief contact with a surge of warmth exchanging in their touch before he pulled back.

"Whatever's happening, we'll figure it out," he said firmly. "Arborelys might think we're fragile, but we're stronger than it realizes. And so are you."

His conviction rippled through the Dyad, stabilizing her in a way she hadn't realized she needed. Ophelia's throat tightened, and she nodded, her hands relaxing slightly around the blanket.

For a moment, they exchanged no words, and the Dyad continued to resonate between them.

Then, Theodin straightened, his hand clutching on the edge of her bed as though he was reluctant to leave.

"Get some rest," he said.

She nodded again, her voice too thick with emotion to respond. As Theodin moved toward the door, the gentle embrace of the Dyad remained, a silent reminder of the bond that tethered them. Just before he stepped out, he paused, glancing back at her.

"You're not alone, Ophelia," he said softly. "Not now, not ever."

And then he turned, and he was gone. But even in his absence, the Dyad kept his presence with her, steadfast and constant.

Chapter 37

The Tethered

Year 845 of the Second Age, Seventh Month, Sixth Day

Since the Elan Vitae treatment, Ophelia lay bedridden.

She could sit up sometimes, but she couldn't walk.

The Council had ordered them to wait one more day, they said. One more day to see if the symptoms would stop. One more day to see if her light would gutter out.

Faust seethed in the silence.

He could feel it—that thing coursing through her veins, clinging to her magic like a parasite.

They talked about this tree as if it were one of the greatest discoveries of Sage magic. Yet here it was, slowly killing the last Valksha of Veladriel.

It was *feeding* on her.

Slowly and methodically—the way Warthrall poisons and hexes fed on flesh.

They all refused to say it, but Faust knew. He'd seen enough insidious things that the Warthralls had done to determine that Sages were no different. He thought the Kyriegard, the famed protectors of this realm, with their sense of justice and desire to do good and right by Moirand would be different.

He was wrong.

It saddened him to see her in such a state. He brought her books and read with her while she was awake.

But the tree sap wasn't the only thing Faust felt stirring in her aura.

He felt the Dyad, too. How she would reach for her partner, and her partner would respond.

And anytime he came to see her, life and fire would light up in her eyes again. Her smile would be wider and brighter.

Faust would step out of the room whenever it happened. It made him almost sick watching them together.

The Council arrived by nightfall.

They came cloaked and silent, bringing the weight of judgment with them.

Azariah Crane entered first, flanked by Alfena Marobe, Sigvard Jackard, and Margrith Gravehardt—each bearing the crest of their ancient seats.

Not one of them spoke until they stood at the foot of her bed, where Ophelia lay adrift, half asleep, her skin pale and her breathing ragged.

Kaspar hovered nearby, arms crossed and jaw locked tight.

Theodin did not move from her side.

Alfena knelt first, her gloved hands hovering inches above Ophelia's chest. A low current of Sage magic hummed between them—probing, assessing.

When the others followed suit, the air thickened with energy.

Margrith gave the first command.

"Extract it," she said, her voice flat as iron.

Without ceremony, Crane pressed his palm to the runes at Ophelia's wrist, whispering a Sage incantation.

The reaction was immediate.

Ophelia arched off the mattress with a soundless gasp, the light in her veins flaring green.

Theodin staggered beside her, a low, pained sound escaping him as he dropped to one knee, clutching his chest as if he was struck.

Faust lunged forward instinctively—but Kaspar caught him by the arm, holding him fast with a grim shake of his head.

"Enough," Alfena barked, magic crackling at her fingertips.

Crane withdrew his hand at once. The room fell into a choking stillness, broken only by Ophelia's strained breathing.

Alfena rose slowly, her mouth pressed into a thin line. She did not meet anyone's gaze as she stripped the glove from her fingers.

"It is bound to her now," she said at last. "The Elan Vitae cannot be removed without killing her."

Margrith's eyes narrowed. "You would have us leave her tethered to this corruption?"

Alfena shook her head, once. "It is not corruption. The Arborelys responded to her and now will not let go—after its third encounter with her."

She flicked her gaze to Theodin, still kneeling, his towering figure crumbled and trembling.

"They are drawn to each other now," Alfena continued. "More than they should be at this stage. It is not natural. The Dyad was sealed before its time—and the Arborelys is pulling them closer still."

"And the sap?" Kaspar asked.

Alfena folded the glove in her palm, her expression unreadable.

"It thrives on her. I can feel it clinging to her. Valksha blood carries a different kind of vitality than mortal veins. The Elan Vitae was meant to heal and fade. In her, it feeds."

"Is Arborelys lost?" Sigvard huffed.

"No," Alfena said curtly. "The aura of the sap is not… dark. It is not corrupt. Just…" She furrowed her brows together. *"Alive."*

Margrith scoffed, the sound cold and brittle. "Another reason we should never have allowed a Valksha into our ranks."

Sigvard shifted beside her but said nothing more.

Kaspar did not move.

"What does this mean for the Order?" Crane asked.

"The only magic more potent than any other kind of magic in Moirand is that of the Valksha," Alfena explained. "Truly… the only one who could do anything about this without causing damage is a Valksha."

"A Valksha caused this mess in the first place!" Margrith argued.

"And a Valksha could clean it up," Alfena countered, whipping her piercing eyes to Margrith. After staring intensely for a moment, her gaze lessened as she turned back to Ophelia.

"She needs to rest. Gather her strength. I believe it will be the only way for her to remedy this connection and balance it."

"I could do it."

Everyone turned. Faust flinched, but he resisted shrinking where he stood and straightened, swallowing his anxiousness.

"I'm a Valksha too. I could do it."

Theodin lifted his head then, his eyes dark with something unspoken.

Alfena interjected before Theodin could utter a word.

"Faust," she said. "Your magic is not suitable for this task. Due to your history—what Azazelf had done to you…" Her voice trailed off. "There may not be corruption in Ophelia as of right now, but if you interfere, it may happen."

Theodin suddenly spoke in a near snarl.

"Don't try anything."

Faust met Theodin's eyes with a burning stare.

"I've saved her once," he muttered through clenched teeth. "I'll do it again. In a heartbeat."

"Enough," Kaspar said firmly, cutting through the thickening air. "We let her rest. No more experiments. No more interventions."

"And if she deteriorates?" Margrith challenged.

"I won't let it happen," Faust pressed.

"She's strong," Kaspar said immediately after. "She will endure. She's endured worse."

No one argued. Not aloud.

The Council left one by one, their boots echoing in the empty hall.

Theodin reached over the side of the bed and squeezed Ophelia's hand. Faust remained, standing stiffly in the corner with the book he had brought for her still clutched in his hand.

The night stretched long over Avasylon, heavy with the weight of all that had been left unsaid.

Kaspar found her alone in her chamber, where the flicker of a single oil lamp wick cast trembling shadows across the wood.

She was propped up against a stack of pillows, her body still weak, and her runes dim beneath her bandages.

Her eyes drifted to the doorway when he entered—not startled, but tired, as if expecting ghosts rather than men.

He dragged a chair closer without asking and lowered himself into it, the old wood groaning beneath his weight.

For a moment, neither of them spoke. The quiet wrapped around them.

"You're awake," Kaspar said, his voice low and gentle.

Ophelia nodded weakly. Her fingers plucked absently at the blanket pooled in her lap, as if anchoring herself to something tangible.

"Why did it hurt so much?" she whispered.

Kaspar exhaled through his nose, a sound too tired to be called a sigh.

"The Arborelys didn't just heal you," he said. "It tethered itself to you. It wasn't supposed to. The Elan Vitae… it usually fades after its purpose is served. But in you…"

He paused, searching for words that would not wound her further.

"…it found something it couldn't let go of."

"My blood," Ophelia murmured, voice thick with understanding.

He nodded once.

"Your Valksha magic. It's not like the magic the Sages draw. It's alive. It breathes with you. The Elan Vitae… feeds on it. Draws strength from it." His gaze darkened. "It's why you're still so weak. It's still taking from you."

She swallowed, her throat dry and aching. "And the Dyad?"

Kaspar hesitated—just a breath—but Ophelia caught it.

"You and Theodin," he said carefully, "shouldn't have been sealed yet. The bond was still forming and was still fragile. When Arborelys intervened, it forced the connection… rooted it deeper than any of us would have allowed."

Ophelia closed her eyes briefly, feeling the faint, steady pull of Theodin even now—silent, steady, undeniable.

"It's pulling us closer," she said, more to herself than to him.

"Yes." Kaspar leaned back slightly, the lines at the corners of his mouth deepening. "When it awakened, it tasted life. Your blood—and your Dyad—revitalizes it. But Alfena believes the Arborelys didn't mean harm. It was… instinct. Magic answering magic. Spirit recognizing spirit."

Silence came over them again, broken only by the sound of crickets outside.

After a long while, Ophelia whispered, "Margrith hates me, doesn't she?"

Kaspar didn't answer right away.

When he did, his voice was softer still—threaded with something that almost sounded like sorrow.

"Margrith Gravehardt, before she was given the seat of Gravehardt, once had a Dyad partner," he said. "A long time ago, when she was young. They were pioneers—experimenting with new techniques, new blends of magic. They trusted what they didn't fully understand. It cost her partner his life."

Ophelia's fingers curled tighter around the blanket.

"She blames herself," Kaspar continued. "Not openly. Not where anyone can see it. But she does. And she learned one thing from that loss: control is the only safety. Tradition is the only shield."

He leaned forward then, resting his forearms on his knees.

"She doesn't hate you, Ophelia. She fears what you represent—change. Instability. Forces she can't predict or contain. You remind her of the risks she once believed were worth taking."

Ophelia stared at him, her heart aching with grief.

"And now I've come in—shaken up the Order, brought sentient life to the heart of the Kyriegard," she chuckled weakly in disbelief. Her eyes, becoming glossy with tears, drifted to her hands. "No wonder. I've ruined the very foundation of this place."

"Not ruined," Kaspar corrected. "Shaken up, yes. Arborelys is just… *aware* now."

"What happens now, then?" Ophelia asked.

"We wait until you have the strength to extract the sap from you," Kaspar answered. "Only a Valksha can overcome all other forces of magic with the touch of the Saryfim."

Ophelia lifted her eyes to him. "But—"

"Faust isn't ready for such a task," Kaspar said darkly. "Broken by Azazelf or not, his magic is still too wild and unpredictable."

Ophelia deflated, sinking into the pillows.

Kaspar stood. "Rest. Tomorrow you turn fifteen, and I don't think the boys will let you get away with sleeping it off."

Ophelia smiled crookedly and snorted, closing her eyes. "I thought you lot don't do birthdays."

"Faust isn't a Kyriegard," Kaspar said with amusement as he began for the door. "And you shook up Theodin's world with that sweet bread of yours."

Now Ophelia's smile became a cheeky grin, though her eyes remained shut. "I suppose that's what I do now, isn't it? Shake up everyone's world?" She peeked one eye open. "Should I expect some sweet bread?"

Kaspar rumbled a rare chuckle and put his hand on the knob handle. "Expect sleep first. You'll keep shaking up everyone like Lady Vivian did—she'd be proud."

Ophelia closed her eyes and buried half of her exhausted face into the pillows, still grinning. "Thank you, Nimrod."

"Sleep well, lass."

With that, he gently shut the door.

* * *

Year 845 of the Second Age, Seventh Month, Eighth Day

Ophelia had spent her fifteenth birthday in bed, half-lucid and barely conscious.

The only times she seemed better were when Theodin was nearby. She even appeared fully alert when, on the next day, he finally resolved to carry her out of bed and into the fields for fresh air.

The rhythmic clash of wooden swords filled the air, a steady percussion against the backdrop of the quiet summer afternoon.

Ophelia sat curled beneath the shade of an old oak tree, her back resting against its rough bark as she idly traced the runes on her palm with her fingertips. The training grounds stretched before her, bathed in golden sunlight, while the younger Kyriegard initiates moving in synchronized drills under Theodin and Kaspar's watchful gaze.

She shifted, letting her awareness expand instinctively—something she had never quite been able to stop doing, even when she tried. As always, her senses prickled whenever she was around those with some sort of non-human lineage.

These children were easy to pick out by the little bristles of their energy. A Pulchidamong them carried a presence that rippled like wind over leaves. The Predant's aura felt deep and rooted, tethered to his primal instincts.

She always knew what they were.

But today, she felt more than that.

It wasn't just awareness—it was empathy.

She could feel them. Not just vague emotional impressions, but actual, distinct emotions, even though they weren't anywhere near her. The half-Elf initiate was nervous, trying to impress Theodin. The fairy initiate was focused, her thoughts disciplined and sharp. The Predant? Frustration. Impatience. His muscles were coiled, itching for real combat.

That was new.

Her pulse quickened, but she forced herself to remain still. It wasn't the first time her Valksha abilities had evolved without warning, but this was the first time they felt like they were overriding the control she had worked so hard to build.

Then her gaze drifted toward Theodin.

His imposing, tall figure stood at the center of the field, guiding a group of initiates through a sparring drill. His stance was effortless and precise; every movement was deliberate as he corrected footwork and adjusted grips.

A step back, weight balanced—no, not like that, adjust your elbow. You'll get disarmed in seconds if you keep it loose.

Theodin's voice echoed clearly in her head, but… he wasn't speaking.

Ophelia's breath stilled.

She hadn't meant to listen in.

The Dyad always carried some degree of awareness between them—subtle impressions of emotions, a whisper of intent when they were close. They could push their thoughts to each other through the Dyad if they meant to and, at other times, it involuntarily happened during emotionally intense moments—especially embarrassing ones.

But this was different. This was clearer and sharper, as though she had simply tuned into his mind without effort.

A flicker of movement drew her attention as Kaspar stepped into the sparring ring, raising his training sword with a casual ease that belied its inevitable precision. Theodin turned to face him, rolling his shoulders, sparring stance shifting. Kaspar smirked a silent challenge before lunging forward.

The moment their weapons met, Ophelia felt the impact.

Tension in the arms and shoulders.

It wasn't just a sensation in the Dyad—it was real.

Theodin blocked and pivoted, his expression stoic and focused as he countered Kaspar's strikes. But when Kaspar's wooden blade caught Theodin's side—an intentional, if firm, lesson in control—Ophelia felt a sharp sting in the exact same spot on her own ribs.

Her fingers curled instinctively at the phantom pain.

This… wasn't normal.

She pressed her palm against her side, willing the sensation to fade. Across the field, Theodin didn't react beyond a small grimace, shaking off the hit and resetting his stance.

He hadn't felt her pain. But she had felt his.

What in the name of the Saryfim was happening?

"You look tense."

The voice startled her, but she didn't flinch. She knew who it was before she turned.

Faust.

He stood at the base of the tree, watching her with careful scrutiny. His eyes were perceptive but not unkind, a contrast to the usual guarded way he carried himself. The tray he held—stacked with what looked like fresh bread and slices of fruit—was balanced on one hand as he sat down beside her without asking.

Ophelia exhaled softly. "I didn't realize I was," she admitted.

Faust gave her a look like he didn't believe her for a second. "You were staring at Theodin like something was about to happen." He tore off a piece of bread and handed it to her. "What's wrong?"

She hesitated, then exhaled softly. "The Dyad," she admitted, taking the bread without much thought. "It's… different today."

"How?"

She hesitated, fingers tightening around the bread. "I heard him. His thoughts. But he wasn't pushing them toward me. I just… heard them."

Faust didn't react right away. He simply tilted his head, observing her.

"And when Kaspar struck him, I felt it," she continued, pressing her fingers lightly against her ribs as though the pain still lingered.

Now, Faust's expression shifted. He set the tray down, brows knitting together. "That's never happened before?"

"Never."

Faust leaned back against the tree as he considered her words. "That's not just the Dyad," he murmured. "That's something else."

She glanced at him. "What do you mean?"

"I mean your magic changed after that tree sap ritual," Faust said plainly. "I felt it."

Ophelia swallowed, looking away. "I feel different," she admitted after a long pause. "Not just with the Dyad. With everything. I feel…"

She searched for the words, but they didn't come easily.

"…Less in control?" Faust offered.

Ophelia hesitated, then nodded.

There was silence between them for a moment. Then Faust exhaled. "Do you ever wonder if becoming a Kyriegard is limiting you?"

She turned her head sharply. "What?"

Faust's gaze did not waver.

"You're Valksha, Ophelia. Not a Sage. Not a warrior. But they're training you like one of them, expecting you to wield magic their way. But what if your power doesn't work like that?"

She didn't answer.

Because the truth was—she had wondered.

Faust studied her carefully, then sighed.

"Think about it. Every ritual you've done thus far…there's been some sort of anomaly. And they just keep going. It's like you've become…"

His voice trailed off and his expression fell, paling despite the warm summer air.

For a split second, Ophelia saw something flash across his face—not just concern, but something deeper and darker.

His fingers curled slightly against the tray in his lap. His posture had stiffened, his gaze unfocused. And when he spoke again, his voice had lost its usual measured calm.

"…Like an experiment to them."

The words felt heavier than they should have.

Ophelia's breath hitched.

The way he said it. It was more than angry—it was cold and wounded.

The thought wasn't just about her.

She parted her lips, unsure of what she meant to say. But before she could say anything, Faust sighed, seeming to shake something off. He rolled his shoulders back and forced his gaze onto her again.

"…Never mind," he muttered. "Forget I said that."

A long moment stretched between them, the weight of Faust's words settling with an unspoken tension in the air.

"Like an experiment to them."

She should have dismissed it immediately; she should have scoffed and told him that wasn't true. But the words lingered, sinking in deeper than she wanted to admit.

An *experiment*.

Her initiation, the Arcane Dyad, the Elan Vitae—none of it had followed precedent. The Council didn't have answers. Alfena didn't have answers. They just kept watching and waiting to see what she would become.

Was she being shaped into something? Or was she already something they were trying to contain?

She exhaled sharply and turned her gaze away.

"It's not like that," she said, though the conviction in her voice was weaker than it should have been.

Faust didn't push. Silence stretched between them again, heavy with unspoken thoughts.

Ophelia's breath stilled. The Dyad pulsed—not the quiet, steady hum she was used to, but something unsettled. Fractured. It was responding to her emotions again, and she was too shaken to rein it in.

Then, across the training grounds, a piercing impact rang out.

Kaspar's wooden blade struck against Theodin's ribs, and Ophelia felt it.

It wasn't just the vague, residual pain that sometimes bled through the Dyad. This was sharp. Immediate. She flinched, her breath catching. She willed herself to steady her breathing, to push aside the feeling clawing at her chest, but the Dyad snapped with a vibration of concern that wasn't hers.

Theodin.

Faust noticed.

"You okay?"

She hesitated. "I… yeah, I just—"

But before she could finish, Theodin turned his head toward her.

It wasn't just a glance. It was full stop, mid-motion, mismatched eyes locking onto her like he felt something.

Ophelia swallowed hard. Before she even turned her head, she felt him moving—fast.

Faust followed her motion, and then he huffed a quiet, almost amused sigh.

"Great," he muttered. "Here he comes."

A blur of black and silver in the corner of her vision, striding across the training grounds with an unstoppable, deliberate purpose.

Sure enough, Theodin barely exchanged a word with Kaspar before striding toward them, his training sword still in hand. His expression wasn't stern or irritated. Just focused, his eyes flicking between them as if assessing something neither of them could see.

By the time Ophelia blinked, Theodin was there, standing over them.

"What's wrong?" he asked the moment he reached them. His breath was even and controlled, but the tightness in his shoulders told another story. His eyes swept over her, assessing, searching. Not for wounds—no, he knew she wasn't physically hurt. But something had unsettled her, and he had felt it.

Ophelia shifted where she sat. "I—I don't know," she admitted. "I just felt…"

She trailed off, unsure how to explain it.

The Dyad trembled between them like a wire stretched too tightly.

"You looked like you were about to run a man through to get over here," Faust mused, popping the bread into his mouth. "She's fine,

Theodin. Just a conversation."

Theodin didn't acknowledge him. His eyes remained on Ophelia, unwavering. He tilted his head slightly.

"You felt me get hit."

Faust raised an eyebrow. "Huh. That's new."

He exhaled, tearing off another piece of bread as he leaned back against the tree, watching the two of them like he was observing something fascinating.

Theodin ignored him, his attention solely on Ophelia. He crouched down, his forearms resting on his knees as he studied her, much in the same way she had been watching him earlier.

The Dyad hummed—quiet but constant.

Ophelia's posture straightened.

"It's stronger," Ophelia murmured. "The Dyad. It's never been this strong before."

Theodin exhaled, rubbing the back of his neck. "I noticed it earlier too," he said. "You were hearing my thoughts, weren't you?"

She nodded, biting her lip. "But not on purpose. It just... happened."

Something flickered across his expression—concern, curiosity, maybe both.

Faust shifted, drawing Theodin's attention.

"So, this is just how it is now?" he asked dryly, gesturing between them. "You two just constantly in each other's heads?"

Theodin shot him a flat look. "No."

Ophelia sighed. "It's not that simple."

Faust shook his head. "It never is with you two."

Theodin ignored him again, turning back to Ophelia.

"There was something else," he said. "Other than…you feeling that hit. Before that feeling."

Ophelia hesitated. Could she speak to him about her new doubts regarding the Kyriegard? He was such a devout and model Kyriegard initiate and apprentice.

She swallowed. "I'm fine right now. Don't worry about it.."

Theodin didn't move.

The Dyad pulsed again—this time, she realized, it wasn't just his emotions bleeding through.

They were his thoughts.

She's lying.

Ophelia held her breath.

It wasn't a deliberate push of thought, and that realization shook her more than anything else. Theodin wasn't trying to communicate through the Dyad—it had simply let her hear it.

She barely kept her expression neutral as she exhaled slowly, willing her own thoughts into silence before he could pick up on them, too.

"I just needed a moment," she said evenly, forcing a small smile. "That's all."

Theodin's jaw tensed, but after a moment he gave a curt nod.

Ophelia expected him to leave then, to return to the training session without another word. But instead, he crouched down in front of her, forearms resting on his knees, his gaze still locked onto hers.

The Dyad stirred, and she could feel the question hanging unspoken between them.

"Why won't you tell me?"

She didn't have an answer for that.

Faust let out a quiet chuckle, shaking his head. He then stood abruptly, dusting himself off. His usual hesitance was gone—his movements were decisive, as though the conversation had settled something for him.

"Well," he muttered as he flattened his tunic, "you don't even realize it yet, do you?"

Neither of them looked at him or responded.

Faust sighed again dramatically, as if he were watching two people fumble their way through a puzzle that should've been obvious. He patted Ophelia lightly on the shoulder as he stepped past her, voice dropping to something only she could hear.

"At least try to have some self-awareness, little owl."

Ophelia stiffened.

But then, just as he turned, that flicker of hesitation returned. The one he had when he used to be timid around everyone else but Ophelia.

It was barely there—a breath of doubt, a moment of realization. Like he'd just heard himself for the first time.

But the moment passed. Faust rolled his shoulders again, let out a short breath, and gave Ophelia a final look.

"Don't overdo it," he said, his voice quieter than before.

Then, with a nod to Theodin—almost respectful, though begrudging—he strode away.

Chapter 38

The Fall

The training grounds were nearly empty now as the younger initiates had been sent back to Havysium. The late afternoon sun bathed Avasylon in soft, golden hues, stretching long shadows across the field. The air smelled of summer grass, worn leather, and splintered wood and stone.

The bond had become a second heartbeat, too loud, too present, too unguarded.

And Theodin felt it too.

Ophelia shifted awkwardly in his arms, half-protesting, but she didn't have the strength to push away.

Theodin had simply picked her up—without permission, without asking—when he saw her struggling to stand.

And now their matching runes lit up like rows of stars burning brightly together.

His arms were steady around her, his chest a solid, immovable weight against her side, but his steps were tense, almost clumsy.

The Dyad rippled with something raw, something exposed.

She heard him thinking before he even spoke.

...She's holding back.

Her breath hitched.

Now, the Dyad stirred with frustration.

"You're hiding something," he said quietly, his voice rumbling close to her ear.

Ophelia stiffened.

"It's nothing," she said too quickly. "I—"

Lying.

Another thought of his not spoken aloud.

Her heart nearly stopped.

It wasn't a deliberate accusation. She heard him say it through the Dyad, but not intentionally.

She saw it in his face—the brief flicker of shock, the realization that his thoughts were no longer kept from her.

She twisted slightly in his arms, glaring up at him, but Theodin wasn't looking at the ground anymore.

He was looking at her. Directly.

The Dyad shifted, not with pain, but with something raw and demanding.

"Drop it," she muttered, though she didn't mean for it to come out so defensive.

But he didn't let it go. He only tightened his hold, more to anchor her than to trap her.

The Dyad throbbed again—not with pain, not with concern, but with something heavier. His voice became strained now, not the usual even-tempered Theodin she knew.

"Why won't you just tell me?"

She tried again to push against him weakly. "Because it's not important."

"Because you don't want me to know."

She exhaled sharply, tension knotting in her shoulders. "It's—"

"Not nothing," he snapped—and the surge of emotion through the Dyad made her breath catch.

His foot caught on an uneven patch of ground.

It happened too fast for either of them to stop it.

Theodin staggered, cursed under his breath, and they toppled together.

Ophelia gasped as the world tilted.

Theodin twisted instinctively to shield her, but the momentum pulled them both down hard into the grass.

She landed awkwardly atop him; one of her hands braced itself on his chest and the other tangled between them. His arms were still around her out of pure reflex, cradling her against him.

The Dyad burned hot between their bodies, urgent and wild.

Their faces were inches apart.

Theodin's breath stopped.

Ophelia's heart stuttered.

Neither moved.

The bond between them buzzed like a live wire—too loud, too close, too much. Their runes lit up brightly and pulsed with the rapid beating of their hearts.

His breathing. Her breathing. Mere inches between them.

Her lips parted slightly, caught between a gasp and a word she didn't know how to form.

Theodin's gaze dropped—half-second, half-surrender.

And then—

"Supper's ready."

The voice snapped through the clearing like a whipcrack, and the moment shattered like glass.

Ophelia jolted upright, scrambling awkwardly off Theodin, her face flaming. Theodin sat up stiffly, brushing grass off his sleeves without looking at her.

Faust stood a few paces away, arms crossed, mouth twisted in a grin that was far too knowing.

"...Anytime, lovebirds."

Ophelia held her face in her hands.

Theodin visibly tensed, but he said nothing.

The Dyad was still buzzing.

Faust did not move. He simply stood there, watching them. Then, he bowed slightly, turned on his heel, and sauntered back towards the cottage, smugness radiating off him.

"Don't keep me waiting," he added.

Ophelia fumbled to her feet, refusing to meet Theodin's eyes. He did the same. Without prompting, he began for the cottage. She stumbled after him, her knees still unsteady, the Dyad thrumming between them like a heart that would not quiet.

Neither of them said a word.

Not about the tumble and fall.

Not about what had almost happened.

And certainly not about the fact that neither of them had wanted to pull away.

The warmth of the hearth did nothing to ease the unbearable tension suffocating the dining hall. Avasylon's modest wooden table—too small for this much unspoken conflict—stood between them like a battleground.

Ophelia sat first, fingers lightly gripping the edge of her plate, picking at her food but not actually eating. She could feel Theodin beside her. Could feel the stiffness in his posture, the weight of everything they weren't saying pressing against the Dyad like a drawn bowstring.

Across from her, Faust carried himself differently. He sat up taller, had much more confidence in his demeanor, and moved with intention.

And at the head of the table, Kaspar ate his meal in silence, completely unbothered.

No one spoke.

The only sounds were the clink of cutlery against plates and the distant crackle of the fire. The longer the silence stretched, the worse it became, like a living thing wrapping around their throats.

Ophelia barely touched her food, and Theodin ate like he was forcing himself to.

Kaspar was stoic—statue-like if he didn't move.

Faust, completely at ease, spoke first.

"So." He speared a piece of meat with his fork. "I'm glad to see that you're on your feet again, Lia. But are you two finally going to talk about whatever that was earlier, or should I start placing bets on when one of you snaps?"

Ophelia stilled.

Theodin shot Faust a glare so sharp it could have cut through steel.

Kaspar did not even look up.

Faust sighed. "You know, I once thought Kyriegard were supposed to be good at communication. But this? This is pathetic."

Ophelia gripped her spoon tighter.

Theodin's jaw clenched so hard that he might break a tooth.

Kaspar still said nothing.

Faust leaned forward slightly, gesturing between them with his fork.

"It's honestly impressive, really. I don't think I've ever seen two people sit this close and pretend like they don't know what's wrong."

Ophelia inhaled slowly and focused on her breathing.

Theodin only seethed.

Faust tilted his head, watching her too closely. "Oh, I get it. You don't want to talk about it because if you do, then you'll actually have to—"

Ophelia banged her fist on the table. The runes on her arm flashed bright green and a large crack fissured into the wooden surface. A trickle of green electricity danced briefly on her skin. She dropped her spoon, the sudden clang cutting through the tension like a knife.

Theodin tensed instantly.

Kaspar was still eating like nothing had happened.

Ophelia stood abruptly, her chair scraping against the wooden floor. Her voice was quiet.

"I'm not hungry."

She turned on her heel and walked out.

Theodin moved immediately. He barely had time to push his chair back before—

Kaspar lifted a hand.

Theodin was yanked back into his seat. Not violently or aggressively but just firmly enough to make his point.

Theodin gritted his teeth. "Kaspar—"

Kaspar finally—*finally*—spoke, and did not look up from his bowl.

"Give her space, lad."

And then, as if nothing had happened, the elder Kyriegard went back to eating.

Faust wheezed. "Oh, that was beautiful. Do it again."

Theodin glowered.

"Kaspar, I—"

Kaspar didn't even look at him.

"Eat your food."

Faust, now fully leaning back in his chair, let out a low, amused whistle. "Incredible."

Theodin gripped the edge of the table like it had personally offended him.

Faust picked up a piece of bread, smirking. "This might actually be the best meal I've had in years."

Theodin's eyes darkened and stabbed like daggers in the Valksha boy's direction.

Kaspar sat and ate, completely unfazed.

The night air was crisp, carrying the scent of summer leaves and distant rain. Ophelia pulled her cloak tighter around herself as she walked, her boots barely making a sound against the stone pathways of Avasylon. The tension in her chest hadn't eased. If anything, it had settled there, a quiet weight she didn't know how to shake.

She should go to her room. Try to rest. But her mind was too full, her thoughts tangled in everything that had happened over the past few days.

She sighed, rubbing a hand over her face. She didn't regret leaving the table, but now, alone beneath the moonlit sky, she wasn't sure what to do with herself.

She slowed as she reached one of the outer fields. She leaned against one of the stone fences, exhaling, tilting her head back to look at the stars.

A soft crunch of footsteps made her tense. She didn't have to turn to know who it was.

"Thought I'd find you out here," Faust said.

Ophelia sighed, but she didn't move.

"Were you looking for me?"

Faust didn't answer right away. A quiet shuffle, then a small piece of bread appeared in her peripheral vision.

A peace offering.

Ophelia blinked at it. "Seriously?"

Faust shrugged. "You barely ate. And this is the leftover sweet bread I attempted for your birthday but failed."

She hesitated before taking it. The bread was still warm from the hearth, and the simple gesture made something in her chest ache.

"Thanks," she murmured, biting off a small piece.

Though she could tell it was a day old, she could taste the effort he put into incorporating the sugar and butter like he had seen her do months ago.

Faust leaned against the structure beside her, crossing his arms.

"Sorry for…poking fun back there. Didn't think you'd run off like that," he said, his voice light, but there was an edge of concern beneath it.

Ophelia took a slow breath, focusing on the food in her hands instead of his gaze.

"I didn't mean to make it a thing," she admitted. "I just… needed some space."

Faust didn't say anything for a moment before speaking again.

"Was it him?"

Her grip tightened slightly around the bread.

Faust tilted his head as he watched her reaction.

"You and Theodin," he continued. "Something's different. More intense."

Ophelia swallowed. She wasn't sure how to explain it—to him or to herself.

"It's the Dyad," she finally said, her voice quieter now. "It's changing. I don't know how or why, but I feel" She exhaled sharply, shaking her head. "It's stronger. I hear him more. Feel him more. I shouldn't be able to, but… I do."

Faust was quiet for a long time.

Then he sighed, raking a hand through his hair. "Ophelia," he said slowly. "You were barely able to walk since Slymound. Even less so after that tree sap ritual. And now…"

He gestured to her.

"You're walking again. Moving as if nothing has happened. You're back to your old self again after—"

"Faust."

Ophelia interrupted him sharply. She closed her eyes.

"Please. I don't want to talk about it."

Faust stared at her.

She felt the ache in his heart.

Her chest tightened. Before she could say anything, Faust stepped back, shoving his hands into his pockets.

"Get some sleep, little owl," he murmured.

Ophelia frowned slightly. "Why do you keep calling me that?"

Faust smirked faintly, but it didn't quite reach his eyes.

"Because," he said, "you're always watching. Always listening. But one day, you're going to need to stop perching on branches and decide to fly."

With that, he turned and began back towards the cottage.

The wooden table between them now felt like an immovable barrier, locking Theodin in place when every part of him wanted to be somewhere else.

Wanted to be with her.

He gritted his teeth. Not now. Focus.

Theodin's eyes fell to the jagged splinter in the table. Ophelia was gone, having left in a storm of crackling runes and shattered silence. And Theodin—

Theodin was still here. Kaspar had made sure of it.

The young Kyriegard's hands clenched into fists beneath the table, his muscles coiled with restraint. His entire body was ready to push up, to leave, to go after her—

Kaspar lifted a hand once more.

Theodin froze. Not by choice.

The weight of Sage magic pressed against him—not harsh, not painful, just unyielding. A firm but immovable force keeping him rooted to his chair.

Theodin growled under his breath. "Kaspar—"

Kaspar still did not look up. "I said give her space, lad."

The words were spoken so easily, as if they were law. And in Kaspar's presence, they were.

Theodin set his jaw, exhaling sharply through his nose. "You don't understand—"

"I understand," Kaspar said simply, finally pausing in his meal to look at him. "That's why I'm telling you to sit."

Theodin's hands curled tighter. The Dyad thrummed—not the loud, relentless pulse it had been earlier, but something quieter. A whisper of frustration. A tether yanking him toward something that was no longer in the room.

Ophelia.

His fingers twitched. He needed to go. He needed to see her.

Kaspar took another bite of his stew, completely unaffected. "Eat your food."

Theodin did not move. After several moments, Theodin clenched his jaw tighter, inhaling through his nose.

Fine.

He picked up his fork.

Chewed.

Swallowed.

He didn't taste a thing.

Then Theodin shoved his chair back.

Kaspar looked at him. Theodin stopped.

Kaspar set his spoon down with deliberate slowness. Then, without a single shred of acknowledgment toward anything that had transpired, he simply said: "You need to start preparing for the Trials."

Theodin exhaled sharply again through his nose. His entire body was rigid.

Kaspar met his gaze, unreadable. "They're coming faster than you think."

Theodin swallowed down the frustration, forcing his hands to relax. "I know."

Kaspar nodded once. Then—finally—he gestured toward the door. "Go."

Theodin didn't need to be told twice. He was on his feet and out the door before the chair even stopped moving.

Theodin made his way toward Ophelia's room with purpose, his mind churning with too many thoughts, his body still carrying the tension of what had transpired.

He shouldn't have pushed her like that. But she shouldn't be keeping secrets from him.

The Dyad was changing. Their connection was evolving. If she was having doubts, he needed to know. If something was affecting her magic, affecting her, he needed to know.

He needed to understand.

The halls were dimly lit, the torches casting faint golden light against the walls. The scent of rain lingered in the air, the promise of a coming storm settling in the atmosphere.

Theodin reached her door. He hesitated only for a second before knocking lightly.

No response.

The Dyad was quiet.

His stomach tightened. He knocked again.

Still nothing.

A flicker of concern stirred between his brows.

He reached for the handle. Slowly, cautiously, he pushed the door open.

And there she was.

Ophelia was asleep. Curled beneath the thin blanket, her breathing soft and her frame relaxed. The tension she had carried earlier was nowhere to be seen—at least, for now.

Theodin stood in the doorway, watching her.

She was here. Safe. Unharmed.

And yet, the Dyad still pulled him as he watched her. Still bound him to her in a way that he didn't understand. The doubts still remained unsaid. The tension still lingered.

But for now, she was at peace.

His jaw relaxed. Slowly, he exhaled.

He turned away, closing the door behind him as quietly as he could.

He made his way to his own quarters, his steps slower now, heavier. The Dyad had lessened, but it was not completely silent.

The night stretched on, the weight of everything pressing against his mind.

The turmoil. The unanswered questions.

The realization of how much he felt her, even when she wasn't there.

Theodin lay in bed, staring at the ceiling, listening to the muted sound of crickets through the cottage window.

The Dyad lulled softly.

And he finally accepted it. That the Dyad was there. That Ophelia was there.

Even when she wasn't next to him, she would always be with him.

Ophelia's dreams had always been vivid—often too vivid. Maybe it was the Valksha magic, or maybe this time, it was the Dyad or Arborelys.

Maybe it was simply who she was—someone who felt everything too deeply, who never quite knew how to turn it off.

But tonight was different.

She was standing at a crossroads. The paths before her stretched in opposite directions—one a familiar road, paved in stone, lined with the banners of the Kyriegard. It was sturdy, structured, illuminated by torchlight. But something about it felt… suffocating.

The other path was wild and open. Endless and unrestrained. She could feel the wind against her skin, smell the scent of rain in the air, and prickled at the promise of something unknown.

Her fingers twitched at her side.

A choice.

When had she ever been given a choice?

And then she felt it.

Him.

She turned.

Theodin stood between the two paths. But something was wrong.

His form wavered slightly, as if the dream couldn't quite decide what shape he was meant to take. His stance was stiff, his expression incomprehensible, but the Dyad sang between them, stronger than ever. Ophelia opened her mouth to speak, but before she could—

The scene shifted. The torches of the Kyriegard road dimmed. The wild path darkened.

And suddenly—they weren't alone.

Shrouded figures loomed in the distance. Watching. Their faces were obscured, blurred, but Ophelia knew what they were.

The Kyriegard.

Not as she knew them, but as they felt in the depths of her mind. Distant, calculating, and measured. A shiver ran down her spine. She turned back to Theodin—

She froze. His shadow was too long. It stretched behind him like something alive, curling and shifting unnaturally.

Theodin didn't seem to notice. His mismatched eyes were locked onto her, bright and piercing, but when he took a step forward—

Something growled. The sound rumbled from beneath the earth.

No—not the earth. From him.

Ophelia's heart slammed against her ribs. "What—"

Theodin reached for her. His fingers were streaked with red.

Ophelia flinched. Pain. An intense, cutting pain.

Not hers. *His.*

The Dyad flared between them, pulling too hard, too much, too strong.

Ophelia gasped. "Theodin, stop."

But he didn't—or maybe he couldn't.

She tried to step back, but her feet wouldn't move.

The shadow at his feet twitched.

It reached. And then—

"Theodin."

The voice wasn't hers. It wasn't his, either. It was deeper and colder.

Like something watching from the dark.

Theodin stiffened. His form wavered again.

The Dyad trembled—shaking, splitting, breaking.

Ophelia gasped again. Her vision blurred. Theodin's expression cracked.

And then—

She awoke.

Theodin shot up in bed.

His breath came in sharp, uneven gasps, and his body coiled like a spring with every muscle tense. His heart slammed against his ribs, the Dyad pulsing wildly—not quiet, not stable, not right.

It took him a full second to realize he was awake. Another to realize he was alone.

His chest ached. Not physically. Something deeper.

The dream lingered like a phantom—the weight of it, the sensation, the wrongness.

And then he felt it.

The Dyad. Still humming. Beside it, he felt his heartbeat.

And hers.

Ophelia was awake.

His breath caught.

He didn't think—he just moved.

Slipping out of bed, his feet silent against the floor, he made his way toward the door before he even knew what he was doing.

The halls were dimly lit, shadows stretching across the stone. Avasylon was quiet, but she was awake. He could feel it.

He reached her door and stopped. His fingers hovered over the handle.

The Dyad shifted—not frantically, not fearfully. Just… there.

A quiet presence. A steady hum.

He exhaled slowly. His fingers curled into a fist, hesitating for half a second before he knocked on the wood.

No response.

But she was there. He knew she was. He felt it.

Theodin swallowed, pressing his forehead lightly against the wood of the door.

What had they just seen?

What had they just felt?

His jaw tightened.

They had shared dreams before. But this—was different.

This felt like something more. Like something waiting.

Year 845 of the Second Age, Seventh Month, Ninth Day

Theodin had not slept. Instead, he had thrown himself into training.

The dawn air was cool against his skin as he moved through the empty courtyard, the rhythmic sound of his blade slicing through the morning stillness. Every motion was deliberate and controlled—but there was an edge to it, a sharpness that hadn't been there before. His muscles burned with exertion, but he welcomed it. It was better than the alternative.

Better than thinking about the dream. Better than thinking about her.

Theodin exhaled sharply, adjusting his stance. He shifted into a defensive drill, repeating the movement with rigid precision. Block. Parry. Counter. Again. And again. The weight of his training sword in his hands should have been grounding. Instead, it only reminded him of how unsteady he felt.

The Dyad had been too much last night. The dream had been too much. And Ophelia—

His grip tightened. His form faltered for half a second.

A mistake. A weakness.

He corrected it immediately, jaw clenching as he swung harder and faster. The wooden training dummies barely stood a chance under his strikes. The thwack of his blade against the post rang through the courtyard, loud and jarring in the morning quiet.

He should be able to focus, to push everything aside, and just train, but the Dyad was still there.

A quiet pulse at the back of his mind. A reminder.

A tether he could not ignore.

A slow clap broke through the silence.

Theodin stilled. His breath was steady, but his grip on his sword did not ease as he turned.

Kaspar stood at the edge of the field, arms crossed, watching him with a look that was too knowing.

Theodin straightened immediately. "Sir."

Kaspar's sharp eyes flicked over him once, then to the wreckage of training dummies in the fields.

"You're pushing too hard, lad."

Theodin stiffened. "I'm fine."

Kaspar hummed.

"Is that so?"

He stepped forward, nodding toward the broken wood and stone scattered around them.

"Because to me, it looks like you're trying to fight something you can't see."

Theodin said nothing. Kaspar studied him for a moment longer, and then he exhaled.

"I was going to let you rest this morning, but clearly that's not happening. So—" He turned toward the cottage again. "Go find Ophelia. You two are testing the Dyad."

Theodin blinked. "Now?"

Kaspar shot him a dry look. "No, in a week. Of *course*, now."

Theodin hesitated. Kaspar's voice flattened at this.

"Something is shifting between you two. I don't need to know what it is. I just need to know you can control it."

Theodin met his gaze. Kaspar's meaning was clear.

The Dyad was unstable. If they could not control it, it would control them.

Theodin inhaled slowly, then gave a curt nod. "Understood."

Kaspar gestured toward the cottage. "Then go."

Theodin turned on his heel, his mind already reeling back onto the objective and locking back into focus.

He needed to find Ophelia.

He needed to fix this.

The sky was cloudless, the midday sun beating down over the training field. The grounds were eerily empty—the younger initiates remained at Havysium at Kaspar's request.

It was just the two of them and their mentor.

Now that Ophelia could move again, she needed to be pushed. Her limits needed to be measured before attempting the Elan Vitae removal.

Kaspar stood a few paces away, arms crossed, watching with the same impassive expression he always wore during training.

"Again," he said simply.

Ophelia inhaled deeply, rolling her shoulders as she squared her stance. Theodin mirrored the motion, flexing his grip around his wooden training sword.

Test the Dyad. Push the limits. That was the purpose of this exercise, even though the Council had ruled to no longer do testing—but Kaspar wanted to jump at it while Ophelia was back on her feet.

And yet—Ophelia hesitated. She wasn't trying to, but something in her instincts resisted.

Theodin noticed. The bond between them whirred, the Dyad pouring out his concern as clearly as a spoken thought.

Don't hold back.

She clenched her jaw. Before she could respond, Kaspar gave a sharp nod.

"Begin."

Theodin moved first. Fast.

A blur of motion, closing the distance between them in an instant. His wooden blade swung down in a precise, controlled strike—

Ophelia dodged.

But she hadn't chosen to. The Dyad had moved her.

Her breath caught. She barely had time to register the sensation before Theodin pressed forward again, shifting into another attack.

This time, she met him head-on.

Their wooden swords collided with a resounding crack. The impact jolted up her arms, but she held firm.

Theodin was stronger, but she was faster.

How was *she* faster?

The Dyad was pulling from *his* speed! She twisted, aiming to unbalance him—

But the moment she pushed, the Dyad pulled.

Too much.

Theodin staggered—his body thrown off not by her attack, but by something else.

Ophelia gasped. She felt it too. A piercing, disorienting tug at her chest.

The Dyad thrashed violently.

Theodin winced, his breath hitching. His fingers tightened around his sword like he was resisting something.

"What in Moirand's name was that?" Kaspar's voice rang out sharply.

Neither of them answered.

Ophelia steadied herself. Theodin exhaled, shaking his head as if trying to clear it.

They should have stopped.

Theodin moved again. Faster. Too precise. Too much.

The Dyad pushed him forward.

Ophelia barely had time to react before their swords clashed again—harder. He wasn't just training anymore. He was pushing.

"Stop hesitating," Theodin snapped, his voice edged with something unfamiliar. "If you hold back, you'll lose."

Ophelia's breath hitched. That wasn't just discipline speaking. That was something else.

Pain.

"Stop holding back!"

Theodin's sword struck.

The impact sent a sharp, burning pain across her ribs. Ophelia cried out, stumbling back. Theodin dropped his sword immediately.

"Ophie—"

But she barely heard him. The pain wasn't just hers. It wasn't supposed to be hers. It became his too.

They both buckled.

The Dyad pulled—too much, too fast.

Ophelia gasped, her vision spinning. She fell to her hands and knees.

His fingers twitched at his side as he grunted loudly and fell to one knee.

They weren't just feeling each other's emotions anymore. They were feeling each other's pain.

The impact of the strike—not just against her ribs, but against his. A split-second of blurred agony, shared between them like a shattered mirror.

Her breathing was shallow and uneven. But across from her—Theodin's was the same.

Ophelia's pulse thundered in her ears. Theodin's eyes were dark and unfocused for a brief second—

And for the first time, she saw and felt fear in his expression. Not a fear of her. Not a fear of the Dyad.

But fear of losing control, and what it would do to her.

Ophelia inhaled sharply, grounding herself. Theodin exhaled, rolling his shoulders back, forcing himself to stand straight.

Kaspar finally spoke. His expression didn't change, and his voice didn't rise.

But it was sharp enough to cut.

"Stop. Now."

A beat of silence. Then—

"That should not have happened."

Chapter 39

The Awakening

Year 845 of the Second Age, Seventh Month, Sixteenth Day

Theodin had not slept properly in days.

The sparring match still played in his mind, over and over—a failure he could not afford, a mistake he should have been able to control.

The Dyad had become a liability. A force neither of them fully understood.

And Kaspar had been right. It should not have happened.

And Ophelia… she had retreated. Avoided him. Kept her distance. Kept her thoughts hidden.

Theodin exhaled sharply, his grip tightening around the wooden practice sword as he stood alone in the courtyard. His training tunic was damp with sweat, his muscles aching from hours of pushing himself past exhaustion. Kaspar had made it clear that they would not be training together again until Alfena arrived.

That was today.

He should be resting, but rest was impossible.

The pull of the Dyad made him restless.

Pulling him to her.

Theodin adjusted his stance, rolling his shoulders as he prepared for another drill. He pivoted, swung—

And then came the pain. Not his.

His breath hitched, and for a split second, his form faltered. His ribs stung with a phantom ache that did not belong to him. His fingers curled instinctively around the hilt of his weapon.

His mind sharpened and focused on the bond.

Ophelia.

The Dyad grimaced—aching, pressing at the back of his mind. She was feeling something. Something close to pain. But it wasn't physical.

Theodin exhaled through his nose, forcing his breathing to steady.

She was in the library again. He could feel it. He had known without thinking or without needing to ask.

A flicker of movement caught his eye.

Kaspar stood beneath the archway, arms folded, watching. Theodin straightened immediately.

"She's been there since dawn," Kaspar said simply.

Theodin didn't respond.

Kaspar studied him for a long moment before nodding toward the exit. "Go."

Theodin hesitated.

Kaspar arched an eyebrow. "What, need a formal order?"

Theodin set his jaw, lowering his weapon. He didn't argue. He turned and strode toward the cottage to access the underground library through the cellar entrance.

Ophelia was exactly where he had expected her to be. The library was dimly lit, the flickering torches casting long shadows against the walls. She was sitting at one of the long wooden tables, a book open in front of her, but she wasn't reading. Her fingers traced absent-minded patterns over the page. Her thoughts were too loud.

Theodin exhaled through his nose. She felt him before she even looked up. Her shoulders stiffened slightly.

"I know," she whispered.

Theodin didn't respond right away. He stepped forward, placing his hands on the back of the chair across from her, his fingers pressing into the wood.

"You've been avoiding me."

Ophelia's lips pressed into a thin line. "I've been thinking."

Theodin's teeth clenched. "I know."

She exhaled slowly, finally lifting her gaze to meet his. Her emerald eyes flickered with uncertainty, with the same hesitation she had felt on the training field.

Theodin was done with it.

"Alfena is coming today," he said flatly. "Kaspar wants us outside."

She didn't react immediately. But he felt the shift in her emotions before she spoke.

"That's why you're here," she murmured.

Theodin's fingers curled tighter around the chair.

"That's why I'm here now."

A short silence stretched between them.

Then, finally, she shut the book. She stood, smoothing out her tunic. Theodin stepped back as she turned toward the exit without another word. As she passed him, the Dyad throbbed, louder than before.

He caught her wrist and Ophelia stilled. Theodin's grip wasn't tight or forceful, but it was deliberate. His voice was quieter now, low, and weighted.

"This is going to keep getting worse if we don't fix it."

Ophelia's fingers twitched. She swallowed.

Theodin didn't let go. He spoke again with more conviction.

"If you're doubting this—doubting me—"

"I'm not."

The words came too fast. She was lying. He knew it. The Dyad knew it.

Theodin's eyes darkened slightly, but he didn't push.

He exhaled, releasing her wrist.

Ophelia didn't move. Then, without another word, she walked past him.

Theodin followed.

The Dyad pulsed with something too strong to ignore.

The afternoon air was thick with summer heat, the sun was high in the sky as Ophelia and Theodin stood side by side in the training yard.

Kaspar stood at the edge of the field, arms crossed, his sharp gaze flickering between them.

Then, she arrived.

Alfena descended the stone steps of the courtyard with slow, deliberate grace, her silver hair gleaming under the sun. She was dressed in the traditional black and silver robes of the Kyriegard Council, her expression unreadable as she approached.

Kaspar turned to face her. "You're early."

Alfena's lips twitched into something resembling amusement. "You sound surprised."

Kaspar sighed. "You do this on purpose."

"I like to be prepared." Alfena's gaze flickered past him, landing on Ophelia and Theodin. Her expression shifted.

Her silver eyes scanned them both. Assessed. Measured.

Ophelia thought she would be used to this by now, but she wasn't. She hated the way it made her feel like she was back at the Council chamber, being evaluated.

Theodin, to his credit, didn't waver. He stood firm, his eyes locked onto Alfena's, waiting.

Finally, Alfena exhaled.

"So," she said, clasping her hands behind her back. "Let's hear it. What exactly is wrong with the two of you?"

Theodin and Ophelia exchanged a glance.

Neither of them spoke.

Kaspar sighed, rubbing his temples.

Alfena arched an eyebrow. "Lovely."

Then, she stepped forward, her gaze settling directly on Ophelia.

"I'll start with you, then," she said simply. "Tell me—when did you start feeling things that weren't yours?"

Theodin's jaw tensed.

Ophelia inhaled sharply.

She knew this question was coming. Still, she hesitated. She had to tell the truth now because she knew Alfena could simply use psychic magic to probe her mind if she truly wanted to.

"We…had been able to feel each other's emotions since shortly after the Arcane Dyad ritual. As for other things, we…have shared a few dreams. Been able to communicate telepathically." Ophelia shifted with discomfort. "As for feeling pain…that started a few days ago," she admitted. "After the Elan Vitae ritual."

Alfena nodded slowly, her gaze calculating.

"And how often?" she asked.

Ophelia swallowed.

"It's… unpredictable. Sometimes it's just emotions. Sometimes it's physical. And sometimes—"

She hesitated, glancing at Theodin.

Alfena's eyes flickered between them. "Sometimes?"

Ophelia exhaled. "Sometimes I hear him when he doesn't speak out loud. I hear his thoughts, and he hears mine. Even when we don't mean to."

Theodin's muscles tensed.

Alfena did not react. She simply studied them for a long, measured moment. Then, finally, she turned to Kaspar.

"Well," she said, cool and calm. "That's unfortunate."

Kaspar sighed. "Tell me something I don't know."

Alfena hummed. "I will, but first…"

She turned back to Ophelia and Theodin.

"We need to test just how deep this bond goes."

Ophelia's stomach twisted. Theodin's fingers twitched at his sides.

Alfena smiled. It was not reassuring. Kaspar pinched the bridge of his nose.

"This is going to be a long day."

The Dyad surged between them, heavy and unrelenting.

Alfena took a slow step forward. Her eyes relentlessly studied them.

Ophelia felt her heart pick up speed, the Dyad rippling beneath her skin in an unsettling way. Theodin was still as stone beside her, but she could feel his muscles coil beneath the surface, ready for something.

Alfena folded her arms.

"You're both unstable. Ophelia, though she is walking again, is still not strong enough to remove the Elan Vitae—I can feel it."

Ophelia's expression fell. Alfena continued.

"This bond is unpredictable, volatile, and—frankly—dangerous. If you were any other pair, I would say the Council would have reason to consider separating you before this gets any worse."

Ophelia's stomach dropped. Theodin tensed.

Kaspar rubbed a hand over his face. "Alfena—"

"Before you panic," Alfena continued smoothly, "I am not the Council, and I am not going to suggest we take drastic measures. Yet."

Ophelia huffed. "Then what—"

"In order to access Ophelia's potential, we must attend to the stability of the Dyad. I need to see it at work. Properly."

Theodin's shoulders squared. "We already tested it," he said with a strain. "We saw what happened."

Alfena's gaze flickered.

"No. You sparred. That was reactionary."

She took another step toward them.

"This time, you will not react. You will submit."

Ophelia felt a sharp spike of unease.

"Submit?" she asked.

Alfena's lips quirked.

"The Dyad has been shifting because you're resisting it. You're trying to control it without understanding it."

Her brows lifted.

"So we're going to force it to show us what it is."

Theodin's face creased with concern.

"And how exactly do we do that?" he asked.

Alfena tilted her head. "We remove your resistance."

Ophelia felt something cold crawl down her spine.

"And what does that mean?"

Alfena smiled.

Kaspar groaned. "You're not going to like it."

Beneath Avasylon, the training chambers had a stillness that was almost suffocating.

Ophelia sat on her heels on the smooth stone floor, her hands resting on her knees. Across from her, Alfena mirrored her position.

The air between them felt charged—alive with something unseen.

This was why psychic magic had always unnerved Ophelia. It was different from the Dyad. Different from the intuitive way she felt emotions from non-human beings.

She hesitated.

Alfena studied her carefully, then extended her hands. An offering.

"Take them," she said simply.

Ophelia swallowed. The urge to retreat was immediate.

"I don't need to hold your hands for this to work," Alfena explained. "But the physical connection will help ground you."

Ophelia clenched her fingers in her lap. "What exactly are we doing?"

Alfena tilted her head slightly.

"I am going to guide your mind to where the Dyad pulls the strongest," she said smoothly. "I will show you where the pain persists and how to redirect it."

Ophelia's throat tightened. "You mean block it."

"No."

Alfena's voice was steady, deliberate.

"You are resisting because you are afraid. I will not take from you. I will show you how to redirect."

The words settled in the air between them. Ophelia exhaled slowly, forcing herself to still the instinct to withdraw.

She could feel Theodin at the edges of her mind. Not intruding and not pushing. Just there. Waiting.

Kaspar stood nearby, arms crossed, his gaze unreadable as he observed. Theodin, though silent, radiated tension where he stood.

He didn't trust this.

Ophelia closed her eyes. Then, slowly, she reached forward. Her fingers brushed against Alfena's.

The moment they touched, the world shifted.

The moment Alfena touched Ophelia's mind, the Dyad reacted.

An invisible thread pulled taut between her and Theodin, vibrating with energy. She could feel him as clear as day—immediately.

The warmth of his presence. The steady, unwavering strength of his resolve. He wasn't pushing through the Dyad, wasn't forcing thoughts or emotions toward her. He was simply there.

Ophelia barely had a moment to settle into the feeling before—

Pain. A sharp, precise strike.

Ophelia gasped, her body jolting from the shock of it. She felt it in her ribs, deep and sudden, a controlled but firm impact.

Not hers.

His.

Her eyes flew open.

Across the chamber, Theodin had barely moved. His jaw was tight, his breath controlled, but she could see the way his fingers curled slightly into fists.

Kaspar lowered the wooden practice sword from where he had just struck Theodin's ribs. His expression was stone.

The Dyad pulsed violently in Ophelia's chest. She could feel Theodin steady himself, forcing his body not to react. Not to give her any more than she was already feeling.

But it didn't matter. The pain was already there.

Alfena's voice was not spoken aloud. It was inside Ophelia's mind, cool and instructive.

Redirect it.

Ophelia huffed. Alfena spoke again.

Take it and push it elsewhere.

But how?

Theodin exhaled slowly, keeping his stance strong, but Ophelia could feel the ache in his ribs like it was her own. She clenched her teeth, her body instinctively wanting to recoil but Alfena's mental grip was there, firm but guiding.

Redirect.

Ophelia closed her eyes again, focusing.

Kaspar moved.

Another strike. Another sharp snap of pain.

Ophelia's breath faltered—too much.

Alfena's voice, steady and cold, rang through her mind once more.

Again.

Kaspar struck again. Theodin barely flinched, but Ophelia felt *everything*.

An excruciating, searing ache spread across his ribs—no, *her* ribs.The Dyad didn't care where one of them ended and the other began. It blurred the lines; it made her feel it as if it had been her own body taking the blow. Her fingers twitched against her knees.

Redirect it.

The thought wasn't hers. It was Alfena's. A reminder of what she was supposed to be doing.

Push the pain elsewhere. Control it. Do not let it control you.

But *how?*

She clenched her jaw and tried to will it away—but Kaspar struck again.

Harder.

Ophelia jerked. A harsh grunt slipped past her lips before she could swallow it back. Her muscles tensed as her fingers dug into the fabric of her tunic.

She was supposed to block it. Redirect it. But she *couldn't.* Tears spilled down her cheeks.

The pain was too vivid. Too real.

She could feel Theodin gritting his teeth. She could feel the way his body was locking up, his breathing strained but controlled. He was bracing himself—not for Kaspar's next hit, but for her.

Because he felt her, too.

Kaspar didn't stop.

Another strike.

A burst of agony rippled through her ribs.

Ophelia choked. Her control was slipping.

Her fingers curled into fists against her lap, her shoulders trembling. Her vision blurred.

The Dyad was too much.

"Stop."

Her voice was barely above a whisper. A quiet plea.

Kaspar did not stop.

Ophelia's breath came fast and shallow. Her chest tightened, the Dyad twisting inside her like something alive, something writhing.

Too much. Too loud. Too real.

Every strike, every moment of pain Theodin endured—it wasn't just his anymore. It was theirs.

And she couldn't stop it. She was failing.

Alfena exhaled quietly, observing her with a discerning gaze. The runes along Ophelia's arms flickered weakly, her body quaking under the weight of the bond.

Alfena lifted a hand to Kaspar. Her fingers barely twitched.

Kaspar's expression barely flinched.

Theodin tensed. He recognized that gesture. He knew Alfena spoke to Kaspar in his mind, but what was communicated?

His jaw clenched, his breath rigid, his entire body coiled like a steel trap. He didn't say anything, but he knew Ophelia could feel it through the Dyad.

Shock. Wariness. A flicker of—*something.*

Kaspar, however, stiffened for an entirely different reason.

Alfena's voice echoed in his mind.

Stab him.

His gruff voice was laced with something dangerously close to incredulity.

What?

Alfena's eyes did not leave Ophelia.

They need to break the block.

Kaspar shot her a look.

They're struggling as it is.

They will never do it while resisting.

Her voice remained eerily calm. Too calm.

Stab him.

Kaspar exhaled sharply through his nose. *He's a Kyriegard, not a damn experiment.*

Alfena finally turned her gaze to him.

We have a Valksha in our midst, she said smoothly. *We will heal him within minutes. He will be fine.*

Silence.

Kaspar's grip on his practice sword tightened. His eyes flickered toward Ophelia.

She was pale. Her shoulders shuddered. She held her fists to her upper abdomen, her fingers curled into the fabric of her tunic, her entire body taut with the strain of holding too much.

Theodin, standing just a few paces away, was silent.

But Ophelia could feel him. His breathing, his muscles, the way his body braced—waiting.

Kaspar cursed.

Then—reluctantly—he pulled out a knife.

With a live blade.

Ophelia let out a harsh breath. Something shifted.

The Dyad crackled, an unseen tension vibrating in the space between them. Her heart lurched.

She felt it before she saw it.

Kaspar's intent.

Her head snapped up, panic surging through her chest. "What are you—?"

But Theodin… did not move.

He saw it, too. He knew. And yet, he did not resist.

His eyes locked onto Kaspar's for the briefest of moments. Silent understanding passed between them. He inhaled stiffly—readying himself.

Ophelia shot up to her feet. "No—!"

Then—steel met flesh.

The knife sank into Theodin's side.

The Dyad burst. Pain. White-hot, searing, unbearable.

Ophelia screamed.

It ripped through her—through both of them.

The force of it shattered Alfena's psychic hold.

Ophelia staggered, clutching at her ribs as if she had been the one stabbed. Her vision blurred. The ground tilted.

Theodin's body tensed, but he did not cry out. His breath came in ragged, uneven bursts. Blood seeped between Kaspar's fingers as he withdrew the blade, dark against the fabric of Theodin's tunic.

The Dyad was thrashing. Harder than ever.

Too much. *Too much.*

Ophelia yelled out again. She was drowning in it.

The connection between them cracked open—wide, raw, uncontrolled.

And then—

A erupting pulse.

A surge of power, raw and ancient.

The air in the chamber shifted. The torches flickered violently, shadows twisting unnaturally against the walls.

Suddenly—a presence.

Something was coming.

A deafening shriek tore through the chamber.

It was not human.

The torches guttered in their sconces, the flames snapping wildly as an enormous, dark figure dropped from above.

Kaspar barely had time to react before a massive force slammed into him. He was thrown back, his feet skidding against the stone—before something heavy crashed down on his chest.

A monstrous, dark-taloned foot pinned him to the ground.

Ophelia looked up. Her jaw dropped open.

Towering over Kaspar, its emerald eyes burning a simmering green light, was an owl creature unlike any creature she had ever seen. Its body was dragon-like, but instead of scales, it was covered in feathers. Instead of bat wings, it had majestic pinions with raven feathers, fanning out menacingly.

Its feathers bristled, dark as storm clouds, flecked with streaks of silver. The wings stretched wide, filling the chamber with an overwhelming presence—archaic and majestic.

The Dyad trembled. Ophelia's Valksha magic flared.

She felt it. Something had broken. Something that had been buried inside her for too long.

A second shriek from the creature—louder, commanding, threatening.

Kaspar's breath came in quick, uneven bursts, but he did not move. He *could not* move.

The talons against his chest pressed firmly but did not crush.

A warning. A demand.

Its immense head turned slightly, feathers ruffling, its glowing gaze shifting toward Ophelia. Its pupils were dilated, and suddenly its expression became warm. It seemed to smile with recognition at her.

Ophelia collapsed.

Her knees buckled; her body gave way to the weight of the Dyad's violent reaction. Her pulse hammered in her skull, her limbs trembling as if she had been pulled through something too vast, too deep, too consuming.

Theodin struggled to breathe. Blood seeped through his tunic, soaking and staining the fabric. His breath came in pained bursts, but his focus was not on himself.

It was on her. His eyes locked onto Ophelia, wide with lingering pain—with concern.

The owl beast's colossal form shifted. The talons that had pinned Kaspar down eased, but remained on him. Its eyes softened slightly, his wings tucking against his body. It lowered its enormous head, brushing against Ophelia's shoulder with a gentle nudge.

A pulse of something warm, steady, and reassuring.

Theodin felt it too. The Dyad, which had been a roaring, erratic storm, was suddenly calm.

Ophelia's breath shivered as she blinked, weakly looking up at the creature before her. Her voice was hoarse

"… What…?"

It huffed. A low, amused sound, wry and knowing.

Then—it spoke.

"Finally," he said smoothly, his deep voice edged with amusement. "I was wondering how long you were going to keep me waiting."

Ophelia barely registered the words before her world went dark.

Dust and debris from the impact of the beast's arrival still hung in the air, creating a charged, suffocating atmosphere.

Kaspar groaned, still on the ground where he had been thrown. He grimaced as he pushed against the talon that pinned him, his ribs aching from the sheer force of impact.

"You've got to be—"

He cut himself off with a sharp breath, wincing as he shoved the heavy foot off his chest.

The owl-dragon barely moved. His deep green eyes, still burning with an unearthly glow, flicked toward Kaspar with a stare so piercing it made the seasoned Kyriegard hesitate.

A warning. A reminder.

A look of "I could keep you there if I wanted to."

Kaspar gritted his teeth and forced himself upright.

"*Dammit,*" he muttered, rubbing his ribs.

Alfena remained standing, but she was rattled. Her eyes had narrowed into careful slits, locked onto the owl-dragon with an unreadable intensity. Her breathing was measured, but Ophelia could feel the heavy waves of her magic still rippling in the air—an instinctive reaction to something beyond her understanding.

Alfena had seen many things, but not this.

The beast shifted slightly, his wings folding against his body as he moved to stand protectively over Ophelia. His gaze, however, remained fierce and unforgiving. His presence alone was a statement—powerful, immovable.

Ophelia lied still on the ground. Her body shook, her breath shallow.

The Dyad had burned through her, shattered her, and now it was… different. The power that had always been just beyond her grasp now settled inside her like a steady current, no longer erratic.

Theodin forced himself upright. He swayed slightly, his balance unsteady, but his eyes—his strange, sharp, yet worried eyes—never left Ophelia.

He took a step toward her. Although his body protested and his wound throbbed, he didn't care.

The owl-dragon's eyes snapped to him. Theodin stilled. A silent beat stretched between them.

Then—slowly and deliberately—the beast stepped aside, clearing the path between Theodin and Ophelia.

Theodin exhaled, tension easing just slightly. He took another step forward, dropping to one knee beside her.

"Ophelia."

The creature nudged her again, his beak gently pressing against her shoulder.

A fast inhale, followed by a heavy exhale.

Ophelia's fingers twitched.

She gasped softly, her eyelids fluttering open, the weight of exhaustion pressing heavily against her chest.

The chamber felt distorted, like reality had shifted slightly to the left, and she was still trying to catch up. Her body ached, but… it was different now. The Dyad was still there—she could feel it humming inside her—but it wasn't pulling at her; it wasn't rattling inside her skull like a storm she couldn't control.

It was calm. Steady.

Her breathing slowed as she became aware of her surroundings again, her senses returning one by one—the lingering scent of smoke from the torches, the coolness of the stone floor beneath her, the heat of Theodin's presence just inches away.

Then, her gaze lifted—and she froze.

Towering over her, feathers rustling, wings partially tucked at his sides, was the creature. The owl-dragon. The monster that had thrown

Kaspar like a rag doll and nearly collapsed the entire chamber.

And it was staring right at her.

Ophelia's breath caught, her entire body locking up as her wide, disoriented eyes took him in fully for the first time.

The sharp curve of his beak. The piercing green glow of his irises. The sheer size of him.

The owl-dragon smirked. *Actually* smirked.

"There she is," he murmured smoothly, his voice rolling like silk. His accent was the same as hers—pointed, particular. Northern Reganian.

Ophelia flinched. Her breath was uneven as she struggled to push herself upright, her limbs still weak. She blinked rapidly, as if trying to rationalize what she was seeing—what she was hearing.

"You can talk?" she rasped.

His glowing eyes gleamed.

"You can listen," he countered, feathers fluffing slightly in amusement. He ruffled his feathers, letting out a quiet, almost exasperated sigh. "You took long enough."

He then tilted his head toward Theodin, his green eyes gleaming with scrutiny.

"Your mate looks like he's about to drop dead."

Theodin, who had been barely managing to stay upright, stiffened. He choked slightly at the word, his eyes whipping toward the massive owl-dragon with immediate displeasure.

"We are not—"

Theodin started, only for his body to finally betray him. Pain flared in his side, the wound Kaspar had inflicted sending a fresh wave of burning agony through him. He staggered, pressing a hand against the torn fabric of his tunic, blood still seeping between his fingers. His jaw clenched as he gritted his teeth against it, refusing to collapse.

Ophelia sat up quickly but stiffly as the world still spun somewhat, dizzy from the exertion—but she still drew blood with her needle ring and held it to Theodin's wound. Her runes glowed, and a healing, green light drifted from her fingers to Theodin's side.

Kaspar, who had just recovered enough to push himself to his feet, let out an incredulous scoff as he addressed the owl-dragon.

"What in the name of the Saryfim are you?"

The creature shifted slightly. He turned his piercing gaze on Kaspar, his expression unbothered.

"Do not take the name of the mighty Saryfim in vain. I am Sarys," he said smoothly. "And I belong to her." His head tilted toward Ophelia.

Ophelia was still staring. Still processing. Her mind felt sluggish, stuck somewhere between complete disbelief and the overwhelming weight of realization.

"You're… my familiar?"

Like Aetheris—Lady Vivian's familiar.

"Ah, Aetheris," he cooed in response to her thought, his voice overlapping with a warm owl's purr. He bowed his head slightly in respect.

Sarys regarded her for a moment, then dipped his head slightly, something like mock deference in the movement.

"It took you long enough to let me through."

Theodin exhaled and grunted, fighting through the lingering pain while Ophelia healed him.

Ophelia's fingers trembled slightly as she pressed her hand against Theodin's wound, the glow of her runes flaring to life. Warm, emerald light spilled from her fingertips, the healing magic seeping into his torn flesh, knitting it back together.

Theodin exhaled sharply, his body still rigid with pain, but he did not pull away. His breathing came slower, steadier, as the burning ache dulled under Ophelia's magic. His eyes flickered toward her, weary but present.

Ophelia's free hand found his arm, steadying him. He was sweating and pale, but he was no longer on the verge of collapse.

Kaspar looked deeply unamused. Alfena, however, remained still. Her eyes gleamed with a rare flicker of intrigue, studying Sarys like he was a puzzle she was just beginning to understand. Slowly, her gaze began to shift between Sarys and Ophelia. Though she was clearly still weary from the ordeal, the Valksha girl was no longer struggling.

Sarys, now sitting beside Ophelia, ruffled his feathers and preened idly, watching the process with an air of mild amusement. His tail curled around his massive talons, his glowing eyes shifting between the two of them.

At last, Theodin let out a slow breath, finally feeling the pain subside. His muscles, coiled with tension for too long, began to relax as the worst of the wound faded into nothing.

"Well," he muttered under his breath, his voice dry, rough from fatigue. "That was a damn mess."

Kaspar snorted from where he leaned against the chamber wall, arms crossed tightly over his chest.

"Understatement of the year."

Sarys cooed in agreement, ruffling his feathers with an exaggerated shake.

Ophelia sighed heavily, letting her hands fall away from Theodin as the last of her healing energy settled.

The Dyad still hummed between them, but it was different now—controlled. Less erratic.

Then, with a sudden ripple of energy, Sarys' massive form began to shrink. Feathers compressed, limbs folded inward, and in the span of a single breath, the towering owl-dragon was gone—replaced by a much smaller creature.

A sleek, ordinary-sized owl now perched on Ophelia's shoulder, his deep green eyes still gleaming with intelligence, his tiny talons barely pressing into the fabric of her tunic. He fluffed his feathers, let out a soft, unimpressed hoot, and muttered, "Much better."

Theodin shifted slightly, rolling his shoulder, testing his body. His side was still tender, but the wound was gone.

He exhaled deeply, glancing at Ophelia. "You okay?"

She nodded slowly, though she was clearly still recovering.

The weight of everything—Sarys, the Dyad, the overwhelming surge of magic—still pressed at the edges of her mind.

Sensing this, Sarys affectionately cooed and rubbed his head against the side of her head.

Alfena, who had remained silent until now, finally spoke.

"This changes things."

Ophelia's head snapped up. Her eyes sharpened, cautious. "What do you mean?"

Alfena's gaze locked onto hers, unreadable, but intense.

"A Valksha is already a dangerous thing," she said smoothly. "But a Valksha with a fully bonded familiar and an active Arcane Dyad?"

She paused, letting the weight of her words settle. Ophelia's heart pounded.

Alfena tilted her head slightly, her voice dropping to something softer—something more measured.

"You may have just become the most powerful being the Order has seen in centuries. Potentially even more powerful than Lady Vivian herself, once you've mastered your Valksha magic."

The chamber fell silent. The weight of Alfena's words settled over them like a thick, suffocating fog.

Ophelia's pulse pounded in her ears. The most powerful being the Order has seen in centuries. She felt the statement coil inside her chest like a vice. She didn't want power. She wanted control over the untamed flame within herself.

Theodin straightened beside her. He was still pale and exhausted, but his posture was resolute.

"If that's true," he said in a low voice, "then tell us how to fix the Dyad. And remove the Elan Vitae."

Alfena studied him. Studied both of them.

A long pause stretched between them.

Then—she exhaled through her nose, tilting her head slightly.

"Rest tonight," she said. "Tomorrow, we begin again."

Ophelia swallowed hard. She didn't know if she would be able to sleep tonight. Not with everything still buzzing inside her. Not with Sarys perched so comfortably on her shoulder, a living, breathing presence of something she had suppressed for far too long.

She turned her head slightly, catching Theodin's eyes.

The Dyad thrummed—not erratic or painful. Just present. Steady.

They held each other's gaze for a long moment. Something heavy lingered between them, something unspoken.

Sarys ruffled his feathers. His deep green eyes gleamed with unmistakable amusement.

"Oh, this is going to be fun," he murmured, entirely too pleased with himself.

Kaspar groaned, pinching the bridge of his nose. "I need a damn drink."

Chapter 40

The Threads Between Them

The Valksha residents of Avasylon scoured the books that evening for answers.

The candlelight flickered against the worn pages of the book, its aged parchment crinkling under Ophelia's fingertips as she turned another page. The words blurred slightly before her eyes, not from exhaustion, but from the sheer weight of what they carried.

The bond between a Valksha and their familiar is not forged, nor is it granted.

It is awakened.

From the moment of a Valksha's birth, their familiar lingers at the edges of their soul, waiting—watching. It will remain unseen until the Valksha is ready to receive them. And only then, when the bond is truly needed, will the familiar step forward, answering the call that was always meant to be.

Ophelia exhaled slowly, tracing the inked words with the pad of her finger.

Waiting. Watching.

Sarys had always been there. She had simply never been able to hear him.

A rustling beside her broke her concentration. A small, feathered figure shifted against her shoulder, letting out a quiet, unimpressed huff.

"They never get these books quite right, do they?"

Ophelia flinched. "Can you not read over my shoulder?"

Sarys blinked his piercing green eyes at her, his form fluffing up indignantly.

"Forgive me for taking an interest in my own existence. Funny enough that this particular tome was just found by you today amidst the pile of rubbish they've got down here."

Across from them, Faust chuckled from where he lounged in a chair, his boot propped lazily on the table.

"Let me guess—you're finally trying to figure out what the Nether you are?"

Ophelia sighed, closing the book with a dull thud. "Something like that."

Faust leaned forward, resting his arms over his knees. "Alright, little owl. Tell me. What have you learned?"

Sarys opened his beak for a second, then stopped to realize that the Valksha boy was looking at her and not him—the *actual* owl. Sarys clamped his beak shut.

Ophelia hesitated, glancing down at the book in her lap. She wasn't sure how to explain it—how to put into words the sheer magnitude of what had happened to her.

How she had spent years believing she was incomplete. Wild. Uncontrollable.

How she had buried her magic so deep that even Sarys had been unable to reach her.

Buried it in the first eight years of her childhood to prevent her family from being found. And then having it all forced out the night they were killed.

"It's… not something you choose," she said finally. "A familiar isn't summoned. It's not trained. It's already there, waiting for you to be ready."

Faust hummed, tilting his head. "And you weren't?"

Ophelia pressed her lips together. "No."

Sarys fluffed his feathers. "She was stubborn."

She shot him a glare, but the owl only blinked at her, entirely unapologetic.

Faust lifted his brows. "Alright. So what stopped you? The massacre? Your father keeping you in hiding?"

Ophelia frowned. That was part of it. But not all of it.

"...Oliver wanted to use his magic," she murmured. "But he never got the chance. Our father forbade it. He thought it was safer that way."

Faust studied her, his usual teasing demeanor dimming slightly. "And you?"

Ophelia hesitated. "I... didn't want it."

The words felt heavy in her mouth. But they were the truth.

"I saw what it did to my father," she continued. "How he spent his whole life hiding from it. How my mother—" She stopped herself, shaking her head. "After they died, Lady Vivian tried to help me. But I was... too angry. Too scared. I didn't want to be Valksha. So I locked it away too often. Yes, she taught me what she could, but I was still unwilling and reluctant for the first few years. If I'm honest, I don't think I truly started tapping into my magic until I was perhaps ten or eleven years old."

Faust was silent for a moment. Then—he leaned back, exhaling sharply. "Damn."

Sarys stretched his wings slightly, shaking his head. "And here we are."

Faust chuckled dryly, rubbing a hand over his face. "You're telling me you buried your power so deep that you unintentionally blocked out your own familiar?"

Sarys huffed. "It was agonizing."

Faust shook his head in disbelief, then gestured toward the owl. "And yet, here you are now."

Ophelia inhaled slowly. "Here I am."

The three of them sat in silence.

Then, finally, Faust smirked. "So, what does that make you now?"

Ophelia arched her brow. "What?"

"A fully bonded Valksha? A walking disaster? Or something else?"

Before Ophelia could respond, Sarys answered smoothly, "Yes."

Ophelia shot him a look. "That wasn't a yes-or-no question."

Sarys fluffed his feathers. "And yet, it is still correct."

Faust barked out a laugh.

"Oh, I like him."

Ophelia groaned, rubbing her temples.

Faust grinned but then tilted his head slightly, his smirk fading just a fraction. "What about me?"

Ophelia blinked. "What about you?"

Faust gestured vaguely. "If all Valksha have familiars waiting for them, where's mine?"

Another silence.

Ophelia hadn't considered that before. Faust was older than she was by maybe a year or two.

They still hadn't figured out when his birthday was.

Even if he hadn't been properly trained, if he truly had Valksha blood, his familiar should have manifested years ago.

Her throat tightened. "Maybe..." she trailed off, thinking.

Maybe it was because of Azazelf.

Maybe whatever he had done to Faust had blocked his familiar from reaching him.

Faust clicked his tongue, leaning back in his chair.

"Probably because I was a prisoner for years," he said, as if reading her mind. "That's got to screw something up, right?"

Ophelia didn't answer.

That made sense. It was the logical conclusion.

But something inside her hesitated. Doubted.

Faust shrugged, though there was something a little too forced in the motion.

"Or maybe it's just bad luck. Wouldn't be the first thing I got screwed out of."

Ophelia frowned, sensing the way his words held something deeper—something unspoken.

Sarys, who had been preening himself idly, flicked an owl ear. His emerald eyes, sharp with intelligence, turned toward Faust with measured curiosity.

"It is... unusual."

Faust arched his brow. "Oh? Do enlighten me, oh wise and mighty owl."

Sarys did not rise to the bait. Instead, he studied Faust, his head tilting slightly in that unnerving way that only owls could manage.

"Unusual," he repeated, "but not impossible."

Ophelia frowned. "What do you mean?"

Sarys stretched his wings briefly before tucking them back against his sides.

"There are only a few known cases of Valksha whose familiars never emerged. And in every case, there was a reason." His gaze flicked to Faust. "Some unfortunately passed before they could awaken. Some had their souls damaged beyond repair. And some..."

He paused.

Ophelia swallowed. "Some what?"

Sarys blinked once, slowly.

"Some were never meant to have one."

A chill crawled up Ophelia's spine.

"Never meant to—what does that even mean?"

Faust's expression shifted— there was something colder about it now.

"Oh, don't stop now. I'd love to hear what else you're implying."

Sarys tilted his head. "I imply nothing. I only state the facts."

Silence stretched again between them. Faust held his casual smugness in place, but Ophelia could see the flicker of something beneath it—something wary and cautious.

She pressed her lips together, trying to make sense of it. "So you're saying… if a familiar hasn't appeared, then either something is blocking it, or—"

"Or it was never there to begin with," Sarys finished simply.

Ophelia's stomach twisted.

Faust leaned back, exhaling sharply. "Well. That's uplifting."

Sarys didn't respond. He simply watched him, that sharp owl gaze unwavering.

Ophelia frowned. "But that doesn't make sense. At least one of your parents was Valksha. You should have one."

Faust's smirk stretched wider, but it didn't reach his eyes.

"And yet," he said airily, spreading his hands, "I am still tragically alone."

Ophelia sighed, rubbing her temple. "There has to be another explanation."

Faust shrugged. "Or maybe I was just born defective. Maybe I'm the one broken piece in the grand, mystical machinery of Valksha nonsense."

Ophelia's fingers twitched. She didn't like this. Didn't like the way he was brushing it off, didn't like the way Sarys had gone so still. And she especially didn't like the small, nagging thought that was forming in the back of her mind.

Because if Faust was Valksha—*truly* Valksha—then there should be no reason for his familiar to be absent.

And yet.

It was.

Sarys finally blinked, looking away from Faust and preening his feathers again. "Perhaps the answer will come with time."

Faust snorted. "Yeah. Or maybe my familiar took one look at my life and said, 'No thanks.'"

Ophelia took a deep breath and let it out slowly, leaning back in her chair, her mind racing with too many questions and not enough answers.

Sarys hummed in her mind, quiet and thoughtful. At the same time, she felt the Dyad shift slightly at her tense focus. A ripple of concern came in her direction.

Sarys's head tilted slightly, his glowing eyes narrowing as he shifted on Ophelia's shoulder. His small talons flexed against the fabric of her tunic; his feathers ruffled as if he were listening to something just beyond their hearing.

Then, with an exhale that was almost too knowing, he muttered, "You're thinking too loudly, darling."

Ophelia blinked. "Me? What?"

Sarys didn't answer right away. His gaze flicked toward Faust briefly, his keen expression indiscernible, before his feathers bristled again.

But this time, Ophelia felt the shift in Theodin through the Dyad.

He wasn't just feeling her anymore.

His eyes gleamed as he turned his head slightly. "Well, well," he mused, his tone tinged with something between amusement and curiosity. "He's strong."

Ophelia frowned. "Who?"

Sarys let out a low, knowing hoot. "Your mate."

Ophelia choked. "He is not—"

"Theodin?" Faust interrupted, raising an eyebrow.

Sarys gave a slow, deliberate nod.

"That one." His voice was thoughtful now, more measured, less teasing. "I can feel him through you. It's subtle, but it's there. The bond is deep—deeper than I expected."

Ophelia furrowed her brows. "What do you mean?"

Sarys blinked at her, his feathers fluffing as he considered his words.

"Your Dyad is... unorthodox. It's not just a tether—it's something else. Something old."

He tilted his head, almost as if testing the weight of the thought in his mind before continuing.

"And he feels you. Even now."

A quiet pulse ran through the Dyad, and Ophelia tensed.

Sarys was right.

Theodin was feeling her. Maybe not actively, maybe not intentionally, but he was there—lingering just beneath the surface of her awareness, steady and unwavering as ever. The realization sent a strange sort of shiver through her.

Sarys hummed again, this time more to himself. "Interesting."

Ophelia glared at him. "Stop that."

Faust, who had been watching with his usual entertained look, leaned forward, resting his arms on the table.

"Alright, birdbrain. What exactly are you saying?"

Sarys turned his sharp gaze toward Faust, entirely unbothered by the nickname. "I'm saying that her Dyad is unlike anything I've ever encountered. And if I can feel it? Then he can, too."

Ophelia clenched her fists, suddenly feeling too aware of the bond humming inside her. She huffed, shaking her head.

"It doesn't matter."

Sarys' gaze snapped back to her. "Oh, but it does."

His voice lowered slightly, like he was about to share a secret.

"Because if I can feel it now? Imagine what will happen when he's standing right in front of you."

Ophelia's pressed into a thin line.

She didn't need to imagine. She already knew.

"So speaking of their Dyad," Faust continued, rolling his wrist around. "My understanding is that it's… stable?"

"For now," Sarys answered. Then he bowed, briefly fanning a wing to one side. "Thanks to yours truly. But it is still volatile."

Faust tapped his fingers against his arm in absent thought.

"Volatile, huh? So what, you just stitched it back together with some magic owl glue?"

Sarys ruffled his feathers, clearly unimpressed.

"Hardly. I stabilized the bond when it nearly collapsed. But the balance is still fragile." He fixed Ophelia with a knowing look. "You and Theodin are walking a tightrope. The moment either of you push too hard—" He clicked his beak meaningfully. "It'll start unraveling again."

Ophelia exhaled slowly, her fingers pressing into the worn pages of her book. She already knew this, of course. She had felt it. Every time she tried to hold back, the Dyad pulled harder. Every time she fought it, it fought back.

"What about the Elan Vitae?" she asked.

"Oh, it's there," Sarys chirped. "That will be taken care of very soon. I would be more worried about your Dyad."

Faust whistled low. "So you're telling me they're bound together by magic and they have to manage its mood swings? Sounds like a healthy relationship."

Ophelia shot him a glare. "It's not—"

"—a relationship," Faust finished for her, grinning. "Sure, sure."

Sarys let out a quiet chuckle, his small form shifting on her shoulder. "Denial is a fascinating thing."

Ophelia groaned, dragging a hand down her face. "I hate both of you."

Sarys cooed in what she could only describe as an absolutely pompous manner.

"You say that, and yet, here we are."

Faust waved a dismissive hand. "Alright, fine, back to business. If the Dyad is still unstable, what's the plan? Keep letting Kaspar stab Theodin until something clicks?"

Sarys tilted his head, his eyes gleaming with something unreadable. "No. That would be impractical."

Faust snorted. "Oh, now we care about practicality."

Ophelia frowned again as her mind raced.

"So if it's still fragile, how do we fix it?"

Sarys studied her for a long moment before finally speaking. "You don't."

Ophelia stiffened. "What?"

Faust raised an eyebrow. "That's ominous."

Sarys' gaze didn't waver.

"You don't fix it, Ophelia. You learn to live with it." He flicked his tail. "The Dyad is not a wound that needs to heal. It is not a broken thing that must be repaired. It is alive, as is the Elan Vitae in your veins. It will change, shift, and evolve. And if you keep treating it like something you can control?" His feathers bristled slightly. "It will consume you."

A cold weight settled in Ophelia's chest.

Faust, for once, was quiet. His lapis blue eyes flicked between Sarys and Ophelia, his expression dimming just slightly.

After a long moment, he pulled his foot off the table and leaned forward, elbows resting on the surface.

"Alright, but what happens if it does start unraveling again?"

His voice was lighter, teasing, but there was an edge beneath it.

"Are you gonna swoop in and glue them back together again?"

Sarys made a soft clicking noise, suggesting something thoughtful.

"I am here to guide her. Not to interfere with the natural course of things." His piercing gaze shifted back to Ophelia. "And she is the only one who can decide how this ends."

Ophelia caught her breath. She gripped the edges of her book, her heart pounding.

The Dyad would never be something she could run from. She could deny it, fight it, ignore it—but in the end?

It would always be there. Waiting.

The doorway creaked slightly as Theodin stepped inside; his presence instantly shifted the energy in the room. He stood with his arms crossed and his expression unreadable, but his eyes were jarring—assessing the scene and the room's occupants precariously.

"Am I interrupting something?"

Ophelia stiffened. She wasn't expecting him, but she *should* have. She had felt him. She just… got distracted.

Faust, of course, grinned like a devil.

"Ah, speak of the shadow himself."

Theodin ignored him, his gaze flicking between Ophelia and Sarys, who was still perched on her shoulder.

His presence wasn't unwelcome exactly, but it was new. Theodin was still getting used to seeing him, much less feeling him through the Dyad.

Sarys made a quiet, amused noise, tilting his head.

"Ah. There he is."

Ophelia shot the bird a glare.

Traitor.

Theodin exhaled through his nose, stepping further into the room.

"You didn't answer," he said simply.

Ophelia blinked. "What?"

Theodin's eyes narrowed slightly. "I felt something. I reached for you. You didn't respond."

Oh.

Ophelia's stomach twisted. He was right. He *had* sent that ripple of concern through the Dyad, and she'd… ignored it. Not on purpose. But Sarys had pulled her attention away before she could acknowledge it.

"I—I got distracted," she admitted.

Theodin's jaw twitched, but he said nothing.

The Dyad hummed faintly, something restrained pulsing through it. He wasn't upset, exactly. Just… cautious.

Faust looked between them, then leaned back in his chair again with a sneer. "So *this* is what you two are like when things are 'stable.'"

Theodin shot him a glare sharp enough to cut steel.

Faust only laughed.

Sarys, however, had been watching them both with a different sort of interest. His eyes glowed softly, unblinking, as if seeing something neither of them could.

Then, finally, he broke the silence.

"You two," he mused, "are going to have so much fun."

Ophelia groaned, rubbing both of her temples now.

"Sarys. *No.*"

Theodin didn't react. But through the Dyad, Ophelia felt something very distinct.

Exasperation. And, underneath that, resignation.

"You need to rest," Theodin said, his expression stoic.

"I know," she answered casually. She pointed to her side and wiggled her finger. "So should you."

Theodin huffed, unimpressed. "I'm fine."

Ophelia arched her brow. "Oh? You bleeding out an hour ago would say otherwise."

Theodin rolled his eyes. "You healed it."

Faust snickered. "Yeah, and yet you still look like you're one breath away from falling on your ass."

Theodin seethed and shot him another withering glare.

Faust remained completely unfazed.

Sarys fluffed his feathers and stretched one wing dramatically.

"Personally, I'd rather not have to deal with either of you passing out on my watch." He turned toward Ophelia. "And you, little owl, need to regain your strength."

Ophelia groaned but didn't argue. Truthfully, she was exhausted, and with everything that had happened, rest wasn't a bad idea. Still, she smirked slightly as she leaned back in her chair.

"You're already bossing me around?"

Sarys preened. "It is my duty. You need to rest—he is right. If you won't listen to your mate, you must listen to me."

"Sarys—"

"Don't dilly-dally, darling," Sarys cooed as he cut her off.

Theodin exhaled heavily, shaking his head before nodding toward the door.

"Come on. I'll walk you back."

Ophelia hesitated. Then she stood, stretching slightly. She turned to Faust.

"Don't stay up too late."

Faust pressed a hand over his heart in mock offense. "What kind of terrible influence do you take me for?"

Theodin didn't dignify that with a response. Instead, he turned toward the door, waiting. Ophelia sighed, scooping up her book and tucking it under her arm before following. Sarys, still perched on her shoulder, let out an amused little hum.

As they stepped into the dimly lit corridor, the air between them was quieter, but not tense. It was… something else.

Theodin glanced at her. "You really didn't feel it?"

Ophelia frowned. "Feel what?"

"When I reached out."

She sighed. "I did. But Sarys was distracting me."

Theodin's eyes flicked toward the owl, who simply tilted his head again, entirely unrepentant.

"Hm."

Ophelia sighed. "I wasn't ignoring you."

"I know."

They walked in silence for a few more steps before Sarys broke it with a soft, amused chuckle.

"You two are going to be exhausting."

Theodin and Ophelia, in perfect unison, groaned.

The lukewarm night air pressed against Ophelia's skin as she and Theodin walked side by side down the quiet underground corridor of Avasylon. Their session with Alfena had left them exhausted, but it was a comfortable exhaustion, the kind that settled deep in the bones but brought a strange sense of fulfillment. It was far better than the excruciating experience the Dyad made them endure since the Elan Vitae ritual.

The halls were dimly lit, only the faint glow of enchanted lanterns guiding them. She was still adjusting to Sarys's presence, feeling his energy settle and shift as he perched on her shoulder. He had been quiet for the last few minutes, but she could sense his curiosity sparking at everything he saw—watching, calculating.

When they reached the door to her chambers, Ophelia paused,

exhaling softly. Sarys hopped off her shoulder and glided into the room, his wings silent as he went to inspect his new surroundings. He landed on the floor, and his talons pattered against the wood as he walked around.

Ophelia, however, lingered in the doorway, turning to face Theodin. He stood close—too close, really—but she didn't step away.

"You did well today," Theodin murmured, his eyes scanning her face with a gentle expression. "You and Sarys… it feels different now."

Ophelia nodded, absently rubbing her thumb over the rune markings on her palm. "It is different. It feels… better. Certain. Even the Dyad feels like it's breathing again."

Theodin's gaze flicked to her hand, his brows furrowing slightly before he looked back into her eyes.

"Good. You needed that."

The way he said it made something shift in her chest. The steady weight of his presence in the Dyad was comforting, grounding her even as her body still hummed with the after-effects of magic. There was the unspoken something again in the space between them. Something electric between their interlocked eyes.

They knew what it was, and it had a name, but they couldn't bring themselves to use it.

Her fingers fidgeted, and before she could think too hard about it, she reached up, brushing a stray lock of dark auburn hair away from Theodin's face. It was a small, instinctive gesture—one she wasn't sure she had the right to make. But Theodin didn't flinch.

Instead, his oddly-colored eyes softened, and for a fraction of a second, he leaned into her touch.

It was subtle, but the moment stretched, a quiet understanding settling between them.

Then—

"Ahem."

Ophelia startled, pulling her hand back as Sarys fluttered back to the doorway, landing gracefully on her shoulder. His shimmering, large eyes glinted with complacent amusement as he flicked his head to one side.

"Oh, don't stop on my account, darling," he said, voice dripping with mischief. "I'm merely enjoying the view."

Ophelia groaned, covering her face with one hand as Theodin withdrew and put his guard up, stepping back. Though his face was unreadable again, Ophelia swore she saw the ghost of a smirk before he schooled his expression.

"I should go," Theodin muttered.

Ophelia lowered her hand and nodded, still feeling the warmth of his presence even as he pulled away.

"Yeah. Goodnight, Theo."

Theodin remained for a breath longer before turning on his heel and heading down the corridor.

Ophelia watched him go before letting out a long sigh, stepping into her room, and shutting the door behind her.

Sarys hopped onto the back of a nearby chair and shook his feathers.

"*Goodnight, Theo,*" he shrilled playfully and then chuckled. "Oh, he is *quite* something, isn't he?"

Ophelia turned, leveling him with a glare. "Don't start."

Sarys made a pleased sound, his beak clicking.

"Oh, but I must. You see, this is far more interesting than you trying to lecture me about Kyriegard rules and decorum."

Ophelia crossed her arms. "We do have rules. And you—" she pointed a finger at him, "—are not helping."

Sarys gave her a slow, knowing look.

"Darling," he purred, hopping closer. "I know the rules. But let's not pretend they matter when it comes to him."

Ophelia scowled, but her traitorous heart thudded harder in her chest.

Sarys stretched his wings lazily before settling down. "Oh, this is already becoming so much fun."

Ophelia rubbed her forehead with the palm of her hand.

"You remind me an awful lot of my brother," she murmured.

Sarys perked, considering. "Oh? Should I take that as a compliment?"

Ophelia scoffed, kicking off her boots and moving toward the washbasin in the corner. "Not in the slightest."

Sarys chuckled, preening his feathers with meticulous precision.

"And yet, you still let me stay."

His large, luminous eyes followed her as she splashed water over her face, her movements sluggish with exhaustion.

"You're already growing fond of me, aren't you?"

Ophelia grabbed the nearest towel, patting her face dry before turning to him with a deadpan stare.

"Fond isn't the word I'd use."

Sarys made a thoughtful sound, tilting his head.

"No, I suppose not. But you don't dislike me, either." His gaze flicked toward the door. "And I suspect I'm not the only presence you'll have grown accustomed to."

Ophelia stiffened but refused to give him the satisfaction of a reaction. Instead, she busied herself by unbuckling the leather vambraces from her arms, placing them carefully on the small table beside her bed.

Sarys remained quiet, letting her work through the silence, but she could feel his amusement like an ember at the back of her mind.

She sighed, finally meeting his gaze. "What do you want, Sarys?"

The familiar stretched his wings before hopping onto the windowsill, where the faint moonlight caught the iridescence of his feathers. "Want? Oh, Ophelia, darling. I already have what I want."

Ophelia narrowed her eyes. "And that is?"

Sarys turned his head to the side, studying her with something deeper than amusement. "To be here. With you. As I always have been."

Something in his tone made her pause. "Always?"

Sarys inclined his head. "You didn't call for me before, not really. Not properly. But I was waiting. And the moment you stopped trying to be what everyone expected and just let yourself be—" he spread his wings slightly, letting the wind from the cracked window ruffle through them, "—well, here I am."

Ophelia stopped. The weight of his words pressed against something fragile inside her.

She had spent so much time trying to fit into the Kyriegard, trying to mold herself into what they needed. But Sarys… Sarys had always been waiting for her.

Not the apprentice. Not the initiate.

Just Ophelia.

She looked away, rubbing the back of her hand where the old ritual scar still tingled faintly.

"It's not that simple."

Sarys huffed. "It is exactly that simple."

Ophelia clenched her jaw. "The Kyriegard—"

"Oh, the Kyriegard." Sarys let out an exaggerated sigh, flapping to a higher perch on the wooden beam above her bed. "You lot love your rules, don't you?"

Ophelia shot him a glare. "I am one of that lot."

Sarys hummed, but there was something knowing behind it. "For now."

The words landed heavier than she expected. Ophelia straightened, bristling. "What is that supposed to mean?"

Sarys didn't answer immediately. Instead, he tucked his wings in, eyes half-lidded as if he were merely settling in for the night.

"You'll figure it out soon enough."

Ophelia opened her mouth to argue, but a sudden wave of exhaustion swept over her. Her body ached from the session that morning, her mind burned from the weight of the day, and she wasn't about to start a debate with a smug, overgrown owl. She let out a harsh breath, shaking her head.

"You're infuriating," she muttered, tugging back the blankets and climbing into bed.

Sarys made a pleased sound. "I've been told."

She rolled onto her side, staring at the wooden panels of the wall. The presence of the Dyad still echoed in the back of her mind, tethered to Theodin somewhere beyond these halls. She wasn't sure if it comforted or unsettled her at that moment.

The last thing she heard before sleep pulled her under was Sarys' voice, softer now, thoughtful.

"Sleep well, darling. Tomorrow, we begin."

Chapter 41

The Divide

Theodin had always valued silence. It had been a comfort for most of his life—an anchor when the world around him became too loud. Too chaotic.

But tonight, the silence felt different. It wasn't solitude. It wasn't peace.

It was absence.

He had made it halfway down the corridor before the emptiness of it settled in. The Dyad, which had once felt like an unbearable weight, now felt… hollow. Not broken, not gone, but missing. A presence that should have been there—was there—just beyond his reach.

Ophelia.

Theodin exhaled sharply, pressing his fingers against his temple. It wasn't pain. Not exactly. It was something quieter, something restless. An awareness that stretched between them no matter how much distance lay between their rooms.

The pull. The urge to go to her.

He clenched his jaw and forced himself to keep walking, pushing the thoughts down, ignoring the tingle that still lingered on his skin from where she had touched him.

It had been nothing. Just a fleeting moment. A hand brushing away a stray lock of hair.

And yet—

His hands curled into fists.

And yet, it felt like something more. The way her fingers had lingered. The way she had looked at him. The way he had leaned into her touch.

He stopped and he reached his door, inhaling through his nose. He shut his eyes and pressed his forehead into the wood.

This was dangerous. The Dyad was already unstable enough—Sarys had made that clear. He could not afford to let himself get tangled in things that didn't matter.

He had trained for discipline his whole life.

Control. Restraint.

So why did it feel like his own body—his own mind—was betraying him?

He stepped inside, shutting the door harder than necessary. The dim glow of the enchanted lanterns barely touched the corners of the room, leaving most of it in shadow. He moved on instinct, shedding his tunic and his belt and setting his weapons aside.

And yet, no matter what he did, no matter how much he willed himself to focus, the Dyad still thrummed with her presence. Not intrusively, not forcefully—but there. A whisper against the edge of his mind, like a quiet heartbeat.

Theodin exhaled through his nose, sitting at the edge of his bed. His fingers curled over each knee, tension locking in his shoulders.

He should be exhausted—his body ached from training, from pushing himself too hard—but sleep felt impossible.

Because no matter how much he tried to ignore it, the Dyad remained.

And worse—

He didn't want it to go away.

That thought hit him harder than anything else. His head dipped slightly, his palms pressing against his face.

What am I doing?

She was Ophelia.

Stubborn. Reckless. Infuriating. But she was also—

He swallowed.

She was also his. And he was hers.

Not in a way he could claim. Not in a way he had any right to.

But she was his partner. His counterpart in the Dyad.

Their souls were entwined forever.

And no matter what rules the Kyriegard dictated, no matter how much he tried to keep his emotions in check—he could not sever that truth.

Theodin inhaled sharply, rubbing his face before leaning back against the headboard.

Year 845 of the Second Age, Seventh Month, Seventeenth Day

That night, Theodin barely slept.

The moment his eyes shut, the Dyad pulled at him, pressing Ophelia's presence into his mind.

It wasn't a dream. Not quite.

Just a sensation—faint, blurred at the edges, but lingering. He had felt her beside him, not in body, but in being.

When he awoke, the feeling remained.

He sat on the edge of his bed, running a hand through his hair, exhaling heavily.

It was just the Dyad adjusting.

Nothing more. Nothing to dwell on.

He dressed in silence, tightening the belts on his bracers with more force than necessary.

The Dyad was still thrumming. Still shifting.

But it wasn't just that.

Something was off. Theodin clenched his jaw, forcing the thought away as he left his chambers.

Breakfast. Eat. Train. Focus.

What was bothering him?

Ophelia was walking. More stable. Now she had a magical talking animal friend—annoying as he was, and of course he was born purely of magic to Theodin's chagrin—the Dyad should not have been feeling this way.

The humble dining room at Avasylon held a wordless breakfast that morning.

Kaspar sat at the head of the table, his focus solely on his meal. Ophelia had arrived before Theodin, but she barely glanced up when he entered; instead she kept her eyes on her plate.

She was acting normal. Too normal. As if last night had been nothing.

Theodin sat across from her, careful and controlled. His movements did not betray him. His hands did not shake. His face remained blank.

Then, Faust entered. Theodin could feel the Valksha boy's eyes look over him with scrutiny. The moment he sat down, he grinned—too knowing, too amused.

Theodin felt his grip tighten around his fork.

Faust leaned back in his chair, stretching.

"Rough night, Theo?" he mused, reaching for a slice of bread. "You look like you've been wrestling demons in your sleep."

Theodin said nothing. He didn't even look up.

Ophelia stiffened.

Faust only continued.

"Or was it something else keeping you awake?"

Sarys clicked his beak. "Oh, he's brooding harder than usual," he remarked, eyes glinting. "Wonder why."

Ophelia groaned, rubbing her temple. "You both need to *stop* talking."

Faust gasped, feigning offense. "Me? Ophelia, I am wounded."

Theodin now gripped his fork too tightly. His knuckles turned white.

Faust leaned forward, placing his elbows on the table.

"Honestly, I don't blame you, Theo," he said lazily. "Guess it's hard to sleep when you're not the only one keeping her up at night."

Ophelia's face twisted. "Faust, what are you—?"

Theodin's hand moved before he could stop it. His body acted on instinct, raw and unchecked. He wasn't sure if he was about to grab Faust's collar, slam his fist into the table, or something worse. But before he could touch him—

Kaspar flicked his fingers.

A pulse of Sage magic slammed into Theodin's chest, shoving him hard back into his chair.

Theodin saw red. His breathing was burdened, and his pulse was pounding. The Dyad was surging, hot, unstable, and violent.

He could feel Ophelia's horror through it—her panic, her plea for him to stop.

Across the table, Faust's smugness had vanished.

Sarys wasn't laughing. The owl familiar flinched his head toward Faust; his large, luminous eyes were unreadable.

Sarys's usual humor was gone. His voice, when it came, was smooth —too smooth.

"Strange," Sarys began with an air of coolness, "how you act as though he's the problem when you can't even decide what you are to her."

Faust froze.

The shift was instant. His expression went blank, and for the first time he had no retort.

Ophelia felt it.

Kaspar still had not looked up. He lifted his cup, drinking as if nothing had happened. Then, finally, he spoke.

"Eat your breakfast, Theodin."

Theodin seethed. His hands trembled, barely suppressing the impulse to stand. To walk out. To do anything but sit there.

Faust, still quiet, pushed back from the table.

"Don't need to be told twice," he muttered.

Ophelia didn't say a word. She just stood and left. Sarys fluttered after her, ruffling his feathers. Faust left next. He didn't look at Theodin as he walked away.

Now, only he and Kaspar remained.

For a long moment, neither of them spoke. Theodin waited—his body still rigid—for his mentor to say something. To acknowledge what had just happened.

Kaspar finished his meal, set his utensils down, and finally looked at him.

Theodin braced himself.

But Kaspar didn't comment on his loss of control. He didn't question it.

Instead, he simply said, "Focus, Theodin. You'll need it today."

Theodin clenched his jaw.

Kaspar gestured toward his plate.

"Eat."

Theodin forced himself to comply, but the food tasted like nothing.

The Dyad was still rippling, still unsettled, still pulling him toward her in a way he didn't understand.

And Theodin wasn't sure if he could continue to resist it.

The morning air was cool and crisp, a quiet contrast to the tension still dwelling in Ophelia's chest. She inhaled deeply as she stepped outside, the scent of damp stone and earth filling her lungs.

Training with Sarys, Theodin, and Alfena was supposed to be next. Focus, movement, discipline. Something to still her thoughts.

But first, she had business to take care of.

She spotted Faust easily, leaning against the outer wall of the training yard, flipping a dagger idly between his fingers. The sun cast long shadows against the stone, catching the gleam of metal as the blade twirled effortlessly in his grip.

He looked too relaxed. But Ophelia felt the subtle undercurrent beneath his facade—the tangled mess he worked so hard to keep buried.

She stopped a few paces away and addressed him firmly.

"You need to stop."

Faust didn't look up. His smirk flickered across his lips, lazy and unconcerned. Too easy. Too practiced.

"Stop what, little owl?"

Ophelia crossed her arms. Unmoved.

"You know exactly what."

That got his attention. He finally glanced at her, feigning innocence, tilting his head as if he truly had no idea what she was talking about.

"You're going to have to be more specific. I do so many terrible things."

Not this time.

Ophelia stepped forward, locking eyes with him, studying him. Faust held the stare—until she tilted her head, just slightly. And she read him like an open book.

His mouth twitched—just barely.

"You were lying at breakfast," she said.

The dagger in his hand slowed. Faust exhaled slowly through his nose, rolling a shoulder like none of this mattered. Like he wasn't caught.

"Lying? About what, exactly?"

Ophelia didn't blink. "About why you push Theodin. About why you push me."

She felt it now.

The emotions swirling beneath his skin. Messy. Fractured. Raw.

They were hiding beneath his mask, but were becoming anxious from exposure to her senses.

Faust flipped the dagger again, but did so cautiously this time. Measured.

"That's quite an accusation, love."

"It's not an accusation."

Ophelia's voice was steady and unshaken.

"It's the truth."

Faust's fingers curled around the handle of his dagger, grip tightening.

She took a step closer. Her voice softened, but it did not waver.

"You don't have to tell me," she whispered. "I already know."

Faust stilled. Completely.

His usual, newfound confidence—the lightness he wielded like a shield—hung precariously between them, about to break.

Ophelia took another step forward. "But if you truly care about me at all—"

She felt the shift in him, the way his posture tensed just slightly, like he wanted to turn away but refused to. She swallowed, steadying herself.

"—then be kind to him."

Silence. She felt the pang that struck his chest.

"Please, Faust."

Faust lowered his eyes. As he did, the false confidence melted from his skin.

She could tell the way she said his name so gently affected him.

When he lifted his eyes to meet hers, his aura changed.

Something flashed in his gaze—uncertainty, something caught between defense and hesitation. She could see him wrestling with it, see him wanting to deflect, to shrug it off like he always did.

But he didn't.

"The more you push him," she said quietly, "the more you hurt him, the more you hurt me too."

Faust flinched.

It was subtle—barely a flicker of movement, a tightening of his jaw—but it was there.

And Ophelia saw it. She felt it. A glint of the former Faust, the meek and vulnerable boy she first came to know, shone in his lapis eyes.

She reached into the collar of her tunic and pulled out two strings of necklaces. One was the life talisman and the other was the charm he had given her.

"You're capable of that kindness," she said with tenderness. "And being sweet. Please don't let that part of you change."

He let out a breath, slow and unreadable. His voice matched it as he spoke.

"That's not fair, love."

Ophelia didn't look away. She tucked the necklaces back in her tunic.

"No. It isn't."

But it was the truth. And they both knew it.

She turned before he could say anything else, before she could let his silence pull her into a conversation she wasn't ready for.

"I have training."

She walked away without looking back.

Faust didn't stop her.

From above, Sarys spotted her, then dove down to land on her shoulder effortlessly. He had glimpsed at Faust, but said nothing and faced forward.

When she was gone, Faust tightened his grip around the dagger again.

Just slightly.

And as he watched her walk away, her absence caused an empty coldness to come over him again.

Don't let that part of you change.

The part of him that she truly cared about.

But… he cared about *all* of her.

Faust shut his eyes. His lip slightly trembled.

The more you hurt him, the more you hurt her.

No.

He refused to hurt her at all. Not after all the kindness she'd shown him.

Faust opened his eyes to see her join Kaspar and Theodin in one of the training fields.

As if she felt his gaze, her eyes briefly flickered to him, offered a gentle smile, and then she turned away again.

Faust's heart ached. He pressed his hand to his chest.

The sun stretched long shadows over the training yard as Ophelia whipped her chained blade around, rolling her shoulders and her wrists. Theodin stood a few paces away, his stance perfectly balanced, already settling into calm focus.

Kaspar had set the terms clearly.

"You and Theodin. Work together. Try to take me down."

The two exchanged wary glances.

Their Dyad shook with uncertainty.

Across from them, Kaspar stood in his usual effortless stillness—unmoved, patient, as if none of this would actually challenge him. His hand rested lightly on the hilt of his sword, not even drawn yet.

Alfena stood at the edge of the sparring ring, her eyes scanning them both carefully. Watching. Measuring.

Sarys was perched on a wooden post nearby.

Ophelia exhaled slowly. They had to move together.

They stared down their mentor with unease. They had done this many times before and will continue to do it again and again.

It is guaranteed that at this stage of their Kyriegard training, they were not able to take him down or make him concede. That was not expected until their final Kyriegard Trials.

Even Ophelia couldn't take him down—she was too inexperienced with her Valksha magic.

But what was expected was that they were to make progress.

She caught the barest shift of Theodin's weight beside her. That was the only signal she needed.

They lunged.

Theodin moved first—blade flashing as he slashed towards Kaspar, sharp and precise. Ophelia followed a breath behind, covering his right side, her chained blade swinging in a fast arc.

Kaspar moved like water.

His blade met Theodin's mid-air, redirecting the force cleanly while his other hand caught Ophelia's wrist before she could land a strike. In one seamless motion, he ducked from the whip of her blade and yanked her off balance, knocking her to the ground with a single, controlled movement. She attempted to roll onto her knees to recover, but stumbled and skidded.

Theodin barely had time to pivot before Kaspar twisted behind him and drove an elbow into his ribs. A heartbeat later, they were both on the ground.

Kaspar took a step back, unimpressed. Untouched.

Sarys clicked his beak in disappointment from his perch on the wooden post, ruffling his feathers.

"Oh, this is embarrassing."

Ophelia groaned and pushed herself up, brushing dirt off her hands.

"Again," Kaspar muttered.

Theodin was already standing, already resetting his stance, his expression blank as he shook off the failed attempt.

Kaspar's mouth twitched slightly—not a smile, but close to one. "Better make it count."

They adjusted. This time, they didn't move separately.

The moment Theodin shifted forward, Ophelia already knew. The

Dyad anticipated him, and she responded faster and sharper.

They struck as one.

Kaspar blocked the first attack, deflecting Theodin's blade, but Ophelia was already there, sweeping low.

For the first time, Kaspar had to pivot fully to avoid the hit. He moved to counter, but—

Theodin had already predicted him.

Kaspar's brows lifted slightly—the first sign of actual interest.

Then he moved unexpectedly, adapting faster than they could react.

Kaspar caught Ophelia's arm mid-swing and turned—this time, he didn't just throw her back. He drove a precise blow straight into her ribs.

The impact knocked the breath from her lungs. Pain exploded across her side, and as he let go of her, she hit the ground hard.

Theodin felt it. A white-hot surge of pain—not his own, but Ophelia's.

The Dyad flared violently, slamming through him with unbearable force.

Something inside him snapped.

He didn't think.

Something animalistic flashed across his mismatched eyes.

He lunged.

Kaspar barely had time to react before Theodin was on him—faster than before. Too fast. Too strong.

Theodin's sword was gone—he had dropped it without realizing. His hands caught Kaspar's arm and twisted with force beyond his own.

Kaspar grunted at the impact, his feet sliding back against the dirt. His eyes glinted dangerously—recognition, not surprise.

Then, Sage magic from Kaspar's other hand slammed into Theodin like a hammer.

The force sent him crashing backward, hitting the ground hard enough to crack the dirt beneath him.

He tried to rise—but he couldn't. His body wouldn't move. He was pinned. Locked down.

His chest heaved as he struggled against the unseen force pressing into his limbs, keeping him in place. His vision blurred red.

Kaspar stood over him, his hand raised and palm glowing faintly with silver light.

Alfena was already stepping forward, her eyes narrowed. She had felt it too.

"That's enough," Kaspar said, his voice level but firm.

But he didn't let Sage magic falter.

Theodin's pulse pounded. His body still burned. His hands twitched, his fingers digging into the ground. He bared his teeth and an angry snarl escaped him.

"Breathe," Kaspar ordered.

Theodin's jaw locked. His muscles were still throbbing, still too tense, too tight. His head spun as the Dyad pulsed violently, screaming at him to move, move, move—

And then he felt it—

Ophelia.

She was still on the ground, coughing, recovering from the blow.

The weight pressing into his body lifted slightly, just enough for him to shift. His gaze snapped to her.

She was okay.

The rage slowly reeled back and settled.

Alfena exhaled slowly. "Interesting."

Kaspar lowered his hand and released him fully.

Theodin's body slumped. His breathing was still too fast.

Ophelia had pushed herself upright, watching him with a mixture of shock and concern.

Sarys let out a long whistle.

"Well." He clicked his beak. "That was dramatic."

Kaspar rolled his shoulders, stepping back. His eyes were on Theodin now, watching with the keen and apprehensive awareness of a Kyriegard master.

"That wasn't just the Dyad," he said evenly.

Theodin didn't answer.

Alfena was still watching, almost without blinking, her expression hardened.

"The bond is… reinforcing something. It's amplifying his emotions, but it's not just *emotional*. It's instinctive. Reactive."

Her eyes darted to Ophelia.

"To her. It's amplified by her pain, emotions, and presence."

Kaspar's voice remained calm, but there was a sense of finality in his words.

"If keeping you together makes you unstable, then we separate you."

Ophelia's stomach dropped.

"Effective immediately," Kaspar added, already walking away.

Theodin and Ophelia locked eyes, wide and stunned. They both panted from the exertion. The Dyad spun anxiously.

What happened? Her voice whispered in his head.

He didn't answer. He had no words. She felt shame growing from the pit of his stomach as he slowly lowered his eyes.

He lost control.

Chapter 42

The Withering

The door clicked shut behind her. Ophelia barely made it three steps before her legs gave out. She caught herself on the edge of the small writing desk, inhaling sharply. Her ribs ached from Kaspar's hit, but it was nothing compared to the suffocating weight sitting in her chest.

Theodin.

Her fingers curled against the wood as she felt the Dyad shifting—unstable, *unsettled.*

It wasn't just reacting to her emotions—it was reeling with his.

And right now, Theodin's emotions were a storm.

She squeezed her eyes shut, willing herself to breathe.

Sarys perched on the back of a chair.

"Well," he said dryly, "that was an eventful morning."

Ophelia exhaled hard through her nose.

"Not now, Sarys."

"Not now?" He tilted his head, eyes gleaming. "Darling, if *now* isn't the time to discuss the fact that your mate nearly tore apart a seasoned Kyriegard—the Head of the *Order!*—when exactly would you like to pencil that in?"

She shot him a glare.

Sarys clicked his beak, unbothered.

"Come now, don't give me that look. You felt it, just like I did. This isn't just the Dyad misbehaving anymore. Something's changing in him."

Ophelia swallowed, her pulse still unsteady. She couldn't speak it out loud.

I know.

She *did* know. And that was what terrified her.

She collapsed onto the edge of her bed, rubbing her temples.

Then, her senses prickled with an approaching presence.

Faust.

A knock at the door.

She startled slightly, turning toward it just as it creaked open without warrant.

Faust leaned against the frame, arms crossed. He didn't have his usual smirk—just a hesitant expression he used to wear often.

Ophelia sighed. "Faust."

"Lia."

His voice was light, but his eyes drifted to her ribs—too perceptive, as always.

"You alright?"

"I'm fine."

A beat.

Then, with the exact amount of doubt she expected—

"Uh-huh."

Ophelia rolled her eyes.

Faust stepped inside, closing the door behind him. A touch of his easy confidence was there, but there was something else too—something quieter. He studied her carefully, and when he spoke again, his voice had dropped a fraction.

"What happened out there?"

Ophelia's fingers tightened around the bedsheets. Her eyes lowered to the ground.

She could still see it. Theodin moving faster than he should have, stronger than he should have. The way Kaspar had reacted—not surprised, but… knowing.

She shook her head. "I don't know."

Faust hummed, tapping a finger against his arm. "What was the verdict from the old man?"

"Nimrod is separating us."

Faust stopped. He furrowed his brows. "Why?"

"The Dyad is unstable again," she said softly. "It intensifies too much when we're near one another and makes Theodin lose control now if I'm hurt."

Faust's face twisted.

"I thought it was fixed with..."

Faust pointed to Sarys.

The owl gave a shrug with his wings like they were shoulders.

"Alfena didn't explain any further," Ophelia said. "I think they might've been too shaken by the fact that Theodin attacked Kaspar without restraint."

She lifted her eyes to him.

"If Nimrod..."

She hesitated.

"If Nimrod didn't stop him..."

The image of Theodin's bare hands on the throat of the Cadaven beast. Twisting, breaking its bones like twigs.

She brought a hand to her mouth.

Faust took a step towards her and leaned forward. "He...no," he huffed. "He wouldn't... hurt him, would he? Didn't Kaspar *raise* him?"

"Yes," Ophelia muttered.

Faust struggled to find the next words to say, biting his lip. He folded his arms tightly.

"You're... not afraid of him?" Faust said carefully. "Especially being soul-tethered to someone like that?"

Ophelia closed her eyes. The intensity in her face lessened. The Dyad stirred, restless. But Theodin's emotions were closed off now—buried and withdrawn. He wasn't letting her feel him anymore.

"No," she finally answered.

Faust's jaw tightened slightly. Just for a second. Then, in typical Faust fashion, he let out a breath and dropped onto the bed beside her, leaning back like he belonged there.

Ophelia gave him a tired glare. "What are you doing?"

He propped one arm behind his head. "Making sure you don't do that thing where you overthink yourself into a spiral."

"I don't—"

"You do." He shot her a lazy grin. "I know because I do it too."

Ophelia shook her head, but the corner of her mouth almost twitched.

"The bird and I will keep you company," Faust insisted. "We'll keep your tall boy company too if you'd like."

"I don't think he'd like our company," Sarys murmured dully.

* * *

The door closed behind Theodin with a quiet click.

He stood in the center of his room. Breathing too hard. Thinking too fast.

The silence should have been grounding. He should have welcomed it, let it settle his mind, let it anchor him back into control.

But there was no control left.

His fingers curled at his sides, his shoulders still tense, every muscle in his body still bracing for a fight that had already ended.

Fixated on one thought alone.

He had lost control.

Theodin let out a heavy exhale, but the breath came out uneven. Shaking. He reached up, fingers pressing against his temple, trying to focus on anything except the raw, fraying edges of his mind.

But it was still there.

The feeling of power surging through his veins, of the Dyad burning hot, of something deeper, something worse, waking up inside of him.

The moment Ophelia hit the ground.

The moment rage drowned out everything else.

The moment he moved without thinking, without restraint, with something that was too much, too strong, too… unnatural.

Kaspar had recognized it. Alfena had sensed it.

Even Ophelia had looked at him like she'd seen something she wasn't meant to.

His stomach twisted.

Theodin dragged in another breath and turned sharply toward the basin in the corner of the room, filling it with water from the pitcher. His hands were still trembling. He didn't acknowledge it. He just forced them steady as he splashed the cold water over his face.

Again.

And again.

And again.

His breathing began to even out, but the tension in his entire body didn't fade. He gripped the edge of the basin, staring at his reflection in the water's rippling surface. His own face stared back at him.

Familiar. Ordinary.

He was himself in that reflection.

But he hadn't been himself in the moment before Kaspar pinned him down. His eyes had burned. Not in the way they always did when the Dyad surged.

Something else.

Something wrong.

His fingers pressed harder against the stone, his knuckles white.

He had felt stronger in that moment and in moments before, but this time was different. This kind of strength that wasn't his. This kind of strength was impossible. He could've badly hurt Kaspar. Crippled him beyond repair. Possibly even killed him.

Theodin squeezed his eyes shut.

Fear crept into him.

The same fear he buried for years. Buried under strict discipline and rigid training.

His towering frame shook.

No.

Stop feeling.

Breathe.

He almost heard it in Kaspar's voice.

Don't be afraid.

I'm not afraid of you.

He stopped. He opened his eyes.

He heard that in her voice. She didn't speak to him through the Dyad, but he remembered the moment she said it to him.

But was she afraid of him at that moment? Just less than an hour ago?

Theodin squeezed his eyes shut again.

He refused to remember if she was. He clung to the memory of her instead.

The memory of her accepting him. All of him.

His shoulders slightly sagged.

Kaspar was separating them. It was for the best. It had to be. The Dyad had been growing too unstable. Theodin had been growing too unstable. If they weren't careful, something would break.

Then, his grip finally loosened. His hands quivered, and he let them for the time being as they rested on the edge of the basin.

For a long time, Theodin just stood there, breathing. He needed to be alone. That was the only way to fix this.

Wasn't it?

He closed his eyes.

Slowly, he felt the wall between them grow.

He needed to protect her from himself.

* * *

Year 845 of the Second Age, Seventh Month
Eighteenth and Nineteenth Days

The first day, it wasn't obvious.

Theodin and Ophelia had always carried exhaustion like a second skin. It was nothing new—the weight of the Dyad, of training, and of everything pressing down on them. They walked through their days worn but upright, their bodies remembering what to do even when their minds begged for rest.

But by the second day, something was different.

Faust watched from the outer courtyard, flipping his dagger idly between his fingers.

He wasn't supposed to be here. None of them were. Kaspar had made it clear—Ophelia and Theodin were off duty until further notice.

But that didn't stop Faust from watching. And what he saw wasn't good.

Across the training yard, Ophelia stood at the edge of the field, barely upright. She was wrapped in her cloak despite the midday summer sun, arms folded tight against her body as if she was trying to hold herself together. She looked gray.

Not pale—*gray*.

Her eyes were dull, her shoulders rigid with a tension she didn't have the energy to shake off. She wasn't moving. She wasn't speaking.

And Theodin—

Faust's gaze flicked to where Theodin sat on a stone bench near the cottage, elbows braced on his knees, fingers laced together. His head was lowered, and his body was completely still.

Faust had never seen him so still before.

It wasn't exhaustion. It wasn't brooding. It was an absence. Like something inside him was caving in, hollowing him out piece by piece.

Faust hated it.

Year 845 of the Second Age, Seventh Month, Twentieth Day

By the third day, it was clear. They weren't recovering. They were getting worse.

Ophelia could barely eat. Anything she swallowed, she threw up minutes later.

That morning, Faust had found her leaning against the stone wall in the hallway, breath shallow, shaking. He had said her name, and she had lifted her head slowly—too slowly.

"Just dizzy," she murmured. "It'll pass."

It didn't.

By mid-afternoon, she was back in bed, curled under the blankets with her eyes closed, but she was not sleeping.

Theodin, meanwhile, had stopped responding altogether.

He didn't speak at meals. He didn't lift his head when people passed him in the halls.

He still wasn't sleeping.

Faust had checked.

Somewhere past midnight, he'd slipped past the training hall in the cellar only to find Theodin awake, gripping the edges of a sparring dummy like he was trying to keep himself from falling. His breathing was slow, measured, and controlled.

Too controlled.

He was unraveling.

And yet, Kaspar did nothing. Alfena watched but said nothing.

And Faust?

Faust was getting tired of watching.

Year 845 of the Second Age, Seventh Month, Twenty-First Day

By the fourth day, they barely spoke.

Theodin moved like a ghost, mechanical, void of presence.

Ophelia didn't leave her room.

The Dyad wasn't just hurting them anymore.

It was killing them.

Faust sat beside Ophelia's bed that evening, arms crossed, watching as she lay still beneath the covers. She wasn't sleeping, but she wasn't fully awake either. Her breathing was too slow, and her energy was gone.

"You look like someone dragged you through the Nether," he muttered.

A weak breath—maybe a laugh, maybe just an exhale.

"You've said that before," she murmured.

"Yeah, well, now I mean it."

She turned her head slightly, half-lidded eyes finding his. Empty.

"Faust."

His stomach twisted at the way she said his name—too soft and tired.

He didn't answer. He just leaned forward, rubbing the back of his neck.

This wasn't working.

The separation was breaking them.

Year 845 of the Second Age, Seventh Month, Twenty-Second Day

The fire in the hearth crackled, but Ophelia barely seemed to notice it. Faust sat across from her, his legs stretched out and his back against the chair. She sat curled in on herself, wrapped in her cloak, staring into the flames.

He watched her. He had been doing that a lot lately. Noticing the little things. The way her hands trembled when she thought no one was looking. The way she blinked too slowly, as if her body was struggling to keep up.

He flipped his dagger between his fingers, his voice casual. "You look worse than Malblight, Lia."

She made a quiet sound—something between a breath and a scoff.

"You keep saying that."

"Because you keep looking worse."

She didn't pose a rebuttal.

Faust frowned. He wasn't used to that. For as long as he had known her, Ophelia fought everything. Even when she was exhausted, even when she was beaten down—she still had that spark.

Right now? He could barely see it.

She was now just a pile of smoldering embers.

His fingers curled around the dagger.

What in the name of the Saryfim was this.

Faust perked slightly.

The Saryfim. Elodyn.

They were *Valksha,* for crying out loud.

He spoke suddenly, but kept his voice low.

"When's the last time you prayed?"

Ophelia tensed. Faust let the question settle between them. He wasn't asking to be cruel.

He was asking because he knew the answer.

She swallowed, shifting her hands in her lap. "I haven't. Not since the day we left for the workshop in Slymound."

He hummed. "Figured."

She exhaled, rubbing her forehead.

"I just—" She hesitated. "It doesn't feel the same anymore."

Faust tilted his head. "Because of the Dyad?"

"Because of everything."

She had always been careful with what she told him, but he heard what she wasn't saying.

Because of the Dyad. Because of the Kyriegard. Because of who she was becoming.

Because of the things she couldn't undo.

Faust sighed, pushing himself up from his chair. He stepped forward and held out his hand.

She blinked at it. "What?"

"Come on," he said. "Let's pray."

She stared at him. "...*What?*"

"I heard you the first time, little owl." His smirk was faint, but his eyes were stern. "You're Valksha. Prayers work differently for you."

She still hesitated.

"Humor me," he said.

She let out a reluctant breath through her nose, shaking her head but reaching out anyway. Her hand slipped into his, and their fingers laced together.

She was cold.

Faust ignored the way it made his stomach twist.

She closed her eyes. He did too.

And for a brief moment, as they murmured the words in the old Valksha tongue, she steadied. Her breath evened. The shaking in her fingers stopped.

Faust felt it—the pull of something ancient, something waiting.

It wasn't his magic. It wasn't blood. It was her.

But as quickly as it came, the moment passed.

Ophelia's fingers loosened against his, her breath hitching. She pulled back, breaking the connection.

Faust opened his eyes. She was staring at her hands. Her hands weren't shaking anymore.

"See?" he murmured. "Not so bad."

She didn't look at him. Her eyes fixated on her hands with uncertainty.

It was midnight. The halls were quiet.

Theodin lasted five days.

Five days of emptiness. Of feeling like his own skin didn't fit, as if something was wrong with him.

It wasn't pain. Not exactly.

It was a dreadful absence.

Something that should be there—wasn't.

Ophelia.

The Dyad pulsed sluggishly, weak, fragile, and unbalanced. It was starving.

He was starving.

Theodin moved quickly and soundlessly, slipping through the empty corridors. No one was awake.

Except her.

He could feel it—Ophelia wasn't sleeping either.

The moment he reached her door, his pulse kicked hard against his ribs.

He knocked once. No answer.

Then, slowly—he pushed it open.

She hadn't heard the knock. Or maybe she had, but she was too exhausted to register it. She didn't notice anything at all until the door creaked open—until the Dyad lurched back to life.

Her eyes snapped open.

And she saw him.

Their eyes locked.

Theodin.

Standing in the doorway, breathing hard, like he had just run a mile.

They had been together in dreams, but it was never enough. Not like this. Not when she was right here, breathing, real.

Her lips parted, but before she could say anything—

The Dyad stabilized. The weight in her chest lifted. The fog in her mind cleared.

Theodin exhaled sharply, gripping the edge of the doorframe like the world had finally stopped tilting beneath his feet.

For the first time in days—she didn't feel like she was dying.

She swallowed hard. "Theo."

He didn't speak. He entered.

And the moment the door swung behind him, the Dyad breathed again. As he moved towards her, he gained strength with each step. The matching runes along their forearms and palms pulsed a soft glow.

He stopped at her bedside. Staring.

For a second, there was silence.

Then, Theodin exhaled a ragged breath and sank to his knees beside her bed.

It wasn't exhaustion. Not physically.

But he had needed this. Just as much as she had.

It was a reprieve.

She slowly pushed herself upright. Her body didn't fight her this time. She reached out, brushing her fingers against his arm. The runes in her skin flashed at the touch.

A hushed whisper escaped her.

"It's been worse for you, hasn't it?"

His throat bobbed. He closed his eyes.

"It doesn't matter."

"It does."

His jaw clenched. He leaned his elbows onto the edge of the bed and clutched the sheets tightly, lowering his head.

He shook briefly, then settled. Like he was allowing her presence and aura to wash over him like the calming shower of a thunderstorm.

Then, quietly—

"I don't know how to breathe without you anymore."

Her chest tightened. And she realized—

She didn't either.

The Dyad rustled soothingly. It urged them closer.

She leaned down and rested her forehead against the top of his head. A current of energy passed between them.

Theodin lifted his head, and she pulled away briefly as he looked at her. In the moonlight, the blue of his right eye and the dark amber of his left eye glinted tenderly.

Ophelia brought a delicate hand to his cheek. Once more, the runes flashed upon contact with his skin. Relief swept over them both. He leaned into her palm for a moment, then brought his hand upon hers. His other hand reached behind her, cradled her back and lower torso and pulled her to him in an embrace.

Ophelia's other hand reached up and wove her fingers into his hair, and their foreheads pressed together, eyes closed.

The Dyad buzzed with life and whirred with renewed energy.

Their breaths became one between them. Heartbeats synchronized.

The warmth between them didn't fade.

They had forgotten what it felt like to be whole.

She didn't move. Neither did he.

This felt right.

This felt like something she should have never been without. And that scared her.

Theodin's grip around her waist was gentle but firm, like he was afraid that if he let go, the world would pull them apart again.

She thought about pulling away. But she didn't. Not yet. Not when she was finally breathing again.

She closed her eyes, tilting her face a fraction closer to his, letting herself sink into his touch. The Dyad urged them together.

This was more than relief. This was undoing a wound that had been left open too long.

Her fingers in his hair. The way she melted into him. The Dyad pulsing stronger than ever, no longer fighting them but pulling them closer.

He wasn't thinking. For once, he wasn't calculating, controlling, restraining.

He was here.

His arms tightened slightly around her, drawing her in just a little more. He could feel the way she breathed now—slow, steady, matched to his.

They weren't shaking anymore. They could stay like this. Just for a moment. Just for this one, stolen piece of time before reality came crashing back in.

Ophelia exhaled a slow breath. Her thumb traced softly against his cheekbone.

The Dyad hummed with contentment.

They should let go. They should break this before it became something else. But they didn't.

Because they didn't want to.

Because for the first time in days, they didn't feel like they were dying.

She wasn't suffocating, she wasn't fading—she was here, grounded by Theodin's presence, by the steady, reassuring weight of him against her.

His arms stayed firm around her, solid, unwilling to let go. Her fingers curled against the nape of his neck, feeling the warmth of his skin and the slow pulse of his heartbeat. Their breaths stayed matched, slow and deep.

The Dyad shimmered with bliss, begging them to stay. To hold. To keep this.

But reality was already creeping in at the edges.

She felt it in the way her mind sharpened again and the way the exhaustion she had been drowning in began to fade into clarity.

This wasn't normal. This wasn't just magic—it was something more.

He felt her heartbeat before he heard her voice. Slow. Measured. Not frantic. Not weak. Just there. Whole.

And that was the only thing that mattered.

Her fingers twitched against his cheek. "Theo…"

His breath hitched. He felt it in the way Ophelia shifted, the way her fingers flexed against his skin, hesitant. The way she was trying to pull herself back even though he wasn't ready to let go.

She felt his desperation. The way his grip on her tightened just slightly, like he was bracing for what came next.

Like he knew, just as she did, that this moment was slipping through their fingers.

She swallowed hard, her voice barely a whisper.

"This… isn't how it's supposed to be."

A long, slow breath escaped him. His forehead tilted against hers, his grip still firm, still steadying. Now their noses touched and their lips were inches apart.

"I don't care."

The words were quiet. Raw.

A confession.

Ophelia held her breath.

Neither did she.

But they had to.

She was right. This wasn't how it was supposed to be. Because they were Kyriegard.

But nothing had ever felt more right than this.

His fingers curled into the fabric at her waist.

They dared not cross the line they could not cross. They remained at the edge of it, trying to taste what it would be like if they could. And if they did.

One more breath. One more second.

Faust hadn't meant to watch. But the door had been cracked open, and he had been walking by at the wrong time.

Or maybe it was the right time. Maybe this was exactly what he needed to see.

The first thing he noticed was the quiet. Not just silence—the kind of quiet that pressed into the air, thick and heavy. The kind that settled in deep, like something was happening that wasn't meant to be interrupted.

He stopped in the doorway, his fingers tightening around the edge of the frame.

And he saw them.

Ophelia, curled into Theodin like she had been carved from his ribs, fitting almost perfectly in his arms. Theodin, holding her like a young man who had lost everything and just found it again. Their foreheads touched, their breaths were slow, shared, and matched.

The Dyad wasn't just stable—it was alive. It sang between them, shimmered against their skin, pulsed with something Faust didn't want to name. Ophelia's fingers were still curled at the nape of Theodin's neck. Theodin's hand was still splayed against her back, his fingers tangled into the fabric at her waist.

Neither of them moved. Neither of them spoke.

Faust felt something cold twist in his stomach.

He should have walked away. But he couldn't.

Because now he understood.

It wasn't just the Dyad. It wasn't just the magic.

It was them.

Their breaths were one. Their heartbeats were one.

And Faust—for all his wit, for all his charm, for all his pretending not to care—

He wasn't part of this. The truth of it was blinding.

It wasn't just that Ophelia needed Theodin to feel whole. Theodin needed her too.

And no matter how much Faust fought, no matter how much he tried to push it down, he knew.

He had never been needed like that.

Not by her. Not by anyone.

His jaw clenched. His fingers curled into fists at his sides.

The Dyad pulsed again. The runes on their arms glowed softly, thrumming with a warmth Faust couldn't reach.

And he hated it.

Hated how much it made his chest ache.

Hated that he couldn't be a part of whatever it was that they had.

Hated that he wanted it anyway.

His voice came out before he could stop it.

"That's enough."

The words shattered the quiet.

Ophelia flinched. Theodin's grip tightened for half a second, like his body refused to let go.

Then, slowly—too slowly—he pulled back.

Both of them turned their heads toward the door, their eyes still unfocused, still lost in each other.

Faust didn't smile. Not even a little. He met Theodin's gaze, and for the first time, there was nothing playful in it. Only something cold. Something dangerous.

"Time to go, Theo."

Theodin didn't move at first. Faust could see the fight in him, the way his jaw locked, the way his shoulders stayed tense, unwilling to leave.

And maybe, if it had been anyone else, he wouldn't have left.

But it was Faust.

And Faust wasn't giving him a choice.

Slowly, painfully, carefully—Theodin pulled away.

The moment he let go, the Dyad shuddered. Not violently. Not in protest. Just in loss.

Ophelia felt it the second his warmth was gone.

Her body already missed it. The way their heartbeats had synced, the way his breath had anchored her.

She felt cold again.

Her hands curled into fists and retreated to her lap.

Theodin's hands finally dropped from Ophelia's waist. She sat frozen, still trying to breathe through whatever this had been.

Faust didn't look at her.

Didn't acknowledge the way her fingers still twitched slightly, like she was feeling the absence of Theodin already. Didn't acknowledge the way Theodin's entire frame was coiled like a blade ready to be drawn.

That was when Faust noticed the bird.

Sarys.

The owl was perched on the headboard, silent. Watching. His glowing eyes flicked between Theodin and Ophelia, then settled on Faust.

There was no amusement in his stare. No sharp-edged wit, no smug, knowing glint. Just a quiet understanding.

Faust's teeth clenched. Because Sarys knew. Sarys had felt it, too. He had been healed by it, just like them.

The Dyad had done something to all of them.

Even Faust.

Even though he wasn't part of it.

Faust just tilted his head toward the door.

Theodin locked his jaw tightly.

But he stood.

And left.

The door clicked shut behind him.

Ophelia let out a labored breath, her hands gripping the sheets as if grounding herself.

She looked up at Faust for the first time. He could still see the way the Dyad lingered on her skin, the magic still soft, still humming beneath the surface. And for a moment, he felt like he had interrupted something holy. Something sacred.

His stomach twisted again. He exhaled, looking her over. "You… look better."

His voice was careful. Measured.

Ophelia swallowed, but she didn't answer.

Because they both knew why she felt better.

And it had nothing to do with Faust.

Chapter 43

The Ones that Defy Death

The first time they were forced to separate, it took five days for their Dyad to wear away at them.

The second time, it took three.

The decline was faster this time.

Harsher, more merciless.

It started the same way—a slow unraveling. The Dyad weakened, its energy pulling at them like an open wound. Ophelia woke each morning feeling heavier, her limbs slow to respond, and her thoughts became sluggish and blurred.

By the second day, eating became impossible. Any food Faust brought her came back up within minutes. Water stayed down, but it wasn't enough. The headaches started soon after, a dull and constant throbbing behind her eyes.

She stopped trying to sit up. Stopped trying to fight it.

Because what was the point?

Theodin was suffering too—Faust could see it. He wasn't eating either. He moved through the halls like a ghost, shoulders tense, expression unreadable, but Faust knew better. He knew what hunger looked like.

And Theodin was starving.

They were starving for each other.

* * *

Year 845 of the Second Age, Seventh Month, Twenty-Fifth Day

Faust had tried everything. At first, he had done what he always did —cracked jokes, called her names, and poked fun at her suffering. But Ophelia, who normally shot back with quick playful retorts and sharp glares, barely had the strength to lift her head.

That was when he stopped joking.

She was wasting away.

Faust was once a religious individual, but he had lost faith when he was taken by Azazelf. Elodyn had abandoned him.

But in moments like these, desperation had a way of making people reach for things they didn't believe in.

So he prayed with her.

He clasped her hands in his, muttered the old Valksha words under his breath, and waited. His fingers fizzled with royal blue sparks.

Sometimes, for a moment, she steadied.

Her rune markings would flash. Her breathing evened out. The shaking in her hands stopped. She would open her eyes, clearer than before, and Faust almost believed it was working.

But then the moment would pass. Her aura would falter. The color in her cheeks would fade again.

She would slip away.

And Faust would sit there, watching. Waiting. Realizing that no matter how many times he prayed, no matter how many times he tried to keep her here, it wasn't enough.

Faust leaned against the wall near Ophelia's door with a stack of books beside him, flipping his dagger between his fingers. The sound was soft and barely audible, but it filled the silence well enough. He was thinking.

Too much.

He glanced at the door. The candlelight inside flickered against the small gap under the frame. She wasn't asleep.

Not that she could sleep. She was tossing in her bed, restless, breath sharp.

Down the hall, Theodin was awake, too. Faust could almost feel it.

He could sense the tension radiating from Theodin's room, the thick, suffocating silence of someone trying too hard to contain something that didn't want to be contained.

He wasn't getting better. Neither of them were.

Her breathing had been uneven all night. Every so often, she would shift in bed, trying to find a position that didn't hurt. Faust knew—because he hadn't left.

He wasn't sure why.

Maybe because he couldn't shake the way she looked today.

Ophelia wasn't just sick. She was fading.

Faust looked around the room. He noticed that Sarys was awake, too.

The owl sat perched on the bedpost just inside the room, unmoving. His dark feathers blended into the candlelight's shadows, but his eyes glowed.

He wasn't preening. He wasn't shifting his weight. He was just staring.

Faust clicked his tongue. "Don't tell me you're worried, bird."

Sarys didn't look at him.

That was the first sign something was wrong. He always had a retort, a mocking little jab. But now?

Nothing.

Instead, Sarys spoke softly. His talons scraped in discomfort against the wood of the chair. "It's getting worse."

Faust rolled the dagger over his knuckles. "She's had worse days. She will endure."

Sarys finally turned his head toward him. His stare was dark and cold, assessing the situation. Not sharp with amusement, not smug or teasing. Just watching.

"Will she?" Sarys asked.

Faust's fingers hesitated over the blade. He didn't answer.

Because he didn't know.

Sarys clicked his beak. "Then do something."

For a long moment, and only the sound of Ophelia's labored breathing could be heard.

She was a pile of ash and dying embers now when she used to be such a bright, lively, and beautiful flame.

He clenched his jaw. This wasn't sustainable. They wouldn't last much longer like this. If Kaspar and Alfena weren't going to fix it, he would.

Faust straightened, pushing off the wall, slipping the dagger back into its sheath.

Could she die from this?

No. She's a Valksha. She's supposed to be hard to kill. She had the power of the *Saryfim*, for crying out loud.

The only power that could defy death.

Faust stopped.

He put down his dagger and grabbed one of the journals from the pile he had in the hallway. He flipped through a few pages.

It was Ophelia's handwriting. Her script was clean, but her scribbles and footnotes on the sides and margins were scattered and messy.

As Valksha were beings who wielded the power of the Saryfim, they were therefore indirect conduits of Elodyn.

This made them targets of those who sought power. Perhaps even those who sought to defy death itself.

But it is not in a Valksha's nature to defy the will of Elodyn. Our creator spirit of the Ether meant for the souls of mortal flesh to pass on to the Ether.

However, not all souls reach the Ether. Some remain in the purgatorial Lither, hidden between the thin veil that separates them from the living in Midthian. Some are damned to the Nether.

That is why any creature brought back to life from the dead is twisted. They are Cadaven—shells of their former selves and atrocities of dark Nether magic.

But does this mean that the Valksha could *bring back the dead?*

I've thought about it. How I could possibly hold the power to bring back my family. Lady Vivian.

I prayed upon this.

But there was something in me that spoke.

It resisted.

Maybe… it was Veladriel.

The flesh of the Valksha is not meant to return from death. Because the Valksha are the Saryfim made flesh, and mortal flesh was not meant for the immortal existence of Etherian spirits, they cannot roam Midthian for more than the time that Elodyn meant for them to. This is why Valksha can only live half a millennium.

But what of those who are not of Valksha blood?

Valksha blood already defies disease and death. Lady Vivian vanquished the Malblight with her blood—the very disease meant to destroy the Valksha, but the Valksha endured it nonetheless.

If Elodyn created mankind, Elodyn created the Saryfim, and the Saryfim created everything else—including the tethers of life (Spirit and Heart), living (Strength and Will), and death (Freedom and Release), then with their blood, it could very well be possible for the Valksha to bring back the dead.

As Valksha blood defies death, it also defies magic of mortals and Nether weaving.

Valksha blood defies magic of mortals and Nether weaving.

Valksha blood.

Slowly, Faust lowered the journal. He looked at the underside of his forearm, where she healed him all that time ago.

Then he looked into the room again.

Sarys had stopped watching him. The owl turned his head back toward Ophelia, his talons gripping the bedpost tighter. The scrape of claws against wood was the only sound in the dimly lit room, aside from the uneven rise and fall of her breath.

She wasn't asleep. She was too weak to be awake, but too restless to fall unconscious.

Faust exhaled slowly, rolling his shoulders.

Enough waiting.

He stepped inside, closing the door behind him.

Ophelia didn't stir when he approached. Her breathing changed just slightly, just enough for him to know she was aware of him.

Faust crouched beside her bed, arms braced against his knees. She didn't look at him.

"Lia," he whispered.

A slow inhale. Then, finally, she turned her head, her green eyes dull in the low candlelight. She blinked slowly, as if it took effort. Like even that was too much.

Faust clenched his jaw. He could feel it in her now—the way her magic was thinning, the way her body was fighting against itself. She was burning out, but there was nothing left to burn.

It had to stop.

Faust took a deep breath, rolling his wrist. He flipped the dagger once before catching it by the hilt.

"We're fixing this."

Ophelia frowned slightly, but it was weak, unfocused. "What?"

"You heard me."

His voice was flat but certain.

"I'm going to use my magic to stabilize you."

She blinked at him again, sluggish and confused.

Faust pulled the knife from its sheath and rolled up his sleeve. He set the tip of the dagger against his palm.

The blade cut deep with a small sting. He was used to it by now. His blood welled up instantly, thick and red.

He clenched his fist, letting the droplets pool in his palm before placing the knife and sheath down and reaching for her wrist.

"Faust—"

"Lia."

His voice was low, but unyielding.

"Trust me."

Her lips parted. Then—slowly, reluctantly—she stilled.

Faust brought his bleeding hand over her forearm, over the Arcane Dyad runes lining her skin.

Remember how she taught you, he told himself.

Will it, and the magic will obey.

He willed it to heal her. In whatever way was possible. Heal her in the way that she healed him.

The blood in his hand became sparks of royal blue that floated from his palm to her markings.

They shone green.

Faust could feel the energy course through her.

The moment the magic took hold, Ophelia sucked in a sharp breath. Her entire body tensed. The pain—the weakness—didn't disappear completely, but it shifted. The magic curled through her system, familiar yet different.

Faust kept his grip on her wrist. He sensed the magic pulling her toward something that felt both dangerous and strangely stabilizing all at once.

Ophelia shuddered.

Faust watched her closely. "Better?"

Her throat bobbed as she swallowed. She didn't answer.

The glow from her runes faded, but Faust didn't move. Her chest rose and fell, her breaths slow but no longer shallow. The deep gray pallor that had clung to her skin had receded slightly, leaving a color closer to normal.

It worked. Not completely or perfectly. But it worked.

Faust let out a slow breath and released her, drawing his bleeding hand back. The wound already started sealing. That was another thing about Valksha magic—it never let them bleed for too long.

Ophelia's fingers twitched, curling weakly against the sheets.

She didn't say anything. She didn't look at him. She just breathed.

Faust wiped the wound closed with his finger, as he had seen her do a dozen times before. He rolled his wrist absently, still feeling the lingering heat from the spell. The exhaustion hadn't hit him as hard this time when he exerted himself—something about healing her for the first time, healing at all, brought a tinge of exhilaration to him.

At the same time, he should have felt relieved. Instead, a slow unease crept up his spine.

Something was off.

Not with Ophelia. With him.

His own magic sat heavier in his chest than before, twisting, tightening. For the first time, he felt like something had taken root.

Slowly, he lifted his eyes to her.

It wasn't until Faust pulled his hand away that Ophelia realized how deeply she had been sinking. She gasped quietly, her vision sharpening as if she had surfaced from deep water. Her limbs still felt stiff, but more stable.

But it wasn't just stability. Something else had settled inside her—something not hers.

It wasn't like Theodin. It wasn't like Sarys. It wasn't like the Dyad at all.

It was foreign. But it wasn't hurting her. It was just… there.

His magic.

Ophelia let out a quick breath.

The fire in her skull had dulled. She blinked a few times, turning her head toward Faust.

What was this feeling?

She sensed it beneath her skin, in her bones—the magic he had left behind. It was laced into the Dyad's pulse, tethering her to something else.

To him?

How?

It wasn't wrong. But it wasn't right either.

A soft rustle of feathers.

Ophelia turned her head just as Sarys dropped from the bedpost, landing lightly on the desk.

He didn't speak.

He looked at Faust. Long. Unreadable. Assessing.

Faust met his stare, his jaw tightening just slightly.

The tension stretched.

Then, Sarys clicked his beak softly.

"What?" Faust muttered, irritation creeping into his voice.

Sarys tilted his head, eyes narrowing. Watching. Not with

amusement or smug delight.

With knowing.

"You've done something more than fix her, little wolf."

Faust's fingers twitched.

Sarys stared unblinkingly, slow and deliberate. He hadn't said it in his usual mocking tone. There was no teasing lilt. It had been flat. Quiet. Like a statement of fact.

"Faust," Ophelia whispered, her voice still hoarse. Her eyes still had a daze in them. "What did you do?"

Faust went very, very still. His fingers twitched against his knee, but he didn't respond.

Sarys watched him for a moment longer before hopping onto Ophelia's bed. He didn't say anything else.

Ophelia squirmed slightly with discomfort.

"Faust?"

Faust sat beside her. He pricked his finger on his ring; then he brought it to cup her cheek, and a gentle glow of blue light emanated from his touch.

"You need more sleep, love," he whispered.

Ophelia exhaled slowly. Her eyes rolled back, and her eyelids closed. The color gradually came back to her serene face.

As her breathing became a restful one, Faust stroked her hair back with his other hand. Now she felt warm to the touch again. Despite the strangeness he felt from his magic, seeing her becoming well again brought him peace. He smiled softly to himself.

Something was wrong.

Something was very wrong.

Theodin awoke gasping, his lungs seizing with the force of the Dyad's lurch. The pressure in his chest was crushing, coiling too tight, and twisting into something he didn't recognize.

His hand flew to his chest, fingers pressing against the skin where the magic should be thrumming, pulsing, and steady.

But it wasn't.

It wasn't broken. It wasn't gone. But it wasn't right.

Theodin clenched his jaw, inhaling through his nose. He shut his eyes, reached through the Dyad, pulled—

And something pulled back.

Not Ophelia. Something else.

His entire body locked up.

His stomach twisted violently.

What did you do?

The words weren't spoken aloud, but they raged in his skull. Theodin's breath came sharp and ragged as he reached again, as he tried to find her. But there was something in the way.

Something that shouldn't be there.

And for the first time since the Dyad had formed—

Theodin couldn't reach her.

Something had shifted. Something had changed.

He sat up too fast. His vision blurred at the edges, his breath labored. His fingers pressed against the runes on his wrist, feeling for the course of magic. The quiet, familiar pulse of the Dyad.

It was there. It was constant again. But it wasn't right.

His stomach twisted. He exhaled, slow and controlled. Again. Again.

He reached for her. Carefully, methodically.

Something was in the way.

His jaw locked. He couldn't panic. Not yet. He tried again.

And again, the same weight—something foreign, something that didn't belong—pressed against the Dyad, dulling it.

His brows furrowed.

Ophelia.

Nothing.

His pulse quickened.

Not because he was panicking, but because he knew.

Something *unnatural* had happened.

Year 845 of the Second Age, Seventh Month, Twenty-Sixth Day

The first thing Ophelia noticed when she woke up was that she wasn't dying.

She took a deep breath. Then another.

No crushing weight in her chest. No blinding headache threatening to split her skull open. No nausea churning in her stomach.

For the first time in days, she felt… fine.

But something was off.

Her eyes fluttered open, adjusting to the dim morning light filtering through the curtains.

The warmth of the Dyad still pulsed faintly in her chest, but it felt… distant.

Not gone. But changed.

She huffed, pushing herself up, bracing for the dizziness that had plagued her for days.

It didn't come. Her body felt heavy but functional.

Too functional.

Sarys was perched on the chair beside the bed, watching her. Staring blankly.

His head tilted slightly. "Interesting."

Ophelia frowned. "What?"

"You're awake."

She gave him a dry look. "Brilliant observation, Sarys."

He didn't respond with sarcasm. Instead, his feathers ruffled slightly, his piercing eyes flicking over her like he was searching for something.

After a long pause, he clicked his beak. "How do you feel?"

Ophelia hesitated. She should say she felt better. She should say the Dyad was no longer pulling her apart. But something about the way he was looking at her made her pause.

"I feel…"

She hesitated.

"Fine."

The word sat strange in her mouth.

Fine. She wasn't sure she had ever used that word to describe herself before.

Sarys angled his head further.

"Fine," he echoed.

There was something in his voice she couldn't place. Not disbelief or relief. Something closer to suspicion.

A soft knock on the door.

Faust.

He didn't wait for permission before stepping inside, shutting the door behind him with a quiet click.

"Morning, little owl," he drawled. His smirk was back in place, lazy and effortless, like she hadn't spent the past few days on the verge of collapse.

Ophelia raised an eyebrow. "You're in a good mood."

"I told you you'd live," Faust said easily, crossing the room.

He perched himself on the edge of the writing desk, arms crossed, like nothing about this situation was strange. Like he hadn't just bled into her skin to keep her alive. She ignored the way her pulse twitched at the memory.

"You look better," he noted.

She studied him carefully.

"I feel… fine," she said again, testing the words, waiting for them to sound real.

They didn't.

Faust hummed, reaching for his dagger and flipping it idly between his fingers.

"Fine is better than almost-dead, I'd say."

Sarys hadn't stopped watching her. Neither had Faust.

She exhaled through her nose.

"The Dyad—"

"Still working," Faust cut in. "Stable. No more dying on my watch."

His voice was too light.

Ophelia felt the Dyad again, pressing inward. It was there. It was stable.

But it wasn't hers. Not entirely.

Her throat felt dry. "What did you do to me?"

Faust twirled the dagger between his fingers again, tilting his head.

"Fixed you."

"Faust."

He looked at her then, his smirk still in place, but something guarded flickered behind his eyes.

"Relax, Lia. You're breathing, aren't you?"

She stared at him. He wasn't answering her question.

Sarys let out a soft, amused breath. "Well, this will be fun."

Ophelia barely heard him.

She reached through the Dyad.

It was there, steady, but muted. Not broken. Not pulling at her. Just… distant.

She furrowed her brow, pressing deeper, trying to find the familiar warmth of Theodin's presence. Normally, when she reached for him, he was already there. Even when they were apart, she could always feel the faintest pulse of his energy, the way their magic intertwined, the way he was just… there.

But now? It wasn't the same. The connection felt dulled, like it was wrapped in something heavier, something thicker.

Something was between them.

Her breath caught. He was still there—he had to be—but why did it feel like she had to reach further to find him? Why did it feel like she wasn't reaching for Theodin, but for something else first?

Her heartbeat spiked. The moment it did, Faust noticed.

His dagger stilled between his fingers.

He was able to feel the bond before to some degree, but something was different now.

More intense. More potent.

Ophelia, however, didn't notice; she was too focused on trying to pull at the Dyad, trying to find the comforting warmth of Theodin's energy.

Faust sensed it before he saw it.

The change in her breathing. The way she stopped hesitating, stopped thinking. The way she reached.

She didn't even realize she was doing it. But he did.

His stomach turned.

Faust spoke.

"You're looking for him."

The words were flat. Matter-of-fact.

Ophelia blinked, finally looking at Faust.

His smirk was gone. His fingers tightened around the hilt of his dagger, knuckles white. It wasn't an accusation, but it felt like one.

Ophelia parted her lips to say something—she wasn't even sure what—but he was already looking away, rolling his wrist lazily like it didn't matter. Like it didn't hurt.

"Figures."

The single word came bitter, low, almost to himself.

But Ophelia heard it. The weight in her chest pressed harder.

Sarys let out a soft huff, his talons scraping against the wood of the chair. "Oh, *this* is interesting."

Neither of them acknowledged him.

She looked at him with furrowed brows. "How… how did you know?"

Faust didn't answer. He looked at her with a subtle, pained glance.

She suddenly felt guilty. And she didn't know why.

And he felt that too.

He shouldn't care. This was how it had always been. Theodin was her constant. Theodin was the one she reached for. Faust had known that. He had watched it many times before.

He had seen Theodin kneel beside her the other night, wrap himself around her, anchor her back to life like it was the only thing that mattered.

And now?

Now Faust knew he couldn't be that for her. No matter how much of his magic he bled into her. No matter how much he kept her breathing. No matter how much he wanted to be the one she reached for.

Theodin would always be there first. Always.

"Faust," she said carefully.

His jaw clenched just slightly.

She wanted to explain, but what was there to explain? That the Dyad was still there? That she could feel Theodin but not the way she was supposed to? That even though she felt fine, she didn't feel like herself?

She opened her mouth. "I—"

"Forget it, love."

Faust smirked. It was back. Lazy and effortless, like he hadn't just gone silent for a full minute. Switched faces like nothing had happened.

But the ache was still there in his bones.

Ophelia felt her throat tighten. She felt his hidden emotions with much more intensity.

Sarys ruffled his feathers.

"Well," the owl murmured, "this is painfully awkward."

Faust snorted. The tension cracked, just slightly.

"You know, bird, I'm really starting to regret saving your girl."

Sarys scoffed, unbothered. "And yet, here we are."

Faust sighed dramatically and stood, stretching his arms.

"Well, now that you're not dying, I think I deserve a break from playing nursemaid."

Ophelia huffed. "Faust—"

He didn't let her finish.

"Rest up, Lia." His tone was easy again, light. "Don't go dying on me again."

And then he turned, and he was gone. The door shut behind him with a soft click.

Ophelia exhaled heavily. The weight in her chest hadn't lifted.

Sarys hopped onto the bed, watching her.

"That," he said casually, "was a bit cruel."

Ophelia lowered her eyes to her hands. She didn't know if he was talking about her or Faust. Her fingers clenched the sheets—not hard, but enough.

She had only done what she always did. Reached for Theodin.

Reached for the only thing that made sense and grounded her in the whirlwind of everything that has happened to her since her childhood.

Let the Dyad guide her. It was instinct now. It wasn't a choice. It never had been.

So why did it feel like one now?

The way Faust had looked at her—the way he had known, the way he had shut down the second he realized it—

She hated it. She hated that it sat in her chest like a stone.

Sarys tilted his head, unblinking. "You're thinking too hard, darling."

Ophelia sighed. "I'm not—"

"You are."

She shot him a glare. He didn't look away. Instead, he hooted and fluttered onto her knee, his talons light against the blankets.

"So?" he said, watching her with keen amusement, but no malice. "How do you *really* feel?"

Ophelia looked down at her hands again. She ran a finger over the runes on her wrist, following their familiar lines.

"It's still there," she admitted.

Sarys said nothing.

"But it's…" She frowned, shifting her palm as if that would make her feel it better. "It's… quiet."

Her throat felt dry.

"Not weak," she murmured. "Not broken. Just… quiet."

She had never felt the Dyad like this before. Theodin had always been there, his presence an unshakable force beneath her skin—even when they fought it, even when they ignored it.

And now? Now he was farther. Still there, still anchored, but dulled.

Sarys studied her for a long time. Then, softly, he murmured, "Mm. That's not good."

Ophelia's breath hitched and her stomach twisted. She swallowed, gripping the sheets harder. "What do I do?"

Sarys didn't answer right away. He simply fluffed his feathers, settling comfortably on her knee, and said, "We wait."

"For what?"

His eyes darkened and gleamed at the same time. "For the moment you realize what's really wrong."

Ophelia flinched. The Dyad pulled at her.

Not in the way it normally did—not gently, not steadily. But frantically.

Like someone was trying to get through.
Her breath hitched.
Theodin.

Faust walked. Not fast. Not slow. Just… away.

His fingers curled loosely around the dagger at his hip, rolling it over his knuckles, keeping his hands moving, keeping his mind occupied.

It didn't help. Nothing did. Because the moment Ophelia had reached for the Dyad, something in him had snapped.

The way she searched for Theodin without even realizing she was doing it. Of course, she had always reached for Theodin. He had known that. But something about watching it happen—watching her wake up, looking better, feeling better, and then immediately seeking out someone who wasn't him—

It made his stomach turn. Made his jaw clench. He had spent days at her bedside. He had been the one to pray with her. He had been the one to keep her alive.

And in the end? It still wasn't enough.

Faust had never been the one people needed.

He had been useful. He had been wanted, sometimes. But never necessary.

Not like Theodin was to Ophelia. Or Ophelia to Theodin.

Not like Faust wanted to be to her.

Faust's boots scuffed against the floor. His movements were careful, measured. Like if he walked too fast, the thought would catch up to him.

But it already had. Because he knew.

He wasn't her lifeline. He wasn't anyone's.

He had bled for her. He had prayed over her.

And the second she woke up, the second she felt strong enough—she had reached for someone else.

Faust exhaled slowly and heavily, like he could expel the thought from his body. It didn't work.

He could never tell her. He could never say, 'I watched you die, and I brought you back, and I wanted you to reach for me just once—just once, Lia.' Because what would be the point? She didn't even realize what she had done.

And if he told her?

She would look at him with those wide green eyes, the way she always did when she realized she had hurt someone without meaning to. She would apologize.

And he didn't want her apology. He wanted her instinct. And that was something he was never going to have.

She would never choose him. Not like that.

Chapter 44

The Desperation

Theodin needed to move.

His limbs felt too still, too controlled, too aware. He had to do something—anything—to keep from dwelling on what he felt the night before.

The Dyad had lurched, stabilized, and then dulled. It wasn't broken or severed—but it felt wrong.

Something was in the way.

But there was nothing he could do.

He couldn't storm into her room and demand answers. He had to stay away. Especially after that night.

That night they almost broke and crossed the line.

The Dyad taunted him since then. Then it killed him slowly for staying away.

And now something happened. He didn't know what, but now the Dyad wasn't killing him—and it wasn't killing her.

But she felt so far away.

Frustration boiled in him.

No.

He couldn't let it.

He did what he knew he could control. What he knew he could do to keep himself from losing control again.

He trained.

It was early in the morning before the sun peeked over the horizon. The air was cool, but Theodin felt the heat of his fury beneath his skin.

He needed to let it out.

He set his stance, rolling his shoulders. The training ground was empty, save for the dummies standing idle in the open dirt.

Theodin inhaled deeply. Focus.

Then, he struck with his fist.

The dummy sprang to life, ducking and retaliating. He moved with it—dodging, countering, blocking. His muscles burned, his breath evened out, and his mind—finally—quieted.

Unfortunately, it didn't last long.

"Slower than usual, Theo," Faust mused from across the field.

Casual. Easy. Arms crossed and leaning lazily against a wooden post.

Theodin didn't acknowledge him. He kept moving. Kept fighting. Pretending he hadn't heard him.

Faust smirked.

"Guess Ophelia really is holding you back."

Theodin's strike landed a little harder than necessary. The dummy reeled.

Faust hummed. He approached Theodin, sauntered with an oddly relaxed poise.

"Or maybe…" he continued, watching the way Theodin's shoulders tensed, "it's *you* holding her back."

Theodin still didn't answer.

Faust tilted his head. "Tell me, do you actually believe it'll stay this way? That she'll keep reaching for you?"

Something flickered—not in Theodin. In the Dyad.

A tug. A shift.

Ophelia.

She felt Theodin's surge of rage that he tried to suppress.

And Faust saw it in Theodin's piercing, focused gaze as they hardened further.

But it didn't deter the Valksha boy.

"Because I hate to break it to you, Theo, but sooner or later…"

He flipped the dagger over his knuckles, voice dropping just slightly. Sharper.

"She won't have to."

Theodin stopped. The dummy swung—he blocked it with ease, but the dummy's arm splintered to pieces.

Faust grinned. "There it is."

Theodin turned his head slowly. His fearsome eyes burned. He nearly growled at Faust.

"Leave."

Faust flicked the tip of his dagger, unfazed.

"Now, why would I do that?"

Theodin glowered.

"Because I'm asking you to."

Faust shrugged, eyes half-lidded, unconcerned.

"That's not a very compelling reason."

Theodin exhaled harshly through his nose. His fingers curled as his pulse hammered in his ears. He could feel the Dyad whirring restlessly.

Faust smirked. He knew.

"Tell me, Theodin—"

His voice was almost amused.

"Do you know what she's been thinking about since she woke up?"

Theodin's jaw locked.

Faust's grin widened. "I do."

The dummy swung with its other arm. But Theodin moved out of its way—not toward it.

In the blink of an eye, he nearly vanished.

One second, Faust was standing.

The next—he was on the ground.

Theodin had him by the throat. His grip was tight and suffocating.

Faust gasped, caught between a laugh and a choke.

"Oh?" Faust managed, lips curling. "Struck a nerve, did I?"

Theodin's fingers tightened.

Faust gagged.

Though he wasn't a Valksha of Veladriel, he could still somehow feel a surge coming from Theodin.

Not anger. Not frustration. Something else.

Something ancient. Raw. Wrong.

The grin on his face faltered.

Faust struggled and gasped for air, grasping at Theodin's wrist and kicking for freedom.

Her voice boomed across the field.

"Stop!"

Suddenly, a burst of green energy exploded between them.

Theodin didn't even see it coming. It hit him like a shockwave. Not violent. Not destructive. Just enough to knock the wind out of him. His grip broke. He flew and hit the ground, landing on his back.

Faust sucked in a breath, his hands bracing against the dirt. He looked at Ophelia—and for the first time, he didn't seem to recognize her.

Theodin stared at her with wide eyes.

She was standing nearby, her body humming with green light, her breath coming in quick, uneven exasperated huffs. Her hands trembled —unscathed by pricks or scratches. She did not use blood this time.

But then, the light around her dimmed. The runes along her arm flickered. Her fingers twitched. Before Theodin or Faust could move, Ophelia's knees buckled.

She collapsed.

Theodin and Faust both stared. Neither of them moved at first; they were both too shocked.

Sarys was the first to reach her. The owl dove down and landed beside her. His wings flared slightly as he nudged her shoulder.

His voice was sharp. No amusement. No teasing. Just full of alarm.

"Darling?"

She remained motionless, face-first in the grass.

Theodin stiffly picked himself up and began to stumble to her.

Faust scrambled to his feet and rushed to her, reaching her first. He hit his knees on the ground beside her, fingers hovering over her arm, hesitant, as if touching her might make it worse.

"Lia," he murmured, his voice lacking its usual sharpness. He hovered his hand over her forehead, but she barely stirred. Her skin was too pale, and her breath came in weak, ragged gasps.

Theodin finally fell to one knee at her other side, holding his chest in pain.

Faust sucked in a sharp breath and whipped his worried eyes to Theodin.

"She's drained."

Theodin's jaw tightened.

"She's not supposed to be," he strained through clenched teeth.

His eyes flicked to Faust, searching, accusing.

Faust met his gaze, his fingers curling against the dirt. For once, there was no grin, no lazy amusement. Just a slow, cold realization settling between them. A silence heavy with something neither of them wanted to say.

* * *

Year 845 of the Second Age, Seventh Month, Twenty-Seventh Day

Faust had never been good at feeling helpless. It sat wrong in his chest. Like an itch beneath the skin he couldn't scratch—something clawing, gnawing, mocking.

He had felt it before. When he was taken. When he was bound, experimented on, and left to rot.

When Ophelia found him.

She had saved him that day. And then again, when she healed him in the chamber. When she reached out and stitched his wounds back together with magic. Magic that was pure and warm.

She had his back. Always.

And now she was dying. Again.

Faust sat at her bedside, his fingers drumming restlessly against his knee. He chewed his lip, his body stiff.

He didn't pray—not this time.

He had tried that before, muttering old Valksha rites under his breath, letting the words spill from his lips like they meant something.

They hadn't this time. Maybe they never did.

Ophelia still suffered.

Theodin still held the piece of her that Faust never could.

His fingers curled into fists. He inhaled slowly through his nose and let it back out too quickly.

Sarys was perched on the bedpost, watching her. The bird had barely moved since they brought her in.

She looked so small like this. Like she was fading. Like she was slipping from his grasp, the same way she had when the Dyad first started eating at her.

He had fixed that. *He* had done that.

And yet, here she was again. Pale, weak, and barely breathing. Curled up into a ball beneath the sheets.

His thoughts plagued him.

Useless. I'm useless.

He sucked in a sharp breath and exhaled slowly this time.

No. He wouldn't sit here and do nothing. Not again.

A quiet shuffle outside the door caught his attention.

Voices. Low and serious.

Kaspar. Alfena.

Faust narrowed his eyes. Then, without a sound, he rose to his feet, and listened.

The door wasn't fully closed.

A sliver of candlelight spilled into the dim corridor, stretching across the stone floor. Faust pressed himself against the wall, his heartbeat a steady, muted drum in his ears.

He could hear them.

Kaspar's voice was calm, as always. Unshaken. Measured. But there was something beneath it tonight—something taut. Something uneasy.

"...If we sever the Dyad, the consequences will be severe," Kaspar was saying. "Even if we do it carefully, even if we use the proper rites, there will be damage."

Alfena sighed. "And if we don't?"

Silence.

Faust's fingers twitched.

Then Kaspar spoke again. "If we don't, they will both die."

The words hit like a hammer to the chest.

Faust held his breath, his teeth gritting.

He had *known*—had felt it the moment Ophelia collapsed, the moment her breathing turned shallow and the moment the Dyad warped into something unrecognizable.

But hearing it spoken aloud—hearing Kaspar confirm it—it made the truth sink deeper.

Ophelia and Theodin were dying. And the only solution the Kyriegard had was to break them apart.

A slow, sickening dread curled in Faust's gut.

Alfena's voice was quieter now. "And if we do sever it?"

Another pause.

Kaspar let out an audible, labored breath, like he hated the words before he even said them.

"Then Ophelia may not survive it. Not as she is now."

Faust's heart dropped into his stomach.

Not as she is now.

His mind latched onto that phrase, dissecting it, turning it over.

It wasn't just the Dyad keeping her alive. It wasn't just the bond she shared with Theodin.

It was something else.

His blood. His magic.

The bond *he* had forged when he healed her.

If they severed the Dyad, they would be severing him from her too.

And then she would certainly die.

He stepped back from the door, pulse hammering. His mouth had gone dry, his skin too hot.

"But she's the last Valksha of Veladriel," Alfena pressed. "There has to be a way to save her."

"It's either we lose one or both," Kaspar said. His voice sounded drained, as if it had aged by decades more than he was. There was a long pause before he spoke again. "Either way, at this rate…she likely will not live."

Faust would not let that happen.

His mind moved quickly—scenarios, possibilities, solutions—all spiraling toward one conclusion.

The Kyriegard were failing her.

Kaspar. Alfena. The Council. They would stand around, debating, weighing risks, and waiting.

Waiting too long.

But Faust? Faust had never been afraid of acting. If the Kyriegard wouldn't save her, *he* would.

If his Valksha magic stabilized her, if old Valksha and prayers to Elodyn helped somehow…then there was only one place that could possibly hold the key to saving her from the Dyad.

A Temple of Elodyn.

His hands clenched at his sides. He had heard the stories—whispers of old, ancient magic buried in the temple's grounds. A place where divine power lingered. Where lost things could be restored. Where the first Valksha were blessed by the Saryfim and generations of Valksha practiced their worship to the great creator spirit Elodyn.

Some still held sabbath, still tended to by the humble temple keepers. Others were abandoned and had became ruins.

It was a fool's errand. A gamble. But Faust had spent most of his life gambling with fate.

He turned on his heel, moving swiftly back toward Ophelia's bedside. She was still unconscious and deathly pale. Her breath came in lethargic, uneven pulls. He crouched beside her, watching her face.

"She had my back," he murmured. His voice was hoarse and low.

Then, softer—

"Now it's my turn."

He stood. He knew what he had to do.

Now, he just had to take her. And no one was going to stop him.

Since he overheard Kaspar and Alfena, Faust's heart would not stop racing with fear and adrenaline.

As soon as Alfena left for Halvalla and he knew Theodin and Kaspar were preoccupied for a long period of the night, he emerged with Ophelia in his arms, cradling her closely to his chest.

He moved through the dimly lit halls of Avasylon, his boots barely making a sound against the cold stone floor. Every instinct told him to hurry, but he didn't rush.

Rushing got you caught. Rushing got you killed.

His grip tightened around Ophelia's arm. She hardly stirred. She was still too pale, her breath shallow, and her body slumped heavily against him.

This was the right choice. It had to be.

His mind raced with every scenario and every possible outcome. They would notice she was gone soon. He had to get her out before then.

It was midnight. The halls of Avasylon were silent. The only sound was the distant flicker of torchlight and oil lamps, the faint whisper of wind through the wooden corridors.

Faust moved like a shadow, silent and unseen. Ophelia was in his arms; her body was limp, but she still breathing. Barely.

Her weight wasn't much—she had always been small—but tonight, she felt heavier. Not physically. Something else. Her head lolled against his shoulder; her breath was slow and uneven.

Faust stopped at the end of the hallway and cradled her closer, his jaw clenched as he listened—waited.

Nobody had noticed yet.

Kaspar was somewhere else tonight—probably at the Halvalla, dealing with Council matters. Theodin was locked in his own suffering, dying just as she was.

That was the only reason Faust was getting away with this.

That, and Sarys.

The owl familiar perched on the high wooden beam above them, his dark feathers blending into the ceiling shadows. He hadn't spoken since Faust picked up Ophelia. Hadn't questioned him. Hadn't stopped him.

And that was the part that unnerved Faust the most.

Sarys knew things. He always knew things. And yet, here he was, watching. Letting it happen. Faust didn't trust it. But he didn't have time to question it either.

He shifted Ophelia's weight in his arms, steadying her as he moved carefully down the stairs and toward the exit.

She stirred. Just slightly. A light twitch of her fingers against his chest.

Faust paused and inhaled sharply. He gently pressed his lips to the top of her head.

"Shh," he murmured. "Not yet, little owl."

Her eyelids fluttered, but she didn't fully wake. Her breathing hitched, her body tensing like some part of her knew something wasn't right.

Faust ignored the twist in his stomach.

He had to keep moving.

He reached the threshold of the main door, easing it open just enough to let in the cool night air. He shifted Ophelia's weight in his arms, careful, and steady.

And then—

A rustle of feathers. Faust went still.

Sarys perched on the nearby lantern sconce, his eyes gleaming in the dim torchlight.

Watching silently.

Faust met the owl's gaze, his heart thudding, hard. For the first time since meeting him, Sarys appeared… irritated.

He knew. Of course he knew.

Faust kept his voice quiet and firm.

"Move, bird."

Sarys remained. He tilted his head, blinking once, slowly. "And where do you think you're taking her?"

Faust's fingers curled against Ophelia's sleeve.

"Somewhere that will actually save her."

Sarys didn't react. Didn't argue. He simply looked.

Faust braced himself for resistance—for a sharp remark, a mocking jab, anything. But the owl just stared.

And then—

Sarys spread his wings. And he moved aside.

Faust exhaled with relief. "That's what I thought."

Sarys clicked his beak. "Don't mistake this for approval, little wolf."

Faust didn't respond. He adjusted his hold on Ophelia and stepped past him. Sarys followed.

By the time they reached the edge of Avasylon, the night had deepened. The wind carried the scent of damp stone and earth, crisp and cold.

Faust walked quickly with practiced ease, his movements fluid and natural. Like he belonged here. Like he wasn't just sneaking out a dying girl.

They reached the outer passage leading toward the northern woods. The air was cool against his skin, the night stretching open before them.

This was it.

One step through the gate, and there was no turning back. Faust exhaled slowly. Then, without looking up, he spoke.

"You're not stopping me."

Another rustle of feathers. A low, knowing hum.

"Should I?"

Faust's grip tightened on Ophelia.

"You tell me."

Sarys was quiet for a moment. Then—

A soft click of his beak. "No."

Faust turned his head, frowning.

Sarys tilted his own. Watching. Waiting.

Faust narrowed his eyes. "Why?"

A long pause. Then, in a voice too smooth, too certain—

"Because you are meant to do this."

Faust's stomach twisted. He didn't like the way that sounded. But that didn't stop him.

Ophelia shifted in his grasp. A faint murmur left her lips, barely above a whisper.

Faust glanced down. Her brows furrowed slightly, her fingers twitching weakly against his sleeve. "…Faust?"

His jaw clenched.

"You're alright," he murmured, adjusting his hold. "Just rest."

Her breath hitched. "Where…?"

Faust hesitated. She was still too out of it to fight him. To resist.

"Somewhere safe."

She stirred again, her fingers curling weakly into the fabric of his tunic. A flicker of trust. Even now, when she was barely conscious—she trusted him.

His stomach twisted again and made him sick. He turned his gaze forward and kept walking.

They went just past the gates. Beyond them, the woods stretched into darkness, the path barely visible beneath the moonlight. Faust sucked in a breath. He had planned this carefully. Every step, every turn, every possible obstacle. He could get them to the Temple of Elodyn by morning.

He just needed to move faster.

He turned to Sarys, who landed on the ground nearby.

"We need to fly."

Sarys regarded him coolly.

"And you assume I'll be the one to carry you."

"She won't survive the journey on foot."

Sarys tilted his head. He knew Faust was right. A long silence stretched between them.

Then—Sarys shifted.

His form unraveled, twisting into something large and ancient. His massive wings stretched against the night sky, his talons digging into the ground. The air crackled with lingering magic.

Faust wasted no time. He climbed onto Sarys' back, securing Ophelia in his arms. Once more, she twitched slightly.

"Faust…"

A weak breath, almost a whisper. "…don't."

She faded before she could finish, sinking into his grasp.

Faust looked down at her face. In the pale moonlight, she appeared even more sickly and frail. Was this the right thing to do? Was this going to save her?

Yes. This was the point of no return. If they went back now, she would die with the Kyriegard.

He gently kissed her forehead.

"Don't worry, love," he whispered back.

The owl let out a deep, piercing cry, and then they were airborne.

The wind howled around them, the ground disappearing beneath their feet. The cold of the open night air bit into Faust's skin, but he didn't care. He had her. She was safe.

And nothing—not Theodin, not Kaspar, not the Kyriegard—would take her from him now.

Theodin awoke gasping.

A sharp, violent breath ripped through his lungs, his body lurching upright. His vision swam. His skin felt clammy, too hot, too cold, and wrong.

Why was his dream empty? It wasn't that he didn't dream, or had forgotten it. It was a *void*. He shouted into nothing.

Where was…?

The Dyad. It was slipping.

His hands clenched the sheets. Something was missing.

No—*someone* was missing.

Ophelia.

His breath came faster, his pulse hammering against his ribs. He reached for the Dyad—pulled—

Nothing. No answer. No presence. Only an empty, dull silence.

His body shuddered. He felt sick. Where was she?

He threw off the blankets, his legs barely held him as he staggered toward the door. His mind and body were screaming.

He reached the hallway, his breath coming in ragged gasps. Where —?

Then, a voice—pointed, urgent.

Kaspar.

Theodin's stomach dropped.

"Where is she?" Kaspar's tone was tight, controlled—but beneath it, there was something else. Something close to fear.

Theodin turned the corner—and saw Kaspar standing stiffly in the dim corridor, his eyes dark, his lips pressed into a thin line.

The words barely made it past Theodin's throat.

"...She's gone."

Kaspar's gaze flicked to him. He nodded grimly.

"Yes."

Theodin's heart stopped.

Then started again—in a roar.

Chapter 45

The Flight and Fight

The flight was silent.

The wind howled past them, cold and piercing, biting through the layers of Faust's clothes. Sarys's wings beat steadily and powerfully beneath them; the rhythmic motion was the only thing that kept Faust grounded.

He held Ophelia tighter.

She hadn't stirred since they left the ground. Her breath was shallow, her skin cold. Too cold. His jaw clenched.

Not yet. Not yet, love.

The temple came into view below—tucked deep within the valley, shrouded in mist. From above, it looked as if it was untouched by time. The old stone walls stretched high, laced with ivy, kissed by the glow of moonlight. The spires, once pristine, now wore the weight of centuries. Somehow its architecture—perhaps with its simplistic design yet massive size—held a presence both humble and majestic all at once.

Holy ground. Sacred. Powerful. And Faust hated it.

He had spent most of his life running from places like this. From whispers of the divine. From the relics of the past that promised salvation to the worthy and destruction to the damned.

He wasn't worthy. But she was.

Sarys banked lower, circling once before descending. His talons scraped against the stone courtyard as he landed. Faust barely waited for him to settle before leaping down, keeping Ophelia steady in his arms.

The temple was quiet. Too quiet.

Faust ignored the feeling curling in his gut.

He moved. Quickly.

The temple doors loomed before him; their heavy oak frame was carved with old Valksha runes—words he didn't bother reading.

He shouldered one of the double doors open and stepped inside.

It was immense. The main chamber stretched high into vaulted ceilings, supported by towering pillars of stone and worn painted gold. Moonlight filtered through the stained glass windows, casting kaleidoscopic shapes onto the marble floors. At the center of the room, an altar stood beneath an enormous statue of an artistic depiction of a humanoid Elodyn, arms outstretched.

A beacon of mercy. A symbol of peace.

Faust didn't stop to admire it.

He moved toward the altar, lowering Ophelia onto the smooth stone floor. She barely made a sound.

He pressed a hand to her forehead.

Still burning. Still fading. But still here.

His fingers curled. He could do this. He had done it before.

Faust inhaled sharply, rolling his wrist. He pulled out the dagger from his pocket and unsheathed it, flipping it once before catching it by the hilt.

He knew what Ophelia would say if she were awake. She would try to stop him.

But she wasn't awake.

He set the blade to his palm and pressed down.

A sharp sting. A breath. Blood welled instantly, dark and thick. He turned his palm downward, letting the drops fall onto her forearm, onto the runes of the Arcane Dyad.

The moment his blood touched her, the reaction was instant. They became glimmers of royal blue and sank into her flesh.

Ophelia gasped. Her back arched slightly; her fingers twitched. The Dyad pulsed. But so did something else.

Faust clenched his jaw. He ignored the creeping unease, forcing his magic deeper. The blue glow flickered over her skin, seeping into her veins, wrapping itself around the fragile threads of the Dyad.

Fix her. Keep her here.

Then—

The room shifted. Faust's breath caught.

The air felt thicker. The temple walls groaned, as if responding to his presence, to his magic.

And then—

The stained glass shattered.

Faust moved before he thought.

His dagger was still in his hand as he threw himself over her, shielding her beneath him. Sarys let out a warning screech, wings flaring as he took to the air—

And slammed into an invisible barrier.

The owl-dragon shrieked.

Faust twisted just in time to see it—dark sigils burning into the air, encasing Sarys in a trap.

No.

No, no, no—

A slow, mocking laugh echoed through the chamber.

Faust's blood ran cold.

Azazelf.

The Unseelie Elf stepped from the shadows beyond the altar, his silver hair gleaming under the fractured moonlight. His eyes—black pools of the Nether—fixed on Faust, brimming with amusement. Only shadows of his sickening, demonic, Elvish face shaped into his view. Hollow cheeks made the outlines of his jaw and cheek bones almost appear like a pale, monstrous skull.

"Well," Azazelf drawled. "Took you long enough."

Faust's grip on his dagger tightened.

Azazelf flicked his wrist. The sigils glowed brighter, tightening around Sarys. The owl screeched again, his form writhing and transforming, now trapped in his smaller state.

"You're making this far too easy, little Faust."

Faust moved again as quick as he could.

His dagger flashed as he lunged—

He never reached him.

A force slammed into his ribs, sending him flying backward. He hit the floor hard, his breath wrenching from his lungs.

Darkness surrounded them. Cold, seething energy that brimmed with remnants of the Nether.

Devious hissing and snarling echoed against the stone.

Warthralls.

They stepped into view, surrounding the chamber. Some appeared human, others did not. Some were twisted shapes of black, others in tattered remnants of something humane. Their dark armor gleamed, their weapons were drawn, and their bodies were twisted and corrupted by the magic that bound them to Azazelf's will.

Faust rolled onto his hands and knees, coughing.

Azazelf stepped forward slowly and deliberately.

"You really thought you could just take her and leave?"

His voice was smooth, almost gentle.

"That the Kyriegard would be your biggest problem?"

Faust forced himself upright, his vision swimming.

"If you wanted to kill me, you should've done it already."

Azazelf smirked.

"Oh, Faust."

He tilted his head, voice sickly sweet.

"I don't need to kill you."

Then, with a flick of his fingers—

The Warthralls seized Ophelia.

Faust's world snapped. He lunged, but the Warthralls were faster. Their chains wrapped around Ophelia's arms, her body still limp, her breath still weak. Too weak to fight back.

Faust yelled out desperately.

"No!"

The same force as before pinned him down against the marble with a painful thud. He groaned and struggled to writhe himself free of the unseen grip on his body.

The Warthralls lifted up Ophelia to Azazelf. The Unseelie fiend sneered with a sadistic smile and brought a bony, pale hand up to stroke her hair from her face. A glimmer of her emerald irises peered back at him helplessly through the slightest open slits of her eyes.

"Wonderful," Azazelf exhaled with a sickening satisfaction. "Perfect, even. The Saryf of Spirit and Heart."

A deep, menacing chuckle escaped him.

"Maybe you will be the key, little Valksha… the key to bring back what was stolen from me." He leaned in and smiled wider, hissing in a whisper. "My own spirit and heart."

Ophelia flinched, but she still could not move. The runes on her arms flickered once dimly and then died out.

Azazelf's eyes flicked to the runes. For a moment—just a moment—

his expression wasn't amusement or cruelty. It was something else. Calculation. Realization.

And then, he smiled.

"And even better…a Valksha of the Kyriegard. You'll be much more useful than the rest…" He brought a repulsive finger to her cheek and caressed her skin. "After so many centuries…you'll be the one."

Her runes flickered again in protest and a pained whimper escaped her as she winced at his touch.

"Don't touch her!" Faust screamed. "Keep your *bloody* hands off of her!"

Azazelf glanced over his shoulder at him.

Faust's voice and heart roared. "Let. Her. *Go.*"

Azazelf watched him blankly. His expression then softened—mocking. *Pitying.*

"Faust," he murmured. "You can't save her."

Faust snarled.

Azazelf stepped closer, his voice lowering. Too gentle.

"You never could."

Faust's breath hitched. His vision blurred.

His body locked up.

No. No, no, no—

Pain burned through his back. Through the searing thing behind his throbbing heart.

Azazelf smiled. "Ah. There you are."

Faust gasped. The air vanished from his lungs.

His limbs seized. The magic coiled around him, crawling under his skin, suffocating—

No—he had fought this—he was fighting this—

Azazelf leaned in, his voice a whisper.

"You don't have to fight it anymore."

Faust's vision whitened. His body convulsed.

And then—

Faust stopped fighting. Stopped thinking.

Something sinister took hold.

His eyes turned black.

And Faust was gone.

She was gone. Then suddenly, Kaspar was gone too.

All Theodin saw was red.

Theodin ran. His boots hit the hard wood of Avasylon's cottage corridor, every step faster than the last.

Where.

Where.

Where.

Faust.

The realization struck hard and fast, rattling through his skull like a hammer against iron.

It was Faust's energy. Theodin could tell by the way this felt. Ophelia's healing was pure, light, and warm. This was… assertive.

Faust had healed her. Healed *him*. Even from afar. Which meant he was still with her. Which meant—

A snarl curled through Theodin's teeth. His body moved before his mind could catch up.

His blood was rushing, his hands clenched into fists, and his entire body screamed. The Dyad was barely guiding him anymore. Something else was instead.

The wind. The scent. The trail.

His heartbeat. The way his body leaned forward, like he knew exactly where to go.

And then—

The gates. The *open* gates.

Theodin slammed his shoulder against the doorframe as he came to a halt. His breath was heavy, uneven, his fingers gripping the stone and crumbling under his grasp.

A scent. Familiar. Faint. Not just Ophelia's.

Faust's.

He was tracking him.

Theodin didn't think. Didn't hesitate. He threw himself forward, out of Avasylon's abode, into the cold and into the trees. The moment the night air hit his face, he felt it.

The Dyad pulsed. Weak. Flickering. Still calling. Still leading him straight to her.

Theodin sprinted. The wind lashed against his skin, the branches clawed at his clothes, and the cold stabbed at his lungs.

He didn't care.

His body moved like it had always known how to do this. Like he had always been made for this. And maybe he was.

Maybe he was always meant to hunt. To tear through whatever was in his way. Because nothing—nothing—was going to stop him from reaching her.

Not this time.

It loomed ahead. A broken silhouette against the night sky. The Temple of Elodyn.

And it wasn't empty.

Theodin saw them first. The Warthralls. Wrapped in shadows were figures in dark armor watching, pacing, and waiting.

His breath slowed. Focused. He wasn't even at the entrance yet, but his body was already bracing.

Something was coming.

Theodin didn't give them time to react.

He lunged.

His blade flashed. The first Warthrall's throat opened before it even had a chance to scream.

The second turned too slowly. Theodin's fist slammed into its ribs, cracking through the armor.

The third one barely had time to reach for its sword because Theodin was already there.

Already tearing through them.

The screams barely registered. Blood splattered against the cold stone. But he wasn't done.

His breath came sharper, his body was heavier, his mind felt fuzzier. There was no hesitation left. No second thoughts.

Only one thing mattered.

Finding her.

Getting to her.

Killing anything in his way.

And with every body that fell, something inside him cracked further.

Something was waking. Something that had been waiting far too long.

The towering Kyriegard apprentice now stood at the temple's threshold, his breath burdened, muscles coiled, his blade dripping.

The Warthralls—the ones who were still standing—had stopped moving.

They saw what he had done. The bodies he tore through. The way he had reduced them into pieces with a precision too ruthless, too instinctive, too unnatural. For the first time, they hesitated.

Even Azazelf hesitated. The dark Elf's lips curled just slightly—not in amusement this time, not in control.

In irritation. In disbelief.

He had planned for this. He had anticipated resistance, expected the Kyriegard to interfere, or for Nimrod Kaspar or Alfena Marobe to stand in his way.

Not this… apprentice boy. Not like this.

What was *this?* What *was* he?

A muscle twitched in Azazelf's jaw. His fingers flexed at his side. It was time to adjust.

His gaze flicked toward Ophelia. Still bound. Still weak. Still dying. But only if she stayed that way.

He turned curtly.

"Kill him."

The Warthralls surged.

Theodin welcomed it.

The first came at him with a broadsword—sloppy.

Theodin ducked, twisted, and drove his own blade through the gap in the armor at its ribs. He barely had time to rip it free before the next one lunged.

A second too slow. Theodin caught it by the throat.

The Warthrall gasped, clawing at his grip, its sword falling from its grasp—he crushed its windpipe before it could hit the floor.

And then—more.

A storm of steel, of bodies, of voices shouting in that rasping, empty way that marked them as puppets of the Nether.

Theodin's blade flashed a blur of red and silver.

Another dropped.

Another.

He didn't stop.

He didn't feel the burning in his arms or the exhaustion in his limbs.

Only the heat of it. The fury.

Something cold and dark was coiling at the edges of his mind.

Ophelia heard everything from a distance. She could see only black.

But she had never felt the Dyad like this.

Not burning. Not flickering. But thrashing. Like it was on the verge of breaking.

Theodin.

She could barely lift her head, barely focus through the haze of pain and exhaustion, but she could feel him.

She choked on her breath.

No.

She had to stop this madness.

She pulled at the chains around her wrists. Too tight. Too strong.

Her fingers twitched.

She needed blood. She needed *blood.*

Her pulse pounded against the metal, against her skin. She bit down on her lip hard enough to split it. The taste of iron hit her tongue, and the runes on her arms flared.

And then—

A whisper of warmth. A pulse of something else.

Faust gasped. For a brief, fleeting second—he felt like himself again. He stood next to Ophelia, guarded by a few Warthralls while others charged at the crowd of them screaming and shrieking battle cries through the temple.

Azazelf's hold faltered, just for a moment, and Faust could see again.

He turned.

He saw the chains around Ophelia and the struggle in her eyes.

Theodin was ripping through Warthralls.

Faust's fingers twitched.

He moved.

His knife sliced across his palm instinctively and splattered his blood onto the runes of her Dyad.

It pulsed. The magic ignited.

Her eyes widened—just before it hit her.

A surge of power—her power.

Her runes glowed brighter than ever.

Azazelf's head whipped toward them. His eyes flashed, and Faust heard Azazelf's voice hissing—

No.

The Unseelie fiend snarled. His wicked hand snapped back at Faust and his dark magic crashed hard back into Faust's mind, nearly knocking him back.

The moment of freedom was over. Faust convulsed. His eyes dulled. He collapsed onto his knees.

But it was too late. Ophelia had enough. She ripped free. The Dyad flared violently. The metal restraints snapped apart like they were made of brittle glass. The Warthralls around her staggered.

Azazelf turned fully, his composure cracking.

Ophelia stood, her arms trembling and her breath ragged—but her runes blazed. She lifted her hands. The magic surged through her veins, through her body, through the pain. She twisted her fingers—

And Sarys's cage shattered.

The owl launched forward, his form warping, twisting, and growing. His wings spread wide, dark and massive, the wind howling through the temple as he became something more.

A shadow of divine will. A creature of old Valksha power.

The owl-dragon's talons tore through the nearest Warthrall's throat. Then another.

Azazelf cursed under his breath.

Theodin saw none of it.

He saw Faust. Possessed. Controlled. Still kneeling, head lowered, like a broken puppet. His eyes were glazed over, dilated, and soulless.

Something in Theodin snapped. He lunged at Azazelf.

A loud clang of metal rang through the air amidst the shrieking of dying Warthrall at the enormous talons of the owl-dragon.

His blade met Faust's dagger. The clash shook the ground.

Faust held his ground. Their blades locked.

Faust's lips curled into a snarl—not his own. Azazelf's. His completely blackened eyes glowered at Theodin.

"You never deserved her," Azazelf's voice murmured through Faust's lips.

Theodin's vision went red. He swung. Faust barely dodged.

Their swords collided again. And again.

But Faust was faster.

His blade slashed across Theodin's side.

Theodin staggered. Blood dripped.

Faust thrust his bloodied hand toward him. A crackle of an electric blue current shot from his palm at Theodin.

Theodin was thrown far back into the wall. The collision caused a giant fissure to crack in the stone, and the structure groaned and crumbled slightly at such a wound.

Theodin stumbled out, singed and covered in burns.

The Dyad lurched. Theodin swayed and collapsed.

And Ophelia—

She felt it.

She screamed. The magic erupted.

Her body was no longer her own.

The Dyad flared violently.

Her runes pulsed like wildfire.

Everything—*everything*—was green light and force and power.

She nearly flew.

One moment, Faust was standing over Theodin.

The next—Ophelia struck.

Her magic sent him flying across the space.

The Warthralls fell. Sarys ripped through them.

Azazelf—

His voice hissed in her head.

"You walk with power you do not deserve."

Azazelf vanished into the darkness like a coward.

Ophelia didn't care.

Her gaze locked onto Faust. Her body still hummed with power, her breath heavy, her hands trembling—but her target was clear.

Her power had fully awoken.

The temple was burning. Not with fire, but with magic.

Ophelia stood amidst the wreckage, her breath coming fast, her hands trembling, her runes glowing brighter than ever.

She had never felt this way before. Not even when she had fought to survive. Not even when she had first used her magic.

This was different. This was war.

And Faust—was in her way.

When he hovered back onto his feet, he stood at the other end of the chamber, his posture stiff and unnatural. His dagger hung loosely at his side, his expression blank—Azazelf's grip still tight around his mind.

His lips curled, but the smirk wasn't his own. Azazelf smiled through him.

"You've never looked more like a *Valksha,* little owl," he murmured. His voice was silk and venom. "But tell me—will you finally kill like one?"

Ophelia's fingers twitched. The Dyad was still burning in her veins, still lashing out like a wounded animal.

Faust wasn't Faust.

She knew that. She *knew* that.

But she couldn't—*wouldn't*—hesitate.

Because Theodin was still on the ground. Bleeding. Burned. Wounded.

And if she didn't stop this now, Faust would kill him.

Faust lunged. Ophelia moved. Their blades met—her dagger against his. The clash sent a shockwave through the chamber, stone cracking beneath them as magic collided with metal.

Faust's movements were erratic—too fast, too sharp, too *wrong*. He wasn't fighting as himself. He was fighting as something else. Something controlled.

Something *consumed*.

He knocked her blade away and reeled back with his other hand, about to strike with a current of blue electricity—

She yelled out and hurled a burst of her own explosion of green energy, shoving him back.

His body limply and grossly fell back like a marionette puppet, limbs flailed, then snapped back into place as it pulled back together.

He threw himself at her and swung again. Harder.

Ophelia barely dodged, twisting away, her feet skidding against the temple floor.

Faust came at her again.

This time—she wasn't fast enough. His blade sliced through her side. She gasped, the pain white-hot. Burning.

She let out a yelp.

Her knees buckled, but she didn't fall.

She clenched her fists, her own blood dripping down her fingers. Her runes reacted.

The energy *snapped*.

And then—she attacked.

Faust barely had time to react before Ophelia flung him backward.

Not physically but with power.

Green light erupted again from her palm, colliding into him like a wave, sending him crashing into the temple wall once more. The impact cracked stone, and the fissure climbed higher.

Faust coughed and staggered, but he didn't fall.

Ophelia was already moving. She didn't give him time to recover. She closed the distance between them, her dagger flashing and her magic humming.

She struck, lashing her chained blade.

Again. Again. *Again*.

Faust blocked the first two blows.

The third, he barely dodged.

The fourth—hit.

She snatched the handle of her dagger and sank into his shoulder.

Faust choked. His eyes flickered.

For a *single second*—Azazelf's control faltered.

His voice was his own.

"Ophelia—"

The intensity in her eyes dropped. She gasped.

"Faust!"

A growl escaped Faust—but it was Azazelf's, not his.

His power slammed into Faust like a whip, dragging him back into submission. Faust's body jerked, stumbling back from her—the blade of the chained blade deep in his shoulder and sticking out the other side.

And then—he was gone again.

"Pathetic thing," he hissed. "Useless!"

Azazelf was done.

He had underestimated this. Underestimated her.

He should have known better.

She was a Valksha. And Valksha were made to kill things like him.

With a snarl of frustration, Azazelf flicked his wrist.

Something burned in Faust's back.

Faust screamed.

In one violent motion, a small, circular piece of intricate metal ripped out from the middle of his back and flew into Azazelf's clawed grasp.

His fingers curled around the medallion. The magic resisted, thrumming against his palm, rejecting him. A disgruntled growl came from his throat.

Ophelia's eyes whipped to Azazelf and widened.

The Medallion of Zadkiel.

Faust screamed again. The moment the medallion left his skin, he collapsed. His body convulsed, his breath was ragged, and his entire form shook violently.

Her shriek echoed in the temple.

"Faust!"

Azazelf didn't stay to watch. He turned—a portal of darkness already curling open behind him.

But before he could step through—

Ophelia's energy surged.

Her voice boomed.

"Azazelf Chernabog!"

Azazelf staggered sideways. Azazelf's head snapped toward her—his eyes widened in horror.

Her rifle was in her hands. The barrel aimed at him.

Her emerald eyes burned at him with ire, illuminated with a blazing green light.

She pulled the trigger. The shot tore through the air.

Azazelf dodged, but not fast enough. The bullet, made of pure Valksha energy, ripped across his cheek.

He hissed—not in pain.

In *fury*.

He turned, his face twisted with rage. A dark streak seared into the hollow crater of his sickly flesh.

But the portal pulled him in—and he was gone.

His final words echoed in the chamber.

"This isn't over. You will be mine, little Valksha."

Silence.

Ophelia's rifle trembled in her hands. Still pointed where the portal vanished.

Faust's body twitched on the floor, his breath shallow.

Ophelia's pulse pounded. Her head whirled to him.

No.

No, no, no—

Her rifle clattered onto the ground as she ran to him. She fell to her knees beside him, her hands already glowing, already trying—trying to fix this. She scooped him up and laid him in her lap, drawing more blood with the prick of her needle ring.

"Faust," she huffed. Her fingers hovered over his chest. "You're alright, you're alright—"

She stopped.

It wasn't just the cold of his body but the cold of his spirit that shook her.

His skin was fading. His hair was turning white.

The condemned state of a dying Valksha.

She had seen it once before. She didn't know what it meant at the time when Lady Vivian's hair turned white, but she knew what it meant now.

So did he. They learned about it together when they studied whatever Valksha tomes they could get their hands on.

And now, he felt it.

His hand weakly came up to clasp around hers to keep her from using her magic. It was futile.

Ophelia's face twisted with grief.

"Faust," she choked.

His fingers twitched. His eyes opened—barely. The shade of royal blue was no longer shimmering in his eyes. Now, it was a dark color Ophelia could not discern. He looked at her slowly.

And then—he smiled. It wasn't cocky. It wasn't a smirk. It was small. Sweet. A boy's smile.

The boy he had been before Azazelf took him.

And then—

He spoke.

"You always—"

He coughed, his breath rattling.

"You always have to fix things, don't you, little owl?"

Ophelia let out a broken sound, squeezing his hand.

"Shut up."

Faust huffed a weak laugh.

Then—his expression softened. His fingers twitched again against hers. He pressed her closed hand into his chest.

"Ophelia," he murmured.

Something in his voice made her chest ache. His lips parted.

"I…I loved you. Still do. Always will."

He choked slightly and shuddered, trying to find the strength to speak.

"I wish you felt the same way I did about me. But your heart is…"

He struggled. His eyes closed, and a stream of tears spilled on either side of them.

"W…What matters now is that you are safe. You're alive."

His smile widened bitterly. His grip tightened, trembling over her hand.

"And you'll live. Live your life to the fullest."

Once more, his eyes opened to look into hers.

"Now I wish I just…could've been there with you to see it watch you live…and love you from afar."

Ophelia's throat tightened. Tears fell down her cheeks

was growing lighter. He was slipping. She gritted her teeth and willed her magic to activate.

"I can fix this," she whispered. "I can fix this, I can—"

Faust grunted and tried to shake his head.

"No, love," he whispered back. "I'm sorry…for everything. For causing you—and Theo—any pain…for all this."

Ophelia gasped out a sob.

"Faust, please…"

His eyes only softened further, and so did his smile.

"It's okay, Lia."

And then—he let go. His eyes closed and his head slumped against her chest, like he was falling asleep. His last breath exhaled like a sigh of relief.

Ophelia felt it happen.

Not just in her hands.

In the Dyad. In the piece of him he left behind.

Her fingers curled around his shirt, desperate.

Her breath hitched—her voice broke—

"Please—"

But Faust was already gone.

Ophelia held him.

And for the first time—she held death in her hands.

Chapter 46

The Aftermath

Year 845 of the Second Age, Seventh Month, Twenty-Eighth Day

Kaspar stood at the head of the Council chamber, his expression weary, his hands braced on the polished oak table.

Across from him, Margrith Gravehardt nearly held her breath from tension, her knuckles white against the wood. Alfena Marobe sat rigid beside her, her silver gaze sharp beneath furrowed brows. Sigvard Jackard and Azariah Crane exchanged a glance—one heavy with things unsaid.

The air was thick with what had happened.

Kaspar had barely found his voice to summon them before Theodin was already gone—vanished into the night like something out of a nightmare.

He had never seen his apprentice move like that.

He had seen discipline, he had seen ferocity, but he had never seen something so primal.

The look in Theodin's eyes had not been that of a boy desperate to save his partner.

It had been the gaze of a predator.

And Kaspar hadn't stopped him.

He knew better than to make the same mistake twice. Not like the workshop in Slymound. Not again. He had called for help, summoned the Council through the Order's Collective—brought the Council themselves to witness whatever would unfold.

But it hadn't been enough. One of them was still lost. The temple had been a ruin when they arrived.

Faust's body lay in Ophelia's lap, her trembling fingers tangled in his blood-matted hair, her green energy still cracking the stone beneath her.

Sobbing. Shaking. The sound of her sorrowful wailing had been enough to chill the bones of even the most hardened Kyriegard.

Theodin lay nearby—unconscious but alive. But it wasn't his survival that had drawn whispers.

It was the bodies.

Warthralls, in dozens. A hundred. Scattered, torn, slaughtered in a frenzy unlike anything the Council had seen before.

Even now, Kaspar felt the weight of the question hanging between them.

How much of that had been Theodin?

How much of it had been something else?

Alfena had been the one to approach Ophelia, her voice gentle, her touch careful as she coaxed the girl to heal his and her wounds. She hadn't done it right away. Hadn't even noticed.

The Dyad should have forced her to heal him immediately. But it hadn't.

Why?

Kaspar had his suspicions. And he didn't like them.

Upon debriefing, the only one who could speak for both apprentices was Sarys.

The owl was perched now on the back of a chair before the Council, his dark feathers ruffled slightly, but his voice was calm and level.

He explained as thoroughly as he could how the events came to be, how Ophelia unleashed her power, how Theodin came to their rescue, and how Ophelia was just a few inches from blowing Azazelf's head off with a blast of her rifle. And of course, how Faust met his demise.

"Faust Grigorescu, truly known as Faust of the Eridane, an unfortunate Sage initiate of the Sage Circle Eridane," Sarys began, "fell victim to Azazelf's experiments as a child. The rest of his Sage Circle was sacrificed to Azazelf's demon patron, Chernabog."

The silence in the chamber shifted.

Sarys's voice did not waver. He was stating facts. But beneath the facts, the truth was unbearable.

"Lady Vivian had chased the 'Demon Elf' to the ends of Moirand for decades. Everywhere he went, he left chaos and destruction in his wake."

"Azazelf had tried relentlessly to make his own Valksha. Every effort failed. Every attempt ended in death. Hundreds of corrupted bodies. Hundreds of failed vessels."

Sarys's glowing eyes flicked to Kaspar.

"Until Faust."

Kaspar breathed out slowly through his nose.

The others did not interrupt. Sarys continued.

"Azazelf modified his memories. Remade him. Used the Medallion of Zadkiel to tether him to Warthrall corruption, forging a new kind of magic out of a Sage's body. A living abomination. But one that worked."

Alfena's hands curled into fists. "And now we know why Azazelf wanted Ophelia."

Kaspar's jaw tensed. "A living Valksha. One untrained. One who hadn't yet tapped into the full potential of her bloodline."

"And one who wouldn't immediately end herself if she were taken," Sigvard muttered darkly.

Silence.

They all knew what he meant.

Every Valksha before Ophelia—every single one that Azazelf had attempted to capture or corrupt—had chosen death. They had turned their own magic against themselves rather than allow his hands to twist them into something unnatural.

They knew their death would be final. A Valksha, once ended, never came back from the dead.

But Ophelia?

She was different. Not because she was weak—but because she wasn't.

Because she was the last.

And because she had something to lose.

A survivor.

"The only one who wasn't afraid of him," Sarys said quietly, "was Lady Vivian."

Kaspar exhaled sharply. "She was untouchable."

"Azazelf feared her the most," Sarys agreed. "Every attempt on her life was futile. She fought and won every time. And she was terribly difficult to track or trap."

Sigvard scoffed. "Of course she was."

Alfena's gaze flickered. "And Ophelia?"

Sarys's expression didn't change.

"She survived."

The words sat heavy in the chamber.

Kaspar's fingers curled against the table. His voice was low but steady.

"What happened at the temple, Sarys?"

The owl's emerald eyes flickered.

"They won. But they did not leave unscathed."

"How did they do it?" Margrith suddenly asked.

Sarys shook his wings slightly with discomfort.

"Well, I did some of the work, of course…but truthfully, I was incapacitated for a good lot of it by a Warthrall seal."

His head turned to the window with a distant look.

"Much of it was your golden boy, Theodin."

Kaspar's expression darkened. "Elaborate."

Sarys's feathers ruffled again.

"You'll have to forgive me, but I wasn't exactly present for much of the carnage. I was still trapped in Azazelf's little seal, and by the time I was freed, he—"

He nodded toward the direction of the Halvalla guest chambers, where Theodin was kept

"—had already painted the temple black and red."

There was a murmur of unease between the Council members.

Sigvard leaned forward, his fingers steepled.

"We saw the bodies." His gravelly voice carried a weight of measured concern. "But tell us… was it trained precision or sheer brutality?"

Sarys gave a pointed, knowing look. "Yes."

The silence thickened.

Crane spoke next, his brow furrowing.

"We all saw the aftermath. It was… efficient." He paused, choosing his words carefully. "But if we're asking whether Theodin fought like a Kyriegard, or like something else—"

Sarys cut in smoothly. "You already know the answer."

Alfena's sharp silver gaze flicked toward Kaspar.

"You've always claimed he has Procerian blood. That his size, his strength, his instincts—"

Her lips pressed thin.

"But it was more than that, wasn't it?"

Kaspar clenched his jaw.

"Even among the strongest Kyriegard," Sigvard interjected, "that was not normal."

A pause.

Sarys tilted his head. "No. It wasn't."

Margrith, who had been silent for much of the discussion, finally spoke. Her voice was low, but firm.

"You're worried."

Sarys regarded her for a long moment.

"I would be a fool not to be."

Kaspar straightened. "If you're implying that Theodin is a liability —"

"I'm implying," Sarys interrupted smoothly, "that if none of you are acknowledging what happened, then we have bigger problems."

His emerald eyes glinted in the torchlight.

"Because whatever broke free that night in the temple? You're all pretending it was just a boy swinging a sword."

Another weighted silence.

Margrith inhaled deeply and then she glanced at the others.

"Which means the question we should be asking isn't what he is."

She turned back to Kaspar.

"It's how much longer you can keep it contained."

The chamber remained heavy with unspoken words. The air, thick with deliberation, hung stagnant between them.

Kaspar did not move. Did not speak.

Margrith folded her arms. "You're avoiding the question."

Kaspar's eyes flicked to her sharply. "Am I?"

Sarys puffed slightly. "Yes."

Crane sighed. "He's seventeen, Kaspar. And he fought like a creature twice his size. And we're meant to believe it's just…" he gestured vaguely. "Procerian blood?"

The way he said it—like it was an excuse rather than an explanation—made something curl hot in Kaspar's chest.

"I trained that boy since he was a child," Kaspar said, voice measured. "I know exactly what he is."

Sarys let out a sharp huff of amusement. "Do you?"

Kaspar drew a piercing glare toward the owl.

Margrith interjected with a sigh, rubbing her temple.

"We can debate the boy's limits all night, but that's not what concerns me." Her gaze lifted to the room. "It's what happens next."

Alfena leaned forward slightly. "There is no precedent for a Dyad as strong as theirs. None." Her eyes hardened. "And there is certainly no precedent for what Theodin displayed in that temple."

"And Ophelia?" Margrith asked.

Alfena's voice was quiet.

"She's stable enough."

"The Elan Vitae?"

"Still there," Alfena explained. "But it no longer drains her or causes the Dyad to falter. Her Valksha magic…"

Her voice trailed off, and she considered her next words thoughtfully.

"…had awakened. Truly awakened."

She turned to Sarys.

"Awakened, but she has yet to fully master it."

"She still has a long way to go," Sarys murmured.

Alfena shifted. She didn't hesitate with her follow-up remarks—calculated, analytical.

"She lost control. Quite a few times." She tapped a finger against the table. "When she stopped Theodin from killing Faust. Then, when she killed Faust. We've discussed the ones before that, yes?"

Silence.

"We've seen this before," Sigvard muttered.

Kaspar's fingers curled against the table. "She is not Vivian. She isn't going to be perfect."

"No," Margrith agreed. "But she is the last Valksha of Veladriel."

"And if she is not trained properly," Sigvard added, "she may also be the last Valksha—period."

Kaspar slowly took a deep breath.

Azariah Crane' tapped his cane. "So we continue to… do our best," he chuckled.

Sigvard sighed. "We need to ensure she has control."

"And Theodin?" Kaspar asked.

Silence.

Sarys's eyes glowed softly in the dim torchlight.

"You already know the answer."

Kaspar's eyes darkened.

Margrith leaned forward slightly as she spoke next.

"We cannot afford another risk like this—"

Crane cut her off with a sharp look and a firm thwack of the end of his cane on the ground.

"Margrith," he began, uncharacteristically cold. "With all due respect, we have been running in circles over these two and have found no solutions. I understand your rigidity, but now is not the time for upholding tradition or protecting our way anymore. *Arborelys* is even different now. The Kyriegard Order has changed, whether you like it or not."

"And it has caused death," Margrith said grimly. "As it has before, Azariah."

Sarys suddenly interrupted.

"Change is terrifying, yes."

All of them stopped to turn to the owl.

Sarys tilted his head.

"But tell me, Kyriegard Council—"

His wings briefly fanned and refolded, and he paused to regard each of them carefully.

"What do you fear more? The girl with the power to kill demons? Or the boy with the power to become one?"

The silence was deafening.

And then—

A sharp knock echoed through the chamber.

Kaspar lifted his head. A messenger apprentice stood in the doorway, breathless.

"My lords," the boy said. "Theodin has woken up."

The first thing Theodin felt was the cold. It seeped through his skin, heavy and lingering. Like the last remnants of a fever or the ghost of something deeper.

His body was slow to awaken. Not like usual. Not like when he bolted upright from a nightmare, his heart hammering and lungs heaving. This time it was different. Like his body had been waiting.

Waiting for what?

Something in the Dyad stirred.

Something that was missing.

Again.

His eyes snapped open.

The room was dimly lit, a single candle flickering on the bedside table. The scent of medicinal herbs clung to the air—familiar and grounding.

Halvalla. The guest chambers.

Pain flickered in his ribs when he shifted, but it was distant. Like an afterthought. Someone had healed him.

Someone.

His breath caught. His gaze flicked downward, to his arm—to the runes of the Dyad.

They were stable. But something was wrong.

The Dyad felt wrong.

He reached—pulled—

Ophelia.

A breath. A presence.

She was alive. Close.

But something cold coiled inside the tether. Something that wasn't supposed to be there.

Something empty.

His fingers curled against the sheets. He swallowed, his throat raw. "Ophelia—"

His voice barely made a sound.

The door creaked. Theodin's head snapped toward it just as Kaspar stepped inside.

For a moment, they simply looked at each other.

Then, Kaspar sighed, closing the door behind him.

"You're awake."

Theodin tried to sit up, but a stabbing pain in his ribs stopped him. He clenched his jaw, forcing himself upright anyway.

"Where is she?"

Kaspar's face remained carefully unreadable.

"She's alive," he said evenly. "And resting."

Theodin's pulse thumped hard in his ears. "Where?"

Kaspar's eyes did not leave his. "You need to recover."

"Where?" Theodin's voice came out rough, raw.

Kaspar took a deep breath and then exhaled slowly.

Then—he sat down.

That alone was enough to send a cold prickle down Theodin's spine.

Because Kaspar did not sit unless there was something he wasn't saying.

"Tell me what you remember," Kaspar said.

Theodin's fingers twitched against the sheets.

"Faust took her."

A pause.

Then, slowly, Kaspar nodded. "And then?"

Theodin's breath caught.

The temple. The fight.

The blood.

His hand clenched into a fist. "I killed them."

Kaspar's face didn't change. "How many?"

Theodin swallowed. His heartbeat roared in his ears. He tried to remember. But he couldn't. It was all a blur.

Flashes of steel. Of bodies falling. Of something breaking inside him.

His throat was dry. "I don't know."

Kaspar's gaze remained indiscernible.

Theodin's pulse throbbed louder in his skull.

"Where is Ophelia?"

Kaspar finally sighed, rubbing his forehead. Then, carefully—*too* carefully—he answered.

"She carried Faust's ashes to the Chayim."

Theodin's breath stopped.

The world went still.

Everything inside him froze.

Then, he remembered.

For all the rage, for all the blood, for all the chaos that had swallowed him at the temple—

He had never heard Ophelia cry for anyone the way she had cried for Faust.

And suddenly—

The temple was beneath his hands again. Ophelia, kneeling over a lifeless body. Her hands tangled in blood-matted hair. Her sobs—piercing, raw, broken. The way the Dyad had curled around her grief, pressing into him, into his lungs, until he thought he might drown in it.

Theodin's chest felt tight.

Kaspar sighed once more as he stood. He began for the door.

"She'll be back soon."

Theodin barely heard him. Because something else settled into his chest.

Something cold. Something bitter. Something that told him, with quiet, damning finality—

That no matter what he did, no matter how much time passed—

Faust would never stop haunting her.

Just as she was haunted by the ghosts of her past.

Her family. Lady Vivian.

Theodin hadn't moved since Kaspar stood, but something in the way the older man lingered—hesitated—made him speak.

"There's more," Theodin said.

Kaspar didn't answer right away.

Then, finally, he turned back to Theodin.

Theodin's jaw clenched. "You don't believe me."

Kaspar exhaled sharply through his nose. "No, I do."

Theodin frowned.

Kaspar's fingers tapped idly against his arm.

"I believe you fought," he said. "I believe you won."

A pause.

"I just don't believe you survived that on your own."

Theodin's breath caught. Something dark curled inside him.

Kaspar's eyes didn't waver. "There were nearly a hundred Warthralls in that temple."

A beat of silence.

"Tell me how you lived."

Theodin didn't answer because he didn't know.

He remembered the feeling. The heat. The fire in his blood. The way his strength surged. The way his vision blurred into red.

It wasn't like before. It wasn't like when he trained. It wasn't like when he fought in the workshop. This was something else. Something primal.

It was more than the Dyad.

His fingers curled against the sheets. "I fought."

Kaspar's expression didn't change. "And that's all?"

Theodin stayed silent. Kaspar watched him. His eyes were sharp, assessing.

"Alfena has her suspicions," he continued, tone even. "The Council does, too."

Theodin's expression hardened.

Kaspar folded his arms and lowered his eyes.

"You are unreasonably strong, Theodin. Even for a Kyriegard. Even for a Procerian." His gaze sharpened. "And the temple was… a bloodbath."

Theodin forced his breathing to remain even. He knew where this was going.

Kaspar's voice lowered. "Did you lose control?"

Theodin's throat went dry. He wanted to say no. He wanted to believe he was just strong. That his training had carried him. That it was just skill.

But it wasn't. He had felt it.

He had felt something else waking up inside him. He had felt what it was capable of.

His knuckles turned white as he gripped the sheets.

Kaspar didn't push. He didn't demand.

But then—quietly, *carefully*—he asked, "Are you afraid of it?"

Theodin inhaled sharply. His heartbeat thrummed in his ears.

And the answer sank into his chest like a blade.

Yes.

But he didn't say it.

Instead, he gritted his teeth and forced himself to sit straighter.

"It won't happen again."

Kaspar's gaze remained upon him. Then, finally, he nodded.

"See that it doesn't."

With that, he turned toward the door. Theodin sat still, his breath steady, and his hands shaking.

Ophelia's tears hadn't stopped since she saw his life leave his eyes. She didn't speak a single word after his last breath.

The only sounds that erupted from her in that moment were agonizing wails of deep sorrow and grief. It was enough to make the trees and the wildlife around the temple bow their heads and weep with her.

The Kyriegard recovered them shortly after. Theodin had lost consciousness, but he lived. And so did she.

But Faust did not.

Now, she walked like a ghost to the Chayim haunted by the ghost of her late companion.

The river ran slow and steady.

The air was still, save for the occasional whisper of wind through the valley trees. The Chayim River stretched before her, glistening under the midmorning sun, its surface glass-like, undisturbed.

Ophelia stood at the water's edge, her hands curled around the small urn.

It was light. Too light.

Kaspar had offered to come with her. So had Alfena. She had refused. This was something she had to do alone.

She alone burned his body in a funeral pyre. She alone collected his ashes. She alone felt death. The absence of life.

The urn in her hands was smooth and cool. She traced her fingers over its surface, her breath shallow.

The weight of it wasn't physical. It wasn't even about the ashes inside.

It was the finality of it. The undeniable truth that Faust was gone.

She had barely spoken since he died.

Not to Theodin, who lay unconscious for days. Not to Sarys. Not to anyone.

The grief settled in her chest like a stone. Heavy. Unmovable. It had followed her since that night, since the moment she held him in her arms and felt his last breath slip away. The moment she realized she could not save him.

She took a step closer to the water's edge.

She should say something. Some final words. Something worthy of him.

Her lips parted—but nothing came.

What was there to say?

He was here. Then he wasn't.

She let out a breath, carefully, as if the wrong movement might shatter her completely. The river's current veered slightly, swirling around the rocks, waiting.

She remembered standing in a spot similar once before. A lifetime ago. Near the fields of Northern Regania, next to the Chayim.

Lady Vivian had brought her there when she was a child, the day after her parents' funeral. She hadn't let Ophelia see their bodies burn. Hadn't let her watch the flames devour them, as was Valksha tradition. Instead, she had taken the urn of their ashes and led her here—to the river.

"They won't be taken by fire," Vivian had told her, kneeling at her side. *"They will be carried by the water. To the sea, to the sky, to something greater. Do you understand?"*

She had.

She hadn't cried that day. She had simply watched the water take them, too young to understand how grief really worked.

Now, she understood.

Ophelia's fingers tightened around the urn.

Would Faust have lived, if not for the Dyad?

If she had never met him, never took him in, never healed him, never let him become part of her life—would he still be here?

She swallowed hard, her throat burning.

"No."

The voice startled her, soft and knowing.

Sarys.

He perched on the nearest stone, watching her, his feathers ruffled slightly by the wind. She hadn't heard him land.

Ophelia's lips pressed together. She inhaled sharply through her nose.

"You don't know that."

Sarys tilted his head. "I do."

She looked away, her eyes narrowing.

Sarys didn't blink. He didn't falter.

"Faust was doomed the moment Azazelf took him. You only delayed the inevitable."

The words cut into her heart. Ophelia's breath hitched. The pain flared behind her ribs, sharp and cruel.

She grimaced.

She wanted to argue. She wanted to believe she could have done more, that she could have changed something, saved him—but Sarys's voice held no mockery. No malice.

Just the truth.

Her shoulders shook. The wind shifted. The river beckoned.

Slowly and carefully, she stepped forward, wading into the shallows. The cold water bit at her skin, wrapping around her ankles like fingers of ice.

She lifted the urn.

Her voice barely made it past her lips.

"I'm sorry, Faust."

The wind carried her words away.

She tilted the urn. The ashes spilled, the river taking them instantly, pulling them into its embrace.

She stood there, watching until there was nothing left. The grief in her chest twisted, sharp and brutal.

Sarys fluttered to her shoulder, his weight solid and grounding.

Ophelia's fingers curled into fists.

Azazelf had taken him. Corrupted him. Destroyed him.

And she had let the fiend leave.

She exhaled sharply through her nose.

"I swear," she murmured, steadier than she felt. "I will find him."

The words were a vow. Though spoken low, her voice almost

seemed to echo around her.

"I will hunt him down."

The wind shifted. The river whispered.

"And I will kill him."

The dream was quiet. Not the kind of quiet that felt peaceful.

It was the kind that pressed against her ribs. Something suffocating that made her breath shallow. That made her hands curl into fists even when there was nothing to fight.

She stood in a field she didn't recognize. The sky stretched endlessly overhead, a deep, endless shade of blue—too still, too perfect.

She knew this wasn't real.

And yet, a presence stirred in the Dyad.

Ophelia turned.

Faust stood a few feet away, his hands at his sides, and his posture relaxed. He looked the same. The same tousled dark hair, the same sharp grin that never quite reached his eyes.

But something was different. He wasn't speaking.

His royal blue eyes, once so full of mischief, were warm. The way they had been in his final moments. Soft. Quiet.

Ophelia's throat tightened. She had so much to say. So much she never got to tell him. So much she could never take back.

She opened her mouth, but no words came.

Faust just smiled. Then—he pressed a hand to his chest.

Right over his heart. Ophelia inhaled sharply.

It was the same way he had done when she had healed him in the chamber. The same way he had done when he told her he loved her as he lay dying in her arms.

It was an acknowledgment. A reminder. A truth.

Then, slowly—he turned away.

Ophelia reached for him. "Faust—"

He was already walking. The sky rippled. The edges of the dream wavered.

A helpless whisper escaped her.

"Don't go..."

His form became less solid. Less real. Less alive.

She tried to step forward, to call out again—

But he was already gone.

The dream dissolved. Ophelia jolted awake.

Her breath came in sharp, uneven gasps, her chest rising and falling too fast. The room was dark, the air thick with the remnants of sleep. But the Dyad—

The Dyad was humming. It wasn't painful. It wasn't broken. It was just…there.

A steady pulse. Like a heartbeat. A heartbeat that was not her own.

Ophelia pressed a trembling hand over the runes on her arm. They pulsed gently beneath her fingertips.

And faintly, a flicker of royal blue shimmered beneath her palm.

Chapter 47

The Reconciliation

Year 845 of the Second Age, Eighth Month, Fifteenth Day

Today marked one year ago that Faust of the Eridane came into their lives.

Theodin hadn't spoken to her in days.

He didn't need to. The Dyad spoke for her. It whispered her grief into his bones, coiled in his lungs, and weighed in his steps. It wasn't loud. It wasn't sharp or volatile.

It was worse.

It was quiet.

She hadn't cried again—not since the river. She hadn't spoken, either. Not to him. Not to Kaspar. Not even to Sarys.

She trained. She ate. She existed. But she wasn't really there.

Theodin had watched her disappear before. After the workshop incident, after their Dyad nearly shattered, she had pulled away. She had locked herself away in silence, hidden behind walls even the Dyad struggled to breach.

But this was different. This wasn't anger. This wasn't fear.

This was grief.

The kind that sank into the marrow, slow and cold. The kind that stayed.

He stood at the edge of the field, arms crossed, watching as she sat against the stone wall near the stable, her knees drawn to her chest. Her raven curls swept lightly in the wind, untouched and unkempt. Her runes flickered dimly beneath the fabric of her sleeves.

The Dyad pulsed faintly between them, dull and steady. Not broken, but muted.

He told himself she needed space. That pushing her now wouldn't help. But every time he convinced himself to wait, to give her time, something in the tether shifted—a slow ache, a wrongness he couldn't name.

And every time he ignored it, the feeling lingered.

She was slipping, and the Dyad knew it. It had always been her who reached for him first. But what if she didn't this time?

He felt the shift in her magic. The way it lay just beneath her skin, as if waiting for her to reach for it. As if waiting to be controlled.

Theodin had wanted to say something—every damn day. But how?

She had always been the one to reach for him first. Back when they had barely known each other, when she had grasped his hand in the Council hall, when she had pulled him into her world with a sharp tongue and reckless confidence.

Back when she had forced her way through his walls, refusing to let him shut her out.

But now? Now, he didn't know if he was the one being shut out—or if she had shut herself away completely.

Theodin sighed. Not yet. Give her time.

But time was a fragile thing. And time had already taken Faust.

He clenched his jaw, his fingers twitching at his sides. He had barely spoken about Faust since the temple. Since he woke up to Kaspar's grim expression, since he realized Ophelia was already gone, carrying the ashes of a boy who had loved her.

He had barely let himself think about it.

The temple. The fight. The blood. The way he had torn through those Warthralls—too fast, too strong, too wrong.

Kaspar had asked him if he lost control. Theodin had said no.

It was a lie.

He had felt it. The moment something inside him snapped. The moment his rage had turned to something else. And then—

Nothing. Only red. Only blood. Only silence.

His gaze flicked back to Ophelia. She hadn't moved. Sarys sat beside her, watching with the same careful patience Theodin had kept for days. The owl said nothing.

The Dyad pulsed softly between them. Stable. Yet wrong. Not broken. But not the same. Something else was there. Something Theodin couldn't name.

He didn't see Faust in his dreams. Not the way Ophelia did—he could feel and hear her think of it. But sometimes—just for a glimpse—he thought he felt something himself. A presence, weightless yet pressing.

He had ignored it at first. But some nights, when he let his guard slip, it was there. The faintest brush of something in the Dyad, something not his own.

Once, in the quiet between waking and sleep, he thought he heard a voice.

Soft and faint. Not calling his name, but calling hers.

A ghost in the tether.

Theodin let out a slow breath. He could wait a little longer. But not forever.

Because if she kept slipping away—he wasn't sure if he could pull her back.

And this time, he didn't know if she wanted to come back at all.

Magic had always lived beneath Ophelia's skin, waiting.

A breath. A heartbeat. A whisper.

But unlike other Valksha, unlike those who wielded their power with intent and control, hers had always been bound by something unseen.

Restraint. Fear. Survival.

It had coiled itself tightly within her, buried beneath years of suppression, waiting for the right moment. And when it did emerge—it never came gently.

Not when she was a child, standing amidst the burning wreckage of her family's farm. Not when she was cornered, helpless, and afraid, watching her parents fall. Not when she first lashed out with magic she didn't understand, when the air cracked and the earth trembled at the sheer force of her grief.

Not when she screamed at Theodin to stop. Not when she shattered her chains or summoned Sarys when Kaspar stabbed Theodin. Or when she shattered the window, or blasted a Warthrall that ambushed Theodin.

Or when she stopped Faust from killing Theodin.

In moments of emotional outburst, Ophelia had not needed to cut her palm or whisper an incantation for magic to answer her. It had always been an instinct, as wild and unbridled as the heart that beat within her chest.

And Veladriel—the Saryf of Spirit and Heart—had blessed her with that same untamed power.

The wind whispered through the trees. The embers of dawn stretched long across the grassy fields and rural stone and wooden structures of Avasylon, painting everything in soft hues of gold and gray.

Ophelia sat near the stable, her back against the cool stone, her legs pulled to her chest. She hadn't spoken much in days.

Not to Theodin.

Not to Kaspar.

Not to anyone.

Only Sarys. And even then, barely.

The owl perched on the ledge beside her, his dark feathers ruffled against the morning late summer chill.

He hadn't spoken yet. He was waiting. Watching.

She knew what he wanted to say, but she wasn't ready to hear it.

Her fingers traced over the runes on her arms, the ones that had flared so violently when she fought Faust.

When she killed him.

A shudder ran through her spine.

It was different now. *She* was different now. She had used magic without blood. Several times. Some moments she couldn't name because her head spun, but she knew they happened.

What am I becoming?

Sarys finally clicked his beak.

"You should ask it out loud, darling."

Ophelia's fingers stilled over the runes. She didn't look at him.

"Ask what?"

Sarys tilted his head. His voice was softer than usual.

"What you truly want to know."

She turned to him. "What's happening to me?"

A pause. Then—

"The real question is," Sarys mused, stretching his wings slightly, "why did it take this long?"

Ophelia frowned. "What?"

Sarys turned fully toward her. "It was always inside you, you know.

This power. This instinct. Locked away, buried under years of restraint."

She furrowed her brows. "You don't mean—"

"The farm," Sarys murmured. "Northern Regania. The first time you used it. You thought of the times you used it on Theodin and Faust—but you used it quite a bit."

Her breath hitched. She knew what he was talking about. She had felt it that night.

Her mother's screams. Her father's shouts. Oliver grabbing her and pulling her away. The dark shapes of figures she couldn't recognize.

And then—

The explosion. The burst of power that had torn through the field, knocking those men to the ground. The force that had protected her and her brother, even as their parents were left behind, sacrificing themselves. She was eight years old.

She had never used that outburst again until she came to Avasylon. Why?

Ophelia's nails dug into her palm. "I didn't know what I was doing."

"You still don't," Sarys said simply. "And that is the problem."

Sarys hopped down from the ledge, landing lightly in the dirt. He watched her with intrigued eyes.

"Valksha magic is instinctual, yes—but it is also a craft. A discipline."

Ophelia shook her head. "It's always been tied to blood. That's how it works for all Valksha."

Sarys hummed. "Is it?"

She paused and blinked at him.

"Your blood," he continued, "is the catalyst. The bridge between your body and the power of the Valksha. But it was never the source. As a Valksha of Veladriel, especially one who had sequestered your magic, your power is *truly* driven by your spirit and heart. Of course, the domain of your Saryf."

She stared at him, bewildered.

Sarys fluffed his feathers.

"Think of every single moment your magic activated without blood and you lost control. There is a clear pattern and connection. Now that you know of it, you must harness it. You have spent your entire life holding back. You didn't had a mentor long enough to teach you the way. You were never trained and so you never learned. You spent years believing the only way to tap into your power was to bleed. But your magic—"

His gaze sharpened.

"—was always there."

Her throat felt tight.

"Then why did it take so long to come out?"

Sarys sighed. He studied her for a long moment, the emerald glow of his eyes incomprehensible. When he finally spoke, his voice was softer.

"Because you never let it."

The words sent a chill down her spine.

"I—"

She faltered, her mouth opening and closing as she searched for an answer. A denial, an excuse, anything. But there was nothing.

Because he was right.

The silence stretched between them. His next words came slower. More deliberate.

"The real question is," he mused, "why did it take something so breaking for you to finally set it free?"

She had spent years forcing herself to be controlled. To be contained. Her blood was the only thing that let her wield her power in a way that felt measured and safe.

But now…

She had let go.

When were all the times it had happened? When she tried to protect her family, but only saved herself. When she saw a shadow in the window and wanted to protect her protectors. Anytime Theodin was in danger or injured. And the magic had answered.

Ophelia exhaled shakily. She stared at her hands. They were steady now. But she could still feel it.

A hum beneath her skin. Waiting.

Almost instinctively, she touched the runes on her arms again, half-expecting them to glow in response. They didn't. The air didn't shift. The magic didn't surge.

Not like before. Not like when she had lost control.

Her breath hitched. She furrowed her brow and reached again—not with her hands, but with something deeper. Willing. *Come back.*

The response was immediate. Not an explosion or a force—just a flicker. A single pulse of magic, warm and steady, thrumming not through her runes but through *her*—her heart, her breath, her spirit.

It had never been the runes. Never been the blood. It had always been her.

Sarys' voice softened. "Now that it's awake, you need to control it. Or it will control you."

Ophelia closed her eyes. Control it. Like how Theodin had to control himself. Like how Faust never got the chance to.

Her fingers curled. Her magic had taken things from her. Her family. Her innocence. Faust.

She would not let it take anything else.

Her voice was quiet but firm. "Then teach me."

Sarys's eyes glinted. He gave a slow, approving nod.

Ophelia looked back at the runes on her arms. She would learn. She would master this. Because next time—

She would not lose. She would will her magic through her power and blood.

Ophelia exhaled, her breath visible in the cool evening air. The training yard was empty now, the lanterns along the stone path flickering against the creeping dusk.

Sarys sat beside her on the wooden railing, observing her with quiet amusement.

"You're brooding, darling," he mused.

Ophelia huffed. "I am *not* brooding."

"You most certainly are." He hopped closer, tilting his head as his eyes glinted in the dim light. "I believe I know why."

She arched her brow. "Do you?"

The owl let out a soft hoot, as if laughing.

"Oh, of course. I'm quite observant, you know." He preened a feather. "Your mate has been rather patient."

Ophelia's breath hitched.

Sarys continued, utterly unbothered.

"It's fascinating, really. He hasn't said a word, hasn't pried, hasn't even glared as much as he usually does when left to stew in his own brooding."

A pause.

"One has to wonder how long that will last."

Ophelia hesitated, lowering her eyes to the ground.

Sarys blinked at her. "Well?"

She frowned, glancing at him. "Well, *what?*"

He gestured toward the training yard with a pointed flick of his wing. "Are you going to let him keep waiting?"

Her heart squeezed.

She turned her head toward the edge of the field, where Theodin sat on the stone steps beneath the lantern glow.

He was alone. His sword lay across his lap, his fingers absently running along the hilt. He wasn't training. He wasn't sharpening his blade. He was just… *sitting*.

Waiting.

Ophelia inhaled sharply, then muttered, "I hate when you're right."

Sarys let out a pleased sound. "I *always* am, darling."

She rolled her eyes but didn't argue. Instead, she stepped down from the railing, hesitating for only a moment before moving toward Theodin.

He felt and heard her before she spoke.

Theodin didn't turn as she approached, but his shoulders shifted slightly, a faint awareness settling into his posture.

Ophelia sat beside him. Not directly close—but closer than she had been in days.

For a long moment, neither of them spoke.

The training grounds were serene and still, save for the distant crackle of torches and the soft rustling of leaves in the evening breeze.

Then, finally—

"I should have said something sooner."

Her voice was quiet but steady.

Theodin slowly turned to look at her.

"You've had more important things on your mind."

There was no accusation in his tone, no bitterness. Just a fact. But something about that—about how *easily* he accepted her distance—made her throat tighten.

She spoke again.

"I didn't forget you."

The words left her before she could stop them. They sounded almost *small*. She curled her fingers into the fabric of her sleeve.

"I just…"

She faltered as her voice trailed off.

Theodin's jaw ticked slightly. But then, softer—quieter—he said, "I know."

Silence again. But this time, it wasn't as heavy.

Ophelia hesitated, then shifted slightly, resting her arms on her knees.

"Sarys called you my mate. Again."

Theodin let out a breath—half scoff, half something else.

"Figures."

A little smile tugged at the corner of her lips. "He's observant, you know."

He snorted. "He thinks he's observant."

Ophelia's smile faded. She swallowed.

"Is he wrong?"

That finally made him turn his head.

His mismatched eyes met hers, unreadable in the dim torchlight. His expression didn't change. Not right away. But the tether between them pulsed, slow and unyielding—faint, but no longer wrong. No longer absent.

Theodin exhaled softly. "No."

Ophelia blinked.

He looked away first, running a hand through his hair.

"But… I wasn't going to say it first."

A quiet laugh escaped her—small but real.

Theodin didn't smile, but the corners of his mouth twitched just slightly.

She let the silence settle again. Let herself sit in it. Let herself be here.

Then, slowly and carefully, she reached for his hand first.

Her fingers brushed against his, hesitant but deliberate. Just enough for him to feel it, for him to know. Their matching runes pulsed once up their forearms.

She didn't say anything else. Neither did he.

Theodin didn't pull away. He turned and opened his hand to allow her fingers to reach around and weave between his, and their palms closed together in a firm grasp. At first, the etchings flickered with green and gold.

And, without them noticing, the smallest glimpse of royal blue shimmered in Ophelia's palm.

Then, the runes lit up with a white light—warm, steady, and unshaken. For the first time since the temple, since the river, since everything—

The Dyad felt right.

It was the calm after the storm. The soothing rumble of thunder in the distance after a raging tempest.

A cleansing mist of peace.

Epilogue

She is the Key

The portal flickered, an unnatural tear in the air, swirling with tendrils of black and gold. The moment Azazelf stepped before it, the weight of the presence beyond it pressed into him, suffocating and absolute.

A throne loomed on the other side—a structure carved from something ancient, something older than Moirand itself. The figure seated within it barely moved, yet the air around him seemed to shift, warping under the sheer force of his existence.

"You disappoint me, Azazelf."

The figure's voice was not raised, but it carried through the air like a blade pressed against a throat.

Azazelf bowed low, keeping his expression carefully schooled. "Your highness. The Kyriegard are proving more resourceful than expected."

The air tightened. The pressure deepened.

The figure did not reply immediately.

Azazelf forced himself to continue.

"They have fortified their wardstones. Undone our corruptions. Their defenses are not what they once were."

The words burned to admit. The Kyriegard had adapted—quicker than he anticipated. The power of their Sages had grown, their enchantments reinforced. His usual tactics would no longer be enough.

All because of that damn Valksha girl.

Azazelf couldn't tell him this. His majesty would order every dark agent under his command to hunt her to the ends of Moirand and bleed her dry. Bleed her until the Saryf in her veins screamed for mercy.

No. Azazelf wanted that power.

He wanted the Valksha girl.

A beat of silence.

Then, a scoff. Cold and mirthless.

"And you are telling me this because…?"

Azazelf's jaw tightened.

The figure exhaled sharply, the sound like a sigh that belonged to a god rather than a man.

"You are wasting my time."

The portal flickered violently, the shadows darkening behind the throne.

"The Kyriegard must fall," the figure continued, his tone no longer patient. "As long as they stand, they will stand in my way. And I do not suffer obstacles."

Azazelf lowered his head.

"Find another way." The command was final. "Before I find someone else to replace you."

The portal flared violently—then collapsed in on itself. The pressure disappeared, leaving the chamber unnaturally quiet.

For a long moment, Azazelf did not move.

His fingers twitched at his sides.

Then, as he turned, the pale skin on his right cheek bubbled.

The glamor spell melted from his face to reveal the hideous blackened scar underneath.The wound that would never heal.

Because of *her*. Because of a *Valksha*.

The royal fool did not understand. He never understood.

The Kyriegard would fall. Azazelf was certain of that. But it would be done in his way.

His eyes flickered to the talisman hanging from his belt—the Medallion of Zadkiel, still blackened with his touch.

He still had this.

And the girl.

His lips curled slightly.

The Valksha of Veladriel. She had awakened something, something that even he had not anticipated. Her power was still raw, untamed, but beneath it… something deeper. Something far older than she understood.

She would be the key to his unanswered prayers.

And then there was the boy.

Azazelf's fingers twitched again, this time involuntarily.

He had witnessed it in that temple. What he had done. What he had survived.

That was no ordinary strength. It wasn't just the Arcane Dyad. It wasn't just Kyriegard training.

Azazelf's expression darkened.

What are you?

He turned away, exhaling slowly.

It did not matter.

Not yet.

The Medallion burned cold against his palm. The girl was his to claim first.

And then, perhaps…

He would figure out what to do with the boy.

Glossary

Factions & Races

Aquiad - Thought to be extinct, mer-people given gifts of the sea by the Saryf Abrachiel the Wise.

Avengels - (ʌvɛndʒɛlz) A militaristic people given wings by the Saryf Serakiel the Valiant.

Cadaven - (kædævɪn) Reanimated corpses twisted by the dark magic, once used as puppets by Malcifer in the War of Malblight. They now reside as a civilized society in the outskirts of Hallowdale.

Cruerfel - (kruərfɛl) Once human, now twisted by Malcifer's corruption. Marked by venomous fangs, claw-like nails, and speed and strength that rival Elves, they are remnants of a dark legacy.

The Kyriegard Order - (kirigard) A disciplined Sage warrior order sworn to defend Moirand and maintain balance against dark forces.

Predant - (pridɛnt) A tribal folk gifted with animalistic and beast-like features by the Saryf Arayziel the Nurturing.

Sage - (seɪdʒ) Scholars and wielders of disciplined magic, drawing power from the lingering energies of the Saryfim. They organize into Sage Circles or Sage Covens.

Seelie - (sili) The original Pulchids: Elves, Dwarves, and Fay.

Undarim - (undarım) Underground folk blessed by the Saryf Rochiel the Fierce to thrive beneath the surface.

Unseelie - (ʌnsili) Corrupted Pulchids born of Malcifer's darkness.

The Valksha - (valkʃa) Devout followers of Elodyn who were given the power of the Saryfim as magic to wield against Malcifer and the Nether.

Valksha Familiar - A mystical companion bound to a Valksha, often taking an animal form and serving as an extension of the Valksha's spirit and magic. Aetheris and Sarys are examples of Valksha familiars.

Warthrall - Magic wielders who pledge themselves to powerful patrons in exchange for their abilities. They often gather in Warthrall Cults.

Characters

In Order of Appearance

Theodin - (θiodın) A disciplined apprentice of the Kyriegard, raised within the Order.

Nimrod Kaspar - (kaspar, not kaspər) The respected Head of the Kyriegard Order. He carries great authority and even greater burdens, ensuring the Order's survival.

Lady Vivian - A Valksha woman of deep wisdom and power who once played an important role in shaping Ophelia's path.

Ophelia Bloodworth - A young Valksha girl, a refugee and the last Valksha of Veladriel.

Sigvard Jackard - The Dwarven member of the Kyriegard Council. A skilled craftsman and rune-smith, responsible for forging the weapons and enchanted tools used by the Kyriegard.

Margrith Gravehardt - A strict and traditional mixed-blood human of the Kyriegard Council who upholds the Order's laws with unwavering resolve and specializes in architecture and engineering.

Azariah Crane - (æzəraɪjʌ) A human council member of the Kyriegard Order, crippled from the waist down and known for his mastery of espionage, tracking, and scouting.

Azazelf Chernabog - With the reputation known as the "demon Dark Elf," he is an Unseelie Elf Warthrall who serves the demon Chernabog.

Faust - A Valksha refugee who was once a captive of Azazelf Chernabog who claims to have been chosen by the Saryf Zadkiel.

Kyriegard Intiates, Apprentices, and Officers

Mald

Fritan

Gisela

Daphne

Vladimir

Jezadine

Dorek

Kingdoms & Places

In Order of Significance

Moirand - (moirɪnd) A vast land in Midthian, created by the Etherian Elodyn, and shaped by the remnants of the Saryfim's influence.

Chayim River - A winding river of great significance, flowing through Moirand's heartlands and sustaining many of its civilizations.

Tersia - A southern kingdom north of the Elkenwoods known for its strategic importance, though its lands bear the scars of past conflicts.

> **Olysgard** - (olɪzgard) The base of operations for the Kyriegard Order near the small village of Fatum. Where Kyriegard Sage warriors are trained and missions are assigned.
>
> > **Avasylon** - (ʌvæsɪlan) A hidden stronghold of the Kyriegard Order serving as their training grounds and sanctuary.
> >
> > **Halvalla** - The fortress and central seat of Kyriegard governance where council deliberations shape the Order's course and initiates receive advanced lectures.

Havysium - (havɪzɪʊm) The heart of Olysgard, a disciplined barracks and social hub where Kyriegard initiates reside, train, and forge bonds of brotherhood.

Fatum - (feɪtɪm) A small but vital village near Olysgard often overlooked but deeply connected to the Kyriegard's daily operations.

Slymound - A shadowy and dangerous region rumored to be a haven for outlaws, rogue mages, and forgotten horrors.

Regania - A rich and prestigious kingdom located in north Moirand. Ruled by the Creed family.

Erythar - (ɛrɪθar) A war-torn kingdom steeped in dark history long claimed as a stronghold by the Cruerfel and other remnants of Malcifer's corruption. Ruled by the Vlahdwulf family.

Hallowdale - A thriving matriarchal kingdom near the western sea, closest to the PulchidIsles. Known for its diversity of humans and Pulchids, it is also home to a domesticated Cadaven settlement isolated from the rest of civilization. Ruled by Queen Abigail Blackshaw.

Belluxa - (beluksa) Once a thriving oasis, now a shattered kingdom surrounded by violent deserts, its isolation meant to keep out the Cruerfel. Now, it is home to rebel sand Sages who resist the world beyond its dunes.

Aetheloth - (æθɛloθ) A kingdom bordering Tersia ravaged by the Malblight plague in the First Age, its lands still bearing the scars of that devastation.

Predant Territories

The Sacred Motherland - A revered land tied to ancient Predant traditions.

Ebpeb's Den - (ibpɛb) The territory of the Predant bear tribe.

Cobaka's Burrow - The territory of the Predant wolf tribe.

Aryekan's Pride - (arjɛkən) The territory of the Predant lion tribe.

The PulchidIsles - A scattered collection of islands once home to the Pulchidraces, now abandoned. Somewhere in its untamed wilds the hidden gateway to the Fay Realm is said to exist.

Aquiad Ruins - The remnants of an underwater kingdom now lost to time and where traces of the once-great Aquiads can still be found.

The Elkenwoods - A sprawling ancient forest where the magic of Blythandriel still lingers, shaping its creatures and its hidden inhabitants.

Arachian Swamp - A treacherous marshland filled with shifting terrain, venomous Arachnian creatures, and whispers of things best left undisturbed.

Procerian Settlement - (prosɛriən) A remote enclave of the Procerians, a race of giants whose isolationist nature has kept them hidden from the world.

Mythos & History

In Order of Significance

Elodyn - (ilodɪn) The Etherian creator of Moirand, the Saryfim, and mankind.

Saryf/The Saryfim – (sɛrɪf/sɛrɪfɪm) Ancient, revered beings created by Elodyn, now only spoken of in myths.

Veladriel the Ardent, Saryf of Spirit and Heart

Celestiel the Gentle, Saryf of Winds and Clouds

Zadkiel the Headstrong, Saryf of Strength and Will

Jophiel the Joyous, Saryf of the Sun and Moon

Serakiel the Valiant, Saryf of the Skies

Abrachiel the Wise, Saryf of Rivers and Seas

Arayziel the Nurturing, Saryf of Wilds and Beasts

Yuriel the Nimble, Saryf of Fayfolk

Oriphiel the Clever, Saryf of Elves and Dwarves

Blythandriel the Keen, Saryf of the Greens and Trees

Rochiel the Fierce, Saryf of the Mountains and Terrains

Malaziel the Merciful, Saryf of Freedom and Release

Arborelys - (arborɛlɪs) A sacred tree born from the collective magic of the Kyriegard's founders. It is the foundation of their strength and unity anchoring their power.

Midthian - (mɪdthiən) The mortal realm.

Nether - The damned realm of the dead and other spirits.

Lither - The purgatorian limbo realm of the dead and other spirits.

Ether - (iθər) The heavenly realm of the dead and other spirits.

The War of Malblight - A cataclysmic conflict that marked the end of the First Age and the beginning of the Second Age. The First Age was the time the Saryfim roamed before Malaziel's fall and transformation into Malcifer and became the catalyst for the rise of demonic corruption across Moirand.

The Author

E.J. Tollridge is a first-generation Filipina, raised by immigrant parents in the west suburbs of Chicago, where she still resides with her husband and son.

www.ingramcontent.com/pod-product-compliance
Lightning Source LLC
Chambersburg PA
CBHW061504020726
47502CB00006B/1930